HEART OF STONE
VOLUME TWO

Books by K.M. Scott writing as Gabrielle Bisset

Blood Avenged (Sons of Navarus #1)
Blood Betrayed (Sons of Navarus #2)
Longing (A Sons of Navarus Short Story)
Blood Spirit (Sons of Navarus #3)
The Deepest Cut (A Sons of Navarus Short Story)
Blood Prophecy (Sons of Navarus #4)
Blood Craving (Sons of Navarus #5)
Blood Eclipse (Sons of Navarus #6)
The Sons of Navarus Box Set #1
The Sons of Navarus Box Set #2

Stolen Destiny (Destined Ones Duology #1)
Destiny Redeemed (Destined Ones Duology #2)

Love's Master
Masquerade
The Victorian Erotic Romance Trilogy

HEART OF STONE

VOLUME TWO

K.M. SCOTT

HEART OF STONE
VOLUME TWO

Ever After

You fell in love with Tristan and Nina in Crash Into Me, cheered for them as they fought to stay together in Fall Into Me, and watched them finally achieve their happy ending in Give In To Me. For all the fans of the Heart of Stone series who wondered if Tristan's dream at the end of Give In To Me came true, this is for you. Join Tristan and Nina one more time and see how their happily ever after turns out.

Return To Me

What do you do when the one you love is the one you can't have?

Gage Varo had accepted being alone for what he'd done. No one else should be hurt because of him. Then one day Jordan showed up and he fell hard for the beautiful blond who made him believe in love again. But his past returned with a vengeance and forced him to make the hardest choice of his life. He never stopped loving her, though, even as he watched her move on without him.

What do you do when the one you love is the one you shouldn't want?

Jordan Wright thought she found real love with Gage, but it all ended one night with a phone call. Now she's got a chance to have the life she's always wanted with a man who can give her everything. All she needs to do is forget about Gage and she can be happy. The problem is she can't forget the one man who loved her unlike anyone else ever had.

They'll have to put the past behind them if they ever want to have a future, but the past isn't going away that easy.

Forever With Me

For Gage, the past never goes away. All he's done to protect Jordan doesn't erase the failure he can't forget. But he'll have to find a way to overcome those demons that still haunt him to be the man she needs him to be or risk losing her forever.

The only thing Jordan knows to be true is Gage loves her. She doesn't know why Hailey wants her dead or why a billionaire wants to help her kill her, but together with the man she loves, they'll work to unravel the mystery behind Hailey's plan.

But will it be in time, or will she lose him again, this time for good?

EVER AFTER

CHAPTER ONE

NINA

A CRASHING NOISE IN THE kitchen woke me from the nap I'd slipped into, and I sat bolt upright in bed, disoriented and my heart pounding hard against my chest. Looking around, I tried to determine what time it was. The sun was still up, so I couldn't have slept very long. Or had I slept all night and it was already morning of the next day? I had no memory of Tristan coming to bed, but that didn't mean I couldn't have slept all night. With his work at Stone Worldwide intensifying since our return from our honeymoon, he was often up before the crack of dawn after coming to bed after midnight.

My thoughts racing, I shook the sleep from my mind and swung my legs off the bed. Standing up, my legs buckled and everything around me swirled into a blur. Before I knew it, I was on the floor in a groggy heap. This was either the worst wake up ever, or I was having some incredibly realistic nightmare complete with throbbing pain in my right elbow that brought tears to my eyes. Either way, I needed to get up to see what or who was going on in my kitchen.

I lifted myself up to a sitting position to see Tristan standing in the doorway with a look of horror on his face.

"What happened?" he asked as he stepped into the room to kneel down next to me. "Did you trip?"

Shaking my head, I reached over to rub my aching arm. "No. I heard a noise that woke me up and when I went to see what happened, my legs gave out and I landed right on my elbow. Ouch."

Tristan knitted his brows and frowned. "This is the second time this week you've had an accident. We need to get you to the doctor, Nina."

I held onto his forearm as he lifted me up onto my feet, feeling foolish that I'd been so clumsy twice in one week. Smoothing my white cotton skirt down over my thighs, I looked up into Tristan's still worried eyes and smiled, hoping to ease his mind. "There's nothing wrong, honey. I just got up too quickly before I was fully awake. No big deal."

"Are you sure?"

To be honest, I wasn't sure. I'd felt run down for weeks. I hadn't napped this much since I was a child, and even with sneaking extra sleep time, I still felt tired all the time. Instead of worrying Tristan, I'd told Jordan, who had tried to be helpful by suggesting I check out some medical site online. Boy, was that a mistake. Within the first hour, I'd convinced myself I had any number of diseases, including malaria, some variant of the Black Plague, and Lyme disease. Even worse, I'd stumbled onto a page dedicated to leukemia and one of the first symptoms listed was unexplained fatigue.

Nothing like having your heart stop cold for a moment as the possibility that you're dying from the same disease your mother succumbed to weaves its way into your brain. I was so stressed out after reading that I couldn't get to sleep all night. I told myself over and over that I was being foolish, and Jordan had scolded me about taking what I read online with a grain of salt. Since then, I'd tried to put it out of my mind, but every day I felt exhausted, and that tiny niggle of worry sitting in the back of my brain had mushroomed into full blown fear.

I knew it was wrong to keep all of this from Tristan. He was my husband, and I didn't doubt for a second that he'd want to do whatever it took to take care of me. I just couldn't face the reality that after finally finding complete and utter happiness with the man of my dreams it would all be taken away, just like it had been for my mother.

Standing on my toes, I placed a tiny kiss on the tip of Tristan's nose and gave him my sweetest smile. "I'm fine. No need to worry. So what did you do in the kitchen to make all that noise?"

Tristan raised his eyebrows in fake surprise. "What makes you think I did anything?"

I folded my arms and shook my head. "I doubt it was Maria making all that racket. Unless you hired someone else without telling me—which would be really uncool since that would probably scare the hell out of me when I ran into them and thought the house was being robbed—there's no one else here but us. Since I was busy examining the inside of my eyelids, that leaves you to blame for whatever happened. So fess up."

"It was nothing. I was just checking the pantry to make sure we had Jiffy Pop. I thought a nice night in watching movies would be just what we need since I've been working day and night since we got back from our honeymoon. By the way, we're out of Jiffy Pop, but there's more than enough pie filling and tomato soup."

"Nothing like an avalanche of canned goods coming down on top of you," I said with a laugh.

Tristan winced and rubbed the top of his head. "I'm just happy the Jiffy Pop wasn't next to the huge container of olive oil. I might have knocked myself out."

I laughed out loud. "I can only imagine me finding you lying on the floor of the pantry covered in oil. Definitely not your usual look."

"So what do you say to me picking up a pizza and some popcorn and the two of us making a night of it? I might even agree to some chick flick."

"Bridget Jones?"

A look of pain crossed his face, but he quickly tried to hide it with a sexy grin. "It's a deal but only if I get at least one superhero movie. Maybe two since that Bridget Jones stuff really puts me in danger in losing my man card. This might even require a Clint Eastwood."

"Clint Eastwood? That seems a bit much, doesn't it?" I joked, secretly fine with a Dirty Harry flick but not wanting Tristan to find out. If he did, our movie nights would turn into one long cop and bad guy fest. "I'll agree to Clint if we watch Bridget first. Deal?"

"Deal. I'll be stopping by the liquor store while I'm out. Bridget and I require more of the good stuff. Want me to pick you up the makings of your chocolate cake martini?"

"Sure. I haven't had a martini since we got back, so I think one would be good tonight. But we need some birch beer for the pizza, so don't forget to grab that at Tony's."

Tristan kissed me gently and pulled me close. "Got it." He was quiet for a long moment, and then he finally said, "By the way, did I tell you how much I love you today?"

I slid my hands around him and grabbed his ass. "I think our time in the shower this morning included something about that, but I never get tired of hearing it."

He leaned away from me and cradling my face, tilted my head back. Looking down at me with those gorgeous brown eyes, he licked his lips and a sly grin slid across his mouth. "I enjoyed that. Maybe we should make that a daily event. And by the way, I love you even more today, Mrs. Stone."

I felt myself begin to get weak again, so quickly I said, "Me too, Mr. Stone. All this talk about food has gotten me hungry, so let's get that pizza and get this movie party started."

He kissed me and my stomach did that flipping thing it always did when his lips touched mine. Even now, as we stood there as a married couple used to each other, he had that effect on me. At least I hoped it was that and not some horrible disease slowly sapping the life from me.

Pulling away, he whispered next to my ear, "Your wish is my command, my lady. I'll be back in a few. Feel free to begin Bridget

Jones before I get back."

I looked up and saw his smile telling me how much he really didn't want to sit through one of my chick flicks. That he would and be so cute about it meant a lot to me. "And miss a moment of our movie time together? No way."

✦ ✦ ✦

TRISTAN'S HEAVY BREATHING BEHIND ME signaled he was fast asleep, so I pressed Stop on the remote and curled up against his chest. A light sleeper, most nights he really only dozed, but these days he barely did that. Wrapping his arms around me, he squeezed me tightly to him and murmured, "Did I miss Bridget?"

I hugged him and laughed at his joke. "Yes, and that's not fair if you're going to wake up just in time for your movies."

"It's in my DNA. As soon as the Man of Steel is even mentioned, men naturally wake up. Who am I to fight nature?"

His voice grew less sleepy with every word, and I looked up to see him wide awake. "I'm calling shenanigans on this, Mr. Stone. I should put Bridget in again."

Kissing me on the forehead, he whispered, "Bridge is tired. You know how much that girl drinks. Let her sleep it off. We've got better things to do than hang out with her."

"Like spending the next two hours with Superman?"

Tristan got that look on his face that he wore when he had sexier thoughts in mind. Pushing his hips off the couch, he slid his hands down my back to cup my ass. "I think we can leave Superman for another time. Right now, I think we should go back to acting like we're still on our honeymoon."

"Mmmm....I like that. Got anything specific in mind?"

He kissed me, lightly snaking his tongue into my mouth and making me want him right there in the media room. Unbuttoning the remaining buttons on his dress shirt, I slid my hand over his muscular torso, loving the feel of the taut muscles under my fingers. His body never failed to thrill me.

"I had planned on taking you in my arms to the bedroom, but on second thought, right here will do just fine," he said on a groan as he worked to slide my T-shirt over my head. "Your clothes seem to be working against me tonight, though."

I sat up and wriggled out of my shirt and skirt, leaving me in my bra and panties. "I wonder if Superman needs help to get his wife's clothes off," I joked.

Tristan rolled his eyes as he pulled me back on top of him. "Only if Lois Lane is wearing Kryptonite underwear. But she wouldn't look as incredible as you do right now."

Straddling his hips, I sat up and unhooked my bra as he lightly teased his fingers along the waistband of my panties. "Even if she didn't match like me?"

He licked his lips and stared at the path his fingers traced over the crease of my leg. "I wouldn't care if you wore a burlap sack. You'd still be the most incredible woman on Earth." Looking up, he winked. "Luckily, you're mine. Superman's going to have to find his own woman."

Pulling me down to lay on top of him, he hooked his thumbs on the sides of my panties and jerked them off my body. "Hey! I like those panties. They weren't built to withstand the caveman thing."

With a grunt, he slid out of his pants and boxer briefs. "I'll get you a new pair. Now stop talking and let me show you what I was thinking about during my afternoon meeting."

He captured my mouth with his and kissed me hard, as if he'd missed the feel of my lips for weeks. Already rock hard, it only took a slight tilting of his hips and he was pushing into me. My body craved his, craved the feel of him inside me touching parts of me that only he knew how to excite. An expert at knowing exactly how to make my body sing, he stroked into me slowly, like the sensation of each inch of his cock entering me was something to be relished and appreciated, even now after we'd known each other as intimately as any two people could for over a year.

My fingers pressed into the back of his neck as I clung to him, loving the feel of our bodies joining as much as I had the first time we made love. Whatever exhaustion I'd felt just hours before was gone, replaced by a renewed need for that wonderful feeling being with him created in me.

Tristan cradled my face and grimaced sweetly as he stopped, filling me completely. "God, Nina, I wasn't sure we'd ever find our way to this place we're at now."

His eyes were so full of emotion I wondered if there was something wrong, something bad he had to tell me. I waited, my body clinging to his as he stared up at me, each second ticking by making me sure there was something wrong. "Tristan, is everything okay?"

With a smile that made every worry I had fade away, he said, "Everything's perfect."

He said nothing more as we continued to make love, and as he took my body to that place only he could, I closed my eyes and thanked God for my husband. As he came, he held me tightly and kissed me, whispering how much he loved me.

"Promise me we'll never turn into people who forget why they got married," I asked, loving moments like this. "I never want this to end."

"I promise," he whispered into my hair. "No matter what, we'll be the people we are right now.

His heartbeat slowly returned to its normal rhythm as I rested my head on his chest, his strong arms wrapped around me, protecting me as his promise eased my soul. No matter what, I hoped we'd always be the people we were at that moment.

HOURS LATER, AS HE SLEPT quietly next to me in bed, I sat awake, exhausted yet unable to sleep because of the fears that had settled into my mind. Something was wrong with me. I knew it. I needed to see a doctor and face whatever this was.

Tristan left for work early, and I pushed away my fear to call for a doctor's appointment. As if fate knew I'd be on edge until I find out what was making me sick, I was lucky enough to get one that afternoon. Hopefully, I'd find out all my fears were for nothing.

Hopefully.

Chapter Two

Nina

Dr. Anshon's waiting room teemed with people, all of us struggling to find something to read to avoid making small talk as we sat there stressed out about whatever sickness we each had. A dog-eared copy of Marie Claire was all that was left on the table in front of me, so I picked it up and pretended to read about the best hairstyles for last year's holiday season, all the while unable to concentrate on anything but the fear that what was wrong with me was what took my mother from me all those years ago.

I had so many things I wanted to do. After all Tristan and I had endured to be together, I'd hoped we'd have a child or even a house full of children. Ever since he told me about his dream of those twin girls—our twin girls—I'd hoped that we'd be blessed, but every month my period came just as it always had since I was fourteen and every month I consoled myself with the idea that there was no need to hurry.

That we had our whole lives to look forward to, and of course, we'd have children eventually.

Now I worried that our time had already been cut short, and we'd never have a family. Just the thought of everything being taken away from me brought me to tears, but as I sat there in that waiting room with others wearing the same look of concern, I had to remind myself that all this was just speculation. I could just need a B12 shot, or I might need to get more exercise. I had gained a few pounds since we returned from Europe, so that might be it.

Feeling better for the moment, I looked around at the waiting room's décor. On the pale teal blue walls hung pictures of nature scenes, each one focusing on an exotic location. The one closest to where I sat looked to be a tropical setting, and the artist had chosen iridescent blues and greens for the water lapping up on the beach. It consumed my thoughts for a few minutes as I fantasized about us taking our next vacation to an island just like it, and then I was back to worrying.

"Nina Stone," a voice called out, and I looked to my left to see Dr. Anshon's nurse Jana smiling at me.

I stood and as we walked back to the examination room, we made small talk, mostly about my name change, which she had read about in the paper. No matter how low key Tristan and I had tried to make our wedding, it had ended up on Page Six, minus any pictures, of course.

Jana pointed at the scale in the room. "Let's see how much you weigh, Nina."

I removed my shoes, hoping to shave off any extra pounds I could. It was no use. I knew I'd gained some weight. My clothes told me every morning. I just didn't know how much.

"135. Okay, hop up on the table and let's get your pressure and temperature."

As the evidence of my brand new ten pounds resonated in my mind, I took my seat on the paper covered examination table and Jana attached the blood pressure cuff to my right bicep. My arm felt like it was going to explode, but I was preoccupied with my weight gain. Ten pounds would certainly explain my feeling run down. Dragging around extra weight like that would tire anyone out. It was salads for me from now on.

Jana told me my blood pressure and temperature, but I didn't pay attention. I was too busy feeling relieved. This wasn't going to be so bad, after all.

The door opened and Dr. Anshon came in, her bright smile easing any leftover concerns that still plagued me. I'd seen her since

I'd first moved to Brooklyn, and every time her warm smile had made me feel better. A petite woman with dark brown hair and brown eyes, she was beautiful in an unconventional way since her eyes were too small for her face, but that smile of hers made up for that slight imperfection.

"Mrs. Nina Stone, I presume?" she teased in a sweet voice. "Jana told me she saw the write-up about your wedding to none other than Tristan Stone himself, Nina. She didn't show me a picture, though."

A blush warmed my cheeks. Lowering my head, I couldn't help but smile. "We tried to keep it small, but everything about Tristan seems to attract the attention of the gossip pages."

"From now on, you should expect that everything you do will cause them to wag their tongues too, Nina," Jana said from the chair next to me.

She wasn't wrong. I knew all too well that the paparazzi would be all over me visiting a doctor, so my two new bodyguards had made sure no one saw me and I'd even gone in the back door to the building, just to make sure. It all seemed ridiculous to me, but what did I know? I didn't care one bit about anyone's doctor's appointments but mine.

"Yeah, well, I'm just me. There's nothing interesting to report on me, so they can stick to writing about real celebrities."

Dr. Anshon sat down in front of me on her rolling stool and looked up. "So what are you here for today?"

All of a sudden, everything I'd worried about flooded back into my mind and I choked up as I tried to explain what I'd been feeling. "I'm sure it's nothing…I mean, now that I know I've packed on a few pounds, I'm sure it's that."

"Just tell me what's going on and we'll figure it out," Dr. Anshon said in her comforting voice.

I took a deep breath and let it out slowly, allowing my shoulders to sag as I tried to relax. "I'm tired all the time. No matter how much sleep I get, I'm exhausted. As you see on my chart, I've gained ten pounds. I know I probably shouldn't have, but I went online to try to find out what's going on with me and other than being relatively sure I don't have the Plague, I don't know what's wrong."

Just saying it brought me more relief than I thought possible. Dr. Anshon nodded and asked, "Are you pregnant? It sounds like the early months of pregnancy."

I shook my head and frowned. "No. I haven't missed a period, so we can rule that out."

She stood up and patted me on the shoulder. "Well, I think I know what you're worried about and while I can't say for sure it's not what your mother had, I can say let's get some blood and see what's going on so we can get you back to feeling on top of the world, just like a newlywed should, okay?"

"Okay. Sounds good."

She scribbled something on my chart and turned to speak to Jana. "Please escort Nina to the lab. Tell them I want these back ASAP."

Dr. Anshon turned back to face me. "Don't worry about my putting a rush on these tests. It's just that I don't want to see you worried any longer than you have to be. Give me a couple days and I'll give you a call when I find anything out. Until then, go home and enjoy that new husband of yours, okay?"

I nodded, thankful for her kind gesture and for making sure we found out what was going on as soon as possible. As I left with Jana to head down to the lab, I hoped what she found out was something simple and not the one thing that would put an end to all my dreams and happiness.

✧　✧　✧

JORDAN STOOD NEXT TO ME holding up a shirt in front of her. "Is it me?"

I examined the floral pattern next to her face and shook my head. "It's a little hippie for you, isn't it?"

Shrugging, she hung the shirt back on the rack. "I don't know. I thought maybe I should find a new style, but you're right. I'm not a flashback kind of chick."

"Why do you need a new style? I like this Jordan."

She frowned slightly and shrugged again. "I don't know. I just figured maybe I should change something up. You know, since Gage is out in LA with all those beautiful people, I thought maybe I should change things up a bit."

I smoothed her long blond hair away from her face and shook my head. "He's only gone for a little while, Jordan. That doesn't mean he's going to get all Hollywood on you. He liked you like this. Why would you think you should change?"

"I don't know. Just feeling insecure, I guess. I'm so very…well, New York, but what if he wants a sunny California girlfriend instead?"

"First of all, you do remember who we're talking about, right? He's more down-to-earth than any man I know. Second of all, you being New York is exactly what makes you so fantastic. This is the greatest city in the world, and you are its finest example of that greatness. You're gorgeous, smart, and genuine. No one talks the talk and walks the walk like you do. Don't change anything, you hear me?"

Nodding, she forced a smile. "Got it. Thanks for keeping me on the straight and narrow, Nina. I guess I was just feeling a little worried about all those stunning actresses he's probably seeing every day and night out there."

"He's got a stunning elementary school teacher right here, so who cares about those starlets? He wouldn't like them anyway, Jordan. More likely, he's simply doing his silent as a statue thing while he guards that kid Tristan got him set up with. It's just for a few months and then Mr. Teen Superstar will be done with his movie and back here and Gage will be back with you."

"You're right. Forget a new style."

I knew what was bothering her. Gage had dated an actress

before he came to work for me, but that was then. Now he had my beautiful best friend in his life. "That phony grin tells me all I need to know. You're worried about him meeting someone out there, aren't you?"

"Not just someone. Her. You told me he seemed pretty sad about her when he told you about them. What if he's not over her?"

Whipping out my phone, I Googled Angela Macaran. At the bottom of the first page of search results I found what I was looking for. Turning my phone toward Jordan, I pointed at the screen. "There. No worries, even though you shouldn't have any."

She leaned in and squinted at the screen. "Actress Angela Macaran on location in Paris with her husband." Looking up at me, Jordan smiled. "Well, I guess that's that."

I pulled my phone back and shut off the screen. "So no more talk of her with Gage. And forget about any of those other starlets. Got it?"

Grabbing another shirt from the rack near us, Jordan saluted me. "Got it, Sarge."

"Good. Now let's get out of here and get some lunch. There's a salad with my name on it."

Jordan began chastising me about my weight obsession, but my phone rang, saving me from her lecture. Looking down at the screen, I saw it was Dr. Anshon's office. "Hang on. I have to take this."

Turning away, I swiped to answer the call and pressed the phone to my ear. My heart raced as every worry I'd worked so hard to conceal came rushing to the surface. "Hello?"

"Nina, it's Jana from Dr. Anshon's office. She wanted me to call you to let you know you have nothing to worry about. The tests came back. You're pregnant."

All of a sudden, the world seemed to come to a dead stop. Pregnant? That was impossible. I hadn't missed a period. How could this be? "Jana, is the doctor sure? I haven't missed a month."

"Dr. Anshon was surprised too since she remembered you

saying that, but that's why she wants you to get checked out immediately. She had me make an appointment for you at a specialist OB-GYN who handles high risk pregnancies. Don't worry, though. It's not that she's convinced anything's wrong, but the fact that you haven't missed your period and the test still shows you're pregnant means this is a unique case. You have an appointment with Dr. Michaelson this Monday at eleven. If you need anything between now and then, don't hesitate to call, okay? And congratulations!"

I mumbled my stunned thanks and pressed End on my phone. The store felt like it was swimming around me, so I grabbed onto the clothes rack and shook my head to clear out the confusion. Pregnant. Tristan and I were going to have a baby.

"Nina, what's wrong? Who was that on the phone?"

"The doctor. She found out why I've been so tired lately."

A look of pure terror crossed Jordan's features, and she grabbed a hold of my shoulders. "It doesn't matter what she said. Tristan's not going to take the word of just one doctor. You've got enough money to fly around the world and find a cure for whatever it is, but I can tell by your face that it's bad."

Slowly, I shook my head. "No, it's not."

Jordan's expression of fear turned to one of confusion. "It's not? Then why do you look like you're going to fall over?"

"I'm pregnant. Dr. Anshon says I'm pregnant."

I'd never seen such happiness in Jordan's green eyes before. "Pregnant? Oh, my God! You're going to have a baby!"

Nodding, I smiled, still unable to believe it was true. A baby. We were having a baby.

"You look like you're going to pass out. Let's find you a seat."

I looked around for somewhere to sit and saw a chair near the dressing rooms. Making my way over to it, I barely kept myself standing my legs were so shaky. Sitting down, I dropped my bag and turned to face Jordan crouching next to me. "I wasn't expecting this. I guess I'm just surprised."

"Honey, I imagine you two have been at it like bunny rabbits, as all newlyweds are. If you aren't on the Pill, it was bound to happen."

"I actually stopped taking it when Tristan left. I was never very good at remembering anyway, so it was easy to stop. Then when he returned, I just never started again."

"Then you could be up to four months pregnant already?" she asked in amazement.

Lowering my voice, I explained, "I haven't missed a period. I wasn't holding out on you. I just didn't know. What if that means something's wrong?"

Jordan gently ran her hand up and down my forearm to ease my worries. "Don't think like that. There are women who go the entire nine months without missing their period. I saw one on the Discovery Channel who never even knew she was pregnant. She just thought she was putting on winter weight. Then one day she felt like she had bad stomach cramps and before she knew it, she was the mother of a perfect baby boy. She barely made it to the hospital. So don't worry. That little boy or girl growing inside you will be just fine."

"Thank God for your love of the Discovery Channel or I'd never know about these things," I said with a chuckle. This was why Jordan was the best kind of friend. Even in moments when I was terrified, she knew just what to say to make me smile and forget my worries.

"Damn right. Somebody's got to watch the medical oddities of this world. You know what this means, right? You don't have to be consigned to Salad Hell. Now you're eating for two."

"Oh, that's good because I wasn't looking forward to that. I should call Tristan and tell him."

"Good. Let's get out of here and get some real food in you. I'm starving too, so it's perfect timing."

I took my phone out and thought about how I'd tell Tristan he was going to be a father. This wasn't something to be done over the phone, so I stuffed it back into my bag. "I'm going to tell him at dinner tonight. That seems like a better way to break it to him."

Jordan took my hand as we walked out of the store. "Break it to him? I'm thinking he's going to be thrilled. I'm thrilled, and I'm only going to be an honorary aunt."

"Honorary nothing, Jordan. You've been more like a sister to me than my own sister ever has, so there'll be nothing honorary about it. From now on, you better get used to Aunt Jordan."

Beaming her trademark gorgeous smile, she nearly bubbled over with excitement as we walked among the crowds of people sharing the sidewalk with us that Saturday afternoon. "Ooooooh, Aunt Jordan. That's got a great ring to it. You know what this means. I have to get my apartment baby-proofed. All those sharp edges have to go. And I'll need to get those outlet cover things— you know, the clear plastic things you put right into the outlets."

"You have time. I haven't given birth to the little one yet."

She turned toward me and shook her head. "Miss I Might Be Four Months Pregnant, I don't have that long. Oh, I just thought of something. You may have missed the entire first trimester. That means you might not have to deal with morning sickness."

"I like that," I said with a smile. "Anytime I can avoid getting sick is good for me." Suddenly a thought tore through my brain. I'd never stopped drinking those chocolate cake martinis! I skidded to a stop and shook my head. "Jordan, I didn't know. I never thought for a second I might be pregnant. I just had a drink last night!"

"Honey, it's okay. You're not an alcoholic. Christ, you barely drink socially. I think you'll be fine even though you had a few drinks in the past few months. Now you know, so you'll avoid them until after when we all celebrate the arrival of the newest member of the Stone family."

"I just didn't know. I hope they didn't hurt the little guy," I said sadly.

"Don't worry about it, Nina. I'm sure your doctor would say the same thing. It's going to be okay. And what's this about a little guy? Am I going to be an aunt to a boy?"

"I don't know. I didn't even think before I said that. Do you think that means something?"

Jordan tugged on my arm to get us walking again. "I think it means you're hungry for a good meal, my treat. Today, we celebrate and we can talk baby names over lunch. Now let's go before all these people beat us to a table!"

CHAPTER THREE

TRISTAN

PULLING THE JAG THROUGH THE security gates at the bottom of the driveway, I ran my fingers over the black velvet box resting on the passenger seat beside me. Hidden inside it was a necklace I hoped Nina would love. Never very good at that kind of thing, I thankfully could count on Angelo, who seemed innately attuned to what looked good.

I turned the car off inside the garage and grabbed the box, stuffing it into my suit coat jacket. I hadn't figured out how I wanted to surprise Nina, but since she'd called me to let me know she was making a special dinner for us, tonight would be the perfect time to give her my gift.

Throwing my keys on the hall table, I yelled, "Anyone home?" as I made my way to the kitchen. The room was empty and there was no sign any cooking had happened there all day. Confused, I walked down the hallway toward our room, wondering if something happened to cancel our date. The fear that Nina had had another accident instantly made me worried, but before I could reach the bedroom, I heard her yell for me from the dining room.

"I'm in here, Tristan! Just give me a second to get everything ready."

Relieved that my worrying had been for nothing, I stopped a few feet away from the doorway, curious about what awaited me. After a long day at the office, I didn't care what food she cooked or what the special occasion was. All I wanted to do was spend time with my beautiful wife and relax.

Nina peeked her head out of the dining room, and I saw that sweet grin she put on when she was up to something. "I have a big surprise for you."

"Good. I have one for you too."

The mischievous expression slid from her face. "A surprise for me? What are you up to, Tristan Stone?"

"Does a man have to be up to something to surprise his wife?" I asked not-so-innocently. In fact, I had a reason to surprise her. I'd received the proceeds from the sale of my share of Club X three days earlier, so today was a perfect time to give her a present to show her how much I loved her.

"Yes, he does. That's okay, though, since I'm up to something too," she said with a wink. "Come in."

As I walked into the dining room, I saw our ordinary table and chairs and the same dinnerware we always used. Nothing looked different, as far as I could tell. Nina wore a yellow sundress, which was more formal than we usually were for dinner, but even that wasn't really different since she was barefoot, like she always was around the house. I took a seat and crossed my arms to pretend I was angry at her keeping secrets, even though I knew she was planning something sweet in her typical Nina way. "So what's this thing you're up to?"

Nina sat down in her chair to my left, just as she had that first night we'd had dinner together all those months ago. She looked just as she had that night, and for the first time since then, I wanted to replay that moment. Taking the serving fork in my hand, I served her a slice of ham. After scooping out some sweet potatoes and cauliflower onto her plate, I smiled at the recognition on her face. She remembered that night too.

As I filled my plate, she said quietly, "You better give me some more ham. I'm feeling like I need to eat some more now."

Never a big eater, Nina sounded like she was trying to tell me something with that, but if I was supposed to figure it out, I was missing the point. I placed another slice of ham on her plate and took a long look at her. Nope. She didn't look any different, but there was definitely something she was hiding.

"Suddenly a fan of ham tonight?" I asked. "I figured the ham was for me since it's my favorite."

"It is. I just think I should eat more."

I cut up a piece of ham and served it to her as I tried to figure out her cryptic hints, but it was no use. I had no idea what she was up to. "I hope I'm not ruining your surprise, but I don't know what I'm supposed to be getting here. Maybe we should begin with my surprise?"

She seemed to consider the idea for a moment and nodded. "Okay. I'm pretty curious what surprise you could have for me, so I can wait to give you yours."

Taking the jewelry box from my jacket, I slid it across the table toward her. "Surprise."

Her eyes grew wide at the sight of the black box in front of her. "What is this? What's this for?"

"Being you. I sold one of my businesses, and since I sold it for you, I thought it would only be right to get you something."

She opened the box and saw the diamond necklace Angelo had sworn up and down she'd love. Not that I doubted his choice, but it was a little extravagant for her taste. A diamond studded choker, the necklace dropped down to showcase three one caret diamonds that Angelo said would land just above her cleavage. Five carets total, it was fancier than what Nina usually wore, but I wanted her to see herself as I did.

As a goddess. My goddess.

"Oh, my…it's gorgeous, Tristan," she said in a voice full of awe as she lifted the necklace out of its velvet box.

I stood and walked behind her to help fasten it around her neck. "Here, let me help. Angelo says it's called something like a Venus necklace."

Nina held her hair up, and after I closed the clasp, I walked around to look at her wearing my gift. Just like a goddess. "I hope you like it."

She looked down and lightly ran her fingers over the diamonds resting on her tan skin. "Oh, it's beautiful." Looking up at me, she asked, "Why did you get me this? Not that I don't love it, but what's the occasion?"

"I sold my part in that club in Florida—the one I went in on with Chase. After I told him about wanting to get out of Top, I decided I didn't want to be in Club X with him either. So I contacted the other owners and they were happy to buy me out."

"So you just went out and bought me a necklace because of that?" she said with a shy smile, not seeing the connection.

"I wanted out of those businesses because of you. I'm a happily married man now, so I didn't want to be bothered with clubs and Chase."

"Was this Club X like Top?"

I knew where she was going with that question. "Not exactly. I just didn't have any interest in being involved anymore."

"You said the owners were happy to buy you out. What about Chase?"

Nodding, I explained, "Chase got himself into some tight spot with money, so he was happy to hear they'd buy him out too. Everyone won and everyone was happy."

Nina ran her fingers over the necklace again. "How come you never took me to this Club X like you took me to Top?"

Always with the questions. "Well, in the first place, I should never have taken you to Top, but I never took you to Club X because you meeting Chase was bad enough. I didn't want to introduce you to the owners, three eligible bachelors, one of whom reminded me of myself."

Arching one eyebrow, she looked at me intrigued. "So you worried I might like this man? I think you're crazy. There's nobody like you, Tristan."

"Well, not exactly like me, but the oldest brother Cassian

reminds me a little of me when I was younger. I couldn't be sure you wouldn't fall madly in love with him and never want to come back."

Nina rolled her eyes and made a clucking sound with her tongue. "You're silly. I would never do that. It's nice to know you were worried, though. Makes you even more charming, if that's possible."

"Good. I can always use a little more charm, especially with you, Mrs. Stone. So now you can tell me what you're up to with this surprise dinner."

From under the table, Nina pulled out a baby's onesie like the one we'd found in the attic and placed it on the table. Inside near the collar was my name sewn in so the nanny had known it was mine. I picked up the tiny blue outfit and ran my fingers over the fabric, noticing how soft the cotton felt. Lowering it, I looked at Nina, confused. "Did you find something in the attic today?"

Shaking her head, she smiled sweetly. "No. I just thought you should see that."

I looked down at the onesie and back up at her. "Okay. Now I'm feeling really stupid because I have no idea what you're trying to tell me, Nina."

"I just thought you should get used to seeing that around. We're going to have more around like that, but maybe in pink. I don't know yet."

Nina's words filtered through my brain, and my jaw dropped as her meaning became clear. A baby? She was having my baby. "When? How? How long have you been thinking you're pregnant?"

"About five hours. I had no idea. I went to see Dr. Anshon because I've been so tired these days. She did a battery of tests, including a pregnancy test, and her nurse called me today with the news. I was as stunned as you are. I hope after the stunned goes away you'll be happy, though."

I stood from my chair and pulled her into my arms. Cradling her face in my hands, I looked down into those beautiful, sweet eyes staring up at me in anticipation. "Happy? I'm out-of-this-world happy. I'm the luckiest-man-on-Earth happy."

"It's so early, though. We just got back and you're so busy at work. We never even discussed this and now it's possible we're a third of the way to becoming parents."

"A third of the way? Really?"

"It could be. I don't know how this happened." She stopped and a sexy smile spread across her lips. "Well, I know how it happened, but I never missed a period, so I had no idea."

Bending down, I kissed her on the tip of the nose. "All the better. Any guess as to when the big day is?"

She shook her head. "No idea. I don't know when we conceived. Dr. Anshon made an appointment with the OB-GYN for Monday, so hopefully I'll have some answers after that."

"Well, until we know, we're still in honeymoon mode, so I think I know exactly how I want us to spend the rest of this night."

She looked behind her at the table full of my favorite foods. "What about dinner?"

I slid my fingertips over her shoulders and down her arms as I nuzzled her neck. "I like the idea of breakfast in bed more. We can spend the entire night making love, and in the morning, I'll make your favorites and serve you right in bed."

Turning to face me, she gazed up into my eyes in that way that made me want to push aside the platter of ham and bowl of sweet potatoes and take her right there on the dining room table. I kissed her hard, loving the fact that this woman I adored was going to give me a child. That she was going to be the mother of my son or daughter. I didn't think I could love her more, but now as I stood there with her in my arms after what she'd just told me, I adored her truly as the goddess of my world.

"You have a way of sweeping me off my feet, Tristan Stone. I can't say no to you."

"Why say no to a night of incredible sex and then breakfast in bed?" I asked, unsure if she was kidding or that she actually considered saying no.

"Well, I have been pretty tired."

I knew from the lilt in her voice that even though her expression was serious, she wasn't. I liked teasing her as much as she liked teasing me, though, so I knitted my brows and said, "That's true. Perhaps I should tuck you into bed and get some work done. I have a few projects that really need my attention."

Nina stared up at me with a look of disappointment in her eyes. Finally, after a long moment of trying to figure out if I was teasing her, she asked, "You're not serious, are you? I was just kidding about being tired."

I shrugged and shook my head. "I don't know. You have been a little rundown lately."

"I do know, and I say we should head to the bedroom right now."

No matter how I tried, I couldn't keep the smile from my face. I loved when Nina acted like this. "So you're not tired?"

Slipping from my hold, she grabbed my hand and pulled me toward the hallway. "I've never felt more awake." Then she stopped and turned to face me. "And I knew you were teasing the whole time, by the way."

"You don't know teasing. I'll show you teasing, princess."

"Is that a threat, my dear husband?" she asked, her eyes wide as she looked up at me and her fingers toyed with the buckle on my belt.

I shook my head. "No threat. Just a warning."

Nina unbuckled my belt and pulled both ends of the leather out in front of me, tugging me toward her. Licking her lips, she smiled. "Oooh, you're in a playful mood. First one to the bedroom gets to tell the other what he has to do."

She turned to set off toward down the hall, but I caught her by the arm and held her there in front of me. Her playfulness made me want her right there, and I didn't want to wait. "Not tonight, baby. Tonight, we do it my way right here. I think this is probably the only room we haven't christened since we got back from our honeymoon, so it's about time."

I slid off my jacket and unknotted my tie before I began unbuttoning my shirt. All the while Nina stood there watching me with a wide-eyed look like she had that first night I brought her here. I threw my clothes over the back of the nearest chair and took her by the hand. She slid her hands across my chest and up over my shoulders and whispered, "Right here? All that food just gone to waste?"

Shaking my head, I lifted her by the waist and positioned her above my already rock hard cock. "No. Wrap your legs around me."

She did as I commanded, but added, "I still have panties on, Tristan."

I reached behind her as she clung to my shoulders and with one quick tear, ripped the cotton panties off her body. Throwing them onto the floor, I thrust my hips upward, sending the tip of my cock through her wet pussy. "Not anymore. Any more questions?"

"Just one. What are you waiting for?" she said with a sexy smile.

I slid my hands down to her ass and held her above me. Another thrust against her pussy and over her excited clit elicited a needy moan from her, and I said quietly in her ear, "Teasing, remember?"

She nudged up my body trying to outmaneuver my hold, but she was no match for my strength. "Don't tease, Tristan. You know I hate that."

Another thrust of my cock up over her clit and then back down again, this time so close to sliding inside her I had to pull her body away for a moment. In the past with other women, I could play this game for hours, enjoying the feel of them wanting something so badly it hurt and hearing them beg for my cock inside them, but Nina was different. Even when that part of me that loved control wanted to come out and play, I had no choice but to give in to her.

I adored her too much to not give her everything she wanted.

"I thought you wanted to play a little tonight," I said as I gently eased her down onto me.

She buried her face in my neck and whispered, "No more playing. Just give me what I need. Please."

Cradling the back of her head, I turned around to face the wall and gently pushed her back against it. I leaned back away from her and looked into those eyes so full of desire. "Don't let go."

She nodded, weaving her fingers together behind my neck, and I placed my palms flat on the wall as I looked down at her. Her expression was a mix of need and impatience, and so her. Those big blue eyes stared up at me and she bit her lower lip as I made her wait just a few seconds longer before I pushed my hips forward to send my cock deep inside her waiting cunt.

Her nails dug into the back of my neck as I plunged into her wet and willing body over and over, her heels pressing hard against the base of my spine urging me to fuck her faster and harder. My lips devoured hers. Each ragged thrust of my cock into her brought that tiny grunt into my mouth I loved to hear her make. I wanted to please every inch of her, to experience every part of her body that made her feel good.

She moaned, "Yes," against my lips, and I knew she was close. I slid my hands down the wall at the first twinge of her cunt tightening around me and cupped her ass to keep her on me as we rode each other toward that final moment when the two of us came. Her losing control and giving in to what I made her feel pushed me close to the edge. Biting my lip, she cried out as her release tore through her, and I watched as the woman I loved exploded around me, drenching my cock with her juices.

As the tiny tremors of her release began to subside and Nina eased her hold on my neck, I pushed her hard against the wall one last time, burying my cock inside her as I came so hard my legs nearly buckled underneath me. My fingers dug into her cheeks while I held on as my cock released into her.

Sweaty but satisfied completely, I looked down and kissed her on the lips, softer now. "And they say married sex is boring."

Nina smoothed the damp hair that clung to my forehead and pressed her lips to mine in one of her gentle kisses she always gave me after we'd made love. "They don't know this married couple, I guess."

Pressing my forehead to hers, I said quietly, "No, they don't. What do you say to continuing this in our bedroom, Mrs. Stone?"

"Well, since we christened this room, I guess we could head into the bedroom. Have anything particular in mind?"

Slowly, I slid out of her and placed her on her feet. "I think you on top would work," I said with a smile.

She stood up on her toes and kissed me, whispering, "Your wish is my command. Lead the way, Mr. Stone."

CHAPTER FOUR

TRISTAN

WITHIN A WEEK, NINA AND I received the good news that even though her pregnancy had been unconventional up to that point, she was fine and everything was going just as it should, except for the fact that we'd missed the first three and a half months of it.

And then she had her first ultrasound and our lives were instantly turned upside down.

I'll never forget the words the technician spoke as she slowly pressed her probe against Nina's abdomen. "I think we're looking at twins, Mr. and Mrs. Stone."

Twins. Two babies just like I'd dreamed about on our wedding night. The tech couldn't tell us the sex of the twins, but we were having two children. I shouldn't have been surprised. Twins obviously ran in my family, but I guess I'd always believed the general idea that they skipped a generation.

Nina looked up at me wide-eyed and squeezed my hand. "Twins! Just like that dream you had that night. Wouldn't it be incredible if it was twin girls, Tristan?"

"It would," I mumbled as I tried to decipher the small forms on the screen in front of us. Our children. Our daughters or our sons. Right there growing with each moment as we spied on them. Would they look like Nina with her soft blue eyes and light brown hair? Or would they be tall like me and have my eyes? Would they tend toward being quiet or would they have their mother's trait of loving to talk?

All of these thoughts raced through my mind as those two grey spots became real to me in that moment.

Nina beamed her happiness as the technician talked about how great a view we were getting and how our children seemed to be naturals at mugging for the camera. There were jokes about their innate good looks and charm too. All the while I stood there holding her hand amazed at the reality that we were going to have two tiny souls to add to our family in just a few months.

I drove us home as Nina talked and giggled about the babies. Still stunned, I headed in for a shower, hoping the water would help me get my head around the fact that our life together would be only us for a short time longer. I wished I didn't have to spend so much time at work. It would be years until we would just be Tristan and Nina again, but a vacation wasn't in the cards. Stone Worldwide needed me at the helm, especially with the new heart drugs making such great progress.

Nina sat on the edge of the bed gently running her hands over her belly and smiling like she had since the technician had given us the news. Looking up at me as I rubbed a towel over my wet hair, she said, "I still can't believe it. Can you? Twins. It's just so wonderful. I called Jordan while you were in the shower, and she nearly came through the phone she was so happy for us."

"I have to admit I'm having a hard time believing it," I said as I stepped into pajama pants. "I think we have some decisions to make."

"Like what?" she asked, her eyes filling with fear.

I sat down next to her, and cradling her face in my hands, kissed her on the forehead. "Do we want to keep this house or move? If we want to stay here, where do we want the nursery?"

Nina's fear evaporated and smiling again, she said, "I like this house. I know that sounds crazy since I hated it at first, but I want our kids to grow up here. As for the nursery, what's wrong with the room down the hall from this one? It will be perfect."

"When they get a little older, it won't be big enough, especially if they're girls."

"Then we'll buy another house, right?" she said as she ran her fingertips over my damp shoulders.

"Whatever you like. What about a nanny? We need to begin looking now."

Nina shook her head. "I told you I didn't want a nanny. I want to stay with the babies. The idea of a nanny makes me feel lonely for me and them."

I ran the towel over my chest and stood to throw it in the hamper. "Nina, two babies at the same time is a huge job for just one person. Why wouldn't you want some help?"

She thought about it for a moment. "I guess some help would be okay, but I don't want to be one of those moms who never spends any time with her kids. You never know how long you have on this planet, Tristan. I want to make sure my kids know I love them and like being around them."

Her veiled reference to her losing her mother worried me. Taking a seat next to her again, I asked, "Is there something you're not telling me—something the doctor told you?"

"No, but I was afraid I might have what my mother had and that made me realize I don't want to waste a minute of the time we have together with each other or our kids."

"Speaking of that, you know it's going to be a very long time before it's just us again. At least eighteen years. We'll be nearly fifty by the time the twins are off to college and we're back to being just the two of us."

Nina leaned back on her elbows and looked up at me mischievously. "What makes you think we'll just have two children, Mr. Stone? Maybe I want more."

I raised my eyebrows in not-so-fake surprise at the thought of a houseful of children. "You're talking to a man who until quite recently never thought he'd have any kids. Now it's more than two?"

"You're the perfect kind of man to be a father, Tristan. You say very little and when you do speak, it's usually some kind of order or something else serious. You'll be great!"

I leaned over to kiss her, loving the feel of her soft skin beneath my lips as I made my way over to her ear. "You make me sound like I'm no fun at all."

Nina ran her fingers through my hair and held my head where it was near her neck. "Mmm….I never said that. What you're doing right now is pretty damn nice."

Running my tongue over the shell of her ear, I nipped it with my teeth. "Well, I think we should see what else might be pretty damn nice. Don't you?"

Her hands traveled down my back, her fingernails gently raking my skin. In my ear, she whispered, "I like the way you think. Anything in particular you have in mind?"

I raised myself up on my hands and hovered over her as I slid my hard cock over the front of her already damp panties. Staring down into her eyes full of need, I smiled. "A few things. Maybe I can change your mind about being that serious guy."

✧　✧　✧

THE JAG FELT GOOD, LIKE I hadn't been in the driver's seat for ages and now I was back where I belonged. Every inch of the interior shined like new, and I slid my hand over the console to the paddle, ready to take this perfect blend of machine and beauty on the ride of my life. The highway stretched out before me begging to be mastered. The engine revved as I stepped my foot on the gas pedal, but I needed more speed. Wanted more speed. I shifted into third gear and the force of the car lurching forward pinned me back in my seat, the leather enveloping me as I pushed the speedometer past ninety toward a hundred miles an hour.

Nothing in this world—not money, not sex, not anything—made me feel this alive. The Jag hugged the road, eating up the asphalt as it flew by cars like they were standing still, each one a different colored blur as I raced toward some unknown destination.

Music played on the car's stereo, but the sound of my heart pounding from pure excitement drowned out whatever song was on.

Every ounce of me melded into this machine to make us one. It controlled me as much as I controlled it. I pushed it past a hundred and ten miles an hour, and the car took me along, holding me in to feel the rush of power as the wind slid over the roof, no match for the Jag or me.

I watched out the windshield as we passed trees that looked more like green and yellow streaks against the perfect blue sky that never moved. It alone held dominance over our speed. My hands gripped the steering wheel tightly, but tiny beads of sweat formed on my palms as my brain screamed, "Too much! Slow down! You can't handle this!"

It didn't matter if I could handle this. The Jag could. I shifted into fourth gear and the car topped a hundred and fifteen. Never before had I pushed it so hard to go so fast. I didn't know where I was going or why. All I knew was that I needed to go faster.

Over the sound of my heart pounding in my ears and my brain screaming warning after warning, I heard a tiny voice say my name. It was so quiet, but like a gentle whisper, it sounded like it was part of me.

"Tristan."

It repeated my name, adding, "Don't let us get hurt." I took my focus from the road for a mere second and looked to my right to see Nina sitting in the passenger seat. Her belly swelled from pregnancy, she looked up at me with those soft blue eyes, and even though I expected to see fear, I saw trust in them. She trusted me not to hurt her or the babies.

I opened my mouth to tell her she couldn't be there now, that I was driving too fast and one slip up could kill us, but before I could, I felt the car begin to lose control. What had been the smoothest ride I'd ever experienced quickly ended as the tires rode over rocks and gravel on the side of the road. We were out of control.

I was out of control.

Nina sat quietly as I fought to correct the car, but it was too late. The front bumper hit the guardrail, sending us into the air. She never screamed or cried. All she repeated again and again were the same three words. "Don't hurt us."

I didn't know how long I got to sit there staring into her eyes so full of trust and belief in me. Everything that had been so fast now seemed to move in slow motion. I reached out to touch her, knowing it would be the last good thing either of us would feel in this lifetime, and as I took her hand in mine, she whispered, "Tristan, save us."

THE BLACK JAG LAY IN a mangled heap in front of me. I had no idea how I could be standing there in one piece after the accident. Was I dead? My eyes quickly scanned every inch of the remnants of the car for Nina. She didn't seem to be anywhere in the car, but I couldn't move from where I was standing. My feet were like two blocks of cement.

"Nina! Where are you?"

She didn't answer. Was she out of the car somewhere like I was? Were we both dead? I lifted my right foot to take a step, and to my surprise, I could move it. Tearing around the tangled mess that was the Jag, I searched for her. Blood covered everything where she'd sat in the passenger side, and I stumbled back in terror.

"Nina! Don't leave me like this. Where are you?" I screamed but got no response.

I stood staring at the wreckage knowing what I'd done. Nina was dead, and I'd killed her. I'd denied her the one thing she'd asked.

People suddenly appeared surrounding me and the car. A man in a police uniform began to ask me questions about the accident. Was there anyone else in the car with me? What was my name? Was I hurt?

His words jumbled in my mind, and over and over I tried to respond but nothing came out. I cried out in pain, pointing at the blood on the car, but he simply walked away as he casually muttered words that chilled my heart. "Whoever it is, you killed them. You and your need for speed killed them. Happy now?"

And then I heard that same tiny voice call my name. "Tristan, help me..."

Pushing past the people still walking around the car and giving their opinions on the accident, I saw a hand in the brush a few yards away. Afraid at what I'd find but needing to know if Nina was okay, I slowly walked toward where the hand lay, seeing for the first time what I'd done. Her body lay mangled like the car, twisted into a form I barely recognized. Gashes carved into her face from when she crashed through the windshield seeped blood, but her eyes still stared up at me with that gentle look of trust in them.

"Tristan, help me," she whispered.

Her words hit me with a force that knocked me back onto the ground, and I put my hands out to break my fall, feeling wetness beneath them. She repeated her plea as I lifted my hands to dry them only to see them covered in red. I was sitting in a pool of Nina's blood.

Horrified, I scrambled to my feet, but it was no use. The blood continued to flow from her, rising inch by inch up my legs until it covered her and I couldn't see her anymore.

"Nina! Nina!"

I woke up covered in sweat, my heart pounding in terror as I struggled to escape my dream. Quickly, I turned to see if Nina was okay. She lay silently asleep with her hands curled under her chin like always, a tiny snore coming from her to tell me she was all right.

Pulling her toward me, I held her in my arms, afraid if I let go my dream would return. She mumbled something sweetly as she melded to my body, and then she was back asleep, never knowing the nightmare that had terrorized me.

I lay there for a long time staring up at the ceiling, my mind awash in confusion and fear. I knew what this was. I'd had nightmares for years since the plane crash. Doctor after doctor claimed they were the result of my unconscious mind's need to express the anxiety I kept hidden inside. They always added that if I'd just let out some of what I feared in my sessions with them that I'd surely see some improvement.

Let out some of what I feared. What I wanted to say to them was, "You live through a fucking plane crash and be impaled on a goddamned steel pole so you have no choice but to watch your family die around you, and then you tell me how much you want to relive any of that, assholes."

Needless to say, therapy was never successful and I stopped going after a while, preferring to fight my demons my own way. Then I'd had Rogers to watch over me. Now I was the one who had to do the watching over Nina and the babies, and somewhere deep inside me a tiny voice whispered that I couldn't do it. That I would fail them as I'd failed everyone who'd ever depended on me.

✦   ✦   ✦

"TRISTAN, ARE YOU PLANNING TO come to bed?"

Nina looked over at me as I sat at the desk staring out the window instead of doing the work I'd claimed I needed to do. I hadn't looked at my laptop for nearly twenty minutes. After my dream the night before, I wanted nothing more than to avoid sleep.

Padding up behind me, Nina wrapped her arms around my neck and whispered, "You look exhausted. Didn't you get any sleep last night?"

I turned to kiss her, loving the feel of her body next to mine. "I slept."

"Don't lie to me," she said sweetly. "I know you were tossing and turning for hours, and you weren't there when I woke up. Something wrong?"

"Not a thing," I said in my best lying voice.

She looked directly into my eyes. "You sure?"

"What could be wrong? I've got everything a man could want. Gorgeous wife, happy marriage, a couple kids on the way."

Nina studied my expression and after a moment gave me one of her gentle smiles. "I just thought maybe something at work was bothering you. You know if there was you could talk to me, right?"

"I know, but work is fine. Nothing going on there but the usual."

Moving around me, she nestled into my lap. "I know you, Tristan Stone. You're worried about something, so just spill the beans."

She stared into my eyes with a look so intent I knew I wasn't going to be able to brush her off. There was no way I wanted to tell her about my nightmare. Whatever madness my mind was cultivating had nothing to do with her and everything to do with me. Saddling her with it wouldn't do any good.

With as genuine a smile as I could muster, I took her face in my hands and pressed my forehead to hers. "There's nothing to worry about, Mrs. Stone. Your husband is fine. I have a lot of work to finish, so you better get yourself to bed. You're sleeping for three now, you know."

My attempt at being cute garnered a giggle from her, the kind that never failed to make me truly happy. "I don't think that's how it works. If that were the case, I'd never get out of bed."

Leaning back, I tapped the tip of her nose with my forefinger. "Well, then you better get yourself to sleep. I'll be there in a little while. Don't worry. I'll just be over here working hard."

She kissed me softly and nodded. "Okay. If you need anything, I'll be right over there. Don't stay up too late."

"I promise. I'll be there in just a few."

Whether Nina believed my lie or not, she headed back to bed and fell asleep in minutes. I wanted to be there next to her, holding her in my arms as I drifted off to sleep, but my terror at what thoughts my mind would create kept me fast in my chair. The numbers and details in the Ryder Pharmaceutical report on my laptop's screen swam in front of my eyes after a while as I fought against the need to sleep, but it was no use and I felt my eyelids begin to slowly lower.

The sound of Nina's muffled cries made my blood run cold, and I ran through the house yelling her name, praying I wasn't too late. My heart slammed against my chest at the fear I wouldn't find her before they hurt her.

"Nina! Where are you?" I shouted over and over, but all I heard in

response were her quiet pleas to find her.

I stopped at every doorway, my eyes frantically searching for any sign of her, but she was nowhere. No matter which way I ran, her voice remained the same soft cry so full of fear.

"Tristan, help me!"

Images of them pressing their hands hard over her mouth to stop her from letting me know where she was raced through my mind, filling me with the purest fear I'd ever felt. I saw her blue eyes wide with terror begging me to find her. I had no idea who they were or why they wanted to hurt her, but I knew they would.

I tore down the hallway toward our bedroom, but as I turned to enter the room, the door began moving away from me. I stuck my hand out to turn the doorknob, but it was just out of my grasp. "Nina! Come toward the door!"

Suddenly, her voice became clear, and she screamed, "Don't let them take me, Tristan! Save me!"

I ran full speed at the door, but it continued to move away from me, always just out of my reach. Nina still screamed her plea for me to help her over and over, but I was powerless. No matter how fast I ran, the door never came any closer. I pushed my legs to their limits, my muscles feeling like they were about to explode out of my thighs, but I was too slow.

Finally, a piercing scream stopped me dead in my tracks, and I looked down at my feet to see Nina's broken body lying there in a heap. Her blue eyes looked up at me so full of pain, still pleading with me to save her. She was so small there, so in need of my protection, and I'd failed her. Her dress hung flat against her hips, a sign that our children were no more.

I'd failed them too.

I fell to the floor and took her in my arms, but she was limp. They'd killed her and our children. They killed them and I couldn't stop them. Pressing my lips to her cold cheek, I kissed her and as the tears rolled down my cheeks, I whispered, "Nina, I'm sorry. I'm sorry. I tried. I swear I tried. Don't leave me like this. I tried. I tried."

CHAPTER FIVE

NINA

I WATCHED AS TRISTAN GRADUALLY began to look like all my pregnancy books said women typically felt. He never seemed to sleep, even though he came to bed each night exhausted. Every day I felt more wonderful than the day before, and he grew more and more worn-down. Finally, after weeks of him doing his walking dead impression, he came home with a renewed love of life. He sat down next to me on our bed, barely able to contain his smile.

"Hey, baby. You look like the cat that ate the canary. Did Stone Worldwide's stock go through the roof or something like that?"

Beaming, he shook his head. "No, nothing like that. Something even better. I have to go to London to handle some business, and I thought it would be a perfect trip for us to take together."

Tristan began to explain all the places we could visit after he finished working each day. I'd never really had any interest in London, but he made it sound so incredible that I couldn't say no, even though I wasn't sure a pregnant woman in her second trimester should be flying halfway around the world.

I took his hands in mine and raised them to my lips in a kiss. "Okay, you've convinced me. London it is. When do we leave?"

A look of complete relief washed over his features. "We'll leave tomorrow. The pilot already has his orders. All I needed to do was convince you. We'll be there for a week. I can't wait for you to see the London penthouse. It's in the West End and surrounded by great museums you can visit while I'm working, accompanied by bodyguards, of course. You'll love it!"

I hadn't seen him this excited in nearly a month. This was the side of Tristan I adored more than anything else in the world. When I saw those soulful brown eyes light up in delight like this, I couldn't help but love him even more. I wanted to make every day as good for him as life was at that moment for me.

"Then I can't wait! I'm wondering if I should contact my doctor first, though. I am carrying twins, and that isn't something necessarily commonplace. I don't want to put them in danger, Tristan."

Nodding, he appeared to get lost in thought. "Of course, of course. We need to call him tonight and find out. I can assure him that unlike on commercial airlines, I can have a doctor there for you every step of the way, if that's what you need." Jumping up from the bed, he moved toward the door as he continued, "I'll find out who can travel with us right now while you call your doctor. That way, no matter what he says, we're covered."

In seconds, excited Tristan seemed to turn to almost frantic Tristan. This wasn't like him at all. Standing, I grabbed hold of his arm before he raced out the door. "Hey, relax. We're good. I'm sure the doctor will say everything's a go. Just give me a little bit since I'm sure I'm going to get his service."

Taking my face in his hands, he nodded quickly. "This is going to be great for us. Just what we need. Some time away never hurt. I'll make a few calls so if your doctor says he's concerned at all, I can assure him it will all be okay."

With that, he was off and tearing down the hallway to arrange everything for our trip. His enthusiasm was contagious, and as I dialed Dr. Michaelson's number, sure I'd get his answering service, I had to smile. I was damn lucky to have a husband who surprised me with gifts and trips like Tristan did.

"Hello?" a male voice intoned into my ear.

"Dr. Michaelson? This is Nina Stone. Do you have a minute?"

"Of course, Nina. Are you feeling all right?"

"Oh, yeah. I'm fine. It's just that my husband wants me to go on this trip to London with him, but I wanted to make sure it's okay. I mean, I feel fine. I just don't want to do anything to endanger the babies, that's all. He said he can have a doctor with us for the trip, if you think that's necessary."

"Well, you're around five months pregnant. Usually I don't suggest my patients take long trips like that, especially with multiples, because it puts a lot of strain on your legs and feet."

"Oh. We won't be traveling commercial, so I'm sure I'll be able to get up and stretch whenever I need to."

As I said those words, I cringed a little. They sounded so pretentious. Traveling commercial. Who said that? Before I met Tristan, I'd never even flown on a plane, commercial or otherwise, and now I sounded like some Park Avenue snob.

"I was thinking that might be the case," Dr. Michaelson said with a chuckle. "I'm doubting the doctor will be necessary, but I think I'd feel better if I knew you had them along. How long will you be gone?"

"Just a week, so not too long."

"Okay, check in with my nurse when you return, and if you run into any problems, I want to hear from the doctor traveling with you. Other than that, take it easy, rest when you need to, and enjoy your trip."

"Thank you! I'll be sure to call the nurse as soon as I get back. Have a great night, Dr. Michaelson."

I ended my call feeling good about our mini-vacation. If my OB-GYN had been concerned, I would have reconsidered the trip, as much as I knew it would disappoint Tristan. The two souls I carried were everything to me, and if that meant I had to stay home, then I would have for their sake. London would always be there.

"Tristan!" I called as I made my way down the hallway. "Where are you?"

As the last word left my mouth, he came racing toward me with a worried look on his face. "Everything okay?"

"I'm fine," I said, trying to reassure my suddenly very nervous husband. "You're like a cat on a hot tin roof tonight. Are you sure everything's okay with you?"

Shaking his head, he smiled. "I'm sorry. I guess I'm just excited about this trip. What did the doctor say?"

"He's fine with me going. He likes the idea of a doctor being around, though, so if we have one that would probably be better. It's the twins thing, I think."

"It's all arranged then. We leave tomorrow morning. I'm going to do some work tonight, but you get some rest."

He turned to walk away, but I grabbed for his hand. "Wait a minute! You just got home. Can't we at least have some dinner? It's barely eight o'clock. I'm not tired yet."

"I'm not hungry. I'm sorry, but I have a lot of work to do. I need to be up-to-speed when I get to London."

Suddenly, a terrible thought crossed my mind. Tristan was acting weird. Was he doing coke again? Unlike the wife I knew a lot of women would be, I wasn't going to make myself sick wondering because I wanted to avoid some silly confrontation with him. If he was going to act bizarre, I was going to ask why.

Pulling him back toward me, I asked point blank, "Are you back to doing coke again? If that's what this acting crazy business is about, I won't tolerate it, Tristan. I told you I can deal with a lot of things, but a cokehead for a husband and father to my children is not one of them."

As if my words had alarmed him, he stopped moving and stared down at me. After a long moment, I finally heard him say what I needed to hear. "No, it's nothing like that. I've just got a lot on my mind lately. I promise I'm not back to the coke."

I wanted to believe him, but I knew there was something else, something more than work or things on his mind. That he wouldn't or couldn't tell me about what was troubling him made me sad. "Tristan, no matter what you're dealing with, you can tell me about it. I'm always here to lean on. I hope you know that."

Bending down, he pressed his forehead to mine and closed his eyes. "I know. You have enough to handle being pregnant. You don't need to hear me complain about work and other nonsense."

I wrapped my arms around him in an embrace and held him to me. "I don't care what it is or if you think it's nonsense. If it's bothering you, it's important," I whispered near his ear. "I hope you know that."

He squeezed me tightly, and I knew he was dealing with some burden, even if he didn't feel like talking about it yet. "Don't worry about me. I'm fine. You're the important one in this group, remember? I'm not the one carrying our children."

His hands slid down my body to cradle my baby bump, and he smiled as he looked down at it. "Speaking of that, we need to get to work deciding on what their nursery is going to look like after we get back from London."

I watched as he gently moved his thumbs over my stomach and smiled. "We don't know what the sex is, Tristan. I don't want to make it all pink and frilly, and then we have two boys or design it in all blue with trucks and airplanes, and then we have two little girls."

"Isn't there some unisex color for babies? What is it, green or yellow?"

"Yellow could be good. Maybe ducks?" I asked, knowing he was trying to get my mind off his odd behavior.

"Ducks? A room full of ducks?" he asked, looking up at me.

"It's cute. We can decide when we get back. Right now, I want to sit down and spend some time with you before you become chained to your desk again."

I didn't know what part of that upset him, but a darkness crossed his face by the time I finished my sentence. He forced a smile, but I knew something was wrong. I'd just have to wait for him to tell me.

✧　✧　✧

THE RICHMONT LONDON WAS JUST as wonderful as I expected it to be. I'd pumped Tristan for information about the room décor for hours on our flight, and for once, he seemed happier to be on the plane than he had back home. Far more formal than his other properties, the London location still impressed me. As at all his hotels, the staff greeted us with warmth when we arrived, and we were quickly shown to our penthouse suite.

Exhausted from the trip, I made a beeline to the nearest bedroom and flopped down on the king size bed, loving the feel of the firm mattress under my aching back. This having babies business was tough on the body, and Dr. Michaelson hadn't been wrong about me needing to stretch my legs on the flight. Even though I had gotten up and moved around a few times, for the first time, a plane ride had really tired me out.

I stretched my weary body as Tristan lay down next to me looking the very picture of relaxation. As he weaved his fingers in mine, I couldn't help but comment on this new Tristan. "I don't think I've ever seen you so happy after a flight. Is there something about London I should know because it seems to have a wonderful effect on you?"

Nuzzling his lips to the spot on my neck just under my ear, he chuckled. "No. I'm just happy to be here with you. That's all."

He trailed kisses over my skin to my shoulder as I took in the gorgeous design of the Royal Albert Suite. The canopy bed sat on the dark hardwood floor in the middle of the enormous room, surrounded by cappuccino brown walls on three sides and a full bank of windows on the fourth wall covered in pale gold sheers. Above our heads, the gold and paprika red colored canopy completed the design, making me feel warm and secure. The designer had done a wonderful job of making what could have been a sterile, large space quite welcoming, and I felt myself falling in love with this latest hotel of my husband's.

"Your properties are really stunning, Tristan."

"Our properties, princess. Ours."

I rolled over and saw him grinning at me. He said those words so easily, as if they were second nature to him, but I continually had a hard time thinking of anything he owned before we married as part mine. You could take the girl out of the middle class, but you couldn't take the middle class out of the girl.

"I don't think I'll ever get used to that, you know."

Tristan kissed me softly on the cheek and whispered, "Yes, you will. The hard part will be to make sure our kids don't get too used to it."

He was right. I'd always been so thankful my father had grounded my upbringing in our middle class values. I knew what it meant to work hard and achieve things. I was forced to account for my behavior, and when that meant I got in trouble, I didn't get what I wanted sometimes. But Tristan came from a world that smacked of entitlement. He'd always had everything he wanted.

"How are we going to do that? How did you learn to work hard and earn things?"

"My mother," he said with a smile. "She always made sure Taylor and I knew as easily as things could come to us, they could be lost. Unfortunately, my father had more influence over Taylor, but because I always gravitated toward her, my mother's ideas about money and possessions became my ideas."

Climbing on top of him, I sat across his stomach and looked down at the serious expression he always wore when he spoke of his mother. "She did a good job, Tristan. Money and things come and go, but it's the people we love that matter. We just have to make sure that our kids know that too."

He gently ran his palms over my rapidly expanding stomach and nodded. "We will. I promise I won't spoil them too much."

I twisted my face into a fake scowl as I remembered how he spoiled me from practically the moment we met. "I know you, Tristan Stone. When you care about someone, they always benefit. I just want you to promise me our children will understand the value of people as much as they do things. I want them to be like us, not your brother."

"Don't worry. They'll be wonderful, just like their mother."

Bending down, I smooched his cheek. "Such a smooth talker."

Sliding his hands around my waist, he settled his palms on my ass and pulled me into him. "Only with you, princess."

"Don't you have work to do, Mr. Stone? We didn't come to London to make love, did we?"

"Not really, but I just figured since we're here and in bed…" he said with a sly, sexy look in his eyes.

Just then, his phone vibrated in his pants' pocket. Rolling off him, I said with a giggle, "Perfect timing."

Tristan rolled his eyes and swung his feet off the bed as he answered his phone. "Yes?"

The person on the other end began to speak, and I instantly saw my husband's expression grow serious. He walked out of the room, leaving me alone in the Royal Albert Suite to think about how lucky I was.

TRISTAN'S MEETINGS TOOK UP THE entire next day as he worked to solve some problem that had occurred between the hotel and some high level government official on his last stay at the Richmont London. Apparently, a nervous hotel employee had unceremoniously nearly outed the man and his mistress, and now he was calling for an investigation into the legality of Tristan's ownership of the hotel in the UK under some arcane law no one had thought about for over a century. His attempts at business diplomacy left me with an opportunity to visit a museum or two, and I was drawn to one nearby, Pollock's Toy Museum.

A tiny building painted red and green on the main floor, it was actually two houses joined by three narrow staircases. As I walked through looking at the wide assortment of toys, everything from board games to Russian nesting dolls, I found myself in the Teddy bear and doll house room. The stuffed animals seemed to cover every inch of space, and near a tiny window a family of tan bears sat around tea cups having their very own tea party.

The room began to feel hot, and I knew I'd overexerted myself with all those staircases. As much as I wanted to stay and see the rest of the museum, my thighs began to cramp, so I quickly bought a Teddy bear in the gift shop and made my way back to the hotel, worried that I'd put the babies in danger because of my need to wander around instead of waiting for Tristan in the room.

I laid down on the bed, instantly feeling better as the pain in my legs eased, only to hear my phone ring. Lifting it off the night table, I saw it was Jordan and swiped my phone, happy to hear from her. "Hey, you! I was just resting after visiting a museum. What's up there?"

"Nothing. I just wanted to talk to a friend."

Her voice trembled, like she was holding back tears. "Jordan, what's wrong? What happened?"

"It's over," she said as she began to sob unlike I'd ever heard her before. "I just got off the phone with him. He's not coming back."

"Oh, honey, I'm so sorry. Why would Gage be acting like this? Did you have a fight?" I asked, heartbroken to hear two of my favorite people hadn't been able to make it work together.

"I don't know, Nina. I think he's found someone else. Maybe that woman he was with before." Jordan began to cry harder, making her words impossible to understand.

I hated hearing her like this. "Shhh, don't cry. It's going to be okay."

"I hate to be a bother, but I really need a friend at this moment. Would you be okay with me coming out there to hang out for a few hours? I'll leave before Tristan comes home so he doesn't have to deal with my weepy ass self, but I don't want to be alone now."

"I'm not at the Dutchess County house, Jordan. I'm sorry. Tristan surprised me with a trip to London."

Jordan sniffled. "Oh. Okay. It's no big deal."

It was a big deal, though. My best friend was sobbing into my cell phone over losing someone she cared about, and all I could tell her was that my husband had whisked me across the Atlantic Ocean on his private jet to his five-star hotel in London. All the times she'd listened to my sob stories and lent me a shoulder to cry on, and the best I could do was help her long distance.

"That doesn't mean I can't talk, though. I'm all ears."

"It's okay, Nina. I mean, it's got to be the middle of the day there. You have better things to do on your vacation than talk to me about something silly. Tell Tristan I said hello and call me when you get back, okay?"

"Jordan, it's all right. I'm just lying here resting up a bit. I have all the time in the world."

The phone fell silent for nearly a minute, but in the background I heard her crying again. When she returned, all she said was, "I have to go, Nina. I didn't mean to impose. I should just be a big girl about this and accept that it just was never meant to be. I'll talk to you when you get back. I love you."

Before I could assure her she hadn't imposed and I wanted to talk, she hung up. A lump formed in my throat at the idea of how sad she sounded. Why had Gage broken it off with her? I hated the very possibility that I'd brought them together thinking he was a great guy, but now he'd left her high and dry. Had he gone back to that Angela woman? As my mind launched into best friend mode, I thought about calling him but decided against it. That would only make things worse. I called her three times, but her phone went directly to voicemail.

She'd moved into hibernation mode. I knew all too well how that went. Alcohol, ice cream, greasy fast food, and too much TV on top of lying in bed and listening to sad songs would be on the menu for the next few weeks. There would be a constant loop of that Goo Goo Dolls song and Sarah McLachlan song from the City of Angels soundtrack, two of our favorites when we felt like love had kicked us in the ass once again.

As I imagined her alone in her apartment feeling like she didn't have a soul in the world to turn to, Tristan returned from his meeting all smiles. My frown stopped him dead, though, and racing to my side, he asked, "What's wrong? Did something happen? Why are you in bed?"

"Jordan and Gage broke up. I just got off the phone with her. She's heartbroken."

Tristan's shoulders sagged and he let out a deep sigh. "Oh. You had me scared there for a minute, Nina. I thought something had happened."

My frown deepened. "Something did happen, Tristan. Jordan is a mess about this. She really cared about him and he broke up with her over the phone from LA."

"I'm sorry. I get it. She's always been there for you. Why don't you call her back?"

"I tried. She's turned her phone off. I feel terrible for her. I set them up, and now he's bailed on her."

Pushing my hair back from my face, Tristan leaned over and kissed me. "It's not your fault, Nina. Maybe they just need some time apart."

I turned my face away from him. "Do you know what I would have said if someone told me that when we had any one of our fights? What would you have said to someone who said that to you?"

He gently pulled my face back toward him. "I would have told them to stay out of my life. I imagine you would have been more colorful."

"Tristan, I want to go back home. You won't miss me since you're in meetings most of the day, and to be honest, I'd feel better being close to my doctor. I went to a museum today and felt pretty rundown by the time I got through only half of it."

"Were the bodyguards with you? Are you okay now?" he asked, those brown eyes of his filled with concern.

"They were, but I didn't need them. I'm fine, but I think being close to Dr. Michaelson would make me feel better. We were only going to be here a week, so it's no big deal. We can come back after the babies are born. You won't miss me too much."

"Yes, I will, but I can't blame you for having a kind heart. I also can't blame you for wanting to be at home. Every female at the meeting today gave me a nasty look when I announced my wife who's five months pregnant came with me."

"I wanted to come, but I'm glad you understand why I want to go home early. You'll be back in a couple days anyway, and maybe I'll ask Jordan to stay with me until you return. That way no one is hanging out alone."

"Except for me," he said with a grin, teasing me.

"Are you trying to make me feel guilty?" I joked.

"No. Let's get you ready to go home. The sooner you're off the plane and back on New York soil, the better."

CHAPTER SIX
NINA

TRISTAN WAS RIGHT. BY THE time I got back to New York, I felt so much better. Being in my own house and my own bed, even if I was without Tristan, made me more comfortable. He'd be home in just a few days anyway, so I'd have a chance to spend some time with Jordan and help her ease her broken heart.

I called her as soon as I woke up the morning after getting home and convinced her to spend a few days out of the city with me. Indian summer had settled into the countryside around the house, and for late September, it felt more like the dog days of August. We could hang out in the garden during the day, swim a little in the pool, and relax at night as we figured out alternatives to ducks for the nursery, all the while I'd be doing what I could to make sure she didn't crawl into a hole of depression I already heard traces of in her voice.

Jensen opened the car door, and Jordan stepped out into the sun, her hand shielding her eyes like she'd already made a home inside that hole. Slowly walking toward me, she looked so dejected. Her normally bubbly self, that spitfire everyone knew and loved, seemed absent, replaced by someone so full of sadness.

I opened my arms to hug her, and she hung her head and just leaned into me. Wrapping my arms around her, I held her tight as she quietly sobbed. I couldn't help the tears as they welled up in my eyes. Jordan was always so tough, and now she felt so small next to me.

As she continued to sob, I whispered, "Hey, no crying allowed, lady. I'm a pregnant woman. I might just break down into a pool of hormonal mess."

Jordan leaned back away from me and shook her head, a tiny smile creeping onto her lips. "Pulling the pregnant lady in distress card on me? Lame."

"Come into the house and get yourself settled into your old room. Then you and I are going to relax like we're at the beach in this heat. How did you end up convincing your principal to give you three days off in the middle of the week?"

"I get a handful of days off a year, so I just told her I needed to use them. I must look like a truckload of shit because she didn't even ask why. She just gave me that fake smile she puts on for the parents and went back to shuffling through a stack of papers on her desk."

"Well, I think you should look at this as a vacation from real life. You name it and we'll do it. Deal?"

I bent down to pick up her bag and a twinge of pain shot up my right thigh. Grabbing my leg where the charley horse started, I groaned a little louder than I meant to. Jordan quickly took the bag from my hand. "You okay? That didn't sound right."

Straightening my back, I took a deep breath and shook my head. "No big deal. Just pregnant lady stuff. You try gaining nearly twenty pounds and see how you feel."

Jordan looked me over and nodded. "You really do look pregnant now. How are my two nieces doing these days?"

I ran my palms over my belly and grinned. "They're just fine. You do know they could be your nephews."

"I'm not doing so well with males these days, so I'm hoping for girls," she said in a voice tinged once again with sadness.

Before we both began crying right there on the front doorstep, I took her hand in mine and pulled her into the house. "Come on. We've got relaxing to catch up on and I want your help with picking a design out for the nursery."

As she walked through the entryway with me, she mumbled, "Since they're going to be girls, I say go with pink. Case closed."

I twisted my face into a grimace and rolled my eyes. "Just come on."

LYING ON MY SIDE ACROSS Jordan's bed, I listened as she explained her breakup with Gage and tried to figure out what had happened to something that had started out so great. Every word was laced with the familiar insecurity every female of dating age experienced, some more than others, when a relationship broke up and there wasn't a shred of closure to be found.

"I thought we were good together, Nina. I mean, I never gave him a hassle about being out in LA, even though I missed him a ton. I may have felt insecure because of all those stunning women out there, but I didn't think I was screaming 'I'm needy' all over the place." Jordan turned her head and stared out the window. Lowering her voice, she said quietly, "Maybe I was and I just didn't know it."

Reaching out, I squeezed her arm. "Don't do this, Jordan. Of all the people I know, you are the least needy."

She turned back to face me wearing an expression filled with pain. "Then maybe that's it. Maybe I didn't need him enough. Was I supposed to tell him I missed him and couldn't wait until he came back all the time? That's just not me. I missed him and told him that, but I wanted him to know he had space to do what he needed to."

"What did he say when you talked to him the last time?"

"He was acting weird. I heard it in his voice. He sounded distant, but I didn't want to think it was anything. I knew something was wrong when he picked a fight with me. All I did was ask how things were going and when filming would be done, and he blew up at me."

"What did he say?"

"He said, 'I can't say, Jordan. Maybe we should just play it by ear, and when I get back to New York, we can get together and talk. I don't really have time for this right now.' You know me. I wasn't going to let it go at that. I said that I thought we were more than just phone pals who may or may not talk when he returned, and then it just escalated from there."

That Gage would say he didn't have time for her didn't sound like him at all. What the hell was going on with him? I didn't want to say it, but my mind immediately went to the idea of him getting together with his ex-girlfriend and then feeling guilty. Trying to sound sympathetic, I said, "It doesn't sound like it's totally over, though. Maybe he was just having a bad day."

She shook her head and frowned. "No. When I told him that I thought he was acting strangely, that all of this seemed so sudden, he accused me of not trusting him. Before I could say anything, he said this wasn't working for him and hung up."

"Oh." That definitely didn't sound like the Gage I knew. And it didn't sound good.

"Yeah, oh. So your single friend Jordan continues to be single. Forever, it seems."

I sat up and shook my head. "That's nonsense. If you want to not be single, there are millions of men who would bow down at your feet to help you with that. Don't let this one get to you."

Jordan nodded her agreement, but I knew she didn't think that way. Love just always seemed to elude her, even though I couldn't imagine another person deserving it more.

"I just don't know, Nina. I thought Gage could have been the one. We had a good time once we finally got to know one another. It felt right. He wasn't some asshole who expected me to play dumb to make him feel like a man or some guy who just played around. I just don't know what happened. That's the worst part. One day we were okay, and then the next day we're done."

"I know it's hard to believe now, but he's not the only guy out there. You're the greatest person I know, Jordan. I mean that.

You're smart and funny, and you have a heart like no one else."

Wiping a tear from her eye, she said quietly, "Then why is it everyone else has found someone but me? You know what I want? I want what you have. Not the money or all that, but someone like Tristan. He's so crazy in love with you. I want that. I want a guy who calls my friends like he did when he called me that night you left for Italy. I heard something in his voice then that I've never heard in any man I've ever been with."

I tried to lighten the mood a little. "It was probably utter frustration with me. I was such a fool for doing that."

"No, it wasn't that. It was…" She stopped and thought for a moment, and then she got an intense look in her eyes like she was searching for something. "You should have heard him, Nina. It was like he'd lost part of himself, like he'd lost something so dear to him he couldn't go on unless he found it. I want that."

Instantly, I missed Tristan more than I had since Jordan came to visit. He'd be home in a little over a day, but at that moment, I wanted to feel his arms around me as we lay in bed and I talked his ear off about something or another while he just smiled at me, all the time quietly listening.

"You're lucky, Nina. Tristan would protect you with his life. You mean as much to him as he means to you. That's the real thing. I want that."

"You'll get that. You will. Just because it wasn't Gage doesn't mean it's not out there for you, but I'm not convinced it's totally over with him either."

Sadly, she said, "I wish it wasn't."

I took her hand in mine. "Remember what you always say— good things happen to good people."

"I want to believe that. I do believe that. I just don't know why when everyone else around me is finding love, I'm still the same old single Jordan."

"When it happens, you'll see that it couldn't have happened at any other time. Then it will be everything you deserve."

As the tears rolled down her cheeks, Jordan smiled. "Is this what happens with pregnancy? You get all philosophical?"

I stuck my pregnant belly out and with a chuckle said, "I'm doing my best mom work here. How's it sound?"

Jordan wiped her eyes and sniffled. "It sounds like my nieces are going to have a great mom."

"Speaking of the babies, you need to help me figure out something other than ducks to decorate the nursery. It has to be unisex, so any ideas?"

"Why unisex? Aren't you finding out the sex of the babies before they're born?"

"No. Tristan and I decided to leave that a mystery until that day."

"New age hippies," she said with a laugh. "Well, if the unisexual ducks aren't good, we'll have to come up with something else."

"You up to checking out some nursery designs? I'd like to get going on this soon. I only have a few more months, and that's assuming they don't come early. Twins often do, so I may not make it to full term."

She swung her legs off the bed and reached out to take my hand. "Lead the way. Those ducks have met their match."

Her words were still tinged with sadness, but I hoped that sometime soon she'd see that even though Gage and she broke up, love was still out there for her as long as she believed it was.

Jordan and I spent hours searching for ideas for the nursery, and we were shocked at how much grey was popular in unisex nursery design. Grey and white, grey and yellow, grey and green—it all looked like some depressing winter palette had taken over the baby world.

Clicking on a page that claimed to be the Latest in Nursery Design, I saw more grey. I turned to Jordan sitting next to me at the dining room table and said with disappointment, "Why are all these babies' rooms designed to look like January in the northeast? I think

I'd grow up depressed if I had my first months in a room like this."

"You can't put my nieces in a room like this, Nina," she said as she pointed at the grey and mustard yellow design on my laptop's screen. "Damnit, you can't even put my nephews in that room. I think the Puritans had more colorful nursery ideas."

Everything was so washed out. I wanted a nursery with flair, and all I saw page after page was blah. I clicked on another link and saw a jungle themed room. Tristan might not be crazy about green, but this design was cute. I could imagine our children in their cribs surrounded by monkeys, giraffes, and elephants all frolicking in their jungle habitat.

"What do you think of this one?" I asked as Jordan leaned in to check it out. "The room could be painted white with a dash of vibrant greens and yellows."

"It's sure as hell better than that washed out stuff we've seen for hours. I say go with this one. At least it won't lead to your kids being depressed."

"It's settled then. Jungle it is. As soon as Tristan gets home, I'll show him and convince him that jungle is a good look for the nursery. We're going to have to go shopping for baby furniture too. I doubt he'll want to do that with me, so I hope you're up to it."

"You know me. I'm always up for shopping. We'll make a day of it and do lunch too."

Jordan seemed more upbeat than she'd been since she arrived. I didn't have the heart to tell her that just touring a tiny toy museum had worn me out, so a day of shopping probably wasn't going to happen. Instead, I just nodded and listened as she happily planned our day out, pleased she was focused on something other than the breakup with Gage.

✧   ✧   ✧

"NINA, THIS BUSINESS HERE IS much more involved than I thought it would be, so I'm not going to get home tonight like I planned."

Tristan's news right after I woke up the next morning started my day off pretty badly, but I understood. It didn't mean I was happy about it, though. Rubbing the sleep from my eyes, I asked, "When do you think you'll be home? We have a doctor's appointment soon."

"That's not until right before Halloween, so I'm sure I'll be home by then. That's nearly three weeks from now. I'm hoping to be back by next week."

"Oh. Okay. Jordan's here with me, so I have company. We picked out a nursery design. I'd hoped to show it to you since we have to go shopping for furniture soon. I want to get that done and completed before I get too far along."

"Don't be sad, princess. I promise it will go by fast. In the meantime, we can get the room designed by anyone you want. Pick a designer and let them go at it."

"Trying to buy my happiness?" I asked, sounding sharper than I'd intended.

"Don't be upset, Nina. I won't be gone long, and I'm only a phone call away."

"You're thousands of miles and a huge ocean away, Tristan."

"We can Skype, if you like. How's that sound?" he asked, being so sweet I couldn't stay angry at situation.

"Okay, but it's not the same. I don't think cuddling up with my laptop is going to be like lying here with you."

"I know. I miss you too. I'd rather be there waking up next to you, watching you snore as you sleep and holding you in my arms. I promise it won't be long."

"Okay, but I don't snore. We need to establish that before you hang up the phone and go into another meeting," I joked, trying to make up for being so surly just a minute before.

"You do snore, but that's all right. I love that part of you too. Tell Jordan I said hi, and I can't wait to be back with you as soon as I can."

"I love you, Tristan. When we Skype you'll see I'm getting as big as a house. The babies must be getting big now. At least I hope that's it or I'm just getting super chunky."

"I'll call you later, and don't worry about what you look like. You're gorgeous, so you have nothing to worry about."

I told him I loved him again and heard him say it one more time before I pressed End on my phone and laid back on my pillow. At least this time our time apart wasn't going to be for any terrible reason. I hated that he would be gone for another week, but he was the CEO of Stone Worldwide. I had to understand this kind of thing was going to happen once in a while. As long as we were together for the babies' births, we could handle a few days apart as I busied myself with designing the nursery and bolstering Jordan's spirit.

AND THEN ONE WEEK TURNED into two. And two weeks turned into three.

By the time late October came around, the jungle themed nursery was complete and Jordan was back on her emotional feet again. She'd even gone out on a date with a guy she'd met one night at Tony's Pizza Heaven. It hadn't been the beginning of a whirlwind romance, but it was a new beginning for her.

I had gained at least another five pounds, but other than feeling like a beached whale, I was happy, except for missing Tristan. Each day I hoped when he called that he'd say he was coming home, but the laws of the UK continued to make that an impossibility.

Jordan had to go back to school after our first few days together, so I spent my time doing what all the pregnancy books called "nesting." Most days it involved an odd need to clean and straighten things, which confused Maria, but she was sweet about it, even if she couldn't understand why I trailed behind her tidying up rooms she'd just finished cleaning.

I also spent an hour or so swimming each day. I'd read in one of my library of pregnancy books that it was a great activity for pregnant women since it allowed them to get exercise, but it wasn't hard on the body.

So every day right around two in the afternoon, I put on my maternity one piece bathing suit and marched myself down to the pool. Just a few laps at a time with a rest in between each set, but it made me feel good, especially concerning the cramps in my legs, which had become an everyday occurrence. Sometimes the babies would move around as I swam, making me feel like the three of us were getting exercise. I'd talk to them and tell them how much their father and I couldn't wait until we finally got to see their sweet faces, the sound of my words echoing in the pool area.

Like every other day, I climbed out of the pool after my swim on the last Friday before Halloween, tired but feeling good. Looking up at the clock on the far wall of the room, I saw it was close to three o'clock. Jordan would be back within two hours, and Tristan would be calling soon, hopefully with the news that he was finally coming home.

Grabbing my towel from the lounge chair, I bent down to dry my legs and feet, barely able to reach my toes because of my belly. As I wondered if I'd ever get back to my pre-pregnancy size, the room began to spin. Slowly I raised my head, remembering that lightheadedness was normal for pregnant women and all the books had said to move slowly to avoid making the dizziness worse, but it was no use. I reached out for the chair to keep my balance but missed it. The last thing I saw was that chair at eye level and the Italian tile floor of the pool deck coming up to greet me.

CHAPTER SEVEN

TRISTAN

DARKNESS SURROUNDED ME AS I felt my way along the smooth wall, unsure of where this was or how far away the exit was. The heat pressed down on me, making it hard to breathe, and sweat rolled down from my scalp into my eyes. I stopped to wipe my forehead with the back of my hand and then continued feeling my way, hoping my fingers would touch a doorframe or corner sometime soon.

My eyes strained to sense even the tiniest speck of light, but there was none. This was like swimming in a pot of black ink. I called out for Nina and the kids, hoping to hear their voices to lead me out of this darkness, but my pleas went unanswered. I had no idea how long I'd been here. Hours? Days? I didn't have a clue. How far I'd walked down this hallway I didn't know either. My legs ached, but I didn't know if that was because of the heat or how far I'd gone.

My drenched collar rubbed against the skin on the back of my neck, and with each step, sweat rolled down my back beneath my shirt. Why was it so hot?

"Nina! Where are you? Can you hear me?"

Again, there was no answer from the darkness.

I felt the wall end and stopped, hope springing up inside me. Pushing my hands out in front of me, I searched for another wall or anything to guide me, but I felt nothing. I spread my arms to my left and right, but suddenly the wall that had been there for so long was now gone.

"Nina! Answer me! Tell me where you are!"

The faintest sound of a baby's cry hit my ears and sent my body into overdrive. Nina and the kids were there, somewhere in the distance, and I had to find them. I lunged forward and felt the ground drop away beneath me. Flailing to grab onto anything, I fell through the darkness as the baby's cry became louder and louder with each passing second.

The sound of my phone ringing pulled me from my nightmare, and I sat up trying to shake the memory of it from my mind. Every time I laid my head down I had a different version of the same nightmare—Nina needed my help, and I couldn't find her, no matter how hard I tried. This one included a baby, but it was the same nightmare that had haunted me for weeks.

Swiping my finger across the face of my phone, I held it up to my ear and heard a female voice. "Tristan? Tristan, are you there?"

"Nina?"

The voice on the other end fell silent. When I heard it again, I knew something was wrong. "It's not Nina. Tristan, it's Jordan. There's been an accident."

Suddenly, it felt like all the oxygen had been sucked from the room and I was left hanging suspended in midair with nothing to grasp onto. One thought ran through my mind—I had to get home. Jordan began explaining what happened, but I wasn't listening anymore. Everything was moving in slow motion, even though I was racing around the room mindlessly throwing things into my suitcase. It was like moving under water in one sense and fast forward in another.

"…but I don't know how long she was there. She usually took her swim between two and three, so I don't think it was long. I don't understand why this happened. She told me you hired more security, so why didn't they see her lying there on the floor?"

I stopped dead and stared at the Teddy bear Nina had gotten me from the toy museum. Quietly, I answered Jordan's question with the terrible truth. "Because of me. I turned off the security cameras in the pool area months ago." I reached out and ran my finger over the soft fur of the stuffed animal staring up at me. "Because of me."

Jordan's voice shook with fear. "They brought her to the hospital near the house, but her doctor wanted her at Lenox Hill. I'm here, and her OB-GYN is in with her now. Tristan, you need to get here."

"I'm coming. Tell her I'll be there as soon I can."

"Tristan, didn't you hear me? She's unconscious."

I let the suitcase slip out of my hold onto the floor next to me. "What?"

"I don't know how long she was lying there, but she was unconscious when I found her. Just come now. Please."

My head felt like it was spinning as each word sank in. Nina needed me, and I was an ocean away. My pregnant wife had returned home alone, and I'd done nothing but give her excuses why I had to stay in London.

Swallowing hard, I said, "I'm coming, Jordan. I'll be there as soon as I can."

"I'll be here right by her side, so don't worry about her being alone. I'm here. I'll see you in a few hours."

The phone went dead, and I mechanically slipped it into my pocket, my brain shutting everything else out but thoughts of Nina and how once again I'd failed her when she needed me most.

✧   ✧   ✧

"Mr. Stone, it's good to see you," Dr. Michaelson said in his bedside manner voice. "Let's talk."

I looked past him through the hospital room doorway and saw Nina sitting up in bed. Relief washed over me as she smiled and waved. "Can I see my wife first?"

"I'd like us to talk before we go in and see her," he said in a tone that told me something was wrong.

I turned to face him and studied his expression. A middle aged man with salt and pepper hair and faded green eyes, his forced smile didn't reach up to those eyes, a telltale sign he was putting on a good face in front of Nina. Nodding, I followed him to a lounge down the hall and sat down across the table from him.

"Today's episode wasn't a major event. Nina's blood pressure fell, causing her to pass out. Her blood pressure is routinely low, but I've monitored it since she arrived here, and it's not in a range I'd like."

"What are we talking about, Doctor?"

"I'm going to order her to stay home for the remainder of the pregnancy, assuming the ultrasound we do tonight is okay. She's going to fight this, but I want you to be vigilant about it. I'd feel much better about this if we could get those babies to at least seven months, but I'm worried that won't happen without her staying put."

"And if the ultrasound isn't okay?" I asked with a lump in my throat, terrified at what he'd say next.

"Then I'm going to admit her."

"Okay. Assuming she's on bed rest, I'm going to move us to the penthouse at the hotel. I want her close in the city to me at work and the hospital here."

"I think that's a good idea. Now let's go deal with Nina, who I'm pretty sure is going to put that pout of hers on when I tell her the good news."

"Don't worry, Doctor. I'll figure out some way to make her happy with the arrangement."

Dr. Michaelson was more correct than he could have imagined. While Nina only showed him a little of her disappointment at his news, it wasn't long after he was gone from her room that her typical Nina pout was out in full force.

"He's going to make me stay in bed for weeks, or even worse, stay here," she said sadly. "I should be at home, not in the hospital."

Jordan took a seat next to her on the opposite side of the bed and leaned in to kiss the top of her head. "It's okay. It's just for a few weeks, Nina. My nieces are homebodies. They just don't want to go out anymore."

Nina wasn't buying any of her friend's attempts to make the situation lighter. Frowning, she mumbled, "Staying at home all day will be like being in prison."

"If you're on bed rest, we'll move to the penthouse. That way, you're closer to me at work and the hospital when it's time," I said, hoping she'd see we could make the best of a less than perfect situation.

Her eyes flashed her unhappiness as she turned to face me. "The penthouse? That's not home. I've never spent more than a few days at a time there." As she began to cry, she buried her face in her hands. "Now I don't even get to go home if they let me out of here."

I softly stroked her cheek, but she just shook her head. "It'll be okay, Nina. It doesn't matter where we are as long as we're together, right?"

She just continued to shake her head and slunk down under the covers. "I guess."

Jordan signaled she wanted to speak to me, so I kissed Nina and followed her friend outside into the hallway. She looked almost as sad as Nina standing there with her arms folded and a frown on her face.

"Nina seems really depressed, Tristan. What can I do? Tell me what to do. I hate seeing her like this."

I wasn't sure what to do. Nina was always the one whose bright outlook kept me positive. Seeing her so down unnerved me. "Whenever you can come by the penthouse, you're always welcome, Jordan. She needs you now more than ever to be the person you've always been. She needs to hear that good things happen to good people."

Silently, I admitted to myself I needed to hear it too. I'd thought nearly dying in that plane crash had been the most frightening thing I'd ever have to face, but the news that something had happened to Nina and the babies made my blood run cold as I stood there in that hotel room thousands of miles away. I never wanted to feel that helpless again. I needed to believe we'd all come out of this okay.

Jordan lightly squeezed my arm, bringing me out of my thoughts. "It's okay, Tristan. She's going to be fine, and soon there will be four in the Stone family out there in the country. Don't worry."

"Thanks. I hope you're right."

I gave her some time with Nina, hoping that she knew something to bring her out of her funk. I hated seeing my wife like that and not having a goddamned idea how to make her happy. I couldn't go against her doctor's orders, no matter how much I wanted to whisk her away to Venice or even London and hole up in one of our hotel rooms, pushing the world and all its troubles away as we lay in bed in each other's arms.

As I stood in the doorway watching Jordan try everything to bring a smile to Nina's face, the nurses came to take her downstairs for an ultrasound. I followed, praying to God we'd find out everything was okay with the babies, not only for their sake but for Nina's. Bed rest in our penthouse would be hard enough. Bed rest in a hospital would be torture for her.

Either way, I'd be there right next to the woman I loved. If it was in a hospital, then Lenox Hill would have to get used to me sleeping in the chair next to her bed.

While the ultrasound technician readied herself for Nina's examination, I took her hand in mine and brought it to my lips in a kiss. Bending down, I whispered in her ear, "No matter what, I'll be by your side. If you have to stay here, so do I."

She looked up at me and her face looked so sad. "You know you can't do that, Tristan. You need to be at work."

With the pad of my thumb, I wiped a tear from her cheek. "I need to work, but this is the twenty-first century, Mrs. Stone. They call it telecommuting. As long as I have a laptop and Michelle helping me at the office, I can handle everything I need to. But even if I can't work here, if you're here, I'm here."

Nina closed her eyes and whispered, "Oh, Tristan. What if something's wrong with the babies? What if they make me stay here for weeks? I hate being in the hospital. The hospital is for sick people."

I cradled her face in my hands and placed a kiss on her forehead. "We can't do anything but what we have to, Nina. We can handle this. The four of us will be together, no matter what."

Sniffling, she opened her eyes and nodded. "Okay. Together, no matter what."

The technician tapped Nina on the shoulder. "You ready? Let's see what these two are up to these days."

Just like before, she squirted the ultrasound jelly across Nina's very pregnant belly and began running the tool across her skin. Quickly, we saw our two children, perfect and content on the screen, but something was wrong. I saw it in the technician's expression. She continued to do the test, concentrating on the left side of Nina's stomach with a back and forth movement as the sound of the baby's heartbeat seemed to grow faster and faster.

Nina sensed something was wrong too. "What is it? Is there something wrong with her?"

"You already found out the sex?" the ultrasound technician asked, clearly trying to calm us as she moved her tool to the other side of Nina's belly.

"No. We're going to let it be a surprise," Nina said with a tiny smile.

"What color are you making the nursery if you don't know the sex?"

Nina looked up at me. "It's a jungle theme with monkeys and hippos and giraffes. Lots of green grass and blue skies, perfect for a boy or a girl."

"I think if I could do it all over again, I'd wait until my son was born to find out he wasn't a she," the technician said as she slowly guided her tool back to Nina's left side. "In the end, it doesn't matter anyway when you look at your baby for the first time and realize there's a little version of you right there in your arms. Boy or girl, they're the light of your life."

As she spoke, the sound of the left baby's heartbeat grew faster as once again she ran her exam tool over that part of Nina's stomach. I knew even though she was trying to keep Nina distracted, she was concerned about something.

Suddenly, she stopped and turned off the machine. "All done. Your doctor will have the report in a little while. Let me get the nurse to take you back to your room."

And with that, she left.

"I think the one on the left is a little jumpy," Nina said with a nervous chuckle as she eased herself off the exam table and into the wheelchair. "Not much for being on the small screen."

"That one is more like me then," I said with a wink.

We waited for another hour to see Dr. Michaelson, but in the end, he saw no reason to keep Nina in the hospital. The heartbeat of the left baby was a little fast for his preference, but with regular doctor visits, he believed if there was a problem, we could handle it.

Alone together in the hospital room, I sat on the bed as Nina got dressed to go to the penthouse, exhausted but relieved. She came out of the bathroom and without a word, she walked right toward me, and I took her in my arms.

"Tristan, I was so afraid something had happened to them. I don't want to mess this up. I'm sorry."

Leaning back away from her, I shook my head and looked into her beautiful blue eyes so full of concern. "You have nothing to be sorry for. You did nothing wrong. We're going to the penthouse and everything's going to okay. I promise. You better get used to me being around a lot. By the time these kids get here, you're going to be sick of me."

Nina kissed me and hugged me tightly in her arms. "I could never get sick of you, Tristan. Never."

CHAPTER EIGHT

TRISTAN

NINA LAY SLEEPING NEXT TO me, all curled up like always, her head tucked into the crook of my neck and her warm breath against my skin. "Good morning, beautiful," I whispered next to her cheek as my alarm sounded it was time to wake up.

Mumbling something into my shoulder, she rolled onto her back. "It can't be morning already. I swear somehow nights are shorter now that I'm as big as a house."

"That's because you were up and down all night going to the bathroom," I said with a smile as I placed a kiss on the tip of her nose.

She turned her head to face me and frowned. "You were up all those times too, and now you have to do work all day."

I lifted her chin to kiss her full on the lips. "Don't worry about me. I don't plan to work all day. Not with you right here with me."

"But don't you have things to do? I don't want to ruin anything in your work. They expect you to be the CEO."

"Exactly. I'm the CEO. If I want to take a few hours off to watch a movie with my wife in the middle of the day, then that's what's going to happen."

"A movie?" she asked with a smile. "Is that what you have planned for today?"

I sat up and swung my legs off the bed. Turning back toward her, I nodded. "Yes. Well, that's one thing. That reminds me. I better make sure room service has Jiffy Pop. Can't have a movie without popcorn."

Nina's eyes filled with tears. "Jiffy Pop? That's so sweet. Come here, you incredible man, and give me a kiss."

I twisted around to kiss her and then leaned over to place a kiss on her swollen belly. "And that, my sons, is how you do it."

"Sons? Did you see something on the ultrasound?" she asked, her eyes wide with eager curiosity. I knew it was killing her not to know, but I'd gotten her to agree to suppress her very natural urge to know their sex until they were born.

Sitting up, I shook my head. "No. Just something that felt right to say. By the way, since the doctor believes you probably won't go to term, maybe we should talk about names."

Nina shrugged. "I thought we had names already. Diana and Tressa. I liked the way that sounded from your dream, so I just figured we'd handled that issue."

"What if they're boys?"

Her expression twisted gently as she thought about my question. Sighing softly, she said with a smile, "I hadn't thought about that. Two boys instead of two girls. We could always do our fathers' names."

"Maybe as middle names," I said, not wanting to explain why naming a son of mine after my own father filled me with dread. I didn't want my children to be like my father or brother. If I had sons, I wanted them to grow to be Stone men I could be proud of.

"I think I'm going to need some time to think about this, Tristan. Any ideas to help me?"

"Nothing yet, other than staying at home with my wife is exactly how I want to spend a Monday."

Nina looked down and rubbed her stomach. "Do you two hear this? Your father is one smooth talker."

I leaned over again and chuckled. "See boys? The women love smooth."

"Don't go teaching my boys how to be players, Tristan Stone. Smooth only works if the man is wonderful underneath."

My wife's naiveté could still charm me, even after all we'd been through. Placing a tiny kiss on the tip of her nose, I whispered, "Smooth works all the time, princess. I'm off to the shower. Care to join me?"

The smile faded from her face, and Nina shook her head. "I'm sorry. I'm just worried that if we do anything we could harm the babies. You understand, don't you?"

"Abstinence it is, I guess."

Licking her lips, she slid her hand down my chest to palm my cock. "I didn't say anything about abstinence."

"Well, that's a different story." Her hand stroked me to hardness as she pulled me down toward her with her other hand. "Mmmm....I didn't realize pregnancy included this stage. Is this the horny stage?"

With a wink, she smiled. "I have no idea. This is my first time doing this. All I know is that if I keep feeling like this, you might not want to sleep in the nude anymore."

Maneuvering around my legs and her pregnant belly, she rolled over on her side and took me into her mouth. My head rolled back on my shoulders as she slowly slid down every inch of my cock. "No more clothes anywhere near this room," I moaned.

Coming up to the tip, she let it pop from between her slick lips and looked up at me. "I'm thinking you should take advantage of this, dear husband. My pregnancy books talk a ton about hormones making expectant mothers cry but nothing about them making us want to jump our husbands' bones."

She wrapped her lips around my cock again, and as she continued to stare up at me with a look that nearly took my breath away, I moaned, "Well, then, thank you hormones."

BY THE TIME I RETURNED from the gym an hour later, Nina had finished dressing and room service had delivered breakfast. I sat waiting for her at the table covered with every kind of pastry, pancake, and egg dish, hoping I'd covered every possible choice. I hadn't been sure what she'd want, but I needed to make sure she ate to keep herself and the babies healthy.

She walked into the room looking stunning in a dark blue and white print dress and coming to a dead stop, opened her eyes as wide as saucers. "Tristan! What is all this?"

"Breakfast." I stood and escorted her to her seat. "You need to eat."

"Me and what army?" she looked up at me and asked.

Walking around to my side of the table, I explained, "I realized when I went to order from room service that I never asked what you wanted. I had no idea what to order, so I got some of everything."

Nina picked a tiny piece off the side of a coffee cake and popped it into her mouth. "That's because you're usually at work when I eat breakfast. I have to admit, though, you really know how to put out a spread."

"It's the least I can do for the woman I love."

Cutting a square of the coffee cake, she placed it on a plate in front of her. "I do believe, Mr. Stone, that the bigger I get, the smoother you get. How did I get so lucky to have such a wonderful husband?"

"Fate, I guess. I ask myself the same question about you all the time."

She looked over at me and saw I had nothing to eat. "You're not planning on having me eat all of this by myself, are you? I feel like Henry VIII over here."

"I'm not much for breakfast, and I'm happy to just watch you eat."

"Said the man with the six pack to the lady who looks like she's swallowed a barrel."

"Do you want to watch any particular movie today? It's ladies' choice."

"Tristan, I know you want to keep an eye on me, but you don't have to stay here with me. I know you have work. We can watch a movie tonight."

I reached across the table and took her hand in mine. "Nina, I want to spend the day with you. I can keep an eye on you from anywhere in the world. I prefer to be here with you."

She stopped eating the piece of coffee cake and looked at me with a confused expression. "What do you mean you can keep an eye on me from anywhere in the world? Are you talking about the two new bodyguards you hired?"

"No. I'm talking about the cameras I had installed in every room here at the penthouse."

"What? Are you saying every room is monitored? Why?"

Her voice was that tone I knew all too well. She wasn't happy. "Because your accident happened at the pool and no one knew you were there. If I hadn't turned that camera off when you got angry with me last year, the bodyguards would have seen you there and gotten help."

"Tristan, what happened wasn't your fault. It wasn't anyone's fault. I don't want to be watched twenty-four hours a day."

"It's for your safety, Nina. I'm not going to let anything happen to you and the babies."

"Nothing's going to happen to us. We're fine. It was just a fainting spell. I think you're overreacting, and the thought of me being on camera in the bathroom or anywhere else in my own house creeps me out."

"Nina, I promise as soon as the babies are born, I'll take down every last camera. Until then, they're staying."

"And that's that? I have no say in it?"

"You know I'm not going to take the chance of you getting hurt again. What's wrong with taking precautions?"

She stood up and pushed her chair out from behind her. "I feel like you're spying on me and I don't..." Before she could finish her sentence, she fell back into the chair with thump.

"Nina!" I jumped out of my seat and ran around the table. "What's wrong? Tell me. I can have the car here in minutes and we can be at the hospital in no time."

She shook her head slowly as she took a deep breath. "No, it's okay. I just stood up too fast and got lightheaded."

I crouched down next to her and held her hand. "Do you see now why the cameras are needed? What if you fell and I wasn't here? What if you couldn't get to your phone? How long would you be on the floor this time before I found you?"

Nina looked down into my eyes and smiled. "I know. I just hate feeling like an invalid. Pregnancy shouldn't mean I have to be watched all the time, Tristan." She stopped and took a sharp breath in. "Oh…one of the babies kicked! Put your hand on my stomach right here."

She took my hand and placed it near her left hip. My palm pressed softly against her skin, I waited for another kick and then it happened. A tiny push against my hand. A foot or hand or even an elbow pushed out into my hand, touching me for the first time, leaving me speechless.

"Did you feel it? She's a busy one, that girl," Nina said with a smile. When I didn't say anything, she asked, "You felt it, right? It was a kick."

A lump formed in my throat, making me choke up, and I said quietly, "That was incredible. One of our kids just touched me."

"Isn't it great? In just a few months, that foot and that body will be someone we hold in our arms."

My mind filled with thoughts of that little person kicking my hand. What did he or she look like? Did they feel me like I felt them? Never before had just the idea of meeting someone thrilled me like it did at that moment. I simply stared at the spot where my hand had felt his or her touch, unable to tear my gaze away from my child right there with me.

"Are you okay, Tristan? You're not saying anything."

I looked up to see Nina staring down at me. "I'm great. I guess I just didn't realize it would be like that."

"Like what?"

I struggled to find the right words to explain how I felt. "I didn't know such a simple thing like a baby's kick could make me feel so connected to him. Or her. It doesn't matter which they are. It just matters that I felt them touch me."

"This is really happening. Pretty soon, it won't be just you and me anymore. We'll be four instead of two. Are you ready for that?"

If I were to be honest with her at that moment, my answer would have been no. I thought I was, but with one touch that baby had made everything so real that all my romantic thoughts of having kids flew right out the window, replaced by a reality filled with worry and the need to make plans. I couldn't tell Nina that, though. She was already dealing with enough. She didn't need to hear me talk about my sudden need to visit my lawyer to make sure those souls she carried were taken care of, no matter what happened to me. She didn't need to listen to me worry about how wrong the penthouse was going to be for children, and how there was no way I could believe that we were ever going to be able to do this without a nanny.

"We'll be fine," I lied, hoping she couldn't see right through me.

"I think I've come up with a name for a boy. What do you think of Ethan?"

I couldn't help but smile. "Yeah, Ethan sounds good. Ethan Stone. Good strong name for a boy. What do we do if it's a boy and a girl? Diana or Tressa?"

"I think we should decide that when we meet our little girl. If she has blue eyes, she'll be Diana. If she has brown eyes, she'll be Tressa. She's bound to look more like one of us than the other."

"So it's settled then. Ethan and Diana or Ethan and Tressa. But what if we have two boys?"

"What about your middle name, Rider? We could do Ethan and Rider. I like the sound of Rider Stone. What do you think?"

I could live with that. I only hoped he could. "Okay," I said as I stood to kiss the top of her head. "Since we have that taken care of,

I think it's time for a movie. You continue eating while I get everything ready."

She looked up at me in surprise. "Tristan, it's ten o'clock in the morning. We're going to watch a movie now? Don't you have work to do?"

"I can work later."

"Well, what if we watched a movie later too? I was thinking maybe we could go out for a little bit. Maybe shopping?"

"Nina, you're supposed to stay at home. You just had another fainting spell."

Nina's bottom lip quivered and her adorable pout appeared to signal her disappointment. "Tristan, I can't stay here until the babies are born. Please don't treat me like this. We have things to buy before they get here."

I hated seeing her sad, and that pout of hers never failed to do exactly what it was intended to do. "Nina, what if you pass out while we're shopping? What if the babies are hurt because we had to find some mobile with dancing hippos?"

"Don't minimize this, Tristan. I'm practically a prisoner here, stuck in my home, which isn't even my home. I wanted to get the babies' layette. My books say now's the time to get the things they need when they first come home, and since we aren't having the baby shower until after the babies are born, we won't have anything for when they get here."

I had no idea what a layette was, whether it be furniture or some kind of bottles, but the sadness in Nina's face told me she knew what it was and it was important to her. I wasn't comfortable relenting on her going out to shop, but there were ways around that for someone like me. I rarely took advantage of that fact, but now seemed as good a time as any to use my power and wealth.

"Give me thirty minutes. If I can't find a way to make you happy in that time, we'll go. Okay?"

A look of disbelief filled her eyes, but she nodded her agreement. "Thirty minutes? Okay."

I kissed the top of her head. "I have a few phone calls to make. You keep eating, and I'll be back."

Quickly, I headed to the bedroom and made my first call to Angelo. Always able to handle my shopping with ease, he hopefully could do the same for my children. He answered on the second ring in his usual chirpy voice. "Tristan Stone! How is the soon-to-be father?"

"You must be reading my mind, Angelo. That's exactly what I need your help with."

"Really? I don't recall men having to wear anything different during pregnancy," he joked.

"Not me. I need something called a layette."

"A layette? Why on earth do you need a layette, whatever that is?"

Sighing, I closed my eyes and tried to keep calm. "I don't have time for twenty questions, Angelo. Nina wants a layette for the babies, but in her condition, she can't go shopping for it, so I want the shopping to come to her at the penthouse."

"Oh, I see. Give me a few hours to see what I can come up with. I know the owner of a baby boutique who I think would be happy help."

"You have thirty minutes. I'm depending on you, so don't let me down."

"Thirty minutes? Tristan, I'm used to you giving me much longer lead time."

"That's for my clothes, Angelo. This is my wife and kids we're talking about, so get going and set this up for me."

"Okay, okay. I'll get on it now."

"Good. Call me with the details."

Angelo's tone told me he'd get the job done. I could always rely on him. Barely ten minutes later, he was giving me the details about how happy Elise Weston of Petits Coeurs would be to help us. "Thanks, Angelo. I won't forget this."

"I hope not. And, by the way, Elise says a layette is clothes.

Well, clothes and whatever else she decides to bring. She'll be there by eleven."

"Perfect. By the way, I'm going to need some things for the events after the babies are born, like the christening, so here's your lead time. You have at least a few weeks."

Angelo chuckled. "Now that's the Tristan Stone I'm used to. I'll get to work so you're ready when those little bundles of joy arrive. Happy shopping!"

ELISE WESTON ARRIVED EXACTLY AT eleven, just as I got Nina settled in the living room. I'd kept my plans a secret, so when the concierge rang to announce her arrival, Nina's eyes grew wide in surprise. "Did he just say Petits Coeurs? Oh, my God! I'm not dressed to shop there, Tristan!"

"Thanks, Frederick. Make sure security on the floor below checks everything out and then send her up." I sat down next to Nina on the sofa and held her hand. "Shhh…you look incredible. And you're not shopping there. They're bringing a layette here to *you* and you'll decide if it's what you want. And if it isn't, I'll get another one to do the same thing until you get what you want."

Nina shook her head and smiled. "You crazy man. You got the most exclusive baby boutique in town to come here to show me a layette?"

"You wanted to shop for a layette, and I want to keep you safe and secure. Now we're both happy."

Hugging me, she whispered against my chest, "I love you so much, Tristan. Thank you for this."

I kissed her and squeezed her to me. "I love you too, princess. Now let's get these kids their layette."

CHAPTER NINE

NINA

I FELT LIKE A REAL life princess as Elise showed off newborn clothes, blankets, and every possible item a baby could need. With Tristan egging me on, I picked out two of every item I liked, and by the time she left, our living room was full of what every newborn needed in those first weeks of life. I knew since our twins would probably be small or even preterm, we might have to wait a while to put them in those adorable little onesie outfits decorated with giraffes to match their nursery, but that was okay. The very fact that Tristan had arranged for the owner of the most exclusive baby boutique in Manhattan to come to our house made the day more special than even he probably knew.

Tristan worked hard to make sure every day was as wonderful as the day that Elise Weston brought me most of her shop to pick and choose from. Sometimes we enjoyed a simple movie and popcorn, and other times he brought in chefs to create meals that bordered on banquets. Each morning, I awoke to flowers on my nightstand. Roses, daisies, and lilies, they made the start of each day wonderful. Even as I felt bigger and more uncomfortable by the moment, I couldn't help but feel like I was the luckiest woman in the world.

We spent a quiet Thanksgiving at the penthouse with Jordan, who was happy to have someone to celebrate the holiday with instead of sitting around her apartment alone. I remembered those days after my father died and how lonely they'd always felt, so when

Tristan asked me what I wanted to do to celebrate Thanksgiving, having her over was top on my list. Plus, by that time, I couldn't help feeling I wanted to have the two people I cared most about around me. I wasn't due until late January, but something told me it wouldn't be long before the babies came.

December in New York brought a winter storm that nearly crippled the city. I watched out the penthouse windows as people hurriedly moved along through the snow with their shoulders up around their ears toward the warmth of stores and restaurants, and for the first time in weeks, I didn't mind not being outside with them. Work on the heart drug to replace Cardiell took up most of Tristan's time, and as much as he wanted to spend his days with me, being CEO meant he had to spend his hours at his office.

I watched him dress in his usual suit look, coming up behind him to adjust his tie as he looked in the mirror in the bedroom. Barely able to reach around him because of my very pregnant belly, I straightened his look and gave him a hug, like I always did before he left for work. "What time will you be home tonight?"

Tristan stared back at me in the mirror and smiled. "I'll be home for dinner by six tonight. What time is Jordan coming by this morning?"

"She'll be here by ten. That leaves only one hour for me to cause mischief here," I teased as I walked around to face him.

He took me by the chin and frowning, shook his head. "What am I going to do with you? I spend all day worrying you're going to go into labor and I'm not going to get you to the hospital in time, and you make jokes about being alone here."

I looked up into those brown eyes now so concerned as they stared down at me. "My oh-so-serious husband. Smile. We're going to be parents soon. Then you can wear your serious face all the time like all good dads do."

"If that's the criteria for being a good dad, I should be the best then," he said with a tiny smile that told me he wasn't sure of the father he'd be.

But I was. Standing on my tippy toes, I kissed the corner of his mouth. "You're going to be a fantastic daddy. You're going to spoil our kids rotten but be the one who does all the glaring when they misbehave. Don't worry. You got this covered."

"Thanks for letting me know my role," he joked. "Now that I have the job description…"

I turned to head for the bathroom and felt something wet on my leg. Instantly, my mind raced through all the pages of my pregnancy books, and I knew it was time. Looking down, I expected to see water or something like it on the floor, but there was nothing. My gaze trailed up my leg and there, in the middle of my thigh, I saw a line of bright red blood.

Terrified, I spun around to face Tristan. "There's something wrong. We need to go to the hospital now!"

His eyes followed mine to my leg and then everything began to move so fast. I heard him say something like everything was going to be okay, but my mind was filled with fear. I had no idea what was wrong, but I knew blood wasn't a good sign. He guided me to my coat, all the while working to keep me calm as he called Dr. Michaelson, and I just nodded over and over, unable to speak. I wanted to believe it was okay—that the babies were fine and we'd be okay—but I had a bad feeling.

By the time we arrived at the hospital, my heart raced in fear that I'd done something wrong to make this happen. Turning to Tristan as we walked through the emergency room doors, I grabbed his hand and squeezed it tightly as I spoke the first words since telling him something was wrong. "I'm sorry. I swear I didn't mean for this to happen."

Pressing his lips to my cheek, he kissed me. "You're going to be fine, Nina. I won't leave your side. I promise. We're going to get through this fine, and in a little while you and I are going to meet our children."

Dozens of people hurriedly moved around me in the operating room, barking out words that all blended into one big stream of noise, but throughout it all Tristan stood next to me holding my hand and smoothing my damp hair off my face. No matter how frantic everyone else looked, he remained calm, his expression full of love, as he whispered over and over, "Don't be scared. I'm here."

I wasn't scared. I'd prepared myself for the real possibility that I'd have to go through an emergency C-section. Twins rarely were born naturally, so this was nothing to be frightened of. Even if I was, Tristan smiling down at me and squeezing my hand would chase all my fears away.

The tiny sound of a baby's cry broke through the cacophony of voices around me, and I looked down to see our child in the doctor's hands. Was it a boy or a girl? I looked up at Tristan, my eyes pleading for the answer.

"Say hello to your daughter, and her sister is coming right behind her," Dr. Michaelson said in a voice full of joy.

Tristan bent down and in my ear whispered, "Two girls, Nina. Diana and Tressa."

I opened my mouth to speak, but suddenly the room felt like it was spinning out of control. My eyes couldn't focus, and then I heard a voice say something about blood or bleeding out and heard machines begin to buzz and chime frantically, and I felt Tristan let go of my hand. Everything spun around me, but I saw his face twist in terror as he was led away. Why was he leaving me there with all those strangers when I needed him most?

And then everything went dark.

I opened my eyes and saw I stood in a yard of green grass lined by flower beds filled with yellow and white daisies. The sun was shining like it was a gorgeous summer day. I looked around confused. I knew this place, but from where? I walked toward the middle of the yard, unsure of what I'd find but somehow knowing there'd be something familiar there. I stopped as my foot landed on a stepping stone. Crouching down in the cool grass, I saw in the center of the grey stone a yellow and orange painted sun, the kind a child would make.

I'd made that picture. The memory of that week at summer camp the year my mother died came rushing back to me. The hours I spent in the art building while the other children played tag and kickball. The happiness that week had given me after months of living in my house as my father and sister mourned my mother's death, me being too young to understand what had happened but feeling the pall that hung over every room and every moment of our lives.

I ran my fingertip over the sun, feeling the warmth of the rock as I traced the ridges worn into it by weather over the years. Closing my eyes, I remembered the look on my father's face as I showed him my stepping stone I'd made for my mother, not understanding the sadness in his eyes as he pretended to love my creation. Tears began to stream down my cheeks as the realization of what this rock meant dawned on me.

Just like my mother and father, I'd died.

"Don't cry, Nina."

I knew that voice. Soft, feminine, it filled my heart with warmth and happiness. Opening my eyes, I saw her for the first time in nearly twenty years. My mother, gone since I was just a little girl, stood there in front of me as she had so many times when I played in our backyard. Beautiful, with long brown hair and blue eyes just like mine, she smiled at me.

"Mom? Is that you?"

"Yes, sweetheart. I'm here."

"How? What is this?"

"I've missed you, Nina. I've missed you every day since I had to leave that morning."

Tears filled my eyes again. Why was this happening? "What is this, mom? Why am I here? Am I dead?"

She reached out to touch me, caressing my cheek with her palm. I felt it as sure as I felt my own hand cover hers, so I knew she wasn't a dream. Whatever this was, it was real.

"So many questions. Always so many questions with my Nina. Give me a few minutes and all your questions will be answered."

Holding out her hand, she nodded, and I had the surest sense I needed to follow her. I placed my hand in hers, and she led me down the stone path toward the end of our yard. There was no fear, no dread. Just love like I'd only felt with one other.

Tristan. Oh, God! Where was he? Turning to face my mother, I pleaded with her for answers. "Is Tristan here? Where are the girls? I can't leave them there. I need to get to them. Can you help me?"

She shook her head, and a tiny frown turned down her lips. "He's not here, Nina."

Tears filled my eyes, making my vision blurry. As they rolled down over my cheeks, I sobbed, "I have two little girls who need me. Why am I here? Mom, tell me how to get back to them."

"Your daughters are beautiful. Your children are all beautiful, Nina. Tristan is taking care of them now. Not to worry."

"I want to go back. Please tell me how to get back to them."

My mother cupped my cheeks in her hands. "We all get only a small amount of time with those we love, honey. Sometimes it's less than we planned, but hopefully, we've been there long enough to have them remember us."

My heart ached at the sound of her words. "How will my girls remember me, Mom? They never even got to meet me. I was taken from them right after they were born."

"Don't cry, sweetheart. Don't cry."

I turned my head, searching for a way out of this place. For as far as my eyes could see, there was just grass and my childhood backyard. "How can I get back to them? I need to be back with them!"

She gently pulled me back to face her. "I'm so proud of you, Nina. You're everything I always knew you'd be. I didn't get enough time with you, and for that, I'm sorry. I'm sorry I wasn't there for your art classes so you knew how talented I thought you were. I'm sorry I missed your graduation from college and your first day of work at the gallery."

"I always wanted you there, but I know why you weren't. I don't blame you for leaving."

"And now you're all grown up with a husband and children of your own. Your life is everything I always hoped it would be."

Her words eased my mind, and I remembered how she knew Tristan's mother when she was young. "My husband is the son of Tressa, the girl you knew in college who got you and Daddy together. I never met her, but I think he's like her—kind and caring."

My mother smiled warmly, as if what I'd said caused a long forgotten memory to reappear. "We always said how wonderful it would be to be related to one another, the sisters neither of us ever had."

I stood watching her for a moment, loving how wonderful just being next to her made me feel. But I couldn't stay there with her. I had to get back to Tristan and the babies.

Squeezing her hands, I begged, "I need to get back to my family, Mom. Tell me I can get back. I don't belong here yet. Tristan and the girls need me."

"And you need them, Nina. But promise me something before you go."

"Anything."

"Remember that at any time everything you love can be taken from you, and then all you can do is watch from afar as they continue to live after you're gone. Promise me you'll live with no regrets."

"I promise. I miss you so much, Mom. All those times I wished you were there so I could talk to you."

My mother kissed my cheek and whispered, "I was there, honey. Every time you doubted yourself, I was that tiny voice in your head saying you were brave enough. Every time you asked for a sign, I was there to give you one. I'll always be there."

Before my eyes, the light began to fade away, taking my mother with it. I reached out to hold on to her for a moment longer, sad I was losing her from my life after such a short time again. As she slipped from my touch, I watched as she blew me a kiss like she always did when she said goodbye to me as a little girl.

"I wish you could see the babies, Mom."

As she faded into nothingness, I heard her whisper in my head, "Thank you for making Tressa and me sisters this time, but I have no advice for him. Tressa would know about that. I love you, honey. Take care, and know that I'm always there."

And then she was gone and I was floating in a sea of darkness.

"Baby, wake up. Wake up and look at me."

I heard Tristan's voice pleading for me to wake up, but why? Was something wrong? Slowly, my eyelids fluttered open, and I saw his face just inches from mine. I opened my mouth to speak, but no words came out between my parched lips. What was going on?

"Nina! God, honey, I'm so happy to see your beautiful eyes open. Hang on, let me get the nurse."

Tristan moved to leave, and I saw I wasn't in our bedroom. Where was I? I grabbed his wrist, afraid to be left alone in this strange place, and tried to speak again, but failed.

He sat back down in the chair next to me and cradled my face in his hands. "It's okay. I just want to let the nurse know you're awake. I won't leave, though. I'm right here."

"Tris…" I tried to say his name, but my throat felt bone dry.

"Don't speak. Let me get you a drink of water." He poured a glass for me and raised it to my lips. "Here, drink this. You'll feel better."

Never before had water tasted so incredible. It felt like I hadn't had an ounce of moisture pass my lips in ages. What was going on?

"Does that feel better?" Tristan asked, his voice full of concern.

I nodded and looked around at the room I was in. Boring cream colored walls with some kind of brown and pink wallpaper border near the ceiling surrounded me. Looking down at the twin bed with its institutional footboard, I had my answer. I was in a hospital.

But why?

"Tristan," I croaked out. "Why am I here?"

He smoothed my hair off my face and smiled down at me. "You don't remember? Do you remember anything?"

I saw in his eyes the fear that I'd forgotten everything again, like before, but I knew who he was and who I was. I just didn't know why I'd need to be in a hospital. I slowly shook my head. "No. What happened? How long have I been here?"

He pretended to smile, but I saw the disappointment all over his face. "Almost eighteen hours. I've been here the whole time waiting for you to wake up."

Then it hit me what had happened. Like a flood of memories, it all came back to me. I pushed myself up to sit and clutched at his hand. "The babies! What happened to them? Where are they? Tristan, where are the girls?"

"Nina, it's okay. They're here with us in the hospital. I've seen them…"

"I remember everything. I saw my mother. She was in our backyard. Well, not our backyard, but my backyard from when I was a kid. She told me she was always there with me. She knew about the girls too. Oh, Tristan! It was so wonderful to see her again."

"Nina, I have something to tell you, so I need you to lay back down, okay?"

Shaking my head, I moved my legs to get out of bed. "No, I don't want to stay here. I want to see Diana and Tressa. Where are they?"

Tristan stood up and gently held me in place so I couldn't move. "I need to talk to you before you see the babies. They're tiny, Nina. The doctor said it's not surprising since they came so early, but that's not all."

My emotions became all jumbled. I wanted to cry. I wanted to scream, "Let me go see them!" I saw in his face something had happened, and I wasn't sure I wanted to know. I remembered the blood running down my leg at the penthouse. Something bad had happened to the babies, and now he had the job of telling me. Tears welled in my eyes, and I shook my head, not wanting to know. "No, no! Don't tell me something happened to them. Please don't say that!"

Holding his phone up in front of me, he showed me a picture

of the first baby. "That's Diana. She's the littlest one. The doctor says she needs help breathing, but that happens to preemies a lot."

I stared at the tiny being with a head full of dark hair in the picture with all those wires and tubes attached to her. She couldn't have been bigger than one of my shoes. "How big is she?"

"She's a little over two pounds, honey, and she's beautiful, just like her mother."

With terror in my heart at what his answer would be, I asked, "What about Tressa? Do you have any pictures of her?"

He scrolled to the next picture on his phone and held it up in front of me. "Meet your daughter Tressa. A little bigger than Diana at about two and a half pounds, she's tougher and look at all that hair. The doctor thinks she'll be fine too, though."

Tressa looked stronger, even though she was hooked up to a machine too, and I imagined she was the baby who'd been doing all the kicking. Not afraid anymore, I took a deep breath, but I remembered Tristan leaving as the girls were born. Something had happened. Turning to look at him as he scrolled through to the next picture on his phone, I asked, "What happened during my C-section? Why did they take you out?"

He looked up and smiled. "Well, you began to have difficulties and then we found out about this." Lifting his phone again, he said, "This is Ethan, Nina. Born two minutes after his sisters, he's over three pounds and nearly sixteen inches long. And look, just like his sisters, he has your adorable pout."

"Three? Three babies?" I asked as I began to feel like my head was swimming. Three children. Triplets. A boy.

Tristan nodded and beamed down at me. "Three. He was hiding on all the ultrasounds, so that's why we never knew. He was probably the one kicking you."

"But why did they send you away then?"

"Things got a little dicey there for a while. The doctors didn't want me to be there if things got bad. Don't worry, though. Dr. Michaelson says you'll be fine now. They had to go in and stop the bleeding, but you were out a long time. I didn't leave your side, except to go see the kids. Sorry about the pictures being so far away. They don't let you take cell phones in. Not sterile enough."

"So you named them all without me?" I asked with a pout, a little disappointed I hadn't been a part of that first important event in their lives.

Tristan's mouth twisted into a sly smile. "No, not officially. I waited for you since I didn't know what we wanted the middle names for the girls to be. I had no idea about Ethan's either."

"Ethan. We have a son, Tristan. Your dream was only partially true."

Shrugging, he said, "Well, I never promised it would be one hundred percent true. Dreams are funny that way. Like the one you had about your mother."

"That wasn't a dream, Tristan. I talked to her for the first time since I was a little girl. I touched her, and she was real."

I saw he didn't believe me entirely, but it didn't matter. I knew what I'd experienced. After all those years, I'd finally gotten the chance to tell my mother how much I loved her.

CHAPTER TEN

NINA

THERE ARE SOME THINGS A person never forgets. Their first day of school. Their first kiss. The first time they fell in love. For me, the day I met those three incredible souls will always be a moment in time that changed me forever. Tristan followed as the nurse rolled me up to the NICU in my wheelchair, his hand holding mine. If we'd been alone, I would have told him how my heart was pounding in chest at the thought of meeting my children. I didn't say anything, though, keeping my fears to myself.

I'd spent hours reading my pregnancy books, but nothing could have prepared me for the reality of the NICU. Instead of a softly lit delivery suite, the setting for the first time I saw Diana, Tressa, and Ethan was bright and sterile. And cold. No matter how warm the temperature may have been, all the room made me feel was cold. White walls, bright lights, and all those people milling about made the NICU intimidating, and I wished I could run away with Tristan with our children in our arms to a kinder place where no machines beeped and buzzed and no barriers kept up apart.

The nurse chatted with Tristan about how exciting our lives would be from now on as we entered the area just outside the NICU, her perky happiness almost too much for me. We donned masks and gloves, making sure to cover every inch of our clothes before we entered the room the children were in. It felt like I was being prepped for going into one of those radiation chambers they always put in disaster movies. This wasn't how a mother should see her children for the first time.

Even worse, I realized I wouldn't be able to hold any of them. The nurses spoke their rehearsed laundry list of do's and don'ts for spending time with the babies, the most important one being we couldn't touch them too often to avoid upsetting them. I knew they weren't trying to ruin this for me, but all I could feel was sadness. No matter how hard I tried, all I wanted to do was cry the entire time I sat in that NICU room.

For Tristan, just being there clearly meant the world to him. I watched as he gently stuck his fingers into the incubator to touch Diana's tiny hand, all the time beaming a smile that lit up the room. So patient, he stroked her little arm with his forefinger as he whispered how he couldn't wait for the day she'd be able to sit on his lap and how he'd tell her the story of the day she was born.

The nurse explained how I could touch Tressa and Ethan just like Tristan was with Diana, but it felt awkward when I put my gloved hand in my daughter's incubator, like I was an intruder in her tiny world invading her space. My finger grazed her wrist, and I recoiled at the thought of possibly hurting her tender body.

I looked around to see if anyone had seen me and noticed Tristan coming toward me. He'd seen my inability to bond with Tressa. I wanted to run and hide.

As he took his place behind me, he leaned down to whisper, "It's a little difficult at first, isn't it? Don't worry. They love it as much as we do."

I forced a smile as my hands sat in my lap. I didn't love this. In fact, it took everything in me not to break down and cry. "She's so tiny, Tristan."

He slowly slid his hand into Tressa's incubator and touched his fingertip to her pinky. "Tiny Tressa. Something tells me she won't like it if that nickname sticks."

The way he so effortlessly bonded with both girls when I seemed incapable of even touching Tressa's arm made me wish I could be like him. All I felt was failure.

A nurse slowly moved Ethan's incubator back into the room, and I watched as Tristan's eyes lit up with joy. "There's my little guy. How's he doing this afternoon?"

I closed my eyes to stop the tears from falling as the nurse explained how well Ethan was doing, and like all the others, congratulated us on our new family. Tristan made his way over to his incubator while he chatted the woman up about needing one more of everything, every word filled with so much happiness.

"Nina, come over and see him. He's as gorgeous as his sisters," he bragged.

Slowly, I made my way to where he sat and stared into the incubator my son lay in. Tristan's finger touched his wrist, lightly stroking the skin in a way that seemed totally foreign to me. He talked about what they'd do when he got older, and I sat there silently, unable to say anything for fear I'd explode into tears.

"Tristan, I don't feel well. Can you get the nurse to take me back to my room?" I quietly asked, sure everyone heard the truth in my voice. I didn't know what to do with my own children—how to even touch them.

"Sure. It's probably a good idea we leave now anyway. We don't want to excite them too much."

He was trying hard, but he didn't understand why I wouldn't want to be there. Why should he? I didn't understand, to be honest. All I knew was that if I could run away, I would.

✧ ✧ ✧

BY THE END OF THE first week, I was released from the hospital, but Diana, Tressa, and Ethan had to stay so Tristan and I continued to live in the penthouse. Day after day for weeks, I walked hand in hand with Tristan down the NICU corridor to see my children, and day after day, I went with a smile on my face but on the verge of tears. I had no idea what was wrong with me. At first, I'd thought I'd just been unsure of myself as a new mother. All the books had said that could happen and not to worry, but every day I waited to feel better, and I never did.

I knew Tristan wondered what was wrong with me. No mother who cared about her children felt like this. I was broken, defective, and no matter how much I wanted to be the right kind of mother, I wasn't. I didn't know why. I just wasn't.

Even visits from Jordan felt forced. Her happiness for us was so genuine, but every time I saw her, I felt like a fraud. I wanted to feel the happiness she felt. I just didn't. I didn't know why either. By the time Christmas arrived, it was all I could do to get out of bed each morning. Jordan came over to spend the holiday with us, but I begged off as soon as I could, claiming to be sick with the flu so I could go hide away in bed. At least there, I could close my eyes and pretend I wasn't myself in my dreams.

Getting up from the table, I pushed my still full plate away from me and forced a smile for Tristan and her. "I must be coming down with something. Probably the flu. I'm going to head to bed. Tristan, they're not going to let me see the babies until I get better, so I want to kick this as soon as I can."

He stared up at me with eyes full of fear but merely nodded, forcing his own smile onto his lips. "Anything you need, just say the word."

I turned toward Jordan and shook my head. "I don't want you to get whatever I have, so no hugs today. Sorry to be such a party popper. I'll give you a call this week, okay? Merry Christmas."

"Okay, honey. Merry Christmas. Feel better."

I left them and climbed into bed, loving the solitude it offered. Pulling the covers up over my head, I closed my eyes and waited for sleep to come and take me away.

A HAND ON MY SHOULDER roused me from my nap, and I rolled over to see Jordan sitting on the bed next to me. Rubbing my eyes, I sat up against the headboard. "Hey, what's up?"

"I want to talk to you, honey. I think it's time we admitted something's wrong, don't you?"

"It's just the flu, Jordan. I'll be okay in a few days," I lied.

"I don't think so, Nina. Your husband may not know what to do about how you feel about visiting the kids, but I do. You're suffering from post-partum depression, sweetie. My brother's wife had it after Caleb was born."

"I'm not depressed, Jordan. I have everything any woman could want—a wonderful husband, a beautiful house, this penthouse, three beautiful children."

"Who you don't want to go see."

Her words hit me like a fist to my face, and I tried to avoid her stare, but she wasn't letting me go on this. "Look at me, Nina. Don't look away, honey."

Tears streamed out of my eyes and over my cheeks as I turned back to face her. I couldn't deny the truth anymore. "I don't know what's wrong with me," I sobbed. "I love them, Jordan. I do. I love them more than I ever thought I could. I was so worried when Tristan first told me about them, but there's something wrong with me. I thought by now I'd feel better about visiting them, but I don't. I'm terrified of going to that hospital, and I don't know why."

Once I began crying, I couldn't stop. Jordan took me in her arms and held me as my sobs wracked my body. For the first time since waking up after my children were born, I didn't feel like I had a hundred pounds of worry on my back. I'd kept this secret inside me for so long, and now as I cried my eyes out on her shoulder, the heaviness that had weighed me down faded away.

"Honey, there's nothing wrong with you. You're going to be okay. Sandy felt a lot like this too, but she's fine now and she and Caleb are closer than she ever imagined they could be."

I leaned back against the pillows and hung my head. "I worry all the time that I've ruined this for Tristan. You should see him with them, Jordan. He's so loving and caring. I don't know what to do."

"You haven't ruined anything for him, Nina. He's worried sick about you. He doesn't know what to do, so I told him I'd talk to you. Tristan wants you to be as happy as he is."

"I want to be that happy. I see him touching them and talking to them and I think to myself how much I wish I felt like that. What if I never feel that way toward my own children, Jordan? What kind of mother feels like this? I messed up their birth, almost killed them, and now I can't even be there for them."

"You didn't mess up anything. Is that what you think? That you did something wrong?"

"I must have. Why would I have started bleeding if I didn't?"

My body heaved from crying, and Jordan took me in her arms to hold me. "Oh, Nina, you didn't do anything wrong. You were carrying three babies. That was hard on your body. And it's no wonder they wanted to come out early. They knew how wonderful you were on the inside, so they wanted to meet their mom on this side."

I held onto Jordan as all the insecurities I'd lived with for weeks flowed out of me. It felt so good to believe that someday soon I'd be the mother I wanted to be. "I don't know what to do now, Jordan."

"You need to talk to Tristan, Nina. He doesn't know what's wrong, but if you tell him, he'll be there for you."

She released me, and I dried my eyes. "What if he can't forgive me for feeling like this? What if he thinks I'm a monster?"

Jordan pushed my hair off my face and gave me one of her terrific smiles that never failed to make me feel better. "He would never think that. He just wants you to be happy, Nina. That man of yours is a good guy. Tell him what you told me."

"Okay," I said through my sniffles. "I will."

"Good. Now I'm going to jump in the car with Jensen and head back to Brooklyn, and you're going to tell Tristan everything. Don't worry. It will be okay. I promise. Remember what I always say. Good things happen to good people, and you Stones are the best kind of people."

"Thank you, Jordan."

She rose from the bed and smoothed the covers over my legs. "He loves you, honey. Let him know what's going on and he'll be there for you." Leaning in, she kissed my cheek. "My work is done here. I'm off to Brooklyn. I'll see you later this week."

As she left me there alone with my thoughts, I worked to tamp down my fear of telling Tristan everything I'd told Jordan. I wanted to believe he wouldn't hate me for feeling like this, but what if he did? What if he couldn't understand what I was going through since I couldn't even understand it?

I saw him appear in the doorway and pushed down the overwhelming urge to burst into tears again. He slowly walked toward the bed and sat down next to me, those beautiful brown eyes searching mine to figure out how to act so he didn't upset me. He deserved better than to live like this, like every day was walking on eggshells.

Looking down at my hands in my lap, I began quietly. "Hey, I need to tell you some things, and I don't know how you're going to take it."

Tristan lifted my chin with his fingertip and shook his head. "You don't have to worry about how I feel about anything. This is about you. Whatever's going on, Nina, you never have to feel like you can't tell me."

"I don't know why I feel like I do, but I want you to know I didn't mean for this happen. I mean, I have been depressed before, but not like this. I promised my mother I'd live with no regrets, but that's all I have. I have everything to be happy about, but I'm not."

I couldn't stop the tears from flowing again. They drenched my face and ran into my mouth, and before long I was sobbing even as I tried to get the words out. Tristan pulled me close and held me as my crying continued. He said little, but every so often whispered, "Let it out, baby. Let it out."

Once it started, I wasn't sure I could stop letting it out, but I didn't try. I just let my emotions take over as Tristan rocked us slowly back and forth, easing my heart in the process. When I finally felt like I had no more tears inside me, I kissed his cheek and said quietly, "I love you, Tristan, and I love our kids. I promise from this point on I won't be sad."

He stroked my back and was silent for a long time. Finally, he said, "No one expects you to never be sad, Nina. I want you to be happy, but if you need help, we'll get you help."

I leaned back and took a deep breath. "I don't know if talking to a stranger would help, and I don't want to take any drugs. Just sit and talk to me. That's better than any doctor or medicine there is."

Tucking a lock of hair behind my ear, he smiled and nodded. "I want to tell you something I've been keeping to myself for a long time. When you first told me you were pregnant, I began having nightmares again. In every one, you were hurt and needed me, but I couldn't get to you. I'd wake up in a cold sweat terrified that the nightmares would come true. It's the reason I hired more bodyguards out at the house. When you left the hotel in London, I had another one. Same thing as always. You needed me, and I wasn't able to save you, but that time you had already had the babies and I couldn't save them either. And then I got the call that you'd blacked out at the house, and it seemed like every one of those nightmares was coming true and I was thousands of miles away."

"Oh, Tristan. Why didn't you ever tell me you were having nightmares again?"

"I didn't want to give you something to worry about. You already were dealing with having twins. You didn't need your husband telling you about his silly nightmares."

"They weren't silly to you."

"No, but I think they were my brain's way of telling me I wasn't sure I could handle fatherhood."

I brought his hand to my lips and kissed it. "You are so good with them, Tristan. It's like you were meant to be a dad. You never had anything to worry about."

"Maybe, but I don't think either one of us knew what this would be like. My mind dealt with it by creating nightmares based on my biggest fears. Your mind is dealing with it in your way."

I sighed heavily, wishing my mind wasn't like it was. "Why is my way like this?"

"Nina, I don't know. What I do know is that there's not a sweeter, more caring person in the world. Before you were a mother or my wife, you were Nina—sweet, gentle, kindhearted Nina. You're still that person. Don't forget that. I think if we just take this one day at a time, we're going to be okay. Don't worry about the kids. They're thriving, and soon they'll be home with us out at the house. For now, I want you to focus on getting better."

"I'm sorry you have to deal with this, Tristan. You deserve to be happy at this time, not dealing with a basket case like me."

Without saying a thing, he stood and walked around the bed, climbing in to lie next to me. He gently pulled me to him, wrapping his arms around me. "You don't have to apologize. I love you. When you feel bad, I feel bad. That's what being in love is about."

I pressed my ear to his chest and listened to his heartbeat so strong and steady. "I was afraid you'd think I was a monster."

He kissed the top of my head and whispered, "You could never be a monster. I don't know what this is you're going through, but you don't have to do it alone. I'm here. I'm not going anywhere."

"I love you, Tristan."

"I love you, princess. You gave me the greatest gift you could when you gave me your heart, and now you've given me three wonderful children. The only thing that could make me happier is if I knew you were happy."

"I want to be happy. I do."

"Then that's my job now. To make you happy."

The real fear that I'd never be happy again had settled into my brain during the weeks since the babies' births, but now as I lay in Tristan's arms after telling him my deepest, darkest secret, I believed I would be happy as a mother and wife. Maybe not that day or even the next, but with all the wonderful gifts I'd been given, I had to believe it would happen someday.

Epilogue

Tristan

"Open your eyes, sleepyhead."

Looking up, I saw Nina standing over me with her Mom look on. "Let me guess. Time for my fun in the sun to end?"

"And time for theirs to begin," she answered with a smile. "Not that I'm not totally loving the view of you relaxing in the sun with just shorts on, but we'll save that for later."

I reached out and pulled her by the arm down on top of me as I lay on the chaise lounge. "I don't want to wait for later, so let's see what we can sneak in before the kids come down."

Nina squirmed in my hold, giggling as I playfully smacked her on the ass. "Tristan! I need to get up. I can hear Tressa coming."

"So? What's she going to see? Her parents madly in love? She better get used to it. I plan on this being the norm for a long, long time."

My words stopped her wriggling, and she kissed me full on the mouth. God, I loved times like this when we stole moments together. Even five years after having triplets, my wife's kiss still had the effect on my cock that it had since that first night together.

Looking down my body, she shook her head and smiled. "Three children and a nanny coming any second, and you're hard as a rock. What am I going to do with you, Mr. Stone?"

"I can think of a few things," I said as I lifted my hips off the chaise lounge to graze the front of her swimsuit.

She pushed herself off me, leaving me hard and committed to

spending an afternoon at the pool with the kids. Life was tricky sometimes. A towel came flying at my head as she said, "Cover yourself, at least. Cara will think we're some kind of pervs."

Not that what some middle aged Italian woman thought mattered much to me, but I could see Nina's point, so I quickly threw the towel over my lap and attempted to look nonchalant as the nanny and our kids came bounding down the pathway toward me.

"Daddy! Look! I have my swimmies on!" Diana screamed as she led the three of them toward the edge of the pool, proudly showing off her pink inflatables wrapped around each bicep.

"No jumping in yet!" Nina barked, trying to stop the stampede of children to inspect them. "Diana has her swimmies on, but Ethan, where are yours? And Tressa?"

The only other male in the house frowned and looked over at me for help. "Daddy, tell Mommy I don't need swimmies. I'm not like Diana and Tressa. I know how to swim."

"I know how to swim," Tressa protested with her hands on her hips, which then encouraged her sister to give her opinion on her swimming abilities, causing all three of them to talk at once and saving me from having to insert my opinion on swimmies into the conversation.

Nina held her hands up in the air and loudly announced, "Enough! Anyone who has swimmies on can swim. No swimmies, no swimming."

Cara held out two sets of inflatable arm swimmies, pink for Tressa and yellow for Ethan, and both children grudging walked over to accept them as Diana jumped into the pool to do her best cannonball. Personally, I didn't feel the urgent need to have everyone wear inflatables in the pool, but Nina did, so worn they were.

When Mama was happy, everyone was happy.

"Daddy, come swim with me," Diana pleaded as she bobbed near the edge of the pool. Nina shot me glance as if to warn me about what was going on under my towel, but the introduction of our children and their nanny had made any sexy thoughts instantly disappear from my mind, taking my hard-on with them.

"Only if you promise to swim in the deep end with me," I teased as I stood and made my way to where she floated.

She looked up with that adorable little grin I liked to think she reserved just for me. "Okay, Daddy."

From behind me, I heard the sound of feet slapping on the concrete and then a duo screamed, "Cannonball!" Diana's eyes grew as wide as saucers as her brother and sister jumped into the pool next to her, nearly swamping her tiny body. Quickly, I slid into the water to grab onto her before she was swept away with the cannonball tidal wave.

"Tressa! Ethan! No more splashing your sister like that!" Nina ordered from behind me.

"Sorry, Diana!" they said in tandem as they swam toward the center of the pool to grab the beach balls.

Wrapping her arms around my neck, Diana clung to me as I began to walk toward the deep end of the pool. I saw the fear in her eyes as the water crept up inch by inch over her torso and whispered near her ear, "Trust me?"

In a tiny voice, she said in my ear, "I trust you, Daddy."

"We should get Mommy in the pool," I said, knowing that's all Diana would need to begin the prodding that her brother and sister would quickly join in on.

"Mommy, Daddy says you should be in the pool. Please come swimming this time," she pleaded.

I turned to look over at Nina and smiled, hoping she'd join us. "Yeah, come on in. I'm sure there's a pair a swimmies you can wear."

Nina gave me the raised eyebrow look and slid into the pool next to us, kissing Diana. "Big girls don't need swimmies."

"Mmmm…what do big girls need?" I joked, receiving a glare in response.

"Yeah, Mommy. What do big girls need?" Diana asked innocently.

Rolling her eyes, Nina tickled Diana on the ribs. "Big girls need a big kiss from their daughter. That's what they need."

Diana kissed her sweetly on the cheek and turned back in my arms to face me. "How about a kiss from Daddy too?"

"Mommy! Ethan took his swimmies off!" Tressa reported loudly from across the pool.

Jabbing me gently in the ribs, Nina winked. "Saved by the tattle. Looks like no kisses for you." Turning away, she warned, "You two better behave or you won't be able to see Aunt Jordan tomorrow."

"Aunt Jordan is coming!" Tressa squealed in joy. "Yay!"

Nina swam away toward the other two children as I called after her, "Don't think I won't get you later!"

AT EIGHT O'CLOCK, ALL THREE kids had finished their baths and were ready for bed. Nina sat on Tressa's bed with one of her mother's clay animal sculptures in her hand as she told them the story of how my mother and hers were best friends and how Diana and Tressa were named after them. As she finished her story, she kissed them all one by one and said, "Okay, time for bed."

Ethan spied me in the hallway, and intent on squeezing out every moment awake he could, asked, "Can Daddy tell us a story tonight? He never gets to tell us any."

A five year old's guilt trip is one of the most powerful things in the universe. The boy was destined to be a captain of industry with manipulation techniques like that. Nina looked up at me and waved me in, reluctantly submitting to Ethan's request if the look on her face was any indication of her opinion on my storytelling that night.

"A story? I don't really tell stories very well," I teased as I sat down on the bed next to Nina.

Tressa jumped up on my lap and looked up at me with a

plaintive look in her deep brown eyes. "Tell the story about the day we were born. I love the part about Ethan."

Diana and Ethan climbed onto Nina's lap and settled in for the best story I had. "I was a surprise," he said, quickly jumping to the exciting part, as far as he was concerned.

"Yes, you were a surprise. Your mother and I thought only your sisters were going to be born that day. Imagine our surprise when the doctor said, "Mr. and Mrs. Stone, congratulations, you have three children.""

Unsatisfied by my storytelling, Tressa tugged on my shirt to get my attention. "Now you have to tell another one. That one doesn't count."

"How about the one about the first time I met Mommy?"

My son's face told me he was unimpressed with my choice, but Diana and Tressa's eyes lit up like they always did upon hearing I'd tell the story about that first night I met their mother. Nina just smiled, secretly loving the story, even if she didn't believe it was the absolute truth.

"One night I decided to go to an art gallery, even though I don't like art, and your mother was there. I saw her and fell in love at that very moment."

Diana looked up at her mother and said, "And you didn't even notice him, right Mommy?"

"Well…"

"No, she didn't, honey," I said, cutting Nina off before she ruined my version of our meeting. "I tried to get her attention, but she looked right past me. I left the gallery sad that I hadn't gotten to speak to her, but when I came back because I just had to know who that beautiful woman was, I finally got my chance to say hi."

"And as soon as she got to talk to you, she fell in love too, right?" Tressa asked, her eyes wide in anticipation.

"I don't know. Did you?" I asked Nina as I looked over at her.

"Did you, Mommy?" Diana asked.

"Of course," Nina answered with a smile. "Now it's time for

bed for all my munchkins. Let's go."

Tressa climbed off my lap and into bed as Nina placed Diana into her bed. As I tucked Tressa in with her Teddy bear, she said, "Tomorrow when we go swimming, I'm going to go to the deep end like Diana."

I gave her a kiss goodnight and smoothed her dark brown hair over her pillow. "It's a date then. We'll go to the deep end together. I love you, Tressa."

Nina and I exchanged children, and while she said goodnight to Tressa, I kissed Diana goodnight with her Teddy bear. Her little hands reached up to cradle my face, and she whispered, "I like your stories, Daddy. I'm glad you're going to come swimming again tomorrow."

"Goodnight, sweetheart. Sweet dreams. I love you."

As the girls curled up underneath their blankets with their stuffed animals tightly in their little arms, Nina and I took Ethan's hands and walked him to his room next door. Jumping into bed, he scooted under the covers. "Why do you always tell girl stories, Daddy?"

Nina chuckled and kissed his forehead as she placed his bear next to him. "Good night, honey. I love you."

I stood next to his bed, and when she was out of earshot, I leaned over and kissed him goodnight, whispering, "We're in the minority here, buddy. There are more girls than guys, so a lot of times, we have to deal with girlie stuff."

Ethan's tiny bottom lip jutted out into a pout like his mother's. "I don't like that."

Smoothing his light brown hair off his forehead, I nodded. "It's just the way it is, buddy. It's not so bad, though. Girls are okay."

Twisting his face into a grimace, he reluctantly agreed. "I guess."

"Goodnight, Ethan. I love you."

"Goodnight, Daddy. I love you too."

I found Nina lying across the bed looking exhausted after a

long day. Still as beautiful as that first night at the gallery, she smiled as I approached her. "What did Ethan want to talk about?"

Sitting down next to her, I said, "Too many girls in the castle."

"Do you think he gets sick of spending all of his time with females? Maybe I should look for a playdate for him with one of the boys at school."

Leaning back, I turned to kiss her. "I think that's nice, but he just wants more manly stories. Maybe I could tell him the Iron Man story next time."

Nina raised her eyebrows in disbelief. "He's not even six years old, Tristan. Iron Man seems a bit much."

"It's never too early for a man to learn about heroes, Nina, and there's none cooler than Iron Man."

"He's got a cooler one right here in his dad," she said sweetly.

I pulled her on top of me for a long, deep kiss. Between work and being the parents to three very active children, I couldn't remember the last time I'd had the chance to just be myself with my wife.

Looking into my eyes, she gave me a devilish grin. "I think you might need another towel. You never know who's going to come in to interrupt us."

I ran my hands down her back to cup her ass. Pulling her into my body, I shook my head. "No towel this time, lady. I can be ready to go in ten seconds after I lock the door. You give me the sign, and we're on."

Nina slowly ran her tongue over the shell of my ear and whispered, "Lock the door."

I'd locked the door and peeled off my clothes before I even got back to the bed. Nina was still in her bra and panties, but I made quick work of them, happy to take advantage of the two of us in the mood and not exhausted, a rare thing since the kids came along.

"Somebody's ready," she said with a giggle as I gently pushed her back onto the mattress.

"I have a gorgeous wife who I want to make love to right now.

We don't get too many opportunities like this anymore."

Trailing my mouth down her neck, I kissed my way to her breast and took her nipple between my lips. I sucked gently, loving the feel of the tender skin pebbling against my tongue.

Nina held my head in place, moaning as I moved to the other nipple. "I hope you know I wish we could do this more often too."

I popped the pert nipple from my mouth and looked up at her. "No talking. Just sex, Mrs. Stone."

As I returned my tongue to flick her hardened nipple, I heard her above me say, "I mean, it's not like I don't want to a lot more, Tristan, but with your work and the kids…"

Sliding up her body, I kissed her hard on the mouth to stop her from explaining. "No more. I want to make love to my wife tonight, so let's just forget we're the parents of those three kids and remember how much in love we are with one another."

Her hands slid down my back as I positioned myself over her, and she pulled me into her. Nothing ever felt as incredible as when I was deep inside her wet cunt. Nina sighed softly and wrapped her legs around my waist, taking me into her even deeper. Slowly, I thrust in and out of her body, loving every touch of her hands on my skin and every whimper and moan as my cock slid over that spot I knew drove her wild.

"Oh, God, yes…don't stop…"

I loved it when she talked like that. The needy sound in her voice told me she was close. Thrusting my hips faster, I pushed into her searching for that sweet moment when her body came apart beneath me. Dragging her nails down my back, she panted near my ear. "Right there, Tristan. Don't stop. Fuck me…"

"Let yourself go, baby. Let me feel you come."

Her cunt contracted around my cock, squeezing it gently as she began to orgasm, and I drove into her hard, desperate to come and feel her give in to her body. "Oh, God! Yes…yes!"

Nina's body shook, her release sending tiny tremors rolling over my cock as I came inside her. Every ounce of energy I possessed left my body as I let myself get lost in the feeling of making love to the woman I adored.

She stayed silent for a long time, and then placed a single kiss just below my ear as she whispered, "I love you, Tristan. I've missed this."

Rolling over onto my back, I pulled her close. With her head on my chest, she traced her fingernail over my stomach, making my skin flutter beneath her touch. "I've missed this too. Between my work and the kids, we forgot us for a while."

Looking up at me, she asked in a small voice, "Do you ever wish we had waited? I mean, I love our kids more than life itself, but I miss being able to just lie here, naked in your arms after making love without expecting a knock on the door."

Bringing her hand to my lips, I pressed a soft kiss into her palm and looked into those gentle blue eyes. "I know. I miss this too, but I wouldn't trade a minute of our time with the kids either."

"I wouldn't either, Tristan. I know the five of us had a rocky start, but you were there for me every minute of every day. You were their dad from day one, but I needed your help to become their mom."

I cupped her face in my hands and gazed into the eyes of the only person who ever truly brought out the good in me. "You were always their mother, Nina. You just needed to believe in that. That's all I did."

"Someday, Tristan, I'm going to tell the kids the truth about that first night, about how the real story is that it was me who fell for you first."

I shook my head. "Don't. I don't want our daughters thinking they should fall for a guy because of a nice car."

Nina chuckled and pressed a kiss onto my lips. "You're okay with our kids not ever knowing the truth?"

I wrapped my arms around her and held her close. "They already know the truth, Nina. You do too."

She mumbled something about honesty against my chest and

drifted off to sleep as I held her in my arms. As I stroked her soft brown hair, I knew whatever the truth was of how we fell in love and who fell in love first, since that first night Nina had been the only person to ever make me want to take a chance on a life built on love.

I looked across the room to the portrait we'd had taken right after the kids' fifth birthday and saw the family that love had given me. In front of Nina and me sat our beautiful children, each one with something special from both of us. Diana, with her dark brown hair and eyes but a smile just like her mother's, leaned back against me with her tiny hand wrapped around my finger like she'd done since she was a baby. On the other side in front of Nina sat Tressa, her sister's identical twin but as different as night to her day. Just as in my dream, Tressa was a Stone through and through. And in the center sat Ethan, the perfect melding of his mother and father with Nina's light brown hair and my brown eyes. Quieter than his sisters, he was his father's son in that way, but I hoped that one day years from now, he'd meet someone who made him want to say those words that could change his world like his mother had done for me.

Nina snuggled against me, and just as I closed my eyes, I whispered into the darkness of the room, "I love you, Nina."

Lifting her head to look up at me, she smiled sweetly. "I love you too, Tristan. And it was me who fell first."

"Sweet dreams, princess."

Return To Me

CHAPTER ONE

JORDAN

THE SOOTY SMELL OF A campfire fills my nose as I race through the woods toward the tent I'm sharing with my sister Kayla for the next week. It's a hot summer night, and the heaviness of the humidity hangs in the air, weighing me down, but I reach the tent safely and zip the flaps closed to a chorus of laughter from Kayla.

But I turn around and it isn't my sister sitting behind me but my mother. I shake my head in confusion and ask, "Why are you here? Where did Kayla go?"

Her expression turns serious, scaring me. She says nothing but points toward the outside of the tent, a look of terror filling her eyes.

"Mom, what's wrong? What's out there?"

"He's out there."

Her words come out in cryptic monosyllables as her look changes to sadness. I'm confused. Who's out there?

"Was Dad able to get off work and come with us?"

She just shakes her head. "He's out there."

I opened my eyes and struggled to remember the details of the dream as I slowly eased back into consciousness. Reaching for my phone, I scrolled through my contacts to find my mother's number and called her. It was silly, but after having the same dream over and over for the past week, I figured I should mention it to her. Maybe she knew what my subconscious mind was up to.

"Jordan, is everything okay?" she asked in her usual sweet voice.

"You didn't get mugged, did you? I worry about that with you living there."

"No, mom. I didn't get mugged," I said, stifling a yawn. "I just had a weird dream and wanted to know if dad's okay."

"Of course he's okay, honey. He already left for work, but he's fine. Why?"

I rubbed the sleep from my eyes as I thought about the dream and wondered why my father never appeared in it even though my mother kept saying he was out there. My mind clearly thought someone was out there, and if it wasn't my father, then who?

"No reason. I've just been having this strange dream where Kayla and I are camping and you show up saying that some guy is outside the tent. I ask you if it's dad and you say it isn't but you keep saying he's out there."

"It sounds more like a nightmare to me. Imagine me out in a tent in the middle of the woods. Just the thought of it makes me feel like bugs are crawling all over me. I did it once. No thanks."

Laughing, I sit up in bed. "I don't remember you ever going camping with us. That's why I was calling to ask about dad since he's the one we always go camping with."

My mother remained silent for a moment and then quietly said, "Well, I'm sure it's nothing. Nothing at all. You probably saw some show on TV that had camping in it and that's what's playing on your mind."

"Probably."

"Anything else new, honey?"

"Just the engagement party. I can't wait to see you two there. It's going to be great."

"Oh, I'm sure it will be, Jordan. We'll see you and Brock Saturday night. I'll tell your Dad you miss camping with him too. Maybe you two can get out to the woods before school begins again."

"I'd like that. Okay, I'm going to get moving with my day, Mom. I'll see you Saturday. I love you."

"Love you, honey. See you then."

I pressed END on my phone and set it down on the bed next to me, my mind occupied with the idea of what my mother's only time camping must have been like to ruin the experience for her forever. I wished I could remember, but I must have been only a baby then.

Maybe it was all that fresh air. She'd always been more of the air conditioning type.

THE MESS OF MY LIVING room stood as proof positive that I'd need to change my ways once I became Mrs. Brock Hannon. Mrs. Brock Hannon. I loved the way that sounded. Jordan Hannon. Not bad. Maybe something hyphenated would work. Jordan Wright-Hannon. That sounded pretty good too.

"Nina, which sounds better—Jordan Hannon or Jordan Wright-Hannon?"

Looking up from the magazine she was reading, a slow smile crept into Nina's usually placid expression. Tilting her head so her warm brown hair tumbled over her left shoulder, she said, "Well, I don't know. I've always liked your last name, so maybe the hyphenated one could work."

I pushed aside the pile of bridal magazines on the couch and plopped myself down. "I like that one too. Okay, it's settled. Hyphenated it is."

"Jordan, I can't believe you're getting married. It's still hasn't sunk in."

"I know. It's just so wild, isn't it? It's a nice feeling, though."

Nina stayed silent for a moment. "It is. I think it's great. I just thought…"

Curling my legs under me, I waited for her to finish her sentence. When she didn't, I asked, "What? You always thought what?"

She got a sheepish look on her face and I saw in her eyes she had something to say. Did she not like my future husband? "Nina, what is it?"

"I just always thought you'd marry someone else."

"Who? Have you been holding out on me? Does Tristan have another brother because you know I'd be open to that," I joked.

Knitting her brows, she shook her head. "No."

"Well, I was teasing anyway. I wouldn't just dump Brock that way, even for someone as great as Tristan."

Nina gave me a weak smile. "Jordan, I thought that you and Gage would end up together."

Her words landed like a flaming bag of shit right there in the middle of our conversation. Gage? Why the hell would she think I'd ever end up with him?

I crossed my arms and leveled my stare on her. "Why would you think that? The man broke up with me over the phone and never even bothered to call me when he came back here, assuming he came back and didn't hook up with some Hollywood tartlet instead."

"I know, but I guess I just always hoped that I got you together with the guy you'd end up with."

"Well, Gage lost out. His problem, not mine. We weren't very good together anyway. Not like Brock and I are. Now that I'm with someone like him, I see Gage and I could never have worked out."

Nina shifted her gaze down toward the magazine in her lap. "Oh."

"Oh what? Don't you like Brock? He's wealthy, smart, hot, and everything I've ever wanted. All Gage had going for him was hot."

"I don't think he was dumb, was he?" she said in defense of the man who'd broken my heart.

"No, but he wasn't Brock smart. He was just bodyguard smart."

"Oh, okay."

"Another oh? What is up with you? You don't like Brock, do you?"

She avoided my gaze and shook her head. "No, it's not like that. I like him. I do. He's got everything a girl could want. Looks, money, intelligence, success…he's the whole package. I can definitely see why you'd be crazy about him."

Something in the way her voice sounded tentative told me that's not all she thought of the man I was set to become officially engaged to in just days. "Is there something you need to tell me, Nina? Did you have Tristan investigate him and you found out he's a serial killer or something? Tell me. You have to tell me! As my best friend, you can't let me marry someone who's a serial killer."

"No, I didn't have Tristan check him out. I don't know anything about Brock other than what you've told me and what I've seen in the times we've all hung out together. He seems perfectly nice. Just the kind of guy you deserve. I have no doubt that he'll make a fantastic husband."

"Okay. As long as he's not an ax murderer, we're all good," I said with a chuckle.

Leaning toward me, she got a playful look in her eyes and whispered, "You've never mentioned about the goods. How come?"

Nina never ceased to surprise me. No one would ever know to look at her, but she had the ability to see into someone in a way that other people couldn't. In truth, Brock's goods were…well, less than stellar. I'd never really talked about him that way because even though his skills in bed were definitely passable, the reality was that sex between us wasn't the best I'd ever had.

But then again, the best sex I'd ever had was with someone who thought so little of me he broke up with me over the phone and never called back.

"He's fine. You know. Everything is in working order and we have a great time together."

Wow. Even I knew that sounded lame.

"Oh. Well, that's good. Working order is definitely good."

Lots of goods. Except the ones we were talking about.

"Sex isn't everything in the world, Nina. We're not all as lucky as you are with Mr. Incredible Guy who has all any woman ever wanted."

That came out a whole lot more defensive than I'd intended.

Nina reached over and gave me a sympathetic arm squeeze. "I'm sorry. I didn't mean to say anything to upset you. I'm sure you and Brock will be very happy, Jordan. That's all I've ever wanted for you. If Brock's the one to give you all the happiness you deserve, then I'm his biggest fan."

"No biggie, honey. I know you love me and want to see me happy. I think Brock can do that—make me happy, you know? Maybe I'll get my happy ending like you did."

She tilted her head and smiled. "Definitely. So what kind of progress have you made on the wedding gown? You know, it's never too early."

I picked up one of the half dozen bridal magazines that sat between us and began to absentmindedly flip through the pages. I'd breezed through a bunch of them a few times, but nothing had jumped out at me. None of the dresses seemed right. I wasn't reed thin and tall like so many of the models or cute and shapely like Nina. I was too toned to wear the thin girl or the curvy girl dresses.

"None yet. I still have time."

Nina grabbed another of the magazines and turned to a page where she'd found one I might like. "What about this one? It's got great lines and with your body, it will look incredible."

I turned my head to look at a form-fitting white gown with a draped neckline and a body hugging cut. "Not horrible."

"It would be great on you. I could never wear that." Nina looked down her body and frowned. "Even before having triplets."

"Says the woman whose wedding gown nearly took her husband's breath away that day."

Nina blushed that cute way she always did when someone complimented her, and the apples of her cheeks turned pink. "Well, then we need to find you a gown that will do the same for your husband-to-be. Should I fold this page down?"

I glanced down at the dress again. "Yeah, it's fold-worthy."

"Good. We're making progress. I think if you can find ten fold-worthy dresses in this mass of glossy magazines you'll be in good shape."

"Nina, you know I'm only getting engaged in a few days. We're not getting married until next year. I think I have time."

She pointed at another magazine near my knee. "You can never be too early with the gown, according to an article I read in that one there."

"Well, the oracle has spoken then. Will twenty by Tuesday be okay with American Bride?" I joked.

Rolling her eyes, she made a clucking noise with her tongue. "You're not taking this seriously, Jordan. Brock is an important man. You're going to have a big wedding with lots of important people there. You can't leave the dress to chance."

The way Nina talked about my wedding made me queasy. I didn't really want a big wedding. I liked the way she and Tristan did it. Intimate and cozy with just a few close friends. The idea of some big shindig with hundreds of people who were little more than strangers surrounding me on my big day wasn't my style.

"Well, does that mean I can't have a wedding that's right for me? Does everything have to be right for him?"

Nina's blue eyes opened wide in surprise. "Is something going on that you haven't told me?"

I shrugged and waved away her concern. "No. I get that Brock is different than me. I'm all about shooting straight from the hip, and he's diplomatic and professional. I laugh out loud at funny things, and he can barely stand watching comedies. I get that. But shouldn't our wedding be a reflection of both of us and not just him?"

"Jordan, what's going on? Do you want to marry him?"

Her question hit a little too close to home, and I quickly answered, "Of course I do."

I couldn't answer that question as easily as I would have liked. I was crazy about Brock, no doubt. He'd swept me off my feet the very night we met. There I was standing outside school on the curb in the pouring rain deciding if I wanted to go home to my lonely apartment or stay in Manhattan for dinner by myself, and out of nowhere he pulled up and his limo drenched me with a puddle. Jumping out of the car, he ran to me and quickly stripped off his coat to try to dry me, like some fairytale hero.

But it was no use. I looked like a drowned rat. He gazed at me with those beautiful hazel eyes of his and introduced himself, and I thought maybe I was dreaming. When he offered to give me a ride home, I accepted, not even knowing his full name, and by the time we made it to Brooklyn, I hoped that one encounter wouldn't be our last.

He pursued me with a vengeance, sending gifts and calling me at all hours just to say he was thinking of me. By our third date, I knew we had something special. He doted on me like no man ever had, and for the first time in my life, I wanted to believe a relationship would last.

But for all that, something inside me made me worry that it would all go away as quickly as it came into my life, leaving me alone once again. This time that little voice inside me that always feared the worst seemed to be able to whisper louder than my positive side and its Good Things Happen To Good People mantra.

Now as we got ready to celebrate his asking me to marry him, my worries that something would make this all go away plagued me more than ever. What if I wasn't enough? I'd never been enough for anyone else. What if he woke up one day soon and realized that he wanted someone like him—wealthy, proper, and subdued.

Someone not like me.

I folded a glossy page with a long silk gown better suited to the type of woman Brock Hannon should probably be with. Needing to change the subject, I mumbled, "I had that same dream again."

"The one with your mother?"

Nodding, I looked up and pretended not to be frightened. I'd had the dream all week and still couldn't figure out what it meant, if it meant anything. But my gut told me it wasn't a good thing.

"Yeah. It's so weird because my mother wouldn't be caught dead camping," I joked.

Nina chuckled at the thought of my mother anywhere near the outdoors. My mother was the last person on Earth I'd expect to find camping or doing anything like that. In fact, the running joke in my family was that she was the inspiration for the giraffe from the Madagascar movie and his fear of nature.

"Your mother's a sweetheart, Jordan, but she's definitely not a woman who does the camping thing."

"I know! All those bugs and wild animals and no decent bedding. She'd crawl right out of her skin if she had to spend ten minutes in a tent."

"Was it the same dream as before?"

"Yep. She keeps saying some guy is out there. She never says who or if it's my father, even though it makes sense that she'd be talking about my dad since he's the one I've gone camping with for all my life."

Looking up toward the ceiling, Nina seemed to think about it for a moment and shook her head. "I have no idea. Keep in mind that not all dreams mean things. It could just be that you miss going camping. Maybe you and Brock should take a weekend and spend it in the outdoors."

Now it was my turn to chuckle. "Brock and my mother are cut from the same cloth. He'd no more spend time in a tent camping than she would."

"Then maybe that's what it means! You love camping and because he's so much in love with you, Brock comes to see you out in the wilderness, even though he hates it."

I couldn't help but smile. "Always the romantic, huh? Well, if that's what it means, why don't I ever see him in my dream? And why does my mother keep saying he's out there instead of saying Brock's out there? She knows Brock's name."

Nina stood from the couch and leaned over to kiss me on the cheek. "I didn't say I had all the answers. I'll keep thinking about it, but I have to get back to the house. Cara and the kids will be back from the park by the time Jensen gets us home. When are you coming out to see them? Ever since they started walking they're even more fun to hang out with. I can grab Cara and we can take them to the zoo. They'd love that. What do you think?"

"Sure. We can do it before I go back to school. I still have a few weeks, so it's a date. Give them all a kiss for me, and be sure to tell Tristan I said hi."

Grabbing her purse, she turned toward the door. "Call me. I know we'll be seeing you Saturday night, but call me anyway. I get lonely for our talks out there."

I followed her to the door to see her out. "I will. Tell Jensen not to drive too fast, that maniac."

Nina rolled her eyes. "Jensen is no more a maniac than I am. We're all boring out in the country. Just think, that's going to be you in a few months."

I kissed her goodbye and as I closed the door, I thought about what she'd said. I didn't consider her and Tristan boring in any way, shape, or form. After all they'd gone through before they got married, they deserved some calm times. My life had always been pretty boring, though, until Brock.

Would that all change when we married?

✧　✧　✧

I STOOD IN THE LIVING room of Brock's penthouse apartment as he paced back and forth talking on the phone about some business issue that had come up just as we were set to leave for dinner. Dressed in his usual black suit, he looked every bit the businessman he was. The owner of a web startup company, he'd rocketed to the top of his field in just three short years. He'd branched out into other areas of business I had to admit I didn't know a lot about, but the main source of his income remained the internet startup.

It was that business that preoccupied him at the moment, making him rake his hands through his light blond hair in an obvious sign of stress. The frown on his face deepened with each pass by me, and I worried our night might be ruined by whatever bad news he was dealing with.

"Riley, I don't give a damn what you think. This needs to happen and I expect it to happen this week. Do you understand me or do I need to explain it again? I assume you're bright enough to take care of this. Am I wrong in that assumption?"

The sharpness of Brock's tone made me feel sorry for poor Riley on the receiving end of his anger. For as sweet as he could be, my future husband had an edge to him that could cut anyone to the quick.

He passed me again, still grimacing, and bit out, "I'm going out tonight, and if I get back and find out this hasn't been handled, you're going to be out of a job. I don't think I can make this any clearer, Riley, so get it done."

And with that, he shut his phone off and stuffed it into his pocket.

Brock stopped in front of where I sat and looked down at me, the serious expression still on his face. "Jordan, I'm sorry that took so long. I had to take that call."

Looking up at him, I put on my sweetest smile. "I understand. It's no biggie."

He lifted my chin with his forefinger. "So sweet. Thank you."

"I did feel a little bad for poor Riley." Standing, I straightened his grey tie. "You gave him a pretty stern warning there."

"I understand," he said, his hazel eyes staring deeply into mine. "You're far nicer than I am. Riley probably wishes you were his boss. But sometimes you have to crack the whip."

"I'm sorry. I understand."

"No need to be sorry," he said sweetly. "So how hungry are you because I'm starving."

I loved when he was like this—when he shed the serious

businessman part of himself and just let himself be who he was with me.

"I'm famished. Where are we off to tonight?"

He tapped me on the tip of my nose and winked. "How about that Brick place near your apartment?"

"Wanting to slum it tonight, huh?" I joked. "Okay, I'm good for it."

Brock smiled and kissed me softly on the lips. "Good. Just let me change out of these clothes and we can go."

As he took off his business suit, I looked out the floor to ceiling window at the city below. For the first time ever, I felt like I'd really found someone who wanted me. Even though we were truly as different as night and day, we worked.

"Did I tell you Nina came over today to get me moving on the wedding gown?" I said loudly toward the bedroom.

He walked toward me dressed in jeans and a button down shirt, and I saw the slight frown that always seemed to come across his face whenever I spoke about Nina. They'd only spent a little time together and nothing of note had happened on any of those occasions, so I couldn't figure out why he wouldn't like my best friend.

"Nina? No, you didn't mention she came by to see you."

I encircled his neck with my arms and leaned in to kiss him, planting a tiny kiss on the center of his lips. "Yeah. She's coaching me on how I should be focusing on the dress since I'm marrying such an important man."

"An important man? Did she say that?" he asked.

"Yes, she did. She thinks I need to take the whole wedding gown issue far more seriously. I'm not having any luck finding the right one yet."

Brock turned away from me and walked over to the bar to pour himself a drink. "That's nice of her, but I wouldn't worry about that quite yet. We have time. We aren't even announcing our engagement until this weekend."

A hint of disgust hid just under his pleasant words, and I wondered if I should ask why he didn't like Nina. She and Tristan had never been anything but perfectly nice to him every time they'd be around him, so I was baffled. Nobody ever disliked Nina.

"Is everything okay, Brock? Nina doesn't mean any harm. She just wants to make sure our wedding goes as smoothly as can be."

Taking a sip of his bourbon, Brock shrugged. "No, everything's fine. I'm sure she's just trying to help. I just wish you'd come to me with any issues about our wedding instead of her."

I moved over to his side and shook my head. "No, there are no issues. Nina isn't trying to intrude, if that's what you're thinking. She's my best friend, so it's natural that she'd want to be involved in the happiest moment of my life."

He pressed a smile onto his lips. "I'd always thought that two people who want to be husband and wife would be best friends."

"I'm sorry, Brock. I didn't mean it that way. It's just that Nina and I have been like sisters since college. That doesn't mean she's more important to me than you are, though."

Instead of making things better, that only made them worse. "I certainly hope not. After we're married, I hope to move to Dallas so it's just going to be me and you then."

Something in the way he said that made the hairs on the back of my neck stand up. I'd been a New York girl for so long and near Nina since freshman year in college, and the thought of leaving the city I'd grown to call my own for a brand new one without a friend anywhere close made me uneasy.

I was just being silly. Brock offered me the world, and all I had to do was accept that I couldn't continue to live the life I'd lead as a single girl all these years. I'd wished for this for so long, and now all my dreams were coming true all because of this wonderful man.

So why did the mere mention of him taking me away terrify me so?

Brock reached out and took my hand in his, almost petting my skin. "I'm sorry. I didn't mean to be like that. It's my work and

Riley's screw up. Let's just go to dinner and forget all this."

I smiled, even though his remark about leaving and it being just the two of us continued to echo in my mind. This was what my life was now. If I ever wanted to move out of that Brooklyn apartment and have nice things like Nina had with Tristan, I needed to be willing to make compromises. Brock could offer me everything a girl could want, if I could compromise.

No one got everything they wanted.

Right?

CHAPTER TWO

GAGE

FINISHING THE REPORTS FOR THE month, I clicked SEND to make sure my accountant had everything for July and sat back in my office chair to read over the letter that had kept me up most of the night before. I'd done exactly what they'd demanded every time they'd sent one, convinced that if I did they'd leave my life, but now they'd returned with more threats.

She still isn't safe, Gage.

I closed my eyes and swallowed hard at the thought of Jordan being hurt because of my failures. I'd left her with no explanation, making her think she was the reason I'd basically turned my back on her but willing to be that kind of bastard if she'd be safe.

The memory of the hurt in her voice that night when I broke up with her over the phone made me cringe now, months later. I couldn't give her a reason for leaving, knowing when I didn't that her imagination would take over and fill in the blanks.

I could be a real dick sometimes.

That I did it to protect her didn't matter when I heard her quiet sobs and her pleas for some answer to why I could be so callous to her. If I told her, then she'd be in danger too, and I couldn't risk her life because I'd made one stupid mistake.

Since that day, I'd lived with the guilt of knowing the one woman I loved hated me and had good reason to. She'd gone on with her life, probably getting hooked up with some great guy through Nina. If I knew Nina, she found her friend a man with all the things I couldn't offer her.

Money. Power. All the things Jordan deserved and I'd never have to give her.

"Boss, we're off to the Becker party. You coming?"

I looked up from the letter and smiled at John, one of my workers at the tiny business I'd started from the money Tristan had given me after I'd returned to New York. Saving someone's life came in none too cheaply, and with the money I'd built Varo Security. Tristan had helped me by referring some clients too, so it didn't take long before I'd gotten back on my feet again.

"I'll be there. It's just a birthday party, so unless Becker has pissed someone off, it should be mostly making sure no one put their hands on him. The man has a real problem with people touching him. I told him I'd be stopping in after the party begins, but if you have any problems, just call my cell."

"Got it. See you there."

John left me sitting alone in my tiny office with my memories and my guilt. As I did every night, I typed in Jordan's name on my computer to search for any news of her. Not that anything would have changed since yesterday. I knew that, but it didn't stop my need to see if today was finally the day I'd learn that she'd moved on.

The usual came up on Google. A shopping trip with Nina. A picture of her with Nina and Tristan standing near their triplets on one of their days at the playground near the house in Dutchess County. An older picture of Jordan from college, her blond hair much longer but her eyes the same gorgeous, unforgettable green.

I'd seen all of these before, but it didn't matter. I had to make sure.

Not that I'd be able to do anything if one day I saw an engagement announcement with her name. The people black-mailing me had sworn that if I ever even tried to contact her again, they'd hurt her. I didn't doubt them either, so even if I wanted to do my best impression of the famous scene in The Graduate and try to stop her from marrying another man, I couldn't.

I couldn't risk them hurting her because of their hatred for me.

I sat there staring at the pictures of her on my laptop screen, my mind drifting back to the night when I first stopped over at her apartment in Brooklyn. That night I knew I'd fallen hard.

Jordan sat cross-legged on the couch wearing shorts that showed off her tanned, toned legs and a pink t-shirt, her long blond hair tied up in a messy ponytail. She had an All-American girl look that said the boys at the high school football games had watched her as she cheered on the sidelines each Friday night, every one of them secretly in love with the bubbly blond with the beautiful smile.

"I was a little surprised to see you at my door," she said quietly, her green eyes staring at me with a look that made me think she'd see right through any tough guy act I'd try to pull.

"Well, I was in the city, so I thought I'd stop in."

Not exactly the truth, but I wasn't about to tell her I'd been thinking about her for weeks and as I drove down the Taconic I'd finally decided to take a chance on whatever we could be instead of living in the past.

Her cheeks turned a deep pink color that only made her more beautiful, and she smiled. "I'm glad you did."

We sat there awkwardly trying to be cooler than either of us were about the obvious attraction between us. I'd fought it day and night when we'd lived together out at Tristan and Nina's house, convincing myself that being with her would be a conflict of interest. I couldn't let another client down because my attention was on my desires instead of their safety.

Jordan hadn't fought it then, though. Every evening, rain or shine, she'd pretend to walk around the grounds exercising, as if I didn't know exactly what time she worked out in the gym inside the house every morning before going to school. She'd wave and smile as she walked toward us, and I'd pretend I wasn't thrilled to see her there for me. Most nights I'd stand practically silent as she and West talked, but no matter how bad my day had been, just seeing her made it better every time.

"Do you miss living out at the house?" I asked, more nervous than a teenage boy on a first date. Christ, even my palms were sweaty!

Jordan looked around her small apartment and sighed. "In some ways, yeah. I miss living with Nina. We've lived as roommates for so long that it feels weird here without her. That was one good thing about living out in the sticks. And the gym Tristan has out there is first rate. I loved that! Now I have to haul my cookies eight blocks to get a decent workout. I definitely miss the gym."

"Eight blocks at the crack of dawn could be dangerous around here," I considered out loud, more than mildly concerned about her walking that far so early in the morning.

A sly smile spread across her lips. "Crack of dawn? How did you know when I worked out?"

"I...I just assumed since you work all day and you're probably exhausted after dealing with all those little kids all day."

Hopefully gorgeous women loved rambling because that's what I was offering at the moment.

"You knew when I worked out when I lived at the house, didn't you?"

I shrugged, attempting to be nonchalant. "I was security for the estate. I was supposed to know what was going on there."

"With Tristan and Nina, Gage. Not me."

"I was thorough."

"You knew when I worked out. You liked me."

I nodded, unsure of what to say. I had liked her, more than I wanted to admit at first and then much more, even as I tried to fight it.

"Why didn't you let me know you liked me? I was convinced all those times I tried to get you to talk to me that you didn't even like it when I came around."

"I didn't think I should start anything when I was watching Nina, Jordan. I didn't mean to make you think I didn't like it when you came around."

She gave me one of her gorgeous smiles and bit her lip lightly. "It's okay. I survived."

We sat there staring at one another, neither of us knowing what to say next. The beginning was always hard. Two people who've noticed they like the world a little more because the other person is in it realize they want to say all those things they've heard in songs but are too afraid to in case they've misread the signs.

Jordan stood from the couch and pointed toward the next room. "You thirsty? I'm going to grab a glass of soda or something. Want one?"

"Sure. Thanks."

I watched her walk to the kitchen and something inside me said it was now or never. Time to bite the bullet. If I didn't make a move now, we'd sit there in her living room talking around our attraction to one another by retelling stories of the one person we had in common. As much as I liked Nina, I didn't want to spend the entire night talking about her with Jordan.

Rounding the corner, I found her standing at the counter pouring a glass of soda. I watched her catch a drop as it slid down the side of the glass, smacking her lips as her finger touched her lips. She put the bottle of soda back in the refrigerator and stopped to look at herself in the glass front cabinet door next to the sink.

I walked up behind her and whispered, "You look beautiful."

As she spun around, her hands ran into my chest. Startled, she took a step back and hit the counter. "I didn't know you were standing there. I was just looking…getting the drinks."

"You look beautiful, Jordan."

She looked gorgeous. Her blond hair hung in long wisps around her face, escaping the confines of her hair tie that held her ponytail and making her look messy in a sexy way. She never wore much makeup, so her skin had a natural look to it, a glow that made her look healthy. Then there were those green eyes, a green unlike any I'd ever seen. They weren't dark like pine green or vivid like emerald or Kelly green. They were more like deep moss green, the kind of color you could get lost in trying to figure out where in the world you'd seen that exact shade before.

She blushed at my compliment and smiled up at me. "I never noticed how much taller you are than me. I guess since I was always in shoes, but I wore sneakers a lot, so—"

I stopped her talking with our first kiss, soft and unsure but thrilling nonetheless as I watched her eyes slowly close. Her lips yielded to mine, and she slipped her arms around my neck. Her touch against my skin sent chills up and down my spine. I'd waited for this moment for months, unsure I'd ever be able to go through with it and sure I'd fuck it up when the time finally came.

I didn't want to fuck this up like I'd fucked up with everyone else in the past.

Pulling back, I cupped her face in my hands and watched her as she kept her eyes closed. "Why won't you look at me?"

"Because you're so close and so right here that I'm afraid I'll open my eyes and see you don't like me as much as I want you to."

"Open them, Jordan." Still they remained closed. "Open your eyes and look at me."

She took a deep breath and winced as if she was in pain. Then she slowly lifted her eyelids to show me those beautiful moss colored eyes looking up at me.

"Okay."

"I love it when you look up at me like you are right now. You did that the first time I met you. Did you know that?"

A tiny smile made her mouth turn up slightly and she shook her head. "No. I didn't know."

"I remember it. I remember wondering what it would feel like to have you give me that look if we were ever alone together. I told myself if the chance ever came around that I'd make sure I took it."

Her eyes grew wide as I spoke, like hearing the words made her want to see more of me. She looked away and began to speak, but I took her chin and made her look at me again. "It's okay. Don't look away."

"I think I should warn you. I don't have a good track record with men. It always starts out good, but then it always ends."

"My track record isn't great either, so I guess I should warn you too. At least we know going into this, right?"

She nodded. "Yeah. We gave each other fair warning. That's all anyone can ask for."

I kissed her again, loving the feel of her lips on mine. We stood there in her kitchen for hours talking and kissing as she sweetly scolded me for ignoring her the entire time she lived at the house and I teased her about how I thought for a while she might have liked old man West instead of me. The entire night was comfortable and easy, like we'd known each other forever and could tell one another anything.

I looked around my tiny office to see I'd been daydreaming about Jordan for an hour. I could have spent the rest of my night sitting there at my desk remembering how she made me feel, but Becker was expecting me, so I had to go.

Duty called.

✧   ✧   ✧

"GAGE VARO, GOOD TO SEE you! How are you?" Mitch Becker asked as he ushered me into his Upper West Side penthouse. "Your guys are already here, so head out to the terrace and have a drink."

Mitch Becker looked like nearly every client Tristan sent me. Tall, lean, with perfect hair and perfect teeth and always wearing a suit, no matter the occasion. They all seemed to reek of inherited money, but unlike Tristan, most of them were insufferable. I could deal with Mitch, though. He acted more human than the others.

"Thanks, Mitch. Any problems I should know about?"

He flashed me a big toothy smile. "No. These people are mostly friends, so they know the rule about touching. You'll know if there's a problem."

"Got it. I'll circle back in a few, Mitch."

Backing away, he pointed toward the doors leading outside. "Sounds good. Tristan Stone and his wife are out on the terrace."

I smiled like this was good news, but seeing Nina and Tristan always brought back more memories and at that moment, I didn't want to think any more about Jordan. I couldn't avoid at least saying hello, though, and heading out to the terrace, I saw Nina wave her arms in the air to get my attention.

"Gage! I didn't know you'd be here!" she announced with a smile as she moved through the crowd toward me.

"How's my favorite power couple doing?" I asked, truly happy to see her and Tristan again, even if just the sight of them made me think of Jordan.

Nina hugged me and took me by the hand to join Tristan, who seemed to be enjoying the party as much as a trip to the dentist. Shaking his hand, I said, "It's good to see you again. How's life out in good old Dutchess County?"

He leaned in toward me and whispered, "Better than here. If I didn't have to attend parties like this, I'd much rather be sitting with the kids and Nina watching the Care Bears movie."

Nina beamed her happiness at hearing him say a night of cartoons was better than a swanky party in Manhattan, and I couldn't blame her. They'd been through so much they deserved a quiet life in the suburbs.

It wasn't what I'd want for my life, though.

"How's the security business going? I hope some of my references panned out."

"It's going well. Thanks for referrals. They've been working out great so far."

"That's wonderful, Gage," Nina said as she gave my wrist a sympathetic squeeze.

I knew what was coming next. Nina and Tristan knew too. It always happened this way. Every time we saw each other, we made some small talk, and then there came the uncomfortable lull, which meant none of us wanted to mention the person we all had in common, even though we were all thinking about her. But Nina would end up saying something about her and I'd have to pretend just the mention of Jordan didn't hurt like hell.

This time I wanted to leave before any of that happened, though. "I need to get going, but it was nice seeing you guys again." I extended my hand to shake Tristan's again. "Keep those referrals coming."

"Always," he said in that genuine way I knew meant he'd keep on sending me work.

They both smiled as I turned away and I was sure I'd escaped before any mention of Jordan, but Nina caught up with me just as I walked back inside and took my hand. "Hey, Gage. I wanted to tell you that Jordan is—"

I looked down and saw sadness in Nina's eyes. Suddenly, terror raced through me. "What's wrong? Did something happen to her?"

Frowning, she said the words I'd dreaded hearing since I lost Jordan. "She's getting engaged. She and her fiancé are announcing it this Saturday. He owns a web startup company. I'm sorry, Gage. I just thought you should know."

In an instant, the room felt like someone had picked it up and shaken it like a snow globe. Everything seemed to float around me as Nina's news sank into my brain. Jordan getting engaged. I mumbled something about thanking her for letting me know and quickly made my way through the crowd of party guests to get outside. I needed to escape that world that had just taken the woman I loved away.

Jordan had moved on and in just a few days she'd be engaged to be married to another man. What I'd feared every day since I broke up with her had finally happened.

And it hurt even more than I ever thought it would.

I HEADED DOWN COLUMBUS AVENUE, unsure where I was going. I didn't want to go back to the office, but it didn't matter where I went. Everywhere in the city made me think of her. What the fuck had I been thinking when I moved back here?

My chest felt like someone had just hit me square with a

sledgehammer. I tried to take a deep breath in, but I couldn't. Nina's news threatened to smother me right there in the middle of Manhattan. My legs continued to move, but my brain was preoccupied with one thought.

Jordan marrying another man.

A half hour later I was in a cab headed toward her apartment for the second time that week. I knew I couldn't talk to her or I'd risk putting her in danger, but maybe if I could see her as she left her apartment for the night I might not feel like my chest was being squeezed until I couldn't breathe.

Who was I kidding? Seeing her would only make this feeling worse, but I didn't care. At least if I saw her, even for just a fleeting moment, it could feel like I was still in her world and she was still in mine.

"Hey, slow down past these buildings," I ordered just as the cabbie turned onto Jordan's street. On the sidewalk, people stood talking and laughing, never knowing that for one guy in a cab he would have given the world to see the woman he loved for even a second.

The car slowed down to a crawl, and as we passed her building I looked up toward her windows. Dark, except for the light from the lamp in her living room she left on whenever she went out, it looked empty and lonely.

Like me.

She was probably out with her soon-to-be fiancé planning a life together. My chest contracted at the truth that finally Jordan had moved on. I'd promised myself that as long as my past put her in danger, I wouldn't try to be part of her life anymore, but the reality that come that Saturday she'd be officially engaged to another man made me want to forget all those promises I'd made to myself and finally tell her the truth of why I'd had to leave her.

I told the cabbie to take me back to my office as the hard truth settled into my brain. I couldn't tell her any of that if it meant she'd be in danger. So she'd get engaged and I'd remain what I'd always been since that first night at her apartment.

In love with her more than I thought it was possible for one person to love another.

CHAPTER THREE

JORDAN

JENSEN PULLED UP IN FRONT of my apartment at eleven sharp, and I headed down the stairs to join Nina for our noon mani/pedi appointment at our favorite spa, Roget's. A treat from Nina to celebrate my engagement, it was also a chance for us to spend time together like the old days.

"Nina, any chance we can stop for a coffee before we go to Roget's? I'm dragging without caffeine this morning," I said as I climbed into the back of the car. Turning to face the front seat, I tapped Jensen on the shoulder. "Hey, Jensen! How are you today?"

"Very good, Miss Jordan. It's good to see you again."

"It's good to see you too. Just like old times."

"Can you wait until we get to the spa? You know they have those delicious scones I love," Nina said as we pulled away from the curb.

"Any coffee shop will do," I pleaded. "I ran out of coffee yesterday and you know how I am without my morning nectar of the gods."

Giggling, Nina said, "I haven't forgotten all those mornings we lived together. Jensen, there's a Dunkin Donuts on the next block. Please stop there so Jordan can get some caffeine in her and become human again."

"Thank you. I promise once I get my coffee, I'll be the same old wonderful Jordan I always am."

Nina began talking about the day ahead of us, full of

enthusiasm for our spa time and the final fitting for the gown I'd wear just two nights from then. I loved how excited she was for me and my big event. I just wished I felt as terrific about it as she did. It all felt like so much more than I was used to, but then again, I was marrying a successful man, so it was all new to me.

The car stopped and I jumped out to make a beeline for my morning go-go juice. Thankfully, the line was short and I only had to wait a few minutes to become human again. With coffee in hand, I climbed back into the car and we were off to Roget's for a day of pampering.

Bumper to bumper morning traffic into the city held us up, and as we sat waiting to move again, Nina said quietly, "I saw Gage last night at a party. He was working."

Just hearing his name made my heart skip a beat, and suddenly it felt like all the air had been sucked out of the car. Trying to act cool, I said in my best nonchalant voice, "Really? Who's he guarding now? The same teenager as before?"

"No. He's got his own security firm. I didn't tell you because I didn't want to upset you, but he's been back in the city for a while."

Back in the city for a while. So not only had he broken up with me over the phone, but he'd been back for a while and never bothered to even call me?

"Have you seen him before last night?"

"Yeah, a few times. The first time you were still pretty broken up over him so I didn't want to say anything. Then the other times you were already with Brock. Tristan sees him more than I do since he's been trying to help him get his business off the ground."

"Oh, well, that's nice," I said as all the pain of him leaving rushed back into my mind. "Nice to get his business off the ground."

Nina took my hand and squeezed it as if she'd just told me someone I loved had died. I didn't want sympathy. I wanted to forget Gage Varo, but every time I thought I'd finally put him out of my head, something reminded me of him and all those feelings came back with a vengeance.

God, I didn't want to feel that way anymore.

"I told him you were getting engaged, Jordan. He looked like he'd lost his best friend and then he left the party."

I turned away to look out the window so Nina couldn't see the tears in my eyes. "I don't know why he'd look like that. We were never friends. We were never much of anything by the way he could leave me with nothing more than a goodbye and never talk to me again."

"I'm sorry. I didn't know if I should tell you, but I figured since you're getting engaged to Brock, you wouldn't be upset like this. Jordan, what's going on?"

I wiped under my eyes and turned back to face her. "Nothing's going on."

"Then why are you so upset about me seeing Gage?"

"I'm not. Feel free to tell him I said hi the next time you see him."

Jensen stopped the car in front of Roget's and as I climbed out behind Nina, my entire world turned upside down. It was as if the universe was trying to hammer the idea that I needed to suffer into my head. There on the sidewalk in front of a boutique just two doors from the spa stood Gage with a stunning brunette in a red and white sundress. Nearly as tall as him, she looked like a wealthy debutante or supermodel with her gold jewelry and designer purse draped over her arm.

My brain told my legs to move, to follow Nina, but I stood there watching him smile and laugh with the woman and felt as if my feet were encased in cement. For nearly a year, I'd promised myself if I ever saw him again, I'd tell him how shitty a person he was. I'd finally show him how I overcame what he did when he left me without even a word of explanation. But now that I saw him there just a few yards away, none of that was in my mind.

All I could think of was how much I'd missed him.

His dark hair seemed longer than the last time I'd seen him, just brushing up against his collar now. It still looked soft, though, and the feel of it against my cheek as we lay in bed on Sunday mornings, relaxing on the only day of the week we both had off work, rushed back into my head.

He looked good. I hated that he looked good. I wanted him to look like shit because he missed me so much, but I didn't have that kind of luck. No, he looked like he always had.

Masculine and strong. The kind of man who would protect the woman he loved.

I felt the tears well in my eyes. He hadn't protected me. He'd been the one to hurt me, and now he got to stand there smiling and joking around with some beautiful woman while I stood frozen on the spot desperately wishing I didn't fucking care about him anymore.

"Jordan, honey, you okay? What's wrong?"

I tried to speak but his name got caught in my throat. Swallowing hard, I whispered, "Gage."

Nina followed my gaze to where he stood and quickly pulled on my arm. "Oh, sweetie. Let's go inside."

I looked back at the car to see Jensen watching me with concern and I turned to face Nina. "I need to go. I can't do this now. Get me out of here, Nina."

She hurried me back into the car, ordering Jensen to drive away quickly. I sat there staring at Gage, needing to see his eyes. Those dark blue eyes I'd loved. All I needed to see were his eyes. If I saw his eyes and he looked happy, I'd have to admit to myself that whoever I'd been in love with hadn't loved me. But if I saw something in his eyes that told me he wasn't as happy as he looked, maybe I'd find some solace in that.

Maybe I could believe he missed me like I missed him.

As the car drove past him, I lowered the window and he turned to look at the car. For a moment, there was only him and me in the world. His gaze met mine and I saw he recognized me. Those blue eyes stared into the car, and I searched them for any shred of a chance that he still cared. I wanted to believe somewhere inside him he missed me like I missed him, but the man who looked at me now wasn't like me.

Everything in his eyes told me whatever love I'd felt hadn't been mine in return.

The moment ended and Jensen sped down the street, weaving in and out of traffic on his way to wherever Nina had ordered him to go. It didn't matter. Wherever we went, I'd still feel the same.

"Jordan, what's going on? What happened back there?"

Losing the battle against my tears, I hung my head, embarrassed as they began to roll down my cheeks. "I always thought the first time I saw him I'd be able to be cool about things, but just seeing him standing there with that woman laughing and joking was too much to handle."

"Sweetie, why do you care? You're getting engaged to another man in a few days. What does it matter who Gage is talking to?"

"I don't know. It's been months since he broke up with me and I thought when I met Brock that I'd gotten over Gage, but you mentioning him the other day when you said you thought I'd marry him brought all those feelings back. And then you said you told him I was getting engaged and he looked bothered. I guess I just hoped that when he saw me he'd look like he missed me."

"I think you're wrong, Jordan. Every time either Tristan or I mention your name, he gets a look on his face like he's fighting some kind of awful pain. But if you feel this way about Gage, what are you going to do about Brock?"

I wiped my tears away and straightened myself in the seat. "Nothing. We'll get engaged this Saturday and then I'll begin planning a big society wedding just like he deserves to have."

Nina's face twisted into an expression of horror and confusion. "What do you mean nothing? You can't marry him! You still love Gage."

"Love has nothing to do with it, Nina. Brock can give me a good life. Gage obviously doesn't even care enough to tell me he's in the same fucking city as I am."

The car turned toward Brooklyn, and Nina leaned up against the front seat. "Jensen, please keep driving. We're not going back to Brooklyn just yet."

"Yes, we are, Jensen," I interjected, ready to go back to my bed and forget this day had ever happened.

"No, we aren't, Jordan. We need to talk."

"What's there to talk about? He doesn't care! End of discussion. Now poor Jensen can stop driving to random places and get me back to my apartment where I can crawl under the covers and call it a day."

"I'm talking about Brock. You can't seriously think you should say yes to marrying him if you're in love with another man. You'll be miserable."

Nina touched my shoulder and suddenly I couldn't stop myself from crying. I looked away and mumbled through my tears, "I'm already miserable. At least with Brock I'll be wealthy and miserable."

"Oh, honey. I don't want to see you miserable, and money won't make it any better."

"You don't understand, Nina. You have everything. A fabulous husband, three wonderful children, houses, cars, someone to drive you around wherever you want to go. You don't have anything to worry about."

"It hasn't always been that way, but I will admit I have a great life. I want that for you too, and I don't think Brock will give you that."

"Then I won't be getting it because other than Brock, no other guy has ever offered me much other than a few months and a quick goodbye."

"Is money that important?"

I couldn't help but look at her with disgust. "Spoken like someone who doesn't have to worry about money."

She sat back against the seat and sighed. "I could say that's not fair, but I see your point. But Tristan knows lots of wealthy, single men. You give me the word and I'll have him round them up."

"What does it matter? It will just end like it always does with me. What I want to know is why you don't like Brock and why you never told me before today."

Nina suddenly grew quiet and wouldn't look me in the eye, so I repeated my question and waited for some kind of answer. My best friend obviously didn't like the man I planned to marry, and I intended on finding out why.

"Well?"

"I don't know. I have a gut feeling about him and it's not good. There, I said it. The first time we met I felt it."

"That's because you're a diehard romantic and think I should be with someone else."

"I'm not going to lie. I like Gage. I always have, and I hoped you two would work out. But if you feel like you do and can't even see him without falling apart, why are you even thinking about marrying Brock?"

"Because I've never had a chance with someone like Brock, okay?" I screamed. I saw Jensen's look of surprise in the rearview mirror and lowered my voice. "I'm afraid if I don't take advantage of this I'm going to end up alone."

"Jordan, you're never going to be alone. Look at you. You're gorgeous. When we go places, men don't look at me. They look at you. The blond hair, the green eyes, the great body. You've got it all, and on top of all that, you're smart and funny. You're the whole package. Please don't sell yourself short and think you can't have any man you want."

"I can't," I said quietly, admitting a truth I'd tried so hard to avoid since that last time I heard Gage's voice tell me he basically didn't care enough to keep dating me.

"Why didn't you tell me you still cared for Gage? I could have invited the two of you out to the house and you could have had a chance to speak to him."

"Nina, he knows where I live. He's been back in the city for months and never once has he made the effort to see me. He doesn't want to speak to me. He never cared for me like I cared for him."

"I think you're wrong. I don't know why he hasn't called or come by, but I see the way he looks when I bring you up. He looks lost."

"Not lost enough to find me, though," I said, hanging my head.

We rode along in silence with the unavoidable truth there with us. If Gage had wanted to see me, he would have. It was that simple.

And since he hadn't, I had to accept that he didn't care about me anymore, if he ever really had, and I had a man who did care about me who wanted to marry me. All my romantic notions about Gage meant nothing compared to the reality that Brock loved me and had asked me to be his wife.

So he didn't make me feel like Gage did. So my best friend and the person I trusted more than anyone else in the world thought there was something hinky about him. That wasn't enough to throw away a chance at a good life with a man who could give me everything I'd ever dreamed of.

Especially not for a dream of someone who couldn't offer me anything the way Brock could.

"Jordan, please tell me you're going to reconsider this whole engagement thing."

I shook my head and took a deep breath. "No. Brock has asked me to marry him and I've said yes. On Saturday, he and I will be there with nearly a hundred people to celebrate our engagement. I hope you'll still be there."

Nina wrapped her arms around me and hugged me tightly to her. "Of course I'll be there. I just wish you'd think about this."

"There's nothing to think about."

She leaned back and sighed. "What about Brock? Do you think

it's fair to him? How would you feel if he still loved someone else but was getting married to you?"

"Stop trying to make me feel bad. People get married to people they aren't madly in love with all the time. Not everyone gets the white knight like Tristan Stone. Some of us have to settle for a regular guy on a horse. Brock's more than just that regular guy, so all in all, I'm making out pretty well, if you think about it."

"Well, if you put it that way…"

"Sarcasm in my moment of need isn't what my best friend should be doing."

"Jordan, you talk about getting married like it's a negotiation. Marriage isn't like that. I'm afraid if you aren't crazy about Brock now, you're going to be forever unhappy. Why not just put off the whole engagement thing for a while? Tell him you need some time."

"No. I can't do that to him."

"Why? Is there some reason you have to get engaged now?"

"The party's all planned. It can't be changed. So we better get going to the spa and my dress fitting."

I didn't want to tell Nina that I was still uncertain about marrying Brock. When he asked me, I hesitated at first, unsure we should marry so quickly since we'd only known each other for a few months. His insistence on getting engaged as soon as possible because we loved each other reassured me, even if I wondered if we were rushing things. No one had ever wanted me enough to even consider marriage, though, so I said yes.

Did I love him? I wasn't sure, but he was the kind of man who could give me a life I'd dreamed of, so why shouldn't I marry him?

It wasn't fairy tale perfect, but it was real life pretty good and that was okay too.

Chapter Four

Gage

Before I had the chance to sink into my own head over Jordan's impending engagement, a call came in about a job and I dove into work. Anything to get my mind off the news I'd dreaded for months. The addition of an uptown party for the well-known socialite Janine Truman to my crew's schedule made the weekend a tight one, but thankfully my people were as eager to see Varo Security succeed as I was. At least I hoped they'd still feel that way when I told them about this late change to their Saturday plans on a Thursday morning.

Seated on the edge of my old oak desk, I braced myself for my staff's possible mutiny. The seven men and one woman in front of me chatted about their weekend plans and a Yankees doubleheader a few of them had snagged tickets for while I sipped the last of my morning coffee trying to think of a nice way to upend their days off.

There was no time like the present, so I cleared my throat and began.

"Okay, I've got good news. A new client contacted me last night and even sent over a check this morning, so we have a new job."

Casey Dawson, the only female with the company, smiled and gave me the thumbs up sign. Deceptively strong for her just over five feet height and at least as tough as any of the guys, she'd taken on the role of workplace cheerleader almost as soon as she started working for me. Casey often reminded me of those female gymnastics champions who barely weighed a hundred pounds but could throw a man halfway across the room if they had to. Behind the pretty brown hair and blue eyes, she had that kind of quiet spunk about her. Sometimes we got a drink after work, and the boss-employee relationship between us had gradually morphed into a friendship like I had with my sisters.

"But—"

"There's always a but, isn't there, boss?" Jack said from the back of the room.

One of my first hires, he was young and a bust ass, but he was right. Good news always seemed to come with a hitch.

"Yeah, and this one's a big but. She needs security for a party this Saturday."

I let the news sink in for a moment before I continued, and within a few seconds, the realization that their weekend plans had just been shot to hell came over the people in front of me and the happy faces that had just been smiling at me grew dark.

As they grumbled about bad timing and missing the Yankees beat up on the Red Sox, I held my hands up in surrender and nodded my understanding of all their complaints. "I know, I know. And I'm sorry, but I need everyone on this job. It's a big one."

Not that I truly understood having my weekend ruined by Janine Truman's party needs. All I ever did on Saturdays and Sundays was either sit in my office or sit at home watching TV, spending too much time in my head and no time out in the world the city offered.

"We understand, Gage," Casey said in her best sympathetic voice. "I can see the Yankees another time. I think everyone else agrees we signed on to Varo Security because we wanted to be a part of this company. Weekends come with the territory."

I looked around and saw the rest of the group nodding. "Thanks. I appreciate this, everyone. It's the Royale, so we're doing the big time now. It's a birthday party for Janine Truman, so unless she's the world's worst person, I'm not thinking we'll have much to really worry about. Just the usual issues with drunk party guests and the birthday party version of wedding crashers."

"What time does the fun begin?" Will, my newest hire, asked.

"We need to be at the Royale for five, and the party begins at seven. I'll be heading over there in a little while to meet with the hotel's security so we can coordinate our efforts."

"Boss, why does this lady need more security than what the Royale can offer? They've got a crack staff there, and they're used to high society parties and their problems."

I shook my head because I had no idea why Janine Truman had wanted to hire security, or why she'd wanted my company in particular. It must have been Tristan's influence, but it still seemed like overkill.

"No idea, Casey. I just know the lady wants us and she's willing to pay. Maybe Varo Security is getting a good name out there."

"Why not? We're the best!" she cheered in an effort to rally the troops.

"Alright, let's get going. We have work to do today before our big debut at the Royale."

✧   ✧   ✧

THE GRAND BALLROOM OF THE Royale Hotel had been decorated to within an inch of its life with silver and white decorations, silver silk bunting, and enough burgundy to make it my new least favorite color. Wait staff buzzed around with armfuls of napkins in that very color followed by more staff with dishes and silverware for what looked like an army.

If this lady had enough people for all that at her birthday party, I could only imagine how popular she was. Money certainly talked in this city. I hadn't thought about it before, but as I watched the preparations continue around me while I checked out the nooks and crannies that could present issues during the party, I wondered if she was more than just some Upper West Side wealthy woman. She had to be someone important to warrant all this effort.

The sound of my crew coming into the ballroom distracted me from any more thoughts about Janine Truman's net worth and I turned to see them staring in awe at the room and all its decorations.

"Who is this woman, boss?" Casey asked, her eyes wide as she took in all the silver and burgundy surrounding her.

"Someone more important than us, Case. Try not to get blinded by the splendor of it all," I joked. "Let's check out where we all need to be stationed. The gift table appears to be over there in the corner of the room farthest away from the door, and other than that, there are all these archways and alcoves that could present us with issues if someone wants to cause trouble."

"You seem to know an awful lot about this kind of thing, Gage," Will said with a grin.

He wasn't wrong. I'd spent enough time with Angela at events even bigger and more impressive than this to know a thing or two about how the other half lived. Not that I ever felt comfortable in their world, but I knew enough to navigate through.

"Yeah, I've lived an exciting life," I said with a laugh. "Always a bridesmaid, never a bride. Time to get to work."

BY SEVEN O'CLOCK, MOST OF Janine Truman's guests had arrived, and I could tell this woman had some serious money. Her friends and family all had a telltale air of old New York penthouse wealthy to them. From my spot in one of the alcoves, I noticed the women all seemed to have tightly pulled faces like they'd had too many facelifts and Botox treatments. Or maybe that was what women born into money looked like. For their part, the men seemed looser in every respect, from the way they talked to the amount of alcohol they drank. The party had barely begun and more than a few already looked half in the bag.

Looking down at my black suit, shirt, and tie, I couldn't help but compare what I wore to the guests' clothes. Intended to make me as invisible as possible to the partygoers, my clothes gave me an almost funereal appearance compared to the women in their dresses of virtually every color and the men in their formal black tuxes and white shirts.

Not that I cared what I looked like. I was there to do a job. This wasn't a social event for me. It wasn't my style.

My style was a few beers at a neighborhood tavern with me in a pair of jeans and a t-shirt, and I definitely wouldn't be there with any of the women at this party.

As I watched for any trouble, out of the corner of my eye I caught a glimpse of a familiar face and turning, I saw Nina walk past the ballroom doors as a group of partygoers entered. Was she a friend of Janine Truman's? That would explain how Varo Security got the nod for this job.

I quickly made my way through the crowd and caught up with Nina as she began to walk away from the room. "Nina, the party's in here."

She spun around and her eyes opened wide. "Gage, what are you doing here?"

Gesturing toward the ballroom filled with Janine Truman's hundred or so closest friends, I explained, "I figure I got the job because you and Tristan are friends of the birthday girl. I'll have to thank him when he gets here. Where is he?"

Nina's face contorted into an expression that looked like she was in pain. "Oh, Gage, I'm sorry. I don't know how this happened, but we're not going to that party. We're going to…uh…to the one next door."

"Oh, no problem. I just figured Tristan was the reason I got this job," I explained with a shrug.

She frowned, as if what I'd said upset her, and as I opened my mouth to ask what was wrong, she said, "We're going to Jordan and Brock's engagement party in the main ballroom, Gage. I'm so sorry."

Suddenly, it felt like all the air had been sucked out of my lungs. Jordan was right there in the same building celebrating her engagement to another man. I quickly made sure my face didn't show how much Nina's news hurt and forced a smile. "Small world, huh? Well, please tell her I said congratulations. I better get back inside just in case any of the guests get out of hand."

Reaching out to squeeze my arm, Nina tried to be chipper as Tristan joined her. "I wish it wasn't like this."

"Gage, nice to see you again and so soon."

Nina shook her head quickly. "He's working a party right next to Jordan's, Tristan."

He looked at his wife and then at me with a curious expression. "Sorry, Gage. Hell of a coincidence."

"Yeah. I better get back in there. Have a nice night."

I got away before either one of the Stones could apologize again. I knew they meant well, but being pitied wasn't what I wanted at that moment. What I really wanted was to get the hell out of town and never look back.

The people attending Janine's party made me question why she'd even contacted me about extra security. Other than drinking more champagne than I'd ever seen anyone drink, they were a pretty calm group of middle-aged New Yorkers. The most excitement I saw in the next half hour came from her two twenty-something kids and their friends who decided to pretend like their mother's birthday was a good time to get hammered.

Casey joined me at my post after gently separating a few of the younger partiers who had gotten out of hand on the dance floor. As we watched for any more antics by Janine's kids, she nudged me and said, "So this is how the other half lives. I'll still take a few beers at the ballpark over this."

I nodded, wishing I was sitting behind home plate instead of anywhere near the Royale. "I hear that."

She continued to talk about the scene in front of us, but my mind was in the room next door where the woman I loved was announcing her engagement. I couldn't stop it, but that didn't mean I didn't hate it. I'd stayed away from Jordan for fear that if I didn't she'd get hurt, but we'd left everything between us unresolved. I always thought I'd get the chance to explain myself—or at least I'd always hoped I would.

Now that she was getting ready to marry another man, that chance was gone.

Casey gently elbowed me in the side. "Hey, boss, did you hear me?"

I looked to my right and saw her staring up at me. "No, sorry. I was a million miles away there for a moment. What's up?"

"I just said you look beat. You can leave, if you need to. We got this. I doubt this group will get much wilder than what we saw from those kids before."

"No, I'm good," I lied.

She looked me up and down and shook her head. "Gage, you don't look good. Maybe you're coming down with something. Whatever's going on, take the night off. I'll make sure everything is handled to your standards."

I knew I shouldn't leave the party, but the need to talk to Jordan one last time and at least try to explain why I'd done what I did pressed on me enough to take Casey up on her offer. Knowing I could trust her, I headed over to the ballroom next door and hoped I'd get the chance to set things right.

FOR AN HOUR I WATCHED as Jordan greeted guests and charmed them with her gorgeous smile and grace. She was the most beautiful woman in the room, and one of the best things about her was that she wasn't like these uptight society wives who looked like they had no idea how to have fun or be good people.

Her fiancé spent little time next to her, instead glad-handing and schmoozing the men in the room. He didn't bother to pay much attention to the woman who was supposed to share the evening with him, and it made me dislike him instantly. Not that I had a whole lot of love for him anyway. He had a cheap look about him, like some kind of millionaire who'd only gotten his money through winning the lottery.

I waited for Jordan to be alone after she'd finished greeting the long line of people dying to speak to her. All I needed was a few minutes to at least show her that letting her go hadn't been as easy or painless as she thought.

She finally came close to where I stood hiding in an alcove, and I took my chance. Grabbing her by the arm, I pulled her into a room off to the side and closed the door. But if I had thought she'd be happy to see me, the look of pain I saw in her eyes instantly told me otherwise.

"What are you doing here?" she asked, her voice full of sadness. "Why would you come to my engagement party?"

"I needed to talk to you, Jordan. I needed to see you."

"No! Why would you do this to me? I've finally found someone who actually cares about me and now you come back and act like I should want to talk to you?"

I held her gently by the shoulders, afraid if I didn't she'd leave and I'd miss my chance. "Jordan, please listen to me. I need you to forget what I did and hear me out."

Tears welled in her eyes. "I can't forget. I can't, so whatever you need to say to me, you should have said it back when you had me in your life. Now let me go."

She pushed me away and went for the door, but I grabbed her hand and squeezed. "I just want a chance to explain. I don't want to ruin anything for you. If you love this guy, I wish you nothing but happiness."

"You drag me into this room to tell me you want to explain? Explain what?"

"Why I broke up with you like I did."

Tears welled in her eyes, and she shook her head. "No! I won't let you do this to me again. I can't listen to this. Do you know how many nights I cried myself to sleep because of what you did? You broke my fucking heart, and now you think you can just make up for everything by explaining yourself? Go away, Gage. I finally got over you and found someone who really loves me."

"I still love you."

It felt as good as it always had to tell her that. Her response, on the other hand, made me feel like shit.

"Well, I don't love you. Go away and let me be happy."

"I just want you to listen to what I have to say."

I touched her arm and she yanked it away from my hold. "Don't touch me! You don't get to do that anymore."

Her rage surprised me. I'd expected anger, hurt, even sadness, but not the level of rage I felt coming at me. I couldn't let that deter me from telling her the whole truth, though.

"Jordan, you deserve to know what happened. I hope you'll hear me out."

"This is for you, Gage. Not me. If you wanted to do something for me, you would have done it that night you broke up with me over the phone and didn't call back. You would have done it on my birthday a month later when I waited for you to call to let me know you remembered me. You have done it when you returned to New York and lived close enough to see me whenever you wanted to. What truth am I supposed to know other than those?"

"I can't fix what I did. All I can do is tell you the reasons why I did those things."

"So now you want to tell me your excuse for breaking up with me over the phone like I never meant a damn thing to you? As I sat there and pleaded with you to tell me why you were doing this to me and all you said was it just wasn't working out for you."

"I couldn't tell you the truth. I never meant to hurt you. I didn't think I had a choice. All I was thinking of was keeping you safe."

Jordan closed her eyes, shutting me out, and said in a low, sad voice, "You always had a choice. Always."

"I didn't. Someone was threatening me and said they'd hurt

you if I didn't stop seeing you."

She looked up at me with a complete look of disbelief in her eyes. "Really? This is what you expect me to buy as the reason you dumped me? Okay, I'll bite. Did he tell you to break up with me like a callous dick, Gage? Did he? Did he say to call me on the phone and act like I meant nothing to you? Did he tell you to give me nothing to go on so I'd naturally think you'd gone back to your ex-girlfriend the actress?"

"No. All I knew was if I didn't let you go, you could get hurt because of me. I couldn't let that happen."

"So you hurt me instead."

I wanted to look away, to avoid the indictment in her eyes as she stared at me with the purest hate I'd ever seen. I had hurt her, and as far as she was concerned, I was still hurting her.

"You just think I'd willingly hurt you?"

"Whether it was willingly or not, the end result was the same."

"Jordan, is it that you doubt how much I loved you or that you just will never be able to forgive me? Because at least if it's the first one, I can try to prove to you how I feel, but if you can never forgive me, I don't know what to do about that."

She shook her head and opened her mouth a few times to speak, but no words came out. Finally, she spoke, and I felt like someone had kicked me hard in the gut.

"It's both. I didn't realize until now, but it's both. I don't believe you loved me. You couldn't have and done what you did. And I don't know if I can forgive you, Gage. I don't know if I have it in me."

"I can't believe that."

"You can't believe that because you don't know how much it hurt when you broke up with me. Let me try to explain to you what it felt like to hear the man you loved tell you things just weren't working for him. To have him tell you that over the phone while he was three thousand miles away surrounded by women who already had made her insecure."

"You had no reason to be insecure, Jordan. You're more gorgeous than any of those Hollywood actresses I met guarding that kid."

"You knew how I wondered about your ex and you being in the same town, and you broke up with me with that vague bullshit line of things not working for you. What did you think I'd think?"

"I didn't. All I could think about was making sure you were safe. If I stopped dating you, then the person threatening me would go away. That's all I was trying to do. I never meant to hurt you."

"You keep saying that, but that's what happened! You called me up and over the phone broke up with me like we hadn't spent all that time together. Like we hadn't given each other everything we had inside ourselves. You knew more about me than even Nina did. I told you things I never told anyone else in the world."

She couldn't hold back the tears anymore, and as they rolled down her cheeks, she sobbed, "All those hours we lay in each other's arms after making love and all you could say was things weren't working for you?"

Christ, she was tearing my heart out. I wanted to take her in my arms and find a way to make up for all the hurt I'd caused her then and now. As she stood there sobbing, I tried to figure out a way to fix things.

"Jordan, I loved you. If they had done anything to you, I wouldn't have been able to go on."

"And then you never called back. It was as if I'd never meant a damn thing to you. You went on with life, and I could barely get out of bed. Then I went out to live at Nina and Tristan's and all those memories of you were there too. I couldn't go anywhere without seeing you or remembering something we did. All those months together suddenly meant nothing. And every time you said you loved me hurt like someone was carving into my chest."

"I couldn't call. If the person threatening me found out we were still together, you'd be in danger."

"You were three time zones away. How did you know I wasn't

in danger?"

"I knew."

"How? How did you know I wasn't in danger?"

"I knew."

She wiped the tears from under her eyes and shook her head. "More stalking."

"It's not stalking if you're watching the woman you love."

"No, then it's worse. Then it's letting her believe you don't care anymore and seeing her fall apart and still doing nothing."

"In my defense, I wasn't watching you myself. I had a friend who also works security watch you until I knew you weren't in danger anymore."

Her expression twisted from disgust. "So what, did he take pictures of me, sort of an album of my falling apart after you left me?"

"It wasn't like that. He made sure you were safe and no one harmed you."

Jordan wiped the last few tears from her cheeks. "Well, since he didn't let you in on how I really was, let me tell you. For the first couple days, I didn't get out bed. I just laid there feeling like everything I loved had been taken away. My phone never left my side just in case you called. I was sure you'd call and say you were sorry or at least explain why you didn't want to see me anymore."

"Jordan, I never—"

"Yeah, you never meant to hurt me! I got that, Gage. But you did. So after those first few days when I felt like I wanted to crawl into a hole and die I hurt so bad, Nina brought me out to the house. All that did was bring back all those memories of when you lived there. I'd go for walks back near the carriage house and remember how you looked when you'd stand there like a stone while I flirted to get your attention. Then I'd remember that first night you came to my apartment and we laughed about all those times I came to see you and you thought I might like West."

I wanted to tell her I remembered all those times too, and every day it felt like I was missing part of me. I wanted to tell her every night I'd lay in bed and think about her sitting on her couch in a pair of shorts and a t-shirt with her hair in a ponytail drinking her diet soda looking more beautiful than any woman I saw in LA.

I didn't say any of that. I just let her talk, knowing I deserved everything she threw at me.

"On my birthday—the day you and I had planned to meet at Brick Fire because that's where we had our first date after that night at my apartment—I waited for you to call. I sat in my apartment on my couch with my phone sitting on the coffee table and waited. I lied when Nina asked if I was okay and pretended my heart wasn't broken. I lied when my mother called to wish me happy birthday and told her I didn't sound good because I was getting over a cold. I sat there for hours waiting and you never called. You never even texted happy birthday. The day came and went and I ended my birthday alone crying myself to sleep."

"I'm sorry, Jordan."

Shaking her head, she held her hand up to stop me. "Save it. Want me to continue? My days and nights were basically the same for months. During the day, I pretended not to be so heartbroken all I wanted to do was die, and at night, I spent my time with the covers over my head wishing something could take all the pain away."

I didn't know which was worse—her anger or her sadness. Both cut me to the core.

"And then one day as I stood in the rain a man came into my life and for the first time I didn't hurt as much. Brock made me feel like I might be able to go on. He listened to me when I talked, took me wonderful places I'd only dreamed of before, and wanted to marry me. And then you showed up and ruined everything."

"We can still be what we were. I still love you."

Her mouth hung open in shock for a long moment and then she shook her head violently. "Are you out of your mind? You tear my heart out by breaking up with me over the phone and now you show up at my engagement party and claim you still love me after living in the same city for months without bothering to call me even once? Do you hear yourself? He loves me. He wants to marry me. You broke up with me long distance over the phone to go fuck around with Hollywood starlets! Who do you think I should go with?"

"I didn't break up with you to go with anyone. I had to. For you."

Jordan's eyebrows shot up in disbelief. "For me? You broke up with me for me? Are you high?"

I knew what this sounded like. I had to find some way to explain what I'd done without sounding like a madman.

"Please, just listen to me. I had to break up with you to make sure you didn't get hurt."

"Uh, I'd say you failed epically then because I got hurt. I got hurt bad, Gage. Now let me go and rejoin the party so I can celebrate my engagement to my future husband."

"That's not what I meant. I know it sounds bizarre, but I'd been getting letters threatening your life if I didn't leave you alone."

"Really? That's the best you can do? Some crazy story about letters threatening me unless you left me? And yet here you are endangering my life because you wanted to tell me you love me. I've heard enough. Goodbye, Gage. Have a good life."

She tugged her arm from my hold, but I couldn't let her go. Not with her finally standing right there in front of me after all those months. "Tell me you don't miss my touch. Leave here with me right now. I'll go anywhere with you, Jordan. Please."

Closing her eyes, she bit her lip in that way that never failed to make me want her. When she opened them, those beautiful green eyes were filled with pain. Pain I'd caused. "I don't miss you at all. You left me. Now I'll do you the same favor. Goodbye, Gage."

Her lips were so close I couldn't stop myself. I pulled her into me and kissed her long and deep, the way I'd fantasized I'd kiss her if I ever had the chance again. For a moment, she melted into my arms and all the feelings I'd kept bottled up began to surge through me after so long. She was my Jordan again.

But then she pushed me away and pointed her finger at me. "No! I won't let you do this to me. I won't! I have someone who loves me and wants to marry me."

"He doesn't love you like I do."

She flashed her enormous engagement ring in front of me. "Really? He gave me this diamond ring because he doesn't love me?"

Looking down at the giant rock on her left hand, I felt my jealousy begin to overtake me, knowing full well I'd likely never be able to give her anything close. "Nice. Who wouldn't want a diamond the size of their fist?"

Jordan recoiled from my sarcasm and shook her head. "You had your chance, Gage. Goodbye."

I reached out to hold her there with me, but she turned and in a moment was gone from the room, leaving me to figure out how I'd convince her the man she planned to marry didn't love her as much as I did.

How was I going to make her see that no matter what I'd done, I was the man she should be with?

CHAPTER FIVE

JORDAN

I GOT THE HELL OUT of that room and away from Gage's accusations that Brock didn't love me as much as he did before I started to believe him. See, that was the problem. All it took was being close to him and one incredible, knee-buckling kiss and I wanted to believe every word that came out of his mouth.

At least my heart did. Thank God my brain still had some control over me or I'd really be a mess.

Making a beeline to Nina who stood next to Tristan alone in a corner of the ballroom, I apologized to him and pulled her aside, barely able to contain my shock at what had just happened. "Gage is here. He just pulled me into a room to tell me that Brock doesn't love me and that I should be with him."

Nina's blue eyes stared at me in stunned amazement. "What? Gage is here?"

I began to nod frantically, as if my head couldn't stop telling her he was there. "He is. He just pulled me into a room and tried to convince me to leave here with him because he's still in love with me. The man is insane!"

"Calm down, calm down. What did he say exactly?"

I took a deep breath in and let it out slowly. "He said that Brock doesn't love me like he does and that he left me because he was getting letters threatening my life. It's craziness, Nina. The man is crazy. Why would he do this to me on the night of my engagement party?"

"Hang on. Let me get Tristan." Nina pulled Tristan from his quiet corner and told him what I'd just told her. "Do you know what he's talking about?"

"No, but I only know Gage through his work for me. What did the letters say?"

I stared at Tristan in shock. Was he actually taking Gage's outrageous tale seriously? "I don't know. What does it matter? Letters or no letters, he broke up with me and never bothered to even come see me until tonight."

Nina tugged on her husband's arm the way she always did when she was excited about something. "Go find Gage and ask him what this is all about. Please. Find out what he's talking about."

Tristan looked at me for a moment and left before I could tell him to forget asking Gage anything. "Nina, why did you do that? Now Tristan is going to hear all about Brock not loving me as much and all of Gage's nonsense."

"Jordan, we have to find out what this is all about. Would you have rathered I go find Gage and leave you here with my husband?"

Sighing, I had to admit that would have made things worse. "No. Even on his best days Tristan says very little to me. I'm not in the mood for making small talk about the weather or how he looks in his tux at a time like this. That strong, silent type thing isn't what I need at the moment. I need someone to talk to now."

"See? There's method to my madness. So did anything else happen when you talked to him?"

I pressed my lips together to relive the memory of our kissing and looked around before I whispered, "He kissed me. I shouldn't have let him, but I did. I couldn't stop myself, Nina. Oh, God! Why did he have to come here tonight?"

"I told you he still cared! He wouldn't have kissed you if he didn't," she said with a huge smile. "Now you can't marry Brock. You got your wish. You know Gage still misses you. Call this whole thing off and get back with the man you love."

A few of the guests standing nearby turned to stare at us with a look of confusion on their faces. I forced a smile and pulled Nina away toward the next alcove. "Are you crazy? No! That man broke my heart and left me in pieces. You should know. You had to pick them up and put me back together how many times since then?"

"But you can't go through with it, Jordan. This was a sign. Don't try to ignore it."

"I'm going to start ignoring you if you don't stop with this craziness. You're as bad as Gage. So we kissed and it felt good. Well, actually great. So what? That doesn't compare to the chance at a life with someone like Brock."

Tristan returned and looked at me like he'd just heard all my deepest, darkest secrets. "I found him, and he says the letters began coming while he was in LA with the teenager he was guarding. He still doesn't know who they're from, but they stopped when he broke up with you. But recently he began getting them again."

"The man's insane! I don't care about what letters he's getting. This ship has sailed."

"He's worried, Jordan. I don't know Gage as well as you do, but I can see he's worried," Tristan said quietly. "He also seems genuine when he says he's still in love with you."

Nina tugged on my arm now. "See? He still loves you and you still love him."

"Honey, you two are starting to sound as mad as Gage. Brock loves me. It may not be the love story of the century, but he cares for me and I care for him. This whole thing is Gage's attempt to—"

I couldn't finish that sentence. I had no idea why Gage would show up at my engagement party. Did he really still care for me? Was this his way of trying to win me back?

No! I couldn't let myself think those kinds of things. He'd proven how little he cared for me by leaving me without even the most basic excuse and then letting me make up my own reasons why I wasn't good enough to stay with. And he'd lived in the same city as me for months, even seeing my closest friends, and never even bothered to try to see me. He didn't want me back. He just wanted to hurt me again.

"I have to go deal with my guests. My parents probably think I'm avoiding them. Don't worry about me."

Squeezing my arm, Nina said quietly, "You know you don't have to go through with any of this, Jordan. It's just an engagement party. There's still time to change your mind."

"I know, honey. I'm fine. All this nonsense from Gage made me a little nuts for a few minutes, but I'm fine. Enjoy the party, and be sure to stay until Brock and I make the official announcement."

Nina stopped me dead with the most serious look she'd ever given me. "Okay, but let me ask you one thing before you run off. Who are these people to you? The only people I recognize other than my husband and you are your parents. Where are your friends from school? Where is your sister? Why does it seem like everyone here is here for Brock and not you?"

I looked around the ballroom filled with strangers and saw what my best friend saw. Almost no one there had come for me. I'd let Brock handle the guest list, assuming he'd just include all the names I'd given him, but instead he'd packed our engagement party with his guests and invited only my parents and Nina and Tristan. Even my sister had been left out.

But I couldn't admit that without feeling foolish. So pressing a smile onto my face, I lied. "Kayla had to return to school early since she's a senior RA this year. It's no big deal. Like you said, it's just an engagement party. Everyone will be at the wedding. I have to go now, but please don't leave without saying goodbye."

Nina opened her mouth to speak, but I left to rejoin my guests and my future husband, standing by his side for the rest of the night. When Brock toasted to having the best woman in the world as his fiancée, I smiled and believed every word. Then out of the corner of my eye I saw Gage standing in the shadows of a far alcove toward the back of the room watching me and the look in his eyes wasn't the same as the one in the man I stood next to.

That sadness I'd looked for days before as Jensen drove us away from the spa was telegraphed as clear as day now as he stood there staring at me from behind a column. All that I'd needed to know every night and day for months I now saw in those dark blue eyes.

I remembered when I thought he'd be the man I could marry. All those dreams of a happily ever after and us riding off into the sunset to live together in married bliss were just that. Dreams. The harsh reality was that Gage Varo dismissed me with one phone call and never thought about me again until he found out I was happy and someone else wanted me.

The party wound down and people lined up to kiss me and Brock to wish us congratulations before leaving. Nina took me in her arms as Tristan wished Brock all the best and in my ear she whispered, "I'm only a call away at any time. I may be out at the house, but I can get into the city in no time or have you out to the house just as quick. If you need anything, call me."

I turned to look at Brock and smiled. "Thanks for coming both of you. It means so much to us that you were here to share this with us."

Nina leaned forward to hug Brock, who gave her a brief embrace before letting her go. "It was nice of you to join us. Thank you for being a part of our big night."

I saw in Tristan's eyes a slight disapproval for Brock now. Had Gage changed his mind about him? But always the gentleman, he extended his hand to shake Brock's and said, "It was a great party. Congratulations to the both of you."

"Remember, call me so we can talk more about your wedding dress. We need to get on that," Nina said with a forced smile as she pretended she didn't want me to call her to talk about Gage.

As they left, Tristan leaned in to kiss my cheek and whispered, "Let us know if you need anything."

I smiled as if he'd merely wished me well and moved on to thank the next guest for attending, but I couldn't help but think that the two people I was closest to in the world believed what Gage had said.

I couldn't, though. The hurt he'd caused me made it impossible.

✦ ✦ ✦

BROCK POURED HIMSELF A DRINK and stood by the window looking out at the city below. I waited for him to offer me one, but as usual he didn't, so I got myself a glass of bourbon since it was a special occasion. Gulping down a swallow, I felt its effect immediately as my body began to warm all over. Never much of a liquor drinker, I definitely understood why Brock drank this stuff.

I padded up behind him and pressed my cheek to his shoulder. Raising my glass, I offered a toast to our engagement. "To a wonderful night, don't you think?"

Instead of toasting us, he took the glass from my hand. "I don't like women who drink. You know that, Jordan."

"I just thought since it's a special night that we could share one. It's no big deal. I don't like drinking anyway."

Brock tipped his glass and swallowed the last inch or so of alcohol before pushing past me to fill up his drink. His coldness confused me. After such a wonderful celebration of our engagement, I couldn't understand why his demeanor had changed from the party.

I followed him over to the bar and wrapped my arms around him. "It was a lovely party, wasn't it?"

"It was. I saw you spending a lot of time speaking to your friends and family. You didn't think that was rude to the rest of our guests?"

"I didn't really know anyone else."

Staring straight ahead, he groaned. "Like I did?"

I stood there confused. The way he'd said it, he hadn't known most of the guests at our engagement party either. Weren't they all his business associates and friends?

"I don't understand, Brock. If they weren't there for you, then why did you invite them?"

He shrugged and took another gulp of his drink. "I didn't mean it that way. Nevermind."

"Nina and Tristan were the only people there for me other than my parents. I wanted to make sure they knew how happy I was to see them there for our big night."

Brock turned his head and glared at me. "I told you my feelings on them. You're going to have to remove yourself from them once we marry, so you might as well begin now. And what could you possibly need from Tristan Stone?"

I knew what he meant. He wanted to know why he'd said to let them know if I needed anything. I quickly shrugged and tried to make it seem like I didn't know why he'd offer help as he and Nina left the party. "Nina and I will be shopping for my wedding dress soon. She says it's never too early. And there are a lot of plans that have to be made for the ceremony. He knows Nina wants to help."

Brock slowly spun around to face me, and I saw in his eyes I'd angered him with my answer. "You'll have a personal shopper for that, Jordan. There will be no need for Nina to accompany you as you look for your wedding gown."

"Nina's my best friend, Brock. She's going to be my matron of honor in the wedding. I have to have her with me," I said, practically in a panic. I hadn't taken his comments about weeding Nina out of my life seriously until that very moment and suddenly his behavior frightened me.

He let out a frustrated sigh and kissed me on the cheek. "We can have this discussion another time. I have a long day ahead of me tomorrow, so make sure to turn the lights out when you come to bed."

I wanted to say we'll have this conversation now because you need to know I'm not abandoning my best friend for you or any man. I wanted to say that, but I didn't. Instead, I put on my nice girl smile and played the role I knew I'd have to play for the rest of my life.

That didn't mean never seeing my best friend again, though.

No matter what he said, Nina would be with me forever. We may not end up growing old together like we'd planned, two old ladies sitting on the front porch of the nursing home checking out the hot doctors, but she'd be part of my life until the day I died.

Friends like her you didn't just toss away, not even for a husband.

Brock left me standing there alone looking out at the city below and feeling especially lonely. I poured myself another drink as the memory of Gage and I kissing began to root around in my mind. I'd tried so hard to get rid of every trace of feeling I had for him, and on most days, I didn't think of him much at all. Maybe a passing thought if I heard a song that reminded me of something we'd done together or a faint yearning brought on by my seeing a place we'd gone to that faded as fast as it came.

Seeing him at my engagement party made every feeling, every longing for him rush back so I couldn't think of anything else. Why couldn't he just leave well enough alone? All those crazy things he'd said about Brock not loving me as much as he did and letters threatening me—who made those bizarre accusations? He hadn't backed any of them up with facts. They were just the ramblings of a crazy person.

I wanted to believe that because if I could, then I could dismiss him. I could dismiss that kiss that had taken my breath away just like when he'd kissed me the first time in my kitchen that night. I could dismiss the look of longing in his eyes that made me want to take him in my arms and whisper, "I forgive you."

Swallowing a gulp of bourbon, I felt a rush of warmth cover my arms and legs and knew I was getting buzzed. Not good. One of the reasons I didn't drink much anymore was alcohol always made me reminisce. It didn't take much for my mind to wander back to Gage, so instead I usually just remained sober. Better to avoid the temptation to take that walk down memory lane than feel the pain all over again.

God, I was truly a mess.

I didn't want to be this way. I'd been dumped before by boyfriends. Why did he make me feel like I'd lost everything when he went away?

Maybe Nina was right. Maybe tonight was a sign, and the fact that just one kiss made me want Gage all over again, even after he broke my heart, meant something. Or maybe she was just her overly romantic self, as usual, and I needed to forget all this nonsense from the past and focus on the present and the future.

A present that included a gorgeous wealthy man who wanted to marry me. A future that if only I could get my head out of the clouds could be what I'd always wanted.

I finished the last of the bourbon in my glass and poured myself another drink. If I could get drunk enough, maybe I'd pass out and all those thoughts of Gage and me rambling around my brain could go away.

There was just one problem with that idea.

I wasn't that kind of drunk. If anything, drinking made my brain kick into overdrive, so by the time I'd finished my second glass of bourbon I couldn't think of anything but the craziness Gage had dumped on me hours earlier. The story he told was so fantastic that I couldn't believe it.

Letters threatening me. What bullshit!

And if these letters did, in fact, exist, why did he feel perfectly fine endangering my life tonight, of all nights?

Jesus Christ! This was what Gage Varo did to me. He made me crazy and filled my head with nonsense. Flopping down on Brock's black leather couch, I reached for my phone and considered calling Nina before I did something incredibly stupid and called Gage.

But talking to Nina now would only mean more discussion of the person I was trying to forget.

Tossing my phone aside, I leaned back against the cool leather and breathed deeply, already feeling entirely too drunk from the bourbon. I hoped I wouldn't have to change that part about who I was when Brock and I got married. Then I remembered his admonition about not liking women who drank. No, I definitely wouldn't have to learn to handle my liquor.

Or wear jeans, which he hated on women.

Or hang out with my best friend because he disliked her and her husband.

It didn't sound like I'd be much of the Jordan I'd always been when I became Mrs. Brock Hannon. But who wanted to become a drunk anyway?

Lately, I wondered if he wasn't different from the person I'd met that rainy night. Now that I'd agreed to marry him, something had changed between us. At first, he'd showered me with flowers and gifts and complimented me all the time. But all Brock seemed to compliment me on these days was my blond hair. That he loved.

Gage had loved my blond hair too. Closing my eyes, I remembered the time he and I drove to Vermont on an impromptu ski weekend. Wet from a day on the slopes and nearly frozen to the bone, we made love and then lay in each other's arms in front of the fireplace as he played with my hair, telling me it was just one of the things about me he loved.

I shook my head violently to rid my brain of that and every other memory of him. Why did the mind only save the good stuff? Why couldn't I remember all the bad stuff about him so I never wanted to think of him again? Like how he often didn't say a word when I talked about work, instead just sitting there watching me as I talked. Who wanted that kind of guy?

Or the way he liked to sit around in that damn beat up Broncos jersey of his and drink beer while he watched football games on Sunday afternoons instead of visiting museums or going to see concerts in the park? What kind of woman would want that type of man?

Or how he broke up with me over the phone, not even giving me a decent reason why he didn't want to continue being with me. Who the fuck wanted that kind of boyfriend in her life?

CHAPTER SIX

JORDAN

I REACHED FOR MY PHONE and stared at it, debating whether I should do it or not. Should I finally call him and tell him what I thought of him and everything he'd done? If I didn't, I'd never be rid of him, and if I ever wanted a life with Brock, I needed to put Gage and that part of my life behind me. Unsure if I should do it, I went into my contacts and scrolled down until I found his number under the secret title I gave him when Brock and I began dating.

V.

Pressing my fingertip to his name, I put the phone to my ear and took a deep breath. I didn't have to think about what I would say. I'd rehearsed it in my mind a million times since that night he broke up with me.

I heard him say hello and felt like my stomach dropped inside my body, sending butterflies fluttering everywhere. Mustering every ounce of courage I had, and even some the bourbon had supplied me, I said quietly, "I'll never forgive you for trying to ruin my engagement party, Gage."

Not exactly the way I'd wanted to begin, but it worked for a start. I had more things to say, but then he spoke and so many of those things went to wherever those butterflies had gone.

"Jordan, I need to know you're okay. Tell me you're at your house and I can come over so we can talk."

"I was okay, or at least I was getting better at pretending I was okay until I saw you on the street the other day with that woman," I said suddenly unable to keep my emotions from spinning out of control like some goddamned whirling dervish.

"What woman? Where?"

"I know you saw me, Gage. Right outside of Roget's Day Spa. You were standing there with some gorgeous woman with a designer bag. Do you know so many women now that you can't figure out when I'm talking about?"

"Jordan, you know me well enough to know that describing her as someone with a designer bag doesn't help me. I don't notice those things. But I know when you mean. I did see you. Why didn't you come over?"

"And say what?" I asked too loudly and heard Brock stir in the next room. Lowering my voice, I moved toward the window and whispered, "And say what, Gage? Hey, what's new with the guy who dumped me and broke my damn heart?"

"Jordan, I'll be happy to explain myself if you tell me you're at your apartment and the doors are locked."

"No, I'm at Brock's apartment. He is my fiancé, Gage. It's not odd that I'd be with him after our engagement party."

"Then meet me somewhere. I'll go anywhere. Just pick a place."

"I will not. I'm happy with him and your story about whatever bullshit you were spewing earlier doesn't change that. Brock loves me and I love him. I just wanted you to know that."

I thought I heard his breath catch, and then there was a long silence before he finally said in a much quieter voice, "If you love him so much, why are you calling me on the night of your engagement party?"

I didn't have the answer to his question. All I knew was I needed him to know I'd moved on. If only I had. Looking toward the bedroom to make sure I hadn't awoken Brock, I sat down on the couch. "I have to go, Gage. I just wanted you to know I haven't forgiven you."

"Let me come get you and take you up to Nina's. Tristan has a solid security set up there, and you'll be safe. Tell me where you are."

I stood and began to pace, my drunkenness pushed away by the adrenaline pumping through my body. Who the hell did this guy think he was? Why would I ever go anywhere with him ever again?

"You're not hearing me, Gage. I'm not leaving Brock. He loves me, and if any of this threatening letter bullshit is even true, he'll protect me."

"Jordan, I'm not lying about the letters. They began when we were dating. I finally started to believe that the only way to keep you safe was to break up with you. I never meant to hurt you. I meant to protect you. And now that they've started coming again, I'm beginning to wonder if your fiancé has something to do with them."

This guy just never gave up, did he? "You're out of your mind. You just want to see me miserable and alone. I don't know what you think I ever did to you, but I don't deserve this. Goodbye, Gage."

He began to say something again about needing to believe him, but I clicked END and threw my phone away from me. All those months I'd waited for him to call me and say he missed me were all a waste of time. He'd never missed me. He'd never even cared about me, no matter what he claimed about loving me.

I willed the tears away, but they came anyway, and as they rolled down my cheeks, I hated myself. Why did he have such power over me? Dozens of boyfriends had come and go since I moved to New York, but only he still stayed in my mind. Why?

The worst part of all of this was the seed of doubt he'd planted in my mind. True, Brock and I weren't a perfect match, and no, he didn't light my world on fire. But Gage's claim that Brock didn't love me as much as he did made me look at my fiancé's behavior toward me in a new light, and what had just been concern that the people I cared about the most didn't like my future husband was quickly snowballing into my worrying that I was marrying him for all the wrong reasons.

What if what Gage claimed was really true? What if I was still in love with him and marrying Brock was a big mistake?

God, why was this happening now? Why couldn't he just leave well enough alone? It wasn't bad enough he'd broken my heart, but now he had to ruin the rest of my life too?

Gage had never been cruel. This wasn't like him.

Slumping onto the couch, I felt my stomach roil from the bourbon sloshing around in there as I couldn't stop myself from remembering when Gage and I had been happy and in love.

The evidence of our time together lay strewn around the room, like some path showing the progression of Gage's seduction of me hours before. His shirt and pants in a pile near the door. My t-shirt and pink bra hanging off the back of the chair in the corner. His boxer briefs and my pink lace panties beside the bed.

Not that I had been an unwilling participant. I'd loved him since that first night he came to see me at my apartment. Maybe I'd loved him since we all lived out at Tristan and Nina's house in the country. It didn't matter when I fell in love with him because once he came to me that night, he was all I could think of.

"I could stay here forever and be the happiest man on earth, you know that?" he said in a low voice as he nuzzled my neck.

Rolling him over, I straddled his hips and balanced myself on top of him with my hands on his chest. God, he was beautiful! Never before had I been with a man so masculine. His body seemed to be all hard muscle, from his strong shoulders to his carved abs. I slowly ran my fingertips over his soft skin covering all that hardness and couldn't help be impressed. Gage Varo was definitely the most gorgeous man I'd ever been with.

"I think we might get sick of each other if all we ever did was have sex," I said with a smile.

He lifted his hips off the bed, sliding his hard cock through my pussy. "I think we should see if that happens. I'm good for the next week, so that could be a good start."

Gage's hands roamed down my sides until they reached my waist. His touch tickled me, and I giggled as I said, "I don't have the next week. I have to be back by Monday or my students won't have anyone to teach them."

"Substitute teacher. Your students will love you for it. Kids love it when they walk into class and see a substitute."

I leaned down and pressed a tiny kiss onto his nose. "You promised me we'd go running this morning. Remember? I've been looking forward to it."

Although it sounded strange to say that, I had been looking forward to going for a run with him. It was one of the many things we had in common, which was rare for me since I never seemed to date men who did anything I liked.

Gage grinned and slowly ran his finger between the swell of my breasts. "I like a good run as much as anyone else, but you can't say this isn't better than a jog through the park. We can go this afternoon."

I shook my head. "Nope. It's supposed to rain this afternoon. So we need to get out of this bed and get moving."

"I see I'm not going to change your mind, but how about a compromise? We make love once more and then we go for a run," he said as he moved his hands down to my hips.

"Can you remember one time sex with us didn't go for hours?" I asked with a grin, quickly coming around to his idea of what to do with our day.

"No, but that's why we should just forget about the run and stay right here."

His lack of logic made me chuckle. "That makes no sense. I can't even follow that line of reasoning."

Gage pulled me down on top of him and kissed me long and deep until any thought of leaving that spot had faded away. "It's not about reason, Jordan. It's about two people in love enjoying each other."

For a moment, I stared into his eyes, stunned by what he'd just said. Even though we'd been dating for over a month, neither of us had used the L word. But now he'd said it so casually that I wasn't sure I should say anything.

But I had to say something. He'd just told me he loved me.

Quietly, I said, "In love?"

He smiled that sexy Gage grin that never failed to make me go weak and nodded. "Yeah. In love. I love you, and I think you love me, right?"

"I do love you," I said, unsure if admitting that would be the kiss of death to our relationship as it had been to so many other ones I'd had in my dating life.

His blue eyes sparkled. "Good. So about that staying in bed all day..."

Closing my eyes, I tried to convince myself that every moment I spent with him wasn't some of the happiest of my life. That Gage wasn't the only person, other than Nina, that I felt completely and utterly at home with.

But it was no use.

The reality was that I still loved him, no matter what lies I tried to tell myself. I missed his sexy grin and the way he made me smile after a long day at school. I missed how we could just spend hours in each other's arms watching TV. I missed feeling like the happiest woman in the world because of him.

Not that it mattered. I'd said yes to Brock and would marry him in seven months, as we planned. He offered me a life I'd always dreamed of, and whatever romantic dreams I'd had for Gage and me had to be forgotten. I couldn't give up surefire happiness for a past that should stay right where it was.

Grabbing my phone from the other end of the couch, I typed a text to Gage, even though I knew I shouldn't.

I'm marrying a wonderful man who loves me. I would have married you if you didn't dump me like I was the least important thing in the world. Your loss.

I'd hoped saying that would make me feel better, but it didn't.

Maybe calling myself the equivalent of garbage wasn't the way to cheer myself up. Normally, I was so much better at dealing with this kind of thing. It must have been the bourbon. I definitely wasn't a happy drunk. That was sure.

My phone vibrated against the couch cushion, and I looked down to see a response from Gage. *Don't.*

Don't? That was his entire answer to me saying I was officially never going to be his again. Don't. Quickly, I typed out another text.

That's it? You must really love me, Gage. Nice way to fight for the woman you love.

I didn't know why I was continuing this conversation. I didn't want him to fight for me now. It was too late. I had Brock in my life now, so what the hell was I doing? It definitely was the bourbon.

Again, my phone vibrated as Gage's next text came in.

I never stopped loving you. Come to me tonight and I'll protect you.

Ah, now I understood. This whole thing wasn't about any kind of romantic feelings. This was about him keeping me safe from those crazy letter writers. I couldn't do this anymore.

Goodbye, Gage. I don't need a protector now. I have Brock.

He texted back, but I didn't read the message and instead deleted it. There was no point. I was with Brock, and in a few short months I'd become Mrs. Brock Hannon and begin a life only he could offer me.

I SLID INTO BED NEXT to Brock and wrapped my arm around his waist to pull him close to me. He murmured something in his sleep and took hold of my hand as his body melded to mine, kissing my engagement ring. Pressing my lips gently to his bare shoulder, I closed my eyes and loved the sense of security he gave me just being there.

"Hey you. You asleep?" I whispered in his ear.

Brock rolled over and looked at me through bleary eyes. "Everything okay?"

"It is now. I just wanted to tell you I love you and can't wait to be your wife."

His sleepy face lit up as he smiled. "Good. I love you, Jordan. And I promise I'll never let anyone hurt you."

"Why would you say that?" I asked nervously, praying to God he hadn't heard any of my conversation with Gage in the next room.

"No reason. Just feeling protective of the woman I love tonight. I have a big day tomorrow, so I need to sleep, but I promise after my meetings we can pick up right where we're leaving off tonight, okay?"

As he kissed me on the tip of my nose in that way he loved to do just before he went to sleep each night, I couldn't help but feel loved and cared for.

"Okay. It's a date."

Brock rolled over and fell asleep as I told myself I'd made the right choice. He offered me security, a good life, and love. Those things were important. So maybe we weren't what anyone else would call madly in love. That kind of thing was overrated anyway.

What we were was secure and comfortable, and I liked that. For the first time in my life, I felt cared for, and no matter of great sex or unforgettable romance was better than that.

So I'd marry Brock and make compromises for the greater good. And I'd forget Gage Varo and all the feelings he brought out in me.

CHAPTER SEVEN

GAGE

FOR HOURS, I LAY IN bed reading over Jordan's texts and wishing she was in my arms instead of miles away in another man's bed. I'd promised myself I'd stay away from her to make sure whoever was after me didn't hurt her, but now that I'd seen her again all those pledges to let her go forever had gone out the window.

I should have never gone to her engagement party. What the hell was I thinking?

Rolling over, I buried my face in the pillow. I knew what I was thinking. I wanted to really see that she had moved on from what we'd had. That she had moved on from loving me.

Well, I guess I got what I wanted. She'd definitely gotten over us. Her future husband wasn't much to speak of, though. Sandy blond hair, weak chin, and beady eyes were his best features, and that wasn't saying much.

Not that it mattered one fucking bit. Whatever romantic dreams I still harbored about getting back together with Jordan someday were just that. Meaningless dreams I had to forget. I couldn't let her get hurt because I was too selfish to stay away from her.

Her life was more important than my missing her, even if missing her felt like someone was ripping my heart out of my chest every night. She didn't deserve to pay for my mistake.

AFTER A FEW HOURS OF restless sleep, I woke up with a new focus. I needed to make sure Brock Hannon was who he claimed he was. If I had to give Jordan up to some guy, I had to know he wasn't part of whoever continued to send me those letters threatening her.

I got to the office and there waiting for me slipped under the front door was a white envelope sent from Texas and addressed to me. Turning it over in my hand, I saw no evidence that it had actually been delivered by the post office, so this was meant as a clear warning since I'd seen Jordan just the night before.

But who had sent it? More and more I began to think the person behind these letters was none other than Jordan's fiancé himself, Brock Hannon. I needed to find out just who the hell this guy was.

Since it was a Sunday, I had the place to myself. An hour's worth of searching online only resulted in the party line on Brock Hannon. Wealthy entrepreneur with an internet startup worth multi-millions, he seemed perfect in every way. No bad press, no former relationships with unhappy ex-girlfriends or spouses. Not even a speeding ticket in one of his dozen or so luxury sports cars.

But nobody was that perfect. I just needed to find the right kind of help to dig up the real goods on Hannon. I only knew of one person who could find out all the dirty details about a person, and all it would take was one phone call to find him.

It had been a while since I saw the guy, but with the right help, he'd get me what I needed. I dialed Tristan's cell and hoped he wouldn't mind me interrupting his Sunday morning in the country.

"Hi, Tristan. I'm hoping you can help me. I need Daryl's number."

He remained silent for a long moment, and then in a quiet voice barely above a whisper, he asked, "Are you going to have him check out Jordan's fiancé?"

"Yeah. Did you already have him do that?"

Another long pause. "Not exactly. I did a basic check of him and found nothing. He seems like a decent guy."

I heard hesitation in Tristan's voice. "But? I hear a but in there somewhere."

"He seems too good to be true, to be honest. I've wondered if I should check deeper, but when I mentioned it to Nina a couple weeks ago, she told me Jordan's happy. Something just seems off about him, if you know what I mean. And last night seemed strange. He and I don't necessarily travel in the same circles socially, but I would have thought I'd know at least a few of his guests. I didn't know anyone."

Tristan's words sent up all sorts of red flags in my mind. "That's why I want to have Daryl dig up whatever there is to dig up on him. I just don't feel like she knows all there is to know about this guy."

He gave me Daryl's cell number and as I thanked him, he said, "Good luck, Gage. I hope you find what you're looking for."

"Thanks. Say hi to Nina for me."

I keyed in Daryl's number as the thought of finding what I wanted passed through my mind. If I did find out that Brock Hannon wasn't all he claimed to be, Jordan would be heartbroken. Again, I'd be the one to ruin her happiness.

But that was a chance I had to take. I couldn't take the risk that Hannon was involved with whoever was threatening her. She could hate me all she wanted. As long as she was safe, I could live with her hating me.

Daryl answered with his usual relaxed way of making someone feel like he knew exactly what they wanted from him before they said a word. "Hey, Gage. Tristan just texted me that you would be calling me. I assume it has to do with that pretty blonde friend of Nina's you used to date marrying another man?"

I sighed at his succinct assessment of my problem. "I guess I'm thankful Tristan gave you the rundown. At least I won't have to go through the preliminaries for you."

"Tristan didn't tell me a thing, other than saying you wanted to talk to me."

"Then how did you know I needed your help with something involving Jordan?"

With a chuckle, he said, "Because that's my job. I'm supposed to know things, buddy. So what can I do for you?"

So I would have to go through the details. Better to get it over and done with so he could move on to actually finding out about good old Brock.

"I need you to find out everything you can about Brock Hannon. And I mean everything—not just what it says when you Google the bastard."

"Well, I was right then. You do want to know about your girl's fiancé. At least you're smart enough to know you can't believe the bullshit you find when you do a search for him. He's a fucking millionaire. He can afford to keep the dirt hidden and hidden well. I'm sure he has someone like me on his payroll like Tristan does, and it's that guy's job to make sure when people look into his boss's past that nothing but roses come up."

Daryl's mention of Tristan and hidden dirt made my mind wander for a moment as I wondered what he could be hiding and if Nina knew. What exactly was the perfect guy keeping buried?

"Thankfully, I'm better than the guy Brock Hannon has, so whatever he's hiding, I'll find out."

I had to laugh. Daryl was always so confident, even if everything about how he looked inspired anything but confidence with his unkempt bushy mountain man beard and almost troll-like appearance.

"That's big talk. You sure this guy's dirt will be that easy to find?"

"If I didn't know this was for a good cause, I'd hang up on you right now for that insult, Gage. But I'm an incurable romantic, so I'll let that one slip up slide."

"No offense intended, Daryl. Just worried this guy has pretty crafty people on the case and his past might be a hard nut to crack."

"I've never met a nut I couldn't crack, so don't worry. Here's the thing, though. Do you have any idea what you think I'll find?"

I cringed at the thought that this Brock guy might be associated somehow with anyone who wanted to punish me for my past. While I didn't want to discuss the dirt I was hiding, I didn't really have much of a choice.

Clearing my throat, I said quietly, "He might be connected to something that happened with me years ago."

"The girl who got killed on your watch? That something?" he announced casually, as if everyone had the murder of a girl in their past.

"Yeah. That."

"So why would you think he's connected to that? Seems like an odd coincidence, doesn't it?"

I opened my desk drawer and lifted out the stack of letters. "Because a year or so ago I began getting anonymous letters threatening Jordan's life if I didn't leave her. And then she meets this guy out of the blue and he sweeps her off her feet? And now I've begun getting more letters."

Daryl suddenly sounded genuinely interested for the first time in the conversation. "Hmmm, the plot thickens. I think I want to see these letters before I go digging. I'll be at your office in twenty minutes. Make sure there's coffee because I'm no good without caffeine."

"Okay. I'll be here with the coffee."

He arrived in just under a half hour, and after a few gulps of coffee, Daryl focused on the pile of envelopes in front of me on my desk. "Those the poison pen letters?"

I nodded. "Yeah. I started getting them when I was out in LA. When I broke up with Jordan, they stopped, but recently they started up again."

"So what's changed?"

Daryl's question confused me. "Nothing changed. I'm still doing what I do every day. Same shit, different day."

He shook his head, his red hair and shaggy red beard moving

with it. "Nope. Something changed. That's the only reason for the letters to start coming again. Tell me exactly what was going on when you began getting them the first time."

"I was watching that kid Tristan helped connect me with out in LA. He was filming a movie and I spent most of my time making sure teenage girls didn't get close enough to touch him. Other than that, I spent all my down time at the hotel at his beck and call and in my room."

"That's it? Sure do know how to live, don't you? You're out in La La Land and you spend your time in your hotel room."

"I was there for a job. Nothing more."

"No extracurriculars with your ex Angela while you were there?"

Surprised to hear Daryl bring up her name, I leveled my stare at him. "How do you know about her?"

He rolled his eyes as I realized of course he'd know about her. Tristan had Daryl check me out before hiring me.

"Oh yeah. Dumb question. Well, the answer is no. I didn't see Angela in all the time I was there."

Daryl pursed his lips and stroked his beard. "Do you remember anything from the day you received the first letter?"

I shook my head. "No. The only thing I remember is being surprised I received any mail at all. Anyone who wanted to communicate with me called or texted me, and my sister handled all my bills while I was there. I had no expectation of receiving any mail."

"Okay. Let me see the first letter."

Handing him the envelope from the top of the stack, I said as a sort of joke, "I hope you're not expecting cut out letters from a magazine. It's nothing that telling. Just some words on a sheet of paper."

He rolled his eyes again and snatched the letter from my grip. "How was your trip back to 1972? This isn't Watergate. You have someone trying to keep you away from that pretty blonde. Simple.

But why is the question."

Daryl turned the envelope over to examine the back flap and then flipped it back to the front. "Sent from Dallas, Texas. Wasn't that where that girl and her father lived?"

Nodding, I swallowed hard as I remembered that day I let her get killed. "Yeah."

"Well, that seems pretty obvious that it certainly could be someone from that period of your life fucking around with you. Let me see what the letter actually says."

As he slipped the plain white sheet of paper out of the envelope, I mumbled, "Like I said, not much."

"Hmmm…done on a computer using basic printer paper. Nothing much to see there. *You let Tiffany die, so how do you think it will feel when Jordan is taken from you? Now you'll feel the pain of losing someone you love.* Subtle," Daryl said with a snort.

"Yeah. I didn't really take it seriously because I think I was just in shock that anyone would refer to her death like that. But when the next one came two days after, I knew I had to do something."

Daryl looked up from the letter. "You mean break it off with her?"

I didn't answer his question and instead just handed him the second letter. "This one is blunter. No mistaking the intention with this one."

"*That girlfriend of yours has no idea the debt you owe. Her life for Tiffany's if you don't end it now.*"

Daryl shook his head, and I saw by his expression that he wasn't impressed. "Any chance this could be an ex of Jordan's instead of someone involved in the incident with the girl?"

I thought about that for a minute, but none of Jordan's exes ever sounded like the types who would do anything like this. At least not the way she described them. "I never got the sense that anyone from her past had any interest in coming back after they'd broken up."

"Hmmm…boys will be stupid, won't they? Pretty girl with a

good job and they don't come back. Okay, so how many of these have you gotten?"

Picking up the remaining letters, I thumbed through them. "Six total, including the most recent ones that began a few weeks ago and the one I found here under the door this morning."

"Well, you say nothing changed, but we know something did, right?" he asked, his voice full of suspicion. "Let me see the last two you got."

Handing him the envelopes, I repeated myself. "I told you nothing changed. I wouldn't keep anything hidden if it could help figure out who the hell is behind this, especially if it's Brock Hannon."

He slipped a letter out and held it up to the fluorescent light hanging from the ceiling. "This one's different. *She still isn't safe, Gage.*" Looking at me, he grinned. "Short but definitely not sweet. And the one from this morning?"

I pushed it across the desk toward him. "From Texas, as they all have been, and the threat is clear. If I don't stay away, she'll get hurt."

Daryl's eyes lit up as he examined the front of the envelope. "This one wasn't mailed like all the others. So something definitely has changed now. Let's see what it has to say." He held the letter up to the light and grinned. "*This is your last warning. Stay away.* Seems whoever's behind these is getting antsy."

"Antsy? Like what? Scared? Nervous?" I asked, hating how he sat there looking at me like I was hiding something from him, something that might be the key to keeping Jordan safe.

Daryl finished his coffee and leaned back in his chair, folding his arms behind his head. "Best for me to just ask the question. When did you start talking to her again?"

"After they started coming again. I'm telling you I didn't change anything. Whatever changed, it changed with the people behind this, not me. That's why I'm thinking it must have something to do with that guy she's marrying."

"No recurring drive-bys of her place late at night after you've had too much to drink that someone might have noticed? No being in the same general area as her when you think no one's looking?"

Even though I was guilty of both of his accusations, I shook my head and rolled my eyes. Daryl didn't need to know how lost I was. "If you're asking if I've been stalking her, the answer is no."

"Okay. I just know how your kind works. That's all."

"My kind?"

"Yeah, your kind. The dark and brooding kind. The still waters run deep and dirty kind. You know what I mean. You don't say much, but you're like an iceberg—most of you is below the surface."

"Jesus, Daryl. I never knew you paid that much attention to me."

His profiling hit a little too close to home, but I still had no desire to admit to him just how much I still loved Jordan. Daryl and I weren't exactly confidants.

He nodded, as if he finally believed me. "Okay, then let's attack this from another angle. What changed with Jordan or this Brock guy recently?"

Only one thing had changed with either of them recently that I knew of. The announcement of their engagement. Hanging my head, I said quietly, "They got engaged."

"How long before that did you begin getting the letters again?"

"A week or so."

"Well, they'd have to plan the engagement party months in advance, wouldn't they to get a decent place in the city? So that doesn't sound like it fits."

I lifted my head as something he said clicked. "I don't think so. They haven't known each other very long, so I don't think it was months in the planning."

"Whirlwind romance, huh?" he said with a grin. "Okay, then maybe there's something to the timing of the engagement being announced and these letters coming to you again. But why? If he's behind them, why start up again? You hadn't seen her recently, had you?"

"No. I stayed away because I was afraid if I didn't that she'd get hurt."

Daryl leveled his gaze on me. "That's not entirely true, now is it?"

"What do you mean?" Jesus, I felt like I was being interrogated.

Picking up the letter I'd found under the door that morning, he waved it around. "Hello? I just told you whoever is behind this is getting antsy. They're afraid you're back in the picture, so when did you see her? Right before the party? Probably not after since the happy couple likely left the party to go home for a wonderful night of celebration for the just the two of them."

His description of Jordan with Brock made me cringe, even if I knew what he thought they did the night before wasn't true. Taking a deep breath, I blew it out slowly and admitted the truth. "I saw her at the engagement party. I was working security for a party in the room next to it and stopped over to see her."

He threw his head back and laughed one of his deep belly laughs. "I knew it! For what it's worth, Gage, you're lucky you didn't have to stand in line behind all those other fools who let her go. She's a beautiful girl. The guy who snags her is a lucky man."

"Yeah, and right now, that's Brock Hannon, but I still think he's no good."

Abruptly, Daryl stood and tapped his knuckles on the top of my desk. "Well, I think I know all I can from you. I'll check out this Brock Hannon. I doubt he's as clean as he comes up in a regular search, but I'm not sure he's going to be connected to the threats against her. By the way, you might want to put one of your guys on her for a while if you aren't already doing it."

"Why?" I asked, terror racing through me at the thought of Jordan getting hurt even after I'd done everything they'd asked.

"Because she's the key here and I'm not sure it's about hurting you so much as it is about hurting her. But maybe it's all nothing but a jealous fiancé trying to keep her ex-boyfriend away. I won't know until I dig up some of his dirt."

"Let me know as soon as you can, okay Daryl?"

"Don't worry, Gage. I'm sure as of right now she'll have the finest protection available. As soon as I know something, I'll call you."

He turned on his heels and headed out the door as I thought about how I'd protect her and still stay far enough away from her so whoever was behind those letters wouldn't see me around her. Daryl was right. Even if it meant my life, I'd make sure she was protected.

CHAPTER EIGHT

JORDAN

ROLLING OVER, I LET MY arm fall onto the empty space where Brock had slept next to me as my head began to pound like a freight train was tearing through it. Never much of a hard liquor drinker, I definitely couldn't handle bourbon. I closed my eyes and prayed to God for some relief from my pounding headache while what I'd done settled into my consciousness.

Drunk texting was literally the worst thing a girl could do, and I'd one upped it and gone old school, adding drunk dialing to my repertoire of drunken stupidity. Well, if you're going to do something, you might as well do it all the way. Anything worth doing is worth doing right.

My inner smart ass didn't make my behavior any better. I should have never spoken to Gage in any way, shape, or form. What was the point? I had Brock now and we were ready to set off on a life of our own.

I looked around on the night table to see if my sweet fiancé had left me a little note just to say hi or when he'd be home from the office, but found nothing. Cute things like that weren't exactly his style, but I had hoped he'd leave me something after our engagement party last night. But that was foolish. Most guys didn't do those kinds of things.

Gage did those cute things.

Ugh!

I needed to get that man out of my head before I began to

sabotage my wonderful relationship with Brock. So what that he used to leave me little sticky notes telling me how much he couldn't wait to see me again or apologizing for having to leave before I got up? It wasn't as if that made him the perfect man or anything.

Cute was definitely overrated. Brock had many other terrific attributes. He was smart, attractive, wealthy, and successful. So cute wasn't one of his qualities. No matter. He made up for it in so many other ways.

I needed to get out of this bed or I'd waste the entire day away. Maybe Nina and the kids could come into town for a visit to the zoo. Pressing speed dial, I waited as her phone rang and wondered where Brock kept his Advil.

"Hey you! You're up early considering last night's party," Nina said in a chipper voice. "What's up?"

"I was wondering if you and the kiddos would like to hit the zoo today."

"Honey, it's Sunday. Aren't you and Brock spending the day together?"

It was Sunday. I'd lost track of what day it was, likely due to my bourbon hangover. But working weekends wasn't anything strange to my fiancé. He seemed to work every day of the year. A man didn't get to be as successful as he was without a little sacrifice.

"No, he's at the office. You know how those Type A executives are."

Nina chuckled, knowing all too well how those types were since Tristan was the same way. "I hear you. We'd just planned on hanging out today, though, but let me call you back in a minute. Maybe we can leave the burbs for a day."

"Okay. I'll be here."

I placed the phone next to me on the bed and covered my eyes with my forearm, hoping the world's worst hangover would soon just be a distant, awful memory. I knew I really should get up to find something for my head, but Nina would be calling back in a few minutes, so I'd just wait.

A few minutes turned into nearly a half hour, and when my phone rang again, it startled me from a sound sleep. Still in a groggy haze, I answered it and heard Nina's happy voice announce that Tristan was taking the kids to the park and then for a drive, so she and I could have a girls' day out. I didn't have the heart to tell her I may not be able to even extricate myself from Brock's bed at the rate I was going.

"Oh. That sounds great," I croaked out.

"Is everything okay, Jordan? I thought the two of us spending some time together would be fun."

Sitting up, I forced myself to come alive from my funk. "It is. It will be. What time do you want to get together?"

"I'm ready now, but you sound like a bus hit you. Can you be ready in an hour or do you need more time to recover from your celebration hangover?"

Groaning, I mumbled, "I wish it was that." I quickly changed the subject, hoping Nina didn't pick up on what I'd just said. "I can be ready in an hour. Do you want to meet somewhere or will Jensen be coming here?"

"Is here at Brock's?"

"Yeah."

"Okay, let's say an hour down in front of Brock's building. I remember where it is. Then you can fill me in on all the romantic stuff you and he did last night."

"Uh huh. Okay, see you in sixty."

I moved the phone from my ear but heard Nina say something. "Jordan, is something wrong?"

Shaking my head, I said, "No. It's all good. Just have a bit of a headache this morning, but some Advil and girl time with my best friend will chase it right away. See you in a bit."

Now I had to get out of bed. Slogging my way to the bathroom, I looked in the mirror and saw my pounding headache wasn't the only physical manifestation of my hangover. My face looked like someone had been beating me with the ugly stick.

I groaned. "Oh. No wonder Brock left without saying goodbye."

Forty-five minutes later, my hair was washed and dried, my makeup was applied so I didn't look like death warmed over, and I wore a cute t-shirt and cut-off jean shorts look that made me feel much better than I had when I woke up.

I put the finishing touches on my face and grabbed my purse, ready for a girls' day out with Nina. As I rode down in the elevator, I couldn't help but think she was the luckiest woman on earth. Gorgeous husband who also had no problem taking care of their triplets? There weren't too many guys like that in the world.

The elevator doors opened and before me stood Nina dressed in a sunny yellow dress with little blue stars. "I was hoping you'd meet me here. I forgot which floor Brock's apartment is on and didn't look forward to going door to door looking for you."

"You're so silly. He has the penthouse. So what should we do today? Shopping? Eating like pigs at our favorite restaurant? Hang out in the park?"

She screwed up her face like she was thinking about our choices and then flashed me that Nina smile that never failed to brighten my day. "How about we grab something to munch on and a couple coffees, and we can decide what we want to do with the rest of the day while we do that?"

"Okay. Sounds like a plan. Onward to find Jensen and our chariot."

WE SETTLED INTO A BOOTH in a little coffee shop a few blocks away from my apartment with our mugs of coffee and blueberry muffins. I missed doing this with Nina. Two or three times a week when she and I lived together we used to hang out in this place with its red Formica topped tables and paper placemats with ads on them, but since she moved out, I hadn't been to any of our old hangouts. It just wasn't the same without her, and none of my other friends enjoyed strong coffee at dive shops like she did.

"So is it okay to ask how you're doing after Gage showed up at the party last night?"

I took a sip and carefully placed the mug on the table. I didn't know if the caffeine was working incredibly fast this morning or if the mention of his name was the problem, but suddenly my hands began shaking. Hoping Nina hadn't noticed, I slid them under the table and pressed them onto the tops of my thighs.

"I'm fine. It's no big deal."

My hands continued to shake as she leveled her gaze on me, as if she were judging whether or not I'd told the truth. Of course I hadn't. It was a huge deal and as much as I wanted to forget everything about Gage, I didn't seem to be able to.

"Well, that's good," she said, but I knew she didn't believe my nonchalant attitude toward what had happened.

I wanted to change the topic, but my head filled with thoughts of him kissing me in that quiet room as my fiancé and all our guests stood celebrating our engagement just outside the door. How long had I waited to know he cared like I did? Too long. But with just one kiss, he had a way of making me fall back in love with him like nothing had ever happened to tear us apart.

But it had. He broke up with me over the phone and I had to remind myself all the time of how it felt for months afterward. God, if only memories brought back how we really felt when things were happening. Then I wouldn't have been sitting in a coffee shop in Brooklyn lying to my best friend about how much I still cared about a man I should have forgotten a long time ago.

Nina tapped on the table, startling me out of my daydreams. "Jordan, did you hear me?"

"No, sorry. This hangover is kicking my ass. What did you say?"

"I just said that I'm happy you're not upset over the Gage thing. I'm sure he was just feeling bad because he lost you, but you're happy now, so too bad for him. Right?"

"Yeah, right."

Why I thought I could pull the wool over Nina's eyes I had no idea. She knew me better than anyone else in the world, except for the very man I wished I could forget, and the expression on her face said she knew I was full of it.

"So are you planning to treat me like someone you can talk to about things or are you going to keep up this charade all day?" she asked with a sharpness in her tone I rarely heard from her.

"Is that your mom voice you're using on me?" I asked, trying to avoid the conversation I knew was inevitable. Sometimes the people who knew you best understood better than you did that talking about it was what had to be done.

"No, but I can whip out the mom voice if you want."

Taking a deep breath, I closed my eyes and let the air out of my lungs slowly. "I got drunk last night and drunk dialed Gage. And drunk texted because if you're going to make a mistake, you should make it big, you know?"

"Why did you do that? I thought you said everything you had to say to him at the party."

I opened my eyes and saw Nina looking at me with confusion. "I guess bourbon didn't think so."

"Bourbon? And how about a better question. Where did you find the time to call or text Gage at Brock's on the night of your engagement party?"

Forcing a smile, I took a sip of coffee and mumbled, "He had an early morning at the office today, so he went to bed early."

Nina sat back against the red vinyl booth seat and stared at me, those cornflower blue eyes looking at me like she was figuring out who or what I was. "Jordan, what's going on? I thought you were crazy about Brock."

I rolled my eyes and looked away from her questioning gaze. "Just because we didn't have sex last night doesn't mean I'm not crazy about my fiancé."

"Don't be intentionally obtuse. You're smarter than that. You know I wasn't referring to the sex thing, which I admit I find odd in people who are supposed to be madly in love."

Another deep breath. "Oh, you mean about the drunk dialing and texting. I don't know. I just felt like I needed to tell him I'm over him."

"You don't think him seeing you announce your engagement to another man took care of that?"

She wasn't buying any of my bullshit excuses. Not surprising since I wasn't buying them either. I couldn't explain it, but I needed to speak to him last night. True, the telling him I was over him was just an excuse, but I felt like it had to be done. The problem was it just made me think of him even more.

My mind felt like it was trapped in some horrible emotional hamster wheel. I thought of him more now than I had for months, just at the moment he should be the last thing on my mind. And the more I thought of him, the more I wanted to speak to him.

Humiliated at how ridiculous I felt, I lowered my head and said quietly, "I don't know why, Nina. I just had to tell him I was happy with another man. It's stupid and juvenile, but there it is."

Touching my arm, she said in that sweet voice of hers, "Oh, honey. I get it. I do. What I don't get is why you're marrying someone else when you obviously can't get Gage out of your mind."

I sighed, exhausted from thinking about him. "Because whatever hold he still has on me, it isn't the same as what I have with Brock. My relationship with him is based on a solid ground. Gage can't offer me the life Brock can. It's just that simple."

A frown settled into her features, marring her beautiful face, and she glanced down at my diamond ring before she looked up at me again. "Why is it you never mention love when you talk about why you're marrying Brock? It's always other reasons, far more pragmatic reasons, but not love."

The older woman at the table near us looked over as Nina asked her question, her eyes trained on me like she needed to know the answer too. Lowering my voice, I leaned over the table toward

Nina and whispered, "Because that stuff only happens in fairy tales."

Confused, Nina asked, "What stuff? And why are we whispering?"

"Because that lady over there heard you ask why I never talk about love when I talk about Brock and I don't feel like having the whole world know my personal life. And the stuff I'm talking about is that true love nonsense you think I should buy into."

"You used to believe in true love. We both did."

"And you got your Prince Charming while I kissed a pond full of frogs."

Nina frowned again at my defeatist attitude toward true love. "I kissed a lot of frogs before Tristan. You know that's true. You met most of them."

"I know."

"But I never gave up, and I don't like that you are. I know Brock is rich and handsome, but where's the love? Without love, it's more a business transaction than a marriage."

I leaned away and considered her description of what Brock and I were doing. Well, what I was doing. Brock seemed to genuinely love me, at least in his own way. "And what's wrong with that? People do that every day. Marriage isn't always about hearts and flowers, Nina."

Her blue eyes grew wide. "Who does that? And I'm not saying it's all hearts and flowers, but where's the passion? Where's the need to be near that other person so much that you get so distracted you can't think of anything else?"

"What you're describing is the kind of thing that gets your heart broken. No thanks. I'll take what Brock and I have any day over getting hurt again."

She began to defend the fairy tale beliefs she still clung to, but I cut her off. "This is just the way it is, Nina. I need you to accept this. I'm making sure I'm taken care of, so no more talk about hearts and flowers and passion. Okay?"

Hesitating for a moment, she let out a sigh and accepted the reality she couldn't change. "Okay. As long as you're happy, I'm happy."

"Good." I took my last sip of coffee and gobbled up the last morsels of my blueberry muffin. "Now let's go have some fun. I start school in a few weeks, so I think we need to do some serious shopping. You up for it or has living out in the country taken all the power out of your shopping skills?"

We stood from the table, and pointing at me, she narrowed her eyes to slits. "You're on. You don't know who you're messing with, honey. I have an entire wardrobe covered in spit up and baby food stains that needs to be replaced. You should be asking yourself if you're up to it because I'm shopping until I drop today."

It was like old times for us, and I loved it. I knew Nina didn't agree with my outlook on love and marriage, but she loved me enough to not press anymore. And more importantly, she knew to let go of the Gage nonsense.

Now if only I could do the same.

AFTER A DAY OF POWER shopping with Nina, I finally returned to my apartment just before five in the afternoon, my body dragging from the hangover and too much exertion the day after drinking. But our time together had been the most fun I'd had in a long time, so although I felt like a bus had hit me, I was happy we'd had our girls' day out.

Just as I closed my front door behind me, my cell phone rang. Dropping my new clothes and shoes on the living room couch, I dug my phone out of my purse as I prayed to God it wasn't Gage calling. I so didn't need the temptation. But instead of him it was Brock calling, just in time to hopefully offer me a great dinner and a night together.

"Hey you! I just got home from a day of shopping. Did you have a good day at the office?"

"I did. But I had a thought I hope you're okay with. I want us to elope."

Elope? We were planning a wedding with nearly five hundred guests. I had four bridesmaids and a matron of honor who were supposed to begin dress shopping in the next few weeks, and we'd already picked a date, for God's sake!

"What are you talking about elope? Why? When? Why?"

"I know it sounds crazy, but I don't want to wait to marry you. We can have the actual ceremony when we planned it, but I don't think we should wait until then. What do you think?"

His voice verged on excited, which was very much not like him. I liked it, though. The idea of someone so eager to marry me that he didn't want to wait all those months made me feel wanted and loved. Why shouldn't we elope? It could be fun.

"Okay. Let's do it! When?"

"Great! We can go to my place in Hilton Head two Fridays from now. It's before you have to go back to school, so we can get in a brief honeymoon too before you return to work."

"You're going to take a week off of work? Really? That's so not like you, Brock."

He chuckled in a way that told me he was nervous. "I know, but you like that, don't you? I've been working hard for a long time. A week off with you is long overdue."

"Definitely! So what do we have to do before we go?" I asked, suddenly aware that actually eloping took a little bit of planning, in reality.

"Don't worry about a thing. I'll take care of everything. I'm going to have to work some pretty long hours beforehand, though, so you might not see me much for the next two weeks. As much as I want to marry you, I can't let the company slip because of my romantic notions. What do you say we plan for me to pick you up at noon that Friday?"

"Oh, I won't see you until then? Okay. I understand. Friday at noon. I'll be the blushing bride standing on my front steps," I joked.

"Good. I can't wait. I'm so glad you don't want to wait, Jordan. But I don't think we should tell anyone. Let's make this our secret."

"Why? I want to tell my family and friends, especially Nina. She's going to be so thrilled, and it would hurt her feelings if I didn't tell her. It would be like lying to her."

Brock's tone turned serious. "Jordan, I don't want the press to get a hold of this news, so you can't tell anyone. We'll have the formal ceremony when we planned, so it's not like your family and friends won't get to be a part of our big day. It's just that our first big day will be our secret."

I didn't like the idea of keeping the biggest thing in my life a secret, but I saw his point. If the press found out, they'd announce it to the world and then our elopement would be news in all the gossip pages. I had to keep in mind that I wasn't marrying some ordinary man, and when Brock Hannon married someone, it would be news.

"Will we at least talk during that time?"

Brock's voice softened. "Of course. I promise we'll talk all the time in the two weeks we're apart. Okay?"

I didn't like the idea that we couldn't see each other for two weeks and that I'd be basically alone during that time. The temptation to reach out to Gage might become too much.

But he offered me nothing that Brock could, so all I had to do was remember that and those two weeks would fly by.

"Okay. I love you and I can't wait to see you on Friday afternoon."

"I love you too, Jordan. How about I ask Monique if she can come up and visit while I'm busy during that time? Would you like that?"

I knew he was trying to be helpful, but since I'd only met his sister once and for just a few minutes right after Brock and I started dating, I didn't know if I wanted to spend the upcoming two weeks with her. I didn't want to hurt his feelings, though.

"That would be nice, but I don't want to impose on her. She likely has things in her own life she has to take care of instead of hanging out with me, Brock."

"Nonsense. She'll love it. She was so upset she couldn't make it for the engagement party. I'll call her right now and let you know when she's coming."

"Okay. I love you."

"Love you too. Just think. This time two weeks from now we'll be a happily married couple."

"I like that. Talk to you later."

We hung up, and I tried to feel good about two weeks apart from him. Maybe having his sister around to entertain would be good for me. Any distraction to make sure I didn't call Gage was welcome. I just had to make it two weeks and then everything would be fine.

Chapter Nine

Gage

DAY AFTER DAY, I WAITED to hear from Daryl, but he never called. Watching Jordan became my full time job, so my crew's assignments had to be rearranged to accommodate my being absent from the office and all other Varo Security jobs. Thankfully, I had the best workers in the business and each of them without knowing why I had to be away picked up the slack and helped me keep my company's commitments.

The doorman at Hannon's building proved incredibly helpful once I got him into a conversation about the Mets. Even though Brock was one of his favorite tenants, Dennis had no problem pushing aside professional etiquette and divulging that on his way out Sunday morning he made a point of mentioning that Miss Wright wouldn't be around much for the next two weeks, so any packages that came for him would have to wait until he returned each night. Although Dennis was sure the two were certifiable love birds, he did wonder if Mr. Hannon had something on the side.

As I made my way to watch Jordan's apartment, I had to question why immediately after announcing their engagement they were to be apart for two weeks. Was Hannon seeing another woman? But if he was, why would he publicize his engagement to Jordan?

Daryl may not have thought there was anything shady about this guy, but I was sure from the minute I heard about this separation that something was going on with Brock Hannon.

At least their spending time apart made watching her easy. From a little cigarette shop at the corner of her block, I could keep an eye on her comings and goings. Like she had since she lived out at the Dutchess County house with Nina, Jordan went to the gym every morning, usually before seven a.m. and worked out for at least an hour. After that, since it was summertime and she hadn't returned to work at school yet, she jogged back to her apartment and stayed there until at least noon. Then depending on the weather or the day, she either walked to one of the nearby grocery stores in her Sunset Park neighborhood to buy lunch or caught the subway to head into the city to grab a bite to eat with girlfriends and shop.

I never got too close but always saw who she was speaking to and what she was doing. To be honest, she didn't seem much like the woman I'd dated all those months. I didn't remember her loving shopping so much, but maybe that was because I hated shopping. Her friends were women I'd never met while we were dating, and I wondered if that was because I wasn't like her fiancé.

Powerful. Wealthy.

But at least they seemed like her. I guessed they were fellow teachers since one day they all left a downtown restaurant and headed to the school Jordan taught at.

By the end of the first week, I hadn't seen Brock stop by her apartment even once and every night she stayed in her bedroom. Through the open window that faced the street, I saw her sitting on her bed watching her favorite TV shows until around midnight. Then she'd turn the lights off and go to sleep.

It seemed like a strange life for someone who was preparing to marry a millionaire.

Beginning on the Wednesday after I started to watch her, one woman began visiting Jordan every day. This woman didn't act like Nina or like her work friends did. Haughty and spoiled, she didn't seem like the kind of person Jordan would want to spend time with at all. While Jordan wore khaki shorts and tank tops with her usual flip flops or sandals, this woman never failed to be dressed in far more expensive designer dresses for the heat of the New York summer. She always seemed awkward around the woman, as if she knew deep down inside she didn't belong with her, but day after day they got together and went to lunch or for manicures or spa dates until nighttime when she returned to Brooklyn alone.

The new woman reminded me of those femme fatales in the old black and white films. She appeared a strange companion for Jordan, who was down to earth and sweet. Her light brown hair was cut in a sharp angle to just above her shoulders, and I couldn't tell what her eyes looked like because she wore enormous sunglasses no matter if the sun was out or not. Lean, she had almost a flinty look about her, like she'd seen things Jordan as an elementary school teacher couldn't even imagine.

It didn't take long for me to dislike and distrust her. On Friday afternoon as I followed them to their second spa appointment for the week, I secretly took a picture of her and sent it to Daryl, hoping he could shine some light on who she was and why she suddenly seemed to need to be with Jordan every day. At the very least, I hoped it would spur him on to call me with any information he might have found about Brock Hannon.

As I watched the front of Roget's Day Spa waiting for Jordan and her new friend to emerge after nearly an hour inside, my cell finally rang with a call from Daryl.

"It's about time," I said, frustrated from not knowing who the hell this woman was. "Any news?"

"Well, hello to you too. That picture you took wasn't exactly photographer level. I couldn't find out anything. What do you have on that phone of yours? A two megapixel?"

"Fine. I'll try to grab another one if they ever come out of this damn spa. Anything else you can tell me, maybe about Brock?"

"Nothing yet. I think if you want to know who this mystery woman is you have to let me put my guy on the case. He's much better than you are at taking pictures, and he'll only need one day to get me what I need. You know, he's got the telephoto lens and all that good stuff."

I watched as the door to the spa opened and yet another woman who wasn't Jordan came out. "Yeah, whatever. Any chance he can do it today? I don't like this person being around Jordan. My gut tells me she's no good."

Daryl sighed. "She didn't look too bad in that shitty picture you sent me. Nice body. What's your problem with her?"

"My problem is she came out of nowhere. I've never seen her around Jordan before, not even at the engagement party. If they were that close that they spend every day together, don't you think I would have seen her before this?"

"Sounds likely. How about Nina? Does she know her?"

I hadn't thought of asking Nina, mainly because somewhere in the back of my mind I didn't want her or Tristan to know I was still so hung up on Jordan. Plus, I knew Nina's feelings on having people guard her, and she likely wouldn't be a huge supporter of my watching Jordan day and night.

"I haven't asked her. I'd like to keep this thing with Jordan between you and me."

"I get that, but if anyone would know about Jordan's friends, it's Nina. She is her best friend."

"True," I said, thinking out loud. "But they aren't as close since Nina began living out at the house and married Tristan."

"I can't deny that, but I still think if Jordan is friends with whoever this woman is that Nina would at least know her name and something about her. I say ask her. What's the harm?"

"The harm is she'll find out what I'm doing," I admitted quietly as I watched two women leave the spa's front door. Had Jordan and her friend snuck out a back entrance? What the hell were they doing in there all this time?

Daryl let out a deep chuckle. "Do you think anyone who knows you two doesn't realize you're still in love with Jordan? Because if you're worried about letting that cat out of the bag, you can put your mind at ease. Everyone knows. You're still crazy about her, and I suspect she's still crazy about you. Call Nina and see what she says. No need to make our job harder, and if this woman is bad news, the sooner we know who she is, the better."

He was right. Whatever fear I had of showing how much I cared for Jordan didn't matter. Nina likely knew I still loved her friend. Crashing the engagement party had probably proved that already.

"You're right. While your guy is doing his paparazzi thing, I'll see what I can find out from Nina about this woman, assuming she and Jordan ever leave this goddamned spa again."

Another chuckle from Daryl only served to make me more irritated about being stuck watching the front door of Roget's for nearly an hour and a half. "I'll call you when I get the pics. Until then, enjoy your day, Gage."

I didn't react to Daryl's busting my ass. As I stood waiting, I thought back to when Jordan and I dated and I couldn't remember her ever even mentioning going to a spa the entire time we were together, other than once when she was a bridesmaid in someone's wedding. The person I knew wore her hair up in a messy ponytail and rarely wore much makeup at all, even when we went out at night. She couldn't be bothered trying to put on airs and pretending to be someone she wasn't.

That's what made her so great, though. It was her genuine way—her realness—that I loved about her. Even with no makeup, her hair undone, and wearing yoga pants and a t-shirt, Jordan still was more beautiful than any other woman I'd ever met before. It was that ease with who she was that made me fall head over heels in love with her.

But now as I saw her leave Roget's Day Spa with this mystery woman, the two of them pictures of perfection in every way, I felt like I didn't even know her anymore. My sadness as I watched them almost made me forget to take another picture, but I pushed it aside and focused long enough to get the best picture I could of her friend. Hopefully, it would be good enough for Nina to identify who she was.

A HALF HOUR LATER, JORDAN and her friend parted ways at her apartment building, and as much as I knew I needed to watch to make sure she was okay, I wanted to see where the mystery woman went to. Maybe that would help Nina tell me her name and what she knew about her.

So I followed her as her driver made his way across the bridge and back to Manhattan. Before long, I saw where she was going. As I watched, she was let into the same building Brock Hannon lived in. I gave her enough time to get to whatever floor her apartment was on and quickly ran across the street to say hi to my favorite doorman and Mets fan, Dennis.

"Hi Dennis! How are you today? I saw the Mets clobbered the Phillies last night. It's a good time to be a Mets fan!" I said as casually as I could.

"Mr. Jones, how are you? I did enjoy my team's win last night. I think they're going to go all the way this year."

"Hey Dennis, I wanted to ask you a question about the woman who just went in. My friend and she were at a spa and the lady left one of her shopping bags with her. I have it in the car, but I didn't catch her in time. Does she live here or is she just visiting?"

Dennis opened the front doors for an older couple and wished them a wonderful day before he turned back to me. "Oh, she's here visiting Mr. Hannon. That's his sister. I can make sure the package is delivered to her, if you like."

"My friend was very specific. You know how women are with their shopping. It's like baseball is to us, right?" I said with a smile, not exactly exaggerating.

"So true, Mr. Jones. I can't let you go into the building without permission, though. I do apologize."

Poor Dennis looked downright unhappy about disappointing

me, so I chucked him lightly on the shoulder and smiled even broader. "No problem. Let me go get the bag. What name do I put on it—hers or Mr. Hannon's since she's staying in his apartment?"

Happy again, Dennis said, "You can put her name on it. Monique Hannon. A beautiful name for such a beautiful lady, don't you think?"

"Truly. Thank you, Dennis. I'll be right back."

As he opened the doors to the building for a group of people exiting a cab, I jogged back across to my car and took off down the street back toward Brooklyn and Jordan's apartment. Traffic on the FDR going toward Sunset Park was a bear even though it was only mid-afternoon, so as I crept along at a snail's pace, I called Daryl to share the information Dennis had given me.

"Gage, did you finally get to leave the spa? Get yourself a mani/pedi while you were there?" he joked.

"Yeah, yeah. I got something even better. The name of the woman with Jordan is none other than Brock's sister, Monique Hannon."

"Monique," he repeated in a singsong voice. "Sexy. I think I'm liking this mystery woman even more."

Daryl could sometimes be too much with his ass busting. Sick of him for the moment, I said, "Just find out all you can on who the hell she is and why she's here in town while her brother seems to be absent, okay?"

"No problem, Gage. I'm on it. I guess this means you don't have to call Nina and ask, huh?"

"Let me know the minute you find out anything, Daryl," I said before pressing END and tossing the phone on the seat beside me.

Twenty minutes later, I crossed into Brooklyn and found traffic thinned enough so it only took me another ten minutes to get back to Jordan's neighborhood. As always, parking was practically non-existent, but I found a spot to squeeze my Jeep into two blocks from her apartment, and beggars not being able to be choosers, I grabbed it and quickly made my way back to near her building.

By eight o' clock, I was sure it would be another night of Jordan in her bedroom watching TV, but a few minutes after the hour she came out of her building and began walking toward the subway. I followed her, keeping a safe distance, but just before she reached it a car pulled up that I recognized immediately.

I crept as close as I could and watched as Jensen stepped out of the driver's side of the black car and smiled toward Jordan. "Good evening, miss."

As he opened the door for her, Jordan patted him on the shoulder. "Thanks a million, Jensen."

"My pleasure, miss. Mrs. Stone has instructed me to take you wherever you need to go."

"Then it's the upper west side for us tonight. I'll show you where when we get close."

Jensen closed the door and walked around the back of the car before he got back in and drove away. I took off toward my car in the hopes that his usually slow driving would allow me to catch up to them so I could see where she was headed.

I had a guess, though. Brock's apartment was in that part of the west side, but why was she going there tonight? It hadn't been two weeks like Dennis had mentioned, but maybe he'd been wrong.

Jensen lived up to his reputation for being a Sunday driver no matter what the day, and I caught up to them just as they pulled up to Brock's building, as I'd expected. Jordan got out, and Jensen waited, which I found interesting. She clearly didn't plan on staying long.

Parking my car halfway down the block, I watched as she entered the building. What was this visit about if Brock had told Dennis she wouldn't be around much for two weeks? Clearly, Nina knew about what was going on since she'd sent Jensen to drive Jordan. I really didn't want to involve her and Tristan in whatever this was, but curiosity got the best of me and I called her.

She answered in her usual cheery way. "Gage, what are you doing on a Friday night calling me?"

"I need some information, Nina."

"Oh. Okay. Do you want to speak to Tristan?"

"No, I'd rather to speak to you since I'm sure you were the one who sent Jensen to Jordan tonight."

The phone was silent for a long moment, and then Nina asked, "How would you know about that?"

"I make sure to know things," I said as I kept my eye on the front doors to Brock's building. "What's going on?"

"I can't tell you, Gage. She'd kill me if she found out I told you."

"Well, I know Jensen drove her to Brock's apartment, even though her fiancé told the doorman last weekend that she wouldn't be around for two weeks. I know she's been spending time with Brock's sister too. So I doubt much of what you know is that secret, Nina."

"You've been following her, haven't you? Why?"

"I can't tell you, but you know I would never do anything to hurt her. Just tell me what's going on with Jordan and why she's suddenly going to his apartment after not seeing him for a week."

"She thinks he might be seeing someone else. Please don't let her know I told you, Gage. She'll be furious. I think she's crazy."

"Seeing someone else? Why?"

"She told me he said he needed some time apart to catch up on work, but she didn't believe him. The guy never takes any time off, so why would he need to catch up? So she asked me if Jensen could drive her a few places tonight. She didn't tell me where. You probably know more about that than I do."

I thought about what the doorman had told me, and I could understand why Jordan might think something was going on with Brock. Right after announcing their engagement was a strange time to suddenly need time apart, even if it was involving work. But if Brock was cheating on her, Dennis didn't know about it, and I had a feeling his opinion of one of his favorite tenants might change if he knew he was being unfaithful.

"Nina, what do you think is going on?"

She sighed, and I heard the sadness in her voice. "I don't know. I've always thought there was something wrong with Brock, but I can't put my finger on it. I intentionally didn't have Tristan get Daryl to check him out because I wanted to believe she could have found a great guy who could give her everything after you two broke up. But it's weird that the day after they announce their engagement he suddenly has to work more, like spending time with his fiancée is something he wants to avoid."

"I'm worried he's not who he says he is."

Nina audibly gasped at my statement. "Why? What do you know?"

"Nothing yet. Daryl thinks it's just me being jealous, but I'm worried."

"Gage, is there something you're not telling me?"

"Yes, but I don't want you to worry. I watch her every day and night to make sure she's okay. I would never let anything happen to her, Nina. I promise you that."

"Is it that he doesn't love her? If that's it, why did he ask her to marry him and then have that big engagement party?"

"I don't know what's going on yet, but I won't let her get hurt."

Just then, Jordan walked out of Brock's apartment building and got into the car. Putting my car into drive, I followed them.

"Nina, I have to go. Just believe me that she's going to be okay."

"I trust you, Gage. I don't know why you broke up with her, but I know you still love her. Just let Tristan and me know if you need anything."

"I will."

Jensen drove directly back to Jordan's apartment, and once she was safely inside, drove away. Parked down the street, I watched her bedroom window to see her watch TV as she had done every night until midnight when she turned out the lights and went to sleep. I had no idea what that night's visit to Brock had been about, but if her expression when she came out of his building was any indication, my gut told me something was wrong.

Very wrong.

CHAPTER TEN

JORDAN

STRETCHING MY LIMBS, I OPENED my eyes and looked around my bedroom as the bright morning sun streamed in through my windows. The DJ on my clock radio said the weatherman was calling for temperatures to soar into the nineties by mid-afternoon. Although many New Yorkers bemoaned the heat, especially when it got up toward triple digits, I loved it. To me, it was just another beautiful day in the greatest city in the world.

Summer was my favorite time of year in New York. True, it often got hot enough that heat waves rippled off the pavement and your feet felt they were melting to the sidewalk. And riding the subway in the scorching summer heat was always an adventure for anyone with a working olfactory sense. But these things didn't matter. The city was still the best place in the world.

I heard children playing outside, and for a moment a feeling of loss passed through me. When Brock and I married, he planned for us to leave and move down south. After all these years here, for the first time I wouldn't have my students to return to once fall came around. I might be able to convince him to stay for this school year, but he had his heart set on leaving New York and there was no way I'd be able to dissuade him from that.

Maybe his sister could, though. Monique seemed to adore the city. Well, at least one part of it. Every day since she arrived in town, she'd dragged me to store after store on Fifth Avenue. The woman could shop, no doubt. I wondered if she had some kind of addiction to spending money because despite my suggestions to visit museums, walk through the park, and check out tourist attractions like the Statue of Liberty and the Empire State Building, all she wanted to do was buy more things.

I cringed at the thought of today being yet another day of shopping til I dropped. One or even two days was all well and good, but every day?

Grabbing my cell off the night table, I looked for a text or missed call from Brock, but there were none. Not that this surprised me. My fiancé wasn't exactly the type of guy who liked to leave cute messages. Brock liked to show his feelings in person more than thoughtful words left on a phone.

I saw a text Nina had sent earlier. *Did everything work out okay last night? Please call me. I worry about you.*

That was quintessential Nina. The opposite of Brock, she loved letting me know she cared. I hadn't wanted to ask her to have Jensen drive me last night, but my suspicious mind got the best of me.

Sometimes I could be so foolish.

I'd gotten it into my head that something fishy was going on with Brock, and being the best friend she always was, Nina jumped at the chance to help me get to the bottom of it all. I didn't know what I'd do without her. Thankfully, Jensen drove me to Brock's apartment, and I saw everything was on the up and up.

How could I have thought there was something going on between Brock and Monique?

For the second time that morning, I cringed, but this time at my own behavior. I should have known better than to suspect Brock would ever cheat on me. He may not have been the type to send cute texts for me to read when I woke up in the morning and he may never be the type of guy who sent flowers often, but he was true.

It's just that Monique had been acting so strange about him that I began to think the most bizarre thoughts. Whenever she talked about him, she got a look in her eyes that I'd only seen before in women when they talked about the man they loved. It was like they began to sparkle when she said his name.

But that was crazy. Sure they weren't full brother and sister, instead becoming family when her mother and his father married when they were only ten. But even that was creepy of me to think. Monique no more loved Brock in that way than Nina did. I knew that deep down inside, but still after nearly a week of her gushing over every part of him—his looks, his intelligence, his success, and his wealth—I'd let myself think that maybe she did feel something more for him than just sisterly love.

God, I really could be an idiot sometimes.

I'd seen that firsthand when I went over to Brock's apartment and found the two of them working on business. Spreadsheets and graphs laid out across his dining room table and the two of them hovered over them told me all I needed to know.

I didn't dare give a clue as to the real reason I was there, so I quickly made up a lie about thinking Monique and I were supposed to meet at a club and I'd become worried when she didn't show up. Brock and I weren't the type of couple to be as sentimental to act like we missed each other in front of anyone else, so I couldn't say that, even though I did miss him during the week. But thankfully, they believed my fib and I got out of there before I made a fool of myself in front of my future husband and sister-in-law.

I dialed Nina's number and hoped she'd be able to talk because I desperately needed to at that moment. By the fourth ring, my disappointment began to set in, and I waited for her voicemail to send her happy voice into my ear. Not that I should be surprised. Being the mother to three children all under the age of two was like a full-time and a half job. I didn't know how she did it some days.

But then just as I expected to hear her message, she answered, her voice barely recognizable between the heavy breaths.

"Jordan, can you hang on a second? I've got to catch Ethan before he..." Her sentence trailed off, and then she yelled, "Ethan!

Honey, don't touch that!"

"Sweetie, this sounds like a bad time. I can call back later."

"No, no. It's fine. Just give me a second and I'll be all yours, at least for a few minutes."

I listened as Nina explained to her son that eating caterpillars wasn't good for him or them. Ethan giggled at her reprimand, but in just a few more seconds, he quietly told his mother he was sorry and through the phone I heard her give him a kiss.

"Okay, that drama is over. Talk to me, Jordan. Tell me something involving adults in the next ten seconds or I might lose my mind."

"I was just calling to let you know what went on last night, but it's not really anything," I said, suddenly feeling foolish for spending any time on my silliness. What Nina did day and night was real. The trials and tribulations of my life felt like nonsense in comparison.

Nina chuckled. "Right now, it's everything to me. I'm literally hanging on by a thread to my sanity this morning, so talking about anything other than eating bugs and who's touching who or who's stealing whose toys is just what I need. Spill the details, woman, and save your friend's sanity."

"If you're sure…"

"I hoped you'd call this morning, so give me the details. I'm all ears."

I sat up in bed and got my thoughts together. "Okay. I had Jensen take me to Brock's last night, but I didn't tell you the truth about why I wanted him to take me there."

"Really? Why?" A twinge of hurt colored her words now.

"Because I was embarrassed. I thought Brock was seeing someone else."

Nina remained silent for a long moment and then finally said, "You're not kidding, are you? But you just announced your engagement. What would make you think he was cheating on you?"

"I'm humiliated to say what it is."

"Well, now you have to, no matter how bad it is."

"I thought he was doing something with Monique."

"His sister?" Nina's amazement at what I'd said couldn't have been clearer. "You thought he was cheating on you with his sister?"

"Step-sister," I said in my defense, knowing it was still a pretty lame reason to not believe someone was faithful. "They aren't related by blood."

"What are we talking about here? Like Cesare and Lucrezia Borgia, for God's sake?"

"They were actual blood relatives, Nina."

"I know that. Whatever. What were you thinking?"

"I don't know. She just seemed so lovey dovey about him every time she mentioned him. I just had a vibe."

"A vibe? Like a gut feeling?"

"Yeah. I can be so stupid sometimes, Nina. I know. But it's okay now. I went over there and saw that everything was on the up and up. It's all good now."

"Jordan, you had a gut feeling about something. I don't think that should be ignored. Remember what we've always said?"

"Yes. 'Go with the gut. It never does you wrong.' Well, this time my gut was wrong."

"Has your gut ever been wrong before?"

I thought back and silently had to admit no gut feeling had ever led me astray before. But I couldn't be right about this. Related or not, Brock cheating on me now with Monique was preposterous now that I'd seen them together last night.

"No, but it was wrong this time. I saw how they acted together, Nina. It was all in my head, probably because I'd just been missing him."

"Jordan, that's weird in and of itself. You two announce your engagement and then he needs to put his nose to the grindstone for two weeks and can't see you during that time? Who does that?"

I couldn't tell her the truth of why Brock couldn't spend time with me for those two weeks, but I wanted to. I didn't like keeping secrets from the one friend who knew me better than anyone else in this world, but I wanted to stay loyal to my future husband too.

"He's just a busy man, Nina. You know how it is. Tristan works long hours too, and there have been times when he wasn't around much. It's the same thing."

"I guess. I don't think about those times anymore because Tristan's always around these days. That's what having three children does to a man. I swear I fully expect him to come home one night and tell me we don't have any money anymore because he's been taking so many weekends off."

Swinging my legs off the bed, I stood up and stretched. "Like that could ever happen. You guys are jillionaires," I joked.

"You're going to be soon too, Mrs. Brock Hannon to-be."

"Maybe, but my husband won't be getting three kids from me anytime soon. He's going to be lucky to get one."

"No big family for you guys?" Nina asked in a tone full of disappointment. "I was hoping all your kids could play with all of mine."

"I'm not like you, honey. I have a feeling I might not even be a good mother."

"Another gut feeling? Well, I can tell you that one is definitely wrong. You'd be a great mom. You're fantastic with my kids. I think you might be Ethan's first crush. Every time I mention your name, his eyes glaze over with that 'He's dreamy, Marcia' look."

Chuckling, I walked out to my kitchen to brew some coffee. "You know I love that little guy, don't you? I love all three of your munchkins, but that Ethan is just such a cutie. Give him a kiss from me when you tell them all I said hi, okay? I've got to get this day going or I'll be late to meet Monique for today's real life episode of Shop Til You Drop."

"Will do. But you seem to be spending a lot of time shopping with Monique. Maybe today she might want to do something other than that."

I scooped the coffee into the filter and started the coffeemaker.

"Yeah. She'll want to go out to eat. That woman has a two-track mind. Shop and then eat. Rinse and repeat."

"Well, call me later and let me know how your day was. I get lonely for adult conversation out here when Tristan is gone to work. I might just chew Cara's ear off, and we wouldn't want that."

"God no!" I teased. "I'll give you a call later and give you the details of my exciting shopping binge for the fifth day."

"Okay, honey. I'll talk to you later. Love you!"

"Love you too!"

As I sipped my coffee, I couldn't help but think about what Nina had said about my gut. It never had been wrong. Not once in my life. How could I have been so off the mark this time? Replaying the entire scene from last night, I tried to think of anything that would make my gut feeling right. Brock and Monique had been casual and relaxed, like a brother and sister would be. Their jokes didn't seem forced or strange. They hadn't touched one another in any suspicious way.

God, what was I thinking? To suggest that they would ever touch each other in any way other than the way two family members would was just insane. That was it. Not only was my gut instinct on the fritz, but I was batshit insane.

"I need to forget this nonsense and get ready for another day of shopping," I mumbled as I finished my mug of coffee. "Because God knows there are at least a few stores Monique hasn't visited yet."

Trudging off to the shower, I worked on forcing myself to remain chipper. Brock's sister was a perfectly nice person, as far as future sister-in-laws went, and if she found some kind of joy from shopping in New York, who was I to blame her?

An hour later, I stood waiting for her on my front steps in a red form fitting dress she'd insisted I buy on one of our trips down Fifth Avenue. A little too tight for my style, I'd planned on returning it as soon as she left town, but when she called and said she couldn't wait to see me in it today, I didn't have a choice.

Even if I felt like at any moment someone was going to stop in the street and ask me what the going rate was.

Monique's driver pulled her car up next to another car, and she rolled down the window. "Come on! Javier is double parked, and I don't want to hang out not one more minute in this neighborhood when there are stores just waiting for us!"

Her sandy brown hair and makeup looked perfect, even in the sweltering heat and humidity that had settled in after a very brief rain shower overnight. Seeing her looking so great instantly made me self-conscious about my hair pulled up in a ponytail and the barely there makeup look I was sporting.

I tugged on the ends of my hair and headed down the stairs to join her in the back of her Town Car. She practically pulled me in next to her as she ordered her driver to head back to civilization, as she liked to refer to Manhattan.

Maybe I should have been insulted about her jabs at Brooklyn and the location of my apartment, but I couldn't deny that being out in the boroughs wasn't everyone's idea of the best place to live. Anyway, I'd be leaving this place as soon as Brock and I married, so it didn't matter much what she thought of it.

"You look so good today, Jordan," she said with a huge smile as she pushed the stray hairs from my ponytail back off my face. "I love how you always look so beautiful with so little makeup and such a casual hairstyle. I'm jealous!"

I forced a smile as I silently wished I'd taken more time to make myself up. "That's me—no makeup and totally casual."

She looked me up and down and threw her arms around me. "And you wore the dress! It's so gorgeous on you. Just remind me when we go to MAC that you need a little more color on those cheeks to pull this off. But you look great!"

As she hugged me tightly to her, I felt less and less great by the second. Clearly, my no makeup look wasn't enough for the dress she'd picked out. For a moment, I felt a little put out, but I reminded myself that this was Brock's sister and it meant a lot to him that the two of us got along. So I sucked up my hurt feelings and hugged her in return.

"Thanks! You do too, but that's nothing new. I love how put together you always look."

She backed away from me and pretended to be flattered, but I had the feeling that was what she expected to hear from people.

"So are you ready to have some fun today? I thought we'd do some shopping and then get a late lunch before I have to get back to Brock's. There's this wonderful little place he took me to a few nights ago and I think you'd love it."

There it was again. That way she had of talking about her brother like he was her boyfriend. She sounded like Nina did when she spoke about some place Tristan had taken her.

"Oh, okay. I'm sure it will be nice. What's the name of the restaurant? Brock and I may have already gone there. We were on quite a fine dining kick for a while."

Monique smiled in a way that looked more like a smirk and waved off my idea. "Oh, I don't think so. We just went there the other night, and I'm sure it was the first time he'd been there. But don't worry. At least it was just with his sister."

She continued talking about our big day out and how much fun we were going to have, but my gut told me something wasn't right. It was impossible what I was thinking, though.

Wasn't it?

CHAPTER ELEVEN

GAGE

AS I WAITED FOR DARYL'S call to find out about who this mystery woman with the shopping addiction really was, I spent yet another day ducking in and out of doorways watching Jordan and her new friend as they visited store after store. A quick text to my sister Lily with the names of a few of the stores filled me in on their objective for the day.

Makeup.

That struck me as strange since Jordan rarely wore much makeup, preferring a natural look over a lot of garbage on her face. As I stood across the street from the third store of the day, I wondered what was happening to the woman I knew. Was it Brock who wanted her to become someone else? His sister certainly wore a lot of makeup. Even from a distance, I saw there wasn't a natural thing about her. Collagen lips, all the signs of Botox, and from where I was standing, those breasts were at least two times the size nature had given her.

Definitely not sexy at all. Not like Jordan.

I watched them walk out of the MAC store and my mouth dropped open. Was today dress up like a clown day? When they'd walked in, Jordan had looked herself. Well, herself in a red dress that she tugged at like it was a straitjacket. Now an hour later, she looked like she'd been jumped by a car full of clowns with the single goal of making her look like she belonged in the big top.

She knew she looked ridiculous too. I could tell by the way she kept her head down as they headed up the street. Something inside me screamed to go yank her away from whoever this madwoman was intent on changing her and whisk her back to her apartment in Brooklyn so she could wash all that crap off her face and return to who she really was.

Pulling my baseball cap down until the brim hit the top of my sunglasses, I blended in with the crowds and followed them as they made their way toward yet another store. I'd guarded movie stars and musicians and none of them ever spent money like these two women. Brock's sister must have been either well-married or independently wealthy because she dropped cash like a champ.

Jordan and she turned into yet another makeup store, this one dedicated to brushes or something, as I wondered how either woman could possibly put more on their faces. Less than five minutes later, Jordan exited the store without Brock's sister. A tiny part of my brain rejoiced, and I hoped that her time with her had finally ended. Any more days shopping with Monique and Jordan might be unrecognizable.

She made her way toward Saks without her friend, so I took the opportunity to get a closer look. I got to within ten yards of her and saw even under all that makeup that the Jordan I knew and loved was still there. As she walked, she adjusted her dress, and I couldn't help but notice how nice it made her ass and legs look. The dress made her look more like Monique than herself, but the body beneath it was still as fantastic as it always had been.

I wanted to come up behind her and pull her away from this street with its painted up women in designer dresses and shoes. She didn't need all of that to be beautiful, and with every minute I watched her, I hated this Brock guy for making her think she had to.

At an intersection, she looked around, probably for her friend, but turned her head back as she crossed the street. Lost in watching her move, I heard someone yelling her name behind me. Quickly, I lowered my head and ducked behind a group of tourists hovered in a circle around a city map as Monique hustled by to catch up with her.

"Why did you leave? I had the perfect brush set I wanted you to get," she said in syrupy tone that set my teeth on edge.

Forcing a smile, Jordan said, "I just needed some fresh air. I guess I didn't realize how far I'd walked."

Monique tugged on her arm to force her back toward where they'd come from. "Well, you have to come back. I want you to see the brushes."

"Another time. I'm feeling hungry now, so I think I'm going to grab a bite to eat. I don't mind waiting for you as you shop, though."

There was the Jordan I remembered. The hint of sharpness in her voice as she told someone she had no intention of doing what they wanted her to do. The forced smile that masked how irritated she truly was. I was happy to see some fire still existed inside her.

Monique had no plans to give in so easily, though. Still pulling Jordan toward where she wanted her to go, she said in a voice almost a whine, "But I don't want to shop alone. Brock would be so disappointed if we didn't have fun together."

For a moment, I saw indecision in Jordan's eyes. Clearly, Monique knew what buttons to push to manipulate her, but that fire I was so thrilled to see still existed in her didn't want to be controlled by Brock or his sister. I waited, not realizing I was holding my breath until I saw her shake her head.

Slowly, I let the air out of my lungs, relieved part of the woman I loved was still in there somewhere.

She hadn't caved.

"I'm just going to get something to eat, Monique. I'm sure Brock wouldn't begrudge his fiancée some food, would he?"

I couldn't help but be proud of Jordan. Monique wasn't the only one who knew how to manipulate.

Brock's sister frowned, obviously unhappy about not getting her way, and I wondered if she'd be able to tear herself away from her gluttonous need to buy things in favor of spending time with her future sister-in-law. I secretly hoped she wouldn't, but something told me she needed to keep close tabs on Jordan.

What I didn't know was if it was for herself or for her brother. And why.

"Well, I'll come with then, but after we eat lunch, I want to go back to the brush store."

Jesus, this woman didn't know how to take no for an answer.

For her part, Jordan seemed to be happy with her win over her friend's demands. Likely, if I knew her like I thought I did, she'd find a way to get out of returning to that store Monique so desperately wanted to go to.

The two of them headed off to lunch, giving me a reprieve from their constant shopping. I'd thought I needed to keep a watchful eye on Jordan to keep her safe from the people behind the threatening letters, but it had turned out that afternoon she was in danger from no one and nothing, except for emptying her bank account with repeated splurges on Fifth Avenue.

When Daryl called just after one, I eagerly answered, desperate to talk to anyone who had nothing to do with shopping or makeup.

"Hey, Daryl. Just the man I hoped to hear from. What did you find out?"

"My guy got me the pictures this morning, so I haven't gotten anything definite yet. Something strange popped in my early search a little while ago, though. There's no record anywhere of Brock Hannon having a sister."

I paid the hot dog vendor for my lunch and took a bite, tasting only bun. "Monique isn't his sister. She's his half-sister. I told you that already."

"Right. But there's no record anywhere of him having a half-sister either. No sister anywhere of any type."

"Are you sure?" I asked, fear suddenly settling into my brain.

Who was this woman?

"I can't find anything yet. But don't jump to any crazy

conclusions just yet. I'm still looking. All I'm saying is that Brock Hannon's sister doesn't seem to exist, as far as I can tell."

"Why would someone be pretending to be his sister? All the woman seems to do is shop and force Jordan to shop with her. I haven't seen her do anything nefarious in the entire time I've been watching them."

"I don't know, but I'm thinking what you were worried about might be right. What was the name of the man you guarded who was the father of that girl?"

"Gregory Michaels." Even saying his name made me feel like someone had just set thousand pound weights on my shoulders.

Daryl repeated the name and mumbled a question about what that would have to do with Brock and Monique and whatever they were up to. "Gage, I'm just not sure these things are connected, but it would be too much of a coincidence if either Brock or his sister had any acquaintance with Michaels. Don't you think?"

Racking my brain for any connection between them, I said, "Michaels is wealthy. That's really the only thing they have in common, as far as I can see."

"Do you still talk to him? I mean, after the incident with his daughter, are you two on speaking terms?" Daryl asked with an uncharacteristic awkwardness to his voice.

Gregory Michaels had every reason in the world to hate me for the rest of his days, but he didn't. He never blamed me for his daughter's death, even if I blamed myself. After her funeral, he sat me down and in his sadness found a way to express to me that he believed everything happened for a reason. That neither of us wanted to accept that about Tiffany's death didn't change the fact she was gone. She had been killed by someone wanting him dead, and he'd have to live with that for the rest of life, like I would have to live with the reality that in choosing to do my job and protecting him, I had unwittingly made it easier for the assassin to still fulfill at least part of his objective. He killed the wrong person, but in some way, he killed Gregory Michaels that day too.

"We haven't spoken in years," I choked out, hating the memories of that moment in time that flooded my mind. "But he never blamed me for her death."

"Good. Good. We may need to contact him if we run into a dead end, and the fact that he's still willing to speak to you might help."

I said nothing in response to the idea that I might have to call Gregory after all this time. It never mattered that he didn't blame me. I blamed me, and all those sleepless nights staring up at the ceiling in my bedroom as I tried to forget that day had done nothing to change that. If I hadn't been so focused on him, Tiffany may be alive today.

And if forgetting was difficult, then forgiving myself was impossible.

"Let me know," I said quietly as I watched down the street for Jordan.

"Will do. In the meantime, keep your eyes on that pretty lady and make sure nothing happens to her. I can't say why, especially since I wasn't convinced when you first told me, but my instincts tell me something's going on with this fiancé of hers and his sister. I'd hate to see something happen to Jordan."

I balled up the foil wrapper and my half-eaten hotdog inside my napkin and tossed it in a trash can. "Yeah, me too."

"Keep your phone nearby. I'll call you when I find something out."

"Thanks, Daryl."

"It's my pleasure. We have to make sure that little lady isn't being used in some horrible way, and if she is, we have to make sure you get to her in time to stop it."

Stuffing my phone in my jeans pocket, I wiped the sweat from my forehead on my arm and pulled my hat back down over my eyes. The temperature had climbed into the low nineties, and even standing felt like an effort in the heat. For the next hour, I watched the front door of the restaurant, at times wondering if I'd somehow lost track of them and they'd slipped by me, but then I remembered Monique's comment about wanting to return to the brush store. At the very least, I would have seen her pass by.

Then I saw them come back out and begin to head directly toward me. Jordan looked different, and as I ducked into a store doorway behind a few shoppers I saw she'd wiped off some of the makeup she'd had on earlier, bringing her face back to its more natural and far more beautiful state. Monique looked irritated, likely because for the first time since they'd begun to spend time together she didn't seem to be having the success she wanted in manipulating her.

As they walked by me, I heard her grumble, "Well, at least come with me to buy a new pair of shoes. These New York sidewalks have all but ruined my Jimmy Choos. We can find some at Saks. Come on. Let's go."

I followed behind them to listen to their conversation and realized the Jordan I had hoped was still inside her somewhere had come back even more, thankfully.

"I'm pretty worn out from this heat, Monique. I think I'm just going to head home."

Clearly, lunch hadn't been all Brock's sister had hoped it would be. And if anyone knew how hard it was to change Jordan's mind once she dug her heels in, it was me. Monique could try, but if Jordan didn't want to do something, it wasn't going to happen. That stubbornness had damn near driven me out of my mind more than once when we were together, but now I prayed for it to return with a vengeance.

Her deep red stained lips drooping into a pout, Monique practically whined like a child. "But we just spent all that time in the air conditioning at the restaurant. Surely, you can't be tired from the heat already." When Jordan didn't budge, her voice changed to its usual scheming tone. "Just one more store. We can go see my brother after Saks, if you want. That would be nice, wouldn't it? I'm sure you'd love to see Brock today."

As I walked behind them, I listened carefully and waited to see if Jordan would take the bait. Monique obviously felt like she was losing control if she trotted out the offer to see Brock, but since he'd even told the doorman he wouldn't be seeing Jordan for two weeks, why would Monique now be wanting to take her to him and in the middle of a work day, no less?

But Jordan didn't bite. "I'm really not up to seeing him right now. Maybe after a shower and a change of clothes into something a little less hot, but for now, I'll just have to settle for his call later tonight."

Whatever Brock's devious sister was up to, Jordan had jammed a monkey wrench into her plans for the day. Maybe Monique was just lonely and wanted a shopping buddy, but I doubted it. She was up to something.

"Well, if that's the way it has to be, I'll get the driver to take you back to Brooklyn."

Jordan smiled and shook her head. "No, that's okay. I can take the subway. I don't want you to have to go all the way out there and then back here. Go shopping. Enjoy yourself!"

I couldn't tell if her words were genuine, but her happiness at leaving Monique certainly looked real. Leaning in to give her an air kiss, Jordan said her goodbyes and turned to head toward the subway, even as her future sister-in-law tried to convince her that taking that way home would be even worse than shopping in the heat.

The woman sure didn't know how to take a hint.

Monique stomped away in her Jimmy Choos and I considered following her to see exactly what she really planned to do, but I had a sense it was nothing more exciting than buying shoes at Saks, just as she'd said. Whatever she was up to, her main concern at the moment seemed to be spending more money on herself.

But whose money was it? Hers or Brock's?

Choosing to stick close to Jordan, I left the puzzle of Monique and her spending for another time and headed toward the subway for the ride out to Brooklyn. But just as she crossed the street to descend down into the tunnel, a black Town Car pulled up, one I recognized immediately.

The window rolled down and Nina stuck her head out, her smile stretching from ear to ear. "Excuse me, ma'am. Did you call for an emergency escape?"

"Thank God! I thought I'd have to sweat it out for real on the D Train."

"Get in. We've got air conditioning and two children dying to see you."

As Jordan got into the back of the car, she asked, "Why only two? Where's the third munchkin?"

I didn't hear where Tristan and Nina's third child was, but it didn't matter as much as knowing that at least for the time being, Jordan was safe. Jensen would take her back home to her apartment in Brooklyn, so I'd have time to get to my car and get out there to begin the night watch.

CHAPTER TWELVE

JORDAN

NINA, DIANA, AND TRESSA FOLLOWED me into my apartment and I quickly excused myself to change out of my ridiculous red dress before I traumatized the kids and their first real memory of their Aunt Jordan was me looking like some high paid call girl. In less than five minutes and after a quick scrub of my face, I was back to my usual casual self in khaki shorts and a white tank top.

The kids played with their wooden blocks on my living floor as Nina lounged out on my couch and looked so at home there it was like she'd never left.

Grinning as I walked into the room, she said, "Glad to see you looking like yourself again. I was beginning to wonder for a few moments there."

"I'm just not cut out for high fashion, I guess. Monique is all about the designer dresses and makeovers."

"You don't need a makeover, unless it's with this apartment and getting some air conditioning. I have to tell you I don't miss the heat in this place during the summer," she said as she fanned herself with a bridal magazine.

Knotting my ponytail on the top of my head, I nodded in total agreement. "I feel you on that. I think one of the few demands I'm going to make in the new place will be air conditioning."

Nina wiped the sweat from her hairline and pulled her hair up off her neck. "I'm sure Brock's apartment has air conditioning already."

"I mean the new place when we move," I said and immediately realized I hadn't told her about moving away.

She sat bolt upright and stared up at me with a look of hurt in her eyes. "Move? Where are you moving? When? Why didn't you tell me?"

"It just slipped my mind, I guess. Brock wants to move to Dallas after we're married."

"Dallas? As in Texas?"

"Yeah. Do you want a drink? What can the girls have?" I asked as I turned toward the kitchen, eager to escape our conversation and the hint of betrayal that had settled into her expression.

Nina followed me, unwilling to let me off the hook with such a vague answer. Leaning against the doorway between the two rooms so she could watch the kids and still grill me, she said, "I can't believe you didn't tell me this. Dallas is so far away. Why does Brock want to move? His business is right here in New York."

I lifted the pitcher of iced tea from the refrigerator door and silently offered it to her. She nodded and I explained, "I didn't intentionally not tell you, Nina. It's just been so busy. I know Dallas is far, but he's got business interests down there and wants to move out of the city. Can the girls have cranberry juice?"

She nodded and sighed, like my news had taken all the air out of her. I tried to ignore how sad she looked as I poured us all drinks, but I had to admit I felt a little like that every time I thought about moving away.

Nina handed me the girls' sippy cups and as I filled them, I said, "It's not like we can't see each other whenever we want. You can fly down to see me on your plane since you're uber rich and own a plane."

My attempt at humor was met with an even deeper frown. "It's not the same. I had hoped when you married you'd move out to the burbs with me so we could be soccer moms together."

I walked past her and gave Diana and Tressa their drinks. Watching them take turns digging more toys out of their diaper bag and sipping on their juice, I knew I'd miss them when I left.

Nina followed and as we sat down on the couch, it was my turn to frown. "I'm not a burbs girl, honey. And you don't live in the burbs. Scarsdale is the burbs. You live out in the country. But that's just not me. I like living in the city."

"Then why are you leaving?"

"Dallas is a city too. I'm sure it will be great. I hear it's a great place to live."

"It's not this city. There's this one and all the rest. If you love living in the city, you should stay here."

"And what about Brock? Are you saying if Tristan didn't want to live out where you guys are now that you wouldn't at least consider moving?"

Nina took a drink of her iced tea and shook her head. "It's not the same. Tristan never wanted to move a million miles away from everyone I was close to."

I couldn't help but chuckle. Nina could be so pouty when she didn't like things. "It's not a million miles away. It's a couple hour plane ride from JFK. Maybe less if you're in your own plane."

"Stop saying that like it changes things. It's more a company plane anyway. And it doesn't change the fact that I'm going to miss you something awful. And who's going to drive into Dallas to pick you up when that awful Monique woman wants to shop the day away and you just want to kick back and put your feet up? See, you can't leave. Jensen can't drive that far."

I squeezed her hand and smiled at her sly attempt at convincing me to stay. "It'll be okay, Nina. Maybe Brock will want to move back here after a while."

"Why does he get to say where you two live?" she asked. "What if you told him you didn't want to move?"

"I do plan to tell him I want to stay until the end of the school year, so it isn't happening right away. This is what happens when you get married. You know that. It's all about give and take and compromise, right?"

"I guess. I just hate the idea of you being down there without any of your friends or family around you."

"It's going to be fine, Nina." Turning toward the girls, I smiled and said, "But for now, I want to see my two most favorite girls in the world. And their names are Diana and Tressa!"

The two girls leaped up from their toys and ran over to me for hugs, but I saw out of the corner of my eye that their mother wasn't able to move past the news that for the first time since we were in college we wouldn't live within a short drive from one another.

As I tickled Diana and then Tressa, eliciting giggles from both of them, I thought about that reality and secretly wished something would happen to make it not come true. Maybe this could be the one thing Brock compromised on.

ALONE ONCE NINA AND THE girls left, I plopped back down on the couch and let the air from the fan in the window blow over me. Mostly just warm and humid, it felt good for about a minute before I began to sweat again, making the fan nothing more than just a noisy box that spread the heat and drowned out the sound of the television.

I wouldn't miss the summertime temperatures in this apartment, but I would miss this place. Filled with memories of all those times Nina and I stayed up late and talked about our jobs, the men in our lives, and every other topic under the sun, it had truly been home for all these years and now I'd be leaving it behind.

My eyes filled with tears at the mere thought of not living there. Leaving felt wrong for some reason. I wiped my eyes and pushed that out of my mind. It wasn't wrong to leave a place for something better. Brock offered me a wonderful life with him, and I was always going to be leaving this apartment, one way or another, whether we moved to Dallas or not.

Leaving had to happen sooner or later. It was for the better anyway since in addition to all those memories I'd made with Nina there were all those memories I'd made with men in my life. I'd dated some winners in my single days, and this couch had seen some wild times. I couldn't help but chuckle at those memories. Sometimes being a single girl in New York had been incredibly fun.

But any thoughts of the past here brought up memories of Gage, and whatever good there had been was always eclipsed by how he'd ended it. This same couch that had seen all those fun times was the spot I cried for days until there were no more tears after he broke up with me. Curled up with a blanket, I sobbed until my body ached at the thought that all we'd had was gone in one phone call.

"No. I can't keep thinking about him," I said in defiance of whatever my heart thought it was up to.

I wanted a drink, but of course in times like this, I had not even a shot of something left in the cabinet. Slipping on my flip flops, I grabbed some money and my driver's license and headed down to the market two blocks away for a six pack. It wasn't exactly high class, but it would do. Nothing like an ice cold beer on a hot summer night.

Living in Brooklyn all these years had taught me to always pay attention to my surroundings, and as I walked back to my apartment with my refreshments for the night, I had the surest sense that even though there were people all around and no one gave me the feeling that I was in danger, someone was following me. Every few feet I'd turn around and look, but I saw no one who looked like they were doing anything more than hanging out with their friends or going out for the night.

I hit my front stairs and just before I put my key into the lock, I turned around one last time to check if my gut feeling was right. Nope. Nothing. Shrugging, I opened the door and walked up the stairs to my apartment to enjoy a cool one.

My gut was clearly on the fritz.

Settling in on my comfy couch, I turned on the television and enjoyed the first refreshing taste of the wheat beer the local market had on stock. Brock and Monique could have their bourbon and champagne. I'd take a beer any day of the week over those drinks.

I'd finished my second beer and something made me go to the window. Maybe it was wishful thinking, but I had a feeling Brock may have come by to surprise me. He hadn't called yet tonight, so it could happen. Looking out down at the street below, I scanned the sidewalk for any sign of him since it was likely he wouldn't find parking anywhere close tonight.

Nope. No sign of him. Just the usual people in my neighborhood out on their front steps having a good time on a summer night. Then out of the corner of my eye I saw someone familiar. Turning my head to look down toward the corner of my block, I saw him.

Gage.

There he was standing against the side of a building like he belonged anywhere near my street or for that matter Brooklyn at all. I knew he saw me too because I watched him slink back toward the shadows, but it was too late. I'd seen him spying on me and after two beers, I was ready to give him a piece of my mind.

I stormed down the stairs and made a beeline to where he stood, surprised he didn't even try to leave. Probably no point in doing that since I'd caught him red-handed anyway. He stood there against the building with his arms crossed like he was Joe Cool or something and had done nothing wrong by lurking in the shadows and watching me like some crazy stalker guy.

"What the fuck are you doing here, Gage?" I asked as I pointed my finger up toward his surprised and all-too-attractive face. "And don't give me some bullshit story because I'm not those dumb Hollywood starlets you hang out with."

With one of his incredibly sexy crooked smiles, he answered, "I don't hang out with starlets, Jordan. I never have."

"Don't smile like that. And don't try to change the subject. I asked what the hell you're doing here in my neighborhood where you know nobody but me."

"You don't know that. I might be waiting here for someone to come out of the store."

His dark blue eyes sparkled as he stared down at me with a look that told me he was enjoying himself. Why I had no idea.

"Well, are you?" I asked as I looked around him for any sign he was with someone.

Quietly, he admitted the truth. Or at least a tiny part of it. "No. I'm not with anyone."

The man was infuriating! "Then the question stands as asked, Gage. Why are you here?"

He took a step toward me and lowered his voice. "I wanted to make sure you were safe."

"What? Why?"

"I can't say right now, but I'm worried you might be in danger."

"In danger of what? Are you still sticking to that crazy ass story about the letters?" I asked, my exasperation quickly rising to a point where I felt like the top of my head was about to blow off.

Gage gently took hold of my arm and moved to guide me across the street. "Why don't we talk about this somewhere more private?"

Why he thought we should talk about anything escaped me. I jerked my arm from his hold and threw my hands up in the air, finished with his madness. "That's it! First you come to my engagement party uninvited to tell me some bullshit story about you still caring for me, and now you're here lurking about spying on me. I'm done with you and your crazy nonsense, Gage."

"Come on, Jordan. Just give me a chance to explain as best as I can and you'll see it's not nonsense."

"You don't get it. The only danger I ever was in was with you. You're the only man who ever really put me in danger, Gage. No one else."

He stepped back, a look of confusion settling into his face. Was there hurt there too? "Me? How can you say that? I would never let anyone hurt you, Jordan."

Suddenly, the effect of the two beers coupled with my feelings of frustration with him and all his craziness rushed through me and I felt like everything around me began to whirl. I opened my mouth to tell him that the only person who ever really hurt me was him, but it was no use. My legs gave out beneath me and I felt myself falling to the ground.

But just as everything began to go dark, I felt Gage's strong arms around me catching me before I fell.

And then he swept me up off my feet and as my head flopped around on my shoulders, he carried me across the street to my building. I wanted to demand he put me down that instant, but somehow the words in my head didn't make it to my mouth.

"I need your key to get us in," he said, his lips way too close to mine.

I didn't know how I did it since my brain felt like it was on overload, but I mumbled, "Right pocket." He gently slid his hand into my shorts and got my key as I tried not to like being in his arms again.

My wits returned to me slowly, so by the time we reached my living room I at least could speak full sentences. He gently lowered me to the couch and smiled, like there was anything to be happy about, but I didn't want to see him smiling at me.

"Don't think this changes anything. It doesn't. I don't know what happened back there, but whatever it was came from having to deal with you and your craziness."

"How are you feeling? Do you want me to get you some water?" he asked and then proceeded to walk toward the kitchen before I had a chance to tell him no.

Sitting up, I yelled in to him, "No, I don't want a drink of water. Why ask if you didn't even care to know my answer?"

Gage reappeared in the doorway of the kitchen with the glass full of water in his hand and that same ridiculous smile he'd worn a few seconds ago. "I think some water would help you. You might be dehydrated from the heat. I'm not surprised considering how you are. All day out in the heat will do that to a person."

He walked over to the couch and handed me the glass as his words sunk in. All day out in the heat? Had he been stalking me all day?

I put the glass down on the coffee table in front of me and watched him as he got comfortable in the chair across from me. "Don't sit. You aren't staying. I have no intention of having a night in with my stalker."

A look of hurt settled into his eyes, but if my words had stung, it didn't show in that smile of his. I tried not to focus on it since I'd always loved that smile. No matter what else he had going for him, Gage could charm the birds out of the trees with that sexy smile. Ever so slightly crooked, it made him look so confident that I'd never been able to deny him anything once he flashed it.

"Take a drink. You look flushed," he said leaning toward me.

"Whatever I am, it's none of your business. And why do I have the sneaking suspicion that you've been watching me all day? That's how you know I was out in the heat, isn't it?"

A slight chuckle escaped his lips. "I know you well, Jordan. You're not the type to sit inside on a beautiful day."

I couldn't have stopped my eyes from rolling if I wanted to, which I didn't. I knew bullshit when I heard it. "Smooth. I didn't realize you were such a bullshitter, Gage. So that's how this is going to play out? You're going to try to play slippery with me and I'm what? Supposed to pretend to be a dumb blonde? Fall at your feet and tell you how much I appreciate you saving me?"

He leaned back in the chair and arched one eyebrow. "I think what you did out there could be considered swooning. That's close to falling at my feet."

"Don't try to smooth talk me, Gage Varo. It won't work. I'm not one of those Hollywood bimbettes you spend your time with."

My sharp reply made his smile fade a little. "How is it that you can be so intelligent with me but with other men you're practically a Stepford Wife?"

"By other men you mean my fiancé, I assume? This jealous ex-boyfriend act you have going on isn't flattering."

A look of concern came over his face and for the first time that night, he was serious. "Jordan, what do you know about him really?"

"I'm not doing this with you, Gage, and you need to just accept my marriage to Brock is happening."

"I'm worried about you. I think there's something strange about him and his sister. He won't see you since last week, and she's all over you like white on rice. Why?"

"Oh my God! You've been following me for days. How do you know Brock doesn't want to see me? He's busy at work and we're planning on—"

I stopped explaining myself just before I let it slip that we were eloping in just days. That's all I needed was to let that cat out of the bag and have Gage go all Sherlock Holmes on me with his theories that Brock was up to no good.

"Planning on what?" he asked. God, he was like a dog with a bone. He wasn't going to let this go.

"Our wedding? Christ, Gage. I'm getting married to the man. We need to plan. A big wedding doesn't come together in a few days or even a few weeks. He's an important businessman. His wedding needs to reflect that."

That same look of hurt flashed in his eyes again, and this time the effect of my words settled into the rest of his face. The time for smiling had clearly ended.

"Ahhh, the wedding," he said in a low tone, his voice catching on the word wedding.

"I think you need to go."

I stood from the couch and began making my way to the door. The sooner Gage left, the sooner I'd stop noticing how hurt he looked at the thought of my marrying Brock. And how sexy that smile of his still was. And how when he took me in his arms just a few minutes ago my body reacted like it had never done with my future husband.

He grabbed my wrist and stopped me before I made it very far. I turned around as a flash of excitement skittered up my forearm from where his fingers touched my skin and looked up into those blue eyes of his, always so intense.

"Don't. Just don't, Gage."

For a long moment, he just stood there looking at me like I was the most important thing in the world to him. Then, in a voice barely above a whisper, he spoke and every inch of my body came alive.

Chapter Thirteen

Gage

"I missed you."

The words came out so quietly I wasn't even sure I'd said them loud enough for anyone but me to hear them. Jordan's eyes filled with something I hadn't seen in so long I wasn't sure I'd ever get the chance to see it again.

Love.

"I don't want to go."

Hanging her head, she said in a whisper, "Please don't say that. I've had too much to drink. I might do something stupid."

"You had two beers, Jordan. Whatever you're thinking of doing has nothing to do with them."

She sighed and let her shoulders droop, like all of this was too much for her. "Then I'm just stupid. Whichever it is, please go."

"You don't want me to go. Just say it."

Her deep green eyes filled with tears, and she shook her head back and forth. "Please, Gage. Just go. If we did anything, it would be a mistake. We're over. For good or for bad, that's the way it is. You made that happen, so own it."

I moved my hands up to cradle her face, but she caught me by my wrists. She may have been afraid of what would happen between us, but I wasn't. Leaning in close to her, I said, "Jordan, I never wanted to leave you. I love you. I've loved you since the first time I kissed you right there in that kitchen. And I don't believe we're over."

"I'm marrying another man. I think that's pretty much a sure sign we're over."

Her blond hair fell over the side of her face, so I tucked it back behind her ear and watched her shiver at my touch. No matter what she was saying, the feelings were still there for her too.

"You never say you love him, Jordan. Why?"

"I say I love him all the time. I love him. I love him." She stopped for a moment and cleared her throat. "I love Brock. There. I said it. Now please go."

I hated hearing her say those words. She couldn't love him. Not the way she loved me. She just couldn't, and I couldn't bear the thought of her not loving me anymore. Desperate to feel her kiss me again, I leaned forward that last inch that had separated us and pressed my lips to hers in a kiss full of how much I missed her.

As much as I knew she'd likely pull away, or even worse push me away, I couldn't stop myself. I'd missed feeling her lips on mine every night we'd been apart, and at this moment in her apartment where we'd spent all those hours together happier than either one of us had ever been before, I couldn't let the chance go by without kissing her again.

But she didn't pull away and she didn't push me away. Instead she kissed me back, and for a long moment it was like all those months apart had never happened and we were happy again.

I felt her let go of my wrists to slide her arms around my neck, and with each second that ticked by her kiss deepened. My body came alive for the first time since I kissed her at her engagement party, and I wanted everything she possessed that had been missing from my life since that night I said goodbye.

Her beautiful smile that lit up every room she entered. The sweetness that hid beneath her strong-willed façade. That sexy look she gave me when she wanted me as much as I wanted her.

I pulled away just far enough that our lips didn't touch anymore and whispered, "I know you missed that as much as I missed it. I don't know why you're marrying him, but I feel in your kiss that you don't love him like you love me."

Jordan wiped her mouth on the back of her hand and hung her head. "I don't love you anymore."

"Yes, you do." I gently lifted her chin to make her face me. "You still love me like I love you."

Shaking her head, she frowned. "No. I don't. I don't love you. I love Brock. See? I said it again. I love Brock. I love Brock. I love Brock!"

Those words made something snap inside me, and I pulled her roughly into my arms. Now my kiss wasn't gentle and full of reminiscing but demanding. I wanted her to admit whatever she felt for him wasn't what she felt for me. I wanted her to be mine again.

Burying my hands in her hair, I tugged her head back and I kissed her and slid my tongue past her lips to tease hers, but playtime was over. I was sick of only seeing her from a distance and living without her touch. I needed to show her what we were still burned as hot as it ever did, and we could get past what I'd done.

"Jordan, I don't care how many times you say it, it won't change the fact that you love me and not him."

"Why won't you just stay in the past where you belong? It wasn't bad enough that you broke my heart, Gage? Now you want to do it again?"

I kissed her and pressed my forehead to hers. "I never meant to hurt you, Jordan. Please know that."

"I have a chance at a great life with Brock. Don't mess that up for me," she pleaded quietly. "Please just go and leave me be."

"I can't do that. I left you because I thought it was the only way to ensure your safety, but now I realize that whoever it is sending me those letters isn't going to give up whether I see you or not. And if that's the case, I want to be around so I can protect you."

She pushed against my chest to force me back away from her and snapped, "This again? Why do you insist on lying to me about why you dumped me? Why not just tell the truth?"

"It is the truth. I would have never left you if it wasn't for those threats I began getting."

Jordan stormed off toward her room. "I'm done with this conversation. What you say makes no sense. People threatening me to you so you break up with me." Turning around to face me, she asked, "Who does that? Nobody. That's who. All of this is some kind of story to fix the fact that you dumped me for some Hollywood bimbo. Probably your ex-girlfriend Angela."

I followed Jordan to her room, pushing the door open when she attempted to slam it in my face. "I didn't break up with you for anyone and I haven't seen Angela for years. Why can't you believe me?"

She folded her arms and turned away. Quietly, she mumbled, "Because if you loved me, you wouldn't have let anyone chase you away, threats or no threats. Therefore, you didn't love me."

"I did love you. I still do. It's never changed for me."

Spinning around, she stared at me with a look like she was trying to figure out if I was telling the truth and finally said, "If only you'd told me that months ago."

"Why?"

"Because then maybe I wouldn't be marrying another man."

I knew she'd just admitted she still loved me too, but I needed to hear her say it. "How can you marry someone you don't love? You love me. Just admit it."

"What I feel for you is inconsequential. Brock and I are getting married, and that's it."

I took a step toward her and shook my head. "Admit it. You love me like I love you."

"No, and you shouldn't be in my bedroom. Leave."

"Admit it," I repeated as I took two more steps toward her.

"Go. Now," she said trying to deny what she knew was real.

Raising my voice, I took one last step to stand in front of her and said loudly, "Admit it, Jordan! Goddamnit, admit it!"

"Fine! I admit it, all right? I love you! I always have. You broke my fucking heart into a million pieces and still being next to you makes all of that disappear because I still love you!"

Her words reverberated off the walls of her bedroom she yelled so loud, and for a moment, we stood there staring at each other in shock. Her for actually admitting she still loved me even though she was getting ready to marry someone else, and me for finally getting to hear that the woman I'd missed for so long still loved me like I loved her.

And then the entire world ceased to matter because she was back in my arms.

She kissed me like she did that first night—soft and sensual with an uncertainty that only made her more beautiful to me. I reveled in the feel of her with me, giving herself to me again. I'd dreamed of this moment every night for months and now it was happening and I didn't want to forget a single thing.

Cradling her face, I returned her kiss as she pulled me to her, any reluctance fading away with each moment that passed. When she finally broke the connection, she looked away and whispered, "Why can't I figure out how to let you go?"

"Because you still love me."

Jordan sat down on her bed and hung her head. "Why couldn't you just stay away? I was okay when I didn't see you. Sad and missing you, but okay." She looked up at me and frowned. "But now I'm not."

"Why? Because you have to admit you love me still? Why is that so bad?"

"I have a chance at a nice life with Brock. So it's not the kind of love we have. That doesn't make it wrong. He's just different than you."

I sat down next to her and stared into those beautiful green eyes so full of emotion. "He's not the man you should be spending the rest of your life with, Jordan."

She chuckled. "You always were such an old-fashioned romantic, Gage Varo. The rest of my life with? I'm not sure I've ever thought I'd spend the rest of my life with anyone. Why should

Brock be so different?"

"You thought that about me."

Tears welled in her eyes. "And where did that get me?"

"How many times do I have to tell you? I didn't leave you because of you or anything between us. I left because I thought I was protecting you."

"Gage, could we at least be honest here? We're sitting in my bedroom for the first time since you broke up with me over the phone as I sat right over there on the edge of my bed. I listened to you coldly tell me you didn't think we were working out. In no way did you sound like a man who was torn up about not seeing me anymore. So if you're going to continue with this craziness about someone threatening me in letters to you, at least remember how it all went down, okay?"

That night replayed in my mind every night as I lay in bed alone thinking about her. I couldn't forget that moment if I wanted to. It existed as the equal only to the memory of Tiffany dying because of me.

"I remember. I remember waiting for you to call and dreading what I knew I had to say. I remember hearing your voice so full of happiness to talk to me, like you always were, and thinking I couldn't do it. I couldn't tell you goodbye. But I also remember getting another letter that day and holding it in my hand as we spoke that night and knowing no matter how much it hurt either of us, I had to do it."

She forced a smile and nodded. "Well, I guess I should thank you. I'm still here, so if these threatening letters are real, your breaking up with me did the job. Thanks."

I heard the sadness in her voice and hated that I had done that. "It tore me apart to do that, Jordan. Every night for months I looked at my phone and thought about calling you. I wished you would text me at least, even though I knew I couldn't answer back, but you'd still be with me if you did. But you never sent even one or called even once."

"Of course I didn't. You know me. No matter how devastated I was at losing you, I couldn't let you see that. I cried my eyes out to Nina, ate about twenty gallons of moose tracks ice cream, and listened to every sad song on my playlists over and over. And then after a while, it wasn't so bad until one day when I thought of you I didn't want to cry anymore."

"I never stopped thinking of you, Jordan."

She cleared her throat and stood from the bed. "Well, that was the past and there's nothing we can do about it. You stopped getting letters and I met someone else. I hope that you can meet someone too."

Before I could say anything, she walked out of the room. I found her in the kitchen pouring a glass of iced tea for herself, her back to me as I stopped in the doorway.

"Is that really what you hope?"

Without turning around, she said flatly, "I wish you no ill will, Gage."

"That's not what I asked. Do you really hope I meet someone and move on?"

She stayed silent for nearly a minute as she stood there drinking her iced tea. Then she took a deep breath and nodded. "Yep. You deserve to be happy."

I heard the trembling in her voice and understood why she wouldn't turn around. She didn't want me to see her cry as she said the words that hurt her as much as they hurt me to hear them. I walked up behind her and put my arms around her shoulders to gently turn her around, and I saw the tears in her eyes.

She didn't want me to move on and be happy with someone else as much as I didn't want her to.

"I don't think you want me to meet another woman any more than I want you to marry Brock Hannon. Why won't you admit that?"

"Because it gets us nowhere."

"A few minutes ago you admitted you still love me. How can

you say you want me to move on to someone else?"

Looking up at me, she asked me, "Do you remember when we were together and I used to tell you all I wanted was you to be happy?"

"Yeah. And I used to tell you all the time I was happier with you than I'd ever been with anyone else before."

"Well, that's all I ever wanted for you. I'm marrying Brock, and I want you to be happy like you were when you and I were together, Gage."

"And what about you? You aren't happy with him like you were with me. You know it."

She nodded. "I know, but life is about compromise a lot of times. I thought I had it all with you, and then you left me and I swore I would never let myself get so lost in someone that I would feel like I had nothing left if he ever broke up with me. Being with Brock means I don't feel a lot of the things I felt with you, but then again, I don't have the risk either."

"What risk?"

"The risk of having my heart broken again."

"And in return what do you get instead of real love?"

"Security. Pretty ironic that it was the one thing I couldn't find with you, huh?"

Her words made me feel defeated, and I took a step back from her. "I guess that's my cue to leave."

"I'm sorry, Gage. I didn't mean to be hurtful there."

I shook my head and swallowed hard to push my hurt down inside me. "No need to be sorry. Have a good night."

She didn't try to stop me as I left, and as much as I didn't want to admit it, she was right. I could protect Tristan's Upper West Side cronies and the wealthy benefactors he sent to me, but for her, the only way I could make sure she was safe was to stay away. As long as I'd stayed away, I'd stopped getting the letters and she'd been okay.

I walked away from her building, but I couldn't bring myself to leave. No matter what she thought about Brock, I still wasn't sure he and his sister weren't up to something, and until Daryl and I found out what that was, I'd still watch Jordan day and night.

I had no choice. I loved her.

Chapter Fourteen

Jordan

Admitting to Gage that I still loved him left me reeling, even if I'd been successful in hiding how it truly made me feel from him. He'd barely gotten out the door before Brock called to see how I was doing and to remind me that it would be just a few days more until our secret elopement. The excitement in his voice made me happy, but to be honest, seeing Gage had made me question if I'd made the wrong decision when I said yes to Brock about running off together.

I tossed and turned all night thinking about all the things we said to one another, just like when we were dating. He had that effect on me still after all the time apart.

Right before eight, my phone woke me up, and answering it I found Monique planning my day once again. Barely awake, I already knew I didn't want to be a part of another one of her shop 'til you drop marathons. The sun was shining, the birds were chirping, and I wanted to spend the day like I usually did during the summer.

Having fun.

"Sorry, Monique, but I can't today. I've got plans already. Maybe tomorrow."

The shock in her voice was unmistakable. "What do you mean you can't? I was so looking forward to spending this week with you getting ready for your big weekend coming up. I know Brock will be disappointed we aren't spending the day together."

I stretched the few hours of sleep from my body and rolled out of bed. "I'll be sure to tell him it was all my fault when I talk to him tonight, but I have to go now. I have about an hour to go before my friend gets here. Talk to you later!"

Before she had the chance to try her hand at talking me into something I didn't want to do, I clicked END and immediately called Nina. For the first time in months, I felt like I wanted to enjoy life, and there was no one better to do that with than my best friend.

"Jordan, you're up early. What's up?"

"What do you say to a day at the zoo with those kidlets of yours? Sun, animals, and more fun than we know what to do with."

"Sure! The kids will love it. Do you mind if Cara comes? Three on three puts the adults on equal footing, so to speak. These type of outings usually go better when there are three of us around."

I made my way into the bathroom to look at myself in the mirror. Scrubbing the night from my face, I said, "Sure! Bring her along. The more the merrier! I'm in love with life today, so bring anyone you like. Maybe Tristan would enjoy a day at the zoo. You know, get him out of that downtown office building and into the wild!"

Nina laughed. "You sound like that zebra from that movie the kids love. The wild! I'm not sure Tristan can go since he's in the middle of that villa deal in the south of France, but the rest of us are good to go. What time should we pick you up?"

"I can be ready in an hour. All I need to do is shower, put my hair in a ponytail, and throw on my clothes and sneakers and I'll be ready for the wild."

"Then I'll get the kids ready and inform Cara that we're going to the zoo. See you in a little bit!"

Nearly ninety minutes later, I watched as Jensen pulled a brand new black Chevy Suburban up to in front of my building and Nina poked her head out of one of the back windows. Her hair pulled up in a ponytail like mine, she looked like she used to when we went to classes together.

Bounding down the stairs, I joked, "New wheels? What happened to riding in luxury?"

"Get in and see what kind of luxury this baby has," she said with a grin.

I climbed in the other side and saw the three kids in their car seats in the last row behind us and Cara sitting up in the front seat with Jensen. Loaded with all the bells and whistles, the new Stone family vehicle was definitely luxury.

"Hi guys!" Reaching back, I tapped on each child's knee. "Tressa, Diana, and Ethan. The three musketeers. How are my favorite kiddos?"

All three giggled and said my name as best they could with Ethan saying it clearest. As Jensen pulled away from the curb, I turned to face Nina. "This is nice. What made you guys get an SUV?"

"The last time Cara and I took the kids out it became perfectly clear that with all their stuff and the three car seats that we needed something more than the Town Car. So we got this the other day. Pretty nice, huh?"

"I'd say so. You Stones know how to travel. But I thought maybe this was a sign you were adding to your family."

Nina reacted to my bombshell of a question by opening her eyes wide, like I'd just announced I had met a Martian. "Uh, no. For now, three's enough. We're quite happy with the kids we have."

We continued to joke around and play with the kids as we rode toward the Staten Island Zoo, a much closer attraction than the Bronx Zoo, where we took the kids last time we visited the wild. A quick trip of about a half hour and we were there, ready to see the animals and have a fun day out.

After unloading all three kids and their diaper bags with all the essentials and getting them into their strollers, we were off. It didn't take long for Nina to bring up Monique, who I was trying to forget about for a day, and as we watched the foxes play in their attraction, she asked, "How did you escape spending the day with your future sister-in-law today?"

"I lied. I'm not above that if it means I get to spend time with you guys."

"From what you told me in the car yesterday, she's a real piece of work. Will you be living near her when you move to Dallas?"

That was a good question. I hadn't thought about it, and Brock hadn't mentioned if we'd be living close enough to her for us to have the chance to spend time together. I hoped not. My brain couldn't withstand much more of her one track mind focused on shopping.

But I didn't want Nina to know I didn't exactly like Brock's sister, so I smiled and shook my head. "No, she lives far enough away that we won't be spending a lot of time together."

Bending down to give Ethan his sippy cup, Nina winked at me. "Good. I was about to get jealous thinking she was going to take my place."

"Are you crazy? She could never take your place. No one can. You're my best friend, Nina."

We walked toward the leopard habitat, and I thought about how I'd just lied to her about Monique. I didn't like lying, but especially not to her. She was my best friend, and unlike virtually everyone else in the world, I could trust Nina.

Desperately wanting to share my news about eloping in only a few days, I leaned over as I kids ooohhed and ahhhed over the leopards and whispered, "Brock and I are eloping this weekend. I promised him I wouldn't tell anyone, but I can't hold it in any longer. But promise me you won't tell anyone, other than Tristan, of course."

Nina's mouth fell open and for a few moments she couldn't speak. Finally, she said, "What? This weekend? But we have an appointment to get fitted for my matron of honor dress next month. Why are you two in such a rush? Are you pregnant? You just said yesterday that you aren't really the motherly type, so what's going on?"

I gently touched her shoulder, hoping to calm her down before everyone around us started staring. "No, it's nothing like that. Brock came up with the idea, actually. He doesn't want to wait, so I said yes and we're going down to his place in Hilton Head this weekend. You're still going to be my matron of honor at the big wedding ceremony just as we planned. Nothing's changed."

"Nothing's changed? How can you say that? I'm not going to be there for your real wedding day! What about your parents and your brother and sister? What about your grandmother? Jordan, she's going to have a coronary if she finds out you got married months before the day she gets to see you walk down the aisle!"

"It's not that big a deal. I thought you'd understand of all people, Nina. You're all about the romance, and what's more romantic than running off and eloping with the man you love?"

That what I was doing didn't involve the man I loved in the way I was making it sound was another lie, but at least it calmed her down. God, I seemed to be all about the lying lately. What was I turning into?

Cara wisely began to guide the children toward the next area as Nina and I followed. For her part, she was the best friend I probably didn't deserve at that moment, and after a minute or so, she gave me that classic Nina smile that told me everything was okay between us.

"I get it. I just wish I could be there. Why does everything with Brock have to be so far away all the time?"

"I'm happy you're good with this, Nina. And don't worry. The big day will still be great. I'll make sure of it."

"Of course it will be. I didn't mean to say it wouldn't be anything less than incredible. Just promise me you won't become like Monique, okay? Promise me you'll always be down-to-earth Jordan and you won't let anyone change you."

"I promise. No one's changing me, so you're stuck with this girl."

"Good."

✧   ✧   ✧

HOURS AFTER NINA AND THE kids dropped me off, Brock called like he did every night. Happy to hear from him, I began to tell him about my day but he cut me off.

"I'm sending my driver to pick you up. I want to see you."

Thrilled that he'd decided to change his mind about us not being together before Friday when we eloped, I said, "I can't wait! I've missed you, Brock."

"I'll see you in a little while. My car should be there in a few minutes."

His statement confused me. "You sent it already? How did you know I'd be home?"

"Where else should you be?"

A nervous laugh escaped my lips. Should be? Why should I be anywhere? We hadn't made plans for tonight. Why would he expect me to be home just waiting for him?

The driver arrived less than five minutes later and just under an hour later I was standing in Brock's living room happy to see him but unsure by the cold expression he wore if he was as happy to see me.

Folding his arms, he cleared his throat and frowned. "Jordan, why didn't you go with my sister today? She was offended by your choosing to go with your friend instead. I thought we talked about you having to let go of your friends when we got married."

His unhappiness with my wish to spend time with Nina stung, and I instantly became defensive. "We're not married yet, Brock, and I've spent every day with Monique since she arrived in New York. One day with my friend isn't a crime."

"Don't you care about how you made her feel? She's going to be family, Jordan. It's not okay to brush her off like that."

"I wasn't trying to brush her off. I'm sorry if she and you felt like that's what I was doing, but I wanted to enjoy a summer day and shopping isn't what I call fun. We always do what she wants to do. If I thought she'd want to go enjoy a day at the zoo or the park, I would have asked her."

Brock remained silent, his face completely placid, but I knew by the look in his eyes that he was displeased. Finally, he said, "Jordan, my sister feels slighted. I think you owe her an apology."

Something in his voice told me that this wasn't a request. I didn't want to fight with him about this, though. Monique was going to be my sister-in-law, not my ruler. All I could hope was that she wouldn't be around much once we were married.

"I'll be sure to say I'm sorry when we hang out tomorrow."

"She's already left to return home."

I walked toward him and slipped my arms around his waist. Looking up into his hazel eyes, I smiled. "I'm sorry, Brock. I'm used to spending my summer days outside, and I missed that. I never meant to offend her."

My apology made his expression soften, and he kissed me lightly on the tip of my nose. "What am I going to do with you? We're so different. Sometimes I forget who you really are."

"I'm just an average American girl. Perfectly average."

He gently pushed my hair off my face and pressed a kiss onto my forehead. "You're anything but average, Jordan. Someday soon you'll see that."

I slid my hands down the front of his shirt and began tugging it out of his pants, wanting more than just vague compliments after being apart for so long. Thinner than I usually liked the men I dated to be, he still had an attractive body and at that moment I wanted to feel it against me without clothes between us.

But he held my hands still to stop me. "Not now. I have a lot of work to do before Friday."

I looked up at him, hurt by his rejection. "We don't have to go for a marathon. Just a little to take the edge off our loneliness. I know you have to be as lonely as I am, aren't you?"

Brock took a step back from me and tucked his shirt back into his pants. "I wish I could, Jordan. I really do. But I have to keep my focus on work—my eyes on the prize, so to speak. It's okay, though. Once we're married, there will be all the time in the world for us to be together."

I didn't understand how that could be true since his job would still require him to work all the time, but even if I wanted to ask him about it, I couldn't since he already had begun guiding me toward the front door.

"Do you have to get back to work so soon? I was hoping we could spend some time together."

With a smile, he shook his head. "I wish I could, sweetheart, but I still have one more project to complete before we can run off and get married."

"Have you taken care of all the necessities? We're going to need a marriage license, two witnesses, and rings. We haven't done anything together about any of those."

Brock kissed the top of my head and hugged me to him. "Not to worry. We can get the license on Friday, and I've taken care of the rings. As for witnesses, I'm sure we'll be able to find two people to stand for us there. Just remember to bring your birth certificate."

Feeling like I was getting the bum's rush, I pushed down my bruised feelings and just smiled, reminding myself that the man I was marrying was busy running a multinational business and I'd have to get used to life being like this. For all I was receiving in return, this compromise surely wasn't that bad.

Even if it felt that way at the moment.

"Okay. I can't wait until Friday, Brock. I've missed you."

I slid my arms around his neck and pulled him to me. Kissing him with all the desire I hoped we'd share soon, for one of the first times I felt him truly return that desire to me. Brock had never been the kind of man I'd call a passionate lover, but now as he kissed me goodbye, I felt something different in him.

He quickly pulled away and his demeanor returned to that far cooler person he usually was, though. "I'll see you at your apartment at noon on Friday."

I wanted to say I loved him, but the coolness in his expression made me stop before the words came out. So I just nodded. "Friday. See you then."

BROCK'S DRIVER TOOK ME BACK to my apartment, and as I sat in my living room watching TV, I couldn't help but feel more alone than I ever had, even though I'd finally gotten to see my fiancé and it was just days until we ran away to become husband and wife. I couldn't put my finger on why, but I felt lonely.

I thought about calling Nina or one of my friends from school, but all of them were married women happily spending time with their husbands and children. I should have been used to it. I'd been the only single girl in my circle of friends for a while, but on beautiful summer nights like tonight when all I could think of was how nice it would be to share a drink with someone as we talked and laughed about old times, the solitude of my life pressed down on me like a weight on my chest.

When life gets you down, sometimes the best person to talk to is your mother, so I called her since I had to get my birth certificate from her anyway. She answered immediately, and just hearing her voice made me feel better.

"Hi Mom."

"Hi honey. I'm surprised to hear from you tonight. I thought you'd be with that fiancé of yours."

"No, he's working," I said, trying unsuccessfully to sound happy about being alone again.

"Well, what's going on? You sound down."

"Nothing. Just tired. I called because I need my birth certificate."

For a long moment, the phone fell silent. When she finally spoke, my mother sounded distinctly distant. "Birth certificate? Hmmm…I'm not sure where it is. I'd have to look. When do you need it for?"

As had become my habit, I lied to yet another person I cared for. "I need it this week for something at school."

Another long pause and then my mother said, "I'll look for it in the morning. I can just send a copy of it to whoever needs it like I did when you first needed it for your job. The lady at the education office said they were fine with that."

Great. Now I had to lie again. "Oh, I think they need to see me with it this time, Mom. I was thinking I could take the train out tomorrow to get it. We can have dinner together."

Quickly, she answered, "No, no. We won't be home tomorrow. We're leaving early and won't be back until late."

"But you just said you were going to look for it tomorrow. I really need it as soon as possible and it's probably a good idea that I have things like that with me now."

"We're having the carpets treated tomorrow, so that won't work. I have to go, honey. Your father is calling for me, so let me go. I'll look for it and let you know when I find it, okay?"

"Is everything okay, Mom? I know you didn't want to give me my birth certificate before because you were afraid I'd lose it, but you know I've gotten much better with keeping things organized since I left school."

"I promise I'll look for it. I'll talk to you later."

Damn, this was the second time that night someone had given me the bum's rush. I was beginning to get a complex.

"Maybe I'll just go out to the Hartford County courthouse and get it myself. I don't want to bother you every time I need my birth certificate. You can keep the original one safe with you just in case. Sound good?"

In a panicked voice, she said, "No! I mean, you don't have to do that. I'll make sure I find it. Your father is still calling for me, Jordan, and you know how he is when he finds something he wants me to see on TV. I'll call you in the morning, okay?"

"Mom, is everything okay? Is Dad all right?"

She sighed into the phone. "Everything's fine, Jordan. I just don't want to see you making the trip all the way up to Hartford if you don't have to."

In truth, I didn't relish the idea of spending four hours of my day trekking up there and back just to get my birth certificate, but I had no choice. If I didn't get it from my mother, I had to get it from the state or I wouldn't be able to marry Brock when we eloped in just a few days.

"Okay, Mom. It's all good. Call me tomorrow and let me know when I can come up for it."

"Okay, honey. I'll talk to you then. Love you."

She ended the call before I could tell her I loved her too.

Talking to my mother had alleviated my loneliness for a few minutes, albeit replacing it with concern about my parents. Something was definitely wrong with my mother. The woman organized things like no one else. Martha Stewart could take lessons on organizing from my mother. The idea of her not knowing exactly where my birth certificate was, which she'd protected all my life like it was the Rosetta Stone, was ludicrous.

I'd just have to make the trip out to Hartford the next day and get it there. The problem was I didn't want to. And there was the truth of it. I didn't want to make the effort to get the one thing needed for me to be able to marry Brock.

I sipped on one of the beers I'd bought the night before and hoped it would help me forget how much I wished I had someone there with me. As much as I didn't want to admit it, the truth was it wasn't Brock who I wished sat next to me on the couch in my tiny living room. My attempt to seduce him at his apartment had been more an expression of just wanting to feel something with him instead of a true desire to be with him in particular.

I knew why I was feeling like this. Damn Gage! It was because of him that I couldn't even convince myself that the compromises I had been so prepared to accept to end my loneliness weren't okay anymore.

Why couldn't he had just stayed away and let me live my life, no matter how lacking it was?

Standing, I walked over to my front window and looked out to see if he was nearby watching over me. People stood out on the sidewalks on both sides of the streets talking and laughing, but there was no sign of him.

When I wanted to see Gage, he was never close. When I didn't want to see him and wished to just pretend I didn't love him anymore, he was all around me. It was the story of us.

But I didn't want it to be that anymore.

I slipped my engagement ring off my finger and placed it in a drawer in the table near the window. Grabbing my phone, I texted him and hoped wherever he was that he'd understand.

Do you remember that July night we sat in Sunset Park and looked out at the city?

It was the first time we talked about a future together. I'd never forget that night. The sun had gone down and the sky still had tinges of orange and purple left over from the sunset. It looked like someone had painted a picture just for us, and as we stared up at it, my head on his shoulder, he bent down and kissed me on the top of my head.

"I can't imagine life without you, you know that?"

We'd never talked about anything but the present, making no plans and keeping everything light and fun. We'd just said the L word earlier that day, and his mention of a future together unnerved me. I had no idea how to react, but as Gage gently ran his fingers through my hair, something came over me and for the first time ever, I didn't feel scared at the idea of letting a man know I didn't want to imagine life without him either.

And when the words came out they sounded more right than anything else I'd ever said before in my life.

"I don't want to imagine life without you, Gage. I love what we are."

He kissed the top of my head again and whispered, "Then I guess you're stuck with me because I'm not going anywhere."

If only that had been the truth.

I closed my eyes and tried to remember how wonderful it had felt to feel his arms around me as we sat there in silence, the two of us finally able to express the love we'd felt for so long. I missed that.

I missed him. I missed how he made me feel like no man had ever been able to before.

My phone vibrated against my leg, and I looked down to see a text from him responding to mine.

Look out the window again.

I did as he said and saw him standing in the shadows right where he'd been the night before. Then another text made my phone vibrate and my heart skipped a beat.

Open the door.

Chapter Fifteen

Jordan

Gage walked past me as I held my front door open and stopped when he reached the kitchen doorway. Smiling, he said, "I'd love one of those beers, if you haven't drank them all."

"Drank them all? What am I, some kind of alcoholic?"

His blue eyes sparkled and he laughed. "You had two last night. I figured you might have had a few more to make you text me tonight."

Shaking my head, I walked to the refrigerator, grazing his muscular chest with my shoulder as I passed. Grabbing a beer, I handed it to him. "Nope. Just one. No drunk texting for this girl tonight."

"That's good to know. Very good to know."

We stood there staring at each in silence, and I wondered what I was doing. What did he have that made me incapable of forgetting him?

"I was happy to see your text."

Gage's voice was low and deep, like always, but it felt like silk sliding over my skin now. I tried to contain my excitement at having him so close, but it was hard.

"I was just thinking about that night. You know, nothing in particular. The sunset. I guess tonight just reminded me of then."

He took a gulp of his beer and I watched his Adam's apple bob as he swallowed. The action had a raw masculinity to it that touched me deep inside and made my breath catch in my chest.

"I remember that night. Actually do you know what I remember most about that night?"

Wanting so badly to know the answer, I squeaked out, "No." I cleared my throat and asked, "What is it?"

He walked toward me and stopped just inches away. Looking down at me, he slid his tongue over his gorgeous lower lip and grinned. "How your hair smelled. Like vanilla. Warm and sexy, like you."

I closed my eyes to hide from his inexorable gaze that felt like he was staring right into the deepest, darkest depths of me. "Don't say things like that…when you're close like this it's no good."

His thumb brushed my cheek as he tucked a lock of hair behind my ear. "All I said was the truth. Warm and sexy is exactly who you are, Jordan."

Shivering from his touch even as a bead of sweat trickled down my neck, I squeezed my eyes shut, sure I shouldn't be doing this. "Gage…I…maybe you should go."

"Is that what you really want?" he asked as his fingertip lightly traced the path the bead of sweat had taken down between my breasts. "You didn't text me just to send me away, Jordan. Open your eyes and look at me if you plan on telling me to leave."

I did as he commanded and saw him looking at me like he used to. There was always something so sensual in his eyes when we were alone back when we were together, and as my eyes met his, there it was again, making me want him even more than I already did.

"So you were about to tell me to leave?" he asked with sex lacing every word.

"No," I heard myself say as I struggled not to slide my hands up under his t-shirt to feel the taut muscles I knew were hidden just underneath the blue cotton fabric.

"Good."

"It's not good, Gage. You make it hard to think straight. I shouldn't be doing this with you."

He angled his hips slightly forward and I felt the gun he always carried press against my lower ribs. Our bodies barely touched, but it was enough to send a shot of electricity straight to my core. I wanted him to kiss me so much.

"Doing what, Jordan? We're just talking here."

Trying to change the subject and regain some control, I looked down at his hip and said, "Still with the gun, huh? Is that necessary?"

"If it means I can protect you better, then yes, it's necessary."

"It makes me nervous."

He grinned at me like he always did when I made a big deal about his gun. "I've been around guns since the day I was born, Jordan. You know this. I come from Wyoming. Everyone grows up around guns there. You have no reason to be nervous."

I didn't want to admit it to him, but I'd never really been uncomfortable because of the gun. Bringing it up was just a way of putting off the inevitable, no matter how much I wanted it.

"Now getting back to us doing something here. I've got some ideas about what we could be doing instead of wasting time with words."

"Never did think much of talking, did you?"

He ran the pad of his thumb against my bottom lip and shook his head. "I'm a bigger fan of actions. You can trust them more."

"Typical Gage," I said as he leaned in just an inch away from me.

"Stop talking, Jordan. There are so many better things you could be doing with that beautiful mouth of yours."

I felt like I couldn't breathe as memories of my mouth on him filled my head, but I croaked out one word to stave off what I knew was just seconds away from happening. "Like?"

He didn't bother to answer, and when he pressed his mouth to mine in a kiss as incredible as any he'd ever given me, my legs felt like they might give out. His lips were so soft, yet he kissed me like I was his to do with as he wished.

And what he wished to do with me I wanted so badly.

My head swam from the feeling of him being everywhere around me as he took me into his arms and pulled me to his body so hard and strong. He buried his right hand in my hair, sending chills down my back in the nearly ninety degree heat that continued to cling to the city, and placed his other hand on the small of my back to hold me to him.

His cock, already hard as a rock, pressed against the front of my shorts through his jeans, thrilling me with a sense of what was to come. This was quintessential Gage—raw, earthy, and commanding our lovemaking from beginning to end.

I'd missed this so fucking much.

He slid his lips down my neck to the hollow at the base of my throat and moaned, "You feel so good. It's been too long."

"Yes," I murmured, unable to think of anything but that single word for what he brought out in me. I wanted to be that sensual being he fostered in me again. For so long, I'd been closed off and fearful, and with Brock those hadn't been changed by his timid, yet perfectly acceptable lovemaking.

I wanted more, though. I wanted this. I wanted what Gage offered.

But as he dragged his tongue over the sweat-damp skin of my neck, a thought sprung up in my mind. I'd become closed off because of him and what he'd done. Pushing his head away, I looked into his eyes full of need for me.

"You made me afraid of love. You know that? When you broke up with me, you tore me in half."

Knitting his brows, he frowned at my mention of that night and the phone call that changed me. "I know. I can never erase what I did, but I want to start making up for it right now. Let me make up for it, Jordan, so you can see you can trust me."

"I'm not that same person anymore, Gage."

His hands moved up to my cheeks, and cradling my face, he shook his head. "Don't say that. You're still the woman I fell crazy in love with. Don't let my stupid mistake change what's so beautiful about you—that unshakable belief that love is worth it, no matter what."

I wanted to say that I'd only really felt that with him, but before I could form the words, he kissed me again and any thoughts of anything but how much I wanted to feel him inside me vanished in a haze of desire and need.

Playfully flicking the tip of his tongue against mine, he teased my mouth as his strong hands slid under my t-shirt to cup my breasts I'd thankfully chosen not to hide beneath a bra. With every caress of my skin with his hard hands, my body yearned for him more and more.

But I had to know something first before I surrendered my heart and body to him again. Leaning back, I savored the taste of beer he'd left on my tongue and pressed my fingertip to his lips.

"I need to know who you've been with since we broke up. How many women since me?"

His face grew serious, and I waited to hear his answer, afraid to find out that he'd tried to forget me through a series of meaningless fucks or even worse, a relationship with someone. Either would hurt, but Gage being who he was with someone day in and day out would crush me.

His eyes narrowed like he was in pain from what he had to say, and in a low voice he said, "None."

"Don't lie to me. That's not what we were all about, so don't start lying now because you want to sleep with me."

Wincing, he repeated his answer. "None. I didn't want anyone else, and it wouldn't have been fair to another woman. I was still in love with you."

"Was?"

"Was. Am. Will forever be."

"Jesus, Gage. When you say things like that, I can't think straight."

"Good. No more talking or thinking. Just doing," he said, the serious expression gone now and replaced by that sexy as all hell look he always wore when we made love.

Scooping me up in his arms, he turned around and carried me to the bedroom with a sense of purpose I couldn't help but love. No other man in the world knew how to handle me like Gage did.

He lay me down on the bed and as I watched him strip his shirt over his head, I couldn't help but be turned on. His body hadn't changed at all. God, he was still as built as ever. My gaze traveled over the muscular peaks and valleys of his torso down to his ruggedly cut abs settled in between hipbones and creating a delicious V that seemed to point directly to his hard cock.

"You just going to lay there staring at my body or are you waiting for me to undress you?"

"The first one. I'd forgotten how much I love looking at you without clothes on."

Tossing his t-shirt at me, he said, "Oh yeah? The second half of the show begins now, so settle in."

I threw his shirt on the chair in the corner and watched in rapt attention as he removed his gun from its holster at his waist and slowly walked around to the opposite side of the bed to place it on the nightstand. Returning to stand in front of me, he slid his jeans and boxer briefs down his legs to reveal his cock settled against his stomach, hard and ready to go. Without missing a beat, he hooked his fingers in the waist of my shorts and tugged them and my panties off my body, throwing them on the chair to join his shirt.

As I slipped my tank top over my head, Gage teased the inside of my thighs with his tongue, sending my body into overdrive. Christ, he had a magical tongue! His touch was always perfect—not too light and never too heavy, he knew exactly how to make every inch he reached come alive. My eyes rolled back into my head with each inch he moved toward my needy pussy.

"Don't look away, Jordan," he groaned from between my legs. "I want you to see me worship you like no other man has."

Oh God, when he said things like that I didn't want to be with anyone else. I didn't want to settle for someone who could give me security. I only wanted to spend the rest of my life with him, the only man who'd ever made me truly believe in love.

His warm breath drifted over my skin, sending shockwaves deep inside me. I wanted to feel his gorgeous mouth with its perfect lips on me, giving me pleasure like only he could, so I lifted my hips off the bed and watched him stare up at me with a devilish look in his eyes.

"I knew that woman I loved was still inside you," he whispered as he kissed his way closer and closer to my core, all the time keeping his gaze locked on mine.

"You're driving me crazy, Gage."

Licking his lips, he grinned. "Good. You should be crazy when a man is about to lick your pussy."

My eyes rolled back in my head at the mere mention of what he was about to do, and then I felt the tip of his tongue touch my needy clit and the world ceased to exist except for him and me and the sensations tearing through me with every second his mouth was on my body.

I had no idea how much time passed as he worshipped me and I reveled in how much I loved the attention he lavished over me. I'd missed this so much. No other man I'd ever met made love like Gage Varo.

Slow. Like he had the rest of time to kiss and adore every inch of me.

Intense. Like his entire focus was on pleasing me.

Raw. Like he knew no boundaries and possessed no defenses when it came to sex.

And I loved every second of it.

My orgasm began to uncoil deep inside me as Gage's tongue flicked against my swollen clit. Stuffing my hands into his hair, I tugged hard to keep him right there as my release overwhelmed me. His hands gripped tightly on my hips as his mouth rode me through every shudder and tremor until finally I released his head and he sat back with a look of satisfaction on his face.

"God, you taste so fucking good."

"You always say that."

He licked his lips and grinned. "You always taste good."

I knew what he wanted now and I wanted to give it to him. Sliding off the bed, I kneeled down in front of him and smiled, knowing how much he loved this. Before Gage, I'd never known how erotic going down on a man could be, mainly because it was always so much work but also because no man before him had made it feel sexy. Mostly it had just felt like a chore.

But Gage was different. His raw sensuality made the act more than just his cock sliding in and out of my mouth. And even though it terrified me to be so under a man's control, I loved it.

All the time apart hadn't made me forget how particular he was with this part of sex. Almost ritual with his tastes, he always stood and I always kneeled in front of him. It was as much about power and control for him as it was wanting to please him for me. While with other men I would have balked at the idea of getting on my knees like this, for Gage it only made the act better.

Like he always had, he stared down at me, his sensual gaze focused on my mouth, and then wrapping his hand around his cock, he slowly fed it into my mouth. Never in my life had anything felt more erotic than when I felt the tip of his cock touch my lips and saw the expression of pure pleasure wash over his face.

Unlike in every porn movie I'd ever seen, I was not to use my hands. I was also forbidden from bobbing up and down on him, as I had always done with other men. What he loved was being in total control until the very end, and what I loved was giving him that.

He set the pace, slow at first as he inched his thick cock in and out of my mouth, his hips barely thrusting forward and his hands buried in my hair gently tugging my head down on him, and then faster as he moved toward coming. It was freeing in one sense and entirely submitting in another. While I did none of what I'd always thought of as the work, I was his to completely do as he liked.

And what he liked was watching me take his cock inside me as fucked my mouth. There was no other way to describe it.

Hands clasped behind my back, I watched as he gradually moved from slowly easing in and out of me to genuinely fucking me that way, perfectly enraptured by how masculine he looked above me. When his movements became shorter and rougher, his cock jabbing in and out of my mouth, his fingers caressed my jaw like a sign he loved what I gave him and wanted to show how much it meant to him.

Never much for words, he spoke little as I knelt before him sucking his cock. Sometimes he'd close his eyes and moan low and deep as I'd flick my tongue around the base. Other times he remained silent, his eyes telling me how much pleasure I was giving him.

He was never more raw than at that moment when he cupped my chin and slid his palm down to tenderly squeeze the front of my throat. He could have roughly thrust his cock to the back of my mouth and I would be powerless to do anything with his hand holding me, but he never did. Always in control of himself and me, Gage knew how hard and fast to fuck me without going too far.

As he inched closer to his release, he groaned and spoke for the first time. "I'm getting close. Just a few more times…"

His words trailed off as I wrapped my hand around the base of his cock, touching him for the first time. Each time he gave me that tiny bit of control, and it meant so much to know that even as he had all the power, he could share some with me and still be more powerful than any man I'd ever been with.

Gage tightened his hands in my hair as he came, the purely masculine taste of him on my tongue as I took everything he had. His face twisted into a look of pain followed by a look of satisfaction, and then he smiled. In the quiet moment when he slid his cock out of my mouth, he gently ran his fingers along my jawline and the outline of my mouth, sensually visiting the place that had given him so much pleasure.

"Come here," he said as he pulled me up off my knees and

kissed me full on the lips.

No other man had ever done that after I'd gone down on them, but that was Gage. Every part of sex between us was shared without limits or boundaries. Of all the things about him, I adored that the most. He gave everything of himself to me when we made love, and I wanted to be that kind of woman for him.

"I missed that," he whispered against my lips. "The feel of your mouth on my cock is like nothing else in the world."

"For a man who doesn't like to talk much, you say the sexiest things," I teased.

Gage groaned and pushed his hips forward so his still hard cock slid through my wet pussy. "Enough talking. We have better things to do."

He slid his hands down over my breasts to my hips and then to my ass, cupping it as he lifted me off the ground. His cock waited for me, and I wrapped my legs around his waist as he slowly eased into my body, filling me completely.

My fingernails dug into his muscular shoulders, and I moaned in his ear as his cock grazed that perfect deep inside me, "Oh God, Gage…Faster…fuck me faster. Please…"

Kissing me hard, he squeezed my ass in his strong hands and pushed into me over and over, grunting with each thrust. His hard body pressed against mine, crushing me, but I loved it. I wanted everything about him.

His hardness. His silence. His rawness. It intoxicated me and made me need him more than I ever thought possible.

Our bodies were covered in sweat from the temperature of my apartment and the heat between us as he fucked me like a man never had before. Every inch of my body pulsated with the pleasure he gave me.

I dug my heels into his back to keep him inside me as I felt the first twinge of my orgasm begin. I wanted every inch of him filling me when I came. With one last hard plunge into my pussy, his cock sent me tumbling over that sweet edge and my body surrendered to him once again.

I was his, completely and without regret, and I knew I'd never be able to pretend not to love him again.

Falling against him, I struggled to find the strength to keep up as he continued to push into me. Wanting to give him what he'd given me, I kissed him long and deep and then clutching his neck, said in his ear, "I love you. Don't ever leave me again."

Gage tugged my hair and kissed me as his cock twitched the first of his release. "Never again. I promise. Never again."

Sated, we fell back onto the bed and I couldn't help but smile. He may not have ever had much to say, but sometimes when he did speak, he said all the right things.

Chapter Sixteen

Gage

The noise outside from the street below woke me, and I opened my eyes to see Jordan's head on my shoulder, her long blond hair covering her face. Lifting my right arm, I looked at my watch to see it was already almost ten a.m. Ordinarily, I'd jump out of bed and race to get a shower if I overslept this late, but this morning I didn't want to move from my place next to her.

The place I was meant to be.

I lightly ran my hand over her shoulder, loving the feel of her soft blond hair against my rough palm. It felt like silken strands teasing my skin.

Lost in how happy I was to be lying there next to her, I didn't notice her wake up and look at me. In a sleepy voice, she said, "Good morning. How long have you been up?"

"Not long. Just a few minutes."

"Do you have to leave? I imagine it's pretty late, right?"

"No," I said with a smile. "I was thinking I'd stay right here with you."

Jordan rewarded me with a huge smile. "Oh yeah? I like that. I know you have a business to run."

I kissed her to stop her talking and then pulled her close to me. "My business is my work and I have very competent people to help me with that so I can be in the arms of the woman I adore when I'm lucky enough to get the chance."

Pursing her lips, she planted a light kiss on my mouth. "Well, when you say it that way… And when did you become so good with the words, Mr. Varo?"

"Sometimes I'm good with them."

Jordan rolled me onto my back and threw her leg over my hips. Resting her chin on my chest, she looked up at me and asked, "So what should we do today? It's a gorgeous Thursday and you've decided to take the day off, so we should do something."

"I thought staying right here all day might be good," I said with a smile. "Maybe get up to grab something to eat and then come right back here?"

She looked up toward the ceiling as if she was thinking about my idea and shook her head. "We need to get out and enjoy life, Gage Varo. No more walking up and down Fifth Avenue with some obsessive shopper for me. I want to throw a Frisbee, take a run—do something that makes me feel alive."

Nuzzling her neck, I groaned, "Only if we promise one another that we'll be back in this spot tonight in each other's arms."

Jordan pushed my head back and ran her hands through my hair. Looking deeply into my eyes, she nodded. "I promise. Every night from now on we can be here together."

As she finished speaking, her expression grew darker and she turned away from me. I didn't know what I'd said or done, but she was different all of a sudden.

"What is it? What's wrong?"

She sighed and said quietly, "I have something I have to do before I can do anything with you out in public."

"Oh." That something tore me up inside. She had to see another man.

Sitting up next to me, she took my hands in hers and brought them to her lips in a kiss. "It's only right, Gage. Brock's never been awful or mean to me. He doesn't deserve to see the evidence that I'm leaving him on the street as he's going out to lunch or traveling to a meeting. He's not a bad man. He's just not someone I want to marry."

"I get it."

I didn't like it, but I got it. Jordan wanted to treat him with respect, and I understood. It was who she was, and I loved her for it. My jealous side didn't give a fuck about how he found out she was leaving him, though.

She caressed my cheek and gave me one of those Jordan smiles that never failed to make me give in. "It won't take long. He's not the type to fight it."

"Then he's fucking crazy because he should be fighting to keep you. Any man who doesn't see that doesn't deserve you. But don't do it today. Let's have today be about us."

"Okay. Tomorrow will work. So I guess you get your wish to stay in today."

I wrapped my arms around her and pulled her down on top of me. "Good. I say we stay in bed until we get hungry and then and only then do we get up. And once we eat, we get right back here."

"I like the way you think, Gage Varo."

BY FOUR O'CLOCK IN THE afternoon, we'd gotten up only once to snack on some potato chips for a few minutes before we headed back to bed. It was like old times between us when we'd lay in bed all day on a Sunday and watch movies on TV. Hours would go by without a word spoken from either one of us, but we never needed to fill our time with constant talking. It was one of the greatest things about being with her.

"Want to watch one of the X-Men movies? Between HBO and Starz, I think we have our choice between like three of them."

"Always a woman after my own heart. You pick your favorite."

As she scrolled through the choices, finally picking X-Men First Class, I leaned back against the headboard and watched her, still in disbelief that I was there again in her bed spending the day with her. I'd dreamed of this very place and the two of us together virtually every day since we'd broken up.

Sometimes when I thought about being with her again I couldn't believe it would ever happen. When those doubts crept in, all I could do was tell myself that I had nothing to lose by never giving up. Life without her wasn't much of a life at all. It was more going through the motions than anything else.

An existence but not much more.

"Did you hear me?" she asked as she pushed on my shoulder, shaking me from my daydreaming.

"Sorry. What did you say?"

"You looked like you were a million miles away. I just asked if you wanted me to make an iced tea run before the movie begins."

"How far do you have to go?" I asked, twirling the ends of her hair around my finger and not wanting her to leave for long.

"Just to the kitchen. I'll be back before you can say Magneto."

"Okay. If you're going for a drink, grab me one. Hanging out in bed all day makes a man build up a thirst."

She stood from the bed and slipped my t-shirt over her head. "I can see that," she said with a giggle. Bending over to kiss me, she joked, "All that lying there and everything."

I tugged the bottom of my shirt and pulled her close to kiss her again. "Actually, I'm planning ahead for later."

"Later, huh? Well, I better hurry then. I don't want to miss what you have planned."

"You won't. It can't happen without you."

Jordan trotted out to the kitchen, leaving me naked in bed as the first scenes of the movie began to play. I loved how comfortable we were able to be with one another again. No other woman had ever made me want to be playful like she could. The lightness in her seeped into me after all those months of being without her, and I felt myself changing even after only less than a day together. The darkness that had made me think I'd lost her for good slowly began to subside, leaving me hopeful that this time we'd make it.

The ice cubes clanking against the glasses in her hands brought me back to the present. She placed them on the nightstand and sat down next to me, snuggling against my chest.

"What did I miss?" she asked as she slipped her arms around me.

I squeezed her to me and whispered in her ear, "I know you've seen this no less than five times. How could you miss anything?"

Turning in my hold, she smiled back at me. "Five times? Multiply that by five, at least."

"Then I'm thinking we should focus on something else."

"Got anything in mind?"

"Yep. I've got a few things in mind, once I get that shirt off you."

Her eyebrows shot up as she pretended to be surprised. "Oh yeah? Well, let me help you out with that so you and I can get going on what you have in mind."

She wriggled out of my t-shirt and straddled me. Instinctively, I slid my hands down her sides and lifted my hips off the bed. My cock, already hard, slid through her wet pussy, grazing her clit, and I gave her nipple a swipe with my tongue.

"Figure out what I have in mind yet?" I asked as she closed her eyes and a tiny moan escaped her lips.

Biting her lip, she moaned again, this time louder. "By the time we're done, I'm not going to be able to walk, Gage."

"Do you want me to stop?"

Her eyes flew open, and she tugged my hair hard so I returned to giving her nipple attention. "Don't stop. Please. I want to feel you inside me again."

I squeezed her hips tightly and lifted her off me to slide my cock into her. One long, slow thrust and I was seated completely in her snug cunt. Jordan arched her back as I leaned forward and dragged my tongue slowly over her skin, tasting the saltiness from the sweat between her gorgeous breasts.

Opening her eyes, she stared down at me with need filling her moss green eyes. "That feels so fucking good. I missed this."

"We just made love like two hours ago," I said with a grin,

knowing what she meant.

"I missed this all that time we were apart, silly."

I slowly pressed her open with my fingers and touched the pad of my thumb against her clit, rubbing it in tiny circles. "No more talking about that. I want to see you ride my cock."

She rolled her hips and kissed me long and deep. "We're going to miss the movie, you know that, right?"

"I'm sure those X-Men won't begrudge me great sex. I'm sure they get their own fair share."

Jordan rose up and slid down on my cock. "I love this, Gage. I've missed this with you."

I knew what she meant. The sweetness and fun as we lay there joined together in the most intimate way two people could were things I'd never found with anyone else.

"Me too. It's not every woman in the world who would be okay with me making X-Men jokes while I'm balls deep inside her."

She wrapped her arms around my neck and began fucking me in earnest. I watched her ride my cock and loved how she held nothing back. There was nothing sexier than a confident woman who knew how to fuck a man. Too many women worried about how they looked or if they were doing something right, but Jordan approached sex like she did everything else in life.

Without fear and with an enthusiasm that only made it better.

But someone so incredible deserved more than to do all the work, even if it was enjoyable for me, so I rolled her over onto her back and moaned, "Enough of that. Time to get yours."

Wrapping her legs around my waist, she dug her heels into my lower back and pulled me into her as she whimpered, "Come back. I need to feel you."

I reared back and buried myself completely inside her as she ran her fingernails across my chest, sending wisps of pain over my skin and making me want her more than I thought possible. Each plunge into her warm, wet cunt felt like heaven on earth. Every inch of my body felt the ecstasy she gave me, and as I inched her closer to coming, I felt my own release begin to build inside me.

"God, I missed you so much."

Looking down at her, I saw that sensuality I'd never found in any other woman that made me want her more than I'd ever wanted anyone. Or anything. She made me believe in good again after years of self-imposed penance that had been nothing more than loneliness. I'd closed myself off thinking I didn't deserve goodness or love, and then one day there she was looking up at me with those green eyes that never failed to enchant me and that smile of hers that could light up a room.

That smile that made me want to see her every morning when I opened my eyes and every night as she fell asleep in my arms.

And now that I had another chance, I wasn't going to let that go for anyone or anything.

Jordan gently sunk her teeth into my shoulder as her orgasm wound through her, and I held her to me, loving the feel of her giving herself to me again. When she finally stopped shuddering, I rolled onto my back and pulled her close.

Breathless, she looked up at me and asked, "Why did you stop? You didn't come yet that time."

I smoothed the blond wisps from her face and kissed her. "I know. I just felt like I wanted to lay here like this."

"Staring up at my ceiling so desperately in need of paint?" she joked.

"No. With you."

"What's the smile about?"

I hadn't even realized I was smiling until she said something about it. Being with her made me so happy I couldn't help but smile.

"Just love being here with you."

Jordan laid her head on my chest and whispered against my skin, "Promise me no matter what we'll always remember this is who we are."

She looked up at me as she waited for my answer. I wanted to believe we could remember. When life got too much and both of us found ourselves stressed out from work and the demands the world put on us, she wanted me to promise that I'd be someone who would shelter her from all that.

Gazing down into her eyes full of love, I pledged to be that man for her. "I promise. No matter what happens."

"You know I never thought we'd ever be together like this again, Gage. It seemed impossible."

I leaned forward and kissed her softly. "I know and I'm sorry about that."

Shaking her head, she smiled. "It wasn't you and what happened that made it feel impossible, though. It was me. I wasn't lying when I said I'd changed. I did. I became closed off after you left. I didn't want to feel good again because I was afraid it would just end up bad. So I just closed myself off."

"I hate hearing that. I hate knowing you changed one of the best parts of you because of what I did."

She shimmied up next to me and pressed her lips to mine in a kiss full of love. "I never thought I'd feel like that again—like my heart was open and willing to love. But then you walked through my door and everything I felt for you came rushing back and for the first time in so long, I was happy. Truly happy."

"I missed this with you. Just lying together talking. The fact that you make me smile just by being next to me."

Tracing my lips, she kissed me again. "I love it when you smile. It's ever so slightly crooked and way too damn sexy."

"I do promise to remember this is who we are, Jordan. I don't want to forget that, no matter what happens."

She sighed and nodded. "It'll be okay tomorrow. He and I were never like we are."

Every time I thought of him with her, I felt like someone had my heart in their fist and was squeezing. I hated the idea of Jordan lying in his arms like she was with me and sharing those little things between two people that made up so much of who they were.

"I just want him out of the picture so you and I can be together again," I said as I looked away. I didn't want her to see how much I hated what she had to do in just a few hours.

But she knew me too well. Pulling my face back toward her, she gave me one of her smiles that never failed to make me love her more. "I never loved him like I loved you, Gage."

"I did this to us. I know. I just hate this whole thing with him."

"I know, but I have to do this tomorrow. I need to know you understand."

Cradling her face in my hands, I nodded, even as my heart felt like that fist was at it again tightening its hold. "I do. I hate it, but I understand it. I don't want to think about that or anyone else tonight, though. Tonight's about you and me."

"You and me then," she said sweetly.

As we made love again, I told her the words I'd never thought I'd get a chance to say again. To tell her I never stopped loving her and no matter what happened, I wasn't going to make the mistake I made before.

When she fell asleep in my arms, I silently swore to finally do what I should have done all those months ago and ask her to marry me. When you found the woman who made your life complete like she did, you married her.

And that's what I intended to do as soon as I could.

Chapter Seventeen

Jordan

Gage's arms held me close to him as I stared out my bedroom window and thought about how I'd break the news to Brock that we wouldn't be getting married. No use in putting it off. It wasn't fair of me to drag it out because I didn't want to tell him. He deserved to know, and even though I'd delayed a day to spend it with Gage, I couldn't wait anymore.

Rolling over, I gently tapped him on the nose and smiled as he opened his eyes. He looked at me still groggy from sleep and said, "I can't think of a better thing to wake up to than your smile."

"Such a smooth talker when you want to be."

He smiled and stretched his arms behind me. "I told you I'm good with words sometimes. What are you doing up so early?"

I sighed. "I have to go to see him. We can't be together while that hangs over my head."

Gage frowned slightly and nodded, even though I knew he hated letting me go. "I know. I don't like it, but I know it has to be done."

"He's not going to cause any trouble. He's not that type of person. But even if he isn't someone who'd die for me, he deserves to be told the truth."

"What time are you going?"

"I'm going to get up now and get ready. The sooner I get it over with, the better."

He pulled me close in a hug and held me to him. "Not yet.

Give me a few more minutes here with you before you go running off to another man."

I wanted to say putting it off only made it worse, but I didn't. Instead, I just lay there in Gage's arms as he pressed his lips to the top of my head and kissed me. No man wanted the woman he loved to go see another man she'd been with. I got that. But no matter how much in love with each other we were, that didn't change the fact that I couldn't intentionally hurt someone. Brock may not have been the man I wanted to marry, but he was a man who had been good to me and that counted for something more than an impersonal phone call to break it off.

"Why does it always seem like one of us is leaving?" Gage quietly asked.

Leaning back, I looked up into his eyes and saw fear. "I'm not leaving. I'm not going anywhere. I'm just doing what any decent person would do for someone they cared about. It'll be a short meeting because I doubt he'll want to spend time with a woman who just broke up with him, and then I'll be back with you."

Gage forced a smile. "I know. Just doing the decent thing. It wouldn't be right to break it off with someone without telling them why."

"I didn't mean it that way, Gage."

"I know. I just can't help but see the difference between you and me."

I kissed him lightly on the lips and cradled his face. "You believed you were doing the right thing. I can't blame you for that."

The fear that had filled his eyes morphed into sadness. "Yeah. I can, though."

"I have to go. There's no use in putting this off any longer."

He said nothing but opened his arms so I could get out of bed. I didn't want to talk about this with him. All I wanted to do was go to Brock and tell him the truth so I didn't have to feel guilty about being in love with Gage anymore.

As I walked toward the bathroom, he said in a low voice, "I'm going to head to my place. I'll have my phone with me if you need anything. Call me when you're finished and I'll meet you."

Turning around, I watched him slip his clothes back on in a way so different from when he'd stripped out of them two nights before. Then he'd been playful and sexy. Now he just looked sad.

I stopped him as he moved to walk past me. "Hey, it's okay, right? You understand, don't you?"

He hung his head and nodded. "I do. I just can't help thinking that all of this never needed to happen. If only I'd done things differently."

"Everything happens for a reason, Gage. You thought you were protecting me. I thought I could move on after losing you, but that wasn't true. Maybe I should have never gotten involved with Brock in the first place since I still loved you. We did what we thought was right. We can't change the past, but I can do the right thing by him now and be truthful. So don't blame yourself."

"I'll be waiting to hear from you, okay? Don't make me wait too long or I might have to come charging in on my white horse because I think I have to save you."

White horse. As I kissed him goodbye and promised to call him the minute I left Brock's, I thought about what I'd said to Nina about a knight in shining armor on a white horse and how she'd found that in Tristan while I'd never found that in any man. Maybe I was wrong.

It seemed like I'd been wrong about a lot of things.

"YOU DID WHAT?" NINA EXCLAIMED into my ear.

"I slept with Gage. Now I'm going to Brock's place to tell him I can't marry him."

Nina was silent for so long I pulled the phone away from my ear to see if the call had been dropped. No, the call was still live. I waited another few moments and said, "I thought you'd be happy."

"I'm stunned. I'm thrilled. I can't believe you did it, though.

Oh my God! Jordan, is everything going to be okay?"

I began pacing back and forth across the floor in my bedroom. "It will be fine. Just fine. You were the one who told me I shouldn't marry a man if I loved someone else. You said it wasn't fair to Brock. That's all I'm doing now. Being fair to Brock."

"I know. I know. And I don't blame you. I'm just stunned about this turnaround. I didn't think you'd ever give Gage another chance, much less call off your wedding to Brock, which I don't think is a bad thing at all. He deserves a wife who loves him, not another man."

I took a deep breath and stopped pacing for a moment. "Thanks, Nina. I needed to tell someone other than Gage, who I know doesn't want to hear about me worrying about Brock's feelings."

"How are you going to do it? What are you going to say to him?"

Pacing again, I passed by my dresser mirror and looked at the woman staring back at me. When did my life become so complicated? I had no idea how I was going to tell Brock the truth. I just knew I had to.

"I don't know. How do you tell someone you're not going to marry them because you're in love with someone else?"

"I can't imagine what I'd say, Jordan. Just remember you're telling someone something they aren't expecting. And just be kind. I think that's all you can do."

Sitting down on the edge of my bed, I took a deep breath. "I've never been on this side of the breakup. I always thought it would be easier, you know? It's not. It's just as difficult, only in a different way," I said as I looked around at the place where Gage and I had made love just hours before.

"You just have to keep reminding yourself that as much as it's important to watch out for Brock's feelings, yours have to be your first priority. He's going to be hurt, but the truth is always better than a lie. I want you to remember that, Jordan."

I listened and knew she was right, even if I felt like the bad guy. "I know. It's just hard."

"Oh sweetie, I know. But it's for the best. You know it. I think you've known it for a while. You just didn't want to admit it."

What I didn't want to admit was something far worse that I couldn't even tell my best friend. I'd been so seduced by the idea that I'd have a life like hers, complete with gorgeous homes, cars, and clothes and the chance to live a life I'd only dreamed of, that I'd intentionally ignored how little there was keeping Brock and me together. I'd let myself believe that things were more important than anything else and forgotten that love was what really mattered.

"I better go, Nina. I have to get over to Brock's and get this over with. I can't put it off any more."

"Okay. I'm only a phone call away, and don't forget that I can have Jensen there for you in no time."

"Thanks. I'll call you after it's all over. At least I won't have to explain to my grandmother that I ran off and eloped instead of getting married in front of her and my whole family."

Nina chuckled. "I know your grandmother. She wouldn't have taken that explanation lightly. She may be in her seventies, but Grandma Mary is a feisty one."

"Thanks for helping me through this. I don't know what I'd do without you," I admitted, truly thankful for having Nina to talk to.

"You don't have to thank me, Jordan. I'm always here for you. I'm just happy you're finally following your heart instead of your head. Remember, good things happen to good people. You said that to me so many times, so now it's my turn to say that to you. Getting back with Gage is a good thing."

I promised again to tell Nina everything about how my meeting with Brock went and ended the call with a feeling that things were going to be okay. Telling him goodbye would be hard, but it was best for both of us.

✧   ✧   ✧

THE DOORMAN AT BROCK'S BUILDING smiled at me like he always did when I passed by him to enter the lobby, but this time I felt like a fraud when I smiled back at him. As I rode up in the elevator to the penthouse, my palms began to grow sweaty and my stomach knotted up like it did whenever I dreaded something. I hadn't felt this nervous since I had to take my teacher exams in my last year of college.

I took a deep breath to settle my nerves, and as the elevator doors opened, my heart sank at the sight of Brock standing there waiting for me with a bouquet of pink roses in his hand. I hadn't told him anything other than that I needed to see him, and he'd mistakenly believed he was meeting with his loving fiancé, not the woman who intended to drop a bomb on him.

"Jordan, I'm so happy to see you. I got your favorite flowers. I know it's been hard these past two weeks, but it's all for the best. I hope you know that."

He handed me the bouquet, and I lifted them to my nose to inhale the sweet fragrance. "Thank you, Brock. This is very nice of you."

"What did you want to talk about, or is it just that you missed me like I missed you?"

Oh, God, this was going to be much harder than I thought.

I placed the roses on the side table in his entryway and took his hand in mine. "About that. We need to talk."

"I know it's been hard, Jordan. I know and I apologize. It's just that my company is relatively new and we're at a critical point in its growth. But that doesn't mean that I haven't been thinking of you all the time in the past two weeks because I have."

We walked toward the living room as he spoke, and with each step I tried to figure out the words to say. I didn't want to be hurtful or cruel. I just wanted to tell the truth and hoped it wouldn't be as bad as I feared.

"I know, Brock. It's just that…"

All of a sudden my brain turned to mush and every thought in my head disappeared. Brock stared at me with a look that told me I was making a complete mess of this. Confused by my inability to even complete a simple sentence, he simply smiled, likely hoping to allay my discomfort.

If he only knew.

He held my hand and gently stroked my arm. "Jordan, is everything okay? You don't look well."

I didn't feel well. My stomach felt like I was about to throw up at any moment, and my head throbbed with a headache that seemed to come out of nowhere. But I had to do this, so I inhaled deeply and slowly let the air out of my lungs before I began to speak again.

"Brock, we need to talk."

The look of concern that had settled into his face instantly morphed into something closer to panic or anger. Which it was I didn't know, but this was already going off the rails quickly.

"Talk about what? We're leaving tomorrow afternoon to elope and I've handled everything for that, so I don't know what you want to talk about."

"About that. I don't think we should elope."

Brock's eyebrows knitted, and he frowned as if he were in pain. "What are you saying?"

I looked away, unable to face him as I said the words. "I can't marry you, Brock. I'm sorry."

Out of the corner of my eye, I saw the shock settle into his features. I felt his stare burn the side of my face and worried I'd never be able to look him in the eyes again. I'd never been the one to break up with someone, and all those times boyfriends had broken up with me it had all looked so easy for them.

Maybe it was, but not for me.

I may not have loved Brock like I should have to marry him, but I didn't want to be like all those guys who'd made this look like a piece of cake.

"What are you talking about, Jordan? Are you joking? I know

you have a different sense of humor from mine, but I don't think this is funny."

Slowly, I turned to face him and shook my head as I slipped the engagement ring he'd given me from my finger. "This isn't a joke. I can't marry you. I'm so sorry. You're a wonderful man and you deserve to be happy. I'm not the right woman for you, though."

The look in his eyes pleaded for me to stop saying these words. "Of course you are. You're Jordan Wright, so you must be the right woman for me."

He tried to smile at his tepid joke, but it wasn't working and he knew it. His shoulders sagged beneath his dark grey suit jacket, and his body hunched like I'd just slugged him in the gut. I recognized that look. It's the same one I'd worn every time some guy had told me I wasn't the one for him.

"I'm sorry, Brock."

Christ, my apology sounded so lacking.

"Jordan, listen to me. I love you. I know it's been hard for the last couple weeks, and I know we're polar opposites like night and day, but we can make this work. I just need you to trust me."

I saw the hope in his hazel eyes and couldn't help but feel like the world's worst person. I wanted to say the truth—that even though I'd honestly and faithfully agreed to marry him, my heart belonged to another man and always had. I hadn't known it or maybe I never wanted to admit it, but my feelings for Gage had never really gone away.

But Brock didn't deserve to hear about all that. Telling him I loved another man would only hurt him, so I told a white lie and hoped it would help him feel better about us.

"You're right, Brock. We're too different, and all that time I spent with Monique showed me that. I'm not the right woman for you. You deserve someone more like you. Like her."

He shook his head quickly. "No, no. I don't want someone like me or Monique. I love how wonderfully different you are from me. I'm so serious all the time, but you're so full of life. I want that in my life."

A noise in the bedroom made me turn my head to look at the door and whoever was in there. "I thought you were alone."

He gently took hold of my chin and turned my face back toward him. "Listen to me. We can make this work. Nothing is ever perfectly smooth sailing for any couple, right? There's too much to lose for us to break up now."

I took his hands in mine, placing the ring in his palm, and brought them to my lips in a kiss. "You have everything a woman can want, Brock. Money, status, great looks, and you're a terrific guy. You won't be alone for long, and you won't be losing much if you don't marry me."

"If I have everything a woman can want, why don't you want to marry me?" he asked with an edge to his voice that told me I hadn't succeeded in hurting him.

"I'm just not the one you want. I know you'll find the right woman and live happily ever after. You deserve that."

Brock stood and walked over toward the bar in the corner of the room. With his back to me, he said in a low, sad voice, "I can't let you go, Jordan. I just can't."

"Please know that this wasn't easy for me," I said as I walked up behind him and touched his shoulder. "I never meant to hurt you. Please know that."

He turned around to face me and handed me a glass of water as he took a sip from his own glass. "I never meant to hurt you either. I honestly didn't."

Cotton mouth had taken me over, so I was glad for the drink of cool water. I took a big gulp and said, "You never hurt me, Brock. You're a good guy."

His gaze shifted behind me as he said in a solemn voice, "I wish that were true."

I opened my mouth to reassure him that my breaking things off between us didn't mean he'd done anything wrong or that he wasn't a good man, but just then my arms and legs began to feel like dead weights and everything grew fuzzy. His lips continued to move, but I didn't understand what he was saying anymore.

Barely able to keep my eyes open, I turned to see Monique standing by my side glaring at me. She said something about me ruining everything, and then the room felt like it was spinning around me.

And then everything went dark.

CHAPTER EIGHTEEN

GAGE

THE VARO SECURITY OFFICE EMPTIED out as my employees all left for their assignments, so I took the time to lean back in my chair and relax for a moment. Not that I expected to have much success at that. I hated that Jordan was at Brock's apartment telling him goodbye. I knew why she had to do it, but that didn't mean I had to like her going there.

My mind raced with what might be happening at that moment. Was he going to try to convince her to stay with him? She wouldn't, but would he try? I imagined him turning on the waterworks right there in his living room as she explained how she wouldn't be marrying him. The mental picture of him crying and begging her to stay made me dislike him even more.

What was he doing home in the middle of the day, though?

No matter. Jordan would tell him she didn't want to marry him and that would be the end of that. Then he'd fade into the past as a distant memory as we began our life together. This time I wouldn't let anyone take me away from her.

Maybe we'd take a trip out to Wyoming to see my family before she returned to school in a couple weeks. I could trust Casey to keep my crew in line, and some time away from the city out in the open spaces of my hometown would be great. No shopping or crowds. Just fresh air and nature.

As I thought about all the fun we'd have, my body began to relax for the first time since I left Jordan's place in Brooklyn. I hadn't realized how keyed up I'd been until this moment as I felt my shoulders retreat from their place up near my ears. Suddenly, my neck and back felt like the weight of the world had been removed from them at the mere thought of heading west.

"Hey, Gage, I don't mean to interrupt—"

I opened my eyes to see Casey standing in the doorway to my office. Wearing her usual smile, she folded her arms across her chest and leaned against the wall as I collected my thoughts.

"What's up, Case?"

"You looked more relaxed than I've seen you in ages, boss. I feel bad that I had to break up whatever you had going on there."

Chuckling, I sat up straight in my chair and moved back toward my desk. "I wasn't meditating or anything like that, so you don't have to worry about interrupting me. Just taking a few moments to get my head together after the last few days."

She nodded her head like she understood. "I'm glad. You looked a little rough at the Truman party that night. It's good to see you back to your old self."

As much as I liked talking about how healthy I was looking, I had a feeling Casey hadn't come to see me to tell me that. "So what's up, Case? You're handling Nestor today, aren't you?"

Casey stepped into my office and braced her hands on the back of the chair in front of my desk. "Yep. His wife told me they were running late this morning, so I don't have to be out there until after one."

"What's on tap for them today?" I asked knowing that providing security for Nestor Ambers and his wife Renee meant being more babysitter than anything else. Obscenely wealthy and friends of Tristan's parents from years ago, they were my first customers when I opened the doors to this business, even though I doubted they truly needed security from much of anything. Everyone loved the Ambers, so I couldn't imagine much danger existed for them.

"It's a beautiful August day, so I believe Mrs. Ambers

mentioned something about a stroll through Central Park and then a nice drive out to the Hamptons where they'll be relaxing until Monday."

I clapped my hands and laughed. "So you're heading out to the vacation spot of the rich and powerful? You must be looking forward to that."

She shook her head so her brown hair bounced around the sides of her head. "You know me, Gage. I'd rather a cookout on the beach or a day at the ballpark, but the work is good and I can't say anything bad about the Ambers. They're nice people."

"That they are. You don't find that in people with money a lot of times, you know?"

"I've learned that in this job, I can tell you that. For every Nestor and Renee Amber, there's someone who acts like we're their personal slaves. But I wouldn't have it any other way. We do good work here, Gage. I know sometimes we all think that the people we're guarding are a pain in the ass, but we do our job well."

I began to speak, but Daryl's ruddy face appearing in my doorway stopped me and Casey quickly excused herself so we could speak. He looked flustered, like he'd run the last few blocks, and any relaxed feelings I'd enjoyed just a few minutes ago disappeared.

He took a seat in front of me worked to catch his breath. "What's up, Daryl? You look like shit."

Tugging on his long red beard, he contorted his face into an expression of pain. "Think you're funny? Just wait till I tell you what I found out. You won't be Mr. Funny Comedian anymore."

"It's okay, Daryl. Jordan and I are back together and she's with Brock right now telling him she won't be marrying him. So whatever you have to tell me is no reason to get that scraggly ass beard of yours all pulled out of shape."

He stopped tugging on his wiry facial hair and leaned back in his chair, instead stroking it gently as if to calm it or himself. "You don't say. Well, I wasn't expecting to hear that when I came here."

I clasped my hands behind my head and leaned back in my

chair. "Yep, so you see, whatever you have to tell me about Brock Hannon isn't important anymore."

"What is this, the pose of the victorious?" Daryl joked. "You look downright gloating. Well, I guess you have every right. The guy had everything going for him. Looks. Money. A ring on her finger. But you're a sly one, Gage Varo. I can admit that."

"No gloating. Just happy. I gave her up once, and now that I have her back, I won't make that mistake again. Brock will just have to go find himself another woman because Jordan's mine and I plan to make that a permanent thing."

Daryl's eyebrows shot up and his eyes opened wide in surprise. "Holy fuck! I stay away looking into things and you two are already racing down the aisle. You work fast, my friend."

"We're not racing anywhere. I haven't even mentioned it to her yet, but I plan to. Nothing big. Just a few close friends and family like Tristan and Nina had. Maybe we'll even do it out in Wyoming."

"Jordan isn't exactly the wide open spaces kind of girl, Gage," Daryl said with a chuckle. "I have a hard time believing she's going to be all about the rolling hills of Wyoming. She's a city girl, my friend. You can't change that. We city people are a breed to ourselves."

"Nonsense. She'll love it. Jordan's the type of woman who can go anywhere and be happy."

Shrugging, he said, "Okay, believe what you want. But I highly doubt when you mention getting married in the mountains that she's going to be thrilled. I see her more on a yacht somewhere than hiking with you out west."

I couldn't help but laugh at Daryl's ignorance. "You really are a city guy, aren't you? I don't think you know one damn thing about Wyoming. Jordan will be fine wherever we are as long as it's together."

"I won't argue with that. Seeing as you're Mr. Love today, I'll let you have your delusions."

"I thought I was Mr. Funny Comedian."

Snorting his disgust with me, he rolled his eyes. "Hysterical. So do you want to hear what I found out or not, smart ass?"

"Sure. Hit me with all the dirt on Brock Hannon," I said as I sat up and readied myself to listen.

Daryl whipped out his tiny notebook and began flipping through the pages. "Him I still have little on, other than some family details. What I found out was about his sister, the lovely Monique."

"Monique with the shopping addiction that's going to land her on an episode of Hoarders someday?" I joked.

Shaking his head, he grinned. "Oh no. She's so much more than a crazy shopper. Just wait until you hear what I found out."

"I'm all ears. Shoot."

"She isn't who she says she is. His mother and father lived happily ever after until their deaths two years ago in a car accident out near Waco, Texas. They were the parents of two children— Brock Jonathan Hannon and Monique Elizabeth Hannon."

I leaned forward and stared across the desk at Daryl. "I thought they were half-brother and sister from when their parents married."

He shook his head slowly and frowned. "Nope."

"I don't understand. Monique isn't his sister, but he does have a sister Monique? What am I missing?"

Flipping a page in his notebook, he said, "Remember that car crash a couple years ago that killed his mother and father? Seems she suddenly became a fixture in his life right after that."

"So who the fuck is she?"

Daryl leaned back and smiled broadly, pulling on his beard again. "Oh, Monique, whose real name is Hailey Sanders, is the kind of woman all wealthy men fear. Born in a small town outside Lubbock, Texas to Nicole Sanders, an unwed teenage mother who had no idea who'd gotten her pregnant, little Hailey grew up around her mother's various lowlife boyfriends who came and went like the tides. Our girl must have learned something from that experience because by the time she was eighteen, she'd snagged herself a local businessman named Jasper Coltrane. Playing the innocent victim of some attack near his plumbing business, she worked her charms on the aging and widowed Mr. Coltrane and got herself a nice life. At least for a while."

"She's a con woman?" I asked, still reeling from the little he'd told me about Monique or Hailey.

"Yeah. She conned Coltrane out of something like fifty grand, but with the way that lady shops, she probably blew through that in no time."

"So how did she end up with Brock Hannon?"

Daryl held up his hand to stop me. "Patience. The story's just beginning. After Coltrane, little Hailey moved on to the big leagues. She and her boyfriend at the time, Kenny Summers, bilked her next mark out of nearly half a million. A wealthy man named Peter Simpson. He owned a luxury car business. You know the kind, import and export stuff. Well, Summers pretended to be the guy's pool boy while Hailey cozied up to him and got him to take her on trips around the world. While he was busy falling for the con, Summers robbed him blind of as many cars as he could steal while she had him in her clutches for a month on some remote island in the South Pacific. By the time the guy got back to civilization, Summers and the cars were gone. A short time later, so was dear Hailey."

"What happened to Summers?"

"Doing fifteen years."

I worked to process all this information about Monique, but it made no sense. "Are you saying she's playing Brock now? I don't get it. Wouldn't Brock know she isn't his sister?"

"This is where things get really interesting. You'd ordinarily think he would know what his own sister looked like, but from all I've been able to find out about Brock Hannon, he was a wealthy recluse estranged from everyone in his family for nearly a decade when they died."

"Where's the real Monique?"

"Dead. That's the really sad part of this story. She got into drugs after Brock left home and disappeared. She was living on the streets of LA, a strung out junkie, and then the all-too-common end for girls like her came just like it usually does when drugs are involved."

"So this Monique Hannon shows up on his doorstep after the accident to mourn the death of their dearly departed parents. This Hailey's a piece of work."

"Exactly. She looks close enough to Monique Hannon and he likely bought into it."

"She wouldn't be happy once Jordan entered the picture, though. Brock planning a life with someone means she'd be entitled to his money. Little Hailey would be cut out of a lot of the money," I said, thinking out loud.

Daryl nodded. "I think that might be what she was doing here in New York, and that would explain why Brock would be away from Jordan for all this time right after their engagement."

"So what was her plan?"

"I have to be honest here, Gage. I haven't figured that out yet. From what I've put together, it seems she glommed on to Hannon after his parents died and just in time for his business to hit the stratosphere. I'm guessing she had her eye on his money, but then he met Jordan and everything she planned was all of a sudden in jeopardy."

I'd never felt any guilt about getting in between Jordan and Brock, but at that moment as I thought about her involved with people like him and Hailey, I couldn't help but be happy that she was walking away from him today. The sooner she got away from people like that the better.

"Then it's good that Jordan's telling him she won't marry him."

Daryl nodded his agreement. "Your lady shouldn't be anywhere near Monique or Hailey or whoever she is. That woman is dangerous, and Jordan was putting all her plans at risk. Now with her gone, Brock can shower all his money on Hailey, just like I bet she wanted."

"I think I feel bad for him now that I know all of this. He's losing Jordan and stuck with the duplicitous bitch who's pretending to be his dead sister and who plans to rob him blind."

Standing, Daryl pushed back his chair and chuckled. "I wouldn't feel too bad for him. He was your rival until a day or so ago. I'm sure he'll figure out Hailey's game. It's just a matter of when and if it's before she takes him for all he's worth."

I stood to shake his hand and thank him for checking things out for me. "You're the best, Daryl. Thanks again for this."

"My pleasure. Want me to keep looking into Brock Hannon too?"

"Nah. No need now. Jordan will be back soon from telling him, and that will be the end of him in our lives. Anything that comes up I'm sure I can handle."

Daryl's eyes lit up suddenly. "Oh, I forgot to mention this interesting tidbit. Hannon isn't the only guy rolling in the dough involved in his companies. Somehow, and I haven't figured out how yet, an even bigger fish is behind him."

"Bigger fish? Like who?"

"My guy found the name Dalton Spear. You know, one of the richest men in America Dalton Spear."

Dalton Spear wasn't just someone with money. The heir to the Spear chemical empire, he consistently ranked as one of the top twenty wealthiest men in America.

"That's some money there."

Daryl puffed his cheeks and blew the air out slowly. "There's money, and then there's Spear level money. I'm just wondering what he's doing with Hannon. Still think I should back off checking him out?"

I shook my head, now more than ever wanting to know what Brock Hannon was all about. "No. It may be just for curiosity, but I think we need to find out about our buddy Brock."

"Got it. Will do." Daryl stood to leave and tugged on the bottom of his beard. "By the way, any more letters? We still never figured that out."

I shrugged. "Maybe it was Monique. She seems like the type to do something like that. Whoever it was, I should have never given in to their demands. Nobody can protect Jordan better than I can, so let them try to separate us again."

"That was probably it," he said as he turned toward the door. He took a few steps and looked back at me. "But that doesn't make sense. If Monique wanted Jordan gone, she wouldn't have driven you two apart."

"Yeah, I guess. No matter. She and I will deal with whoever it was if and when they send any more letters, but their bullshit attempts to break us up won't work anymore."

"Good to hear. Remember, I'm just a call away if you need anything. In the meantime, I'm going to keep working to get to the bottom of this Spear and Hannon business. My gut tells me there's more to this than just a wealthy investor."

"Thanks, Daryl. I appreciate it. Right now, I'm just waiting for Jordan to call me so I can meet her for lunch and forget all of this ever happened."

In a tone of disdain, he grumbled, "Lovebirds. Well, you kids have fun. I'm off to dig up the dirt on a few other people Tristan has me checking into before I get back to your problem. I'll let you know what I find out about your lady's ex."

Daryl left me waiting for Jordan to call and happy to be done with everything associated with Brock and his sister. From now on, we'd live the simple life we'd started back when it was just the two of us, before I made the stupid mistake of leaving the only woman who'd ever truly made me happy.

Never one for daydreaming, I found myself thinking about how great it would be when I got her out to the open country of Wyoming. True she was a city girl, to be sure, but she was so much more than that. The woman I knew would love the fresh air and freedom back home offered.

A FEW MINUTES LATER, MY phone vibrated in my pocket, and I pulled it out eagerly looking for a text from her telling me everything was done and she was fine. Swiping the screen, I saw the text was from her. Slowly, I read the words and suddenly my tiny office felt like the walls were closing in on me.

> *I can't go through with it. I've changed my mind. I'm marrying Brock. Don't try to change my mind. I love him.*

My hands shook so much my phone nearly slipped out of my grip. Over and over, I read the words she'd texted, but I couldn't believe them. She didn't love him. She loved me and wanted to be with me. How could she have spent all yesterday and last night with me making love for hours and then changed her mind?

I quickly typed out a text to her, confused and feeling betrayed.

> *What are you saying? Don't do this. Just tell me where to meet you and we can figure this out.*

For nearly five minutes, I waited for an answer to my message but got none. After feeling so great about us all morning, I now felt like my world was crashing in around me and I didn't know how to stop it. Was she still at Brock's apartment? And what had happened to make her change her mind?

Unsure if I should race over to Brock's place, I called the one person I was sure would know what was going on. Her phone rang four times and with each ring, I worried that even Nina was avoiding me now because Jordan had truly decided to turn her back on us to be with Brock. I knew Nina wouldn't want to hurt my feelings, so of course, she wouldn't want to talk to me.

But she finally answered and when I heard her usual cheery voice, I hoped I'd been wrong about Jordan.

"Hey Gage! What are you calling me for on this beautiful day when I would think you and Jordan would be celebrating?"

"Nina, do you know where Jordan is?"

"Yeah. She told me everything and that she had to go tell Brock it was over. She's probably still there. No need to worry. She just wanted to do right by him. That's all."

I looked down at my phone as I put her on speakerphone and read the message aloud. "I just got this text from her a few minutes ago. *I can't go through with it. I've changed my mind. I'm marrying Brock. Don't try to change my mind. I love him.*"

My chest ached as I read the words.

"What are you talking about, Gage? Jordan doesn't love Brock. I've known for weeks she didn't love him enough to marry him."

I grabbed my wallet and gun out of my desk drawer and started walking toward the door. "She sent me that from her phone just a few minutes ago. I don't know what to think, to be honest."

Nina's voice turned frantic. "Something's wrong. She wouldn't send you that. That doesn't even sound like her. She's crazy about you. We just talked about you and her getting back together and how happy she was about it. Why would she send a message like that? What could have happened?"

Tearing out of my office, I ran up the street not even knowing where to go. "Nina, something's wrong. I have to go find her. Call me if you hear anything."

"I will. I promise. Find her, Gage. Find her and get her away from that guy. He's no good. I just know it."

"Don't worry. I'll find her," I said in between panting breaths as I broke into a sprint at the thought that at that very moment Brock and his scheming con artist sister were doing some horrible thing to Jordan. I had no idea why they would as none of it made sense, but it didn't matter.

Nothing mattered but Jordan and making sure she was safe.

CHAPTER NINETEEN

JORDAN

SLOWLY, I OPENED MY EYES but everything around me appeared cloudy and hazy. My eyes couldn't focus on anything, but studying the blurry shapes in front of me, I had the surest sense I wasn't in Brock's apartment anymore. I heard voices nearby, but all the words were garbled as they hit my ears.

What had happened? I tried to replay the events of the day as best as I could remember them. Gage and I had made love first thing this morning. Definitely not a bad memory to start with. I'd told him I had to tell Brock in person that I couldn't marry him. I'd told Brock the truth and then…

The memory of Monique standing next to me as everything faded away made terror race through my veins. What had they given me? I racked my brain to think of how they could have done it and remembered the glass of water.

Brock had drugged me by slipping something into my drink.

I looked down at my body, but my eyes still wouldn't focus and all I saw was a blurry version of my tan arm and pink t-shirt. Jesus, I felt like a bus had hit me!

I had no idea what they'd drugged me up with, but whatever it was, it had done a real number on me. It must have been some pretty heavy duty stuff if the way I felt was any indication.

Opening my eyes as wide as they'd go, I tried to figure out where I was. All I knew was I was on a couch somewhere. The room around me didn't look familiar, even seeing it through blurry eyes.

It was cold, though. Air conditioned cold, like when you're in a restaurant and they have the temperature so cold that you need a sweater in the middle of summer. I curled up in a ball to get warm as I continued to try to figure out where the hell I was and what the hell was going on.

I was still dressed, which was a good thing and likely meant I hadn't been attacked. Jesus! What was I thinking? Who would attack me?

Working to calm myself, I reminded myself that Brock still saw himself as my fiancé and had never been anything but decent to me. His sister, on the other hand, was an entirely different story. Whatever had happened, I was sure of one thing.

She was behind it.

Since my vision wasn't improving much, I closed my eyes to listen to what the voices I heard were saying. I had the sense they weren't too far away—maybe in a room nearby. But who was speaking?

One person, likely a male, spoke in a low voice. Was it Brock? I concentrated and couldn't figure out if it was his voice. But if it wasn't him, who was the male?

I opened my eyes again but still everything remained blurry. What the fuck had she given me? Anger bubbled inside me. When I got my sight back, that bitch was in for a rude awakening.

One that I'd give her with my hand across her face. Nice Jordan had officially left the building.

I knew I should have listened to my gut when it came to Monique. The woman made me uneasy from the minute I met her.

None of that mattered anymore. Now I had to focus and figure out who was keeping me wherever here was and how to get away. I was smarter than Monique for sure, and while Brock might be incredible at business, he wasn't much for street smarts. That's where I beat both their pampered selves. This chick wasn't merely the smiling third grade teacher I usually portrayed myself to be.

Focusing once again, I listened to the female voice and knew exactly whose it was. No one in the world had a voice like Monique. Whining and insistent all at the same time, it was a voice that made you want to run away, but not before you made her suffer at least a little.

So at least I knew that. Monique and possibly Brock or some other male had brought me to this place. Why, though? Why bring me here or anywhere? And why drug me, for God's sake! Who did that kind of thing?

Shitty people who were likely criminals did that. The problem was Brock had never struck me as a bad man, and even his awful half-sister had never been more than a pain in the ass.

I opened my eyes and slowly waited for things to come into focus, hoping it didn't take too long and Monique found me awake because she'd likely just drug me again. As I waited, my head began to throb like someone had a sledgehammer inside my brain and was swinging it wildly toward the sides of my skull. This was why I didn't do drugs. My head just couldn't handle them.

Gradually, my eyes began to work again and I saw what looked like a living room around me. Someone's living room with seashells and starfish. The room was painted in a pale yellow, and the furniture was wicker and the color blue like every picture of the Mediterranean I'd ever seen.

Was I at the beach?

The pictures on the walls were all seascapes, so figuring out who owned this place by them wasn't going to happen. Nothing else in the room gave me any clues as to who might be behind all of this.

I needed to get out of there and fast.

Then all at once I thought of Gage. He was likely waiting for me to call him like I said I would after I told Brock I couldn't marry him. I felt my shorts for my phone, but it was gone. Suddenly, I became frantic. I didn't know where I was or why Monique and whoever she was with was holding me, and Gage had no idea where I was.

Which meant he couldn't help me. And Nina couldn't either.

I was all alone.

It didn't matter. I was a blond, but I wasn't dumb. I'd skipped out on rotten dates through tiny bathroom windows and escaped unharmed and with all my money from no less than three muggers since I'd moved to Brooklyn. Monique and Brock weren't going to kidnap me and keep me hostage. No fucking way.

I swung my feet off the couch and stood up, too quickly, unfortunately. Not ready to stand quite yet, I fell back onto the couch, too dizzy to try again.

Well, if standing wasn't an option, then I'd crawl. Whatever way I had to, I was getting the hell out of wherever I was.

Carefully, I rolled over and lowered myself to the ground on my hands and knees. The carpet felt like needles jabbing into my legs, but I started to move toward what looked like a door to the outside. It had a window, so at least I hoped it led outside and not into the very room where Monique and the mystery man were still talking.

I hadn't figured out what they were saying yet, and as I moved along the painful carpeting, I tried to decipher the words that floated into the room. She was talking about something concerning a plan. What plan? Was this whole thing planned all along? Why would they plan to kidnap me when Brock just asked me to marry him nearly two weeks ago?

Sure my hearing hadn't returned as well as my vision had, I continued to move toward the door and listened to what they were saying. As I heard the man speak, I began to realize it was Brock in that room with her. My own fiancé had been a part of drugging and kidnapping me!

My knees burned from the pain of rubbing against the scratchy carpet, but I was almost to the door. I prayed to God by the time I reached it I would be able to stand without falling flat on my ass.

And then from behind me I heard Monique snap, "Don't let her get out! Grab her!"

Before I could stand and make a break for it, Brock's hands covered my shoulders to stop my movement forward. I fought him as best I could in my condition, but I was no match for him. Picking me up, he carried me by the waist back to the couch as I kicked and screamed.

"Get your hands off me! You fucking drugged me and brought me to this place! Don't touch me!"

Brock tried to calm me down, but it was no use. No matter what he said, I kicked and screamed and flailed my arms in a pathetic attempt to get away.

Crouching next to me, he said in a plaintive voice, "Jordan, please, I don't want you to hurt yourself. Just calm down. Everything's going to all right."

My blurry vision had all but cleared up, so I looked him in the eyes to see if he could possibly be serious. Everything was going to be all right? How the hell could he think that?

"Where am I? Why did you let her do this to me?" I demanded to know.

His hazel eyes filled with sadness as he shook his head. "I didn't know what she had planned. Please believe me. I love you. I would never hurt you. As soon as I realized what she was doing, I made sure you were safe and in no danger."

"You put something in my drink and filled me with drugs that made me black out. How was that safe?"

His expression sagged into a frown. "I'm sorry, Jordan. I didn't have a choice."

I opened my mouth to say it didn't matter, but Monique barked, "Don't bother coddling her. We did what had to be done. And don't tell her you didn't know what I had planned."

Brock looked past me toward her and narrowed his eyes in anger. "She doesn't deserve to be treated like this. It doesn't hurt anyone or anything you have planned for me to be nice. And I had no idea the stuff you gave me would do that to her, for God's sake."

Monique grumbled and walked into the other room as Brock

returned his attention to me. "I really am sorry. I never meant for any of this to happen this way."

Exhausted after only being awake for less than fifteen minutes, I let my shoulders fall in defeat. "What's going on, Brock? Why did you do this to me?"

"I never wanted you to get hurt, Jordan. I hope you can believe that. I just couldn't let you go."

"So that's it? You kidnapped me to bring me here and force me to marry you?" I asked in horror as my mind frantically sought any other reason why I'd be drugged and brought wherever I was.

"We love each other, don't we? It's not that bad, after all. Right?"

I shook my head in disbelief. "I don't love you enough to marry you, Brock. I told you that."

Brock lifted his hands to cradle my face and looked deep into my eyes. "I think you loved me enough to marry me at some point, didn't you?"

Opening my mouth to explain that I loved Gage and not him, I was interrupted by Monique snapping at Brock, "Stop it with this lovesick puppy bullshit already!"

"You won't get away with this," I said with all the bravado I could muster.

Monique's left hip shot out and her hand landed on it to punctuate her disgust at what I'd said. "We're hours away from the city, sweetheart, so yes, we will get away with this. It's a simple thing, really. When you came to Brock's today to tell him you couldn't marry him, we had to do something. You have to marry him and it has to be today. So we did what was necessary."

I looked at Brock in the hopes that at least he hadn't lost his mind like his sister clearly had. "Don't let her do this. Whatever's going on, it can stop right now and nothing bad will happen to you. You need to stop this."

Brock's face filled with regret, and I knew he couldn't or wouldn't help me. Looking up at Monique behind him, I said,

"People are looking for me right now, I'm sure. My friends will miss me when I don't show up at my apartment."

A sinister smile spread across her red stained lips. She reached into her jacket and held out my phone for me to see. "You're right, actually. Someone is looking for you. That's probably because of the text I sent him as we were leaving the city. *I can't go through with it. I've changed my mind. I'm marrying Brock. Don't try to change my mind. I love him.*"

Barely able to hold back the tears at the thought that Gage had received that horrible text from who he thought was me, I lunged forward to grab my phone from her grip, but she just pushed me hard back onto the couch.

"You have him as V in your contact list, but his name is Gage, right? He certainly seems to care about you, if his text he sent you is any indication. *What are you saying? Don't do this. Just tell me where to meet you and we can figure this out.* He sounds so distraught, don't you think? Not that it matters. He won't find you in time."

Tears rolled down my cheeks as she read Gage's desperate text to me. He thought I betrayed him and still begged me to come back to him. Oh, God!

"Why are you doing this?"

"You know, you have terrible luck with men," Monique said in a mocking voice as she scrolled back through my texts. "I mean, you obviously were fooled this time, and your ex killed a girl, for God's sake. I take it your last name is ironic? Miss Wright? I don't think so."

Looking at Brock again, I pleaded, "Don't let this happen. I'm sorry I didn't want to marry you. Please just let me go."

"I never wanted things to go like this. Honest. But I fell in love with you, even though that wasn't the plan."

"What is this plan you two keep talking about? What plan?"

Brock continued to talk but didn't answer my question. "I mean, I tried to do what I was supposed to. It was no use, though. You really are a sweet person, Jordan. If things weren't like they were, I think we could have been happy with each other."

"Enough! You're like two idiotic teenagers," Monique yelled.

I grabbed Brock's hand, hoping to make him focus on helping me. Whispering so Monique couldn't hear, I said, "It doesn't matter now. It's okay. In a different time and place we might have been happy. I get that. What I don't get is why you have to keep me here. Help me escape. If you truly love me, you can do that."

All he did was shake his head and frown. If I was going to get out of there, he wasn't going to help. A chill ran up my spine at the thought of what this plan they kept talking about could be. Were they going to kill me? That made no sense, though. Why whisk me out of New York to do that?

I looked over at Monique who stood reading my text messages from Gage. A ridiculous smile spread across her evil face as she scrolled through them, as if reading our personal intimations gave her some kind of jollies.

"What is this plan of yours?" I asked, almost afraid of what her answer would be.

She looked up from my phone and chuckled. "You haven't figured it out yet? See, I told this one here you weren't very bright. Clearly brains don't run in the genes. Didn't you find it odd that I suddenly showed up after your engagement party, even after I didn't bother coming to the big celebration?"

"Truthfully, I was happy. You were never someone I wanted to spend any real time with, so when Brock told me you wouldn't be there, I was relieved."

She scowled at my answer and shot Brock a nasty look. He cowered and slinked away to sit on the chair across from me as she continued explaining herself.

"Brock here never did seem to get the full gist of the plan, did you? I showed up because he had actually developed feelings for you and that whole engagement thing was real for him. Well, I couldn't abide by that."

"Abide by what? Him being in love with me? Wasn't that what

he was supposed to be? We were getting engaged."

"He was never supposed to fall in love with you!" she shouted so loud my ears rang. "All he had to do was get you to the altar. That was it. But even that was too difficult for this fuck up."

Brock stood to defend himself but she pointed her finger at him to stop him from speaking. "Don't say a word or you'll see none of the money. Do you understand me or do I need to use smaller words with less fucking syllables?"

I sat stunned at all of this, not understanding why Brock wouldn't or couldn't stand up to her. What money was she talking about? He was a multi-millionaire. Why would he care about her money, and for that matter, when did she get so wealthy that she had any money to give him?

Monique turned her attention back to me. "So today the plan finally comes to fruition, so wipe the mascara from under your eyes and look presentable."

"For what?"

"Your wedding day, of course. You and Brock are about to become the happiest couple in the world. You won't be wearing white, but that's not exactly the color someone like you should be wearing anyway. You're not exactly pure, especially since you spent last night fucking your ex-boyfriend."

Stunned, I mumbled, "My wedding day?"

Brock nodded and hung his head, as if he wasn't just as guilty as Monique for kidnapping me and now forcing me to marry a man I didn't love.

"How can this be legal? Where the fuck did you bring me to that would allow you to force me to marry him?"

With a smile, Monique answered, "South Carolina. Welcome to the south. We do things differently here. Now keep your mouth shut or I swear to God what you got earlier will be nothing compared to what I'll do to you."

She stormed out of the room, but nothing she said made any sense. Why would they force me to marry Brock? I looked at him as he sat defeated in the chair and asked, "Why are you letting her do this to me? To us?"

"I won't let her hurt you, I promise. Just do as she says and everything will be okay."

"What's happened to you, Brock? Where is the man who runs a multinational company and is a self-made millionaire?"

He hung his head and said quietly in a far less distinguished tone than he usually had, "My name isn't Brock. My name is Justin. Justin Archer." Looking up at me, he added, "And I meant what I said. I did fall for you and you are a sweet girl. I'm sorry for all of this."

"What happened to your voice? Why do you sound like that? What do you mean your name isn't Brock Hannon? Who are you?"

He shook his quickly left and right and pressed his lips together. "I shouldn't have said anything. Just do as she wants and I promise you'll be okay. I won't let her hurt you."

"Brock, answer me! What is this all about?"

Just then, a minister and two more people entered the room followed by Monique pretending to be the supportive sister of the groom. "We'll be having the ceremony out on the deck since the sunset is going to be just perfect tonight. Please feel free to walk straight through to outside and the three of us will be joining you momentarily. Just give the lovebirds a few minutes to get ready."

They walked past me with smiles on their faces, and I sat too stunned to tell them the truth of what was going on. As the door to the deck closed, Monique walked up to in front of the couch and glared down at me.

"Play this right and the worst you'll be able to say is that you're married to this man. Play it wrong and you'll be dead, but not before you're married to him. Either way, you're about to become his wife. The choice of what happens after that is up to you."

She turned to say something to Brock or Justin or whoever he was, and all I could think was I was about to be forced to marry this man who wasn't even Brock Hannon and there was nobody who could save me from Monique and her awful plan.

Closing my eyes, I let the tears come as an even worse reality filled my mind. The man I loved thought I'd betrayed him and had no idea where I was to stop this madness.

CHAPTER TWENTY
GAGE

THE STONE WORLDWIDE BUILDING SECURITY guard quickly waved me in as Tristan's assistant waited for me on the other side of the metal detector to escort me up to his office. Michelle and I said nothing as we walked toward the elevator, her shoes making a sound that reminded me of my mother's metronome that used to sit on top of her piano as my sisters took turns practicing their playing. So measured and regular, the tapping of her shoes as they hit the white marble floor strangely calmed me.

At least for a few moments. But as soon as those elevator doors closed and we stood still facing those dull metal doors, all my fears about what might happening to Jordan at that very moment came rushing back.

Fucking Brock and Monique!

We reached the top floor and exited into the executive suite where Tristan was waiting for me in his office. Michelle gave me a gentle pat on the upper arm as she left me to return to her desk, and I walked into the CEO of Stone Worldwide's office hoping to God he could help me rescue the woman I loved from whatever Brock was up to.

Tristan Stone never failed to surprise me. Wealthier than most men his age, he always seemed far more down to earth than his peers who shared his social level with him. This afternoon he looked the same as he always did when I saw him in his office. He wore a dark suit, striking dress shirt and tie, and a look on his face that said he had a lot of money and knew how to wield the power that came from that fact.

But in his brown eyes I saw the familiar warmth he showed those of us he called friends.

Extending his hand, he offered me a seat. "Gage, it's good to see you again, although I wish it were for far more pleasant reasons."

"Thanks for seeing me, Tristan. You're the only person I knew to call once this all began to unravel."

He leaned forward in his office chair and took a deep breath. "I never felt good about that Brock Hannon. Nina and I both had a feeling about him that something was wrong, but I never could put my finger on it. I regret not telling Daryl to check him out for me months ago."

I nodded. "I'm not sure it would have mattered. Brock seems to have hidden all his dirt better than anyone Daryl's ever seen. His sister is a different story, though. I'm sure she's involved in whatever's going on."

Tristan's face contorted into a look of disgust. "Nina's told me all about her. They sound like real winners."

His cell phone rang and looking down at the screen, he said, "I asked Nina to call me when you got here so she could tell us if she remembered anything Jordan told her that might be able to help us."

"Hey, honey. I have Gage in my office right now. I'm hoping between the three of us, we can figure out where Walker should take him. He's got the plane ready, but we need to know where to go."

"Tristan, I have no idea," she said in a frantic voice full of fear. "Gage, I'm so sorry this happened. I told her I didn't think she should marry Brock and when she finally agreed, I was so happy. What do you think happened when she went to see him?"

"I have no idea," I said, trying to remain positive but worried that every minute that went by and I hadn't found her was one that could be her last. "I never dreamed the guy would do anything other than try to convince her to change her mind. I can't believe she did, though."

"She didn't!" Nina said in tears. "I know she didn't. She didn't love him. She knew it. And she loves you. Of that, I'm certain. Please don't doubt that."

"Nina, did Jordan ever say anything about where he has homes or somewhere they might go to get away? I've got men checking his home and office in Dallas, but they aren't there. So where would they go if not there?" Tristan asked.

The phone remained silent for a long moment as Tristan and I sat there staring at each other, and then Nina made a noise that sounded like she'd clapped her hands together.

"Honey, what is it? Did you remember something?"

"Yeah, but I don't know if it's anything. Right after they got engaged, Brock told Jordan he had to stay away from her for two weeks."

Tristan's expression turned to confusion, and I leaned forward toward the phone on his desk. "Yeah, I thought that was weird too. Right after they got engaged he doesn't spend time with her? Do you know why?"

"He said he needed to catch up on work so they could elope. He didn't want to wait until the real wedding, so they were going to elope. She told me the day Cara and I took the kids to the Staten Island Zoo."

"Elope? Are you sure? She never said anything about that to me."

"She probably didn't want you to know, Gage, but she told me he had said to her he didn't want to wait. She thought it was romantic at the time, but I thought something might be wrong. I mean, why not just wait? She wasn't going anywhere, as far as he knew."

"Nina, honey, did she say where they were going to elope to? Dallas?" Tristan asked.

"I'm trying to remember. We were looking at the animals and she was talking about them eloping. Oh God! Why can't I remember? And I can't even ask Cara because Jordan whispered it to me. I'm sorry, Gage. I know she told me, but I can't remember."

Disappointed, I sat back in my chair and tried not to let myself get lost in the despair that threatened to take me over. Jordan had been gone for hours, and God only knew what had happened to her by now.

"Nina, do you think it was out of the country?"

"No. Well, I don't know, but I want to say it wasn't out of the country. God, why can't I remember this, Tristan? She's my best friend and I'm the person who can help her and all I have is mommy brain all muddled with kids' cartoons and what I need to make them for dinner!"

"Don't get upset, honey. Maybe if we just talk for a little bit it will come back to you. If they weren't going to his home in Texas, what about hers? Do you think they'd go to her hometown in Connecticut?"

"I don't think so. Her parents wouldn't be happy about not being at their wedding, and if her grandmother ever found out about her eloping, she'd flip her wig. Her grandmother might be old, but she's spunky and she'd tell Jordan in no uncertain terms what she thought about not being there when she got married."

I was beginning to get antsy just sitting there. Never before in my life had I felt so useless. The woman I loved was out there somewhere with Brock and probably his manipulative sister too, but for what reason? Was he planning to force her to marry him? Because I couldn't believe she truly had changed her mind and wanted to be with him.

Jesus, maybe she was right when she accused me of being nothing but bad for her. First, I left her without even a decent excuse for why I didn't want to be with her anymore and broke her heart, even though I thought I had to do that to protect her. And now, here I sat unable to do anything to save her because I didn't even know where the fuck she might be.

All I knew was that she needed me and I couldn't let her down this time.

"Oh my God! That's it! Her grandmother. That's the answer!" Nina exclaimed into the phone. "I said to her that her grandmother would have a coronary if she wasn't there to see her granddaughter walk down the aisle, but right before that we were hanging out in front of the leopard cages and Jordan said she and Brock were eloping to Hilton Head that weekend. That's it! Hilton Head!"

I looked at the phone like it was something magical I couldn't believe. "Hilton Head? Are you sure, Nina?"

"Yes! I'm sure, Gage. That's where she said they were going. Do you think that's where she could be?"

Tristan already had his office phone in his hand and was dialing a number. "We won't know if we don't try. I'm calling the pilot right now to tell him to take Gage to Hilton Head Island. Once I do that, I'll be home. Love you."

"I love you too, baby. And Gage, go get our girl back."

I practically jumped out of my chair. "I will. Thanks so much for your help, Nina. We couldn't have done it without you."

"Just go get her and bring her back so we can all sit out at the pool real soon and laugh about all this, okay? Get her away from those people and back where she belongs."

"I will."

Tristan put down the receiver and stood to walk me out. "Walker will be waiting for you at Teterboro Airport. He's filing the flight plan right now. Once you get down there, you can use the suite at The Richmont for when you find her. My security chief down there knows everything about the island, so I'll tell him to be at your disposal. Whatever you need—transportation, help locating places there—he's the one who I'll make sure takes care of you."

I stopped at his office door and put my hand out to shake his. "I can't thank you enough, Tristan. I don't know what I would have done without your help. You and Nina."

"Jordan's a good person, and I don't want to see her hurt by the likes of Brock Hannon. Plus, my wife would never forgive me if I didn't do everything I possibly could to help find her best friend, and her happiness means the world to me. Remember, call me if you need anything."

"Can you tell Daryl what's going on? He might have found out something else that could help me find her."

Tristan nodded and flashed me that confident smile of his. "I will. And don't worry. You're going to find her and she's going to be okay."

"Thanks, Tristan. I'll let you know what happens. And thanks for everything."

As I prepared to leave, my phone rang with a call from Daryl. Looking at Tristan, I showed him my cell. "Speak of the Devil."

I pressed the speakerphone button and said, "Hey, Daryl. I'm at Tristan's office. I think Brock and Monique took Jordan to Hilton Head. Why I have no idea, but I'm sure she's in danger."

"It's even worse than that, Gage," Daryl said frantically. "We were all wrong about Brock not knowing about who Monique really is. I just found out he knew his sister was dead. He paid for her funeral, for Christ's sake! Hailey or Monique or whoever the fuck she is isn't playing him. They're in this together, whatever it is!"

Daryl's news shook me to my bones. This was even worse than we'd thought. I took off like a shot toward the elevator to get to Teterboro Airport as quickly as possible. I just prayed I wasn't too late.

✧   ✧   ✧

TRISTAN'S PILOT'S VOICE CAME OVER the plane's speaker, startling me out of the nightmare that had filled my head the entire flight. Over and over, I saw Jordan being harmed by Brock and Hailey, threatened by her and forced to marry him as witnesses stood by and did nothing but watch. The terrified look in her beautiful green eyes stayed in my mind even now as I began to hear Walker explain we were almost to Hilton Head.

"Mr. Stone has arranged for a car to be waiting for you when we arrive. I expect we'll be there within ten minutes, so fasten your seat belt and prepare for landing. The weather's good, so I expect it to be a smooth one."

I nodded, silently thanking him for helping me get to this point. As I sat there alone waiting for the chance to bolt off that plane and begin searching for Jordan, I tried to remind myself of how much Tristan and Nina had gone through and how well things had turned out for them. She'd run all the way to Italy, and he'd found her. That bastard Karl had done everything in his power to hurt them, even trying to kill Tristan in the end, and still they'd come out the other side stronger and better.

If only that could happen for Jordan and me.

I had to believe I could find her, or I'd go out of my mind. I had no idea where to go once we landed at Hilton Head since I'd never been there before. What if I chose the wrong part of the island to search for her, wasting valuable time while Brock and Hailey did whatever horrible things they planned to do to her?

Sagging in my seat, I hung my head. All of this had happened because of me. Because of what I foolishly did. Back when I had a chance to be her protector—to truly be her protector—instead what did I do?

I left her. It didn't matter that I thought I was doing the right thing and that I never wanted to hurt her. I made a mistake and she did get hurt. But even worse, my choices then had set all of this into motion.

If I'd never broken up with Jordan, she never would have gotten involved with Brock Hannon. She wouldn't be in his grasp having God only knew what being done to her. And I wouldn't be getting ready to race off a plane in Hilton Head to drive like a madman to try to find her before it was too late.

Closing my eyes, I silently pledged to her I would find her in time. I wouldn't let her down again.

As the plane began its descent, a terrifying thought wormed its way into my brain, sending a chill down my spine. What if she had changed her mind? What if when she went to see Brock, he showed her the kind of life he could offer her and that desire to have the life she'd always dreamed of overpowered what she felt for me?

What if that text was how she really felt?

The sour taste of bile rose up in my throat at the mere thought that I'd lost her forever this time. I had to believe she loved me. No matter what, I had to have faith in that. Jordan hadn't changed her mind.

But that truth only lead to a more frightening one. If Jordan hadn't changed her mind, had Brock taken her by force and brought her here to marry him? The disturbing thought of him harming her settled into my brain, and as the plane touched down and began its movement toward the hanger, I leaped from my seat, ready to go find her.

It took what seemed like forever to reach the hanger, but finally the plane rolled to a slow stop and the door lowered to allow me to leave. The car Tristan had arranged for me waited nearby, and I made a dash for it to get this rescue on the road. A luxury car, it had all the bells and whistles I'd expect from him.

Inside, the keys were in the ignition and a map of Hilton Head Island sat on the passenger side seat. That's all I needed. Circled in green, Tristan's hotel was located in the Folly Field Beach area not far from the airport, and other parts of the map were outlined in red and blue, along with the main road BUS 278/William Hilton Parkway outlined in black. I looked at it unsure of where to begin, but at the very top of the page I saw a yellow sticky note that read, "Red is residential and blue is commercial."

Now I just hoped I chose the right part to search for her. But I didn't know which one to choose. My gut told me whatever Brock was up to, he hadn't brought her to a hotel. Likely, he owned a home here, so I needed to focus on the blue areas.

I headed out onto the parkway toward Burkes Beach, the

closest area of the island to me where I could find residential homes. Like a stranger in a foreign land, I felt like I didn't even have my bearings yet, but I couldn't wait to get acclimated to the area.

Jordan couldn't wait.

Burkes Beach had a mix of hotels and residences, and with each vacation home I passed, I slowed down and tried to make out if anyone who looked like Jordan stood on the porches or near a window, but I saw no one.

This was like looking for a needle in a haystack. How was I ever going to find her? Even on a small island like Hilton Head, finding her would be next to impossible.

And every moment I spent staring into strangers' homes and not seeing her was another moment she was in danger.

Or worse.

I couldn't give up. I'd done that once before with her because I thought her life would be better, and it was the biggest mistake of my life. I wouldn't give up on her again.

CHAPTER TWENTY-ONE

JORDAN

EVERYONE AROUND ME ACTED LIKE forcing a young woman to marry someone was perfectly normal, like something that happened every day in their world. Had I been transported back in time to the Middle Ages?

Brock gently held my hand, and for every time that I yanked it away, he looked down at it and said nothing, just slipping his fingers through mine once again. Over and over he repeated this until I exploded and barked, "Stop holding my hand! Stop acting like this is normal! Does no one have a problem with the fact that I don't want to marry this man?"

I looked around to see that truly no one cared. Monique just shot me an angry look, a clear threat that if I kept it up, she'd make my life a living hell and likely a very short one at that. Brock simply gave me a sad, impotent look that told me once again that he wouldn't be the one to save me from this and lowered his gaze so he didn't have to face my growing hatred for him. The witnesses behind me looked away when I turned around, a look of discomfort on both their faces as they avoided my desperate stare.

The minister seemed to be the only person around who I saw truly wasn't okay with what was happening, but before I could appeal directly to him, Monique pulled him into another room. When he returned, all I saw was a look of pure fear in his eyes.

He wouldn't be able to help me either.

My heart sank even further as he began to speak the words of the marriage ceremony. Dearly beloved? Beloved my ass! How could this be happening? And why? Why on earth was Monique so eager to see me married to her half-brother? I had nothing more than a decent job teaching third graders and a slightly better than mediocre apartment in Brooklyn, a place she equated with some kind of slum.

I had nothing, so why would Brock's marrying me be so important?

As the minister continued to recite the marriage vows, I turned to look at Brock and whispered, "Please don't do this. I don't know what's going on, but you don't have to do this. You can put a stop to this whole madness right now."

He turned to look at me and gave me a meek smile before he whimpered, "I do."

Coward.

The words coming out of the minister's mouth flowed into my ears, but all I could do was shake my head. No, I did not take this man for anything. I didn't love him enough to even help him if Gage busted in right now and kicked his ass for doing this to me.

Gage. Oh my God, if I married Brock, there would be no way Gage would ever forgive me. Why should he? What kind of person was I that I couldn't see there was something just not right about Brock and his sister? How many times had he said he didn't trust him or her, and I just brushed his worries off?

"Miss, you need to answer," the minister said softly.

He looked at me with true concern in his soft brown eyes, the bushy eyebrows above them making it almost impossible to see how much he didn't want to do what he was doing. While his eyes told the truth, everything else about him showed how terrified he was. His shoulders had risen to just below his ears, nearly touching his frizzy, grey hair, and his entire posture looked tight and fearful.

"No. I do not take this man to be my lawfully wedded husband. I'm being forced to marry this man, and even here wherever the hell I am, if this is still the United States, it's not legal to make me marry anyone."

For a long moment, the room seemed to freeze and everyone around me appeared to hold their breath. Everyone but Monique. Nothing on her froze, and as I watched, her eyes flashed the purest look of hate I'd ever seen in my life.

Then everything began to move in slow motion, and the next thing I knew she lunged at me with her hands going for my neck. Brock let go of my hand and backed away as she tightened her fingers around my throat and squeezed. I flailed my arms as her thumbs pressed into my flesh, my strength fading with each passing moment.

"You aren't going to ruin this!" she screamed as she violently shook me. "No fucking way!"

I thrashed from side to side, grasping at her forearms to escape her hold, but it was no use. No one would stop her and in just a few more seconds, I'd be strangled to death.

"You're going to kill her! We're not married yet!"

Brock's words echoed in my ears, and as my eyes closed and everything slipped away, Monique suddenly released me and I fell to the floor. Choking and gasping for air, I coughed until my chest hurt as everyone watched me lie there. I wanted to scream at the top of my lungs and demand to know what kind of people they were letting all this happen right in front of their eyes.

They had other ideas. I wasn't there for any reason other than to be Brock's bride, so even before I was finished coughing and gasping for air, he picked me up and stood me on my feet. Monique stood next to me, and when the minister repeated his question if I would take Brock as my lawfully wedded husband, the room fell silent as they all waited for me to speak.

But I couldn't speak. I could barely swallow without my throat feeling like Monique's hands were back around my neck squeezing tighter with every moment that ticked by. I opened my mouth, but no words came out. All I could do is croak noises as I tried over and over to say no.

"I think you know her answer," Monique said in a low, angry

voice. "Finish the ceremony now."

The minister gave me one more pathetic look and took a deep breath. In a shaky voice, he said, "By the power vested in me by the state of South Carolina, I know pronounce you husband and wife."

I looked at Brock in horror, realizing the awful truth written all over his face. I was married to him, and now I'd find out the terrible reason why he and Monique had drugged and kidnapped me to force me into a marriage that meant something only to them.

FORCED INTO ONE OF THE house's tiny bedrooms, I watched Monique and one of the witnesses take one last look at me before they closed the door, and then I dashed to the windows to see if I could escape. They'd been left unlocked, but one look out toward the ground below told me I'd never survive jumping the two floors and there were no eaves or ledges to hang on to on this side of the house.

I was trapped.

Sitting down on the bed, I took a deep breath and tried to keep the horrible thoughts that entered my head at bay. Would they kill me now that I'd married Brock? I still had no idea why us marrying was so important, but since neither one of them had mentioned anything besides the marriage I couldn't help but think that now that they'd gotten that taken care of I served little purpose.

But why had they wanted me to marry him in the first place?

None of it made any sense, and I was quickly becoming exhausted from thinking of it. Part of me wanted to cry, but another part of me kept telling the weepy part to shut up. That part wasn't ready to give up, even though the whole marriage thing had happened already.

That part of me had no intention of giving up and shedding any tears just yet.

The sound of the doorknob turning made my head snap to look toward the door, and I saw Brock quickly come in and close it, as if he was escaping from someone chasing him. Confused as to what he could possibly think we might have to talk about, I stood from the bed and folded my arms across my chest.

"Whatever you think you're doing here, forget it. You had your chance to do the right thing out there before that minister married us."

He didn't say a thing, but for a moment I thought I saw a look in his eyes that made me think he had plans to use this bedroom for its most romantic purpose. I backed up toward the far wall, shaking my head.

"No fucking way. Are you going to now tell me you need to have me give you a child too? Forget it. Every ounce of my being hates you, whoever you are, and I'm sure even my uterus would fight with all its strength to expel your sperm, you cowardly son of a bitch!"

Whatever that look in his eyes was, it disappeared when I told him my body would basically intentionally miscarry his child instead of doing what he wanted, and he frowned as he sat on the bed. "That's not what I'm here for."

"Oh yeah? Come to say you're sorry for forcing me into marrying you? Don't bother. I'm pretty sure whatever the hell that minister officiated out there isn't legal in any state in this country, not even this one, so as soon as I get the hell away from here, I'm going to make sure that gets erased from my life, along with you and that bitch sister of yours. If I have my way, the two of you will be living by the motto 'Three hots and a cot' for years to come."

His expression didn't change at my reference to him going to prison for all of this, though, and he just motioned for me to sit with him on the bed. "I don't have much time, so please listen, okay?"

But I wasn't about to budge from my spot next to the wall. "Listen to what? I'm not interested in any more of your excuses, so save your breath."

"Jordan, please listen. What I tell you might mean the

difference between life and death for you."

"Life and death? Oh my God! Your crazy fucking sister is planning to kill me too?"

He shook his head and then stopped. "No. Well, I don't know. Just hear what I have to say, okay? I'm trying to help here."

"Help who? Yourself? Crazy Monique?"

His shoulders sagged, and he stared at me with a look of exhaustion in his hazel eyes. "You. Now please come here because I don't know how long before someone comes in. You already know I'm not Brock Hannon, so Monique obviously isn't my sister."

His words struck me like a slap to the face. In all the commotion, I hadn't even thought about who she really was. "Not your sister? Then who the hell is she and why was it so important for me to marry you, Justin?"

A noise outside the door startled him, and terror settled into his expression. "We don't have a lot of time. I was hired by Monique to impersonate Brock Hannon, but her real name is Hailey. She took him for a shit ton of money and then he died. That's her thing. She's a grifter. Her marks are usually old men, but Brock was different. He was a recluse, so he was the perfect target. He had tons of cash and a company he basically ran from his house. Pretty successfully too, from what I understand."

I moved toward the bed and sat on the end of the mattress. "Did she kill him?"

Justin opened his mouth to speak but nothing came out. Then he shrugged. "I don't know. I just know he was dead when I came into the picture."

"What was the point of all of this? You took over this guy's life for what?"

"To marry you."

The way he said it sounded so matter of fact, like it wasn't the most bizarre grouping of words he'd ever said. More confused than ever about why, I asked, "Why would she want to commit this whole fraud to get you to marry me? I'm nobody. I have no money she can steal, so why?"

He turned to look at the door and then back at me. "Yes, you do. She didn't tell me much, but she wouldn't be out to use you if you didn't have something she wanted, and that's always money."

Closing my eyes, I tried to keep my emotions in check, but they bubbled up to the surface and I began to cry. After all that had happened, I couldn't hold the tears back anymore. Somehow, this crazy woman whose real name I didn't know had gotten me confused with someone else, and now she'd orchestrated this whole forced marriage thing and I wasn't even the right person to scam!

Justin lightly touched my shoulder and whispered, "I'm sorry. I never wanted to hurt you. All I had to do was impersonate this guy, but I really did fall for you. I know you don't care for me, and I get that, but let me try to help now, at least."

With my face buried in my hands, I sobbed, "She got the wrong person. I don't have the money you two think I have. I'm just an elementary teacher with a tiny apartment in Sunset Park. I'm nobody."

He lifted my chin so I had to look at him and shook his head. "We don't have time for this now. She's going to want you to sign something tonight. Do as she says and you might be okay. I'll do whatever I can to help you escape once you sign, okay?"

Wiping my eyes, I tried to understand what he was saying. "Sign what? What would she want me to sign? I just told you she got the wrong person. I'm just a nobody she got mixed up with the real person she wanted to scam. Why can't you get that?"

"Just do as she says, Jordan. Sign whatever she puts in front of you. Once you do that, I'll help you escape the first chance I see."

"Why am I signing anything? If she needs me to sign something so badly, then wouldn't that be my bargaining chip? Why give her what she wants?"

Justin sighed and shook his head. "She's not beyond hurting you, and nothing about this is worth being hurt or killed. You want to go back to your life as a school teacher with that guy Gage, right?

So sign the papers she puts in front of you and then run away when I can find an opening."

Nothing he was talking about made sense. "And what's in it for you? I don't get the feeling you're doing this out of the kindness of your heart, fake Brock. So if I sign, what do you get?"

"I get what I was always going to get. Money. That's why I agreed to this whole thing. Twenty grand up front and twenty more when the deal is done."

"Where is she getting the money? From the real Brock Hannon?"

"We don't have a lot of time left, Jordan. Just listen to me and do as she says. Once you sign, you get your life back and I get paid."

"And she gets what? That's my problem here, pal. That crazy bitch out there is getting something huge out of this, or she wouldn't have designed this whole scheme and ended up drugging me to get me here for our sham marriage. So what does she get?"

He hesitated a moment and then leaned in next to me. "I don't know what Hailey gets, but it's got to be a hell of a lot more than the forty grand she paid me just to marry you."

Before his words could settle into my brain, the bedroom door flew open and there stood Monique or Hailey or whoever she was in all her fucked up glory, a look of pure madness in her eyes. "Time to get some work done, kids. Justin, you better have been able to convince her because I'm not in the mood for any more delays."

I jumped up off the bed and backed up toward the wall again. "I'm not signing anything, Hailey. I don't know what you think is going on here, but you got the wrong person. Whatever you were trying to do, you failed. Your plan didn't work."

Her eyes opened wide for a second, like my bravado surprised her, and then she looked over at Justin still sitting on the bed but now cowering in front of her. "I didn't think I'd be able to trust you, but you didn't let me down. Go out into the living room and wait for us."

The words had barely left her mouth and he was bolting out

into the hallway. Pleased with something he'd done, she took two steps toward me and then stopped. "I bet you have a lot of questions, Jordan. In that way, we're quite similar. I love questions, and I love finding out the answers even more. There's nothing like piecing together a puzzle, right?"

"We're nothing alike, so don't flatter yourself. I don't know what you think you've done, but you're wrong. You made a mistake and whatever this is, I'm not the person you thought I was."

She took another step and stopped less than a foot away from me. Reaching out, she wrapped the ends of my hair around her forefinger and stared at me with the same crazy look she'd worn so often around me.

"I always wanted blond hair like yours, Jordan. Ever since I was a little girl, I wanted hair like this. But I got my mother's hair instead."

Something told me if I didn't try to speak to her now that she might go completely off the rails and try to strangle me again, so I smiled and said, "You have very beautiful hair. I'm sure your mother's was nice too."

My words seemed to calm her for the time being, and she smiled back at me. "You know, I think under different circumstances we might have been able to be good friends. I always wanted a sister, and we could have been like that."

I had no idea what to say to that. She wasn't anyone I'd ever want to spend time with, no matter what the circumstances. Even before I knew she was an out of her mind crazy woman, I didn't like her. My gut had told me something was off with this one.

As always, I should have listened to it.

My gut had also told me she had feelings for Justin too, so despite the fact that I likely shouldn't have asked, I let my curiosity get the best of me. "Are you and Justin together?"

Her smile spread across her face. "Yes, he's mine. Why?"

Trying to keep calm, I shrugged. "Just wondering. I had a feeling that you cared for him more than a sister should, even a stepsister, but I wasn't sure."

She twirled my hair around her finger again, this time tugging lightly as she said, "Yes, Justin is mine, and once we get finished here, he and I are going to ride off into the sunset. You can go back to your life with Mr. V and enjoy teaching those little kiddies their ABCs and colors and all that cute stuff you do, and everyone will be happy."

I had to stifle my urge to correct her ideas about what a third grade teacher taught. What a bitch! Instead, I just smiled and hoped Justin had told the truth because the sooner I got away from the two of them, the better my life would instantly be.

Hailey tugged me by the arm to follow her. "Time to get going, Jordan."

We got out to the living room and I saw Justin sitting on the couch waiting for us with a sheet of paper on the coffee table in front of him. He smiled meekly at me and then looked away as Hailey sat me down next to him.

"Sign on the bottom line and all this ends."

I picked up the paper and saw nothing but my name and Justin's name. No other words appeared on the page. Confused, I turned it over and saw a completely blank page on the back too.

"What is this? What am I signing?"

"Your name. That's it. All you have to do is sign your name and this ends with you returning to your little life with schoolchildren and a seedy little apartment in Brooklyn."

"But I don't know what I'm signing. I could be signing my death warrant for all I know. I could be signing a confession to a crime. I won't sign this."

Justin gently touched my arm. "Just sign it, Jordan. You aren't signing anything that will make you guilty of a crime. Sign it and be free."

I looked at him and wanted to believe what he was saying. I wanted to think that after all that time together that he wouldn't trick me into signing a paper that would hurt me in some way. But everything he'd done at this house told me I couldn't rely on him.

Shaking my head, I turned back to look up at Hailey. "No. You won't get me to sign this, unless you tell me what this is about."

I knew that wasn't she wanted to hear, but surprisingly, she didn't explode with anger. Instead, she just stood there for a moment looking at me and then said, "What you're signing will eventually be a legal document showing that you and Justin are officially married. That's it."

Was she telling the truth? I looked to my left at Justin and saw his expression hadn't changed, so maybe she had. Since I planned on getting this whole sham marriage declared null and void, what harm could come from signing her paper?

"Okay, but with one condition," I said, knowing at any moment this crazy woman might lose her mind and I might lose my life. "I get to go free without any problems from you two."

I carefully watched Justin's face for any sign that he had lied earlier when he told me he'd help me escape, but nothing in his expression told me he wouldn't. Turning to look up at Hailey, I saw her smile and nod.

"Okay."

My gut told me nothing about this was going to end the way I wanted it to, but I didn't have many choices. I could sign her paper and then hope that some slick lawyer could get me out of whatever came from it, or I could refuse to sign it and likely see just how crazy Hailey could get.

Hands shaking, I picked up the pen and felt both Justin and Hailey staring at me as I signed my name. Justin signed his name too and handed the paper to her.

Whatever it was, it was done.

"Now I can go, right?"

Hailey looked up from the paper and shook her head. From behind her back, she pulled out a gun and pointed it at my head. "I don't think so, Jordan. This is where this ends.

"You don't have to do this," I pleaded, silently praying to God to get me out of this terrible mess. "I won't say a thing. Just let me go."

Justin didn't give her a chance to answer and lunged at her, taking her down to the floor, so I grabbed the gun and with my hands shaking so hard I thought it might fall from my grasp, I pointed it at her.

"I don't want to use this, so please don't make me. I just want to leave and forget this ever happened."

Justin pinned her to the floor and looked up at me. "Get out of here! Run!"

Scared out of my mind and unsure what to do, I did as he said and dropped the gun before making a mad dash to the nearest door.

Taking the stairs by two toward the ground floor, I lost my footing and tumbled down them until I hit the last step and landed hard on my back, knocking the wind out of me. Everything in front of me appeared double and I couldn't get a full breath of air into my lungs, but I had to get to my feet and run to the main road before she made it down the stairs to get me.

It took every ounce of strength I possessed, but I grabbed onto a wooden post and pulled myself up. Barely able to stand, much less run, I still had to try and slowly I stumbled step by step toward the road.

Just as I reached the curb, I heard a gunshot from the house and turned to see Hailey running down the stairs like a madwoman. Adrenaline raced through me as I saw her hit that last stair and begin running toward me, her face the picture of rage. I had nowhere to hide and barely enough strength to walk, but I had to keep going.

A car slowly came around the bend just as I stepped onto the pavement, and then everything went dark.

CHAPTER TWENTY-TWO

GAGE

THE HEADLIGHTS SHINED ON SOMEONE stumbling into the road ahead of me, and in a flash I recognized Jordan's long blond hair as she fell to the ground in front of the car. I skidded to a hard stop and jumped out, dreading what I'd find when I reached her.

She lay on the ground, her eyes closed. Terrified she might be dead, I quickly pressed my fingertips to her neck to check her pulse as someone ran toward us in the darkness. It was faint but there, so I scooped her up in my arms and ran back to the car. As I pressed the gas pedal to the floor, I looked in the rearview mirror and saw the person running toward the car was that shopaholic bitch Monique.

I floored the gas, and Jordan slammed back against the seat as we took off down the street. Startled, she sat up frightened and confused. "What's going on?"

"It's okay. Monique was chasing us, but I left her in the dust back there. How the hell did you get away from them?" I asked as I tried to keep the car on the road at the same time as I looked to see if she was okay.

"Justin attacked her after I signed the paper and that gave me enough time to escape."

Jordan slumped against the seat and closed her eyes, so I didn't bother to ask who the hell Justin was. I just took her hand in mine and held it tightly as I drove way too fast over the island's roads toward Tristan's hotel.

As long as we reached the Richmont, we'd be safe.

Brock and Monique may have been able to do as they pleased when it was just Jordan they were dealing with, but I wasn't going to let them hurt her again.

It only took a few minutes to drive to the hotel, and true to his word, Tristan had made sure everything was taken care of. Concierge was waiting to escort us up to our room, and when we got there, a full meal waited for us. I couldn't tell if Jordan was injured and that's why she'd collapsed in front of the car or if she'd just been unable to run anymore.

She sat on the bed and looked like she'd lost her will to live. Hanging her head, she said quietly, "How did you know where to find me?"

"Nina. She remembered you saying you and Brock planned to elope down here, so I took a chance and got here as soon as I could."

Jordan looked up at me and shook her head. "Did you search the whole island? That would be like finding a needle in a haystack."

Sitting down next to her, I slipped my arm around her and pulled her close to me. "I'd hoped I wouldn't have to or I might be too late for whatever they planned to do to you. I'm just glad I picked the right part of the island to search first."

She began to cry and buried her face in my chest, sobbing, "You were too late. I'm so sorry."

What did she mean I was too late? What had they done to her? It took every ounce of strength I had inside me not to let my rage get the better of me and drive right back to that house to punish the two of them for what they'd done to her.

"It's okay. They're gone now and I'm not going to let them hurt you again, Jordan. Tomorrow we'll leave here and go someplace safe for a while."

Her crying stopped for a moment but then began again harder, as if something I'd said had upset her even more. I didn't know what had happened with Brock and Hailey, but it wasn't good.

Looking up at me, she wiped her eyes and looked away. "I'm going to take a bath."

"Okay. I'll put off calling the police until you get out."

She stood bolt upright and shook her head. "No! No police! I don't want to deal with that."

Before I could say anything else, she walked into the bathroom and closed the door. I wanted to go back to that house and beat the fuck out of Brock Hannon for doing this to her. And Hailey? I'd never wanted to hit a woman before in my life, but if she'd been standing anywhere nearby me, I would have taken a shot at her too.

I stood by the bathroom door and quietly beneath the sound of the water running into the tub I heard Jordan's crying. Thoughts of Hannon raping her and every other heinous thing I could think of passed through my mind, and all I could do was stand there because I didn't want to let her out of my sight again.

I'd made that mistake and look what had happened.

After about fifteen minutes of blaming myself, I knocked on the door unsure of what to say or if there was anything I could say to make things better. She didn't reply, so I slowly opened the door and saw her sitting hunched over in the water, her arms, shoulders, and neck showing bruises from someone's hands hurting her.

"I just wanted to see if you needed anything."

She looked up at me and pleaded, "Don't go. Please don't go."

Forcing a smile, I stepped into the bathroom and sat down beside the tub. "I'm not going anywhere. It's okay. I'm here now."

Her long blond hair hung in wet clumps down her back, and just the sight of her made me want to take her into my arms and never let go. I couldn't fight the urge to show her how much seeing her like this broke my heart, so I kissed the top of her head and whispered the only words I could think of at that moment.

"It's going to be okay, Jordan. I won't let them hurt you again."

She began to cry again, quiet sobs that echoed off the beige marble tile all around us. God, it was tearing me apart not knowing what had happened to her. I wanted to ask a hundred questions, but the last thing Jordan needed at that moment was me acting like myself.

We'd never experienced anything like this. Our time together had been fun and at the worst, passionate fighting that ended up in even more passionate lovemaking. I'd never seen her cry, and the only time I'd ever heard her cry was when I broke up with her.

God, would she never stop paying for that? Because that was the truth of the matter. If I'd never broken up with her, she wouldn't have been sitting there in that tub sobbing over what that fuck had done to her. She wouldn't be bruised and beaten.

"I'm sorry you have to see me like this. I should have listened to you when you told me you thought there was something wrong with Brock."

I'd never seen her look so defeated. Those green eyes I loved to get lost in now looked like they'd never lose the fear that had settled into them.

"You couldn't know, Jordan. He seemed like a normal guy," I said, hating how I had to practically defend him.

"His name isn't Brock, by the way. It's Justin."

Her words hung in the steamy air around us for a moment and then my brain processed them. "What? He's not Brock Hannon."

"No. He was just a guy playing him to get to me."

"I thought Monique was the one pretending to be someone else. Some Hailey girl who scams old guys out of money."

Jordan looked at me surprised. "You knew about that?"

"I just found out. I asked Daryl to check both of them out, but he only found out about Hailey by the time I realized you were gone."

Hanging her head, she covered her face with her hands. "I'm so sorry, Gage. She read me the text she sent to you. I can only imagine how much that hurt, and I'm sorry. I didn't have anything to do with it. I was drugged and she took my phone."

"Drugged?"

She lifted her head and nodded. "They put something in my water when I was at Brock's apartment telling him I couldn't marry him. She's crazy, Gage. I think she would have killed me if I didn't get away."

"What was all this about?" I asked, more confused than ever. If Brock wasn't Brock Hannon, and Monique wasn't really his sister, what was their story?

"I don't know. Nothing she said made sense. All I know is that it was paramount that he and I get married."

I gently touched her shoulder, lightly caressing the bruise forming there, and kissed the top of her head. "Well, thank God I found you in time so she didn't succeed with that part of her crazy plan."

Jordan fell silent, and as we sat there the only noise was the sound of the water gently lapping against the sides of the tub. I didn't know everything that had happened to her with them, but just seeing her so broken tore me up inside.

She turned away from me and mumbled, "Just give me a few minutes, okay?"

I stood from the tub and looked down at her bent over hugging her knees. I'd never seen her so frightened. I hated this.

"Okay. I'll be just out there if you need anything."

When she came out of the bathroom in her pink t-shirt and shorts and trying so hard to be strong in front of me, I wanted to take her into my arms and never let her go. She didn't have to pretend she wasn't shaken to the core after what had happened. The fuckers had drugged her and kidnapped her. She had every right to be coming apart.

Tugging on the bottom of her shirt, she looked down toward the floor and quietly said, "I hope you can forgive me, Gage."

Jesus, she was asking me for forgiveness when I was the one who'd messed everything up. I cradled her face and shook my head. "It's not you who needs to ask for forgiveness. It's me. If I'd never been so stupid to fall for those letters, we would have never broken up. This is all my fault."

"Oh, Gage, no! It's not your fault. We've both done things we wish we hadn't, but it's not your fault."

Jordan lay her head against my chest and hugged me tight, like she was afraid I might leave if she loosened her hold. I ran my hand over her damp hair, hating what had happened to her. To us.

If only I hadn't fucked up.

But I had to pretend to be strong for her now because she didn't need some guy with a self-loathing problem dumping his issues on her. When I got my hands on those two assholes, I'd let them deal with my shit.

I couldn't think about that, though. If I did, that would be just another thing between us, and we couldn't handle that now.

"It'll be okay. It will. I promise, Jordan."

She shook her head and sighed. "I don't understand how this could have happened. None of it was true. None of it."

Tilting her head back, I searched her eyes for answers. "What do you mean none of it was true?"

She sighed again and sat down on the bed. Hanging her head, she said quietly, "The whole thing was a set up. This Hailey person wanted me to marry Justin, who was pretending to be Brock. She had us sign a blank piece of paper and then she planned on killing me. None of it makes any sense. Why me?"

"You signed something? What was it?"

"A blank sheet of paper," she mumbled covering her face with her hands.

"Jordan, why did you sign that? You have no idea how diabolical this woman is."

She dropped her hands and stood up to glare at me. "Like I had a fucking choice! I don't know how diabolical she is? She drugged me to make me marry someone and then planned to kill me! Trust me, Gage. I fucking know!"

I wanted to apologize, to tell her I didn't mean to focus on such trivial bullshit like whatever the hell she'd signed, but she spun around and headed toward the door.

"Jordan, where are you going? I don't want you out of my sight here."

She snapped her head back and flashed me an angry look. "This is one of Tristan's hotels, Gage. I'm sure I'm safe here."

The implication that I couldn't keep her safe but Tristan could hit me like a fist to the gut, and I stepped back as my self-loathing began to take me over. I hadn't kept her safe, no matter how much I wanted to. And it was written all over her face that she didn't believe I could either.

"I didn't mean it the way you're taking it, Gage."

I shook my head and tried to act like what she'd said hadn't hurt. "Yeah. You're right. Just be careful."

Jordan turned toward the door and stopped. "I really didn't mean it the way you took it. I just don't...I don't want to fight. I just need to clear my head after everything that happened."

As the door closed behind her, all I could think of was how much I loved her and how much I wanted to find Hailey and Justin and kill them for what they'd done.

My phone ringing saved me from wallowing in my own self-loathing and I answered it to hear Daryl's gruff voice already talking. "...I found out more about our girl Hailey. Tell me you already found Jordan. This Hailey bitch is definitely not someone she should be anywhere near."

"Daryl, I know. I got Jordan away from her, but not only wasn't she who she said she was but Brock wasn't who he said he was either. He was just some guy named Justin."

"What the fuck is going on with these people?"

"Jordan says that Hailey wanted her to marry this guy named Justin. Then she had her sign some blank sheet of paper. I'm sure she's up to something pretty fucking bad."

"No doubt. Thankfully, you got your lady away from those crazy bastards before something really bad happened."

I shuddered at the thought of what could have happened if I

hadn't gotten to her in time. Daryl continued to talk about how happy he was to know Jordan was safe, but then he said, "This is all well and good, but we need to know what was behind all this. Who are these people and why did they want Jordan so badly?"

"No idea. She doesn't know either."

"You know what? Give me a minute to check something out, Gage. I've got a hunch I'd like to check out. I'll call you back in a few."

Daryl left me sitting there in the hotel room unsure about virtually everything that had happened. Not about how much I loved Jordan, though. Throughout all of this madness, that had been the only constant.

I had a second chance with her, and she needed me to be the man I promised her I'd be. And now that we were back together, it was time to make it official.

My phone rang as my mind filled with how I'd ask her to marry me. Looking at the screen, I saw it was Daryl again. Maybe his hunch hadn't panned out.

"Hey Daryl. No luck?"

More excited than I'd ever heard him, he said, "Exactly the opposite. Always trust the gut, my friend. It never steers you wrong. When you told me about the engagement party, you said you didn't think it had been planned for long, but the Royale Hotel doesn't do last minute. Not unless you have the bucks to back up your request."

"That makes sense. Hailey and this guy Justin can't have that kind of money, can they?"

"I didn't think so either, so I made a quick call to the Royale. I know one of the event planners there and asked her who paid for Brock Hannon's engagement party. Too say I'm surprised would be an understatement."

"There's someone behind this bankrolling it, sort of a mastermind?" I asked, stunned that there was more to this story.

"Not just someone. None other than Dalton Spear himself."

"Why would someone like him be involved in this?"

"I don't know yet, but you can bet I'm going to be looking into this. I'll call you as soon as I find something out."

The conversation with Daryl only made me more concerned for Jordan's safety. Knowing that Hailey and Justin had someone like Dalton Spear behind them meant their resources were practically limitless.

And people with no limits were the most dangerous kind of enemy.

CHAPTER TWENTY-THREE

JORDAN

THE HILTON HEAD RICHMONT MAY have been the safest place for me on the island, but all I wanted to do was run away and never come back. Everything I'd been through that day had a surreal feel to it, and as I walked down the hallway I struggled to get my head around the idea that anyone in the world would bother to kidnap someone like me. I was a nobody—one of millions of souls who called themselves New Yorkers and lived day to day in the greatest city on earth but no one of consequence.

Yet there I was, newly rescued from being kidnapped and forced to marry a man who'd been impersonating a millionaire just to trick me into falling for him. Christ, when the hell did my life become such a mess?

And through all of this craziness, Gage had been the man I loved, even if I hadn't wanted to admit it for all those months. Now he sat in a hotel room after saving me waiting for me to return thinking he was to blame for all of this happening to me.

I didn't mean to act like he couldn't keep me safe. The last thing I wanted to do was make him feel unloved. After all the time we'd spent apart, all I wanted was to be back with the man I loved and start over again.

The elevator doors opened and I rode down to the lobby, needing to find a phone. There were only two people in the world I could talk to, and if it couldn't be Gage, then it needed to be Nina. Without my cell phone, I had to hope the concierge would allow me to use their phone to call her.

An older woman with dark skin and long straight black hair smiled at me as I approached the counter. "Can I help you, miss?"

"My name is Jordan Wright and I'm in room—" I stopped speaking as I tried to remember our room number. "I'm sorry. I can't remember my room number. I've had a hard night. I just want to use a phone to call my friend. She's the wife of the owner of the Richmont."

I was rambling, but that was where my head was at the moment. The concierge woman looked me up and down, likely thinking I didn't belong at this kind of hotel with my t-shirt and shorts stuck to my still damp skin and my wet hair hanging in stringy clumps around my face. But instead of turning me away, she smiled again and nodded.

"Ms. Wright, we're happy to help you. Please feel free to use the phone in our office behind me. Just come around the counter and I'll let you in."

A feeling of relief washed over me and I did as she said, hurrying into the room to call Nina. I closed the door behind me so she wouldn't hear about the madness that had been my day so far and dialed the phone. Thankfully, Nina answered on the second ring, as eager to speak to me as I was to talk to her.

"Oh my God, Jordan! Tell me you're safe. Tell me Gage got you out of whatever Brock and his awful sister were doing to you."

"It's okay, Nina. I'm fine. Gage rescued me before any real damage was done. Well, not exactly before, but I'm okay now."

"What happened? Are you sure you're okay? Are you at the hotel?"

"I am. I'm just exhausted from everything that happened, and then Gage and I had an argument and I had to get out of the room for a few minutes."

"Oh honey, you sound terrible. What did you fight about?"

I didn't want to tell Nina about how I had to marry Brock and how awful I felt lying to Gage about it. Just having to think about all that made me feel sick. All I needed at that moment was to hear her say things were going to be okay.

"It's not important. I'm going to head back up there in a minute and apologize for being such an ass."

"Jordan, I'm so happy to hear your voice. I was so worried that something bad had happened. Every minute that I couldn't remember where you said you and Brock were eloping to could have been…"

Nina let her sentence drift off, and I heard the sound of her quietly crying. "Oh sweetie, don't cry. Gage and I are safe, so it's fine."

"I know. I'm being weepy again. Don't listen to me. Now that you and Gage are back together, everything's going to be okay and you'll come back here so I can give you a big hug and the kids can jump all over you and cover you in kisses."

Swallowing hard, I admitted the truth to Nina that I couldn't to the man I loved. "They forced me to marry Brock."

"What do you mean?"

"Well, he really isn't Brock Hannon. I guess I should have known that no real millionaire would ever want to marry me. His name is Justin. And Monique isn't Monique. She's Hailey and she's not his sister. I know this sounds totally fucked up and I'm probably not sounding like I'm making any sense right now, but there was a gun and they forced me to marry him. Oh God, Nina, how am going to tell Gage that?"

She remained silent, likely trying to figure out everything I'd just dumped on her or if I'd received a blow to the head. Finally, when she spoke, I heard in her voice just how bad things were.

"Honey, I know it seems like everything's gone wrong, but it's going to be okay. Good things happen to good people. You always say that. Well, you're my best friend and one of the best people I've ever met, so I can't believe things aren't going to get better."

"Jesus, Nina, if you're giving me the good things happen to good people speech, it must be really bad. He's not going to forgive me, is he? I married another man. How can I expect him to forgive me for that?"

As the tears began to roll down over my cheeks, Nina softly said, "I don't believe for a second that Gage can't forgive you for that. You said they forced you to marry Brock and there was a gun. I bet the whole marriage isn't even legal because you didn't do it of your free will."

"This is why things never work out for me, isn't it? My life is a complete fucking mess. I'll be lucky if Gage is even in the room when I get back."

"Don't talk like that. You're a wonderful person. This isn't your fault, so anyone who wants to blame you is an ass and not worth your time. But Gage isn't that kind of guy. Just tell him the truth. I bet he'll be so supportive, like he always is."

I sagged against the upholstered back of the office chair and took a deep breath in, letting it out slowly in the hope that I'd feel better. It didn't work. I still felt like shit.

"I'm so tired, Nina. It might be the drugs they gave me when they kidnapped me. I don't know. I just know I wish we were all out at your house around the pool drinking some good wine and having some good laughs. Will that ever happen again?"

"Of course it will, honey. Just don't lose faith in Gage. He's a good guy. Tell him what happened. He'll stand by you."

How could I tell the man who'd warned me over and over about Brock that I was actually married to him now? If he told me he'd married some woman instead of me, even if it was under duress, it would eat me up inside. How could I expect him to accept it any better than I would?

"I tried to tell him. I did, but I can't do that to him. I can't. I hate to lay all of this on you, but I need you to help me find a way to get me out of this marriage so Gage never finds out."

"Just tell him, Jordan. He'll understand."

"No, he won't. Please, I need your help. You and Tristan must know lawyers. I need you to find out what I have to do to get this marriage annulled or get a divorce. Whatever it takes, but I can't let Gage know."

"Okay, honey. First thing in the morning, I'll find someone. I'll talk to Tristan tonight and find someone who can fix this."

Sagging against the desk, I closed my eyes and tried to believe things would be okay. "Thanks. I owe you big."

I heard Tristan say something to Nina, and then she said in a frantic voice, "Jordan, the police contacted Tristan's security chief at the hotel. Someone was shot."

"Shot? Who?"

"His man there didn't tell him, but they're looking for you. Why would they be looking for you?"

"I held the gun, but I didn't shoot anyone. Why would they think I did that?"

Instantly, I remembered the only time in my life I'd been fingerprinted—when I applied for my teacher certification in New York. That was how they had my fingerprints on file and how they connected me to the gun.

"Just tell them the truth, Jordan. You're the victim here."

My heart slammed against my ribs as I imagined how I'd explain the bizarre story I didn't even understand myself. There was no way anyone was going to believe me.

"Nina, I need your help. I can't talk to the police about this. My fingerprints are on that gun and they're never going to believe me when I tell them what Hailey and Justin did. And even worse, if I talk to them, Gage is going to find out about the marriage. Please, I can't let that happen!"

"What do you want me to do?"

"Gage and I need to get out of here right now. I need you to get Tristan to let us use the plane again. I don't know where we can go, but I can't deal with the police now."

"Jordan, that means we have to lie to them. Tristan will have to have his security man lie about you being there in the first place."

"Please, Nina! I wouldn't ask if I didn't really need you to do this. I hate having to get you in the middle of all this mess, but please do me this favor."

The phone fell silent, but I heard mumbling in the background. As they spoke, I walked in circles in the tiny concierge office, hoping to God the police hadn't already arrived and spoken to them about me.

Nina returned to the phone and spoke quickly. "Okay, but flying isn't going to be possible since the pilot has to file a flight plan and the police will be able to find out exactly where you're going."

"Then how do we get out of here?"

I waited for Nina to answer but heard Tristan's voice instead. "Jordan, I want you to listen to me. Gage was using one of the Richmont's cars. You can use that and I'll tell my security staff there that they aren't to say a word about that vehicle until the police ask about it. But it might not take them very long. Once that happens, we'll have to find another way to get you where you're going. I'll call Gage now, so by the time you get back up to the room, he'll be ready to leave."

"Thank you so much, Tristan. I'm so sorry you and Nina got wrapped up in all this. I never meant for that to happen."

"Save the apologies for another time. You need to get out of there right now. My guy said the police are on their way."

"Okay. Tell Nina I love her and thanks again."

I hung the phone up and ran out past the concierge toward the elevators. By the time I reached the room, Gage had already spoken to Tristan and stood ready to leave. I saw the questioning in his eyes. He wanted to know why I, the victim, didn't just tell the police everything.

If only I could.

In the few seconds we had, I tried to let him know how much I loved him. Cradling his face, I looked up into his dark blue eyes and said, "If you don't want to do this, you don't have to. You never signed on for this. I know that."

Gage leaned down and kissed me on the top of my head. "What kind of knight in shining armor would I be if I let you drive away from here all alone to deal with all of this craziness?"

Resting my head on his chest for just a moment, I took a deep breath in and sighed. As long as Nina found a lawyer who could get me out of that marriage, he'd never know how truly bad this craziness was.

"We need to go, Jordan. The cops are probably already here."

I looked up at him standing there so strong and protective. "Promise me no matter what happens we'll get through this?"

Gage nodded and smiled in that crooked way I loved. "I promise. Nothing's going to separate us again."

"Okay. Then let's do this. Any idea where we can go?"

"I think it's time to go home," he said as he closed the door behind us. "What do you think of mountains and fresh air for a change?"

"I love it! But I have to be back at school in just over a week."

"We'll deal with that when the time comes. Right now, we need to get out of here or the police are going to find us."

We hurried down the hallway to the nearest stairwell. Halfway down to the main floor, Gage stopped on the landing, a look of fear crossing his face. "I left my phone in the room. If the police find it, they'll know where we're heading because I texted my family we're coming. I have to go back to get it. Wait here. I'll be back in a minute."

I took one last look at him before he tore back up the stairs and knew I couldn't let him pay for my mistakes. Now his family would be involved, and I couldn't let that happen. As the door to the hallway clicked closed, I silently told him I was sorry and began walking down to the main floor.

Where I'd go I had no idea, but this mess was mine and I wouldn't make the man I love pay, possibly with his own freedom. Gage was too good a man for that.

I opened the heavy steel door to the outside and the humid

Carolina air stopped me dead. Catching my breath, I stepped out into the summer heat and saw the flashing red lights of a police car. My heart raced as I quickly searched for a way to escape. To the rear of the hotel lay about fifty yards of grass and then marshland and to the front was the main road, but I didn't dare try to make it past the cops since they likely had a description of me and I'd be caught in a minute.

I had no choice but to head back toward the marshes.

The sidewalk around the hotel led me straight to the grass and the fence that marked the end of the property. In the distance I heard a police radio and raced toward the marshland to escape. Headlights shined on me as I tore across the lawn, and my heart sank at the thought that I'd been caught before I even had a chance.

"Jordan! Get back here!"

I recognized Gage's voice immediately and shook my head as I began to climb the metal fence. "No! Go away!"

Halfway up, I felt a hand grab my right ankle and looked down to see Gage staring up at me with a mixture of hurt and panic in his eyes.

"We have to get out of here now. Get down here!"

I tried to swat him away, but he wouldn't leave. "You need to go, Gage. I can't put you in danger too. Let me go!"

"No!"

Before I could get my footing and climb higher, he wrapped his arms around my waist and pulled me down. Throwing me over his shoulder, he marched back to the car. "Thought you'd get rid of me that easily, huh? Now stop doing stupid things so we can get the hell out of here."

He opened the passenger side door and sat me down in the seat. I wanted to tell him he didn't have to do this, but he just slammed the door and ran around the car. Sliding into the driver's seat, he pressed the gas pedal to the floor.

I regretted the hurt in his eyes when he found me and gently placed my hand on his as he drove. "I didn't want you to get hurt because of me."

As we raced out of the Richmont parking lot and hit the main road on Hilton Head Island, he turned to look at me and smiled. "I'd be more hurt being without you."

"I just couldn't bear the idea of your family being involved too. I never meant for any of this to happen, Gage."

Slowly, one of his sexy crooked smiles spread across his lips, and he turned back to face the road. "Don't worry about that. They'll love you because I love you. Fugitive from justice or not."

The way he said those words made my heart sink. I was now a fugitive from justice. How the hell had my life turned into this?

Gage slid his hand off the steering wheel and laced his fingers through mine. Looking down at where our hands met, I had to admit there wasn't another person in the world I'd feel safer with at that moment than him.

"Thank you for protecting me."

He smiled and nodded. "Always. And once we get to somewhere safe, I'm going to help you figure out what Monique and Brock or whatever the hell their names are were up to and why Dalton Spear was involved with all this."

"Dalton Spear, the billionaire?" I asked in amazement. What on earth would a billionaire like Dalton Spear have to do with petty criminals like them?

Gage brought my hand to his lips and kissed it softly. "One in the same. But for now, we need to figure out how the hell we're going to make it cross country without getting caught because now that I got you back, I'm not losing you again."

I leaned over and rested my head on his strong shoulder. My knight in shining armor. The man I'd loved since the first time he kissed me in my kitchen. The one who'd given me up to protect me.

"I love you, Gage."

As he kissed me tenderly on the top of my head and promised me everything would be alright, I wanted to believe that could be true. I knew he'd protect me with everything he was, and I'd do the same for him.

But as we drove west into the night, I had a feeling before all this was over that those two people who stood in my kitchen kissing for hours would never be the same again.

Forever With Me

Chapter One

Gage

Twenty straight hours on the road made keeping my eyes open next to impossible, but I didn't have a choice. The sooner Jordan and I made it to my parents' house in Riverton, the sooner we would be able to figure out what the hell had happened.

I looked over at her sleeping all curled up in the passenger seat next to me and reached out to lay my hand on her shoulder. Something inside me said she needed to know I was still there with her, even if she was sound asleep. Or maybe it was I needed to reassure myself she was still there with me.

When I marched into that ballroom at the Royale just a few weeks before, I'd never imagined we'd end up being on the run from the police and looking behind us every minute of the day and night like criminals. That was what we were considered, though.

I still didn't know everything that had happened back at that house on Hilton Head. Somewhere in Kentucky as we sat on the side of the road taking a break from the hours of driving, I asked Jordan about what they'd done, but she just shook her head and that frown I hated seeing on her beautiful face came back.

My hands clutched the steering wheel until my knuckles turned white as the horrible idea of what she may have endured at those bastards' hands settled into my mind. I wanted to believe—had to believe if I wanted to keep my sanity—that she hadn't been raped. Maybe that was just wishful thinking.

I didn't know why, but something told me sex played no part

in what Monique and Brock were up to. Or Hailey and Justin. Whoever the fuck they were, I didn't think they'd orchestrated kidnapping Jordan just for sex. No, whatever this whole plan of theirs was, it ran much deeper than that.

But what? I hadn't heard from Daryl since we drove out of the Richmont hotel parking lot in Hilton Head, but I prayed to God he was finding something that would explain what the hell had happened and what those two were up to.

Jordan opened her eyes and turned to give me a sleepy smile as she pressed her cheek to the back of my hand resting on her shoulder. "Where are we?"

"Nebraska."

Scrubbing the sleep from her face, she sat up and looked out the front window at the landscape all around us. Nebraska had the distinction of being the flattest place I'd ever been on earth. Miles and miles of flat seemed to be what the entire state consisted of.

Flat land. Flat road. Flat for as far as the eye could see.

None of it impressed me as being anywhere the good life existed, as the welcome sign had promised when I passed it a little over an hour ago as we entered the state.

"I've never been to Nebraska," she said as her eyes scanned the land around us. "I think I know why."

"Just wait until we get to Wyoming. You're going to love it."

I watched her mouth turn up in a tiny smile, even if it didn't make it all the way up to her eyes. Hoping to keep that good feeling around for a little bit more, I added, "It's the most beautiful place you'll ever see. Mountains, fresh air, blue skies. You're going to love it like nowhere else in the world."

As I moved back to watch the road, she said, "I'm not sure I've ever seen fresh air. I think that's more of a smell kind of thing."

Looking at her, I saw the smile hit her eyes. "Smart ass. You know what I meant."

She snuggled up next to me and slipped her arm around mine. "I know. I just wanted to tease you a little. I thought you could use it since you've been driving for all this time. I can take over, if you want. I'm pretty rested up after that nap."

"I'm good. I'm hoping to find a motel somewhere along this road. I think we've had enough sleeping in the car."

Jordan sighed sweetly. "A motel? Oh, that sounds heavenly, Gage. A real bed and a shower. I love the sound of that."

"Don't get too excited. It won't be anything as nice as the Richmont hotels."

She squeezed my arm and laughed. "I know, but it will be nice to sleep in a bed for a few hours, even if that bed has been the scene of a crime."

"Lack of sleep makes you very dark, Miss Wright," I joked, but instantly I felt her tense up next to me and I knew I'd said something wrong. As she slid her arm from around mine and sat back in the passenger seat, I wanted to ask what made her move away, but I honestly couldn't say I was ready to hear it.

So instead of asking, I simply took her hand in mine and brought it to my lips in a kiss. "I promise the next place I see that doesn't look like it's haunted I'll stop."

"Okay. Sounds good."

I knew by the way she sounded that she was forcing herself to be upbeat. Maybe it was just all the time in the car. Sleeping on the road, no matter how luxury the vehicle was, certainly would make anyone miserable.

Just about twenty minutes later I spotted the first sign for the Circle C Motel a mere five miles away. It definitely didn't sound like it would be a Richmont type hotel, but as long as it had a bed and a shower, it would be perfect.

"I think our wish is about to come true. The Circle C Motel is just a few miles away."

"Is it a ranch or something? It sounds like a place that would have horses."

I couldn't help but smile at her naiveté. "I wouldn't expect any horses. Well, maybe for the continental breakfast, but otherwise, I doubt it."

Jordan smacked my arm. "Gage! I won't be able to eat it if I think it's horsemeat! Gross!"

Turning my head, I saw her face twisted into a disgusted grimace and I couldn't help but laugh. Even like that with her nose all wrinkled up and her mouth screwed into a strange frown, she still looked adorable.

"I was just kidding. We don't eat horses out west. That's a back east thing. And I doubt anywhere called the Circle C Motel would have a continental breakfast."

"Just keep your eyes on the road and let's get to this Circle C place, western boy. Those of us from back east, as you call it, need to stretch our legs and take a nice hot shower. I don't want to show up at your parents' house smelling like I've just spent an entire day straight in a car."

Her apprehension about meeting my family came through loud and clear, but she didn't have to worry. My family would love her just like I did.

"They're going to be so thrilled to meet you that they won't care what you smell like."

"Oh my God! I do smell, don't I?"

Out of the corner of my eye, I saw her lift her arm to check if she smelled bad. "No, I didn't mean it like that. I just meant they'll be happy I brought you to meet them."

"Well, since we dated for all that time and I never met them even once, I'm wondering what they'll think now. Did they even know we dated for months?"

Jordan's question hung in the air like some kind of indictment of how much I felt for her. While it was true I hadn't introduced her to my family, it wasn't for any sinister reasons. I just hadn't. It wasn't like I was a teenage boy who lived with his parents. I hadn't lived with my family since I'd left for the Navy over a decade ago.

But I sensed she felt like there were reasons that reflected on her more than me. Taking hold of her hand, I squeezed it to reassure her.

"I think I told them, but it isn't a big deal. My family isn't like yours."

"What does that mean?" she asked innocently. "Aren't they like you?"

"Yeah, but they live all the way out here. Your parents live in the next state from you. It just never felt like the right time for us to fly out here. Don't worry, though. They're going to love you."

Just then the flickering, half-lit sign for the Circle C Motel came into view and I pointed out the front window. "We made it. Now for a bed and a hot shower."

Jordan was too excited about finally having the chance to really rest and clean up to bother with my lame excuses for never introducing her to my family. It was just as well. I didn't care what they thought of her anyway. This trip wasn't a get-to-know-my-future-wife trip. It was what it had been since we got into the car at Tristan's Hilton Head hotel.

Running away.

I STEPPED OUT OF THE dingy motel shower and stood in a towel staring at the peeling metallic silver and white wallpaper curling down from the seam next to the mirror. Christ, this place was a dive.

"How was your shower?"

Switching the light off, I walked out of the bathroom to find Jordan wearing just a towel and sprawled out across the bed. She stared up at me with a sexy look that made standing there in that crappy motel seem like I was at one of Tristan's swanky hotels.

"Wet and hot. Like a shower should be." I stopped just next to the bed and added, "And the woman I share my bed with."

Arching one perfect eyebrow, she smiled. "I see you're back to yourself again. Good. When I remember this stop on our whirlwind tour, I don't want to think about the disgusting décor or how the people in the next room very well might be ax murderers or meth addicts."

I placed my hands on the bed and leaned down so my lips just brushed hers. "I intend to make sure you won't remember any of that."

Jordan bit her lower lip and smiled. "Mmmm…I like that."

Even though everything that surrounded us was rundown, the feel of her next to me made everything inside me new again. I made quick work of her towel and took her into my arms like I'd wanted to for the last eight hours. "I promise it won't always be like this."

"Great sex between two people who are crazy mad about each other?" she asked with a grin.

"I mean us stuck in places like this."

She kissed me and shook her head. "It's not so bad. It's got something called Magic Fingers so for a quarter it says it will relax us."

Out of the corner of my eye I spied the contraption she was talking about mounted on the corner of the bed. "Well, then I guess if the bed is still working when we're done, it's Magic Fingers for both of us. For right now, I've got other ideas."

"Me too. Like getting this towel off you." She slid her fingers over my skin and unknotted the towel from around my hips. As it fell away from my body, she flashed me a devilish grin. "There. That's better. Now let's see if we can teach this bed a thing or two about magic."

Her fingernails raked down my back as I slid into her body, loving the feel of her snug cunt around my cock. Every time we made love felt like the first time, and this was no exception. There was an urgency that existed between us that had never been a part of anything I ever had with another women before Jordan.

A need that pressed down on us whenever we were together that made the rest of the world fade away. I loved that about being with her. Completely getting lost in the woman you loved was a feeling unlike anything else. For those few moments, I felt like I could take over the world because I had her. She surrendered herself and took ownership of my very soul at the same time.

The old motel bed creaked beneath us as we made love, our bodies joining our hearts as one. But I sensed something different in her eyes as we inched toward that moment of release.

"What's wrong?" I asked, unsure since leaving Hilton Head that I wanted the answer to that question.

The hardness in her eyes that had been there a moment before disappeared, replaced by the sexy look I'd expected to see. Cradling my face, she kissed my lips and whispered, "Nothing. Why?"

I stilled my movement and held myself over her. "I just felt like something was wrong. You know you can tell me anything, right? You don't have to worry about whatever it is. I'm here and I'm not going anywhere."

Sadness drifted through her green eyes for just a moment, and then it was gone and that sexy look had returned. "I never could keep anything from you, so you don't have to worry. Everything I am is right here with you."

I kissed her long and deep with everything my heart felt for her and began making love to her again. When I was buried deep inside her, all the months we were apart faded away and it was like none of the terrible things my foolishness had set in motion had ever happened.

She was my Jordan, just like she'd always been. And I was hers.

Her core squeezed my cock in the first seconds of her orgasm, and then everything we were became focused on that bed in that seedy motel on the side of Route 80 and she and I were again one in the way I'd only been with her.

Completely. Body, soul, and mind.

THE MAGIC FINGERS MACHINE RATTLED against the bed, adding another delightful dimension to the supposedly relaxing experience that had lasted for nearly fifteen minutes. Jordan giggled at the almost surreal feeling of being bounced around for that long, and I couldn't help but think this would be a memory we'd someday tell our kids about.

"This is so great!" she joked as she repositioned herself next to my side. "I need one of these for my bed back home."

Wrapping my arm around her, I felt the bed begin to calm itself as the Magic Fingers wound down. "That weird guy Floyd who lives right beneath you would love it."

"Floyd wouldn't say a thing. He doesn't complain about any noise I make."

I thought back to the one time I saw him as I left after Jordan and I had enjoyed a particularly active night and shook my head. "Not to you, but trust me. He's shown me how unhappy our sex makes him."

She blushed and buried her head in my neck. "Oh, my God! You're not kidding. My neighbors all think I'm some kind of wild slut."

Laughing at her overreaction, I smoothed my hand down over her silky hair and held her close to me. "I'm not sure wild slut was what I saw on good old Floyd's face, but he definitely knew what we'd been up to the night before."

"You're not helping," she said in a muffled voice against my skin.

She turned her head and I kissed her softly on the lips. "I think poor Floyd was just jealous that time. I don't think he's gotten any since the first Bush Jr. administration."

"My neighbors think I'm a brazen hussy. An oversexed brazen hussy. I officially can never go back there again."

And with those words everything we were dealing with came rushing back. Jordan's face clouded over with an unmistakable look of fear and she buried her head in my neck again.

"It's okay. We're going to be okay. I promise I won't let anything hurt you. You know that, right?"

She nodded but said nothing. But I needed her to truly know I was going to take care of her.

"Jordan, I'm not going anywhere without you. You're the woman I love. I'm not leaving you again, so if that's what you're worried about, don't."

Lifting her head, she let out a heavy sigh. "I'm not worried about you leaving or me leaving. That's not it at all. You're a good man, Gage. I know that. You don't have to feel like you continually have to pay penance for what you did. I know you did it to protect me."

"Then what's wrong? As long as we're together, we can handle anything."

She lowered her gaze to meet mine and gave me a look so serious for a moment I didn't know if I wanted to hear her answer. But then she spoke and my heart squeezed at her words.

"I'm just afraid of what's going to happen. The police are after me, I still don't know why all that happened with Hailey and Justin…" Her voice trailed off and she shook her head. "I'm just afraid."

Wrapping my arms around her, I held her tightly to me and pressed a kiss onto the top of her head. "I promise you don't have to be afraid from this moment on. Not of those two or the police. I'll make sure of that."

I felt her sigh against my chest and whisper she loved me, but a nagging thought in the back of my mind bothered me. I wanted to believe I could protect her from anything and anyone that would come after us. Even if it meant giving up my life for her, I would protect her.

But what if the worst danger to us being happy wasn't from outside the two of us? What if it was whatever made that look of sadness cross her face every so often when she looked at me?

CHAPTER TWO

JORDAN

THE PHONE ON THE NIGHTSTAND next to me rang for the third time, rousing me from a sound sleep. Not quite awake, I grabbed the receiver and pressed it to my ear, semi-confused about answering a phone like that since I hadn't used a rotary phone in years.

"Hello?" I mumbled, my eyes still closed. Who the hell would be calling a room at a roadside motel in the middle of the night?

"Jordan Wright?"

"Yeah. This is Jordan Wright. Who is this?"

Instantly, I felt the phone yanked from my hold and opened my eyes to see Gage slam it back down. "Jordan, get up! We need to get out of here!"

He hurriedly slipped into his jeans and grabbed his t-shirt as I tried to figure out what was wrong. "Why? What happened?"

"That call! Whoever called knows we're here because I registered under a fake name. We need to get out of here!"

Adrenaline raced through my body at the realization of what he'd said. How had they found us? And who? The police or Hailey and Justin? My heart slamming against my ribs, I quickly threw on my clothes, my fear nearly exploding out of me.

Gage held out his hand as he opened the motel room door a crack to look out into the night. "Come here. All we have to do is make it to the car. Did you recognize the voice of the person on the phone?"

I tried to remember the voice, but utter terror and the remnants of sleepiness filled my brain. "It was a man, I think. I don't know. I wasn't really awake."

He turned toward me and put his finger to his mouth to tell me to be quiet. "I'm going to take a look outside, but I don't see anyone here yet. Wait here and don't move. And don't open this door!"

Before I could protest and tell him I didn't want to stay in that seedy motel room while he possibly risked his life seeing if the coast was clear, he slipped out the door and left me alone with nothing but fear and dread.

Every terrible thing that could happen tore through my brain, making things even worse. He could get hurt out there. Or killed. Oh God! My stomach dropped at the mere thought of anything happening to him because of me. Please God, don't let that happen.

As I stood there behind the door bargaining with God to let Gage be safe and return to me, I saw headlights shine in our direction and heard tires squeal at the opposite end of the parking lot. Terrified someone had run him down, I opened the door to look out and ran into Gage.

"I told you to not open this door. You don't listen well," he grumbled as he took my hand. "We need to go. I don't know who that was who called, but whoever it was, they know you're here."

I followed him as he led me to the car, my head moving left and right to look for the person who'd called. "What was that squealing noise? It sounded like tires."

Gage let go of my hand and ran over to his side of the car. "It was. Just some kids running out on a wrecked motel room, I'd guess. Get in the car. We need to leave now."

He started the engine and tore out of the parking lot just like the kids had done a few minutes before. In seconds we were back on Route 80 driving west toward his parents' house in Wyoming, but I couldn't think that was a good plan anymore. If someone had tracked me to some dump motel in Nebraska, they certainly could find me at his family's home, and if they did I'd have put them in danger too.

I couldn't do that.

"Gage, maybe we shouldn't go to your parents' house."

He turned to look at me like I'd just said something hurtful, so I tried to explain. "What if the person who found me at that motel tracks me to your house? Your family could get hurt, and it would be all because of me. I don't want that for them or for you."

"We'll be fine, Jordan. Between my brother and my father, there's enough firepower at that house to chase away the entire Wyoming National Guard."

He said that like it was a good thing. "I don't think some gunfight at the OK Corral is something to look forward to, Gage. What about your mother and sisters?"

"They'll be fine. Don't worry. Even Lily can shoot pretty well, so don't worry."

All this talk of guns and shooting people was completely foreign to me. True, I'd lived in Brooklyn for years and experienced the crime that came with a big city, but other than seeing Gage's guns, I'd never seen one in all my time in New York.

And what kind of people were Gage's family if they kept that many guns in their home? My imagination ran away with me as I thought about a whole houseful of people toting guns as they sat down for dinner or watched TV. For a moment, all I could imagine was a family like the Hatfields or McCoys.

"I see by the look on your face you're worried. Don't be," Gage said in his most reassuring tone, his deep voice soothing some of my fears.

"Actually, I was just thinking about what your family is like with all those guns."

For the first time since we'd raced out of that motel room, Gage smiled one of those crooked grins that I loved. "It's not like they sit around with holsters and guns on their hips, Jordan. It's not like that. I know you. You're probably thinking they're mountain people with two or three teeth in each of their mouths and all wear overalls."

I couldn't stifle the giggle that bubbled up at the picture he'd painted me. I hadn't gone that far, but now that he'd described things that way, I felt a little foolish. Wyoming might not be Brooklyn or Connecticut, but it wasn't the 1800s Wild West either.

"I didn't think that. Well, not the teeth part."

Gage reached out to take my left hand in his and raised it to his lips. Giving it a tiny kiss, he looked at me and smiled. "They're just like me, so they're going to love you. As for their safety, don't worry. I'm thinking we'll only stay there for one night and then head up to the cabin we have in the mountains."

"Camping? You know I love camping. If only I wasn't on the run and could enjoy it."

"We're on the run. It's you and me, baby."

He gave me a sexy wink and kissed my hand again as the memory of my dream came rushing back to me. I hadn't had it since Gage and I had gotten back together, but now I wondered if that's what my nighttime brain was trying to tell me. That I should get back together with Gage instead of marrying Brock. That might have been what it meant, but my mother knew Gage's name, so why wouldn't she have just said Gage was outside the tent?

I was too tired to unravel the mysteries of my dreams as we tore down the interstate at nearly eighty miles an hour, so I closed my eyes and tried to push everything out of my mind, except how safe I felt next to Gage. He'd willingly jumped into this mess to stand by my side, and he was right. Now we were both on the run.

I just hoped that it wouldn't end in a hail of gunfire somewhere in Wyoming.

"Jordan, we're here. Wake up."

Opening my eyes, I tried to get my bearings and saw the car had stopped in front of a big house that reminded me of the traditional homes in the suburban Connecticut neighborhood I grew up in. Where were we?

I sat up straight in my seat and asked, "Where are we?"

With a smile, he said, "Riverton, Wyoming. My family's house."

"Oh. It doesn't look like the Wild West. It looks like back home. I thought it would look different."

Unhooking his seat belt, he smiled at my comment. "I told you they're just like me. What did you expect? A ranch with horses and livestock?"

"Nice. Make fun of the groggy girl," I said as I checked my face in the visor mirror. "No, I didn't expect a ranch with livestock. Maybe horses, but that's only because I like them. I just thought it would look different than this."

"Nope. And my family is just like everyone else, so don't worry. And stop fussing over what you look like. You're beautiful."

I pushed the visor up and turned to see him staring at me with that look of pure love he gave me sometimes. At that moment, I really needed it too. I had the face of a woman who'd spent far too much time in a car. Not exactly the way I wanted to look to meet his family for the first time.

"I look like shit, but thank you anyway."

"No, you don't, but we'll have to agree to disagree. Now hang on and I'll come around to get you."

Come around to get me? What was he talking about?

I watched in confusion as Gage walked around the front of the car and came to my side to open my door. Swinging my legs out, I stood up and as he closed the door asked, "What's this about? You haven't opened a door for me since we went skiing that time in Vermont."

He leaned down and kissed me sweetly. "First of all, we haven't been in a car together since until this trip. And second of all, every time we've had to get in or out of the car on this trip, we've been racing away from somewhere. Not a whole lot of chance for chivalry. You know why I open your car door for you, but now that I'm home, if my parents saw you get out of a car without my opening the door, I'd never hear the end of it."

That all made sense. Gage had always been a perfect gentleman in public. I guess I just hadn't remembered the kind of man he was with little things like opening doors for me.

"Well, I'll be happy to tell them you haven't forgotten your manners, except when we've had to flee from the police and two maniacs out to kill me."

Gage leaned closer and whispered in my ear, "About that. Let's go easy on the fleeing talk. I didn't tell them anything about that."

I stared up at him. "What did you tell them, Gage? If I have to lie to them, I should at least know what I'm supposed to say."

"Call it a sin of omission. I just told them you and I needed to get away so we were coming to Wyoming and wanted to see them. So not really a lie."

"For someone who says very little, you sure do know how to parse the truth. What if someone finds us here? Then what?"

He took a deep breath of fresh air and let it out slowly. "I'm hoping that won't happen. We're just going to stay here until tomorrow and then we'll head up to the mountains. If something happens, I guess we'll have to deal with it, but I hope it won't."

Laying my head on his chest, I thought about all that had happened and then realized something even more frightening was about to happen. "I don't know which is scarier—being on the lam from the law or meeting your family."

Gage tilted my head back so I looked up at him and smiled. "That motel room was definitely the scariest part of what we've dealt with so far."

"Don't joke around. This is serious. I'm a fugitive and I'm meeting your family for the first time." And then another thought popped into my head. "Do they know we broke up?"

I saw by the look on his face that they did. "I told my sister Denise. To be honest, I don't know if she told anyone else, though.

She doesn't live here like Lily and Shane."

"Well, at least there's that. Anything else you want to tell me before I walk in there?"

He thought about it a long moment and then said, "My father's just like me, so you'll have no problem with him. My mother hasn't been protective of me since I left for the Navy, so don't worry. And Denise just came out, so it's likely that will come up in conversation if she's not around since from what she told me, my parents don't know what to think about it. To say it was a surprise was an understatement. Ready?"

I wasn't ready for any of what he'd just said, but I didn't tell him that. The eager look in his eyes told me he couldn't wait to introduce me to his family, so I took his hand and a deep breath of fresh Wyoming air and hoped to God I could carry off this sin of omission he'd told them.

CHAPTER THREE

JORDAN

WE'D BARELY TAKEN TWO STEPS on the sidewalk toward the house when the front door opened and a young female came rushing at us with her arms wide open. Tall, thin, with long wavy brown hair, she looked like Gage. As she got closer, I saw she had his same dark blue eyes, except surrounded by makeup, they looked like colored contacts. Her smile beamed her happiness at seeing us, or more likely, her brother.

"Gage! I can't believe you're finally back!" she squealed.

"Lily! You're almost as tall as me! I can't believe you're all grown up now," Gage said sweetly as he enveloped her in his arms.

I stood there praying to God I wouldn't have to boldface lie to her since she clearly was happy to see us. She squealed about how much she'd been dying to see him, how she couldn't wait to tell him all about school, and something about how jealous Denise would be when she found out she'd seen him first.

And then she turned her attention to me and I received the same genuine smile she'd given her brother.

"And you must be Jordan! Gage told me he was bringing someone home."

"Jordan, this is my sister, Lily. Lily, this is Jordan."

His sister wrapped her arms around me and pulled me close. "It's so nice to meet you!" Stepping back away from me, she smiled. "Is this your first time in God's country? You look nearly shell-shocked. Not used to being surrounded by all this country, right? I understand perfectly. Gage belongs here, but you look like a city girl if I've ever seen one."

I wasn't sure if she'd insulted me, but I nodded and smiled, choosing to believe she was as good-hearted as Gage. "It's nice to meet you, Lily. It's lovely here."

"Lovely my ass. I know exactly what you're feeling. I've been feeling it all summer. I can't wait to get back to school in Denver in a few weeks. You should come to see me there if you and Gage are spending any real time here. We could have a great time!"

"Denver? Now there's a city I recognize. I'd love to see the Mile High City."

"Terrific! It's a plan. For now, there's an entire house full of Varos who are dying to see this guy after all these years. Not that they're not wanting to meet you, Jordan. They're definitely curious about you too. It's just that Gage has never brought any female home, so we didn't actually think it would happen."

"Enough, Lily. You're going to make Jordan feel even more uncomfortable than she does already," Gage said as he flashed a supportive smile at me.

He didn't have to worry, though. Lily was just wonderful, and as she hooked her arm in mine and began to lead me toward the house, I felt truly welcome. I just hoped that feeling would continue when we got inside the house and met the rest of his family.

I walked through the front door into the living room of his parents' home and saw four pairs of eyes staring at me. Not exactly the greeting I'd expected, but then again, when the oldest son and brother shows up after years away with someone in tow, it's an occasion to get together.

The male I assumed to be his brother Shane stood at the far end of the room, and I couldn't believe how much he looked like Gage. They could be twins, albeit twins separated by a few years. Dark haired with the same dark blue eyes as his brother, he even wore the same crooked smile as he studied me standing there.

A female I assumed was his sister Denise sat on the couch

directly in front of the door and stood to hug her brother hello. Pretty like her younger sister, she looked about Gage's age. I hated that the only thing I really knew about her at that moment was that she had just come out to her parents as gay. It felt so intrusive to know that about someone before meeting them.

"Big brother finally returned," she said with a smile as she backed away from hugging him. "It's about time we got to see you in the flesh again. Phone calls and texts are good, but nothing beats seeing you again, Gage."

I turned to face him and saw him beam with happiness. Being there did wonders for him, and he looked happier than I'd ever seen him before.

"It's good to be back, everyone. I'd like to introduce you to Jordan."

A chorus of voices said hi to me, and even though I felt a little overwhelmed by the welcoming party that had greeted us, I also felt safe there. Maybe it was the thought of all those guns Gage had mentioned a few hours before or maybe it was because I felt like I was in a house full of people like him, but I liked the feeling of warmth and security I found there.

And then my eyes settled on Gage's mother standing in a far doorway to what looked like a kitchen, her arms crossed and a stern look on her face. Like her children, she had dark hair and the familiar deep blue eyes, but unlike her daughters and younger son, she didn't seem as enchanted by our arrival. On the opposite side of the room Gage's father sat in a recliner with a sly smile on his face. Older looking than his wife, he had grey hair and deep wrinkles in his face that reminded me of the man who fixed the boiler at my apartment building every winter. He winked at me, making me think that even though Mrs. Varo might be a tough sell, he'd already decided he liked me.

Lily broke the brief silence by beginning the formal introductions. Pointing toward her sister first, she said, "This is Denise." Then moving around the room, she said, "Over there is

Shane and, of course, that's my mom and my dad is in the chair."

I put on my best smile and said, "It's very nice to meet you all. Thank you for welcoming me to your home."

His sisters flocked around me and began talking about how wonderful it was to finally meet someone in Gage's life. "We've waited all our adult lives to meet one of Gage's friends, Jordan. How did you meet him?" Lily asked.

I had no idea what Gage had told his family about his life, so I tried to remain as vague as possible. "We met through mutual friends."

"Are you from New York?" his sister Denise asked. "You don't sound like a New Yorker."

"No. I'm from Connecticut originally. Just a transplant to the Big Apple."

"It's nice to see everyone too after all these years," Gage said behind me.

"We can catch up with you later," Lily joked. "Jordan's new."

They peppered me with more questions about how long I'd know Gage and if New York was like it was on television and how long we planned to stay. I could easily have talked about how great New York was and how it wasn't really like it was on Sex in the City, but the questions about Gage were trickier to answer.

Thankfully, he stepped up and saved me from having to say something I shouldn't. "We're going to be here just until tomorrow when we head for the cabin. It was a long trip, so we'd like to get a bite to eat."

He walked toward the kitchen and stopped in front of his mother. "Hi, Mom. It's good to see you again."

As if the clouds covering her expression cleared, she smiled and took him in her arms. "I missed you, son. I'm so glad to have you home, even if it's just for a day."

Gage turned toward his father and stuck out his hand. "Dad, it's good to see you're still holding up after all this time with so many women."

His father smiled and shook his hand, chuckling as he said, "I must have a guardian angel watching over me or I don't think I would have lasted this long with all these women. But Shane I have gotten used to being outnumbered. It's good to have you home, son."

Escaping his sisters, I walked toward Gage's mother and extended my hand to shake hers. "It's very nice to meet you. Thank you for letting me stay here."

She seemed to study me for a moment, her eyes trailing down my body and then back up to my face. For a moment I wished I'd worn something nicer and didn't look like I'd been on the road for nearly twenty-four hours straight, but then her thin mouth spread into a smile and whatever fears I had about her seeing something she disliked faded away.

"It's lovely to meet you, Jordan. My son doesn't bring just anyone home. Well, he's never brought anyone home, so you must be special."

Her words carried a solemnity to them that impressed me. I'd naturally assumed Gage had brought Angela home to meet his family, and as I stood there thanking his mother for her hospitality, I saw in her expression that my being the first girlfriend Gage had wanted his family to meet meant something to her.

If only I wasn't standing there living out that sin of omission.

"Thank you, Mrs. Varo."

Rolling her eyes, she said, "Please call me Sandy. Mrs. Varo is so very formal, and we're not that way in this house."

From behind me, Lily said in a singsong voice, "Ooooh, Sandy. She must like you, Jordan. It's not everyone who gets to call her by her first name."

Before I could say anything, Gage came up behind me and took my hand in his. "Now that you've all gotten to meet Jordan, I'm going to take her upstairs and show her where we'll be sleeping."

The room fell silent, and the look on his mother's face morphed into something that was a cross between angry, confused, and embarrassed. For a moment, I thought about saying I could sleep on the couch or in the car or anywhere not right next to her baby boy, but instead I remained silent as the awkward moment passed.

"Your room is just like you left it when you went away to the Navy," she said quietly.

"I'll grab some blankets from the hall closet since it's only a twin and I'll have to sleep on the floor."

As if his announcement that he'd be sleeping somewhere other than right next to me made the clouds lift away, his mother's expression returned to that sweet one she'd given me a minute before. "Lunch will be ready in a little bit, so rest up. I've made a big meal to celebrate. I hope you like ham, Jordan."

"I love it," I answered truthfully, instantly dying to taste the home-cooked meal I caught a whiff of coming from the kitchen.

CLOSING THE DOOR BEHIND US, he followed me into his bedroom. It looked like it must have when he last slept there with posters of trucks and the Denver Broncos covering the walls. I'd never thought about who Gage was before I met him, but his room made me imagine as a teenager and I couldn't help but smile.

"That wasn't too bad. I told you they'd love you."

I sat down on the bed and looked up at the poster of some very busty cheerleader hanging from the ceiling. "Nice décor."

He chuckled and sat down next to me. "I was a red-blooded American teenage boy the last time I slept here."

Looking at him, I couldn't disagree with his assessment of himself. Gage was a true red-blooded American male. "I'm not sure I can sleep with her and those giant ta-tas hovering over me," I joked.

"You can sleep on top of me then. Problem solved."

"But you told your mother you'd be sleeping on the floor."

Shrugging, he explained what I already knew. "My mother is

old-fashioned. You saw her face when she thought we would be sleeping together. A little white lie about where I'll be tonight was necessary."

"More lies," I mumbled as I looked around at where he'd spent his teenage years.

"I think my mother would handle you being chased by crazy people and wanted by the police better than the two of us sleeping together here, to be honest. It's crazy, but that's how she is."

"You're her little boy, Gage. No mother likes to think of her son sleeping with a woman. No matter how old you are, you're her boy."

Gage grinned like the cat that just ate the canary and pulled me into his arms. "Well, her little boy has every intention of sleeping with you tonight."

"You don't think that's a little weird? I mean, your whole family will be right nearby."

"I'm a grown man here with the woman I love. I'm not a boy anymore, no matter what my mother thinks."

LOOKING UP AT THE POSTER over our heads, I smiled. "Tell Miss D Cups there. She didn't get the memo."

Gage kissed up my neck until his mouth met mine. "I'll take her down. She had a good run, but she's been kicked off the team. There's a new girl in town."

As I kissed him there in his old room where he'd grown up, I couldn't help but smile at the thought of a teenaged Gage. Leaning back on his bed, I asked, "So this was your room when you were a boy?"

Nodding, he smiled. "Yeah. As the oldest boy, I was the only one who got a room to myself. I swear even my father was jealous."

"Do all your siblings still live here? I mean, other than Lily, who's at school."

"No. Shane does, but Denise has a place of her own."

"They must care a lot about you if they all gathered here to see you today."

Gage shrugged. "I think it might have been more curiosity than anything else. They haven't seen me in years, and when I told Lily I was bringing a woman with me, it was too intriguing not to drop everything and come here to see."

"They're really nice people, Gage. You have a nice family."

"Thanks. I wish you were meeting them under different circumstances, but next time we come to visit we won't be on the run."

I took a deep breath and let it out slowly. "That's what we are, aren't we? On the run."

"I think that's the only way to describe it."

"Like Bonnie and Clyde," I said, trying to find something amusing in the reality of our situation.

Gage leaned over me and pressed his lips to mine. "Yeah, except we didn't hold up any banks. So not really."

For a moment, I couldn't help but worry about what would happen to us. Would the police arrest me when they finally found us? Would they arrest both of us? Closing my eyes, I asked him the question that had sat in the back of my mind since we left the Richmont in Hilton Head.

"What's going to happen, Gage?"

I opened my eyes to see his dark blue eyes full of love staring at me. "I told you not to worry. I won't let anyone or anything hurt you. I promise."

"That might be a hard promise to keep."

"Doesn't mean I won't."

He lay down beside me on that tiny twin bed and took me into his arms, and I believed what he said about protecting me. He was my knight in shining armor, after all.

GAGE'S FAMILY GATHERED AROUND THEIR kitchen table, making

feel like I was being surrounded. They didn't mean any harm, and I was the visitor there, but every time one of his sisters looked at me, I had the feeling they were dying to ask me a million questions I definitely didn't want to answer. I hated doing the whole sin of omission thing with people who had been nothing but truly kind to me.

His mother seemed to be disinterested, thankfully. And his father didn't appear to even notice me there three seats away. For that alone, I liked him. He reminded me of my own father, which made me like him even more.

Gage sat next to me, but although I knew he was only trying to help protect me, sitting there just made everyone look in our direction. Each family member passed around dishes of corn and peas to start the meal, making small talk about the weather and how Lily would be heading off to school soon, but they never took their eyes off us. If I didn't feel like I stuck out like a sore thumb, it would have been a very cozy place to be.

As I enjoyed the fluffiest and most buttery mashed potatoes I'd ever tasted, at the opposite end of the table Lily handed her father the salt and casually asked, "So is Jordan going to be the newest member of the family? She fits in, don't you think?"

I nearly choked on my food as the table erupted into outraged women scolding poor Lily and her attempting to defend herself as merely curious.

"Lily, that's no way to treat our guest," Gage's mother chastised. Looking down from the head of the table, she smiled sweetly at me and said, "I'm sorry, Jordan. Gage's sisters and brother are dying to know what their brother has been up to for the last few years. That doesn't mean they should put either of you on the spot, though."

I forced a smile and nodded, unsure what to say as I stared down at the peas I was busy arranging into a design on my plate. Gage took a deep breath in. "For the record, yes, Jordan and I are together."

Unsure what he had tried to set straight by stating the obvious, I looked at him and silently begged for some relief. He just smiled, like this was all perfectly normal, and squeezed my hand under the table.

Everyone lowered their heads to stare at the meal on their own plates. Talk about tension at the dinner table. I would have given anything for some good ole' sibling rivalry to rear its ugly head at that moment.

"So what do you do in New York, Jordan?" Gage's father asked, breaking the awkward silence as he took the platter of ham from Denise.

Clearing my throat, I quietly said, "I'm an elementary teacher at a private school, Mr. Varo."

"Very nice," he mumbled as everyone waited for our conversation to continue. When it didn't, the disappointment in Gage's sisters' faces was palpable. I was relieved. I enjoyed talking about my work, but I'd never felt so on display in my life.

For another five minutes, we all sat in silence eating our ham lunch until Denise looked over at Gage from across the table and asked, "How long do you plan on staying?"

Her question sounded staged, as if she knew the answer already because she and Gage had discussed it.

"We're staying here tonight, and tomorrow we'll be heading up to the cabin."

Everyone looked over toward Gage's mother for her reaction to us staying at the cabin together, but she didn't flinch. Without missing a beat and in a voice that made it seem like none of the meal had been awkward, Gage's father said, "Shane and I cleaned it out earlier this summer, so you should find it pretty comfortable, Jordan. Just remember to stop for food before you head up there, Gage."

And that was that. For the rest of the meal, they all talked about local happenings and who was doing what in the neighborhood in an attempt to bring Gage up to speed, and he politely nodded and smiled with each piece of gossip, although I could see he didn't care. He was still a Varo, but he'd left that teenage boy from Riverton behind when he headed off to the Navy all those years ago.

CHAPTER FOUR

GAGE

JORDAN CLOSED MY BEDROOM DOOR behind her and saw I was already in bed—the bed she was supposed to sleep in while I stayed on the floor. With a smile, she asked, "And if your mother comes in at some point in the night?"

I leaned back on the pillow and put my hands behind my head. "My mother hasn't come into my room unannounced since I was twelve. She knew better."

Rolling her eyes, Jordan walked toward the bed and stopped to look down at me lying naked under the covers. "I'm not going to ask why since I don't want the vision of a teenaged Gage doing God knows what in this bed haunting me for the rest of my life."

"Boys will be boys," I teased as I lifted up the blanket to let her slide in next to me.

Once she got settled, she looked up at me and for a moment I sensed something was wrong. A look I couldn't place crossed those beautiful green eyes, casting a dark haze over them.

"Talk to me, Jordan. What's wrong?"

"I didn't like lying to your family today. I know what you're going to say. They don't need to know, but I still didn't like feeling like I was lying to them. They're good people, Gage. It just felt wrong."

Gently, I touched her cheek and kissed her like I'd wanted to for hours. "They don't need to know that you were misused by those people."

"What if the police come in the middle of the night and bust down the door to get us?"

I tried to stop my smile, but it was no use. "You've seen too much TV. They don't just bust down the door, especially if you open it for them. Also, they have to show a search warrant to come into your house without your permission and a warrant for someone's arrest to take them."

"What if they get those things? Then what?"

"They won't, at least not while we're here. Tristan texted me this afternoon to tell me that the Hilton Head police consider the missing car from the Richmont as a theft, but as of now, they aren't connecting that to me. They don't even know I'm part of this, so there's no reason any police would come here looking for you."

Jordan buried her face in the pillow. "I just want this to be over. Is that too much to ask?"

Pulling her next to me, I tried to make her feel better. "It'll be okay. I promise. When we get to the cabin, we're going to start figuring out what Hailey and Justin's game was and how Dalton Spear figures into it. I've had Daryl looking into it the whole time we were driving here, so he might know something by the time we get up there tomorrow. Then we'll find out what was going on, clear your name, and live happily ever after."

She lifted her head and that same look crossed her face again. Was it fear or sadness? I couldn't tell, and I didn't want to push her to tell me what had happened in Hilton Head. When she was ready, she'd tell me.

In the meantime, it was my job to take her mind off whatever was bothering her, and at that moment, I knew exactly what to do.

I kissed her long and deep, my tongue sliding into her mouth to tease hers with a preview of what I wanted to do to her. She responded with a level of passion I hadn't expected, and leaning back, I looked at her in surprise.

"I figured I'd have to convince you a little more than that."

"You said your mother isn't coming in, right?"

"Right."

Jordan spread her legs and sat up on me. "Well, then I don't see why we shouldn't make love. I'll just have to make sure I don't yell out and alert the whole house to what we're doing in here."

I slid my hands down her sides to rest them on her hips and looked up at the gorgeous woman staring down at me with a look of desire. She never failed to thrill me.

"You're not really a yeller," I said as I nuzzled her neck. "So I don't think we have to worry."

"I know, but you never can tell when it could happen," she said in a faraway voice as I pushed my cock over her already wet pussy. "Like right now, I feel like I want to moan because of what you just did there."

Grabbing her ass, I squeezed as I moved her just enough to give my cock easy access. "Moan away. If anyone hears, I'll just tell them I was doing what I used to do with Miss D Cups."

Jordan stopped the incredible thing she was doing by rolling her hips and sat up straight on top of me. "Not cool. I'm right here and you'd let someone think you were jerking off to that silicone thing above us?"

Her expression told me she wasn't truly angry with me, but I had succeeded in killing the mood. Reaching up to cradle her face, I smiled my best "I'm sorry" grin.

"Just kidding. Of course I'd tell them that we were having sex."

"You're hopeless. Remind me, why do I love you again?" she asked as she rolled her eyes at my joke.

"Because of all my great qualities and because I can do that thing when we fuck that makes your eyes roll back into your head."

She wrinkled her nose and shrugged. "Oh. Well, I guess it isn't every day that a girl can find a hot guy with a great body who makes her happy and can do that thing."

"You make it sound like you only love me for my looks and what Mr. Willie can do. I want to be loved for my brains too," I joked, eliciting a sweet smile from her.

"The fact that you just called your penis Mr. Willie has officially made it impossible to have sex here in your old room. I think you very well might have to resort to giving him a few tugs to D Cups up there."

I ran my hands over her silky soft skin until my thumbs touched her still wet pussy and began rubbing her clit. "It seems like a real waste of Mr. Willie's time to get him all up and ready and then have nothing happen."

Jordan leaned down to kiss me, her blond hair draping over us, and then smiled against my lips. "I swear to God, Gage Varo, if you call your cock that name one more time I won't be able to sleep with you ever again. Now put your cock inside me and no more talking."

"I do love a woman who knows what she wants."

"Good, because what I want is you to fuck me and make me want to scream, even though I can't and I'm still sort of afraid everyone will know what we're doing. Think you're up to it?"

One thrust and I was buried balls deep inside her, loving the feel of her cunt hugging my cock like a glove. "Yeah, I'm up for the job."

She moaned in my ear, and I began fucking her in earnest. I didn't care who heard us or what they thought. There was nothing wrong with a man making love to the woman he was crazy in love with, even in the bedroom he grew up in.

As always, Jordan's body thrilled me like no other woman's ever had. The way she moved in rhythm with my thrusts into her ratcheted up my need for her. She knew just how to make me want her more than even I understood.

And then she whispered in my ear, "Take me from behind."

I didn't need to be told twice to fuck her that way and slid her off me so I could stand on the side of the bed. She rose up on her hands and knees and positioned herself in front of me. Turning her head to look at me, she flashed me a wicked grin.

"Is your bed squeaky?"

Grabbing her hips, I slid into her wet cunt and didn't care what noise the bed made. That's what being with Jordan was like—making love to her made the rest of the world fade away and become insignificant. I didn't care about my family one floor down, the cops who were looking for us, or the two crazy fucks who had tried to take her away from me.

All I cared about was being inside her and making her feel as good as she made me.

With each pump of my cock into her, she bucked back toward me, her body begging for more, and I gave it to her. Lowering her head, she tilted her ass even higher and gave me the angle that would bring both of us to that delicious edge of release.

My hands gripped her hips and squeezed hard as I pistoned into her. With each thrust, she moaned into the blanket, crushing it into her palms as she got closer to coming. I felt her body begin to surrender and stuffed my hand into her hair.

Tugging hard, I leaned forward and moaned into her ear, "Come for me."

Jordan spread her legs wide and arched her back as her release raced through her. My body reacted to her cunt squeezing my cock as she came, and with one last thrust into her, I came just as her thighs began to quiver and buried myself inside her.

When there was nothing left in me, I closed my eyes and slid out of her body to lay down as she rolled over to face me. Her expression still covered in the haze of great sex, she stared into my eyes with those beautiful green eyes of hers and whispered, "I'm pretty sure everyone in this house knows what we just did."

"I don't care." Taking her in my arms, I whispered in her ear, "I love you and part of that is making you come until your legs give out."

Giggling, she said, "Well, I'd say you achieved that just fine. My legs are still shaking."

"Then my job is done here."

With a smile, she asked, "Who are you? Superman?"

"I don't recall Superman using that catch phrase, Miss Wright. You need to work on your superhero knowledge."

The happiness disappeared from her face, and she pressed her head to my chest. "Promise me everything will be okay, no matter what. Can you promise me that?"

I kissed her hair and pressed my cheek to the top of her head. Something was wrong, and I doubted it was anything about Superman or his superhero friends. But I knew Jordan and asking wouldn't get me anywhere until she was ready to tell me what had happened.

"I promise. Someday in the future we're going to laugh about this part of our life together."

She squeezed me gently in her hold as if to tell me she believed what I'd said. In the morning when we traveled up to the cabin, we'd start to dig up the answers to why Hailey had Justin kidnap her and what they'd wanted from Jordan. Once we had those, we could leave those two in the past and begin our future together.

A future that included me asking her to be my wife.

BEING BACK HOME BROUGHT BACK memories of who I'd been when I lived there, including waking up at the crack of dawn when my father got up every day. He'd retired two years ago, but still he rolled out of bed each morning at five AM and began his day just as he had six days a week for forty years. I heard him as he walked down the creaky stairs and slid out of bed to throw on my jeans, leaving Jordan sound asleep under the covers.

My father had never been one for talking much, so I didn't expect a full conversation when I joined him in the kitchen as he stood next to the coffee maker waiting for his first cup of the day to brew. Fully dressed and ready to greet the day, he smiled at my barely clothed look.

"Is the house on fire?" he asked.

I looked down at my jeans and zipped them. "No. I just heard you go down the stairs and thought I'd join you."

Pointing at the coffee maker, he asked, "Want some?"

I nodded and walked over to the cabinet to grab a mug. "Yeah, I could use some caffeine this morning."

He flashed me another smile, and for a moment an odd sense of embarrassment rushed over me. I had no idea why. My father wasn't like my mother. My sleeping with Jordan while he was a few rooms away likely hadn't fazed him in the least. Hell, it probably wouldn't have bothered him if he had been in the same room with us. Less concerned with propriety and things like that, he was a man who accepted life as it was. That two adults would have sex in his house wouldn't be something he'd fixate on at all.

But I still felt strangely awkward around him this morning.

"How's life in New York?" he asked, his suntanned and deeply wrinkled face twisting into a grimace at even the mention of the city.

I leaned against the counter and answered truthfully. "Not bad. I'm making a good living. I have a nice life there."

"Good. That's good. That's where you met Jordan, right?"

"Yeah. Well, not really, to be honest. I met her when I was working out in upstate New York, but she's from the city."

"She looks like the city."

"Yeah?"

A genuine smile brightened his face, and he nodded. "Yeah. There's nothing simple about that woman, but I'm guessing that's what you love about her."

Jordan simple? No way. He was right. There was nothing simple about Jordan, not even on the easiest day.

"She's not that different from us," I said in her defense, feeling like I wanted to explain who she was but not sure how to.

The smell of freshly brewed coffee filled the air around us as the coffee maker completed its job, and my father poured each of us a cup. Pushing the sugar bowl toward me, he said, "I didn't mean to say there's anything wrong with her. She's beautiful, smart, and unless I've totally lost all ability to read people, good-hearted. Nothing wrong with that combination."

He grabbed the milk from the refrigerator and we both fixed our coffee as we liked it before he sat down at the kitchen table. Extending his arm, he invited me to join him, which told me he had something on his mind.

"Heading up to the cabin this morning?"

Knowing my father already had the answer to his question, I guessed that's what he wanted to talk about. "Yeah. I wanted Jordan to see the mountains before we head back."

He took a big gulp of hot coffee and let his roll down his throat. "Your mother thinks you're embarrassed of us because you're only staying one night here."

That my father had chosen to explain that told me he'd been up late listening to my mother worry that her own son didn't want to spend time with them. And as my mother always had, she fell back on her fear that she wasn't enough.

That wasn't the truth, and I didn't like either of my parents thinking we were leaving so soon because of them. So even though I wasn't sure I should, I told my father what I could of the truth.

"It's not that, Dad. We're just dealing with something I don't want to touch you and Mom. Jordan likes you all and I'm sure she wishes we could stay longer. We just can't."

"Dealing with something, huh? That doesn't sound good."

I saw by the sympathetic look in his eyes that he'd misunderstood and thought we were having romantic troubles. As easy as it would have been to let him just think that, I wanted to explain more, if only to assure him Jordan and I were fine.

"She got into some trouble, not of her own doing, and now we have to figure out how to get her out of it."

I'd never been more cryptic in my life. All those words to say very little. My father seemed to understand my reluctance to lay the whole truth on the table and nodded his understanding, whatever there was of it.

"Law involved?" he asked in that rugged way I remembered from when I got into trouble as a kid.

"Yeah, but she did nothing wrong, Dad. I don't want you to think she's to blame. If anyone's to blame, it's me. If I'd never..."

I didn't bother to finish my sentence and took a sip of my coffee instead. I couldn't change the past or the mistakes I'd made. All I could do was everything possible to make sure I didn't make them again and that the future was different.

"You'll make sure she's taken care of. We brought you up right, and even though you've been gone for a long time, I saw yesterday when you got out of the car that you hadn't forgotten all we taught you."

"I will, Dad. I told her you'd never let me hear the end of it if you saw her get out of the car and me not open the door for her," I said with a smile. "She's got a streak of independence in her a mile wide, though."

He took another gulp of coffee and nodded. "I saw that the minute she walked through the door, but don't let that change who you are. She may not think she needs a strong man around, but you have to show her differently."

There was my father, the old-fashioned man who'd never seen any reason to change, no matter what the rest of the world said men should be.

"She's tough, Dad. She can handle herself."

"The point is she doesn't have to with someone like you around. It's okay for her to be tough. Women have to be tough. Childbirth alone shows how tough they can be. But it's our job to make sure they don't have to be all the time."

I couldn't help but smile. It wasn't so much that my father saw men and women as unequal. It was more that he saw them having different strengths with neither sex being better in his mind. That he was totally out of step with the rest of the world didn't even occur to him, and I liked that about my father. My sisters thought of him as some relic from a bygone time best forgotten, but in his own way, he had a heroism in him I was proud of.

"I know, Dad. I haven't forgotten what I learned from you."

"Good, because if that little girl's in trouble, she's going to need you to be there for her."

"I'm not going anywhere, so she's stuck with me," I joked.

My father's expression turned serious. "Don't shortchange yourself, Gage. You're a good man. She's as lucky to have you as you are to have someone like her. You may not be some born and bred city boy, but you have things a person can only get from being brought up away from all that. Those are important, so don't forget that."

"I know, Dad. She does too. Maybe we make a strange couple, but we work, so that's all that matters."

He nodded, even though I wasn't sure I'd convinced him, and for a few minutes we sat there at the kitchen table in silence. I finished my coffee and moved to get up, but he grabbed my arm as I stood and I saw concern in his dark eyes as he looked up at me.

"You remember where I keep my guns at the cabin, right? Make sure you take the key so you can open the cabinet. Can never be too safe."

"I have my 9mm, but it's always good to have some backup."

My father let out a deep belly laugh. "Backup my ass. That gun of yours is nothing compared to what I have up there, so if you get into a jam, make sure you have the key."

"Okay, Dad. I will."

His hand slid off my wrist when I moved to leave, and as I began to climb the stairs, he said, "Next time you two come out here, your mother hopes you'll be married. Just thought I'd give you fair warning."

I stopped and turned to look at him smiling at me. "Tell her I'll see what I can do about that."

CHAPTER FIVE

JORDAN

I HEARD GAGE BASICALLY TELL his father he intended on asking me to marry him and lay frozen in place in his bed. He couldn't ask me to marry him. If he did and I was still married to Justin, I would have to say no, and that's the last thing I wanted to do. It would break his heart hearing me shoot him down like that.

God, this whole thing was a mess. This was why I hated lying. No matter how well I ever thought I did at it, every lie I'd ever told always blew up in my face. I should have just told him the truth when I had the chance, but I never wanted him to think he'd be my second husband.

Not that the whole marriage to Justin would ever be considered legal. Talk about a shotgun wedding. All I needed was a little more time for Nina to get her lawyers in gear and figure out how to make that whole Justin nightmare go away.

The door opened and Gage stepped into the room wearing only his jeans. They hung low on his hips, making him look even sexier than usual. He looked down at me sprawled out across the bed and smiled one of those crooked smiles I loved.

"Any room in there for me?"

"You look like you're up and ready for the day," I said without moving to make space for him. "I should get up too. We need to head out."

Gage crouched down next to the bed so his face was close to mine and kissed me softly on the lips. "I know you feel uncomfortable about my family, but you don't have to. They love you."

"I'm not sure your mother and Denise still feel that way after last night. I got the vibe from them yesterday that they're not really into seeing you as an adult."

"Nonsense. They love you like I do," he said as he tucked my hair behind my ear. "Because you're sweet and kind and beautiful."

Damn, he was so good to me. How was I ever going to say no to him if he asked me to marry him before Nina's lawyers fixed my problem?

"You're going to make me blush if you keep talking like that. Let me up so I can get ready. We don't want to wake anyone else up. I know your father is downstairs already."

I stood from the bed and stepped around Gage, who took my spot on the bed. Lying back, he clasped his hands behind his head and watched me dress.

"Do you like it here?"

Thinking about it for a moment, I nodded as I slipped my jeans on. "Yeah. It's nice here. Lots of fresh air. It reminds me of all the times I went camping with my father when I was a kid. It smells a lot like that. I bet that sounds weird, but that's what it reminds me of."

"Not weird at all. It's the fresh air here. It gets into your lungs and makes everything new again. I told Daryl you'd like it here. He thinks you're too much a city girl for this place."

"Daryl thinks he knows me now? Well, you can tell that crazy mountain man-looking creature that I love the wide open spaces here."

"I told him that. He thought I was crazy when I said that maybe we'd spend some time here. You know, more than just a day or so."

As I wriggled into my t-shirt, I realized what Gage was saying. He'd said something to Daryl about us getting married out here. Oh God! If I didn't stop him, he'd do something incredibly sexy or cute and propose right there in just his jeans that made me focus on his muscular abs and under that giant breasted woman I oddly enough didn't dislike so much after a night sleeping under her.

Pointing toward the hallway, I stammered out, "I...I think...I heard a noise or something, so I'm going to go to the bathroom now before everyone gets up. Lily said she put out a toothbrush for each of us, so I'm going to use that. I'll just be a minute or so and then we can go, okay? Okay. I'll be right back."

Before he had the chance to ask me what was wrong or worse, if I'd marry him, I bolted out into the hallway and raced toward the bathroom to give myself a moment to think. I had to come up with a way to avoid these kinds of conversations with him until Nina let me know her lawyers had a plan to get me out of that awful and undoubtedly illegal marriage to Justin.

I opened the bathroom door and ran headlong into Shane, who looked like Gage's younger twin even first thing in the morning. Wide awake after a shower, he stood there wearing only a towel that hung low on his hips exactly like his brother's jeans. Flustered to find anyone in the one room I hoped to hide out in to get my head together, I stood there staring at him and wishing I hadn't laid around in that twin bed for so long.

"I'm so sorry. I didn't mean to barge in on you in a towel. I mean right after a shower," I blurted out.

Shane smiled and shook his head. "It's okay. I've lived with Lily for practically my entire life. She never lets me have the bathroom to myself. Twenty-two years of living with her means I'm never surprised when the door flies open. I'm just glad I got the towel on before you got to see all of me."

Heat rushed up into my cheeks as I blushed at the thought of seeing even more of Shane than I already had in front of me. Built just like Gage, he had muscles everywhere and a set of abs that could be used to wash clothes. But unlike his brother, Shane clearly knew how hot he was, and I saw in his dark blue eyes he was enjoying this moment.

Looking away, I smiled at his cockiness. I bet lots of local girls in Riverton had their eyes on Shane Varo. "I'm just really sorry. I didn't think anyone else would be awake yet."

As he brushed by me, he said with a grin, "No problem. Feel free to bust in on me anytime."

I closed the door behind me and had to chuckle. The younger Varo brother was just as sexy as the older one, and I imagined Gage at that age just as cocky and just as hot, and for a moment my life didn't feel like it was crashing down around me.

But seconds later, the reality that the very sexy man who waited for me in his teenage bedroom had marriage on his mind came rushing back and whatever amusement at the charm I imagined him having at Shane's age was replaced with my horror of having to tell him no if he asked me to marry him anytime soon.

How was I going to avoid saying no to the man I wanted to spend the rest of my life with?

CHAPTER SIX

GAGE

JORDAN SMILED SWEETLY AT ME as she set her bags down at the edge of the bed. "I'm going to wander about for a bit, you know, explore the cabin. Is that okay?"

"Of course, mi casa es su casa," I said happily.

Things were a mess but for the briefest moment it was just the two of us in the cabin I'd made so many happy memories in. Flashes of me playing with my sisters and Shane while Dad worked on yet another project outside filled me with a sense of calm. I could even still distinctly see the spot on the brown rug in the dining room where Shane had spilled grape juice and thought hiding it for weeks while the stain set was the best plan.

It made me happy to see that the rug was still there, despite the deep purple mark that remained. Sometimes it was important to keep things like that, despite their flaws. My mother had seen red when she finally found it, and the chewing out Shane had gotten was legendary and still brought up when she was angry with him about something.

"Oh, speaking Spanish now are we?" she said flirtatiously, winking at me.

"If it makes you smile and maybe consider checking out the shower with me, sure am," I said as I looked her over. It may have been a joke but if she was going to say yes, I was all on board.

She rolled her eyes playfully, but I could see there was the slightest sign that she wanted that as much as I did. "Maybe in a little while after I check out the place."

"Okay. The Wi-Fi gets a little spotty up here, so I'm going downstairs to the living room. Check out the far bedroom, though. My mother uses it as a study sometimes and she'll have my head if she finds out I didn't show it off to you. She really loves the whole decorating thing."

That was one of the hobbies my mother had that had never stuck with me. To me, if the room had a chair and a table, it was probably good enough. Ask my mother, however, and she'd start in on things called sconces, whatever they were.

"You don't want to come show me yourself?" Jordan asked.

"Trust me. I've seen it. She manages to email me pictures every time she updates the house or the cabin, most likely trying to get me to come home. No, you go explore. I'll be just downstairs if you need me." I reassured her.

Truthfully, I couldn't look at another one of my mother's damned doilies. I loved the woman, but a man could only take so much. My father must have been a very patient man all these years. Either that or maybe true love meant being interested in things not because you truly enjoyed them but because they made the person you love happy.

"All right, don't work too hard. Even you get to relax sometimes, you know," Jordan said, giving me a small kiss on the lips.

Before she could walk away I pulled her back to me and left a long kiss of my own on her mouth. "If it's relaxing we're talking about, I'm going to want a partner for that," I said, winking at her. My version of relaxing was very different from what I thought Jordan had in mind, but I had no doubt she wouldn't mind a little tension relief herself.

She laughed the way I missed so much, that purely happy laugh that made even a man like me have butterflies in my stomach. It was the kind of laugh that if you heard it from around the corner you would feel compelled to go find the source because it sounded like pure joy.

Nodding her agreement, she walked off smiling. I headed down to the living room and flopped onto the black suede couch. This was new. There was no way my mother and father would have invested in suede shoes, never mind a suede couch, when we were kids. If it wasn't Shane or me tripping over something and spilling our drinks, Denise was usually close behind to drop crumbs all over the place. Not to mention that phase she went through with nail polish and getting it everywhere.

As I opened the laptop and settled in, I was greeted by Denise's homepage, Yahoo news. Like a blast from the past there I saw a trending topic, "Gregory Michaels To Head National Banking Consortium."

It had been hard all these years avoiding that name. Gregory Michaels was a great man. It was no fault of his own that I had distanced myself from him, but after that day that had changed both of our lives, there was no way I could keep working for him. He was an everlasting reminder of what a failure I was.

In truth, the man held no ill will against me. He had thanked me for doing my job, even as his daughter lay before him in a casket. He'd repeated the sentiment later when I told him I was resigning, but no amount of forgiveness could make up for what I'd failed to do.

I stood up and tried to shake the memory of that day from my head. It had admittedly become easier over the years. Now instead of punching a wall or screaming, I was able to just put that thought in a box and push the box into a corner somewhere deep in the back of my mind.

Jordan was still upstairs so I crossed the room to the window, hoping looking out at the forest would bring me some peace. Any time I'd had a problem when I lived at home, I'd head up here to clear my mind. The place never failed to make me feel better.

Now as I looked out, the sun shone and the trees swayed gently in the wind as peaceful as any man could ask for, but it didn't do the trick. No amount of fresh pine smell and breeze was going to banish the feeling I had stuck inside me. Maybe if I had the time to go have my existential crisis in the forest I'd be able to get past it, but there was no way merely looking out a window wistfully was going to fix it.

And as always happened, once the memory of that day came back, I focused on the girl herself.

Tiffany had been the most down-to-earth rich girl you could ever meet. She was more interested in the newest book on the shelves instead of clothes and makeup like the rest of them seemed to love so much. She was the opposite of vapid and longed to help others.

Seventeen and wise beyond her years, something about being raised around all that money hadn't turned her into a Barbie doll but instead into an old soul. She used to speak to her father and me about wanting to give back to people who were less fortunate than her like that's what all teenage girls thought of when the weekend rolled around.

I smiled even as my heart contracted at the memory. It had been a long time since I had allowed myself to think of Tiffany in any other way than gone forever. I remembered her running to see the new dog her father had brought home. When the dog crossed the yard it hid a mud puddle, and by the time she was done getting acquainted with the adorable German shepherd, she was soaking wet and filthy, but she didn't care. All she cared about was that dog and how happy she was by her father's present.

She had been brimming with promise, and everyone around her had known it but her. Too smart for her own good, she never got along with most of her peers and instead focused her attention on learning from the adults in her life.

It wasn't surprising then when she started flirting with me. I was older and I'd seen the world she was so eager to explore. The boys her age didn't challenge her mentally the way she craved. They were more interested in what was under her dress than what she had to say or what she thought.

She was out of their league. Even though she wanted them to like her, they couldn't figure out what to make of a girl like her. She dated some boys, but it always ended with them wishing she was as easy to handle as she was on their eyes. Because of that, there was no settling for any of them, even if they did come from money or have good looks. They simply didn't think like she did.

I don't think for her liking me was a sexual attraction, though I had no idea how a teenage girl's mind worked. My own attraction to her was an innocent one but one I scarcely allowed myself to think of, even when she was alive. I'd never do something to jeopardize my job, but more importantly, I would never do anything to jeopardize Gregory or Tiffany. She was young but almost eighteen. That wasn't the reason nothing ever happened for us, though. The simple fact was I was in charge of protecting her and her father. I couldn't let myself be distracted by anything else.

Her kindness was the one part of her I couldn't help but love. I wanted to remember that especially.

Just a few months before she died, that kindness showed itself more than it ever had before. Gregory wanted to take his daughter out shopping for her birthday and had me accompany them. Truthfully, there was little danger that could have presented itself in the small shopping district Tiffany loved, but he wanted me to be there all the same.

I think he knew that I thought his daughter had a crush on me but trusted and understood that I would never act upon it. There was always that small thought of her being eighteen in a short time, but I always shoved that idea aside. It was my job to protect her father, and that meant protecting her too. Gregory trusted me and that trust would be shattered if he found out I was harboring any intentions towards his daughter.

As we walked down the city sidewalk, a dirty and disheveled homeless man lunged out and grabbed at Gregory's leg. With a flash I had gotten on top of him and was ensuring he could do no damage to any of us. I wasn't trying to hurt him, though. I wouldn't have hurt him unless he made me and was only subduing him, but Tiffany had no idea that was what was going on. Most people, if you put hands on them, stop what they're doing unless they're really out for blood, and it was clear this man was not.

"Gage! Stop!" she screamed. I kept him down but looked over at her. Her face was wracked with worry and her fists were clenched at her sides.

"I won't hurt him, Tiffany. I promise. I just needed to get him off of your father," I explained, not wanting her to think I was some sort of animal. My voice was calm and I spoke not only to Tiffany but the homeless man.

He nodded against my chest and weakly said, "I...I was just asking for some change. I'm really sorry."

I released him and helped him to his feet as Gregory pulled some bills from his pocket. Tiffany hurried to his side and began brushing him off. "I'm sorry if he hurt you, sir. He was only looking out for us," she said sweetly, making the man smile.

Like everyone else she cared for, he fell in love with her kindness. Taking the money from her father's hand, she pushed it into the homeless man's palm and closed his fingers around it. "Buy yourself a hot meal. Everyone deserves to have their belly warm with food. Promise me you won't spend it on anything bad, though. Promise?"

The man nodded excitedly. "I promise, miss. A good meal is all I'll splurge on."

"I have money of my own. Here. Take more," Tiffany said as she opened her wallet and put every bill in it into his hands.

The three of us stared at her dumbstruck. Most people would turn their nose up at this man, but she gave him everything she could at the moment and surely would have given more if she had it with her.

"Miss, you...you don't need to—" he began, but Tiffany cut him off.

"I want you to have it. I want you to promise me you'll buy good things with it though, okay?" she said smiling at the stranger.

The man tried to speak but was too choked up, instead nodding vigorously as he shook each of our hands. When he shook Tiffany's, the tears began rolling down his face.

"God bless you all," he choked out before running off.

I had never seen Gregory look so proud in the entire time I'd known him. No amount of business accolades or thanks for his work in the community would ever match the feeling he must have had in that moment.

"Tiffany, that was very kind of you," he said, pulling her into his arms in an embrace.

"Well, you always tell me adults would be a better if we all just made a little more of an effort, and I'll be an adult soon enough, so I better start acting the part, right?" she said, wiggling out of the hug her father held her in.

"Besides, I had to make him feel better after Gage beat him up," she said with a chuckle.

"Hey now, I didn't hurt him. Besides, you'd be happy for my reflexes if he wasn't just a guy asking for change."

"Oh yeah, reflexes like a cat right?" she teased, making fun of how I'd described my abilities once when I first met her.

"Be nice, Tiffany," Gregory chided. "If you embarrass him anymore, I fear he may stay that red color forever."

I reverted to my natural stony silence and Tiffany beamed up at me. "Thanks for always being there, Gage, even if sometimes it's just homeless guys."

She headed off toward a shop, and Gregory rolled his eyes. "She's a handful sometimes, but she means well. She's just young."

I sensed that was the father speaking to me more than the man who paid me to guard him, but I respected that. She was his only child, his pride and joy, and as any good father would, he wanted me to know my bounds. I was, after all, his employee and older than her, so if he treated me with a certain gruffness, he had every right.

In all honesty, he did the opposite. There was always a place set for me at dinner should I choose to stay, and there was always a genuine feeling of caring from both him and Tiffany. When I had a day off and returned to the house, they would ask what I had done in my off time, and when I needed someone to talk to, Gregory never turned me away.

It was three months before she was going to turn eighteen when she caught me quietly standing alone in the garden on the estate. It was something I did whenever I could to escape city life. The days could get hectic and sometimes even doing the same thing over and over got to be taxing. Being from Wyoming made me want to find that escape outside. The natural inhale and exhale of the earth was far more calming to me than spending an hour on a shrink's couch.

Gregory had decided to spend some time in his home gym and had assured me he was not only safe but it would be painfully boring unless I planned to work out too, so I could take a few hours off. So I had done as he suggested and headed outside to clear my thoughts. The house was locked and the gym was on the top floor, so Gregory was safe and most likely enjoying some alone time just like I wanted to.

As I sat there feeling the sun warm my face, from behind me I heard Tiffany ask, "Are you all right Gage? You're so quiet."

I turned around and saw her peeking her head out from behind a tree. Standing from the concrete bench, I said, "Just taking a few minutes to myself. I think I'll be heading back inside."

"You didn't answer my question," she said, walking towards me and sitting down on the grass.

"I'm always quiet. You know me. It's kind of my thing," I joked.

"Why is that?" she pressed as she looked up at me, her brown hair falling in waves around her face.

"There's great power in silence. Just ask anyone who has ever argued with me."

I wasn't dodging her. It was the truth. I had always chosen to stay silent rather than speak in most situations. You learn more about a person and what's going on around you if you watch rather than talk. I was also keenly aware of how often people seemed to insert their feet into their own mouths and wasn't interested in being that type of man.

"Do you think people who like to talk are weak?" she asked, fiddling with a weed next to her foot. I knew she was referring to herself. She may have been vastly different from people her age in many ways, but the talking part was right on par.

"No. I think those people possess a different kind of power. I've just never understood it."

Once again, I was being honest. I had always quietly marveled at those who could speak about anything. I was even more impressed with the people who could do so and still sound intelligent when they did.

She stared at me with a hopeful look in her eyes. "I see. Well I'm glad to know there's nothing bothering you then," she said with a smile.

Her face lit up from that smile and the memory was almost too painful to bear, but my mind pressed on. If I was going to remember her at all, it had to be like this.

"Did you need something Tiffany?" I asked after a lull in the conversation.

She looked nervous, fiddling with that weed in her hand. "I had hoped we could talk. As you know, in three months I'll be eighteen, a legal adult."

I had a feeling I knew where this was going. I had seen that look in a girl's eye before. It was sweeter and more innocent than I'd encountered before that, and it broke my heart to know what I would have to do next.

"I know. It'll be a big day for you."

She nodded awkwardly and bit her lip. "Well, you see, I wanted to talk to you…once I'm, eighteen I was wondering if, well, we could…date," she stammered out.

I froze. There I was a man taught to keep cool in any situation, and this girl was able to render me unsure of how to answer. She looked into my eyes and I could see she already knew my answer, but as she turned in embarrassment and moved to run away, I stopped her.

"Tiffany, stop. I'm sorry. I'm not good at this sort of thing," I said awkwardly. I didn't want to hurt her feelings. Whatever I might have thought about her, I needed her to know my rejection wasn't because of her but because of me.

"Gage, it's fine. I shouldn't have asked. I know I'm too young." The words raced from her lips, but she refused to turn around.

"Tiffany, please look at me."

If we were going to have this conversation, then it wouldn't consist of me speaking to the back of her head. She was about to be a woman, and she deserved the truth.

She turned around, and though she wasn't crying, the tears threatened in her eyes. Her cheeks were red from embarrassment, and I hated seeing her like that because of me.

"You're right. You are young for someone my age, but that's not why I don't think it would work."

"Then what is it? My father? I'm sure he'd love the idea. He thinks of you as family already!" she blurted out before biting down hard on her lip.

"I have no doubt that he would think it was a fine idea, Tiffany, but I work for him. You understand? I can't date the man's daughter and still be expected to adequately protect him. It's a conflict of interest," I explained with a heavy heart.

She remained silent and nodded. I could tell she wanted to say more but something was preventing her from letting the words out.

"Tiffany, the last thing I want to do is hurt you. You're a beautiful and intelligent young woman who deserves to go off to college and have an amazing experience. If you're dating me, it won't happen and you'll always feel like you were cheated out of something that could be great. I'm sorry. I am. I wish there was a way to make it work, but between the age difference and me working for your father, but I just don't think it's possible."

"I understand Gage. Can I ask you something though?"

"Of course."

"If things were different, would you date someone like me?"

I smiled. "If things were different, I wouldn't be with someone like you. I would be with you."

I wasn't sure if it was the right thing to say, or if it would cause her more pain to know that, but I wouldn't lie to Tiffany. A woman deserved the truth. The alternative was to lie to her, and that would be far worse.

She struggled to smile but quickly leaned in and gave me a hug. "Thank you for being so nice," she whispered before pecking me on the cheek and walking away.

I sat there in silence after she left, trying to figure out if I had done the right thing. It was never my intention to hurt her. I had known for a while that she saw me in a way I couldn't let myself see her.

The worst part wasn't letting her down by telling her the truth. The worst part was that I knew she deserved better than me.

I forced myself to stop thinking about it. About her. Remembering did nothing but dredge up all those feelings I'd worked so hard to push down. According to the headline, Gregory was doing well for himself and his company was as strong as ever. That was good. I wished for nothing more than the happiness peace would give Gregory. What he'd achieved since that horrible day would never make up for what he lost, though.

Staring out the window, I waited until I'd successfully put everything I felt about what had happened in that place deep inside and returned to the laptop to begin my search for anything that would explain what had happened with Jordan. The problem was I had little to go on and even more questions than answers. After fruitlessly looking for nearly a half hour, I decided to go check on

Jordan. Whatever was behind the mystery of who Hailey and Justin were and why they wanted her would have to wait a few more minutes.

CHAPTER SEVEN

JORDAN

GAGE'S MOTHER HAD TAKEN CARE to decorate the cabin so it didn't look like a place that could appear in a horror movie, like most cabins I'd been in. No frilly curtains that were supposed to make things look cozy but actually only looked frightening. No exposed outer walls so necessary for psychopaths to paint cryptic symbols in their victims' blood.

Nearly as nice as the house down in town, it was a pleasant surprise to find a jetted tub in the bathroom, and I'd taken full advantage of it for the past half hour. After that cross country ride, every muscle in my body cried out for a massage, but since that wasn't an option at the moment, a nice soak in that tub was a much appreciated alternative.

I sprawled out across the bed and closed my eyes, loving the peace and quiet in the mountains. After living in New York for so long, my brain had gotten used to nearly constant noise, but after being away for a few days, I was starting to like hearing only the gentle sounds of nature outside my window instead of the usual big city cacophony.

"You look perfect lying there like that," Gage said, rousing me from my daydreams.

Opening my eyes, I saw him standing in the doorway staring at me wrapped only in a towel. I loved seeing him look like there was nothing more important in the world than being there with me.

"Did you get tired of working and decide to join me? You're a little late. I just got out of the tub. We could have had some fun in there."

Gage closed the door and stepped forward toward the bed. "I think we can have fun in here too."

"What do you have in mind, Mr. Varo?"

He slipped his t-shirt over his head and tossed it aside. With a glint in his eye, he grinned. "Something I didn't get a taste of last night sounds good right about now."

I opened my towel and crawled over to the edge of the bed. "Now what could you want a taste of, I wonder?"

Gage chuckled and pushed me back on the bed. Spreading my legs, he flicked his tongue over my inner thigh, sending shockwaves of need rippling through my body. "I haven't tasted your pussy in way too long."

As he moved up my thigh, planting light kisses along the way, I let my head roll back on my shoulders and remembered the last time he'd done that to me. It had been way too long, but that would have been the case if he'd just been between my legs a few hours ago. The man had a magic tongue that other men could only wish they possessed.

The first touch of it to my needy clit made my body come alive, but he was only getting started. He pinned me to the bed with one hand and began to taste every inch of me, his tongue dragging up and down my pussy as he slowly fucked me with two fingers, each time stroking my tender skin inside with his fingertips.

I ran my fingers through his hair and tugged hard as my orgasm began deep inside me. "Don't stop...right there...oh, God..."

He kept on licking and thrusting as my release wound its way through me, every touch of his tongue and fingers exciting me until I didn't think I could stand anymore. Finally, he sucked my clit between his lips and I saw an explosion of every color imaginable behind my eyes as I came hard against his mouth. My back arched and my body bucked against him, but he held me fast and rode every moment of my orgasm from start to finish.

Sitting back on his haunches, Gage licked his lips with a smile. "Lunch of champions."

"I think the saying is breakfast of champions, isn't it?" I asked, still practically breathless from the incredible job his mouth had done on me.

"Mmmm, then I guess we know what I'm doing tomorrow morning."

The thought of him giving me that pleasure again made me smile in anticipation. "It's a date."

He leaned forward and kissed me softly on the lips. "For now, though, I don't think we're finished just yet."

"Oh yeah? What do you have in mind?"

Falling back onto the bed, he rested his head on a pillow and stretched his legs as he slid out of his jeans. "Come here."

Even though my legs felt like cooked spaghetti, I crawled over to him and threw my leg over his body. Positioning my mouth above his, I kissed his lips and smiled. "Let me guess. In the mood for a little ride? Since you went commando today, I guess you were planning this."

"You know me well. There are few things sexier than watching you ride my cock."

I loved how sensual and raw Gage naturally was, and when it came to sex, he had a way of talking about it that made me want him more than I thought possible. Climbing on top of him, I spread my legs wide and watched as his eyes rolled back when I slid down his cock.

"Feel good?"

Looking up at me, he nodded. "Not as good as being buried inside you."

Gripping my hips, he lifted me off him enough to give his cock room to ease into me and pushed his hips up. Inch by inch, he slid inside my body until we were joined completely. When he filled me like this, I never wanted to be without him inside me ever again the feeling was so exquisite.

"That feels so incredible," I said as a moan escaped my lips.

"God, you feel so good wrapped around my cock. Ride me, baby," he said through clenched teeth as I rolled my hips and began to do just that.

We moved in unison, up and down and in and out, his body invading mine over and over and mine milking his cock each time as we raced to our shared release. My hands clutched at his muscular body, hard against my touch and beautiful to watch as he fucked me.

Gage rubbed my clit with the pad of his thumb, sending waves of desire unraveling through me. Rolling my hips to feel more of him, I took every inch of his cock.

Forcing his hands into my hair, he tugged me down toward him and kissed me hard. Grunting in my ear, he groaned, "Ride me and don't stop. Don't stop."

I did as he commanded and felt his body tense underneath mine as he came. He stopped thrusting and held me onto him, stilling his movement. I felt my own release begin and held his hand to my clit as it rolled over me like a wave of the most incredible pleasure I'd ever felt.

Collapsing on top of him, we stayed there in each other's arms, his cock still inside me as the two of us got lost in the afterglow of great sex. After a few minutes, he began gently running his fingertips up and down my spine and whispered, "I think that might have been our best yet."

I smiled and rolled my eyes at his brand of keeping track of our sex life. "I give it a nine. The dismount was nonexistent, so points had to come off there."

He kissed me sweetly on the lips and shook his head. "Joke away, but we're Olympic level when it comes to sex. Not everyone is."

Rolling off him, I tweaked the tip of his nose. "Well, thank God we found each other then. I'd hate to be stuck with a bush leaguer with no skills."

Gage pulled me close, and I rested my head on his shoulder. He took a deep breath and let it out slowly before he turned to look at me. "All joking aside, I have a question to ask you."

Suddenly, the fear that he'd ask me to marry him tore through my mind. Every part of my body tensed up, and I scrambled to find some way to distract him from that question he wanted to ask. Sitting up, I swung my legs off the bed and announced I needed to take a shower.

"You just took a bath. What are you doing?" he asked, justifiably confused by my behavior.

"Well, you know. We just had incredible sex, so that means there's a lot of fluids and stuff I should probably clean up."

Even I knew that sounded like bullshit and avoidance.

Gage sat up against the headboard and folded his arms across his chest. "So I tell you I need to ask you a question and you immediately think that's the perfect time to grab a shower?"

As I stood there naked in every sense of the word, I hung my head, unable to face him. "I was just saying it might be a good idea. Maybe not. I don't know. You know?"

"No, I don't know, Jordan. I don't know what the hell is wrong with you."

The anger in his voice upset me more than anything else, and I instinctively became defensive. "Well, I've been drugged, kidnapped, taken hostage, and barely escaped from crazy people, so maybe one of those things can explain what's wrong with me."

"You know what I meant. I'm here, so you don't have to worry anymore. I won't let anything else happen to you. I promise."

"I know you say that, but Hailey and Justin might be right around the next corner and then what?"

As soon as the words left my mouth, I knew I'd made a mistake. It was written all over his face.

His features twisted and contorted from anger and hurt. "What the hell does that mean? Are you saying you don't think I'll protect you if either one of those fucks show up? Is that what you meant?"

"No! I wasn't saying that, Gage."

He stood from the bed and stormed off into the bathroom before I could say anything else. Damnit! All the guy wanted to do was ask me to marry him, and instead because I'd lied to him about being forced to marry that asshole Justin, I had to pick a fight just to avoid telling him no. I had no idea how I was going to fix this, but I had to.

I heard the shower turn on and walked into the bathroom to find Gage standing under the water with his head hung. I hated seeing him like that, especially because I'd made him feel that way.

"I'm sorry, Gage. I didn't mean to make you think I didn't believe in you. That's not the truth at all. I swear."

He said nothing for so long I wasn't sure he even heard me, but then I saw him turn to look at me and shake his head. "I don't know what to do to prove to you I can protect you, Jordan."

"You don't have to. Honestly, you don't."

"Give me a few minutes and I'll be back out, okay? We'll talk then."

I left him standing there in the shower and tried to think of a way to tell him the truth. He'd understand. I knew he would. Gage was just that kind of man. I should have told him when he rescued me, but I felt like it was partly my fault that Hailey and Justin had been able to do that to me. If I hadn't been so stupid to think that some millionaire would want to marry me in the first place, I never would have been in this position.

Disgusted with myself, I sat down on the bed, still naked and wishing everything after our amazing sex session hadn't happened. If only I wasn't such a fool.

Gage returned to the bedroom wearing a towel and grabbed his clothes from around the room. "I didn't mean to storm out like that, Jordan. I guess a shower wasn't a bad idea, after all."

God, he really was the best kind of man there was. There he was standing in just a towel, his skin still glistening in that way that made me want to run my tongue over every inch of him, and instead of being an ass like most men would be, he was actually apologizing for not staying to fight with me.

And even knowing that, I answered, "I just don't think we should be asking any questions of one another right now, Gage. We have enough to deal with and I don't want us to split up over something stupid Hailey and Justin created again."

Gage's mouth dropped open, and he stared at me in angry shock for a long moment. "Split up again? Like when I thought I was protecting you by leaving because of those letters? Do you mean something stupid like that?"

"No! God, I keep saying the wrong thing. I didn't meant that at all."

Fuck. I honestly wasn't sure what I meant now, but I didn't think I'd meant that. Maybe I did. Maybe somewhere deep inside my brain I still resented the fact that he left me without a word of explanation and broke my heart, no matter what the reason was.

He dressed without saying another word or even looking at me. I didn't mean to hurt him every time I opened my mouth. He didn't deserve that. As he angrily jammed his feet back into his shoes, I thought about how I could make things better and hoped that I could.

I sat down next to him and gently touched his shoulder. "Gage, I love you. You know that, don't you? Don't listen to me when I say stupid things."

Turning to face me, he knitted his brows. "Stupid things like you love me? I don't know what to think anymore, Jordan. I know I made some mistakes, but how much do I have to do before you believe me when I say I can protect you?"

"Why is that so important to you? Isn't it enough that I love you and know you love me?"

He shook his head as a look of pain settled into his features. Standing from the bed, he looked away and said, "It's important to me because it's who I am. It's what I need you to know, and you don't give a damn about it. I don't know what to do about it either."

Before I could answer him and explain I did care about that part of him, just not as much as he thought I should, he stormed out and I was left sitting alone on the bed where we'd just made love wondering if he could really handle finding out the secret I dreaded telling him.

CHAPTER EIGHT

GAGE

THERE WAS NO SENSE OF pride or manliness as I slammed the door to the bedroom, leaving Jordan inside, but the pain of realizing she didn't trust me to keep her safe was too much. I loved her more than anything, which was the only reason I had left in the first place. How was I supposed to take care of her if she kept pushing me away? How long was I going to have to keep paying for the mistake of leaving her? With a heavy sigh I turned to walk away and clear my head, and nearly collided head on with Denise.

"Woah! Slow it down, Jeff Gordon!" Denise exclaimed, putting a hand on my shoulder. "Are you okay, Gage? You look like you're about to Hulk out."

"Denise, what are you doing here? Jordan and I are spending the night. I thought we told you that," I said, startled by her appearing right outside the bedroom. I wasn't keen on the idea of my family overhearing our arguments and was even less keen on the idea of people popping up unexpectedly when so much could go wrong.

My sister smiled and patted me on the shoulder. "Relax. I left some work related stuff on that laptop I gave you. I didn't mean to intrude. Old habits, you know?"

I nodded slowly as her explanation sunk in. It made sense that Denise would let herself in. Ever since we were kids, this cabin had been sort of a refuge from everyday life. Whenever my parents had a fight, my mother would pile us in the car and drive right up the mountain to "cool her heels," as she liked to call it.

"It's fine. The laptop is in the living room. I'll grab it for you," I said, moving to the stairs.

Jordan and I could both use a little while to cool down anyway. I knew she wouldn't like me walking away from the argument like that, but I needed to take a minute to do like my parents used to or one of us might say something we'd regret later.

I walked downstairs with my sister to the living room where I'd left the laptop. I quickly closed the open windows and passed it to Denise.

As she pulled out a flash drive from her pocket and began typing, she looked up smiled. "So now that I finally have you alone, how are you?"

Her question was innocent enough, and maybe it was my own guilt over our current situation that made me suspicious, but something in Denise's voice told me she knew things weren't all sunshine and rainbows for Jordan and me right now. Then again, the argument moments before might have given her a clue.

There were a lot of possible answers to her question, and all of them seemed to race through my mind at once. The only appropriate one seemed to be, "I'm good. Things have been a little hectic lately, but when aren't they, right?"

As the hollow platitude escaped my lips, it felt stupid and forced. Worried that my sister would pick up on this I tried to change the subject, "How about you? Anything exciting in your life?"

Denise continued to type as she answered, "I guess hectic is a good enough word for it. Claire and I broke up and that put me in a weird spot for a while."

Claire? Who was Claire? Obviously she had been important because the shadow that crossed Denise's face when she said her name was dark and instantly recognizable.

It suddenly dawned on me how much I had missed being away for all those years. Sure, I had made the correct number of phone calls, but I hadn't really been there for anyone.

Quietly, I said, "I'm sorry Denise. I know that pain and I know the place it puts you in, but I also know you're tough as nails."

It felt like the cliché it was and not nearly as useful as I wanted it to be. I wanted to be supportive, but with everything that was going on, I didn't know what to say.

"Ha! Tough as nails. I thought so too. A few weeks of not managing to get out of my pajamas most of the time proved that wrong, didn't it?"

Her voice had a bitter tone, and it hurt to hear her speak like this. Denise was a realist, for sure, but there had always been a big optimistic streak in her. At that moment, I was having trouble finding it.

"Denise, I'm sorry…I didn't mean to drag up any old feelings." It wasn't my intention to keep hurting the women in my life, but it seemed to be a pattern today.

She finished typing and closed the laptop sharply. "It's nothing to dwell on. I can't fix anything that way. Besides, we aren't talking about me right now."

Sensing that I'd touched a nerve, I reluctantly allowed her to turn the focus back on me. "Sure. Though I think you'll find my life is as uninteresting as always," I lied.

"Oh yeah? Says the guy who mysteriously shows up after a decade with a beautiful woman on his arm, only to whisk her away to the cabin right after we meet her," Denise said with that same edge as when she talked about her ex.

"What can I say? I'm selfish like that. I want to keep her all to myself."

It was beginning to be more and more difficult to keep my family out of what we were dealing with, but they had no part in it. Then again, neither did Jordan or I, but we didn't have any choice. For now, we had to deal with it. My family didn't, and if I could keep them out of the whole mess, I would.

I guess the tug of war in my mind showed on my face because

Denise quietly continued, "What's going on Gage? I haven't seen you this upset since mom said you couldn't date that Landers girl."

A nervous laugh escaped me. That had been one hell of a fight. If only yelling was an appropriate reaction now, but that wouldn't solve anything and would likely make my sister think I'd lost my mind.

"It's Jordan. She's in trouble, but it isn't her fault. She got mixed up with some bad people and I had to get her away. But I know she's innocent. That's why we're here. She needs to stay hidden until we can get all of this sorted out."

As I explained what I'd kept from her and the rest of my family, the weight of the secret lifted from my shoulders. Nothing I said sounded like it conveyed the seriousness of what we were going through, though, and I hated how it sounded like I was making excuses for Jordan.

Denise furrowed her eyebrows. "You mean that woman? The one we met? She doesn't seem like the kind of person that gets in with a bad crowd, Gage. She seems like someone who avidly avoids that, in fact. I mean this in the nicest way, but she's pretty boring from what I saw. I think that's good for you though, so don't take any offense."

I shook my head, "That's just it. She isn't the type at all. I mean she's a school teacher, for God's sake. That's why she needs my help. If they find her…I don't know what they plan to do, but I know it isn't in Jordan's best interest, and therefore isn't in mine."

My mind flashed to a dark place where I imagined what Hailey and Justin might have in store for her and my fists instinctively clenched as my jaw did the same. If they hurt her, I'd kill them. I didn't want to think like that, but no one would hurt Jordan again.

"Well, fill me in. How can I help?" Denise asked.

"I don't know if you can help. I don't know if anyone can."

I hung my head as the truth of those words hit home in that very moment. Who was going to help us? Up until this point, I had a plan, but now I felt like everything was happening so fast that the plan had gone out the window. Where could we go? The cabin was safe and secluded, but other than a remote island I couldn't afford, where would be safe for Jordan?

My sister shook her head. Never one to give up on a problem, she probed for more information. "So why are people after her? Does she owe someone money?"

The thought of Jordan being in trouble because she owed someone money was comical. If only it were that easy.

"No. I told you she's innocent. I'm not entirely sure what's going on yet, but Jordan seems to just be a pawn in it all."

"Ok, so if she's innocent, what are you hiding from?"

Denise was always a bit too pushy and that was evident now more than ever. It annoyed me to have her keep pressing with questions when what I really needed was some support. Denise was never the type though. She would give you a shoulder to cry on, but there would be lecture involved as well.

"You remember I told you Jordan and I were together before, but we broke up?"

"Yeah. You were really torn up about it."

There was an understatement. It had taken me months to try to get over Jordan just to realize it had never really been a possibility for me.

"Well, the reason I left her was because I started getting these letters. I didn't know who they were from, but they all had the same message to deliver. Stay away from Jordan or else."

The memory of those letters, of having to leave Jordan, came back like a crashing wave tearing through me. Sure, I'd left to protect her, but in doing so I had hurt her, had hurt us, immeasurably. I should have just stayed with her and defended her from whoever was sending those letters. Instead, I let her fall into their trap and now she was paying dearly for it.

"You didn't do anything wrong Gage. You were trying to protect her, right?"

"Right...not that it worked, clearly."

"Gage…"

"I know, I know. It's just…"

I couldn't help myself. I had to tell someone, and with every word it was like the magnitude of the situation settled in. Up until this point, everything had happened so fast that sitting down and recapping it made it real for the first time. After what seemed like ages, I finished the complicated story and sat down on the couch exhausted from it all.

Denise sat quietly, her eyes only a little wider than they normally were. She took a moment to absorb everything I had told her and finally said, "Wow, Gage. That's a lot. Honestly, I think it's more than I've ever heard you say at once. So what are you going to do now?"

She stared at me as if I would just magically know the answer after telling her the backstory. Nothing had made sense until this point. What made her think I would suddenly know now?

I looked down at the wood floor, wishing I knew the answer to that question. What were we going to do? I had been so upset at the idea of Jordan thinking I couldn't protect her, but deep down it was my worst fear, and it was starting to seem more and more like a reality. I had gotten us this far in one piece, but we couldn't stay in the cabin forever. I wish we could. Jordan and I holed up in a cabin or an apartment, hell anywhere would be fine as long as I knew she was safe and happy.

"We have to keep her hidden until my guy can get things sorted out. Once all the dust settles, there's no way anyone will be able to say Jordan's guilty of anything."

I knew if we could just get all the facts and connect the dots before someone found us, there was no way a judge or anyone else wouldn't see that she was the victim in everything that had happened.

Denise sat quietly and seemed to choose her words carefully. "I know you love her, Gage, but have you considered this situation she has gotten herself into could get you seriously hurt? Is she really worth it?"

"What the hell does that mean?"

I didn't like what she was saying. None of this was Jordan's fault. All she had done was found someone new and tried to secure a halfway decent future for herself. My glare must have spoken volumes because before I had the chance to say another word, Denise corrected herself.

"Hey, I'm sorry. That was uncool of me to say. I guess going through a bad breakup makes you think less of love as a whole. I didn't mean to upset you," Denise offered apologetically.

She looked nervous, like she worried I would explode in anger any second, and though I wasn't pleased, I knew she was just trying to look out for me. She might know a little of our history, but I'd glazed over the great parts. It was a natural reaction, after all. If she knew the best parts about us, she would understand that nothing I could ever do would be enough for how much I loved Jordan.

I had too much on my mind to sit around being irritable with Denise. "It's fine. I get it. But trust me, she's worth it."

My tone was final as was the discussion as to whether or not Jordan was someone I'd risk my life for.

"Then you must really love her."

Of course I loved her. In my mind, it seemed like I couldn't remember a time when I didn't love her. There had been other women, and I'd even thought I was in love once or twice, but Jordan was the only one who ever made me feel like I couldn't imagine a time without her. Even on the run and unsure of what would happen next, having her in my life again was better than the alternative.

"Well, I want to marry her, so yes, I do," I answered, worried my sister's reaction wouldn't mesh with the positive opinion I had thought she had of Jordan.

Her eyes grew wide. "Wow, Gage. I had no idea. I mean, you clearly love her, but I didn't think there was a girl out there who could get you to settle down."

I smiled as for the briefest moment everything felt normal. I was supposed to be sitting in the family cabin telling my sister how I wanted to marry the amazing woman upstairs. Jordan should be getting to know my mom and listening to old stories from my father, not upstairs scared and alone.

"It seems like you've got a bit of a mess going here. I believe it isn't her fault. After all, look at her. She doesn't look like she could kill a spider. I just hope you can find a way out of this mess for your own sake. You deserve a happy life, not to be caught up in this nonsense."

It felt nice to have someone concerned for me, but even though I knew she wanted the best, all I could keep thinking about was Jordan. My safety was inconsequential compared to hers.

"Thanks for talking to me, Denise. I needed to tell someone about all this. I just hope it's all over soon so I can go back to living a happy life with her."

"I hope so too, Gage. I hate seeing you so worried." Denise stood up and patted me on the shoulder. "Be safe, big brother."

My sister left me alone in the living room trying to come up with any solution to our problem. That was difficult to do considering the woman I was fighting for was also the woman I was fighting with.

I finally decided I couldn't sit on the couch any longer getting lost in my head. Action needed to be taken, and the first step was solving whatever issue was keeping Jordan away from me. Her behavior had been erratic. One moment she was wrapped around me as we made love, and the next she was running away to another room to escape me.

Surely she couldn't believe getting closer to me again was a bad thing. I had left her, but Jordan knew I only did that to protect her. I had been wrong to do it, but it wasn't my intention to hurt her. How could I make her see that? How could I make her understand that I could protect her?

Whatever it took, I needed to make her understand she could believe in me.

Chapter Nine

Jordan

IT WAS SO UNFAIR THAT such an amazing moment had been ruined by yet another argument. It was my fault, I knew that, but as I stepped out onto the balcony off the bedroom and stared at the rolling mountains in front of me, the solution seemed to be as far away as the horizon. The obvious answer was to simply tell Gage the truth, but how could I do that now after I had lied?

This always happened to me. Every single time I had ever tried to lie it had always just blown up in my face. One would think I would learn eventually, yet here I was wringing my hands and trying to find a solution to an overwhelming problem.

It wasn't that I wanted to keep lying to Gage. All I wanted was for this whole terrible situation to be over so I could enjoy the moment where Gage would propose, instead of running away from him in fear.

I wanted to be able to let him get down on one knee and stand there overcome with joy at the idea of being his wife. Instead, I had no choice but to flee from the very idea. This was supposed to be one of the best memories we would share in our lives together. It was supposed to be a story we told friends at the engagement party and to our children one day when they were old enough.

It was not supposed to be a moment that made my stomach twist into knots. If Nina's lawyers could get fix this any minute now, that would be great. If we could figure out what the hell was behind this whole mess, that would be even better.

Then my life could return to normal and I could actually enjoy things like being around Gage and his family. This whole trip should have been so different. If his family found out what was going on, they would probably think I was a mess and way too much work for their son. At that moment as I stared out toward that distant horizon, it didn't seem like they would be too wrong in thinking that. I was becoming far more high maintenance than I ever intended to be.

It felt like Gage was downstairs with Denise forever, but he deserved a break from all of this. Hopefully, talking to her would help him calm down. I also hoped that talking to her didn't make me look too bad. Surely she'd heard us arguing. Otherwise, why would she have come upstairs? This wasn't the image I had hoped to cultivate for Gage's family and getting caught arguing with Gage sure wasn't helping things.

This was as much her cabin as Gage's, but I didn't appreciate the idea of his family members strolling around up here while we were hiding. Didn't that defeat the entire purpose?

I hated putting Gage through all of this. The guy rescued me, did everything to protect me, and now I was lying to him. The charade couldn't go on much longer before what we had was damaged too much.

As all these thoughts swirled around in my head, the door opened and Gage came back to the room. When he spoke, his tone was measured, but there was an undeniable sharpness that lay just underneath.

"Jordan, we can't keep doing this. I know you don't think it's true because of what I did in the past when I left you, but I can protect you and you have to stop pushing me away. How can I help you if you're always keep me at arm's length?"

His sudden accusation stung and I spun around to face him. The stress of the past few days had left me irritable and I responded with more anger than I truly felt in my heart.

"You know? Do you? Well, you're wrong Gage. I don't hold it

against you! I've told you that."

He didn't deserve that from me, but with everything that had happened, I was sick of feeling meek and frail. If he only understood that I knew he could protect me, that I trusted him, and that I loved him so damn much.

"That's bullshit Jordan." The words came so fast and it hurt to know that he so readily thought I was pushing him away.

"I don't. I love you Gage. You know that," I answered. If only he could understand that it had nothing to do with him or what he did in the past. It was just that, the past! I had no doubt that Gage could protect me. I mean, here I was, protected and safe because of him far up in the mountains away from anyone who wanted to hurt me.

"How can you say you love me when you've clearly become more distant? We make love and then next thing I know you're running away from me. That doesn't seem like love to me," Gage said, the pain in his voice evident.

"Gage, I promise you that I do love you. That isn't why I'm being distant." I said, knowing that wouldn't fix a damn thing. It wasn't like I was going to be able to tell him the real reason why I was acting the way I was.

"Then what is it Jordan?" he fired back, abandoning any hope of staying calm.

I hesitated, hoping the silence would magically nullify the sham of marriage I had been forced into. But I couldn't put it off forever. Nina's lawyers weren't going to magically pull through in the next few seconds, so it was now or never.

Unfortunately, never was no longer an option. He had to know the truth.

"They forced me to marry Justin."

The color drained from his face and his shoulders sagged from my words. He said nothing, though, and I could no longer keep everything I'd been hiding inside me.

"I swear to you I said no over and over again, but they forced me and I was afraid you were going to ask me to marry you. I'm so sorry I lied. I had hoped that Nina's lawyers would get it all straightened out before you asked me. That's why I've been distant Gage. I'm so sorry. I knew telling you the truth would hurt you." The words came spilling out before I could stop them, and instantly I wished I could take them back.

My confession hung heavy in the air, making me feel like there was an entire world separating us. Gage looked like he'd been smacked across the face. Finally, after a long moment, he spoke quietly, clearly trying to contain the rage boiling over inside him.

"Jordan, you telling the truth isn't what hurt me. How could you lie to me so many times while I was risking everything to save you?"

He was right. I had no defense. I'd done exactly what he was accusing me of and there was no excuse.

I hung my head. "Gage, I only lied to avoid hurting you. I know it was wrong. I'm sorry."

"I feel like such an idiot. Here I was, ready to stand by your side no matter what, and you were lying to me this whole time. I've felt terrible for lying to you and leaving you, and you turned around and did the same thing to me. I suppose you think I deserved this."

Looking up, I saw his hurt-filled gaze and my heart clenched. "Of course I don't, Gage. It wasn't like that. I didn't want any kind of revenge. I love you."

I had lied, but how could he question my feelings? He knew I loved him, knew how devastated I had been when he left me. I hadn't done this with the intention of pushing him away, but the end result was the same.

"How can you stand there and lie to me in one breath and tell me you love me in another? How can I know you haven't lied about anything else?"

I moved toward Gage in an effort to comfort him, but for the first time since I had known him he recoiled and that was worse than anything he could ever had said to me.

"Gage, you know me. I'm not a liar by nature. I wouldn't lie to you about anything else."

"Do I know you? I thought I did, yet here we stand and I feel like you're a stranger. How could you lie to me about what they did?"

When he spoke of them forcing me to marry Justin, it looked like the vein in his forehead was going to explode at any second. I knew my being married would anger him but this…this was more hatred than I thought Gage could ever harbor in his heart.

"Gage, I didn't…"

"No, Jordan. It's bad enough that they did this to you, but what's worse it that you won't even deal with it to the point that you lied to me about it! You were drugged, kidnapped, and forced to marry a man and you sit there pretending to be fine, except for lying to me."

His fists clenched so hard that I could see the whites of his knuckles. The anger that filled him over what had happened to me was palpable.

In that moment, it was like the cabin, the woods, the world, melted away and all I was left with was the searing pain of Gage's words. Who the hell was he to decide what I was and was not dealing with? It wasn't good to lie to him, that was true, but this was unfair. He wasn't the one who had been kidnapped and drugged. It was me, and I would deal with it how I pleased.

Turning away from his angry stare, I said, "I can't do this right now Gage. I said I was sorry. What else am I supposed to do?"

My world felt like it was crumbling around me. How could all of this have happened in such a short time? All I had wanted was what Nina had, a comfortable life and a man to love me. I hadn't meant for any of this to occur, and now Gage was telling me I wasn't dealing with it? Of course I was, but dealing with something didn't mean obsessing over it every damn second.

"Well, you could start by taking care of yourself and addressing the abuse you've gone through, not to mention the husband you have now."

As soon as the words left his lips I could tell he regretted them. The venom that dripped off every word was too much and my already crumbling world collapsed.

"I...I can't do this right now," I muttered as I rushed past Gage and out the door. He moved to stop me, but I ducked out of the way and kept going.

I had no idea where I was running as my feet carried me down the stairs and to the front door of the cabin. It didn't matter that all that surrounded us was dense woods. I couldn't stay in that room one more second. I let my fear and anger rule me, and my feet followed their orders.

All of this over a lie? How had everything gone from being happily engaged to a millionaire to running out into the unknown outside of Gage's cabin? I was a school teacher, not someone who got kidnapped and forced into a marriage.

With my mind racing faster even than my feet, I didn't notice I wasn't alone until it was too late. With one hand around my neck and the other twisting my arm behind my back, Justin pulled me toward a car parked just out of sight from the cabin.

"Let go of me!" The pain shooting through my shoulder was like nothing I had ever felt before, and every fiber of my being cried out in agony.

Hoping Gage had followed me outside, I screamed his name as best I could through the pressure of Justin's hand crushing my windpipe. The pain was excruciating, and it took everything in me to not just give in and let whatever terrible plan Justin had for me just happen.

I summoned my strength and did my best to wiggle free from Justin's grasp, but every move I made resulted in him constricting my airway further. It wasn't long before my eyesight started going fuzzy and I felt myself slipping away. For the second time in mere minutes, my world was fading away, but this time it was for real. Try as I might to control the situation, Justin was stronger and more determined.

As my vision started to fail, my mind flashed to Gage as I prayed that he would find me before it was too late. If I ever needed him to protect me from something stupid I'd done, it was now. I closed my eyes and saw his face so calm and reassuring like the man he truly was. I knew what I had to do and worked to focus on surviving the way I knew he would.

Jamming my elbow from my free arm into Justin's side, I connected squarely with his ribs. Howling in pain, he pushed me forward toward the car as he cursed me out for fighting him.

Despite my flailing, Justin nearly had me in the backseat when Gage found us. Pulling him off me, he threw Justin to the ground as I gasped for air, finally free from that bastard's hold on my throat. Gage quickly glanced at me to see if I was okay and then went at him like a wild animal, lunging at Justin to pin him on the ground. Rearing his arm back, he punched him over and over until he knocked him unconscious. I collapsed, breathless, onto the backseat as I clutched my already bruising throat.

"Jordan!" Gage cried out, pulling me from the car and held me tight in his arms.

I wasn't aware that I was even crying at first until I saw the mascara on Gage's shirt as I pulled away to look up at him. "Gage, I'm so sorry," I sobbed as I looked away from his eyes.

"Shhh. That doesn't matter right now," he said, using a finger to guide my chin and my eyes up to his. I stared up at him and the rage he'd shown Justin was still in his eyes, those gorgeous dark blue eyes I loved so much.

"We need to get him inside and tied up so we can finally get some damn answers."

His tone was sharp but his hands softly ran up and down my back comforting me. I knew the issue between us wasn't over, but Gage was right. We needed to figure what Justin and Hailey were up to.

"What can I do?" I answered, looking at Justin in a heap on the ground. It was a look that suited him, in my opinion. Though I spoke as if I was resolved to help, in reality I was barely holding it together. My throat was on fire, and it was still difficult to see straight.

"You can stay with me while I carry him back to the cabin. Actually, there's some rope in the trunk of the car. Can you grab that as we go up?" he said.

This was the Gage I knew and loved. He was calm and focused, ready to handle the situation, after I was almost getting kidnapped once again. I hadn't meant to, obviously, but my running away had been foolish and stupid.

I nodded and wiped my eyes as I wondered how Justin had found us here. I thought Gage had said that no one would connect him to me, at least not right away. It seemed like he'd gotten here awfully fast. After all, we'd only been in Wyoming for a day and a half. How had he figured out that not only was Gage helping me, but that he had brought me here? There didn't seem to have been enough time for him to drive here and know exactly where to grab me.

Gage threw Justin over his shoulder like firefighter carrying someone out of a building and gestured for me to walk next to him. I did as he asked and placed a comforting hand on his free shoulder. On the other, Justin's head bobbed lazily as his mouth hung open making him look incredibly stupid.

"I want to keep you in my sight until this mess is over. I'm getting pretty fucking sick and tired of this asshole taking you away from me," Gage said with a small smile that signified he was trying to lighten the mood a little. It was a fruitless effort, but I appreciated it, nonetheless. I was lucky to have a man who, despite all the craziness, still wanted to be with me after the things I'd done. I knew it bothered him just as much as it did me that things between us had become such a mess.

"Thank you for protecting me always. I want you to now that I really am sorry and I believe you can protect me. I don't know what

I would do without you," I said softly. I knew it wouldn't fix the situation at hand, but the look he gave me said he believed me. That was the most important thing.

I must have been running quickly because it seemed like ages until we climbed the hill back to the cabin. I was sweating buckets by the time we reached it, and my hair was starting to mat to my forehead. At my side and carrying a full-grown man, Gage didn't even look winded, although that might have been the adrenaline still pumping through his system.

We tied Justin to one of the dining room chairs and checked his pockets for a cell phone before Gage sat me down on the couch to examine me. Crouching in front of me, he scanned my face as he gently ran his fingers over every square inch of my body. "Does anything hurt other than your throat?"

I shook my head and tried to swallow without wanting to cry out. "I'll be okay. If he had manhandled me for a few minutes more I might not be, but you got there just in time. My throat feels like someone took a blowtorch to it, but I'll be all right. Did you find a phone or anything we can use to figure out how he got here?"

Gage leaned forward and kissed me softly, whispering against my lips, "Shhh. Don't worry about that. I didn't find a phone, but I'll be asking him about how he found us when he wakes up. For now, do you think there's any chance one of these days you're going to stop running so we don't have to keep doing this kind of thing?"

I knew he was trying to make me smile. That was the type of man he was. One minute he was like a superhero, rescuing me from whatever bad guy had descended upon me, and then the next he was sweet and gentle.

"How about I promise not to do that again?" I said with a smile that made him visibly happy. Looking over toward Justin still tied up and passed out, I asked, "What are we going to do with him?"

Gage gently directed my gaze back toward him in front of me. "Jordan, I'm not going to be good guy Gage when he wakes up. Are you ready to see that?"

The intensity in his blue eyes made me worry what he might do to Justin, but I had no fear of who Gage was. "I'm fine with whatever you have to do to get answers from that son of a bitch. He's as much to blame for what happened as Hailey is. He didn't have to set me up like he did."

Standing up, Gage walked over to the gun cabinet and pulled out a pistol to add to his 9mm. Never as comfortable with guns as he was, now I didn't care what he did with it. Justin had nearly lured me to my death. Part of me wanted to see Gage rough Justin up, and I didn't bother to hide that part of me. He deserved whatever Gage decided to dish out to him.

"Are you sure you don't want to go upstairs and stay up there while I take care of this?" Gage asked as he returned to my side on the couch.

"I want answers just as badly as you do, Gage. I'm staying," I answered, mustering whatever courage that hadn't been sapped from me over the past week. There was no way I was about to go upstairs and hide while Gage worked over Justin for information. Of all the people in the cabin, I deserved to know the whole truth of what was going on. More importantly, I wanted to see Justin's face when he gave his answers. I'd looked into those eyes every day for months thinking I saw love in them. Now I wanted to see the truth.

At the dining room table, Justin groaned as he slowly came out of it. His eyes flickered momentarily before they focused on us and the realization that he had been caught dawned on him.

"Wakey wakey, Justin. Time to start talking," Gage said as he slowly walked over to stand in front of him and pointed the pistol to the spot between Justin's eyes.

The look on his face was almost enough to make up for how much my throat hurt.

CHAPTER TEN

GAGE

THERE WAS A STRONG POSSIBILITY that having the gun in my hand was a bad choice after all because as soon as Justin opened his eyes it took everything in me not to pull the trigger and blow his fucking brains all over the cabin's walls.

"You've got to be fucking kidding me," he mumbled, looking down at the barrel of my gun.

"You always did have a terrible sense of humor," Jordan said at my side. "You sit there tied up and with a gun pointed at your head and all you can think to do is be a smart ass."

It was hard not to smile as she showed her tough side. I loved that Jordan was sweet and kind, but I loved that when push came to shove she was ready to push right back. There was always something sexy about a strong woman, and Jordan was no exception.

"I don't know what you hope to get out of this. Go ahead and kill me. I wouldn't have to deal with this stupid bitch anymore," Justin spat back.

His words might have been full of bravado, but I saw by the way he was trembling that he wasn't feeling nearly as brave as he let on. Good. He needed to be afraid. Calling his wife and my future wife a bitch wasn't exactly the way to ingratiate himself with the man fighting the urge to kill him.

Pressing the gun harder to the bridge of his nose, I leaned down to stare into his eyes. "I wouldn't push your luck, Justin. That whole 'til death do us part thing is sounding especially appealing right now, so I would do my best to answer our questions quickly and accurately. Understand?"

I watched as he winced in pain and his body trembled along with his voice. "Listen, I don't know anything, okay?" he whined. "I really don't. Hailey's the one you should be talking to."

To think I had looked at this guy as competition before. Just a short time ago, I had seen a man I had to reluctantly agree might be good for Jordan. It was amazing what an expensive suit did for a guy. As Brock, he held all the cards and the woman I loved.

Now he was a heap of mess tied to my dining room chair and we held the power over him. It was about time something started working in our favor for once. Justin and Hailey were going to pay through the teeth for all they'd done, and this was just phase one of showing them what I was like when someone hurt the woman I loved.

"Oh, you don't know anything? I find that hard to believe considering you've had a big hand in this, obviously," I answered, gesturing towards Jordan with my free hand.

"I...I got as used as she did. It's true! Hailey is the one you should be angry with. I don't know anything. All I was told was to marry her. It was just a job. I have nothing against Jordan, and she's just some woman, no offense. Everything else was Hailey. I'm a pawn too, see?"

Justin looked like he was barely holding back tears. This was a man who had spent months convincing everyone he was an enigmatic millionaire, but just a few minutes with a gun in his face and he returned to who he really was.

A pathetic jackass.

It was nothing impressive, to say the least. No wonder he was a con artist. Being someone who wasn't so sad must have felt good for once.

"Justin, you need to tell us what all this is about, and don't give me any bullshit answer that you don't know. Nobody agrees to marry someone without knowing something about what the hell is going on," Jordan said as she poked him in the chest.

"I swear I didn't know a thing!"

I took a step back and folded my arms across my chest. "See, I don't believe that for a second, Justin. You're the one up here trying to shove her into a car, so you're clearly more than just Hailey's puppet. So I'll ask you as directly as I can. What's going on?"

The idea that he didn't know anything was absurd. I had no doubt that he might lack the knowledge of the finer points of the overall plan, but he was holding out on us. That was obvious.

"I was just following orders," he answered, his voice cracking. That was a half-truth and I could spot it a mile away. He was doing what criminals always did, but I wasn't going to stop until I found out some real information from him. His attempt to tell me just a bit of truth to convince me he didn't know anything else wasn't going to work.

"How did you come to impersonate Brock Hannon?" I asked, not willing to let him idly sit and convince us that he didn't know anything. He was the one who was around Jordan for all that time, so clearly he knew more than he was letting on.

"What does it matter what I tell you? You're just going to kill me anyway, so why the fuck should I tell you anything?"

I narrowed my eyes and worked to control my impatience with his stalling. "Because if you're lucky, I won't kill you. Tell us everything you know and I'll let you go and you can spend the rest of your pathetic life looking over your shoulder for that bitch Hailey."

It may have been a lie, depending on what he told us, but my main concern wasn't being honest with this piece of garbage. It was getting answers so we could clear Jordan's name.

I saw I had bluffed well. While Justin looked elated for the briefest moment, Jordan was obviously confused at my answer. A quick glance in her direction told her I hadn't been entirely truthful. Justin was too excited by the news that he might live to see another day and thankfully didn't notice the tiny smile she gave me to tell me she understood.

"Ok…ok, what do you want to know?" he sputtered.

Criminals like this guy were all so similar. Threaten to kill them and they clammed up, but offer them the possibility of getting away with it and they not only jumped but asked how high.

"What are you stupid? Everything!" Jordan snapped.

"I would listen to her, Justin. I might have the gun, but there's nothing worse than a woman scorned, and I'd say Jordan has every reason to be that," I said, managing to make him shake even more. He knew damn well I was the one to fear, but he also knew enough to fear her wrath. Even the dumbest man could see when a woman wanted revenge. Hell really did have no fury like a woman bent on getting back at someone.

"I'll tell you, okay? Just promise you'll let me go after I do," Justin pleaded.

"Answer the question. How did you come to impersonate Brock Hannon?" I repeated.

"Hailey. She hired me. She said she wanted me to impersonate the guy, but I swear she never told me why," he said.

Justin's eyes darted left and right nervously. It was hard to tell if it was because he was lying or because he guessed correctly that we wouldn't be satisfied with the continued variation on the answer, "I don't know anything."

Hailey. I was so fucking sick of hearing her name already. What I wouldn't have given to have her tied up in front of me instead of this clown.

"Why did she kidnap Jordan and force her into a marriage with you? Why is any of this even happening, Justin?" I asked. The thought of Jordan being married to this useless scumbag made my voice shake with rage I never thought I had inside me.

"I told you, man. I don't know!" he cried out in frustration. Whether I liked it or not, it was starting to seem as though Justin knew barely more than Jordan did.

"I bet you think you're so clever don't you?" Jordan asked,

clearly tired of his stalling. "Do you really think that we're just going to believe that you don't know anything about what's going on and then what, just let you go on your merry way afterwards? If you don't have a bargaining chip, you don't get to keep playing the game, Justin."

"Jordan, don't you remember back in South Carolina? I wanted to help you back there. I tried to. Remember?" Justin said, attempting to appeal to Jordan's good side, not exactly a winning strategy for him.

Her eyes narrowed to thin slits and her mouth tightened into an equally thin line. "I'm finding it hard to recall, though the memory of you trying to shove me into a car while you nearly choked the life out of me is pretty damn vivid right now."

This was getting us nowhere. I understood her anger, but this wasn't working. "Jordan, I want you to stand back by the couch," I said. "Justin and I need to have a man-to-man talk."

She opened her mouth to protest but said nothing. Glaring at him, she stormed away and did as I had told her to.

Justin looked up in terror at me as I slowly circled around to behind him to check his bindings to make sure he was still secured to the chair. When I saw he was, I leaned down so my lips nearly touched his right ear and whispered, "I've had just about enough of your fucking stalling. I'm not a killer by nature, but if you think I won't shoot you right here if you don't start telling me what I want to know, you're wrong. That woman you and that bitch Hailey tricked into marrying you is the woman I love, so if you don't start saying something useful, I'm going to solve the problem of her marriage to you by making her a widow. In fact, you have no idea how much easier that would make both our lives, so I'd think carefully about your next words if I were you, Justin."

He turned his head to face me, a look of pure terror flashing in his eyes. Finally, he understood what his future held if he didn't begin to cooperate. "Okay, okay. Just give me a second to think, okay?"

I stepped in front of him and pointed the gun at the spot between his eyes once again. "I expect to hear something useful from you when I get back."

Keeping my eye on him, I crossed the room to where Jordan waited and quietly said, "Jordan, I don't know if he's lying. He might not know anything."

I hated to admit that. I'd hoped to hear something from him that would help us solve the puzzle of why Hailey had wanted Jordan to marry him instead of continually turning the little pieces we had over and over in our hands.

"But Gage, he's been in on it from the start. This has been going on a while. I mean, think of how long he and I were together. He's got to know something."

Thinking about how long she was with him only made my stomach turn. "I'd rather not, but I get it. It seems like he should know more than he seems to, but Jordan, I know how to spot a liar and my gut says he isn't lying. He may know small details about this whole thing, but I'm not getting a mastermind vibe off this guy. I'm pretty sure Hailey kept him out of the loop, for the most part."

In her green eyes, I saw the disappointment she felt. "I don't necessarily disagree with that, but we should still question him longer to see if he cracks and says something we can use, right?"

"Yes. I'm not ready to give up yet, but I'm not expecting too much from him. He's a tool and that's about it. I just need you to not be distracted when he appeals to you emotionally. He knows you pretty well, after all. He's going to know how to play on your sympathies. Don't let him."

"Okay," she said, nodding her agreement. "I'll try to keep my cool. I can't help it sometimes, though. I trusted him for a long time and thought he was..."

Her voice trailed off, and she hung her head. God, I hated seeing her like that. Jordan believed in people, and this asshole had gotten his jollies off playing her for a fool.

But she didn't need me letting that get in the way of finding out what the hell was going on with him and Hailey, so I stuffed that down inside and pressed a small kiss to her forehead. "Don't let the memory of that get to you. We're going to find out what this is all about and then we're going to ride off into the sunset and live happily ever after, right?"

Jordan forced a smile. "Right."

"Okay. Let me handle this and then we'll move on with what he tells us. Don't worry. I'm not going to let these jackasses do anything more to you."

I saw in her eyes that she believed me and hugging her to me, I kissed the top of her head before we returned to where Justin sat to hopefully pull something useful from him. He must have become convinced that we were discussing whether or not to kill him because when we stepped back in front of him he immediately started pleading for his life.

"Please. Please, I'm just a guy. I only did it for the money and no one ever told me it was going to go this far. I swear you guys, please." He faded off into tears and I snapped my fingers in front of his face to get him to look up again.

"Hey, hey. No crying. If I decide to kill you, I'll let you know," I said coolly, making sure to lower the pistol slightly. Perhaps having it in his face for too long had scared him out of giving an answer at all.

Justin sniffled and sat up a little. "Okay."

"Here's how this is going to go," I continued. "You're going to tell us everything you know from the beginning. I don't care how much you do or don't know about something. If it relates to Jordan and this entire thing, you're going to tell us. Do that, and maybe, just maybe, we'll let you walk out of this cabin alive. But I swear to God, Justin, if I think for one fucking second that you're lying to me, and I will know if you're lying to me, I'll leave you buried so deep in these mountains they won't even know where to start looking. Do I make myself clear?"

There was no room for discussion. My terms were clear and he could decide to not follow them if he liked. I had no problem leaving him tied up miles from here where it would take days for the cops to find him and we'd be long gone from this cabin and him.

He nodded, his hair shaking as he agreed to my demands. I wasn't being entirely untruthful. I might let him walk away with his life, but I wouldn't make it easy for him.

"Well...I don't really know where to start. Hailey hired me, told me to marry Jordan. I was to meet her and make her fall in love with me. I mean it when I tell you that she kept me in the dark."

"Why did she want you to marry me?" Jordan spoke up, her voice raspy.

He turned his gaze toward her and for a moment I could see genuine pain there. He didn't look like he'd enjoyed having hurt her, but that didn't change anything, in my opinion. Just because the guy had decided after he had conned her that he wanted to protect her didn't make him a hero. Frankly, I questioned the reality of his feelings towards her altogether.

"I don't know," he answered feebly.

As much as I hated it, that didn't sound like a lie. I had told the guy that if he failed to tell me something we would kill him. Either he was calling my bluff or he really didn't know anything about why Hailey wanted Jordan. Sadly, I had to admit the latter seemed more plausible.

"So she just said find this woman and make her fall in love with you and you didn't ask a single question?" I found it hard to believe that anyone, even a total idiot, wouldn't ask a few questions when being told to impersonate a millionaire businessman and woo an elementary school teacher.

"It was a lot of money," he offered lamely.

I moved the pistol back to its position in between Justin's eyes.

His eyes opened wide in fear. "Okay, okay. I mean, I had to ask a lot about the Brock Hannon part, but Jordan seemed secondary to me. Pulling off being Brock Hannon was a full time gig, and Jordan didn't come into the picture right away."

"So you asked what about him?" I wondered, remembering that Daryl had said Hannon had died before all this had begun.

Justin blew the air out of his lungs slowly. "You know, his mannerisms, what he liked and didn't like, who the guy was. If I was going to pretend to be him, I had to get him down pat. It took a few weeks, but I got it and then Hailey said it was time to do my part with Jordan."

"And when you did?" Jordan asked quietly.

The pain in her eyes wasn't just because of what he'd done to her throat just minutes earlier. She had been won over by this guy and had been convinced she was on her way to living the life she had always dreamed for herself. I knew she wanted a life like Nina had with Tristan. Hell, who wouldn't? Instead she'd gotten this in return for her trust.

"Well, Hailey had some information on you. Basic stuff like where you liked to eat, what you liked to do, where you worked. Then I got to getting to know you."

Justin spoke very casually about the private and personal details about Jordan's life he had been privy to. In my own line of work, it wasn't unusual to do some digging about the people who didn't like the person you were protecting, but for Jordan it was clear this was huge invasion of her privacy. Her mouth turned into a harsh frown as her eyes filled with tears.

"How...how could you know that about me?" she said, struggling to keep her composure. I wanted to go comfort her, but I needed to focus on Justin and his answers to my questions.

"I told you. Hailey."

"Was she the one who sent me the letters about Jordan?" I asked, drawing his attention back to me so Jordan could gather herself.

He struggled to look past the gun and to my face as he responded, "I don't know anything about any letters." His eyes were wide, but he didn't seem to be lying.

"What was the plan after you married Jordan?"

"I don't know. That part got a little fucked up, you know?" he said like he regretted what had happened to the plan.

I didn't like that he seemed to be relaxing, so I pushed him hard enough to make the chair nearly fall backwards. "You think this is a joke, Justin? You might not know what the plan was, but you and I both know that her plan now is to kill you. There's no way Hailey's letting you live after you botched things up, so you better get serious quick. Otherwise, I'm going to leave you tied up in those woods out there like a prize pig for her to find and do whatever she wants with. Do you read me?" I shouted, watching him wince as he struggled to maintain his balance.

He nodded but said nothing, but my rage wasn't done. It coursed through me as I barked, "I said, do you fucking read me, you piece of shit?"

"Yes! Yes," he sputtered through tears.

I glanced at Jordan and she looked at me frightened. I had warned her that I wasn't going to be playing good cop here. This guy had been a key piece in ruining what Jordan and I had originally had, and he was responsible for so much of her pain. I wasn't going to take it easy on him. Still, I wanted her to know I wasn't some animal, so I struggled to form a half smile and hoped that she would understand.

Thankfully, she seemed to register that I was still in control of myself and nodded back at me for encouragement.

"Let's get back to what you were saying, Justin. You won over Jordan, so why did Hailey come around and start watching over her so closely?"

"Well, we were together, you know, but I'm guessing you don't want to know about that."

I couldn't stop from rolling my eyes. This guy really was an idiot. No wonder Hailey hadn't keep him in the loop. "Spare us the sordid details of your love affair with your psychotic girlfriend. Just stick to what her interest in Jordan was."

"She said she sensed something was wrong. She didn't trust me to handle the situation, so she said she needed to come in and handle it herself. After that she didn't tell me anything, except for when I was supposed to be somewhere to meet with her. I was to stay away from Jordan on business."

"You aren't telling us anything we don't know, Justin. We told you that you needed a bargaining chip if you wanted to keep playing, but you don't seem to know anything. I think we should kill him and move on to dear Hailey, Gage," Jordan said as Justin looked over at her in horror.

Then it dawned on me. I had been so distracted by his attempt to take Jordan that I had forgotten the most important question. "How did you find us here?"

He paused, trying to think of a lie, and I moved closer, pushing the gun to his forehead. "We agreed there would be no lying, Justin. Answer me."

"Your sister, Denise. She's been working with Hailey," he whispered in a shaky voice.

I didn't move as the gun stayed pressed against his forehead and I stared into his eyes searching for a clue that would tell me he was lying. I couldn't find one. But that was impossible. Denise wouldn't be wrapped up in all this. She couldn't be. Not her.

"What did you say?" Jordan rasped.

I stepped back, still pointing the gun at his head. "I said don't fucking lie, Justin. Who really told you we were here?" I yelled.

"I told you! Denise!" he wailed, and the room fell silent.

CHAPTER ELEVEN

JORDAN

IT WAS IMMEDIATELY CLEAR THAT Gage didn't believe what Justin was saying, but he was the one who had said not five minutes before that he didn't think Justin was full of it. It didn't seem to make sense that Justin would be lying right now, not after the threats Gage had made and especially not after being pushed around like that.

"I'm going to give you one more chance to tell us the truth before I put a bullet in that ugly face of yours," Gage said, practically growling in anger at Justin.

He sat there trembling and looked over at me like he was searching for an ally. "You have to believe me. I'm not lying! She's been working with Hailey, but I don't know for how long. I just know Hailey found out from her that you were here!"

I wanted to look into his eyes and see a lie there, but try as I might I couldn't find one.

"Why would Denise sell us out? She doesn't know me and she wouldn't hurt her brother like that," I said, hoping I was right.

I wondered if Hailey had lured Denise in the same way she had Justin. She obviously hadn't been above pretending to be romantically interested in someone just to gain an advantage.

"Hailey told her that she would hurt his family if she didn't give you up," he said quietly, wincing from the rage coming off Gage.

"Shut up! Just shut your face!" Gage barked, clearly letting his anger get the best of him. Every muscle in his body flexed in anger.

At first, it had been nice to see Gage handling the situation. There was an undeniable sexiness in him taking control, but that feeling was starting to fade as Gage was pushed to a new breaking point. The idea of someone he loved doing this to him was more than he could take. I couldn't imagine how it would feel to be dealt such an utter betrayal from a sister, but he needed to focus and not let his emotions get the best of him or we'd never find out what was truly going on with Hailey.

"Gage," I whispered, "What if he isn't lying?"

They were forbidden words but something needed to be said and time was starting to run out. If Hailey knew where we were, it was only a matter of time before she showed up and the situation got one hundred times worse.

"Of course he's lying. That's what he does! He's lied about everything since the day you met him, and now he says my sister is the one who told Hailey where we were and you want to believe him? I'm sorry, Jordan, but between the two of us I'm clearly the one who's better at seeing through bullshit. He's trying to get us to fight with each other and distract us."

I tried to calm him down, but that was next to impossible. I had no choice but to show him what Justin had said was possible. Very possible. "How else did he find out where we were, Gage?"

He looked away and mumbled, "I don't know." It was an important question and one he was clearly trying to answer in his head with someone other than his sister.

"What did you two talk about when she was here? Why was she here in the first place?" I asked.

The pieces were beginning to fit together for me, and if the truth was that Denise had given us up, that meant Gage was going to have some very tough choices to make very soon. I knew he loved me, but if the choice was between his family and me, how could I expect him to choose me?

As Gage's face went white, I knew my answer. There was no

reason Justin would lie about something so egregious with the threat of losing his life dangling over his head. Even if he believed Gage wouldn't carry out his threat, there was no reason he'd choose to blame Denise.

"Gage, we need to speak alone," I said, wishing more than ever this was all over and we were back in my apartment in Brooklyn in each other's arms complaining about the city heat as the not-so-cool air from my junky little fan blew over us.

His only response was a curt nod as he swiftly moved to the closet off the kitchen and opened the door. As Justin whimpered something about telling the truth, he dragged him and the chair both into the closet and slammed the door with a bang.

When he turned around, he looked like he had aged twenty years. Lines crossed his forehead and his mouth was set into a tight frown. "Jordan, I know you want to believe him, but he's full of shit. No one in my family, least of all my sister, would do this to us…to me," he said, running his hand through his hair.

He clearly had a pretty strong bias, but now didn't seem to be the time to say anything like that. "I know you don't want to believe that she would, but how else would Justin have known we were here and get here so fast? We weren't here for even two hours before he showed up," I said, hoping some cold hard facts would bring his always logical mind around to my side.

It wasn't as though I wanted to believe that Denise would have done this to us. I wanted Gage's family to love me. The goal certainly had not been to get them to dislike me enough that they would turn me over to people who wanted to kill me.

It wasn't going to be that easy, though. As I finished speaking, Gage backed away from me, as if the very thought of Denise committing such a sin against him was enough to push him away.

"You don't understand, Jordan. My family doesn't operate like that. We aren't some soap opera family that goes around stabbing each other in the back. Family is important to us, and no matter what, you do whatever you can to make sure they're safe. Denise was raised with the same values I was, and you don't betray family. Period."

He wasn't thinking clearly. That was evident in how he avoided my question. Gage didn't want to hear logic right now. He wanted to return to normality. At this point, it was hard not to wonder if Gage and I would ever return to that state.

Still, I needed him to start thinking clearly, or he wouldn't be considering all of the angles of the complex mess we were both in. "Gage, please. We need to think about this rationally," I started, but before I could continue, he cut me off.

"Fine. Rationally, it doesn't make sense that Denise would this to me."

"What did you two talk about, Gage?" I asked again. I had a strong feeling that I knew why he was dodging the question.

"Jordan, that doesn't mean anything. She didn't do it. End of story."

From the closet, Justin yelled that he wasn't lying, but even as I was beginning to truly believe what he'd said, Gage was nowhere near buying his story.

Ignoring our captive's pleas, I raised my hands to cradle Gage's face. "No, not end of story, baby. You mean to tell me that what you two talked about had nothing to do with what's going on with me?"

His gaze dropped, and I knew the truth without him saying a word. "You two talked about us being on the run, and we're supposed to believe she isn't the one who sold us out? Why would he lie Gage? You threatened to kill him if he didn't tell the truth. You, yourself, said he didn't seem to be lying, so what am I missing here?"

I understood feeling betrayed and refusing to admit the truth. If someone had claimed Nina had done this to us, I would be doing the exact same thing, but if Gage didn't start thinking clearly, it was going to cost us even more than it already had.

The logic of my point was setting in, but he fought it tooth and nail. "No. No, Jordan, I refuse to believe that Denise would do this."

I looked up into his dark eyes so troubled and asked, "Why was she here, baby? All you need to do is answer that and we'll know if he lied or not."

"She needed to get some work off of her laptop," he answered, but the look on his face showed he knew something about that sounded wrong.

"You mean the laptop we were doing all our research on?" I replied.

The anger had taken longer than expected to set in. I was busy trying to get Gage to understand the peril this put us in and I had almost forgotten to be mad. Almost. How could he have been as foolish as to hand over the only edge we may have had over Hailey and Justin. Of course, she had probably done a quick search of the history and figured out exactly what we knew.

"Listen, I don't blame you for telling her what was going on. She's your sister. How could you have known that she was gathering information?"

"Stop it right there," he interrupted sharply. "You don't know what you're talking about."

"Listen Gage, whether you like it or not, we're going to have to face the reality that someone told them where we were and it's looking like your sister is the prime candidate."

He didn't like hearing that, but I couldn't stop to sugar coat it for him. We needed to make a move now or at any minute Hailey or the police would be showing up at the cabin's front door. I didn't know which was worse.

He opened his mouth to speak, but this time I cut him off and raised my hand to stop him.

"No, I know it isn't what you want to hear right now, but you're going to have to deal with that later. Right now, we have Justin tied up in the closet, but we don't know where Hailey is. She could be close. We can't get hung up on whether it was your sister or not. We'll figure that out later."

It wasn't perfect, and I certainly had no interest in dealing with this later as opposed to right now, but we needed to get moving unless we wanted to face serious trouble. Gage didn't want to deal with it later either, but something in what I said must have resonated because he took a deep breath in.

"We'll find out who really did this Jordan. I promise," he said as took my hand.

As I looked into his eyes, I hoped that he was right that Denise hadn't been the one to tell Hailey where we were, but I seriously doubted it. "Of course, but we need to focus right now on what to do next," I said, thankful that he seemed to be returning to his normal self.

"We need to see if there's anything left for Justin to give us. After that, we're going to have to do something with him. It isn't safe and you're right. Hailey is probably on her way and that isn't good. We can't leave him here and get my family involved in whatever Hailey's doing, though," Gage said, his confidence showing in his voice.

I nodded my agreement and he kissed me on the forehead before crossing the room to open the door to let Justin out. "You ready to tell the truth, or do you need a little more time in the closet?" Gage asked as he dragged the chair back to the center of the room. He spoke to the man like an untrained dog, earning a glare from Justin.

Whatever he'd been doing in the closet while Gage and I were speaking, it hadn't included mustering up any courage. When he was settled and the chair had stopped wobbling, he looked up at Gage and pleaded. "I swear I told you. I'm not lying," he whimpered.

"Gage, we need to move on. We don't have time," I said quietly. I knew we couldn't keep fixating on the Denise issue or we would never get any further information before Gage eventually lost it and killed Justin.

He threw me a look that told me he was less than thrilled but he clearly saw the truth in my reasoning.

"Justin, if you've got anything else to say, I better hear it and it better be damn good," Gage growled.

"Hailey...Hailey's mad, and she's on her way," he answered, his eyes flitting around as if he expected her to crawl out of the woodwork.

"Gage, what are we going to do?" I asked from beside him as Justin's description of Hailey sent chills up and down my spine. A madwoman was after me and wanted me dead, and I didn't want to give her a chance to achieve that goal.

"I don't think it's a good idea to talk about it in front of this one," he said with a jerk of his head towards the crying Justin. "I need you to go upstairs and grab the things we brought. We need to get going."

Whatever harm hearing his sister may have been involved in this whole thing had faded, and the man I knew and loved was back. I ran upstairs and grabbed our things, but being out of his sight only made my emotions about Denise come surging back.

Silently, I fumed as I threw things in bags and went back downstairs. How could she do this? What was her problem? I hardly knew the woman and she helped someone who wanted to kill me! I shook it off as best I could and raced back downstairs to join Gage.

"Good. Now grab some bottles of water out of the refrigerator. We'll get food on the way."

Again, I followed his directions, returning to stuff our bags with all the water I could find. Gage stood silently in front of Justin who sat slumped over in the chair as if he'd lost all hope of seeing another day alive.

"Did you knock him out so we could talk?" I asked.

"No, but he's headed in that direction all on his own. Most likely hasn't stopped to eat while he's been pursuing us. He's coasting on fumes," Gage answered stoically.

I had never seen a time before where Gage had lacked any form of mercy. It scared me a little, but I knew he would never display that kind of behavior in regards to me. Still, it was unnerving to see the man who I knew was capable of so much love and tenderness staring at a man who looked like he was dying and not giving a damn.

There was a strangeness in seeing Justin like this too. For almost the entire time I had known him, he had simply been Brock. I was supposed to be in love with this man. I was married to this man, but I had no idea who he was other than a pathetic conman.

I had kissed his lips and far more than that. We had made not only love but memories, moments that now felt cheap and contrived.

I had made plans for a future with this man, and even though I had known deep in my heart he wasn't the one for me, the choice I made had seemed like the safe one at the time. Now as I looked at him after all that had happened, I felt nothing but disgusted at how willing I'd been to discount love for security. I'd gotten neither from him in the end and both from Gage.

"All right, Justin, wake up," Gage barked, startling me out of my thoughts.

"Please, please I'm telling…"

"Yeah, we get it. You're telling the truth. Enough already. We have to move you, so here's how this is going to go. You're going to stay still while I loosen the rope from the chair. Do not move after that. If you do, Jordan will shoot you. I'm going to adjust your bindings and then I'll tell you when you can move again. You fail to follow these instructions and I will kill you. Do you understand me?"

Gage still held the gun and the vein in his head was pulsing. If Justin had any ideas about being brave or daring, I hoped he wouldn't act on them. I didn't give a damn about his welfare, but I didn't want to see the man I loved kill him.

"Yes," Justin said. "I swear I won't do a thing. Just don't kill me." He had given up the tough guy act and seemed to be falling back into his natural state.

A pathetic mess.

And that was just what happened. To my great surprise, Justin followed orders to the letter and didn't try anything stupid. When we were done, he stood, still tied up, and did his best to avoid eye contact with the both of us. He stared at the floor and looked like a fidgeting rat the way he looked back and forth as if counting the floor boards.

"Jordan," Gage said, his tone softening as he looked at me, all the while keeping a hand on Justin's back and shoulder. "I need to get him to the car and I need both of my hands. Are you able to carry our things out and hold the gun?"

I smiled and nodded. "You are looking at the all-time champion of one trip from the car to the apartment with all the grocery bags."

My voice still sounded terrible, and Gage almost laughed before catching himself, which was enough to make me feel slightly better. I didn't know what we were going to do, but more than anything I just wanted Justin out of the picture so Gage and I could have moments of laughter again. Real, beautiful moments, not ones that were cheapened because they were tainted with this mess we were in.

"Right then, let's go." He gave Justin a nudge and he responded by taking a few tentative steps forward. "Just like I said, one foot in front of the other and don't do anything stupid."

We were a motley crew making our way down the mountainside away from the cabin. We reached the vehicle and Justin was clearly surprised when Gage opened the door and gently placed him in the backseat.

"See, that's how you put someone in a vehicle, you animal," he said and shut the door.

When he turned to me he must have seen the anger and confusion in my face because the first words out of his mouth were, "I know this looks bad, but he isn't staying with us. I plan to dump him a few miles outside of town. Since he has no cellphone, it'll slow them down while Hailey looks for him to try and figure out where we're going."

His words were hushed and although I could tell he was thinking of things on the fly, I trusted his judgement.

"And then where are we going?" I asked, earning a concerned look from Gage.

He put his hand out and gently rubbed my cheek. "We'll figure that out after we take care of him. For now, I'm thinking we talk in the car as though we're going to California. If we do that, maybe they'll follow the false trail and it can net us some extra time while we sort out where we're going."

I took a deep breath of Wyoming mountain air and tried to convince myself that wherever we went it would be okay.

"How are you feeling? Are you okay?" he asked.

His eyes showed his concern, and he furrowed his brow as he looked at my bruised neck. I wasn't okay, and neither was he, but now wasn't the time to break down in tears over it. The business with Denise was still in the front of my mind, along with what we'd do about Hailey and Justin, but I knew we had to keep on track. Otherwise, the entire situation would start unraveling around us.

For the sake of the man I loved, I hoped it hadn't been her who told Hailey and Justin where we were. I knew if it came to light that Denise was responsible for putting me in harm's way, Gage would be devastated. His family meant the world to him, even if he hadn't been back home to Wyoming in years. That was the kind of man he was. That loyalty ran deep in him, and if his sister had betrayed it, I didn't know how he'd handle it.

"I've been better. Thinking I may need to pick up a scarf to avoid odd stares in public." My hands instinctively went to my swollen neck and I winced. This was just what I needed on top of everything else.

"I'll find you the best one there is," he vowed as he kissed the top of my hand.

This small moment of sweetness amidst the chaos felt nice. My mother used to say that even in the darkest storm there is hope, and I was trying to believe that. Admittedly, things hadn't gone our way much, but at least we had Justin tied up in the backseat. I couldn't help but think that was a good thing, although it would have been better if Hailey was tied up next to him.

Maybe if we could weather the storm long enough the glimmer of hope flickering inside me would grow into something even better. I hoped so. We'd seen enough bad times to last a lifetime.

CHAPTER TWELVE

GAGE

JORDAN SMILED UP AT ME and for a moment that happiness only she could make me feel returned. She was my Jordan, the complicated, sexy, and entirely maddening woman I couldn't imagine my life without. My gaze drifted down to her neck to see the bruises from Justin's hands choking her already darkening against her tanned skin, and a tiny spark of rage ignited inside me. If I wanted to keep that happy feeling, I would have to get her that scarf and quick.

It was bad enough he had tricked her into falling for him and then helped in her abduction, but the fact that he had nearly strangled her made me want to rip his arms off.

I walked Jordan to her side of the car and let her in before getting in the driver's side myself. Looking up at the rearview mirror, I saw Justin staring back at me with a look that said he wasn't sure I wouldn't toss him out of the car and leave him up here in the mountains to die. A small part of me liked that, so I narrowed my eyes to angry squints and in my best badass voice said, "One problem with you and I'll leave you out here to be eaten by fucking coyotes."

The interrogation hadn't gone as well as I had hoped, a fact I didn't want Justin or Jordan figuring out. In truth, Justin hadn't told us much that we didn't already know and I knew he was lying about Denise. He could cry and whine that he was telling the truth all he wanted, but I knew that wasn't the case. Denise was family, and family didn't hurt each other like that.

The problem I was running into was that I couldn't find the motivation behind the lie. Why would Justin lie about her ratting us out if he knew it would make me angry? Maybe he was more afraid of Hailey than me. She was psychotic, so that would be a real concern since Justin had obviously been screwing things up for her. Odds were that he knew I wouldn't kill him unless truly provoked or out of self-defense.

It must have been clear to him that I would do anything to protect Jordan, but he and I both knew that I couldn't do that if I was behind bars for murder. As I put the car in gear, I looked back at him and couldn't help but wish I'd gotten more information.

It could have gone better, but the important thing was Jordan was still safe. Hurt, yes, but safe, and when I found Hailey I would make her pay for every single pain Jordan had been made to suffer at her hands.

"You ready?" I asked Jordan as I began to drive away from the cabin.

She nodded and even though she was bruised to hell, I couldn't get over how stunning she still was. It was like something about her just radiated a goodness and kindness I craved. Added to those was an undeniable strength within her that I hadn't always been aware of. She might have thought of herself as weak and helpless, but not many women could hold it all together as well as she was after all the shit she'd been through.

"Gage, I think I know where we can go," Jordan said as she turned the radio up just enough to make it seem like we were trying to talk without Justin hearing our conversation.

I liked having her as my partner in crime. While I didn't enjoy the constant danger we were in, it was nice seeing how quickly her mind worked in a situation like this. There was nothing like a beautiful woman who was smart too.

"Well, we're going to have to do something with this one. It's not like we can trust him if he's out of our sight or not," I said just loud enough for our friend in the backseat to hear.

"I thought you were going to just drop him off in the middle of nowhere," Jordan said.

A quick glance in the rearview mirror told me Justin was listening intently, and the news that we might leave him stranded in the mountains terrified him. "I haven't decided what to do yet. One minute I think I'll do that, but every time I look at those bruises on your neck, I can't help but want to shoot him."

Justin made a whimpering noise behind me, and I couldn't help but smile. Fucking weasel. He deserved for me to do my worst. "We need to find someplace to regroup and figure out what we're doing next. Where do you have in mind?"

Jordan turned around to look into the backseat and then leaned over toward me like she was trying to keep what she had to say from Justin. "I have a friend in San Francisco I think could help us."

"San Fran it is. Drive or fly? The nearest airport is a few hours away," I said, feeling Justin's stare on the back of my head as he listened to every word we said.

Jordan pretended to think about my question and then answered, "Fly. That'll be quicker and once we get to the city, she'll never find us."

I lifted her hand to my lips and kissed it. Justin had heard the whole conversation. In a few miles, I'd leave him off on the side of the road to fend for himself, which would buy us time since he'd be more concerned about saving his own hide than finding some way to contact Hailey to tell her where we were headed. Hopefully, she believed him.

We stayed silent for the rest of the drive down the mountain and away from my home town. I drove until I knew we were about ten miles outside of a nearby town and stopped the car on the side of the road.

Turning around to look at him, I glared at Justin and said in a low voice, "This is where you get off."

His face registered his terror. "No, please! I told you I didn't lie!

Please, you told me you wouldn't kill me if I told the truth!"

I sort of enjoyed watching him frantically struggle against the ropes holding his wrists as his knees pressed against the back of my seat and he craned his neck searching for some way out of his impending punishment.

But I wasn't interested in torturing him anymore, so I rolled my eyes, sick of hearing the same damn thing, and got out of the car.

Justin looked up at me with tears rolling down his face. I held the gun and opened the door, gesturing for him to get out of the vehicle. He had difficulty because of the restraints holding his arms together, but with a little steadying he stood in front of me, still begging for his life in the afternoon sun.

"Shut up, Justin. I swear if I have to hear another word out of you I'm going to lose it. Shut the fuck up."

Silence. Nothing but the wind blowing through the yellowed grass on the side of the road and the idling car made a sound as we stood facing each other. I knew he thought I was going to kill him, and I would be a liar if I said I wasn't enjoying the power I held over him. Since the moment I had laid eyes on him, I knew he wasn't right for Jordan and now after all the pain and damage he had helped cause, he stood crying before me. It was a blissful moment of victory.

"Slowly turn your back to me, Justin. I'm going to cut your ropes and we're going to part ways. They say three's a crowd anyway."

Justin looked confused, but he did as he was told. I cut the rope and he turned around to face me, staring at the gun and looking like he didn't know what to do next.

"You...you aren't going to kill me?" he stammered out. His eyes darted from the gun to my face, back and forth.

"Let me make this perfectly clear to you. The next time I see you is the time I kill you. Understand?"

"Yes."

"And you tell Hailey, that bitch's time is running out. I've got Jordan protected, so it doesn't matter what she sends at us. You tell her from me that if she knows what's good for her she'll go run and hide somewhere where I can't find her, because when I do, well, let's just say she won't get the reprieve I'm giving you now."

He chose not to reply and I said to Jordan, who sat watching us with the window down, "Please hand me a bottle of water."

She paused for a moment, and I had the distinct impression she was deciding whether or not to disagree about us leaving him to die of thirst there on the side of a desolate road in Wyoming. Jordan was a good person, though, so after a few moments she handed me one of the bottles we'd taken from the cabin.

I kept the gun pointed and with my other hand tossed the water at him.

Justin stared at me, clearly confused. "Why are you doing this?" he asked.

"Because I'm a good guy."

Knowing what lay ahead of him on a hot August day on a deserted Wyoming road, I might not be considered good. "Well, at least not someone like you. By the time you get into town, you're going to be blacking out from hunger and dying of thirst, so I'd pray to God you see someone willing to give you a ride. Since only about twenty cars a day ever drive up and down this road, I wouldn't count on it, though."

"I didn't lie back there."

With the gun still pointed at him, I walked around the car and leaned up against the side to take one last look at Justin or Brock or whoever he was. "Remember, the next time I see you is when I kill you."

And with that we left him standing there in the hot, summer sun miles away from the nearest town with just a bottle of water. He was lucky I didn't shoot him, but I didn't want his death on my conscience. Jordan and I had a future to get to, and that didn't include being taken away from her for anything.

We may have left Justin behind us. The rest of our problems were still front and center, unfortunately.

I stowed the gun safely under the seat and looked over at Jordan. "You think he bought the San Francisco bit?" I asked.

She turned to look at me with a big grin. "I wouldn't have left him with even a bottle of water. You're nicer than I am, Gage Varo."

"I thought we might need some good Karma points for the future. I promise the next guy I keep hostage at gunpoint won't get such nice treatment."

Jordan leaned over to lay her head on my shoulder. "What do you think of us never doing that again? Do you think we can arrange that?"

Pressing a kiss to the top of her head, I smiled. "I'll see what I can do. For now, we need to decide where we're really going."

She nodded and sat up. "I think we need some help. We need to touch base with someone who knows the situation." Pulling out my phone, she said, "And I know just the person."

CHAPTER THIRTEEN

GAGE

A FEW MOMENTS LATER, JORDAN was holding the phone out between us with it on speaker and Nina was answering.

"Hello? Jordan? Is that you?" Nina asked as she answered the call, her voice frantic and full of worry.

"Yes! It's me and Gage, I have you on speaker phone. We're okay," Jordan replied, trying to mask the pain in her voice from her near strangulation.

"Oh, Jordan, you don't sound okay. What's going on? I'm so glad to hear you're both safe. Tristan and I have been worried sick!"

I knew Nina had likely been pacing back and forth for hours as Tristan had done what he always did—rallied the people he had who could help us.

Jordan looked at me and I spoke up. "Hey, Nina. We're fine. Jordan got hurt when Justin attacked her, but she's going to be okay. I promise."

"What do you mean Justin attacked her? What happened?"

"Justin must have been waiting for me because he grabbed me and tried to shove me into his car. He choked me. That's why I sound like this, but we interrogated him and got away, so I swear we're good."

The phone fell silent, but finally Nina said, "I don't like any of this, but you'll have to tell me more about that later. What are you doing now? What happened to Justin?"

"We left him on the side of the road in the middle of nowhere.

We're driving away from Gage's hometown right now. We're still in Wyoming, but we need to move fast since we don't know how far behind Hailey is."

"Nina, is Tristan with you?" I asked, hoping he was nearby.

We heard a click on the phone as Nina turned her speaker phone on, allowing us to hear Tristan.

"I'm here, Gage. I'm glad you're all right, though it seems like things could be better. How can we help?" There was concern in his tone, but he seemed calmer than Nina was. Tristan knew how to handle a situation, even if that usually meant hopping on a plane rather than getting his boots too dirty.

"We're not sure where to go next. They were able to find us somehow so Wyoming isn't safe, but now we need to figure out where to go."

"What about one of the hotels, Tristan? I know it isn't perfect, but it might be a start," Nina chimed in.

"It's a good idea, but unfortunately, the police have been all over them looking for you two since the concierge in Hilton Head admitted that she'd seen Jordan that night. I'm not sure if they've figured out you're helping her by now, Gage. I don't know if you told Daryl to cover for you, but he's got your staff saying you're visiting family in California."

"I owe Daryl big then. And I'll need to start giving some raises out soon too. So I guess the hotels are no good."

Tristan thought for a moment and said, "I think you two need to head to a bigger city. The small town idea was fine at first, but you need to be able to get lost in a sea of people if you need to. It would also help to have some witnesses around if Hailey catches up to you. She may be less likely to attack you when she knows she'll get caught."

It was a sound idea. Hailey was surely less likely to try anything if there were people around. She may have wanted Jordan dead, but I had serious doubts about her risking her own freedom by being seen doing it.

"That's a good idea," Jordan agreed. "It can't be California, though. We laid a fake trail for Justin that would lead him to California. At least I hope so." With a smile, she joked, "Luckily, we don't know where we're going, so neither does he."

"Well, if you can't go west and you can't come east, you have the south or north to choose from," Tristan replied.

There was a long pause and Jordan and I looked at each other. We were out of answers and starting to run out of time. We needed to make a decision fast but I hadn't spent much time in the south and knew next to no one there, and the idea of running to Canada didn't sound like the answer either.

"Wait. Tristan, didn't your father have a house in New Orleans?" Nina asked.

There was an excited buzz in the air as Tristan replied, "Actually, he did in the Garden District. We've only been there once. It's listed as Stone company property, but we essentially pay the taxes for it to sit there and collect dust, though I do think someone is paid to clean it twice a year, so the dust wouldn't be that bad."

"That could work. That could really work, Tristan," I said, my voice brimming with excitement. Jordan reached across the middle console and held my hand as she smiled at me.

"I'll send someone to the house to open it up for you. Just call me when you get closer to the city and I'll make sure it's taken care of."

Jordan beamed her happiness that once again we had a plan. "It sounds perfect, Tristan. Thank you both so much. I don't know what we would do without you."

"Of course. Do you have a pen and paper for the address? I'll give it to you now."

"I've got a pen and napkin, so close enough," Jordan replied, fishing a pen from her bag.

As Tristan rattled off the address of the home on Prytania Street in the Garden District, I turned the car around to head south.

"Got it. Thank you so much, guys. As usual, you're life savers. We'll call you again when we're closer to New Orleans, Tristan. Nina, can you call my mom and dad and let them know I'm okay. Don't tell them what's going on because they'll be worried to death, but tell them I'm okay and I'll call as soon as I can."

"Of course, honey. Don't worry, Jordan. We're always here for you guys. We love you two. Be safe and if you need anything else, call," Nina said in her usual sweet way.

"Thanks, guys. I can't tell you how much I owe you two," I said somberly, knowing it was a risk for both of them to help us.

"Stay safe, Gage. As Nina said, let us know if you need anything else. I'll tell Daryl what's going on so he can be in the loop too."

"Thanks, Tristan. Talk to you soon."

Jordan pressed END and set the phone down on the console between us. "I don't know what I'd do without Nina, you know that?"

"They're good people. People like that don't come around every day."

Tristan was one of the best men I had ever had the pleasure of knowing and Nina was his perfect match. The two of them lived to see others as happy as they were and they had a family any man would be a little jealous of. I had to admit I'd had more than one moment of wishing I had all they had, especially in those days when I didn't have Jordan in my life anymore.

"Do you think it will work?" Jordan asked, squeezing my hand gently. There was a slight edge to her voice and I knew she was wondering the same thing I was.

Was anywhere really safe now?

I thought about it for a moment and tried to figure out a way Hailey would know we were in New Orleans. "I do. There's no reason Hailey can know we're there," I answered, bringing her hand to my lips to lightly kiss it. "Hailey is the kind of a woman who you think is smart, but take away her edge, and she's nothing."

That there should have been no way for her and Justin to find us in Wyoming remained unspoken. I still had no idea how Justin had found us. For me, there was no doubt of Denise's innocence. However, I had a sinking feeling Jordan didn't see things the same. She hadn't mentioned it after I told her Denise doing anything to hurt us wasn't something I'd even consider, but I knew her well enough. She wasn't convinced.

And at some point I'd have to find out what really happened and if my sister had betrayed me.

Jordan gently moved her hand and mine to her lap. "Have you ever been to New Orleans?"

I turned to look at her and smiled. "Me? No, never saw the allure really. Parades and large groups of drunks don't usually appeal to me unless my job requires me to be there. And even then, they aren't my kind of fun," I joked.

No matter what I'd seen about Mardi Gras, it just wasn't my style. I was always more of a one-on-one kind of guy when it came to having a good time.

She playfully rolled her eyes, "You do realize there's more to New Orleans than Mardi Gras, right? There's a whole culture to New Orleans. The food, the music, the feel of the place. I hear it's all so unique down there."

I wished we could enjoy all the city offered instead of using it as a place to hide out until we found out what was behind Hailey's plans.

That was what I really wanted—the ability to whisk Jordan away to places like New Orleans, Greece, Paris, all over the world. She was a woman who deserved to see so much more than the concrete jungle of New York. She deserved to stare in wonder at the world around her, not run from place to place like she'd had to since we left Hilton Head. I wanted to hold her hand as we explored new places together with joy and wonder, not fear.

"Then I guess we'll have to get you as much of the New

Orleans experience as possible," I said, pretending like we were heading off on one of those vacations happy couples in love got to take. "You mentioned food. I'm always on board for some food," I joked.

In truth, I was starving. I had grabbed a pack of peanuts on the way out of the cabin, but my stomach was starting to pinch from hunger.

"I hear it's incredible! A coworker got to go for a convention and she said as soon as they would break for the day she would rush out into the city and soak in everything she could."

"Did she come back with a bunch of beads?" I teased, earning a playful slap.

"Oh, stop! She had a few, but we didn't talk about it," she answered. "She saw a jazz band and the whole thing sounded so great! I'd love to get to go to a jazz club and taste some authentic New Orleans food."

As I listened to her, I made a mental note to someday make those things happen for her. Maybe they wouldn't on this trip, but we had the rest of our lives in front of us. We laughed about seeing New Orleans for the first time and then fell silent with smiles on our faces. Truly happy, I focused on the road in front of me and breathed a heavy sigh of relief.

"It feels good doesn't it?" Jordan said, running her hand over my leg.

I turned to look at her. "What does?"

"Having a plan. I've been so stressed out that I haven't had a moment to breathe. Sounds like you haven't either."

I paused and looked out the front window at the sprawling mountains around us. She was right. It had been a stressful time, and it wasn't over yet. The last moment I'd had to myself had been a painful memory of the last person I failed, so it hadn't exactly been relaxing. I could use a beer and a comfy chair, but for now I would have to make due with bottled water and the driver's seat.

"It's been rough, but it's been worth it," I finally answered, brushing some hair off her face so I could see those beautiful green eyes of hers. "I know that sounds crazy, but life's better when we're together, no matter how bad it gets."

"That's incredibly positive for you, Gage."

"I can't think of anything else I'd rather do than make sure you're happy, Jordan. For now, that means we have to go through some shit to get to the good times, but I believe they're right up ahead."

I meant it. I knew at that point what I wanted more than anything was to spend the rest of my life with Jordan and use that time to make her happy.

Her cheeks turn red, and she looked down bashfully. "You do, Gage. You really do. And you know what I always say."

"What?"

"That good things happen to good people. I used to tell Nina that all the time, and look at her life now. She and Tristan had to go through some horrible things, but they got through it all and they're happy. We will too because we're good people too. You especially, after what you did for Justin back there."

"That was just being decent. I'd never be able to face my father again knowing I let someone die of thirst on the side of the road, even if he deserved it. It's not right. It had nothing to do with being good, though. Trust me."

Jordan smiled. "Don't bet on it, Gage Varo. You're a good man. You're just going to have to live with that."

Changing the subject, I asked, "Do you want to sleep? I would think you'd be exhausted after today. Your body could probably use it."

Jordan scrunched up her nose and shook her head. "No, I have the hardest time sleeping in cars normally, and I don't think the pain in my neck is going to help with that. Speaking of that, keep an eye out for somewhere I can get that scarf. I don't want to be walking around with people thinking you hurt me."

"Will do. How about the radio, ladies' choice?"

She turned the stereo on and some terrible pop garbage came out and assaulted our eardrums. "Damn, I shouldn't have offered ladies' choice. Who listens to that?"

"What? It's perfect for driving," she said in defense of whatever it was blaring out of the speakers. "I mean, I'm not a huge fan, but it's not bad for pop."

"Oh, I can think of someone who has a weakness for pop music," I ribbed, remembering the Saturday morning when she was living out at the Dutchess County house with Nina and through an open bathroom door, I saw Jordan dancing and singing to some song while she did her hair and makeup.

"Wow. You're really never going to let me live that down, are you?" she asked, pretending to be offended.

"Come on, how could I? Especially with that little butt wiggle move you had going on."

The woman I loved blushed, her cheeks turning bright red, and giggled. It was a welcome sound, far more welcome than our recent conversations.

"All right, I may have my guilty pleasures, but if you think those headphones of yours hide your deep abiding love for Bon Jovi, you're wrong. We could all hear you living on a prayer!"

"Bon Jovi is an American treasure." I said firmly, only causing Jordan to laugh further. "I mean it. Wanted Dead or Alive is a classic. You can't tell me otherwise."

She gave me a playful smack on the arm. "I can't believe we're sitting here debating Bon Jovi."

I chuckled and looked at her. "There's no debate. Bon Jovi are a musical force to be reckoned with."

Jordan once again rolled her eyes and laughed. "Well, at least we can both agree on one band."

"And what band is that?"

"ABBA," she answered with a playful smile.

"You know I only listen to that stuff for you, right? I'd sooner Van Gogh my ears than listen to music like that when I'm alone."

"Really?" She looked completely dejected from my confession. "I thought that was something we shared."

I turned to see her bottom lip quivering in disappointment. "I'm sorry. I didn't ever plan to tell you the truth, but no, I don't like ABBA like you do."

"But you spent all those nights at my apartment listening to their music. Why didn't you tell me?"

"Isn't it obvious? I didn't care about where we were or what music was playing. All I cared about was being with you."

Jordan sat in the passenger seat saying nothing for so long I wondered if I'd made a mistake telling her the truth. Those nights we spent together in those first months dating were some of my favorite times with her, regardless of the crappy music she made me listen to. We'd hang out on her couch for hours each night getting to know one another. Sometimes we'd end up in bed together, but other times we just talked and kissed like people who'd known each other all our lives.

Finally, after about five minutes, she said, "I can't believe you sat through all those hours of listening to every ABBA CD I have, Gage."

"The music was nothing but background noise, Jordan," I said taking her hand in mine. "I wasn't there for the noise. I was there for you. Do you remember that night the heat went out and your landlord wouldn't let me fix the furnace? I'll never forget that night."

She kissed my knuckles and pressed her cheek to the back of my hand. "We spent the entire night huddled together on the couch watching old Star Trek episodes as the temperature got colder and colder because my landlord promised he'd come to fix the damn thing and never showed. You were so pissed you stayed to give him a piece of your mind and he never came over."

I grinned and looked over at her. "I didn't stay to talk to him. You know that, right?"

"Well, I figured you stayed for the extra benefits that came from being under those blankets and afghans with me."

"Damn straight. I don't think I've ever had sex like that before. Between the blankets and the two of us, it had to be ninety degrees on that couch that night."

"We have had some wild times, haven't we?" she said with a giggle.

I pulled her hand to my mouth and kissed it. "And we will again. Don't worry. You can look forward to freaky extra blanket sex the next time it gets cold. We'll turn down the heat wherever we are and get to it."

Jordan leaned over and kissed me softly on the cheek. "I love you, Gage. I always have. And I always will."

As Jordan and I sat in that car driving to New Orleans and recalling our shared memories together, I wished we were back in that freezing cold apartment of hers huddled naked under those scratchy blankets. It was before the letters that drove me form her, before the people who wanted to kill her, before all the madness. Then it was just Jordan and me together with nothing to tear us apart.

She fell asleep before I could tell her I loved her too. As the gentle rocking of the car bounced her head lightly, I brushed the hair from her face and smiled down at the woman I couldn't imagine life without.

Finally, we had a plan. We'd hide out in New Orleans while we worked to figure out what the hell was behind Hailey's desire to kill Jordan and Daryl helped us unravel this whole mystery. Then we'd return to life where it was just the two of us and I'd finally do what I should have done in the first place when I realized there wasn't a life for me without Jordan.

CHAPTER FOURTEEN

JORDAN

I OPENED MY EYES AND looked down at a lovely dark green scarf with a small white bow tied around it in my lap. Rubbing my eyes, I guessed I must have passed out after we grabbed some drive-thru food somewhere in Colorado.

"Good morning, sleeping beauty," Gage said with a cute look that told me he knew how cheesy he sounded.

Sitting up in the seat, I stretched my arms. "How long have I been asleep?"

He looked at his watch and smiled. "Nearly eight hours, I think. You must have been exhausted."

Eight hours! I spent what equaled an entire night asleep as he drove all that time. "Gage, I'm so sorry. Do you want me to drive? You must be so tired," I said, feeling guilty about the poor guy spending the whole trip in the driver's seat.

"Nah, I'm fine, though I think I'll be enjoying the rest we get tonight," Gage answered, always being the hero.

I could tell by his eyes that he was weary from driving, but I knew he wouldn't let me drive. Looking out my window, I knew I'd never been here before. "Where are we?"

"Just past Amarillo, I think. We're about halfway there."

The news that we'd only made it halfway to New Orleans made every muscle in my body ache. I wanted to complain, but I didn't. I'd had eight hours of restful, if not comfortable, sleep, and Gage had been stuck with the thankless job of driving all that way in silence. Knowing him, though, he probably enjoyed the quiet.

"Thank you for the scarf. It's perfect," I said, hanging it around my neck to hide the ugly bruises Justin had left.

"I'm glad you like it. There wasn't much of a choice of decorative scarves at Kmart."

Envisioning Gage wandering around the women's accessories section of Kmart while I slept was too much fun and I laughed lightly to myself. "Did I miss anything big while I was sleeping?"

"Nothing spectacular. I think the trip around Kmart was the most exciting thing I've seen. It's mostly been miles and miles of nothing. There was a fairly scary looking hitchhiker, though, who looked like something out of a horror movie, but I figured it would be better with just the two of us."

He put his hand on mine and smiled. I liked his idea. Just the two of us. No scary hitchhikers. No crazy people chasing us. Nothing but Gage and me and the happiness I knew we could have if life could just calm the hell down.

We deserved to have that feeling after all the crap we had dealt with. I knew it wasn't over. After all, we hadn't even begun to discuss Denise and there was still that whole my being married thing, but for now we were safe in the car together and on our way to a safe haven.

"Do you think we'll be able to see any of the city?" I asked. I knew it was selfish, but I really wanted him to see New Orleans for more than just Mardi Gras.

He sighed, like he didn't know how to tell me the answer was no. "I don't know, Jordan. I want to say yes because I know you want to, but we have to be careful."

"I know." I hated seeing him so serious, so I quickly changed the subject. "Did you know that Anne Rice used to have a mansion in the Garden District?"

Gage turned to look at me quizzically. "Do you mean the vampire lady?" he asked, surprising me that he even knew that much about her.

I chuckled and nodded, "Yes, she wrote Interview with a Vampire among many others. It's one of my favorite books actually," I admitted.

"Well, maybe we can see if there's a way we can sneak a peek of it since you like her so much."

"I'd like that."

Quintessential Gage. Even when he had to tell me no, he found a way to soften it.

✧   ✧   ✧

NEARLY HALF A DAY LATER, we finally arrived in New Orleans after the longest trip I'd ever taken in a car, and that was saying something since we'd driven nearly across the country just a few days before. Even after only grabbing a short nap along the way, Gage still had a smile for me when I messed up the directions and sent us to the wrong street in the Garden District. Aptly named, every house, or more truthfully every miniature mansion, was framed by the most beautiful trees, shrubbery, and flowers. Leave it to Tristan's family to have a house in such a gorgeous place.

Though nearly every home had a small fence either in front of or surrounding it, it was like the original settlers had decided to let the vegetation decide the boundaries of the homes. In some places, the trees intertwined with those from the property next to it, creating an elegant canopy that framed the yard. Many of the homes had pillars that reminded me of Greek architecture.

"What do you think?" I asked Gage as I tried to ignore the pain in my neck in favor of looking at every sight around us. It was impossible not to want to look at every home. Better Homes and Gardens must have had entire issues dedicated to the place, and still that wouldn't have been enough.

"This is impressive and from what Tristan told me of his father, not where I would expect him to have a home," he replied, driving slowly so we could admire the beautiful houses. It was nice to see that he was interested as I was in the area. I liked a man who could appreciate the beauty in life.

"Probably his mother's idea, to be honest. Not that a man can't like a place like this, but I would think a woman would be drawn to it more. Some of the homes remind me of dollhouses. Nina would love this place. Maybe we can all vacation here together one day," I wondered aloud, thinking how great it would be if all of us and the kids could come down here for some time away.

"Maybe," Gage said.

"The Stone kids would love this place. It's a hide and seek gold mine," I joked.

The GPS told us in its monotone voice that our destination would be on our left and I looked over past Gage in anticipation. We pulled into the long driveway and my mouth nearly hit the floor of the car. The only word that came to mind to describe the two story white home was grandeur. Everything about it, from the tall pillars on the front porch, to the regal balcony that adorned an upstairs room and the black shutters framing the windows, screamed status. Large bushes covered in small white flowers lined the front yard, and I could see what looked like a fountain peeking out of the backyard.

"It would probably be best to park back there away from the road," Gage said, all business as always as he directed my attention past the garden to a tool shed in the backyard.

We got out of the car and somehow the back of the house was even more impressive than the front. The porch wrapped around the entire house with white wooden floors that matched the home's paint color. All of the trim was black, including the black wrought iron fence that surrounded the property. It was the very definition of posh and stood in stark comparison to the much more traditional looking Southern style homes that flanked it on each side with their soft yellows and pinks. The Stone residence was regal and stood like a proud woman amidst the more mellow colored houses.

The backyard had a stone path that ran through the middle but otherwise was full of brightly colored plants. We walked along it to the tool shed and saw hidden behind a bush a box with the house key, just as Tristan had told us it would be when we spoke to him a few minutes earlier.

"After you, my lady," Gage said with a bow before guiding me down the path and up the back stairs.

"Shouldn't we get the bags?" I asked, looking over my shoulder at the car.

Gage unlocked the door and looked at me with a smile. "I think we deserve a break that doesn't consist of us being in the car, don't you?"

"Well, when you put it that way," I said as I nodded, leading the way through the back door.

We walked into a large kitchen with more counter space than I had room in my small apartment. In fact, the kitchen alone may have been bigger than my entire place.

"Gage, this is amazing," I finally said after gawking at the place in silence for a few moments. "Nina must have died when she saw these cabinets. This even puts her kitchen to shame, and that's saying something."

I'd always loved a white-on-white kitchen, and this one had it all. An enormous white island with white marble stood in the center of the room, surrounded by tall, white wood cabinets leftover from when the house was first built and stainless steel appliances. It was the perfect mixture of new and old.

We walked through a doorway into what looked like a sitting room or parlor, and Gage ran his hand gently along the back of the exquisite burgundy couch. "I guess we can see where Tristan got his sense of good taste."

I noticed a photo on the mantle and pointed to it. "Look, there's a young boy in this picture. Do you think it's Tristan?" It certainly looked like him with his brown eyes and dark hair. But then again, his brother Taylor had been his twin, so it could have been either one of them.

It seemed strange, though, because there wasn't another one to match it or any with both boys. I'd have to remember to ask Nina about it. Maybe she'd know why.

Gage took my hand and tugged me toward a gorgeous staircase that reminded me of the one from Gone with the Wind. "I think we need to check out the bedrooms."

The look in his eyes told me exactly what he was thinking. I smiled coyly as I agreed. We walked up to the second floor to the first bedroom we found, and as I stepped into the room, I gasped at how stunning it was. The Richmont hotels had nothing on this place.

"Gage, look at this," I said as I stared up at the chandelier hanging over the foot of the dark cherry wood sleigh bed.

The walls were painted warm brown and espresso colored draperies hung over windows that stretched from the floor to just a foot below the ceiling. On the wall opposite the windows was a fireplace painted to match the wood of the bed. The room was all at once majestic and grand while being welcoming and cozy at the same time.

"Too bad it's summer," Gage joked as he nuzzled my neck from behind me. "I think it would be sexy to make love to you with a fire roaring."

I turned in his hold and looked up into his bleary blue eyes. "Aren't you tired? You don't want to sleep?"

A deep moan slid from his throat, and he shook his head. "The last thing I want to do in this room is sleep right now," he said with a grin.

"What did you have in mind?" I teased as he slid my shirt over my head. "We are in The Big Easy, you know."

He looked at me like a starving man. There was a wildness in his eyes that I hadn't seen since that night in my apartment a week before when I'd finally admitted the truth of how much I loved him and didn't love the man I was supposed to marry.

Gage slid his tongue down my neck to between my breasts as he unclasped my bra, ratcheting my need for him higher. Looking up at me, he flicked his tongue over my nipple and smiled. "I don't know about easy. Right now, I'm feeling pretty hard, so get out of those jeans and meet me on that bed in about five seconds."

I did as he ordered as he headed to the bed, peeling his clothes off with every step. By the time I was naked, he was already lying with his arms folded behind his head like he'd been waiting hours for me to arrive.

A quick glance at the bird's eye view the neighbors had through the windows made me a little self-conscious. "Do you think we should close the drapes? It's still daylight out, and even in New Orleans I'm sure people don't expect to see people having sex in the open."

Looking around at the windows, Gage shrugged and then returned his attention to me standing without a stitch of clothes on in front of him. "Forget about the rest of the world, Jordan. Now it's just you and me. I don't care about anyone outside this room. All I care about is you and how much I want to be deep inside you."

If ever there was a typical Gage answer, that was it. When he said things like that, my breath caught in my chest from how sexy he could be.

He held his hand out to take mine and pulled me on top of him in one smooth motion. Setting his hands at my hips, he grinned up at me. "I've been waiting way too long to feel you on my cock. Come here."

I lowered my head and kissed him long and deep, loving the feel of every inch of his hard body against mine. His tongue invaded my mouth, eager and demanding, as he held me to him. A tiny moan escaped my lips into his mouth when he lifted his hips off the bed to slide into me.

Grabbing my ass, he cupped it in his hands, and with each thrust of his cock, I felt all the worry and stress of the past few days melt away. Gage was the only man who'd ever made me feel like this. I didn't know if it was his strength or his quiet belief that no matter what happened he could protect me, but only with him could I lose myself completely and yet have more than I'd ever dreamed was possible.

His lips slid across my cheek to my ear, and he whispered low, "I love how you feel around me."

Together, we rolled across the king-size bed until he was on top of me staring down into my eyes with that Gage look that made my stomach flip with how it seemed like he was staring directly into my soul. He closed his eyes and plunged into me again with enough force to push me up toward the headboard, so I pressed my palms against it and wrapped my legs around his waist.

He was like power and need personified looming over me with desire for all of me in his eyes. Inside, I felt my body begin to surrender to his and closed my eyes to let my release wash over me.

Digging my fingernails into his back, I raked across his smooth skin from his spine to his sides and arched into him. "Yes! Don't stop! Yes!"

I felt his body meet mine, and then there was nothing but pure pleasure as I came. Gage let out a noise that sounded like a growl, and with one last thrust into my body, he came.

Lowering himself on top of me, he sighed and his breath gently skittered past my ear before he whispered, "I could live a million years and never get tired of how incredible you feel when we're like that."

I cradled his face in my hands and smiled up at him. "A million years is a long time. I think you'd get bored."

Gage rolled off me and propped up his head with his hand. "No way. You're not the kind of woman a man gets bored with."

I kissed his lips, loving just lying there with him. "What would you say if I told you I never wanted to leave this very room or this house?"

He kissed me back and smiled. "I'd say I'm right there with you. Now all we need is a couple million and to convince Tristan he should sell us this place."

Neither one of us had that kind of money, so that plan wasn't going to work. "Oh well, I guess we're going to have to settle for my apartment in Brooklyn."

"Does it matter where we live?" he asked, and I heard in his voice that same old fear that he wasn't enough compared to Brock.

I shook my head and sighed. "Nope. All that matters is that you're there with me, Gage. That's all."

He kissed me softly on the lips and pressed his forehead to mine. "Then we're covered because I'm not going anywhere."

And I wasn't going to let him go ever again.

Chapter Fifteen

Gage

I AWOKE WITH JORDAN IN my arms, just the way life was meant to be. Too bad at some point we'd have to deal with the world outside this bed. Thank God the woman had the ability to sleep when everything around us was going to hell because except for a few brief naps, I hadn't been able to get any decent sleep since we left my parents' house.

My cell phone rang, so I slipped my arm from around Jordan and plodded over to my jeans to answer it. Happy to see a familiar name on the screen, I smiled and hoped the next thing I'd hear would be some answers.

"The man, the myth, the legend. How are you, Gage?"

It was a relief to hear my favorite PI sound so casual. At least that might mean he had something good to report.

"Hey, Daryl. How are things?" I asked, working to keep my tone nonchalant.

"Well, I'm not on the run with a pretty blonde, but hey, things are good," Daryl quipped in his usual snappy fashion.

"Yeah, it's been a barrel of laughs."

For a moment I paused and became suspicious. If it hadn't been Denise who told Hailey and Justin where we were, then it must have been someone else and Daryl was a man with a lot of information on hand. Could he have been the one to tell Hailey? The idea instantly made me sick. By all accounts, I had no reason to suspect Daryl, but the idea of it being Denise who had sold us out was still too much of a stretch for me.

"Gage, you there?"

I shook the feeling of suspicion and continued on in the hopes that he wasn't the one.

"Yeah, sorry. It's just been hectic. I'm pretty exhausted, to be honest." It was a good enough answer and seemed to placate Daryl.

"I understand. Well, time to get down to brass tacks. I've got some news."

"Is it good or bad?"

"Well, it isn't bad so much as just information, but that's good, right?"

I had become accustomed to all of my recent news being bad so his answer came as both a genuine surprise and a relief.

"Go on, Daryl. I know you're dying to tell me." In truth I was dying to hear it. Whatever he had to tell me, it was better than not knowing nothing.

"Right. Enough of the feet dragging. Well, it looks like little Miss Hailey has been busy in more than just Jordan's life but her own as well."

I bristled thinking about Hailey's involvement in anything involving Jordan but pushed my anger aside for the moment. "How so?"

"So do you remember when we discussed the wealthy guy, Dalton Spear? Well, they just announced to family and friends that they plan to wed in the next month. And I'll tell you what. He's one hell of a mystery himself. Like our friend, he's got pretty savvy people working for him to keep him exactly that."

More interested in the part about Hailey than Spear, I said, "The girl moves fast. What's the hurry? Is he some ninety year old with one foot in the grave and another on a banana peel?"

"He's dying of cancer," Daryl responded somberly.

"Oh."

"Yeah. So this guy seems to be her sugar daddy, and she's racing down the aisle before he dies of throat cancer. Or maybe it's lung or bone. I've heard a few things."

"Okay, so he's definitely dying of cancer," I said. "What does that have to do with us? None of this explains why Hailey wanted Jordan to be married to Justin and why he'd be bankrolling it all."

It didn't make any sense to me. Jordan was a school teacher from an upper middle class family. She didn't come from money and that seemed to be Hailey's main goal. And what was Dalton Spear's part in all of this?

"That's where it gets kind of weird."

"Are you trying to say the entire situation hasn't been weird from the start? I'm going to have to disagree with you on that one, Daryl."

"Funny, but you'd be surprised at the stuff I see and hear about in this profession. Hell, you guys look like a Norman Rockwell painting compared to some of the shit I've waded through."

That was surprising. I couldn't imagine what other more interesting people had to deal with that was worse than kidnapping, forced marriage, being on the run, and a mysterious wealthy man behind it bankrolling it all.

"Point taken. So what is it?"

"Well, back twenty-some years ago this guy knocked up some lady named Karen Dumond. She had the baby, a boy, in Vermont and gave it up for adoption."

"I still don't see where Jordan and I are involved, Daryl."

"That's the problem. I don't either. That's not to say I don't think they are connected. I do, but how I'm not sure yet. I'm going to speak to this Karen woman tonight. I planned on calling you with the details."

He seemed calm, but I heard an edge in his voice. Daryl prided himself on always being in the know, and it was obvious that not having all the answers was bothering him. That drive was what kept him good at his job. The suspicion I'd had earlier about him faded as I'd listened to him talk about all that he'd learned. A man this invested in helping us find the truth was unlikely to be working against us. I should have known that. He'd proven himself to be someone worthy of my trust time and again.

"Thanks, Daryl. We both really appreciate your help."

"Yeah, don't get all mushy on me. It's not a Lifetime movie. I'm just doing my job," he joked.

"I won't say anything to Jordan about the woman until you let me know what's up. I'm going to see what I can find out about Dalton Spear, but I'm guessing if you couldn't find out much yet, I won't get very far just by Googling him."

"Don't even bother. Trust me. He's got people just like me working around the clock to make sure all anyone finds out about him is what he wants them to find out. Of course, there's always the possibility that there's a chink in the armor, and I think I've found that. Give me a couple more days and I should be able to find out what the hell this entire fucking mess is about."

I didn't want to think about what Daryl's chink in the armor could be. Most of the time, he stayed on the right side of the law, but when it suited him and the job he had to do, he wasn't above taking a step over the line.

Whatever that line may be.

"Okay, in the meantime, we'll stay down here and lay low."

"Good idea," he said with a chuckle. "Stay in that sweet house and get some rest." He paused for a few seconds and then continued, "Or whatever you do when you're in New Orleans with a hot blonde."

Daryl making a reference to my sex life meant the conversation had officially ended, so I said goodbye and headed back to bed where Jordan waited for me, still sleeping.

The mattress dipped as I climbed back into bed. Jordan woke up and smiled at me. "Where did you go?"

Tucking a lock of hair behind her ear, I said, "Daryl called. Did I wake you up?"

"What did he say?" Jordan sat up and rubbed the sleep from her eyes. "Did he find out anything more?"

"Not much yet. Oh, yeah, he did find out that Hailey is supposed to be marrying that Spear guy in just a few weeks. I guess he's dying."

A look of disgust settled into Jordan's face. "She's a real class act. If she's not kidnapping people to force them to marry, she's arranging a hurry-up marriage to some guy so she can get his money. That's classy with a K."

I hated any part of Hailey being in our life. The sooner she was gone from it, the better. For now, at least I could change the subject and get Jordan's mind off her. "I think we should go out tonight."

Jordan's green eyes opened wide with excitement. "Really? I could have sworn I heard you just say something about laying low to Daryl. Now you want to go out on the town?"

"Yeah. We deserve a good time."

"Didn't we just have one?" she asked playfully.

"I mean, we deserve a night out. I say we head out to one of the clubs in the French Quarter tonight."

I saw the excitement on her face and loved that such a simple suggestion had made her so happy.

"That sounds fun, but are you sure?"

"I'm going to get some work done on figuring out what's going on, so why don't you grab a shower? Then tonight, we'll head out into the crowds of the French Quarter. I think it might be safe."

She leaned over and kissed my nose. "Are you doing this because I said I wanted to see the city?"

I nodded and planted a quick kiss on her lips. "Yes, but I do think we need to relax for a night. Unless Daryl suddenly figures out what's going on and tells me in the next few hours, I say we put our worries behind us for a night. They'll be there when we get back."

"I love this idea!" she squealed and then jumped out of the bed. "By the way, have you seen this bathroom yet? Can you say marble for as far as the eye can see? I might have to take an extended bath in here."

As she playfully jogged toward the bathroom, I joked, "Take all the time you need, but be ready in an hour."

In the meantime, I'd see if I could find anything that would explain what Hailey was up to.

Chapter Sixteen

Jordan

Gage stood in the doorway of the bathroom with a grin on his face like he couldn't wait to share something with me. Flicking bubbles at him, I laughed and said, "I'm guessing you found out something by the look on your face."

"I think you're going to like it."

"Really? That good? Well, don't keep it to yourself. What did you find?"

He shook his head, still grinning like the cat that ate the canary. "You have to come out here to see it."

Since he wasn't usually this playful, I was intrigued. Quickly, I wrapped a towel around my body as the suds from my bubble bath still clung to my skin and hurried out into the bedroom to see what he'd found.

"What is it?" I asked as I looked around for his phone to see what he'd found.

He pointed toward the door to the closet and took my hand. "Come see."

I knew Gage hadn't left the house while I was lounging in the bathtub, so what could he have found in the closet? I nervously followed him and when he opened the door, I saw it.

"I'm thinking Nina told Tristan to surprise us."

There in the middle of the walk-in closet hung a gorgeous black dress and a pair of super sexy black heels for me and black pants with a pale blue dress shirt for him. As always, Nina had great taste.

I turned to look at Gage and threw my arms around his neck. Confused, he whispered as I clung to him, "I thought you'd be happy. Now we'll at least get to change into fresh clothes."

Leaning away from him, I sniffed away my tears. "I am happy. I just wish things were back to normal because I really want this night to be one we remember."

Gage pressed a gentle kiss onto my forehead and smiled. "It will be. For tonight, we're going to forget everything else but having some laughs and a good time in The Big Easy. Why don't you get dressed and I'll get a shower so I can look good enough to be with the woman wearing that smoking hot red dress?"

He took his new clothes and headed into the bathroom for a shower as I admired Nina's perfect gift. Grabbing Gage's phone, I quickly called her to say thanks.

"Hey, you didn't have to get us those clothes, but I think you're officially the very bestest best friend of all time now," I said into the phone when she answered.

Nina giggled. "I knew you'd love the dress. How does Gage look in the clothes Angelo picked out for him?"

"I don't know. He's still getting ready. Thank you so much, Nina."

She didn't speak for a long moment, and then she said, "Well...I didn't mean them as a bribe so you wouldn't be angry with me, but I think they've turned out to be that. I did something that I'm worried you're going to be unhappy about."

"What do you mean?" I asked, sure nothing Nina would do could anger me.

"I didn't mean to, but I let it slip that you and Gage are in New Orleans. I didn't think it would be a big deal, but Tristan said I shouldn't have told her."

I couldn't imagine why he would think that. "It's okay, Nina. As long as she knows we're okay, it's fine. It's not like she's going to tell Hailey or Justin where we are, so we're good. No bribes needed."

Nina sighed deeply. "Oh good. I told Tristan it wasn't a big deal, but he worries about things like that. He's way more about secrets than I ever am. Your mother sounded relieved when I told her you and Gage were there and in the house. She misses you, but I think she's okay now that she thinks you guys aren't in danger."

How I wished that was true. "We're still in danger, I think, but at least for tonight, Gage and I are going to get a few drinks in the French Quarter and try to forget this whole mess."

"Just don't get in trouble, Jordan. Remember the police in Hilton Head are still looking for you," Nina said in her usual worried way.

"I won't. Gage will be right next to me the whole time, so I'll be safe and sound. Don't worry."

"Okay. I'll try. Just be careful but have a good time. You two deserve it. Love you, Jordan."

"I love you too, Nina. Tell Tristan and the kiddies we said hi and we'll be back out there at the house as soon as we can, okay?"

I ended the call, happy that my mother believed I was fine, even if that wasn't the exact truth. But we would be fine soon enough, and that's what mattered.

As I daydreamed about what life would be like for Gage and me after all this madness was over, the bathroom door opened and he stepped out into the bedroom looking even more stunning than usual. The light blue dress shirt looked perfect next to this dark hair and blue eyes. For a moment, I wasn't sure I wanted to share him with the rest of the world.

"A quick shower washed away a day's worth of grime, and these clothes look pretty good, if I do say so myself," he joked as he stood modeling his new look.

I walked over to him and ran my hands down his chest. "You clean up nice, Gage Varo."

He looked down at me still standing there in my towel and shook his head. "Just like a woman. Now I'm going to have to wait while you get dressed. The eternal male struggle."

Grabbing my dress and shoes from the closet, I stomped past him and rolled my eyes. "I'll be ready in ten minutes. Eternal male struggle. Hmmph. I might just have to make it fifteen for that remark."

"I don't want to toot our collective horn too much, but we look great!" I announced a few minutes later as I opened the bathroom door and showed off the body-hugging, knockout black dress that hit the middle of my thighs.

It was clear that he agreed with me as he stared at me with a look that said he was having second thoughts about going out. Taking me in his arms, he kissed my neck. "You look incredible, Jordan."

"If you keep this up, Gage Varo, we're never going to make it out of this bedroom," I teased as he ran his hands down my back to cup my ass.

"Fine, but when you look this good, it's hard to keep my hands off you."

He kissed me and my head swum, but I knew if we kept this up, we really wouldn't leave this room, so I said, "You ready to paint the town red?"

"After you, my lady."

THE FRENCH QUARTER WAS EVEN busier than Manhattan, if that was possible, but it was a different kind of busy. In New York, everything was rushed. People rushed from place to place. Cars rushed up and down the streets. Conversations were rushed.

This place was so different, even though we were in the middle of hundreds of people at any given time. Still in the high seventies, the humid Gulf air hung over the Quarter and slowed everything down. People didn't hurry from building to building but meandered down the streets as they partied. The heavy bass of dance music playing in a second floor bar mixed with the soulful guitar coming from a blues club and the drunken chatter of people around us to create a mixture of sound I'd never heard before in my life.

Gage held my hand as we slowly weaved our way through the crowd. Even though my neck still ached, I couldn't stop looking left and right at all the sights around us. The modern neon lights of bar and restaurant signs mingled seamlessly with the French and Spanish architecture of the Quarter, and I couldn't get enough of it.

While I admired my new favorite place, Gage's head was on a swivel too, but for a different reason. I knew we had a better chance of being safe here than we had in Wyoming, especially since Denise wasn't with us, but it was obvious that Gage wasn't taking any chances.

Too often it showed through that Gage was the one with military training, not me. I looked like a tourist even in the city I lived in, whereas Gage always looked like he knew exactly where he was and where everything and everyone else should be.

I spied a club advertising a masquerade party and nudged him. "Look! They're having a masquerade party there. We can wear masks."

"Perfect," he said as I tugged him toward the dark green entrance to the bar.

Inside, we paid the cover and put on our masks. Gage's was white with ornate black trim around the edges. My mask was emerald green with purple lace and flecks of gold around the eyeholes. Both masks covered from our noses up, so only we knew who we were.

"Stay close to me," Gage said low in my ear as we walked past the bar manned by a freakishly tall man nearly seven foot tall clad in a tux and top hat.

Staircases on either side of the long rectangular room led up to second and third stories. Both levels were framed by black wrought iron posts and railings that formed balconies in front of the adjacent hallways. There were places to sit and enjoy a drink or the strange music that didn't seem to be coming from anywhere but could be heard everywhere.

The music became louder as we got drinks and climbed the stairs to the second floor. Taking a seat on a red velvet couch, I looked to my left and saw a man and woman barely keeping their clothes on as they kissed and to my right saw a woman dancing alone to a beat that didn't match the music.

"I think we picked the wrong level," Gage joked.

There was something about the club and the anonymity the masks offered that made me feel like a whole new woman. "Let's go upstairs and see what we find," I yelled over the music, gesturing towards the third floor where balloons and bubbles were pouring down into the center of the club as people danced with bottles of champagne.

Gage winked and held out his hand. "Lead the way!"

It had been ages since I had let loose in a club but a quick finish of my liquid courage had me feeling like I was on cloud nine. Gage finished his drink and joked about trying to keep up with me even though we both knew he wouldn't consider letting himself get drunk when we were still in danger.

I couldn't tell if it was the alcohol, the atmosphere, or our situation, but Gage stuck to me like glue. We danced against one another, and I found myself eagerly anticipating when I would have him all to myself later. The dance we would do in bed would be much better than this one with our masks on.

As we pressed our bodies together, I laughed as he went to kiss me but ended up knocking our masks against one another. Mine went so askew that my vision went dark and I couldn't stop laughing. I looked away to adjust my mask and that was when I saw her.

It didn't matter that she wore a black and gold mask. All it did was make her more frightening. I saw her moving through the crowd and instantly knew I was in danger.

Hailey. I'd spent enough time with that woman to remember how she moved. Like a snake.

"Gage, we have to go," I said frantically into his ear, trying to keep my eyes on Hailey as she weaved back into the crowd. How had she found us here? We had only been in town for less than a day. There was no way unless she and Justin had been tracking us, but Gage had been sure to keep an eye out for that.

"What are you talking about? We just got here," he said into my ear, pressing his hands softly against my back to calm me down.

"She's here, Gage. I just saw her," I answered, my heart pounding wildly as terror filled me.

"Where?" he asked as he turned his head left and right to scan the crowd.

My eyes studied the people around us, but she had disappeared. "I don't know, but I saw her. We have to go."

"Jordan, everyone has masks on, so how could you see her? How could she be here?"

My emotions began to spin out of control and I yelled over the music, "I don't know, but I saw her! She's here!"

Gage cupped his palms on my shoulders to calm me down. "Don't panic. I'm here. Nothing's going to happen to you."

I nodded, but I couldn't stop myself from shaking. The person who had drugged me, kidnapped me, and forced me to marry a man I didn't love before trying to kill me had found us and now she was going to finish what she started.

The party happening around us, which had moments before been exciting in its anonymity, was now terrifying. My hands began to shake uncontrollably and a thin sheen of sweat almost instantly covered me. I was hot and cold at the same time, and I needed to be somewhere safe, somewhere I knew Hailey wasn't going to be.

I wanted to go home.

Not home to the foreign and extravagant house in the Garden District, not to that cabin in the woods. Home to my little apartment in Sunset Park with my goofy refrigerator magnets and oldies seventies music. I wanted my normal life back. I wanted to brew a cup of coffee in my old coffeemaker and eat a scone from the local bakery down the street where the old man always asked me how the kids at school were. I missed my students, my job, and my life. Who had I been kidding coming out to party? We needed to be safe so we could be happy by each other's side, not scared like I was in the middle of that crowded club.

All the joy and excitement had been sucked right out of me. Gage parted the sea of people for me as he led us to the edge of the club away from everyone else.

"Are you sure it was her?" he asked as he began to lift his mask.

Startled, I reached up and stopped him from showing his face. If it was Hailey in the club, the only defense we had was to remain anonymous for as long as possible. Hailey was a bitch, but she wasn't stupid. She wasn't going to approach random people and cause a scene. She would wait until she knew where we were and pounce. No, we had to make sure we stayed invisible in case she hadn't recognized us.

"Leave it on. I'm not totally positive she saw us, so we need to leave the masks on."

Something in what I said convinced Gage that I truly had seen her. He nodded and said, "You're right. Let's get out of here. There will be plenty of people outside to get lost in."

"I just want to go back to the house," I said, wishing more than anything to be back in Brooklyn. What if she found us at Tristan's house in the Garden District? Alone in the house, we would have no witnesses and no one to send for help.

Gage took me by the hand and led me through the crowd down the stairs and out to the street. Happy to be out of the club, I took a deep breath as we walked away toward the house. "It's good we didn't drink that much," I said quietly.

He nodded but didn't say anything as he continued to look around and us. After we walked another block, he turned to look at me and stopped. "I don't think Hailey was in that club. We've been walking for a few blocks now and not a single person has been tailing us. I think you may have been imagining it."

"You think I'm crazy?"

Gage shook his head and put a hand on my right shoulder. "I don't think you're crazy at all, Jordan. I think you're scared. I understand. I just haven't seen any sight of her since we left the club."

People flowed past us as what he said echoed in my brain. He didn't believe me.

"I know what I saw, Gage. I don't care that she was wearing a mask. I felt her there. If you don't believe me, then there's nothing I can say to convince you. But she was there."

I turned away from him and moved to walk away, but he caught me by the arm and held me to the spot. "Jordan, I believe you, but I don't see anyone following us."

"Let me go! I want to get the hell out of here!" I yelled over the noise of the crowd as I tried to yank my hand away.

He grabbed me by the shoulders. "Stop this! You can't just run away this time. We need to stay together."

I knew what he said was right, but at that moment, all I wanted to do was run as fast as I could away from everything. Tears welled in my eyes at the thought that maybe I was wrong about Hailey being at the club. Was I losing my mind?

Gage kissed me and gave me a forced smile. "Let's get out of here. We can talk at the house."

After a tense and quiet walk home, I left him downstairs and headed up to the bedroom. I didn't know what to say to him to convince him because now I doubted that I had really seen her. That he doubted me hurt, though.

He followed me a few minutes later and I saw in his eyes how much he wanted to fix what had happened. I guess I couldn't blame him if he hadn't seen her.

God, every brief moment of joy that came our way was tainted by this awful mess, and Hailey sat spinning at the center of it. I hated her like I had never hated anyone before.

Gage crossed the room and sat down next to me on the bed.

"I'm sorry, Jordan. I wasn't saying you were crazy or you were lying. I just didn't see her."

I buried my face in my hands, wishing we weren't having this conversation. "I think I am going crazy, Gage. I was so sure I saw her there, but maybe I was wrong."

He pulled me to him and held me close as I began to cry. I didn't know why exactly I was sobbing into his shirt, but it felt good to let it all out finally.

Lifting my head, I sniffled and tried to explain myself. "I didn't want to run away back there. I don't want you to think that. I just wish this was all over and we were back to being just Jordan and Gage in my little apartment back in Brooklyn. Is that too much to ask?"

With the pad of his thumb, he wiped the tears from my cheeks and smiled one his crooked smiles that never failed to charm me. "I can't wait to be that again. It's not too much to ask. I wish I could make it happen right now. I do. But until I can, we need to stick together."

I hung my head and nodded. "I know. I was just being a whiny girl. I'm sorry. I didn't mean to make things worse by getting all emotional. I know how much men love when women do that."

Gage lifted my chin with his finger. With a wink, he said, "We don't actually hate that too much, you know. It gives us a chance to be strong and heroic."

That was Gage in a nutshell. Strong and heroic.

"I'm going to do my best to keep it together. I promise."

He smiled at my attempt at bravado, knowing me all too well. As much as I wanted to say I'd be tougher, the reality was emotions were a huge part of who I was.

"Why don't you relax right here for a while? I'll scrounge around in the kitchen and make us something to eat if you're hungry."

"I'm not hungry. I just want to lay down with you and feel your arms around me. Can we do that?"

Gage nodded, taking me in his arms as we lay back on the bed. Closing my eyes, I thought about how great it would be when we finally got back to our life together in New York. Our boring, ordinary life complete with too much heat in the summer and broken furnaces in the winter.

A life I'd taken for granted for far too long.

CHAPTER SEVENTEEN

JORDAN

OPENING MY EYES, I SAW Gage next to me staring intently at his phone. Looking over, he smiled. "Feeling better?"

"I'm beginning to wonder if I'm a narcoleptic. I'm constantly falling asleep on you," I said in an attempt to be funny.

"It's been a rough stretch. I'm not worried about it," he said in that sweet way I loved.

"So what are looking at?"

"I was trying to find something that would give me the answer as to why Dalton Spear would want to marry someone like Hailey."

"He's got a thing for psychotic women who wear too much makeup and spend money like a sailor on leave?" I joked.

Gage chuckled. "That nap seems to have put you in a good mood."

I shrugged, unsure if my mood was as good as I sounded. "I think I might be going crazy, so this could be the first step in madness. I think you should be prepared. It's probably going to get worse."

"You're not crazy," he said, kissing me softly on the lips. "Well, not any crazier than you've ever been."

Looking down at his phone, I saw the webpage he'd been reading about Dalton Spear. "Why does that name sound so familiar?"

He shrugged as he scrolled down the page. "He's rich, so maybe you saw something on the news or in the paper."

"Maybe."

"He owns a chemicals company, but judging by the website, it looks like he's got his hands in a few other things as well. I'm seeing the word conglomerate a lot."

"Is there a picture of him?" I asked, curious to see what this unlucky fiancé of Hailey's looked like.

Gage brought one up, but the man's face didn't register anything with me. "He looks about forty there, but I don't think I know him."

"Me either. I've never worked for him and can't say that I even know anyone who has. He looks intimidating. I'll give him that."

That he was. The man on the screen looked every bit the part of a powerful and wealthy titan of business and had surely used that look to his advantage more than once. I had seen men like him before. They exuded strength. The chiseled jaw. The piercing eyes. The self-assured smile they wore even as they dismantled their competitors.

What he'd want with someone like Hailey and her homicidal tendencies I couldn't imagine, though. Whatever it was, he was supporting her in making my life a living hell, and I found myself instantly resenting him.

"He looks very dark, actually," I said as I looked away from the image of Dalton Spear.

Gage spent a few more minutes searching for information on him before finally drifting off to sleep. After over a day of nothing but catnaps, he deserved a full night of uninterrupted sleep. He looked so peaceful lying there, and for a moment everything else in the world faded away, leaving only the two of us there. If only that were the case.

I wasn't tired, so I kissed him and quietly left to head downstairs.

There was something about Spear that I couldn't get past. His name sounded familiar. I knew it did, and it was unlikely that I only knew it from the news. I didn't spend my time watching news on chemical conglomerates and billionaire older men. That simply wasn't my style.

As I scanned page after page of information about him, I didn't learn anything about the man but only about the image he portrayed. There were awards for his business and him personally for how skillful a businessman he was, and there were plenty of facts about all he'd achieved, but nothing really about who he was other than that.

It made sense to me that Hailey was interested in this guy. Of course, it wasn't love, but anyone with that much money would be of interest to Hailey. What didn't make sense to me was Dalton Spear's interest in her. If he was dying of cancer, what was the point of keeping a hot young wife around?

Nearly twenty pages into my search, I read on an obscure anti-Spear Industries site that he was married once before but his wife died in a fire in Wisconsin on a business trip. The author of the site believed her death had been murder instead of an accident, and Spear had won a ten million dollar judgment against the hotel chain where they'd been staying. It sounded like typical conspiracy theorist ramblings, but it made me dislike Dalton Spear even more.

After losing his wife, he seemed to have focused on his work and nothing else, except for the myriad of charitable organizations he proudly supported and splashed everywhere on his website. There was no information on how he and Hailey met. If I knew her, she'd cleverly found a way to worm her way into his heart. Other than that, he was just some guy who lived in Texas.

That's why I found his name ringing a bell for me so odd. If he'd been a New York bigwig, maybe I would have heard his name in passing, but a Texas businessman wasn't usually what average New Yorkers like me were interested in.

But the more I looked at that picture, the surer I was that I'd heard of Dalton Spear before. The problem was the more I sat there wracking my brain for an answer, the more frustrated I got.

Something about him rang a bell and it wasn't from some

paper I'd seen at a newsstand. Then again, how could I truly know it wasn't? Living in New York City meant seeing thousands of people all the time, not to mention the ones you only heard about from others. Hearing his name or seeing something about him in print or on TV wasn't impossible. I just didn't know. It was like the feeling of knowing the name of a song and having it on the tip of your tongue but not being able to recall it.

"Find anything else on him?" Gage asked as he leaned over the couch, startling me.

"Why are you up already? You keep getting no sleep and we're both going to be crazy before long."

Even though he'd only gotten about an hour's sleep, he looked more rested than he had in days. Taking a seat next to me, he smiled and shook his head.

"I'm good. A few more naps like that one and I'll be all caught up. So what did you find?"

"He enjoys eating at Mandon's Steakhouse and has a house in Hawaii that's estimated to be worth about five million. And neither of these facts help us in any way at all."

I wanted to have more information about the man, but everything I'd found so far truly did revolve around his work, which was probably how he became one of the richest men in the country. It just seemed so strange to me that there was hardly any information about his personal life in the ocean that was the internet.

"Daryl must be right. He said the guy must have a team of people working around the clock to keep his image just as he wanted it to look. It's all about PR and perception."

"One of the few personal bits of information I could find is that he was devastated when his mother died. After attending the funeral, he was out of work for a full week, which was a lot for him apparently."

It was a small anecdote about him but it served to humanize him slightly in my eyes.

Gage seemed to think to himself quietly before nodding. "Yeah, I can understand that. Moms are special." I could tell in that moment he was thinking about his own mother and a look of fear crossed his face.

"Don't worry, Gage. I'm sure your mother's fine. If anything had happened, you would've gotten a call."

I hoped I was right. The idea of this craziness being responsible for any pain in Gage's mother's life made my stomach knot. It had been bad enough that I couldn't truly be myself around her. I wanted everyone in Gage's life to approve of me, not because I needed it but because I knew it would make him happy.

But if what Justin had said about Denise was true, I just hoped he and Hailey hadn't done anything to Gage's family to squeeze some information out of them about where we were.

He nodded and glanced down at his phone instinctually to see if any calls had come in. "I'm sure my family's fine. My mother's tough. If Hailey or Justin showed up looking for us, they'd likely find out how tough all of them are," he said with a smile.

We sat silently on the couch as the thought of Hailey facing the barrel of Mr. Varo's shotgun made me smile. Gage lifted my hand to his lips to kiss it and quietly said, "I'm sorry all of this happened, Jordan. If only I hadn't left because of those letters."

"Gage, please, it's not your fault. It's fine. Well, it isn't, but things could be a lot worse. We're safe and save for a sore throat, I'm fine."

It wasn't a lie. Sure, all that had happened was the stuff of nightmares, but I had a man I loved by my side and the best friends in the world I could rely on.

Gage looked at me as his eyes filled with sadness and furrowed his brow. "Jordan...I just think about everything and..."

"Don't. No regrets for us. Everything happens for a reason, so now all we have to do is find that reason. I don't blame you for any of this, so don't go blaming yourself."

Just as the last word left my mouth, Gage's phone rang.

Looking down at the screen, I saw it was Daryl.

"Daryl, twice in one day?" Gage answered as he put the phone to his ear.

Even without the phone on speaker, I heard him say, "Are you with Jordan?"

"I am. She's right here next to me. Let me put you on speakerphone."

"Hi, Daryl. Long time no speak. How's my favorite mountain man?"

I liked Daryl, for the most part. Other than the bushy, unkempt red beard and the way he seemed to lack even a hint of tact, he was a decent guy who knew how to find out dirt on people like nobody else I'd ever heard of. At the moment, I hoped he'd done just that and could finally tell us what the hell was going on with Hailey that had put a bullseye on my back.

"Same shit, different day. How are you two holding up there on your mini-vacation to The Big Easy?"

Gage rolled his eyes at Daryl's comment. "Did you call us just to bust our chops or do you have something new to tell us?"

"Testy. You'd think after spending time alone with your favorite lady you'd be a little happier there, Gage. Well, along those lines, I'm about to make your day much better."

The excitement in his voice was palpable, and Gage and I sat up straight and looked at one another as we eagerly waited for what he'd say next.

"Gage, did you tell Jordan anything about what we talked about earlier?" Daryl asked, clearly hoping to skip some of the previous details.

"Not everything. Jordan, Daryl told me that there was something about a child of Dalton Spear's being born and given up for adoption. Daryl said it was a little boy born to a woman in Vermont and that he was going to talk to her after we were done talking."

I looked at Gage confused. "Okay, so what does that have to do with us?"

"We know something now. Well, sort of something," Daryl interrupted.

Gage sighed. "I swear to God he never says anything without giving it this ridiculous build up."

"Hey man, I'm just the delivery man. Don't blame me for your impatience," Daryl responded, faking actual offense.

"Okay, okay. Just get on with it. What did that woman say when you went to speak to her?" Gage asked. We were both on the edge of our seats waiting for whatever it was that Daryl wanted to reveal.

"I went to talk to her, but she changed her mind at the last minute and wouldn't answer anything I asked. She stonewalled me."

"So, where does that leave us?" I asked, tired of knowing nothing about what was happening to us.

"I'm getting there. Give me a second. No wonder you two get along so well. You're as impatient as your boyfriend there. So I, being the dedicated guy I am, went to the local courthouse to do some digging and guess what I found out?"

"So what did you find?" I asked, my patience at its end. Daryl wanted to make this dramatic, but he failed to realize for Gage and me, life had already been dramatic enough. We wanted answers, not some daytime drama.

"Nothing at first. That was what struck me as odd. The government is pretty meticulous when it comes to babies being born and adopted. So I hotfooted myself up to Vermont. Bennington to be exact, and unfortunately, the agency that handled the baby's adoption is no more. Thankfully, though, Bennington is a county seat, so I was able to look up some information at the courthouse."

Gage and I looked at each other in utter confusion. What was Daryl going on about? Nothing he'd said made sense or explained what the hell was going on with Hailey, Justin, and Dalton Spear.

"Daryl, what are you talking about?" I finally said quietly. "This whole thing has been so bizarre, as I'm sure you can understand, so I'm finding all of this a little hard to follow. Why should we care about this baby?"

"Because it was fathered by Dalton Spear. One of two children fathered by him, by the way."

Gage leaned in toward the phone with a look terror in his eyes. "You said this child was a boy, right? A boy who was given up for adoption twenty-some years ago, right?"

"Yep, but the records in Vermont said something entirely different than what I thought. The more I dug, the more I realized my source had gotten—"

A loud bang came from the front door, and Gage leaped to his feet. His eyes wide and alert, he said, "Daryl, we're going to have to do this another time."

He grabbed the phone to end the call and handed it to me. "If you hear anything other than me telling you it's okay, I want you to dial 911."

I nodded, but then a thought occurred to me. "But Gage, I'm still wanted by the police. I can't call 911!"

For a moment, he stared at me in silence. Finally, he said, "Call 911 and then go out the back to get to the car and drive like a bat out of hell if you don't hear me tell you everything's okay. Do you understand, Jordan? Don't wait for me!"

Gage ran toward the front door before I could beg him not to leave. I sat frozen on the couch, paralyzed by the fear that Hailey had finally caught up with me, and worse, that Gage might get hurt taking both her and Justin on. I knew what he said was right, but I couldn't let him do it all on his own.

A noise like I'd never heard before in my life made my blood run cold, like the sound of a pipe hitting someone's head, and I waited desperately to hear Gage tell me he was okay. To yell out that he got one of them.

But all I heard were the muffled sounds of voices talking and then the slamming of the front door closing. Terrified, I waited with the cell phone clutched tightly in my hand, and then I saw two men rushing toward me.

I screamed, but it was no use. That noise I'd heard was Gage being attacked. Before I could dial 911, a hand covered my mouth and everything went black.

CHAPTER EIGHTEEN

GAGE

I OPENED MY EYES AND instantly a sharp pain shot across the back of my skull. Wincing, I lowered my head and closed my eyes to avoid the bright fluorescent light shining in my eyes. I tried to move my arms, but I was chained to a pipe with less than six inches leeway.

Where was I? The last thing I could remember was pushing against the front door to keep a man trying to break in from succeeding.

I swiveled my head left and right to see if Jordan was with me now, but I saw nothing but an empty room in what appeared to be some kind of warehouse. Had he gotten to her? Where was Jordan now?

A sinking feeling settled into my heart. I hadn't done the one thing I promised her and now she was God knows where all alone.

I had failed. All those times I'd sworn to Jordan that I would do anything to keep her safe, and in the end, it hadn't mattered because I didn't. Who had I been kidding, whisking her all around the country and pretending to be the big hero? I'd had one job, to protect Jordan, and as she'd feared, I failed. If I was lucky, my captors would kill me quickly so I wouldn't have to know that for long.

All my past failures marched through my mind, playing out in full color as my guilt took over. I hadn't done my job as the man she loved and now she was likely dead, just like Tiffany.

No. I wouldn't let myself go there. It wasn't happening again. It couldn't be happening again. I couldn't handle that a second time.

I shook my head in anger and kicked out towards the wall to my right, but there was nothing to distract me from the memory of that day rushing back into my head. Try as I might, it overtook me and I closed my eyes, slumping on the floor in shame as the past played out in full Technicolor.

She came down the stairs the same way she had practiced for days—slowly, like royalty posing for her fans.

Her dress was white with lace and she hadn't stopped talking about it for days before the party. "Does it make me look like Grace Kelly?" she asked on one of her practice descents down the stairs. "I saw a whole thing about her as a movie star first and then the Princess of Monaco on TV last week. I think it does," she said, twirling around in the dining room as Gregory looked on like the proud father he was.

"Don't tell anyone, but I think even Grace Kelly would have been jealous of you in that dress Tiffany," he answered with a smile.

I watched her walking down the stairs as the entire room looked on. She was everyone's favorite and always the highlight of every party Gregory gave. It had never mattered that she wasn't even an adult. Often guests would end up talking to her more than her father, a fact he was more than pleased to accept.

The mayor's wife leaned in between him and me and whispered, "She's amazing, Gregory. You must be so proud."

His eyes never left Tiffany as he nodded and smiled. "She's my greatest accomplishment."

It was a bold statement. Gregory had the golden touch and seemed to find success everywhere he went, but he meant what he said. On more than one occasion we had stayed up talking and the conversation always turned to how glad he was that Tiffany was growing into a woman her mother would have been proud of had the car accident not taken her years before. For all that he'd achieved in the business world, being Tiffany's father was what he was most proud of.

While her father may have had eyes only for Tiffany, her gaze traveled from him to me and she smiled wide. I nodded in acknowledgement. Any more would have been inappropriate.

Crossing the room to greet her father with a hug, she kissed him on the cheek as the mayor's wife cooed, "You're a vision my dear!"

Always polite and knowing her role, Tiffany blushed and thanked her before telling her how she adored the woman's dress.

Turning toward me at his side, Gregory asked, "Everything going smoothly? None of the others gave you a hard time did they?"

He was referring to putting me in charge of the extra security detail he'd hired for the evening, a fact that made me swell with pride.

"Of course. No problems. I have Johansen here on Tiffany and the rest are stationed where they should be. I'll be on you tonight, like always."

In truth, the men he had hired were a stellar bunch and clearly came from good leadership. None of them had mouthed off in an attempt to prove themselves.

"I wouldn't want anyone else for the job, and I'll be sure to plant myself near the food so you can actually enjoy yourself tonight, Gage," he said with a playful wink. Gregory knew I wasn't one for socializing and had once observed that I always put myself nearest to the food and had made it a habit ever since.

"As long as you're safe, I'll be fine."

If only I had known how wrong I would be.

"Tiffany tells me there's some cheese plate I can't miss. You know how she is with those kinds of things," he joked as I scanned the room for any potential danger spots.

"Gage, hey Gage?" My walky-talky buzzed with the voice of Cooper, the man I had put on the front door.

"Excuse me, sir," I said to Gregory before responding into the speaker. "What do you have for me, Cooper? Everything good up there?"

By all accounts it should have been. The front door was one of the easier jobs since there was a list he had to follow. However, it was one of the first lines of defense, so it was still an important job.

"I think so, but I've got some people up here who say they're here with the food service company but they forgot their badges. I'm going to need you to clear them. I don't have the clearance to do so."

"Did you talk to whoever is in charge of the food service?"

"I did. He says they're good, but protocol states you need to come up here and check them out," Cooper said.

By the book. I liked that. Rules existed for a reason, and it was good that Cooper was following them.

"I know what the protocol says. I'll be there in a minute. Just hold tight and tell them to wait."

I looked back at Gregory to explain, but he spoke before I could get a chance to. "This is why you're a leader, Gage, and why I can rely on you. Hurry back, though. I think the mayor's wife is going to try to coerce me into dancing, and the last thing we need is a repeat of the Christmas party."

"Tiffany would never forgive either of us. She was mortified."

"And for good reason! I have many talents, but dancing isn't one of them. Her mother knew that," Gregory joked, as I remembered his jerking limbs and total lack of rhythm that night.

"I'll be back in just a minute," I said excusing myself. Gregory patted me on the back and I stopped nearby to speak to Tiffany.

"I need to go up front, so I need Johansen to watch both of you. Please stand near him until I get back."

"No problem, Gage, but I'm going to expect a dance after everyone's gone. That's my price," she said with a wink.

"You drive a hard bargain," I said as I walked away. Glancing back, I saw she was smiling.

It was the last time I'd see her beautiful smile. If I had known that at the time, maybe I would have watched longer, hoping to hold onto that moment in time forever where she was alive and happy.

I was still looking behind me as I heard the screams coming from the front door. I turned quickly and could barely make out someone waving a gun around before I heard a shot go off and the screams turned to horrified shrieks. There was blood, but whose it was, I had no idea. My mission became get back to Gregory and Tiffany, so I quickly turned and started pushing my way back to them.

There were too many people running frantically and not enough doors to save all of us. The people near the back door were luckiest and able to escape into the yard, but the food table had been placed toward the front wall near the kitchen. Our only chance was for me to get to them in time and get them to the kitchen and to the service door.

People were screaming and the room became a blur of satin gowns and tuxes pushing against one another in a wave of terror. I focused and saw Gregory covering Tiffany behind the food table. Johansen was nowhere to be found near them.

Running toward it, I jumped over the table and grabbed the two of them.

"Move to the kitchen and stay in front of me!" I yelled over the screams as Tiffany struggled to stay calm.

Gregory crouched and started to move but Tiffany stood paralyzed in fear.

"Tiffany move!" I barked.

My sternness seemed to snap her out of it, and she mimicked her father as I pushed them both along and covered their heads as best I could. If I could just get them to the kitchen and out that service door, everything would be fine.

We reached the end of the table, and I pulled out the pistol on my hip. Glancing back, I saw three shooters dressed in all black, but they were having trouble figuring out where Gregory was. I aimed at the one in front, but Tiffany screamed and I missed when I took my shot.

I turned back and saw Gregory and Tiffany had made it through the door and into the kitchen. I followed and as I entered the room, the putrid smell of burning food still on the stove hit me.

That smell still haunted me.

Gregory ran towards the service door without me needing to tell him, his hand clutched tight around Tiffany's. He threw open the door and pushed her in front of him and turned to me.

"How many of them are there?" he asked frantically.

I had never seen Gregory in a state of panic before. This was the man who was known for his ability to keep calm under pressure. Now his pupils were dilated and his hands shook uncontrollably.

Before I could answer, we heard a piercing scream from outside. We dashed out the door and saw Tiffany struggling against the grip of a fourth man. I tackled him and knocked him unconscious as Tiffany crumpled to the ground and began to cry while her father ran to comfort her.

"We have to go!" I said and grabbed them to move, forgetting to push them in front of me and dragging them towards freedom. If we could make it to the garage, we'd be safe.

We ran and I kept glancing back to make sure they were okay. I felt his hand slip out of mine as Gregory tumbled to the ground. I bent down to pick him up at the same time Tiffany did, and from behind us we heard a shout.

Tiffany stood up and turned towards the sound. Before I could drop Gregory and grab my gun, one of the men from inside had pulled his gun and unloaded two shots into Tiffany's stomach. He smiled smugly and took aim at Gregory, but I put two shots of my own into him.

What happened next all seemed to go in slow motion. Tiffany fell to the ground as Gregory shouted her name, his voice pure anguish.

"Tiffany!" he cried in vain as she landed on the ground next to him. She looked around wildly as she brought her hands to her stomach. It didn't even look like Tiffany there. It was like some stranger I had never seen before was clutching her bleeding stomach.

"Dad, please…I don't want to go," she said feebly as I saw the light start to fade from her eyes. All that hope, all that potential, was rushing away from her as fast as the blood from her body and there was nothing either of us could do to stop it.

I dropped to my knees and applied pressure to her stomach, but it was no use. She was bleeding out fast. I had seen death before, but never like this. Tiffany was innocent in every way. She'd never hurt a soul and hadn't even had the chance to live life yet.

Gregory wept and begged me to help her. "Please, Gage. Please! I can't lose her."

Out of the corner of my eye, I saw another shooter came out of the house and take aim at Gregory. I stood up and shot through tear-filled eyes at him. Three bullets later he was dead on the lawn.

By the time I looked back at Tiffany, the life had left Tiffany's eyes. She was gone.

"Gregory, there were three of them inside. I don't know if the others got the third one, so we have to get to the car," I said, putting a hand on Gregory's shoulder.

He looked up with tears rushing down his face. I had never seen a man look so vulnerable. It terrified me. I couldn't imagine loving and losing someone in the way he just had. Tiffany had been everything to him, and he'd just watched her die.

I struggled to stop my own tears as he whispered, "I'm not leaving her like roadkill, Gage. She's my girl, my beautiful girl."

Saying nothing, I lifted Tiffany off the ground and carried her to the car with Gregory keeping a hand on her head. We laid her down in the back seat of his black SUV, and I drove away to the hospital knowing it was a lost cause.

Sixteen people in total, including Tiffany, were killed that night and the guilt that Gregory bore was tangible. For days after, I shadowed Gregory everywhere, and after the funeral, we sat in his study as he slowly sipped on a glass of scotch. When he finally broke the silence between us, his words were the saddest I'd ever heard.

"I don't blame you for Tiffany's death and neither should you. Your job was to protect me and you did that. Johansen was in charge of Tiffany, not you. I don't want you carrying this guilt with you for the rest of your life, Gage. It will eat you away until there's nothing left. I'd hate to think the memory of Tiffany being that for you."

"*I failed to protect her when she needed me to. That's all I know.*"

"*Gage, you did your job. No one, and I mean no one, blames you for this. If it weren't for you, the two of us would have been shot dead where we stood. Even if we had gotten out, they would have gotten us outside. Thanks to you, I'm alive.*"

I said nothing. What could I say? All that went through my mind as he spoke was because of my failure, Tiffany was gone.

"*Nothing about how you handled that situation was your fault, if that's what you're thinking.*"

Taking a deep breath in, I tried to believe what he said, but it was no use. I knew the truth. "Gregory, I'm sorry, but I have to resign. I've spoken to a friend who can do this job and will be able to meet with you as soon as you're ready. I'll stay a few days to ease the transition, but then I have to leave."

It felt like the coward's way out, but it was what needed to be done. I couldn't stay at that house knowing I'd failed to protect her.

Gregory's mouth fell open slightly and he shook his head. "No. I don't accept this. You belong here. You're the best man for the job. That's evident in the fact that you just saved my life."

"*I can't stay here,*" *I said quietly.*

I couldn't stay and pretend like it wasn't my fault. I couldn't walk the halls and hear the ghost of her laughter echoing after me. As I had wandered through the house earlier that day, it was like her beautiful face was in every corner haunting me. I had walked out to the backyard where she'd died, where I had failed her, and hated every fucking blade of grass where it happened.

No matter what Gregory said, this was my fault. I should have done better, but I'd failed. How could he ever trust me with his life again when I had so clearly failed him?

"*What happened wasn't your fault. What more can I say to convince you of that fact?*"

"*Nothing. I have to stand by my decision. If only—*"

"*You've only made sure I'm safe for years and when someone makes an attempt on my life, you ensure I'm safe. What's the damn problem here, Gage?"*

"Sir. Tiffany."

"Was not your charge, or do I need to drag out the contract you signed?"

"My contract ended a few months ago. I thought you had realized that."

I saw in his eyes he hadn't. That hurt even worse somehow. The man who knew every detail every single time had failed to notice that I had been working without a contract and there of my own volition.

"I didn't realize. Things have just been so hectic lately. But Gage, you have to stop feeling responsible for Tiffany. You did your job and damn well. What happened isn't your fault, Gage."

I knew he didn't blame me for her death, but I blamed me. I blamed me.

I sat there in that empty warehouse chained to the wall alone with the memories of the past and knew it had happened again. I'd failed, and now this time Jordan had borne the brunt of it.

I screamed out in anger and kicked at the wall. It was futile and childish, but in that moment rage filled me and there was nothing I could do to stop it. It didn't matter that Tiffany and Jordan didn't deserve what they'd had to deal with. They got hurt and killed anyway, and no matter what I did, it seemed I was powerless to stop it. All I wanted was to protect the ones I loved, but I was seemingly incapable of even that.

Over and over again I kicked, screamed, and tugged at my chains. Tiffany's lifeless eyes flashed in front of mine, but the more I pushed them away, the more Jordan's beautiful face replaced them. Around and around they went like a carnival ride of sorrow sucking me down into it.

Finally, I gave up. With one more pitiful scream that was more like a growl of defeat, I slumped against the wall and closed my eyes. There was no use fighting anymore, and I succumbed to the depression crushing me.

"Gage? Gage? Are you in there?"

I knew that voice anywhere.

"Daryl! I'm in here!" I yelled back.

I waited for Daryl as a rush of hope filled me. I didn't know how Daryl had found me, but maybe he had found Jordan as well. I had to keep that shred of belief alive.

"The door is boarded up out here. I'll be right back. I need a crowbar or something. Stay there!"

"I'm not going anywhere," I yelled back, happy to at least be hearing a familiar voice.

"I'll be back. You hang tight," he said with a chuckle.

A few minutes later, he came busting through the door and stumbled over to where I sat chained to the wall.

"Christ, Daryl, you look like you went through the war. What happened? Is that blood?" I asked, wondering about the copper color all over his clothes and skin.

"Nope, that would be rust. The whole place is full of it. I'm going to need one hell of a tetanus shot after this," he said as he walked toward me with a pair of bolt cutters.

"Wow, way to come prepared, man. I'm impressed," I said genuinely. I had known Daryl was smart, but I was actually impressed at his readiness.

"I was a boy scout, believe it or not," he said with a chuckle as he broke through my chains. "That is until they kicked me out for being too mouthy. Go figure, right?"

I stood up and stretched my whole body as I thanked Daryl. "You, mouthy? Never would have thought that Daryl."

"Yeah. Well, old habits die hard."

"Enough joking around. Where's Jordan?"

Daryl frowned and shook his head. "I don't know. I just knew where you were."

"How did you manage to find me?" I asked as we began to walk out of the room and downstairs.

He was right about the rust. I was covered in the stuff. It was a wonder the building managed to stand up from it all. From the look of it now as I left, my kicking earlier may have threatened to topple the entire place.

"Tracked your GPS from your cell phone. A little trick of the trade, if you will," he said with a big wink. He was clearly very proud of himself, as he should be. Thanks to him, I hadn't died alone in some rundown warehouse. But Jordan was still out there.

"So you don't know where she is?" I asked, my hope sinking.

Daryl's face grew dark. "I was hoping you would have an idea. I looked everywhere I could think of. I even asked Nina and Tristan if they had any ideas, but there's been no sign of her. She wasn't brought with you?"

I shook my head and pushed through what appeared to be the side door of whatever this building had once been and out into the sunlight. "Where are we?" I asked, using my hand to shield my eyes from the glare.

"Queens, in what I can only guess was where they manufactured rust at one point. Listen Gage, we're going to find her. Come hell or high water, we're finding Jordan."

He tossed me a cellphone and I remembered Jordan had been on mine back in New Orleans when they'd taken me. Quickly, I texted her a message but got no message back.

"Come on, we need to get going."

"Where? I have no idea where Jordan could be. I don't even know where to begin to look, for God's sake," I said as I followed him to his car.

"For right now, we're going back to square one. Home base. Between you, me, and Tristan's resources, we'll find her, Gage."

I hung my head as the possibilities of where she could be began to overwhelm me. Even assuming she was still in the States, she could be any of a million places.

And I didn't know how much time she had left, if she was still alive at all. She hadn't been wrong about Hailey finding us in that club in the French Quarter. If only I'd believed her, maybe we'd still be together.

My phone vibrated in my hand, and I saw someone had messaged me. My heart slamming against my chest, I read the text and knew things weren't any better than I'd imagined back in that warehouse.

Did you enjoy your trip home? You and your girlfriend only put off the inevitable with all that running but I do love when I get to vacation in New Orleans. And just in case you don't know who this is you can call me Hailey. I'll tell Jordan you said goodbye.

Chapter Nineteen

Jordan

"I HAVE TO TELL YOU that guy of yours is just delicious. A body to die for and he's got that romance thing cornered. I bet he's hung too, right?"

Hailey's glee as she described Gage made me want to throw up. Tugging at the ropes holding my wrists tight behind me, I tried to stand but found it impossible. "Shut your mouth! Don't talk about him. He's the only person in this whole mess who's good, and you wouldn't know a fucking thing about a person like him."

She dangled his phone from between her thumb and forefinger, grinning at me like a madwoman. "Maybe I should call him. If I remember correctly, he's got a great voice. Low and deep, it has an earthy, man-who-doesn't-mind-getting-his-hands-dirty kind of vibe. I guess that makes sense with him being from Wyoming. What do you say I give him a quick call and while I have him on the phone, I can finally finish this whole thing? You know, payback for him messing up my plans."

We'd been talking for over an hour, by my estimate, and I had a sense Hailey was near her breaking point. Or at least her sanity was close to it. Exhausted and barely holding onto the smallest shred of hope that Gage would find me, I hung my head and sighed.

"He only did that to help me. When you kill me, I think that will be punishment enough."

She hummed like she was considering what I'd said. "Maybe.

Or maybe not. It won't concern you, though. You'll be long gone, and he'll be heartbroken, but I'm sure he'll move on. There are millions of women who'd love to get their hands on him. That's an interesting question, though. How did you get someone like that?"

I lifted my head and stared into her eyes so full of crazy. "Why are you doing this? Can you at least tell me that before you kill me?"

Stuffing the phone in her shorts, she leaned down so her face was mere inches away from mine and screwed her face into a grimace. "I'll answer your question if you answer mine."

Hailey stepped back away from me, folding her arms across her chest like she intended on judging my story of how I got Gage. I closed my eyes and thought back to the first time I saw Gage and all those months when I lived out at Nina's and he lived just a few yards away in the carriage house.

"Well, Jordan? Quid pro quo. You tell me yours, and I'll tell you mine," she said in a sing-song voice meant to mock me.

"He was my best friend's bodyguard. That's how we met."

"Mmmmm. He really does have that hero thing down pat. Your best friend's bodyguard. She didn't mind you screwing the guy who was supposed to be protecting her? Seems like a conflict of interest, if you ask me."

"I didn't."

She ignored my swipe at her and spun around slowly on the smooth concrete floor. "You know, I've always wondered why anyone would build a garage for his cars and then never put any cars in it. Don't you think that's weird?"

"I have no idea." Clearly, Hailey's mind had begun to leave her.

"So you met that yummy guy when he was a guarding your best friend's body. Nina Stone is a beautiful woman. Why on earth would he even notice you next to her?"

I shook my head, hating every word that came from her mouth. "It wasn't like that. Don't make it sound like they were together."

Hailey spun around again and stopped quickly to face me. "You thought they were, didn't you? Oh, I love that! You were crazy about him, he wasn't about you, and you got jealous. Let me guess. You ran away and sulked like a little girl, right?"

"Shut up!" I screamed with everything I had left in me. "Just kill me already and get it over with so I don't have to listen to your fucking crazy-ass babbling anymore!"

"Tsk-tsk, Jordan. That's not how we play this game. I told you. Quid pro quo. You tell me how you got Gage Varo, and I'll tell you why you can't live anymore."

My emotions swirled inside me. First anger pushed me to lash out, and then frustration sent the signal to my brain that it was time for me to cry. I struggled to hold back the tears as I answered, "I don't know what you want. I found a way to talk to him every day, and then one day he came to my apartment and we began seeing each other."

"So you chased after him? How very modern you two are. I had him pegged as an old-fashioned kind of guy."

Gage was exactly that kind of guy, but I didn't want to discuss him anymore with her. "I told you what you wanted to know. Now why are you going to kill me?"

She closed her eyes and inhaled a deep breath before looking down at me again. "It's interesting, you know. I felt just like you most of my life. Restrained. In the dark about so many things. And then one day, it all became crystal clear. The problem was I couldn't do much about it."

Damnit, I hated the way she talked in fucking riddles. I wanted to tell her to just shut up and forget explaining anything. It wasn't worth it trying to decipher what she meant if these were going to be my last minutes alive.

But she continued to talk.

"Then I found out I wasn't the only one. At first, I was happy. I'd always hated being an only child. I had these fantasies that when I finally found her we'd be like best friends. You know, because we had a shared history. But then I found out how much better it would be if I was an only child again."

"What the hell are you talking about?" I asked, completely confused by her ramblings.

My question appeared to tear her out of a daydream, and she frowned at my interruption. "You, dear Jordan. You."

"Me? Me what? I'm not an only child. I have a brother and sister, so whatever the hell you mean about the only child thing doesn't have anything to do with me."

"I always thought you'd be more like—" The sound of a door opening distracted her and for the first time her eyes flashed pure panic.

I turned to look toward where the sound came from and saw people I'd never seen before. Hailey took one look at them and turned to run, but the four men were on top of her in a flash before she could get away. I watched in absolute glee as they slammed her down and pinned her to the hard floor, thrilled Gage had figured out where I was and sent in the cavalry.

One of the men untied the ropes holding my wrists and ankles. Dressed in a dark suit, he wore a tie that reminded me of the expensive kind Nina bought for Tristan. He smiled down at me as I watched the scene in front of me unfold like a dream and said in a soothing voice, "Are you hurt?"

Shaking my head, I looked around him as the three other men dragged Hailey off kicking and screaming about who she was and how much trouble they'd be in. "I'm okay. Where's Gage?"

The man looked down at me with a blank expression. "I don't know, but when we get to the house, I'm sure all your questions will be answered. Do you need me to carry you, or can you walk?"

"I can walk," I said as he helped me up from the chair. The house? Whose house? Was he talking about Nina and Tristan's? Had they been a part of helping him find out where I was being held?

I had the sense the man guiding me out of the garage wasn't going to tell me. All I knew was Gage had done exactly what he always promised to do. He'd protected me when I needed him most.

And as soon as I had the chance, I was going to show him just how much I appreciated that part of him.

BLINKING, I SLOWLY OPENED MY eyes and as they adjusted to the light, I realized there was someone next to me. I sat up and saw I was on a bed surrounded by decorative pillows. Where was I and whose bed was this?

The room was huge, with high windows and deep red shades pulled halfway down. An enormous mahogany chest of drawers stood on the wall to the right of the bed and on the wall in front of me sat a matching dresser. The bed was a four-poster like the kind that would have a canopy I always wanted when I was a little girl.

Looking to the side, I saw an older woman smiling down at me. She had a grandmotherly look with her grey hair up in a bun. She wore glasses that accentuated the lines near her eyes and gave her a wise look.

"Good afternoon, dear. My name is Helen and I'm just making sure that nothing serious happened to that pretty head of yours. If it doesn't seem crass, I would love to know what conditioner you use sometime. Your hair is just stunning," she said with a genuine smile I liked.

Her comment may have been bizarre, but after all that I'd been through, I had to smile. "It's an argan oil based conditioner. I guess it does what it promises."

"Argan oil? I'll have to get some. Now you just stay here and rest. It doesn't look like they did anything serious harm when they got you. You're safe now."

The way she said that, so comforting and gentle, made me believe her for a moment. However, that same sense of foreboding I'd had for days came rushing back.

"Where am I? Why hasn't Gage come to see me yet? What's going on here?"

"You're in my home in the beautiful city of Austin," a male's voice said from the doorway to my left. I turned my head to look at him and recognized him immediately.

"I'm Dalton Spear, but judging by the look on your face, you already know that," he said as he moved closer.

"No, don't take another step," I said as I pushed myself back on the bed toward the nightstand to grab the lamp. "You think I don't know that it's your fiancé who's been trying to kill me? I don't know what you have against me, but I swear to God you take one step closer and I'll crush your skull with this lamp." Hopefully, my strong words would somehow get me out of whatever new and hellish situation I found myself in.

"Jordan, please, I only just found out what Hailey was doing. I put an end to it. Helen was right, you're safe here. When I received word that Hailey was doing these despicable things, I made sure it all ended," Dalton replied with a pleading tone.

Something about the pain in his eyes and his body language told me he wasn't lying. I looked to Helen for confirmation, hoping she really was the grandmotherly type and not just another person I had to fear.

"He's telling the truth, dear," she said with a smile. "I promise you're safe here."

"I want to see Gage now. Where is he?"

Dalton smiled and shook his head. "I don't know. Hailey won't say where she sent him. I'm sorry."

Unable to stop the tears from coming, I buried my head in my hands and sobbed, "Did she kill him? Is that what happened?"

"I don't know. I wish I did. For now, I hope you'll come with me. There's someone who wants to speak to you."

Someone who wanted to speak to me? Who?

I lifted my head and dried my eyes. "If you're talking about that crazy bitch you're planning on marrying, forget it. I have nothing more to say to her."

He shook his head again and sighed. "No, it's not Hailey. I'm getting tired, so I have to sit down. I hope you'll come and join me. I think it's time we all talked."

"We all who?" I asked, but he ignored my question and simply turned slowly toward the door before leaving.

Helen gently pried the lamp from my hands and placed it back on the nightstand. "I hope you'll do as he asks, but whatever you do, I'm glad I got to meet you, Jordan. You're quite the young lady, and if I do say so myself, you remind me of me when I was your age."

She didn't stay long enough for me to even say thank you for taking care of me. Left alone in a strange bedroom not knowing where Gage was or even if he was okay, I sat there on the bed and hung my head. I had no idea how I'd get home or even why I was there in Dalton Spear's home. Looking around the room, I saw no phone I could use to call Nina either.

I didn't have a choice. Whether I wanted to or not, I had to talk to him and whoever he had waiting for me. Since I had likely lost everything I loved already, why not?

CHAPTER TWENTY

JORDAN

I FOLLOWED HIM TO A room down the hallway and saw it was a sitting room of some kind. Much brighter than the bedroom I'd been in, it was decorated in pale blue and white and had a soothing feel to it. I just hoped this conversation he wanted to have would be as relaxing because I didn't need any more horror added to the nightmare my life had become.

Dalton sat in a high-backed dark blue chair and motioned for me to sit on a white couch across from him. I took my place there and wondered who would be sitting in the matching chair next to him.

"So who is this person you want to join us and what are we talking about?" I asked sharply as I scanned the room, feeling on edge and worried that at any moment Hailey might jump out from behind the door.

"It's me, honey," I heard a familiar voice say and saw my mother step out from next to a bookcase.

"Mom, what are doing here? Did Gage send you? What's going on? Nobody here will tell me anything."

My mother sat in the chair next to Dalton and folded her hands in her lap. I'd seen her do that exact motion every time in my life when she had something she had to say that I wouldn't like. The day we found out my grandfather was diagnosed with pancreatic cancer. The time when my sister broke my favorite necklace trying to walk her turtle. Every time she disliked one of my boyfriends.

"Honey, we need to talk to you about something. I want you to try to understand. Sometimes people do things they later wish they hadn't. Do you know what I mean?"

I looked from her to the man sitting next to her and back to my mother again. "Yeah, I guess. I mean, okay. What's going on here? How do you know this person? I've never heard you or Dad talk about knowing one of the richest men in America. That seems like something I would have heard before now."

Dalton cleared his throat. "I've known your mother for years. Twenty-six, I believe."

I stared at him in complete confusion. "You've known my mother since before I was born, and I've never heard of you, not even once?" Turning to look at my mother, I asked, "What is this? Mom?"

"Honey, I'm sorry. We should have told you years ago. I thought about telling you, but I didn't want things to be confusing for you. Dalton is your father."

I shook my head violently, hoping I could get rid of the words sinking into my brain. "John Wright is my father. Why would you say this man is my father?"

"Because I am, Jordan. John Wright is the man who raised you and clearly did a good job, along with your mother, but I'm your father," Dalton said in a low voice barely above a whisper.

I fought to stop the tears, but they came in a rush, spilling down my cheeks. "How? What do you mean you're my father? Mom, tell me what he's talking about."

My mother pressed her lips together and then began to explain the truth of who I was. "Jordan, we were both very young. Too young, I guess. Things were so different then. We were different people. When I found out I was pregnant, I knew that wasn't what Dalton wanted for his life."

"Don't make excuses for me, Michelle. She deserves to know the truth."

Jerking my head to look at him, I asked, "What excuses? What truth other than the fact that you're my father and I've never met you before today?"

Dalton frowned and cleared his throat again. "I was a spoiled rich punk. There's no other way to describe who I was back then. My family had money, and I had anything and anyone I wanted. Your mother and I dated when I was in college, but when she told me she was pregnant, I told her I wanted nothing to do with a baby. I'm sorry, Jordan. I was selfish."

My chest felt like someone had just placed a hundred pound weight on it. "So you didn't even want to know I existed?"

Reaching across the coffee table, my mother took my hands in hers. "It wasn't like that, honey. He had a life and that didn't include a child. I accepted that, and when I met your father, he loved you from the first time he held you in his arms, so I didn't worry about you not having Dalton in your life."

I pulled my hands from her hold and wrapped my arms around me. "So you never once even thought about me? You got my mother pregnant and never bothered to even find out what your child was like?"

Shaking his head, Dalton answered, "Not until a few years ago when your mother let me know you wanted to go to school in New York and asked me to help."

"Is this true, Mom? You never told me about him, and then you took his money to pay for my school?"

I'd always wondered how my parents, who were typical middle class, could afford to send me to school in New York and pay for my room and board too. God, I'd been so blind!

She sat back, her shoulders sagging. "You had your heart set on that school, and I didn't want to see you disappointed, so I contacted Dalton and asked him to help your father and me pay for it."

"How could you lie to me all my life? And how could a man have a child out in the world and never even want to see her? Jesus

Christ, I'm the product of a liar and a heartless bastard!"

"Jordan!" my mother shrieked.

"Don't talk about your mother like that," Dalton said, coming to my mother's defense. "I gave her little choice but to lie."

I stood from the couch and began pacing in front of them. "Oh, okay. So I'm just the daughter of a heartless bastard. That's great. All my life I thought I was the oldest child of John and Michelle Wright and loved, and now I find out that I'm the daughter of some guy who didn't want to do the right thing and marry a woman like my mother but is the fiancé of a woman who has been trying to kill me. You sure do have some great choices going there, Dad."

"Dalton, what is she talking about? Do you know who has been trying hurt our daughter?"

I stopped and waited for his answer. "Yeah, tell my mother how Hailey, your bride-to-be has been chasing me across the country to kill me. At least now I know why. She certainly wouldn't want some long-lost heir popping up now that you're dying. Dear Hailey is nothing if not a gold digger. I mean, she's barely older than me and she's got her mitts on a man twice her age."

Dalton raised his eyebrows in surprise at my outburst, but he knew I was right. And then he spoke, and I found out I'd been so off the mark about that crazy bitch.

"I asked Hailey to marry me. That's true. I had just found out I had stage four cancer, and she was kind to me. Call it a foolish act by a dying man. I knew next to nothing about her, except that she appeared one day as a nurse sent by the agency. I had no other family to rely on, so I put some of the business in her name to help her take care of things. After all, she was going to inherit it when I died anyway."

He stopped for a moment to take a breath and then continued. "I didn't find out until recently that she'd been stealing from me to the tune of nearly a million dollars or that she wasn't just some nice young woman who cared for a dying man. I guess I should be thankful that my illness made having a physical relationship impossible because she's my daughter just like you are."

My mouth dropped, and I stood there staring at him stunned by what I'd just heard. "So she's not a gold digging woman but another child of yours? How many of us are there and will they all be trying to kill me?"

His eyebrows shot up again, but this time he smiled. "I wish I had met you before this, Jordan. You're exactly the kind of person I can respect. To answer your question, I only have two children, you and Hailey. Now that she's going to jail, you won't have to worry about her anymore."

All I could do was shake my head. What had happened to little old me, the elementary school teacher who just wanted a life with the man I loved and a few nice things to go with it?

"I understand if you can't forgive me, though. I am truly sorry all of this happened."

I took a deep breath and tried to get my head around everything that had happened. "So you had nothing to do with why she was trying to kill me? I thought you did."

"No, I wouldn't do that, Jordan. I've been a son of a bitch all my life, but I never knew what she was doing."

"Hailey and Justin forced me to marry him in South Carolina and sign a document I'm sure was meant to make sure I had no right to anything of yours. I don't want to be married to him. If you're really wanting to make this right, help me get out of that."

His face lit up. "My lawyers will have that document torn up in one court date. Don't worry about that at all. I am sorry about all of this, Jordan. I wish I had known all these years what I was missing. From what your mother's told me, your father provided for you and gave you love. I know I can't make up for what I did and not being around all those years, but I can do what I'm good at in the little time I have left."

It was hard to stay angry at the man. I wasn't ready to start doing father-daughter brunches together, but he really did seem sorry. If my mother had been able to forgive him, maybe I could too. I'd have to forgive her as well, but somehow that felt easier. My parents had lied, that was true, but they had also been damn good parents and that had to count for something.

His cell phone rang and after he listened to the caller say something in his ear, he said, "I'd like for you to see something. I think it will make you feel much better. Come with me."

My mother took my hand and smiled as we followed him out into the hallway to a grand staircase. At the bottom of the stairs, one of Dalton's servants was opening the door for the police.

They walked in and tipped their hats to us at the top of the stairs. "Evening, Mr. Spear. My apologies for our being late," one of the men said.

Dalton smiled and extended his hand out to me. I took it and stepped forward to stand next to him. He looked at me with a gentle glance and whispered, "I think it's important you see this so you understand my true intentions."

"Don't you fucking touch me, you idiot! These nails cost more than your house!" Hailey screamed as Dalton's men dragged her into the foyer.

"That'll be her then?" the chief asked with a grin. From the sound of it, she was throwing a legendary tantrum, but no one seemed to be concerned about it very much.

They handcuffed her as she kicked her legs wildly and bucked to and fro. Justin was in tow also, but had decided to use his right to remain silent and kept his head down in shame. That made me almost as happy as seeing Hailey hauled off to jail. After all the lies and deception, it was he who had to hang his head in shame, not me.

As they were paraded out before me, I couldn't help but feel a sense of victory. After all this time running from them, they now looked like little more than second-rate con artists. Hailey caught sight of us at the top of the stairs and her jaw dropped. In that moment it was clear that everything had really come crashing down on her. The man she thought she'd swindled and the woman she thought she'd get away with murdering were both standing on the balcony of her now former home. It had a wonderful poetic justice to it.

"Dalton baby, please. Don't let them do this to me. It isn't like she says. I swear!" she begged pitifully.

To my immense satisfaction, Dalton didn't say anything. The look on his face screamed volumes, though. Instead of meeting her eye contact or even looking at me, he simply lifted his chin to let her know that she was, in every way, beneath him. It was silent, but it cut like a knife and Hailey felt the snub.

The police started to pull her towards the front door and she screamed about how Dalton needed her and how he could never live without her. Still no one responded to her, only infuriating her further.

With a final twist and jerk of her body, she looked back and make eye contact with me. "I'll make you pay for this you, bitch!" she screamed before the door shut and they were all gone.

Dalton squeezed my hand and smiled. "Jordan, this has been quite the exciting day for me. I lost my fiancé and met you. Would you and your mother mind if I laid down while we spoke a little more?"

He looked a bit pale so I let go of his hand and nodded as my mother did too. "Of course. Lead the way," I said as my mother took my other hand in hers.

The three of us walked to the room next to the one I'd been in and he gingerly eased himself into bed. He reached over to the nightstand cluttered with pill bottles and took a sip of water before settling back in bed and offering me a seat in the plush armchair next to it.

"So tell me about yourself, Jordan. What do you do?" he asked with genuine interest.

"I'm an elementary school teacher, though I've probably lost my job since I was kidnapped and have been on the run," I said, pushing away the stress over my job. Certain things were just going to have to wait.

"I bet your students love you," he said, smiling up at me.

"I really love them and the job."

"And what about your personal life, if you don't mind me asking?"

"I live in Brooklyn in an apartment I used to share with my friend Nina before she married Tristan Stone."

He furrowed his brow. "Why do I want to say I know that name?" he asked, puzzled.

"Tristan's the owner of the Richmont hotel chain."

"Ah, yes. I know of him."

"And then there's Gage. I met him through them. He owns a security company. I figured he was the one who found me with Hailey, to be honest. Do you know what she did with him?"

Dalton shook his head sadly. "I don't know where Gage is, Jordan. I only knew what Hailey did to you. I didn't know someone else was involved until today."

"I need to call him," I muttered. "I know you want to get to know me, but I need him to know I'm okay.

"Use the one on the, on the…" A terrible cough that sounded like it started low in his chest made him double over in pain.

"Dalton? Are you okay?" I asked, but he only coughed more violently in response.

My mother ran to the door and yelled, "Help! Someone help!"

His coughing grew worse, and I saw there was blood on his mouth and chest. He managed to whisper something as two men ran into the room.

"Jordan, I want you to know I'm truly sorry I didn't get to spend more time with you," he said as the men dialed for an ambulance.

"I am too, Dalton." I really was. I wished I had gotten a chance to really know the man who was my father.

"Can you forgive me?"

It wasn't the coughing, or the blood, or anything else in that room that convinced me in that moment that I could. What use was there going through life holding someone's past against them?

"I forgive you," I said, placing a kiss on the top of his hand.

He smiled wide despite the cough that wracked his body. "I need Helen. Please bring her here."

The sweet elderly lady I'd seen when I opened my eyes just a few hours before rushed to his bedside and nodded as he tried to tell her in his last breath all that he'd waited to say.

"Don't be sad. I lived a good life, and now that I got to meet Jordan, I know it wasn't a life that meant nothing. Be sure my lawyers take care of her marriage and my will. They know what to do. I love you. Thank you for being a wonderful mother to me. Get to know your granddaughter so you won't have to say you missed out."

Helen sobbed but promised him she'd take care of everything he asked for. Then she backed away so he could speak to me.

"Listen to me, Jordan. I never got a chance to do the right thing by you and now I can. Today has been the happiest day of my life." he said, pausing to cough again. "Will you stay with me?"

"Of course, Dalton. I'm right here."

He smiled and nodded. "You have green eyes just like me. I like that."

I looked into his eyes and saw how green they looked now. I hadn't noticed that in all the time he'd been right in front of me that day or all that time I'd spent staring at his picture online. I started to tell him he was right, but his coughing started again with a vengeance. I held his hand as he struggled to breathe. Helen returned a few minutes later and sat on the other side holding his other hand and helping to administer some medicine she said would ease his pain. It did for a short time, but the end was coming. About an hour later, the ragged rise and fall of his chest stopped and he was gone.

I was a little surprised when the tears started rolling down my cheeks. After all, I hadn't known this man. Still a dull pain settled into my chest.

"Thank you for giving him such a wonderful last day."

I stood up from the bed and placed one more kiss on Dalton's hand, silently wishing him peace. Looking over at Helen, I smiled even as I continued to cry. "I'm so sorry."

I hadn't known the man for long at all, but he was my father and she was my grandmother, even if we'd just met. As we left his room to let the EMTs do their jobs, I took her hand in mine and we walked down the hallway together with my mother.

It was strange and something I'd never anticipated, but there we were, three generations of my family in Dalton Spear's home. I didn't know what would happen next with us, but it was nice to know I had a chance to meet the man who helped give me life before he was taken from this world.

CHAPTER TWENTY-ONE

GAGE

I SAT IN DARYL'S DINGY office on a battered leather couch while Daryl rallied his resources to find Jordan. It had been hours and nothing was working. It was like Jordan had vanished from the world.

"Get back to me if you hear anything," Daryl said before hanging up the old black telephone on his desk.

"Who the hell still uses a landline?" I asked, busting his balls a little. If I didn't, I was going to go out of my mind. None of my connections knew anything and Daryl's were just as much in the dark.

"It suits me. Makes me look like one of those old gumshoes from the forties," he answered, sounding like some gangster from an old black and white movie.

I couldn't help but laugh. The guy was a lot of things, but more than anything else, Daryl was a good guy. Strange and from another time, but a good guy, nonetheless.

"We're going to find her, Gage," he said quietly, his joking falling away. "Try Nina and Tristan again. Maybe something new has developed."

I did as he suggested and dialed Tristan's number, but just as before, he didn't answer. I started to dial Nina's, but before I could, she called me.

"Hello, Nina?"

"Gage! I'm so glad to hear your voice. I'm sorry we haven't

been answering. Diana had to go to the hospital because of an ear infection, so we've been without cell phone service. What is going on? Is Jordan okay?"

It pained me to have to tell her that Jordan wasn't with me. "Nina, calm down. It's going to be okay. I'm here with Daryl, but we can't find Jordan. Have either of you heard anything? Have you had any contact at all from her since we talked in New Orleans?"

"No, none at all. That's why I'm so worried, Gage. Do you think she's okay? Oh God, what if they've done something to her."

I winced at the idea of Jordan gone from the world. Even the mere thought of it made my heart ache. She had to be okay. If I ever found her…no, when. It had to be when we found her, not if. I refused to accept a world where Jordan was no longer in it, and I once again silently vowed to do whatever it took to have the woman I loved back in my arms where she belonged.

"She's going to be all right, Nina. Is Tristan there?"

"Yes, he's right here. Hang on."

There was a pause and I heard Nina crying in the background when Tristan began speaking. "Hello, Gage. What can I do?"

His tone was even and calmer than Nina's, but I had seen Tristan scared before and there was no doubt that something in his voice told me he was scared right now.

"I'm not sure. I know Daryl was your suggestion in the first place, but do you know anyone else who might have information on where she is?"

"I might. Give me a minute and I'll make some calls."

"Thanks, Tristan."

We hung up after saying goodbye and I looked over at a discouraged looking Daryl. We sat in silence for what felt like ages before Daryl, frustrated, muttered, "I'm putting the game on."

He flipped on the television but instead of the game it was a news story. The bubbly female newscaster was a sharp contrast to my dreary existence and immediately irritated me.

"We have confirmed reports that billionaire businessman

Dalton Spear has passed away from cancer today. Throughout his life he dedicated himself to…" the announcer rattled on but I stopped paying attention. All I could think about was how if Dalton Spear was dead, Hailey had won.

"They didn't say anything about Hailey," I heard Daryl say, but he sounded miles away.

I stood up from the couch and walked out of his office without a word. There was nothing more to be said. If Dalton Spear was dead that meant the odds of Jordan still being alive and us finding her had just disappeared.

It didn't take me long to get back to my apartment. I opened the door and it felt like it had been years since I had been here. Everything around me felt foreign, and the only thing that made sense was the bottle of Jack Daniels on the kitchen counter.

I didn't bother getting a glass but instead opened the bottle and poured a gulp down my throat. Lost in misery from the idea that Jordan was gone, I sat down on the couch and hung my head, letting the tears out for the first time since all this began. Three quarters of the bottle later, my mind had begun to haunt me with the fear and guilt I'd harbored since receiving the first letter threatening Jordan's life if I didn't leave her.

If only I hadn't given in back then, she'd still be alive and with me. We'd be happy. She'd be teaching her students and still living in that apartment in Brooklyn. Or maybe we'd be living together somewhere in the city. Wherever we were, we'd be starting a life together.

A regular life of days filled with work and nights filled with each other.

Sitting there daydreaming about that life was worse than when I had been in that abandoned building. Now the memories didn't have a hint of sweetness to them but instead were cruel as they mocked me. I wasn't chained up this time, but I might as well have been. It wasn't the alcohol that kept me sitting there, wallowing in my memories.

It was regret, and I couldn't see a time ever again when I didn't wish I had done things so differently. If only I had.

I downed one more gulp of booze and checked for any messages from her, hoping against hope she would have sent one. I saw nothing.

Closing my eyes, I threw my phone against the wall, watching it shatter into a hundred pieces, and choked back the utter sadness that filled me. She was gone because I hadn't done the one thing she needed me to do.

Protect her.

CHAPTER TWENTY-TWO

JORDAN

MY FINGERS ACHED AS I pressed the call button on my cell phone again. Under his name, a picture of Gage smiling that crooked, sexy grin of his stared back at me. Once again, the call went directly to his now full voicemail.

"You're going to leave burn marks on the carpet, dear," Helen said softly from across the room.

"I have to know he's okay," I muttered, hitting the call button again.

Helen nodded and walked over to me. Putting a hand on my shoulder, she said, "You wake me if you need me. It's very late and I need to rest."

I'd been so focused on getting in touch with Gage that I'd forgotten Helen had just lost her son. "I'm sorry. I don't want to be insensitive. I didn't meant to act like what's going on here isn't important."

She waved away my concern and smiled. "Dalton and I knew the end was coming. I made my peace with it a while ago. If you need anything just yell and someone will come help you. If you want to talk or need company, I'll be in my room," Helen said with a motherly smile.

"Thank you and good night," I said quietly, still listening to the agonizing sound of Gage's voice telling me to leave a message and he'd get back to me. Something in my heart told me that if his phone was still on, maybe he was alive.

Fucking Hailey! Even when Dalton asked her, she wouldn't say what she'd done to Gage. Had she killed him after deciding he wasn't useful to her, or had she hidden him somewhere to torture until he gave her what she wanted to know about my whereabouts?

For two days, it was all I could think about. Both possibilities made my heart contract in sadness. I had to find him before it was too late.

I dialed Nina's number over and over after filling up Gage's voicemail and got no answer from her either. Was everyone I loved gone from me?

Three hours later, I'd said goodbye to my mother and promised her I'd come home to see her and my father as soon as everything calmed down. Exhausted from everything that had happened and my inability to find Gage or Nina, I lay down on the couch in Dalton's study and closed my eyes to wish for my life to go back to what it used to be.

My ordinary, commonplace life.

When I opened my eyes again hours later, Helen and two men in business suits stood around Dalton's desk shuffling papers.

"What's going on?" I asked groggily as I wiped the sleep from my eyes.

The older man with a grey beard and matching eyes smiled and said, "Good morning, Ms. Wright. As soon as you're ready, we have some papers for you to sign."

Barely awake enough to comprehend what he was saying, I stood on unsteady legs and made my way to the desk. "Papers for me to sign? Why?"

He smiled like he was used to confusing people. "We don't typically meet this way, but your father's last wishes must be observed."

"Last wishes?" I asked as he offered me a seat behind the desk.

"I am Henry Billings of Billings, Billings and Cartwright. We were your father's lawyers, so now we're your lawyers, should you decide to keep us. What you have in front of you are the important documents you may need over the coming weeks as everything is transferred into your name. The house, the cars, the business, and the plane. Your father's company will continue to be run by the CEO, Thomas Spring, and the board of directors will continue according to legal statutes governing corporations in the state of Texas, but your father ensured his shares of the company were transferred to you, so you now hold controlling interest in Spear Industries."

"Excuse me? Did you say plane? I thought I was just getting some shares of the company and the house. What are you saying?" I asked, flabbergasted.

The two men smiled at one another and then at me. "What we're saying is Mr. Spear left you everything, and we mean everything."

My mind raced. What had he said in the beginning? A plane? Next thing, Tristan would be asking me to race him if this day kept going the way it had begun.

"You said plane, right?" It was like a beaming, shining ray of hope had shined down out of the dreary sky my life had become.

"Yes, two of them, actually. Although, I do believe one of them is currently being worked on. Routine maintenance is normal and is usually done in such a manner as to not interrupt your plans. It is best to tell the pilot a week in advance…"

Leaping from the chair, I smoothed my messy hair and straightened my clothes. "I'm sorry to cut this meeting short, but I really need to go do something important. Do you need me to sign something?"

The two men looked confused. "Well, just a few signatures will do for now, Ms. Wright."

"Okay. Someone give me a pen and I'll sign whatever you want, as long as the next thing I get to do is get on one of those planes. Can you tell me where I'd find it, by the way?"

Helen handed me a pen and asked, "Do you have somewhere to go, dear?"

I looked back at her and smiled. "I need to go find the man I love. I need to get to New York City!" I said as I quickly signed my name on every line I was told to.

Everything seemed to move at light speed when you had money, and within a few hours I had landed at JFK. Luckily, the plane had a bathroom I was able to use to freshen up so I didn't look like a stray dog when I returned home.

A driver met me at the gate with a car and a cell phone and was soon waiting outside as I ran up to Gage's place. Sadly, after knocking on the door and getting no answer, I called his phone yet again, but there was no answer there either. So I tried Nina and hoped someone I cared about still answered my calls. The phone rang and I crossed my fingers hoping she'd answer.

"Hello?" I heard as I jumped for joy at the sound of her voice.

"Nina? It's Jordan! I'm here at Gage's place, but he's not here and he hasn't been answering his phone. Please tell me you heard from Daryl and know something about where he is."

"Jordan, oh my God! We thought you were dead. Gage was so worried that awful woman found you and—"

"Nina, where is he? I can't get in touch with him because his phone just goes to voicemail and I tried his apartment, but he's not here. Please tell me you know he's okay."

"Oh, he's alive and well, but I don't know where he is now, honey. Call Daryl. He'll know. He's been helping Gage look for you."

I took Daryl's number and quickly thanked Nina, promising to see her as soon as I could, before calling my favorite mountain man. Never terribly expressive, Daryl sounded like the weight of the world had been lifted off his shoulders when he heard my voice.

"Jordan? Christ, it's good to hear from you. Where are you?"

I looked up and down the street Gage lived on and smiled. "The greatest city in the world and right where I belong. I'm in front of Gage's apartment, but there's no answer. Do you know where he is?"

Instead of telling me where Gage was, he peppered me with questions. "What happened to you? How did you get back to the city in one piece? What happened to Hailey and the whole Dalton Spear connection?"

"I promise to tell you everything as soon as I find Gage. Please, I have to find him, Daryl."

"Yeah, yeah, of course. I forgot my manners there for a second. He mentioned something this morning about smashing his phone. He's been pretty upset. I think he's at his office trying to find someone who can say where you are."

Finally, I knew where Gage was. "I have to go Daryl. Thank you so much!" I said hurriedly as I ran to the car.

I directed the driver exactly where to go, and in a flash, we were heading downtown to Varo Security. When we pulled up, I didn't even let the car come to a full stop.

I burst through the door and saw no one around. I raced toward his office, my heart slamming against my chest, and stopped as my hand touched the doorknob. How was I going to explain to him all the changes that had happened in the last few days?

I didn't know, but I did know I didn't want a life without Gage. Slowly, I opened the door and saw him sitting behind his desk. He looked like he hadn't had a peaceful moment for far too long. I could change that, though. Everything Dalton had given me could be more than just money to buy things.

It could be peace, once and for all. A peaceful life for both of us, just like Nina had with Tristan and the kids.

He looked at me with those dark blue eyes so full of pain and sighed for a long moment. I said nothing, not knowing the right words someone should say when everything in the world has changed.

"Jordan. How? How did you get here?" he asked, shaking his head in disbelief. "I thought I'd lost you forever."

"I thought the same of you too. I'm so happy to see you."

He stood and rushed toward me to take me into his arms.

"What happened to you? Where did she take you?"

I pressed my cheek to his chest and breathed in the soft smell of his laundry detergent. It was a small and seemingly meaningless reminder of a simple act that meant so much. "I don't want to talk about that now. All I want to do is feel your arms around me and know I'm safe again."

Gage pulled away from me and hung his head. "I failed, Jordan. I promised you I'd protect you, and when it came time to prove I could, she got you. I failed."

Cradling his face, I saw the hurt and disappointment in it. He'd spent days thinking Hailey had killed me because of him. I hated that he'd blamed himself.

"You didn't fail, Gage. You were there when I needed you in South Carolina, and you protected me when Justin tried to take me up near the cabin in Wyoming. You made sure we got to New Orleans—"

He stopped me, shaking his head. "Where she found you and took you away to kill you, Jordan."

"Don't do this, Gage. We have a chance to be happy after everything we went through. Don't let your past and whatever happened back there ruin what we can have."

Looking away, he said, "I've spent so long worried that what happened then would happen again with you. I never told you, but I failed before and someone died. A girl who idolized me and believed in me. She thought I'd always be there, and when I had to be to save her, I failed and she died."

I took his hands in mine, worried if I didn't hold onto him that I'd lose him. "I'm not a girl, Gage. I'm a grown woman who doesn't want a protector more than she wants a man who loves her."

He looked down at where I touched him and shook his head. "I was supposed to keep you safe. That's my job."

The heartbreak in his voice tore at me, but I had to show him how wrong he was. "I wasn't a client, Gage. I'm the woman you say you love. If you do, you'll listen to me now. Whatever happened in the past, you have to let it go. You didn't fail with me. You did everything you could to support me, like a man should with the woman he loves. That's all any woman can ever ask for. We don't want superheroes, Gage. We just want a man who takes care of us like we take care of them. I want that. That's you."

I waited as he continued to avoid my gaze, hoping that the words that had come from my heart could help him see how wonderful he was because if they didn't, I wasn't sure what I could say to convince him how much I loved him.

When he finally looked up, I knew it hadn't been enough.

"I love you, Jordan. I do, but I can't stand knowing when you needed me most I wasn't good enough to protect you."

"What are you saying? What does that mean, Gage?" I asked, terrified at what his answer would be.

He sighed and shook his head. "I'm glad you're okay, Jordan. Have a good life. You deserve it."

As he turned away, I grabbed hold of him and cried, "No! Gage, no! Don't do this! We have our whole future ahead of us. Why are you doing this?"

"Because I can't risk failing again!" he bellowed. I stepped back in surprise and he said in a much quieter voice, "You deserve better, Jordan. I hope you find it."

After everything we'd been through and all that had changed in my life over the past few days, I stood there with tears rolling down my cheeks as the truth of who Gage had always been finally sunk in. It didn't matter what I said. Until he believed what I believed, he'd always see himself as a failure and I'd never change that.

Only he could.

Chapter Twenty-Three

Gage

THE SUNSET PARK NEIGHBORHOOD LOOKED the same as it had the last time I'd driven through it nearly three months before right after that day I told Jordan I couldn't be with her. I saw in her eyes she wanted to fight me, to convince me that I was wrong about how big a failure I'd been to her. She couldn't see it. She wouldn't see it, but I worried what if she did someday? What if I stayed with her and she let herself believe she was safe, and then one day when she needed me, I failed again?

I knew now I wasn't that man I'd convinced myself I was. That hadn't changed anything, though. Every day, I thought about going to her. I thought about finally letting myself go to her apartment and begging her to take me back.

I never did, though.

My phone rang and I saw on the screen it was Nina calling. It had been a few months since I talked to her. I'd expected to hear from her after what happened with Jordan, but she never called. I'd seen Tristan a few times since, and he'd been the same man he'd always been toward me.

"Gage? It's Nina. How are you?"

"I'm good," I lied. "How are things at the Stone house out there? I bet those kids are growing like weeds."

She chuckled at my lame comment. "They are! That's why I'm calling, actually. We're having a little party for the triplets and hoped you'd come out here to join us."

"A party?" I asked as I turned the corner to head for the Taconic. "When?"

"Well, this afternoon. I know it's short notice, but I really would love to have you there."

Knowing her penchant for matchmaking, I had to ask the obvious question. "Is Jordan going to be there, Nina?"

There was a long silence before she answered, "Yes, she definitely will be. I hope that won't stop you from coming."

I wanted nothing more than to see Jordan, but what if she'd moved on? "Is she…will she be alone or is she bringing someone?"

"Bringing someone? No, she won't be bringing anyone to the party. So will you come?"

Without hesitating, I said, "I'll be there. What time?"

"Two hours from now. Say three o'clock?"

"I'll be there, Nina. It'll be nice to see you and Tristan and the kids again."

"Great! Oh, I almost forgot to tell you. The party's at the house next to ours. You remember the one closest to us on the left?"

I had to smile. The Stones sure did know how to spend money. "You guys bought that house? Planning on making it a playhouse for the kids?"

"Something like that. See you at three, Gage."

AT JUST BEFORE THREE O'CLOCK, I pulled up to the gates of the new Stone house and was let in by a guard. I drove up the long driveway to the home, impressed by the number of cars I saw. Nina and Tristan must have invited ten people for each kid. It seemed like a lot for people not even five years old.

Two men dressed in all black uniforms waved me on toward the biggest garage I'd ever seen and stopped me in front of the doors. Looking in, I saw six cars parked inside.

Rolling down my window, I said, "Just park anywhere or are we doing a valet thing today, gentlemen?"

"We'll take care of your car, sir," the one said, so I parked it and got out.

"Thanks," I said as I handed him my keys. "I might not be staying too long, so park it somewhere close for a quick getaway."

I was hoping to convince Jordan to leave with me after I'd stayed long enough not to offend the Stones. We had a lot to talk about, but first, I'd have to show her I was different from the man who sent her away all those months ago.

Stopping to look at the house, I couldn't help but be impressed. Slate steps led to enormous dark brown wooden doors, and the cream and brown colored stone façade of the home screamed money. I'd seen this house many times before while living on the grounds of Tristan and Nina's home next door, but now that I was up close, I had to say it rivaled the old one. Maybe Tristan was trying to buy up the neighborhood.

Inside, I passed through a foyer with fifteen foot ceilings, taking a moment to admire the wrought iron and glass light fixture hanging overhead that reminded me of one at Tristan's Garden District house.

The guy sure did know how to live.

Guests mingled in the living room directly ahead of me, so I walked in and looked around for the host and hostess or their children but didn't see anyone I recognized. I headed toward the fireplace on the far wall with stone that matched the outside of the house and stood by the floor-to-ceiling windows that looked out onto a patio and outdoor kitchen area. The barbeque set up alone looked like it cost more than I made in a year, but I had to admit I liked that part of the house.

"Gage! Thank you for coming! Isn't the house gorgeous?" Nina said as she walked toward me.

"It is," I answered with a smile. "Are you guys planning to buy up the whole county?" I joked.

She winked at me and shook her head. "Oh, this isn't our house. It's Jordan's. And since I'm being honest, this isn't a party for the kids. It's a housewarming party for her. She just bought this place last month and finally moved in the other day. I hope you aren't mad about the subterfuge."

What Nina was saying didn't make any sense. Jordan couldn't afford a place like this. A house like this one cost at least a couple million. "Are we talking about the same person, Nina? Jordan's a school teacher."

Out of the corner of my eye, I saw Jordan walk into the room and knew instantly that Nina hadn't been joking with me. She looked like the same woman I'd always known, but there was something different about her now. Something about the way she carried herself looked like she'd found the life she'd always dreamed of.

But who had she found it with? My heart sunk. Nina must have finally matched her up with one of Tristan's wealthy friends.

A waiter offered me a drink, but I waved him off. Turning to face Nina, I said, "I don't know what's going on here, but you've never been cruel before now. I don't need to see Jordan with some wealthy guy who can give her everything her heart desires to know I fucked up, Nina. I'm out of here."

Before she could make some excuse for what was going on, I headed for the door, but just as I made it to the foyer I heard from behind me Jordan say, "I told Nina you wouldn't be interested, but you know her. Always the matchmaker."

I stopped and closed my eyes as she spoke. I didn't want to go, but I couldn't stay and watch her with another man.

Mustering every ounce of courage I had inside me, I turned around and saw her standing there in a black sweater dress that hugged her body perfectly. Her skin was lighter than it had been months ago when we spent those days on the run and her blond hair was longer, but she was still the most gorgeous woman I'd ever seen. Her green eyes focused on mine like she was searching for something in my face.

"You and your husband or boyfriend are very lucky. This is a beautiful home," I finally got out, each word tasting like ash in my mouth as I said it.

Jordan smiled and looked around at the foyer we stood in. "It is a beautiful home, but I'm afraid you're wrong about the other part. This place is all mine. No boyfriend and no husband here."

A few people walked past me as I stared at her, stunned by what she'd said. As she greeted them, I tried to figure out how this had all happened on an elementary teacher's salary.

When her guests had finally left, she took a step toward me. "I guess you're probably wondering how I could afford something like this, right? Well, when you're Dalton Spear's daughter and he leaves you everything, it's not hard."

"His daughter?"

"Yeah. I only got to spend a few hours with him before he died, but he arranged for me to inherit everything he had. Houses, cars, planes, his business. You name it, I got it."

I had to smile. What she always said was true. Good things did happen to good people, and they'd finally happened to her.

"Sounds like the kind of life you've always wanted. I'm happy for you, Jordan."

"Thanks. It's a good life. There's only one problem with it," she said with a sigh.

I looked around and couldn't imagine what that problem could be. She had everything a person could want. "A problem? Seems like the kind of problem most people would kill for a chance to have."

Nina called for Jordan to come into the living room. Flashing me a smile, she squeezed my hand and said, "Please stay. We can talk after, okay?"

"Maybe I'll come back another time. This really isn't my type of get-together."

Her smile faded, but she just turned and left to go into the living room. I walked past a couple as they came through the front door and headed toward my car, disappointed this wasn't ending like I'd hoped it would. I knew it was my fault. She wanted me to stay, but I didn't fit in her world now.

"Gage Varo!"

I turned around just as I reached the garage and saw Jordan marching toward me. The look on her face told me she had a whole lot more to say.

She stopped just a few inches in front of me and took a deep breath before saying a word. And then she let me have it. "You know, you're the most stubborn son of a bitch I've ever met. You push me away when you find out I'm alive that day, and now that you find out I've got a great life all on my own, you walk away without even considering fighting for me. What the hell is wrong with you, or is it you never really loved me as much as you claimed?"

"I've loved you since the first time I kissed you, Jordan."

My answer only served to frustrate her more. Putting her hands on her hips, she twisted her face into an angry grimace. "Then why do you only seem to want to push me away?"

"For what it's worth, I came here to see if you would be willing to take me back. I was an ass and I know it now. I know I needed to deal with my past."

"So what's the problem now?"

"You told me you're this wealthy woman like the Stones and all I could think was I don't belong in your world anymore."

"Why? What's different about me now? I'm not the same woman you fell in love with when she lived in that Brooklyn apartment and taught third graders?"

"It's not that," I said, knowing my answer was lame but unable to explain what I meant.

Pointing her finger at me, she poked me hard in the chest. "You know what you are, Gage Varo? You're a snob. That's what the problem is here. You're a working class snob. I was perfectly fine for you when I was just this struggling school teacher, but now that I've been blessed by one of the greatest gifts anyone can ever get, you don't think you want to be a part of my life anymore, even though you just claimed that's exactly why you came out here today."

"That's ridiculous," I said, turning away from her and all she stood accusing me of.

"It's not ridiculous. We can have the life we've always dreamed of, and instead of being happy about it, you're turning your nose up at it like it's something you're too good for. You're a snob, Gage Varo."

I spun around to face her. "And what the hell would I do in this new life of yours? What am I going to be? Your bodyguard?"

Jordan's eyes grew wide. "This again? My bodyguard? How about my boyfriend or my husband, you fool? You were never someone to just protect me. I'm in love with you. What the hell is wrong with you that you can't see that?"

Her shoulders sagged under the weight of her frustration, and she hung her head. I had to do something to diffuse the situation I'd created. "Maybe it's because you're screaming at me."

"I wouldn't have to scream at you if you weren't being so damn stubborn," she mumbled.

Lifting her chin, I saw the hurt in her eyes and hated that I'd caused that. "I thought my stubbornness was one of the parts of me you liked."

"I love all of you, Gage. The stubborn part, the part that wants to protect me, and even the part that's giving me a hard time about having more money than we'll ever need in this lifetime. You've always been just the man I wanted, even though you make me work way too hard sometimes."

"I make you work too hard? Name once other than right now," I challenged her.

Her eyebrows went up in fake anger, and she pointed toward Tristan and Nina's house, even as she smiled. "Don't make me talk about all those days I tried to get your attention when you were living in the carriage house and got stuck talking to that old bastard West because you stood there like a statue."

She wasn't wrong. We'd known each other for a long time and I had been a difficult man to deal with too often.

"And even after all that, all you had to do was kiss me that night in my kitchen and I was crazy for you."

It was time for me to accept the gift I'd been blessed with too, so I pulled her into my arms and kissed her just like I had that first night. Her lips tasted as sweet as they had then. Nothing had changed in that department, even though we had.

After giving her the kiss I'd waited months for, I leaned away from her and looked down into those beautiful green eyes staring up at me so full of love. "So I guess now we're living next door to Tristan and Nina?"

Jordan smiled and nodded. "The house has fifty acres, so it's not like we won't have privacy. To me, it's the best of both worlds. I get to live with the man of my dreams and next door to my best friend, the man of her dreams, and their kids."

"It's a long drive into the city for my business," I said as I thought about riding up and down the Taconic every morning and night. "I can't just be some househusband who sits around all day."

Jordan looked around and shrugged. "Well, there's telecommuting, and you did hear me mention about the fifty acres, right? So there's more than enough room for you to have an office here."

"Maybe that could work."

Pulling me to her, she ran her hands down my chest to the top of my pants and tugged on my belt. "And as for you hanging around all day, don't worry. I can think of something for you to do each and every day."

I felt myself getting hard at the mere thought of what she might have in mind. "How long is this party supposed to go on?"

Jordan licked her lips and grinned. "Another couple hours, but after that, I'm all yours."

Nuzzling her neck, I closed my eyes and let the feel of her wash over me. "I can't wait."

EPILOGUE

JORDAN

NINA HUGGED ME CLOSE AS the last of my guests began to filter out the door. "We should have gotten out of here by now."

From behind her, Tristan slid his arm around her waist and nuzzled her neck. "Cara won't be back with the kids for another two hours, so what do you say we get back to our own house?"

Giggling, she rolled her eyes at me. "I guess it's really time to go. Call me, okay? And tell Gage we said goodbye."

"I will. I promise."

I loved seeing them still so crazy in love after all they'd been through. When things looked like Gage and I would never be together again, I thought about them and had to believe we would find the kind of happiness they had.

Closing the front door behind them, I headed to the back of the house where Gage waited in the master bedroom. After making polite conversation with my friends and apologizing to Nina for jumping to the wrong conclusion, he'd chatted with Tristan about business for a while before whispering to me that I could find him naked and waiting in my bedroom when the party ended.

I'd never wanted to chase people away more than at that moment, but nearly an hour had passed since then and I wondered if I'd find him not ready and waiting but nearly asleep watching TV.

Not that I could blame him, but it would put a damper on what I had dreamed of for our reunion.

I opened the door to my room and couldn't stop the smile that spread from ear to ear. There he lay, buck naked and definitely ready, with his arms behind his head and one of those classic Gage grins on his way too handsome face.

"Should I take it personally that you made me wait here for nearly an hour naked in your bed?" he asked as he lowered his hand to pat the bed next to him.

Scanning his perfect body, my gaze fell on the muscular ridges of his abs and then slid down to where his cock stood at attention waiting for me. I looked up at him and shook my head. "I had to be the hostess with the mostess. I couldn't just push people out the door because I had a gorgeous man waiting for me to ravage."

He shrugged. "I'm not sure he's interested in whatever ravaging you have planned after waiting so long."

I wrapped my hand around his hard cock and slowly slid up and down for a few strokes. "Your cock says differently. I'm thinking he's the one I can believe."

Gage looked down and shook his head. "Betrayed by my own cock."

Straddling his thighs, I hiked up my sweater dress and lowered myself down to kiss him. "How about I make it up to both of you for making you wait so long? Would that smooth things over?"

He slid his hands over my hips and down my legs, moaning his pleasure at my suggestion. "It certainly couldn't hurt."

"Good. Just let me get out of this dress."

I slid off him, but he grabbed my hand to stop me. "Let me."

Before I knew it, he had the dress over my head and his fingers were unhooking my bra and tossing it across the room. Surprised by his urgency, I wriggled out of my panties and positioned myself on the floor next to the bed, like I knew he loved.

He stood above me like some kind of mythological god I couldn't wait to worship. I raised myself to my knees and ran my palms up his legs, thrilled by the feel of their strength against me. Powerful, the muscles rippled below the skin as my hands inched higher and higher.

Gage smiled at me and gripped the base of his cock. "I can't wait to feel that pretty mouth on me. It's been too long since we could enjoy ourselves like we used to."

I licked my lips and nodded as he waited for me to take all of him. "Now we have all this house to christen."

"I'm liking this house more and more," he said as he guided his cock into my mouth.

His skin felt like silk against my lips as they slid down to the base of his shaft, taking every delicious inch of him into me. Slowly, he eased out of my mouth, leaving only the head of his cock for me to suck, and then with a groan, he gently pushed his hips forward, filling my mouth again.

The entire action had an eroticism to it I craved and had missed for so long.

I closed my eyes and moaned against his skin. Above me, I heard him say in a low voice, "I think I want more after waiting so long."

Confused, I opened my eyes as he backed away and took me by the hand. I stood up, wondering why he had stopped. "I was enjoying that. What's going on?"

"I was too, but I want you to be as happy as I am, so we'll save the mind-blowing blowjob for later."

As he climbed onto the bed, I giggled at the way he said things. "Was that a pun, Gage Varo?"

"No. Just a truthful description of your skills at sucking cock," he explained as he pulled me on top of him.

I straddled his thighs and pretended to curtsy. "I try my best."

Lifting his hips off the bed, he slid his cock through my wet pussy and groaned. "And I appreciate it. Don't think I don't. But I thought since this is our first time together in months that we both deserved to get off. Plus, it's not like I'm getting second best this way, so I think it was a good choice."

I leaned forward and kissed him as I took all of him inside me.

"I like the way you think."

With each thrust into me, my body surrendered to his as he inched closer and closer to release. I'd loved him for so long, and now that the madness in our world had subsided, all that was left was the sweetness that came from our lovemaking.

WITH MY HEAD ON HIS chest, I listened to Gage's heartbeat slowly return to normal and loved the thought that we'd now live a normal life. For so long, I'd wished for some extraordinary life full of action and adventure, but if I could just have him next to me every day like we were at that moment, I'd never want anything more.

"You're quiet. Is something wrong?"

I looked up to see worry in his eyes and shook my head. "Nope. Everything's just like I want it. Perfectly and extraordinarily normal."

"That's some kind of normal there," he said with a wry smile.

"I guess it is."

"So, I'm wondering what my answer should be to you asking me to marry you this afternoon," he said as he lightly ran his hand up and down my back.

What was he talking about? Confused, I sat up and searched his face for an answer before I said, "I don't know what you're talking about. I didn't ask you to marry me."

With a smug smile, he shrugged. "Okay. If that's the way you want to play it, I guess I'll just have to be the one who asks. Will you marry me?"

I didn't have to think twice before answering. Looking into those deep blue eyes that had enchanted me since the first time I met him, I saw he wasn't sure I'd say yes, even after all we'd been through. Then I remembered he didn't know what Dalton had promised his lawyers would do about my sham marriage to Justin.

"Yes, I'll marry you Gage Varo. Of course I will! And just in case you're worried about the whole marriage to Justin, don't be.

Dalton told his lawyers to get that taken care of and I heard from them earlier this month. I'm officially a single woman again."

Gage pulled me to him and kissed me long and deep. Cradling my face, he smiled. "Not for long."

"What about your family? How are they going to feel about you marrying me?"

"What wouldn't they love about it? You're an incredibly wealthy woman and I'll be a kept man," he said with a chuckle.

Every worry I'd had about his family came rushing back as the memory of what Denise did filled my mind. "I'm serious, Gage. Your sister helped the people who wanted me dead. Somehow I don't think that translates into your family welcoming me with open arms into the Varo fold."

My mention of Denise made him frown, and he looked away. "Denise is nothing to me now, and nobody in my family agrees with what she did to us. My parents still love you, and Lily and Shane's opinion of you hasn't changed."

I hated hearing he'd cut out his sister entirely. They'd been close since they were children. I didn't want our future starting out on such a sour note. Gently, I turned his head so he'd look at me. "Maybe you should consider forgiving her. Whatever her reasons were, I doubt she did what she did to be hurtful, especially to you."

He shook his head. "I'm not sure I'll ever forgive her for helping Hailey and Justin get to you. If I hadn't gotten to you in time out there near the cabin…"

His sentence trailed off, and he swallowed hard. "I just don't think I can forgive her, Jordan. She says they found out she was my sister and threatened to hurt my family, but even if that is true, I just don't think I can."

"Look around us at all we have, Gage. We want for nothing now that we have each other again, and it wouldn't take a thing away from our lives to forgive her. You don't have to welcome her back into your life totally, and I can tell you that I probably won't ever be close to her, but I can forgive her. I don't have to understand her reasons or even think they're valid to forgive."

Nodding, he gave me a smile, but I knew he still hurt from Denise's betrayal. "So now that you know what kind of family you're marrying into, do you still want to marry me?" he asked, his tone hopeful.

As if I wouldn't jump at the chance to be the wife of someone like him.

"I can't think of another man I'd want to spend the rest of my life with, and believe me, that's how I see marriage. So if you're looking for anything less than forever, you've asked the wrong girl."

"The answer's simple then. Forever it is."

I chuckled and shook my head. "Simple? Nothing's ever been simple with us, Gage."

Gage kissed me and pressed his forehead to mine. "No, it's been the definition of complicated, but I wouldn't have it any other way. I love you, Jordan, you beautiful, sexy, intelligent, and complicated woman."

After all we'd been through, Gage was still that same man I'd fallen in love with that first night in my kitchen as we talked and kissed. He was my hero, and no matter what happened or what life would throw at us, I'd be by his side.

Forever.

**Exclusively for paperback readers, this book contains
A Heart of Stone Christmas.**

**Continue reading to enjoy that holiday story about
Tristan and Nina!**

A Heart of Stone Christmas

CHAPTER ONE

NINA

THE SMELL OF PINE CONES and cinnamon wafted through the house, even overwhelming the odor of dirty diapers and baby formula I'd gotten so used to in the past twelve months. Tressa, Diana, and Ethan had fallen asleep for their afternoon nap, so I could finally have some time to myself to wrap Tristan's present. For weeks, I'd kept it hidden in the towel cabinet down near the indoor pool, hoping he wouldn't suddenly take to swimming again after his long days at the office. I'd made sure he had better things to occupy his time every night, just to be safe.

Not that making love to my husband was just a diversion, by any means. Even as the father of three infants, he was the same sexy man I'd fallen in love with in this very house. However, I'd gone out of my way to surprise him with my present this year, and even though I knew he hated surprises, he'd love this one.

Sure Cara would hear the babies if they woke, I quickly snuck down to the pool to retrieve the box that contained the watch I'd had specially engraved for Tristan. A stainless steel Rolex with a black face and silver Roman numerals, it was perfectly him—formal, classic, and sexy. On the back, I had engraved the words *To the man of my dreams.*

With the gift hidden behind my back just in case he returned, I quietly crept past the babies' room, looking in on them as I made my way back to the living room. Turning on the stereo, I played Christmas carols low enough so only I could hear the music as I sprawled out all my gift wrapping necessities around me on the floor in front of the Christmas tree.

I opened the gift box and studied the watch. Tristan may have been used to having money, but to me spending a king's ransom on a single item still seemed extravagant. As he often said, my middle class roots ran deep. I knew he appreciated that part of me, but since he'd encouraged me to splurge on myself after the birth of the triplets, I'd taken the opportunity to pick up the gift one day as Jordan and I walked up Fifth Avenue toward our appointment at the spa. Her eyes had almost bugged out of her head when the salesman announced the price. I may not have looked stunned when he told us the watch I was sure would be perfect for Tristan cost more than my first car, but inside I was that same modest person she was and just as shocked that any watch could cost thousands of dollars.

Running my fingertip over the watch face, I admired the Roman numerals. Perfect for my husband, to me they seemed incredibly old fashioned, but that was Tristan to a T. The coolness of the stainless steel band warmed slightly against my touch, and I imagined it against his wrist and peeking out from underneath his suit jacket in some meeting he'd attend as those around him commented on his wife's stunning Christmas gift choice.

I set the box next to me on the floor and rolled out the silver and red foil wrapping paper in front of me. Cutting a large square, I folded it around the box carefully, making sure to make it look as nice as possible, and taped each end closed. A red ribbon would look perfect, so I snipped enough length to wrap around the length and width of the package. Taping it in the center, I used the scissors to curl the ribbon just like I'd learned from my mother when I was a little girl. When I finished, I set the wrapped gift down in front of me and stuck a gift tag with Tristan's name and the words "Love, Nina" next to the bow.

"Perfect."

A noise from down the hall told me my free time had ended,

and I jumped to my feet to head to the children's room to check on them. I found them still sleeping, and chalking the noise up to Cara washing their clothes in the laundry room, headed back to enjoy a glass of red wine and some Christmas carols.

As I stepped into the living room, I was horrified to see Tristan standing in the middle of the room with his present in his hands. Dressed in a dark grey suit and deep green shirt I picked out for him that morning, he smiled at me, but I shook my head and grabbed the package from his hold.

Hiding it behind my back, I asked, "What are you doing here? It's only three o'clock in the afternoon. Shouldn't you be at work or in a meeting or something?"

His smile faded just a little. "If I didn't know better, I'd say you're not happy to see me. I do know better, don't I?"

"Of course I'm happy to see you. I was just…busy doing something. How long have you been here?"

"Long enough to see my gift on the floor and pick it up. I think we should exchange gifts early because I'm thinking I need a new watch right about now."

I hung my head in disappointment. "Oh, Tristan. How did you guess? Now my surprise is ruined."

He took me in his arms and hugged me close. "I'm sorry. I guessed by the shape of the box." Kissing me on the top of the head, he whispered against my hair, "And Angelo heard from the jeweler you went to that you'd bought a man's watch a little while back. I assumed it was for me."

I looked up to see him smiling. "I really wanted to surprise you, though."

"I'm sorry, Nina. I can always pretend to be surprised when I open it."

"It's not the same," I sulked and let my hands fall to my sides. "You might as well open it now."

"I'm sure it's perfect, if that helps."

"A little." I held out the gift to him. "Here. Merry Christmas."

"Why don't we put it under the tree instead? You never know. I might forget in the next two days."

Looking up into his deep brown eyes, I saw he was trying to be cute. I didn't want to let him charm me out of my disappointment, but it was no use. I couldn't help it. I loved him too much to stay angry.

"You know, it's not fair that you have spies all over the city who report back to you about these kinds of things. I never had a chance to surprise you, did I?"

He shook his head and grinned. "Not really spies. Just Angelo, but he's known everywhere as my shopper, so he hears things."

I jabbed him gently in the ribs. "Next time I'm going to shop online."

"As long as you don't know your surprise, I'm happy. How are the kids today?"

"Down for their afternoon nap, and what do you mean my surprise? You're not going to let me know what you got me now that you know what my gift is?"

"No way," he said with a sexy smile. "I love surprising you. You know that."

"I think turnabout is fair play here, Tristan."

"I think I'd rather see your face when you tear off the wrapping paper on Christmas morning."

He kissed me softly on the lips. "I'm going to check on the kids and get a drink. Say I meet you back here in a few minutes and we can relax for a while before they get up."

Just then we heard two loud cries and knew our romantic rendezvous would have to wait for another time. I placed the gift under the tree and wished for a moment that we didn't have to postpone our quiet time together, but this was the life of new parents.

Tristan held out his hand to take mine. "Let's go see how those wonderful kids of ours are doing. I'll tell you about the new hotel opening up in Bucharest on the way."

I held his hand and listened as he told me about the opening of the newest Richmont on the site of the home his mother had fallen in love with all those years ago. The first of the new Richmont Villa hotels Stone Worldwide planned on opening up in the next year, it was particularly close to my husband's heart because of the history attached to it. Just listening to him talk about all the details of the decorating and how much his mother would love the hotel made me love him even more.

"We'll have to go there soon so you can see how it looks. What do you think of right after New Year's?" he asked, his eyes sparkling with interest in his newest project.

"I'd like that. Will all six of us be able to fit in a villa, though? We're like a baseball team now," I joked.

We stepped into the triplets' room, and Tristan picked up Ethan from his crib to calm his crying. Holding him in his arms, he gave me one of those sexy smiles that never failed to make my stomach flip. "I was thinking we might give Cara and the kids one villa and we could have the one next to it. That way we could have some time to ourselves at night."

I took Tressa into my arms and rocked her gently. "I like that. You tell me when and I'm there."

Tristan kissed our son gently on the forehead and winked at me. "Good. It's a date."

✧　✧　✧

SIX HOURS AND THREE BABIES in bed for the night later, I found Tristan lying in bed watching some Christmas special. Wearing only a pair of black silk pajama pants, he looked sexier than any father of three should. If only I looked that good as the mother of triplets.

I looked at the television and saw a Peanuts special. "Enjoying Charlie Brown and his sad Christmas tree?"

Tristan crossed his arms behind his head. "He never gives up, even when that tree of his gets all droopy. I can respect that."

"I think it's Linus who never gives up. Giving up is sort of Charlie Brown's thing, if I remember correctly."

Laughing at me, he said, "I just watch it to see if Charlie falls for Lucy and her football trick. There's a barracuda in the making."

I rolled my eyes. "You're the first person I've ever known who thinks of poor Lucy in those terms."

He clicked off the television and waved me over toward him on the bed. "Enough with Charlie Brown and his droopy tree and women problems. Come here and let me show you how much I missed you today."

Suddenly, my out-of-shape body made me feel self-conscious. Pushing my hair off my face, I shrugged. "I smell like baby food. Maybe if I'm not tired after getting shower."

I knew that wasn't the answer he wanted, but as he sat there looking like he should be on the cover of GQ and I stood there looking like a disheveled, overweight mess, all I could think of was hiding away in the bathroom. I'd been working out since I came out of the post-partum depression, but there was no missing that I was still carrying some baby pounds.

He stood up and wrapped his arm around my waist, refusing to let me go. Nuzzling my neck, he said in a low, sexy voice, "I don't care what you smell like, but if you're really needing a shower, count me in."

"I'm a mess and—"

Turning me to face him, he tilted my chin so I had to look at him. "I know what this is about, Nina. For months you've been uncomfortable in your own skin. You don't have to be. You look as sexy today as you did that first night we drove out to this house, and I'm crazy about every inch of you."

His words brought tears to my eyes. "I feel like a stuffed pig. I still don't fit into my clothes the right way, and then I see you sitting there looking all hot and buff and I can't help wanting to hide away."

Tristan kissed me softly and pressed his forehead to mine like he always did when he wanted to say something sweet. "I love you this way and the way you were before. How I feel about you and why I get turned on every time I lay my eyes on you isn't because of how your body looks, Nina. I get hard just being next to you right now because you're you, no matter what weight you gain or lose."

I hung my head. "I just wish I could go back to the way I looked before. At least then I felt like you were only a few levels above me."

He chuckled and shook his head. "You're crazy. You've never been anything but the most beautiful woman in the world in my eyes. Now let's get into that shower and rinse out all the mess from your hair."

I looked down at the ends of my hair and saw the telltale yellowish-white stain that I always seemed to wear since we brought the babies home. I'd exchanged my favorite perfume for its sour scent for months. Nothing like dried baby formula to make a woman look her sexiest.

"See? I am a mess."

"You're my mess, and once you let me wash your hair and enjoy a hot shower with me, you'll feel like a new woman. Now get in there and let's get this shower going."

I followed him into our bathroom and tried not to let my insecurities run roughshod over what could be a wonderful time with the man I adored. If he was a slightly overweight, pot-bellied man who was losing his hair, it certainly would have been easier. Not that I didn't enjoy the benefits of being married to an insanely gorgeous man. I adored every inch of him just as he claimed the same about my body, except worshipping him seemed easier because of his washboard abs and toned pecs and arms.

Tristan stripped out of his pants and turned on the water before casually walking over to me wearing a grin. "This really works best if you take your clothes off."

Rolling my eyes, I slipped my sweater over my head and pulled my yoga pants off to reveal my usual mismatched panties and bra.

We had all the money we'd ever need, and I still couldn't get my underwear to match. As if I could read his mind, I turned around to let him unhook my bra and said, "Still can't buy the same color bras and panties."

He nuzzled my neck and joked, "I like that about you. It's one of those down-to-earth things that I hope will never go away."

My bra and panties fell to the floor as he wrapped his arms around me. Turning toward him, I pressed a kiss onto his lips and slid my hands down his muscular back. "I guess if you can love me this way, I can too, so let's get into this shower and get this stuff out of my hair before we get freaky, Mr. Stone."

His eyes lit up and he smiled. "That's what I like to hear."

Tristan stepped under the water, and any hesitation I'd had about my body faded away at the sight of him glistening and wet. I could look at him like that forever. Just as stunning as the first time we made love, he was my very own sex god.

"Seeing anything you like out there? Come in and join me," he said with a wink.

The ten shower heads streamed hot water over every inch of my body as Tristan pulled me close. His lips caressed the soft skin beneath my left ear as his hands slid down my body, driving me wild with desire. No matter how insecure I felt, my husband always knew exactly where to touch me to make me want him like I'd never wanted another man.

I pressed my palms to the tattoo on his toned pecs and slowly made my way to the V of his hipbones that pointed like an arrow to his already hard cock. Our gazes locked on one another, I watched his eyes close in ecstasy and heard a soft moan escape his lips when I slid my hand around the swollen head.

Softly, I whispered, "I love seeing you like this. When you aren't worried about work or being a dad but just being the sexy man I fell madly in love with."

He opened his eyes and smiled. "I'm not sexy as those other things?"

"You're always sexy. I just like remembering those early days between us."

Lifting me, he pressed my back against the wall as I wrapped my legs around his waist. "Remember the first time we made love in this shower?"

I looked into those deep brown eyes and let the memory of that first time here flow through my mind. I was in love with him by then, even though we'd only known each other for such a short time. Sexy and mysterious, he'd enchanted me that first night we drove out to this house and I was lost from then on.

"If I remember correctly, you pretty much changed my mind about shower sex that night."

He nodded and covered my mouth with a kiss that made my legs weak. With one firm thrust, he filled me completely and just as he had that first time, Tristan took my body to heights of ecstasy I never knew before him.

Bucking gently against him, I reveled in the feel of his cock stroking in and out of my willing body, even forgetting how insecure I felt. I wanted to be the sexy woman he thought I was. To be that woman he'd fallen in love with in this very house. I wanted to make him feel as desired as he made me.

His hands squeezed my ass, and he pulled me hard onto him. "I've been dying to be inside you all day, you know that?" he said in a voice that hit me deep inside.

I moaned and said in his ear, "I do love you, Tristan."

Holding me close, he thrust into me as he kissed me hard. "Good. I'd hate to think I was in madly in love all alone."

This was why I loved him. How many men could make cute jokes while they made mad, passionate love to their wives?

As we inched toward our climax, I saw in his eyes not lust or even love, but adoration. Just like I adored him, he adored me, and no matter how I felt about myself, looking into those eyes and seeing the person he saw me as made me realize just how lucky I was.

CHAPTER TWO

TRISTAN

THE WINTER SUN STREAMED THROUGH the bedroom window as I silently dressed for work, careful not to wake Nina since the kids were still sleeping. I slipped into my suit coat and straightened my tie in the mirror before I turned around to see her smiling at me.

"I love that shirt on you, you know that? Grey looks great with that red tie too. Very festive."

"I didn't want to wake you. The kids are still asleep, surprisingly, so I figured I could let you have a day to sleep in."

Nina stretched her arms and shook her head as she got out of bed. "I have a ton of things to do today, so no sleeping in for me. Today's Christmas Eve, Tristan. Did you forget?"

"No. Why?"

"Are you seriously making Michelle work on Christmas Eve? Sounds pretty grinchy to me," she teased.

"She's coming in so I can give her my Christmas present you so nicely picked out and then I promise I'm sending her home. I have a little work to do on the villa project, but I'll be home by noon."

Wrapping her arms around my neck, she stood on her toes and kissed me. "I hope she likes the bag I chose. I know she loves Gucci, but I wasn't sure about the color. Do you think she'll like it?"

"I think she'll love it. And I have the note you wrote about the fruit basket she sent, so I'll make sure to give her that too."

"How did I get such a wonderful husband?"

"Luck of the draw, I guess," I said with a chuckle. For all my moments of being wonderful, I knew I worked too much and still said too little too often for the woman I loved.

"So what time will you be home?" Nina asked as she fussed with the knot in my tie.

My instincts told me she was up to something, so I didn't answer and just looked down at her, studying her expression to see if my gut was right. A blush covered her cheeks, and she looked down toward the floor for a moment, confirming what I'd suspected.

"I'll be home by noon. Should I bring anything?"

"No. I'm going to run out for a little while this morning. I was planning to take the kids out today, but I think Tressa has the sniffles. Don't want to make it worse for the holiday."

I arched my eyebrow. "Going anywhere special?"

Nina tilted her chin up and grinned. "Don't trust me, Mr. Stone?"

"Oh, I trust you. I'm just wondering if you're planning to go buy me another Christmas present."

Shrugging, she wrinkled her nose, a sure sign what would come out of her mouth next wasn't the truth. It was her tell. "Why would I do that?"

I kissed her on the tip of her nose. "I don't know, but I get the feeling something's going on."

"That's crazy. Why would you think that?"

"Because you would be the world's worst poker player."

She narrowed her eyes to slits and shook her head. "What are you talking about?"

"Nothing. I just want you to know that you don't have to get me anything else."

"Well, that's good since I wasn't planning on it."

She was lying, which would have bothered me if she wasn't being so cute about getting me a present she could keep a surprise until Christmas morning. "Well, now that we got that settled, I'm off to work."

"You'll be home by noon, right?"

The mischievous twinkle in her eye told me my wife was definitely up to something. Giving her a kiss, I smiled. "Noon. Will you be here?"

"Of course. Where else would I be?"

Out getting me another present, princess.

"I'm off. Kiss the kids for me because I don't want to wake them up."

"Will do. See you at noon."

As I walked out to the garage, I snuck a peek into the nursery and saw all three children still asleep, each one doing that little pout they always did as they slept. It was a rare event. In the past year since they all came home, they'd been awake every day when I'd left for work. It seemed like only yesterday we'd finally placed Diana in her crib with her brother and sister following weeks in the hospital after them, and now they were experiencing their first real Christmas.

I didn't know how much they'd remember of the holiday, but since Nina would take hundreds of pictures like she always did for big events in their lives, in the future they'd see how I surprised their mother with a trip for all of us to the new villas in Bucharest. I'd sworn Cara to secrecy and all the plans had been made, so all I had to do was be home by noon to collect my family and by Christmas morning we'd be in the newest Richmont villas enjoying any luxury we could think of.

"Mr. Stone? Do you have a moment?"

I turned to see Cara poking her head out of the door that led to her wing of the house. Her dark eyes wide, her middle aged face showed her worry about something.

"Is something wrong, Cara?"

Shaking her head, she whispered, "No. Nothing's wrong. I just wanted to mention that I saw on the news this morning that we're supposed to get hit by a big snowstorm late this afternoon. Will that do anything to your plans?"

"No. The schedule is we fly out this afternoon, so we should miss the storm entirely."

"Oh, okay. I just wanted to make sure."

Cara's expression changed to her usual pleasant one free of concern, and I had to ask if my surprise was still that. "Have you had any sense Mrs. Stone knows about my plans?"

"Oh, no. I'm sure it will be an absolute surprise when you spring it on her. I've made sure to pack all the children's things secretly this morning, and if she asks where any of their clothes are, I'll be telling her I'm washing them. Everything's set."

A door closed down the hall and I looked to see if Nina was coming, but the coast was still clear.

"Thank you, Cara. I appreciate your help with this. My wife would come up with a thousand reasons why we shouldn't travel around the holiday, but I'm dying for her to see the new villas so I'm afraid I've had to take to subterfuge to get her there."

"It's my pleasure, Mr. Stone. I hope she can forgive my fibbing."

"Not to worry. Nina's very forgiving, so it won't be a problem. See you around noon, and if anything happens that could upend my plans, please make sure you call my office at the number you have. Michelle knows to put you through any time you call."

"Of course. I'm sure everything will go just as planned and your surprise will be delightful for all of you."

"See you in a few hours, and remember to let me know if anything comes up," I said as I turned to head toward the garage.

Forty minutes later, I pulled into my parking space and made my way up to my office to meet with Michelle and do a final check with the pilot to make sure we were all ready to go. I couldn't wait for Nina to see the surprise I had waiting for her.

My assistant looked shocked as she watched me walk through the office suite door. "Tristan, what are you doing here? It's Christmas Eve. I thought you'd be home with Nina and the kids getting ready to fly out."

Resting my briefcase on her desk, I opened it to give Michelle her Christmas gift and bonus. I handed her the box Nina had specially wrapped and her note about the gift Michelle had sent us. "I couldn't forget you on Christmas. The note is from Nina about the fruit basket, which has been delicious, by the way."

Michelle beamed a smile up at me and politely set the gift aside. "Thank you. I'm sure it's lovely, as always, Tristan."

"You have to open it, or Nina will never forgive me for my lack of details about how you looked when you saw what she picked out," I said with a chuckle.

"You two are so sweet. Thank you," she said as she carefully opened the blue and silver foil wrapping paper to uncover the box containing the Gucci bag. Nina had raved about it, so I assumed Michelle would like it. Personally, I had no idea whether it was great or hideous. Women's purses weren't my field of expertise.

Michelle held her gift up to show me and gushed about how much she loved it, so I'd have something good to tell Nina when she asked for all the details later.

"Tristan, please tell Nina I love it! She has wonderful taste, and you spoil me every year."

"Since I met Nina. I have to make up for all the time I didn't treat you as well as I should have." Reaching into my briefcase once more, I took out an envelope and handed it to her. "This is from me. It's nothing as beautiful as the purse, but I hope you know it's meant from the heart."

Michelle opened the envelope and pulled out the check I'd written for two thousand dollars for her Christmas bonus. When she saw the amount, her eyes opened wide in surprise. "Oh my, thank you! I appreciate this so much, Tristan."

"Good because I appreciate all that you do for me. I'm heading into my office to make last minute calls about the trip we're leaving on in a few hours, so unless you have anything for me to sign or handle, why don't you go home before the storm Cara says is coming rolls in?"

"I didn't see anything about a snowstorm on the news last night. Is it supposed to be bad?"

"Bad enough, so unless you want to have a four hour trip back to Queens, I'd say go home and start the holidays with your family. Merry Christmas, Michelle."

"Merry Christmas, Tristan. Please wish Nina and the babies a wonderful Christmas for me too."

I left Michelle to pack up her things to go home while I called the pilot and Cara one last time to check that everything was set. The pilot had nothing but good news for me. The storm Cara had seen on the weather this morning was heading in from the west, and since we were flying east, it wouldn't affect us. All I had to do was get home and surprise Nina and the holidays could begin.

CHAPTER THREE

NINA

"JORDAN, I THINK SOMETHING'S GOING on with Tristan," I said as I threw on my hat and coat.

"Like what?"

"I don't know. I have a weird feeling about him and Cara. I've heard them whispering a few times in the past week, but he hasn't said anything to me about any problems with her. I can't imagine what they're whispering about. I always deal with her about the babies, so what are they talking about?"

"You aren't actually saying you think your husband, who adores you and acts like you walk on water, is having an affair with Cara, are you?" Jordan asked in a voice filled with sarcasm.

"Don't say it never happens. Powerful men often run off with their nannies."

"Yeah, if they're twenty-two year old blondes with huge boobs! Cara is what, like in her forties? She's got to be ten years older than him, and while I'm not saying she's hideous, I can't imagine Tristan going with her. He loves you, Nina."

"So she is pretty?"

"Yeah, in a sort of stick figury kind of way. She's a little skinny, but I guess you could say she's okay. But that's beside the point. Tristan isn't having an affair with the nanny, Nina. I think you've lost your mind."

"I need to head into the city to find some things out. You're off today, right? Can you come?"

"What do you mean? Are you planning on stalking your own husband to find out what he's up to?"

"I just need to know, Jordan." I hated admitting that, but it was true. If it sounded as sad I as I thought it did, so be it. I needed to know if my husband was sleeping with the nanny.

"Nina, I'm not going to help you snoop on Tristan. This is madness. I think you've had too much country fresh air out there. You need to spend more time in the city."

"Fine, then I'll go alone. I'm going to need to get some time by myself, so will you at least help me shake Jensen?"

"What about the kids?"

"I don't want to drag a trio of one year old babies out into the cold. They'll stay here with Cara."

"You mean you're going to leave your kids with the woman your husband is planning to leave you for?"

"Jordan!"

"Okay, I'm going to stop this craziness right here. Tristan isn't sleeping with Cara. They've been whispering because he's planning a huge surprise that he needed her help in pulling off. He's taking all of you to Romania to the new villas opening at the Richmont hotel in Bucharest. There. Don't you feel stupid now?"

I sat speechless staring out the living room window as Jordan's words settled into my mind. A surprise trip for all of us to the villas he was so proud of? I felt like such an ass.

"I'm so stupid, aren't I?"

"Yes, you are, but we all still love you anyway. Now stop being crazy and have some damn eggnog to calm yourself down. Tristan made me promise not to tell you, but now that I have, you have to pretend like you didn't know. He's really psyched about this trip."

"I know he's so happy about the new villas. I feel awful now, Jordan. I think I'm going to go down to the jeweler near my house and pick up the cufflinks I saw a few months ago to give him as a little surprise from me."

"That sounds nice. Promise me you'll call me when you get

back from your trip, okay? I think you might be going insane out there in the sticks. You need to come back to civilization more often."

"I promise. We can have lunch and you can bring me back to sanity. I'm sure Tristan would love that."

"Good. Enjoy the trip and Merry Christmas, Nina."

"Thanks, Jordan. Merry Christmas!"

I ended my call and stuffed my phone into my pocket as I headed down toward the garage to tell Jensen I wouldn't need the car this morning. Always hesitant to let me go on my own, he'd tell my bodyguards immediately if I let him know I was headed the whole mile to the jewelers on my own, so instead I pretended like I'd decided not to leave the house at all. Thankfully, he believed me so I was free to go buy Tristan's surprise gift all on my own and without my usual shadows.

✦   ✦   ✦

I MADE IT TO MELNER'S Jewelry shop on Main Street in record time for me. Twenty minutes in the freezing cold and light snow will do that to even the most out-of-shape person. Thankfully, the store wasn't closing until noon that day, so I had a few minutes to pick out Tristan's gift and then get back to the house before he returned from the city.

The man behind the counter reminded me of Santa Claus, in a way. Round with a full white beard, he had crystal blue eyes like all those old fashioned pictures of Santa Claus always had. Nearly bald, all the hair on his head had seemed to have migrated down to his face. He looked up as the bells on top of the door jingled and when I closed the door, he smiled and stood up from his stool behind the glass display cabinets.

"Merry Christmas, young lady. What can I do for you today?"

I pointed to the display case at the end of the row farthest from the window and said, "I saw a set of cufflinks a while back that I'd like to surprise my husband with. I'm hoping they're still here."

The jolly jewelry store owner smiled. "I know just the ones. I think I remember you. You were in here with your husband when I saw you, I think. Tall, dark haired young man?"

"Tristan. Yes, that's my husband. We were here looking at a necklace for me then, but I snuck a look at those cufflinks and I think they'd be perfect for him. The onyx next to the gold is just stunning, and I know he'd love them."

Mr. Melner reached in and took out the black velvet display from the case to set it on the counter for me to see. "Yes, here they are. I don't sell too many sets of cufflinks anymore. Young men just don't wear them like we did in my day."

I ran my finger over them and nodded. "I bet they don't, but for his job, Tristan has to get dressed up in tuxes more than most men, so the cufflinks will be used often."

"What does your husband do?"

Looking up from the counter, I smiled and bragged a little about Tristan. "He's the CEO of Stone Worldwide. He owns the Richmont hotel line."

"So that's the Tristan Stone I've heard about in town. Your husband is quite popular around these parts. I just heard the other day that his foundation donated a truckload of toys to the hospital for Christmas."

"It did?" Tristan hadn't mentioned anything about the foundation doing that. I'd known about the center in Poughkeepsie, but not this. And to think that I'd thought that wonderful husband of mine was cheating on me with our nanny. I really was a fool sometimes.

"He's very generous. It's true. That's why I wanted to surprise him with these cufflinks. He's surprising me with a trip to see one of his new hotels too."

The elderly man winked at me. "Sounds like a pretty great guy has a pretty terrific wife too. When are you leaving?"

"Today, I think. I'm not supposed to know about it, but I found out."

He looked out toward the front windows of his store. "You better hurry then. That storm is coming in faster than they thought."

I turned and saw the sidewalks already covered and huge snowflakes coming down at a rate much faster than I'd ever seen. "I didn't even know we were expecting a storm. When was it supposed to get here?"

"I heard this afternoon, but since it's only ten in the morning, I think they might have miscalculated. Let's get you all fixed up here so you don't have to worry about driving on the snowy roads."

"I didn't drive, so I should be okay. A nice walk in the snow will do me good," I joked as I paid for the cufflinks and he boxed up my gift.

"Thank you, sweetie. Have a wonderful holiday. I didn't catch your name, though."

Taking the bag from him, I said, "My name is Nina. Nina Stone. I hope you have a wonderful Christmas too, Mr. Melner!"

Happy I'd been able to buy Tristan the cufflinks I knew would surprise him, I set off in the snow to make it back to the house before he came home from work so I could wrap his gift and get it under the tree without him sneaking a peek at it. I had about an hour, so unless the weather suddenly became a blizzard, I'd be fine.

CHAPTER FOUR
TRISTAN

THE SNOWSTORM SEEMED TO INTENSIFY just in the time between leaving my office and hitting the Taconic. Worried we'd need to leave earlier than planned to reach Kennedy, I called Cara as I drove home.

"Make sure the children are ready, and even if it means you have to tell my wife something that might ruin the surprise, make sure she knows we need to leave as soon as I get home."

"Are the roads that bad?" Cara asked in a worried voice.

I slowed the Range Rover down to around thirty miles an hour as I passed another car pulled off the road. "It's coming down pretty hard, but I think we'll be fine in my truck. We'll just have to leave earlier to take our time getting to the airport."

"Okay, Mr. Stone. I'll get everyone ready."

While Cara made sure everything at the house was prepared for the trip, I made sure the pilot knew we might be a little late but we were coming. Still unfazed by what looked like a blizzard bearing down on New York State, he was ready to take off as soon as we arrived.

At least one of us was calm. With the weather turning bad so quickly, I'd considered postponing the trip until the snow stopped, but if he was okay with it, I trusted him. Flying was horrible anytime I had to do it, but after years of him piloting my plane for me, I knew I was in good hands.

The snow began to fall even heavier as I hit the last stretch of highway before reaching Dutchess County. My SUV may have been built to withstand any kind of terrain, but a few inches of snow an hour made driving difficult in any vehicle. As I concentrated on the road ahead of me, my phone rang and I quickly looked down at the console to see it was Cara.

"Mr. Stone, have you heard from Mrs. Stone?"

"No," I said, instantly worried. "She isn't home?"

Cara hesitated and then said, "No. She didn't say anything to me about leaving, and I asked Jensen and he said she cancelled her plans to go out today. But I can't find her anywhere in the house. The babies are fed and changed so we're all ready, but I don't know where she is."

The nanny's tone quickly moved from concerned to practically frantic, which didn't help my fears about where Nina could be. Trying to calm her down, I said, "It's okay, Cara. You take care of the children. I'll make sure Mrs. Stone is okay."

I hung up with Cara and immediately dialed Nina's cell phone, but it went directly to voicemail. I listened to her sweet voice say she wasn't available but that she'd get back to me as soon as she could and at the beep said, "Nina, where are you? It's snowing out and Cara said you aren't at the house. Jensen doesn't know where you are, which means you didn't tell anyone. I love you, baby, but right now you're scaring the hell out of me. Call me as soon as you hear this."

I got off the highway to find the roads to the house were even worse than the interstate was. It looked like the sky had dumped ten inches of snow since I'd left a few hours before, and it was still coming down hard enough that I could barely see five feet in front of me. Thankfully, no one seemed to be foolish enough to be on the road, except for me, so I didn't have to worry about anything but getting myself home to find Nina.

My phone rang just as I neared the house, and I saw Nina's name come up on the screen. Hurriedly, I answered it only to hear static, but then her voice came through. "Tristan? Can you hear me?

Tristan?”

"I hear you. Where are you? I'll come pick you up."

"I walked to town, but the snow started coming down so quickly I couldn't get home. I don't even have boots on, but I think I'm near the f—house. I can't tell because everything's so white."

Her phone became all static again, but I heard her say something about some kind of house before the line went dead. I called her back three times, but it was no use. Either her phone had run out of battery or the storm was doing something to the calls. I got home to find Cara and the babies all ready to leave, but first I had to get Nina.

I found Jensen waiting for me in the garage with a look of guilt all over his face, as if he'd done something wrong. His grey brows were furrowed, and the serious expression he usually wore had morphed into a deep frown.

"I didn't know she left, sir. She told me she decided against going into the city, so I didn't think she was leaving. The bodyguards didn't know either."

"I know, Jensen. You know my wife. She doesn't see any need for a driver or bodyguards because it's just not her style. The problem is we've got a blizzard going on, and she's out there, so I'm going to head back out again. I'll have the guys search in town, but I want you to search the grounds for me. We'll find her. She'll probably be close by, so don't worry."

Jensen seemed to relax, but inside I still feared that Nina could be stuck out in the snow somewhere, freezing cold because she wasn't dressed for the weather or even hurt from falling. I didn't know what she meant by house, but I had a feeling whatever she meant that's where I'd find her.

Now I just had to figure out what house.

✧   ✧   ✧

ALL THREE CHILDREN LAY IN their cribs for their afternoon naps, and I kissed each one before I left to go find their mother. Cara watched at the door with a frown that told me like Jensen, she too blamed herself for Nina's going out. As I passed her, I patted her on the shoulder to comfort her.

"Don't worry, Cara. I'll find her and then we'll go on our trip. Just watch over the kids until I come back."

"I just feel so bad. She usually talks to me after you leave in the morning, but she didn't today. Was I too busy or did I miss something? Why would she leave without telling anyone?"

This was Cara's first real experience with Nina's impulsiveness, so I knew she probably didn't understand any of what was going on. "My wife doesn't like some of the things that come with being married to me. She especially doesn't like the loss of her independence from having a driver and bodyguards. To Nina, they get in the way. To me, they're important to ensure her safety. She thinks I worry too much."

"But look what happens when they aren't around!" Cara said almost hysterically and then lowered her head. "I'm sorry, Mr. Stone. I'm just worried about her. I shouldn't have said that."

"I understand. No need to apologize. I'll find her. Just watch over the children so when we get back we can go."

I truly did understand Cara's opinion. In fact, I shared it. If Nina had only done as I had repeatedly asked her to, none of this would have happened. That was my fear talking, but it was how I felt.

Changing into clothes and boots more appropriate for the weather, I headed out toward where I hoped I'd find her. She'd said something about a house, but was it a firehouse or farmhouse? I couldn't be sure. There was a firehouse in town, so I'd check there first and if I didn't find her, the only place I could think of looking that even resembled a farmhouse was an old, rundown place off the main road that had been up for sale since before the housing bubble burst a few years ago.

The roads were so slick it took nearly twenty minutes to make the trip into town to the firehouse, but no one had seen her there.

One man thought he'd seen her that morning on Main Street near Melner's Jewelry store, but he didn't know which way she'd gone when she left. The idea of Nina at a jewelry store made perfect sense when I thought about it since she probably went out to buy me another present to surprise me after I'd guessed about the watch.

I didn't know which one of us was worse—me for ruining her surprise or her for insisting on surprising me with another gift.

The snow fell even faster now than on my way home from the office to the point that I almost couldn't see. Every so often a tiny dot of red or yellow from a car ahead of me would appear, but with all the blowing and drifting, the lights quickly dimmed and I was left to guess where other cars on the road were.

Over and over as I drove, I called Nina's cell phone, but each time all I got was voicemail. As I passed one of the last open fields before that old farmhouse I hoped she'd found shelter in, I tried one more time and finally heard her phone ring. Just as I accepted that I'd yet get another turn to leave a message for her, she answered and my heart jumped in my chest.

"Tristan! Are you home? The snow is so bad. Did you get home from the city?"

"Nina, I'm out looking for you. Where are you? I'm near that farmhouse that's been for sale for years, right next to the big open field because I thought you said you were near there. Are you close by?"

Her phone went to static again, but I faintly heard her say she'd made it to the farmhouse. I slowly drove along the road so I didn't miss the turn onto the property. Focused on that, I didn't see the truck flying toward me until it was nearly too late, and when I swerved to avoid it slamming into me, my truck skidded off the road into a snow pile nearly as high as the Range Rover.

After cursing out the other driver, I tried to back up but even in four wheel drive I wasn't getting anywhere. The snow was too deep. I had no choice but to set off on foot and hope that Nina had stayed put in the farmhouse.

CHAPTER FIVE

NINA

I HELD MY CELL PHONE to my ear as tightly as I could, but I still couldn't hear what Tristan was saying. This is what I got for living out in the sticks, as Jordan called it. At least in the city if I became stranded somewhere, I wouldn't be alone with all those millions of people in Manhattan. I'd been able to break into the farmhouse and by some miracle someone had left the heat on, likely to make sure the pipes didn't freeze while the house was on the market. It wasn't exactly balmy, but fifty degrees was better than nothing.

How long had it been since someone lived in this place I wondered. The cupboards were all bare and there were no appliances, but the fireplace looked like someone had used it recently. Crouching down, I lifted one half-burnt page of newspaper out of the grate and saw a date from August of that year. Probably some kids hanging out, or maybe a pair of lovers rendezvoused there. I liked that idea. It reminded me of Tristan and me back when we first got together.

Back before kids and weight gain and skinny nannies.

A loud banging noise startled me out of my daydream about sexier times, and I ran to the window to see what had made such a racket. There at the front door stood Tristan freezing and pounding on the front door as the wind gusted. I pressed my face to one of the windows next to it and yelled, "It's got one of those realtor lock things on it. Go around the back. I found a way in there!"

He trudged off around the side of the house to the back door, so I ran back to open it for him. I couldn't remember the last time I felt so happy to see him. A little saddened by that thought, I opened the door and saw him standing there in front of me covered head to toe in snow. Grabbing his arm, I yanked him onto the back porch and slammed the door to shut out the storm still raging on outside.

"I thought you were driving in the truck? Why are you all snowy?" I asked as I helped him peel off his wet ski jacket.

He slid the hood off his head, sending snow everywhere, and said, "Some jackass pushed me off the road. The truck is in a snowbank right out there."

"Are you hurt?"

"No, but I couldn't get the truck out so I had to walk here. Are you okay? What happened and why the hell were you out in a snowstorm without Jensen or the bodyguards? You have everyone worried, Nina. Jensen and Cara are blaming themselves."

Turning on my heels, I walked back to stand in the living room near the fireplace, angry he'd said those things. Tristan followed me and seeing the fireplace began searching for a way to light the paper. I wanted him to ask me what was wrong, but he seemed far more intent on looking for a lighter or matches, so finally I said what was on my mind.

"I'm not a child, Tristan. I don't need caretakers to watch over me and be your confidants and spies."

He stopped his searching and turned to look at me. Even in the dim room lit entirely by the white of the snow outside the windows, I saw his confusion all over his face.

"What are you talking about? They don't spy on you, Nina, and I don't confide in anyone else in this world other than you."

"You know I don't like them following me. They tell you where I go."

Facing me now, he walked forward to stand in front of me. "Is there any reason I shouldn't know where my wife is at all times? Yes, I can think of one. Maybe things like today wouldn't happen if someone knew where you were."

"Don't talk to me like I'm a child. I gave you three children. I think I deserve the respect accorded to their mother."

"This has nothing to do with that. I worry about you, and you seem to have an issue with me caring where you go. No one treats you like a child. I treat you like the most important person in my life. I don't understand why you don't see that I'd be lost without you, so I want to keep you safe. What's wrong with that?"

I hated when he looked like I injured him. His brown eyes had a way of seeming like they were taking the brunt of my words and reflected how hurt he felt. Turning away, I mumbled, "I thought you were having an affair with Cara."

"What?" he asked, his voice full of amazement.

Spinning around, I said in a loud voice, "I saw you whispering to her all this week, and I thought you were having an affair with our children's nanny."

Tristan's eyebrows raised in surprise. "You thought I was sleeping with Cara? Why would you think that? What have I done to make you think there's any woman on earth I want other than you?"

Looking down at the floor, I answered his question. "Nothing. I didn't say it was logical. It's just what I thought."

He walked toward me and pulled me into his arms, pressing his lips to the top of my head. "Nina, I've loved you since that first night. You're the mother of my children, and I wake up every day happier than the next. That's because of you. But if you really believe I would want another woman, maybe I need to figure out another way to show you how much I love you."

I took a deep breath and looked up at him to see those gorgeous brown eyes full of love for me. "It's not you. It's me. I thought I'd be okay after the post-partum depression was over, but then I just felt uncomfortable in my own skin. You're still the stunning man the whole world adores, and I feel like I'm not good enough. That's why I haven't attended one of your events since the babies were born. I look at the pictures of you in your tux on Page

Six and all those beautiful people around you and think I don't belong there."

Tristan kissed me so sweetly I wanted to cry. In all the months I'd been dealing with these feelings, I'd never told him the whole truth. After all that time, it felt like an enormous weight had been lifted from my shoulders.

"Nina, I knew you were feeling self-conscious about the baby weight, but I didn't know it was like this for you. I'm sorry. But you don't have to change for me or anyone else in the world. You are as beautiful right at this moment as you were when I met you."

"I just don't feel beautiful. I wish I did."

"I thought you were tired from dealing with the kids all day and didn't want to be bothered with my work. I was hoping to change that with a surprise for you, but it doesn't look like that's going to happen today because of the storm."

"I know about the trip to the new villas. That meant a lot to you, and I'm sorry this happened. If I hadn't gone out to get you another gift to surprise you, we would have been on the plane already instead of stuck in this farmhouse in a blizzard. I'm so sorry, Tristan. This is all my fault."

He pulled me close and whispered, "I knew you went to buy me another present. I may not know much about women, but I do know something about my wife."

With my head pressed to his chest, I listened to his heartbeat so sure and steady and said, "I just wish your surprise for me had worked out. I wanted to see the new villas."

"It's okay. We'll just fly out tomorrow. In fact, I'll call the pilot and arrange that right after I call Jensen to tell him where we are."

He kissed me and walked away to make his calls while I looked for something to light the fire so we didn't freeze as we waited for the cavalry to arrive. In the corner of the mantel under some old magazines someone had left a handful of long matches, so I scratched one against the stone on the fireplace front and lit the remaining paper in the grate. There was some wood still left underneath it, so hopefully it would light and give us some warmth.

"Hey, you got the fireplace lit. Good because it's going to take some time for Jensen to get here. He says the roads are impassable."

"Are the kids okay?" I asked, suddenly feeling like the worst mother in the world.

"Yeah, Cara says they're napping, so hopefully we'll be back home by the time they get up."

The fire behind me began to crackle, and I couldn't stop myself from asking him, "Am I a bad mother, Tristan?"

He shook his head and frowned. "No. Why would you ask that?"

"Because for the first months of our children's lives I didn't want to be around them, and now that we're stranded in this farmhouse with nothing but a tiny fire, I'm not wanting to race home just yet. I know I should want to, but as bad as this sounds, it's nice to be out of the house. What kind of mother wants that?"

"I don't think that makes you a bad mother, Nina. You're in the house with them every day while I'm at work. It's not surprising that you feel this way. I know you love our kids, and having three at once isn't easy."

"You're so natural as a father, Tristan. I've watched you with them since they were born, and you so easily slipped into your role. I don't know why I haven't, but I want to. I really do. I don't want our kids to grow up and think that their mother doesn't love them. I love them with all my heart. It just feels nice sometimes to be something other than a mom. You probably can't believe what I'm saying, right? You probably think it's awful."

"No, I don't think you're awful. They're only a year old, honey. They aren't laying in their cribs telling one another you don't love them if you don't spend day and night standing over them."

"You joke, but it all seems so normal for you. From the moment they were born, you were right there holding them and showing how crazy you are about them. I want to be like you, Tristan. I see how you hold Diana and wish I was like that. Or when you tickle Tressa or talk to Ethan about what it's like to be the only two males surrounded by all women, you seem so natural, like this is the role you're perfect for."

Tristan cradled my face in his hands and pressed his forehead to mine in that way that never failed to make me feel adored. Looking at me with those soulful brown eyes, he smiled. "You want to be perfect at this whole mother thing, but all you need to do is be the caring person you've always been and our children will love you. Don't compare yourself to anyone else, even me. Just be yourself."

I rested my head on his chest. "I have gotten better at it since the depression ended. I just always feel like I'm not doing enough."

"You're great with all three of them. And you never favor any of them over the others like I do."

I thought about how clearly Tristan always favored Diana and wondered aloud, "Why do you favor Diana so much?"

With a look of sadness in his eyes, he said, "Because I wasn't sure she'd make it in the beginning. She was so tiny and so frail. I remember holding her in those first days and silently telling her that she just needed to be strong like her sister and brother. That if she could muster up that strength that I'd never let her go. So I still favor her now. I know I have to stop before they get old enough to see it, but I still worry about my little girl."

Taking his cold hands in mine, I brought them to my cheek. "I'm sorry I wasn't there for you then, Tristan. You did all the worrying for the two of us, and I can't tell you how much I wish that hadn't happened."

His face brightened. "You don't have to be sorry. I always knew the Nina I loved would come shining through at some point. I could never do what you did—carry three children and go through the trauma of that C-section like you did. I'm physically strong, but I'm not sure I'd have the strength for that. You did, though. So you needed a little time off after. The least I could do is take over since you'd given me three beautiful children."

"I never thought about it that way."

"Well, you should. You did an incredible thing when you brought those three kids into our lives. And I'm sorry that you think I'm too protective with you, but this is who I've always been. You know that."

"I know, and usually I love that whole protective Alpha male thing you have going on. It's pretty hot actually. It's just that I like being able to do secret things to surprise you and I can't do that if someone's always following me around."

"Being Nina Stone means having people protect you, whether it's me or the bodyguards and driver. I can't change that."

I knew he was right. All the wonderful things that came from being married to a powerful man like Tristan made my dislike for bodyguards and a driver seem pretty minor.

"I know, and I wouldn't change a thing about our lives. I guess I could just shop online. Or maybe I could get myself a shopper like you have Angelo. Then I'd be able to surprise you whenever I wanted."

He smiled in that sexy way that always made me want him. "You know I love surprises, right?"

"That's sarcasm, Mr. Stone, isn't it? What if I told you that I think we should settle in over there right in front of the fire and have ourselves a good time while we wait for Jensen?"

Tristan arched one eyebrow and ran his tongue along his lower lip. "Now that's a surprise I can deal with."

CHAPTER SIX

TRISTAN

THE FIRE HAD BARELY WARMED the room to fifty-five degrees, but I didn't care. The snow continued to fall, so we'd have the abandoned farmhouse all to ourselves for at least a few hours more before Jensen arrived to rescue us. Looking down into Nina's blue eyes, I watched them sparkle in a way I hadn't seen them look in far too long.

"Come here," I said and pulled her by the hand until her body was pressed up against mine. "Do you know how much I love you?"

Measuring out about an inch between her thumb and forefinger, she said, "About this much?"

"More than I ever thought I could love someone. When I was out there driving around looking for you, the thought of what my life would be like if suddenly you weren't in it anymore ran through my mind. For a minute, I felt hollow inside, like there was nothing left of me if I didn't have you."

She stood on her toes and kissed me. "I'm all yours, Tristan. I've always been all yours."

I cradled the back of her head and pressed my mouth to hers in a kiss full of how much I adored her. She made my world complete, even if a few things she did drove me nearly out of my mind. She was the sweetness of life I'd been so sure I'd never get to enjoy again after losing everyone in my family.

Nina pulled her sweater up over her head and giggled. "Like my red bra for Christmas? I was going to surprise you with it and the matching panties later on tonight."

"Matching? It must be a big day," I joked as I gently tugged her jeans down her legs to reveal fire engine red silk boy short panties. "Mmmm….I like these. Have anything specific planned when you chose these this morning?"

She ran her fingers down the front of my shirt and stopped at the top of my pants to unbutton them. Looking up at me, she smiled. "Pretty much what we're about to do now, except I never imagined we'd be in some abandoned farmhouse as a blizzard raged just outside."

"This reminds me a little of that first time we were in Venice," I said, referring to how excited she was making me.

"I loved that trip," she said wistfully as she finished unbuttoning my dress shirt. "It's still one of my favorite times we've had together."

I shrugged out of my shirt into the chilly air and removed her red satin Christmas bra and panties. My fingers slid over her skin, leaving goosebumps in their wake. "This is definitely the coldest place we've ever been together."

Sliding my tongue over her lips, I teased the tip of her tongue as I stepped out of the rest of my clothes and eased her down to the wood floor in front of the fireplace. I sat and pulled her onto my lap to straddle me, wanting to finally feel her in my arms. She wrapped her legs around my waist and eased me into her like we were two pieces of one whole meant to be together.

"You feel so good," she murmured as she slanted her lips to cover mine. I kissed my wife like the goddess I saw her as, loving the feel of every inch of her body as she gently surrendered to me.

"I love it when you ride me like this," I groaned as she rose off my cock only to take me slowly back into her slick cunt, rocking gently against me.

"I miss feeling like this," she said softly against my lips.

With my hands on her waist, I lifted her and then guided her back down onto my cock. "You never have to miss this. I'm all yours."

I lowered my head to take one pink nipple into my mouth, and sucking it between my lips, lightly bit down on her tender skin. Her moans above me as she began to ride my cock faster told me she loved this as much as I loved making her feel this way.

She tugged me back by the hair to look down into my eyes, and I saw the sensual woman that all too often lately had hidden herself from me. "Tristan, this feels so good. Don't stop."

Kissing her hard, I groaned, "I won't stop. I want to feel you come for me."

Cupping the back of her head, I held her to me as she came, loving the feeling of her tumbling over the edge just as I flooded her body. When her thighs stopped quivering, she stilled on me and whispered, "Promise me you'll always be there to rein me in when I get crazy."

"Always. Promise me you'll remember how much I love you when my ways drive you crazy."

Nina gave me one of her sweet, gentle smiles and nodded. "Deal." Sighing deeply, she added, "I can't tell you how much it means to me that no matter what, I know you're right there with me."

"I'm always right there with you, princess. You're my whole life—you and those beautiful kids of ours. I'd be lost without you."

She kissed me sweetly and whispered in my ear, "I didn't have my diaphragm in, Tristan. What if…?

I chuckled. "I was just telling Ethan the other night that we need another male in the house. He'd love a little brother."

"What if we have another girl? Then you two will really be in the minority."

I thought about us adding another baby to the family and couldn't think of a better Christmas gift. "If we're having another child, I don't care what it is. I just want you and the baby to be healthy. That's all that matters to me."

Nina lifted her head and looked over my shoulder out the

window. Standing slowly, she began to get dressed as I stretched my legs. A knock at the front door startled us, and I realized our stolen time alone was over. We dressed quickly and as I let Jensen in out of the cold, I helped Nina into her coat.

He came into the room where we'd been and looked at our fire. "Not exactly blazing. How did you two ever keep warm with such a meager fire?"

Giving Nina a sly smile, I watched her blush as I explained, "It wasn't too bad as long as we sat close to the fire. It'll be nice to get home, though, so lead the way, Jensen."

We rode home in silence, but just before we reached the house, Nina leaned over to whisper to me, "You're pretty slick, Mr. Stone. I bet he knows."

I smiled and kissed her. "Knows what? That two people in love kept warm in an abandoned farmhouse?"

"You know what I mean, Tristan."

"I do, but I don't care who knows. There's nothing wrong with a man showing his wife how much he loves her."

She snuggled up to my side and wrapped her arms around me. "You're right. There's nothing wrong with that at all."

CHAPTER SEVEN

NINA

I WALKED STRAIGHT TO THE nursery the minute we got home and found the babies playing on the floor with Cara. Tressa and Diana sat next to one another looking at their favorite storybook, and Ethan sat perched on one of the three rocking horses Tristan had brought back from his trip to London. When he saw me, he stood on his chubby little legs and squealed, "Ma-ma!" like he always did when he was excited.

Tristan joined me and I crouched down and asked, "How's my baby boy this afternoon? Have you been good for Cara?"

Cara stood and walked over to stand next to me near the door. "Ethan has a surprise for you two. Are you ready Ethan?"

He nodded eagerly and for the first time took three tentative steps before tumbling onto the floor. His best attempt at walking yet, it thrilled me to tears. Opening my arms wide, I scooped him up from the floor and planted kisses on his adorable little face.

"Look at my little man! Three steps today. That's a new record."

Behind me, Tristan rested his chin on my shoulder and tweaked Ethan on the nose. "Good job, Ethan. Pretty soon we'll be chasing you around the house."

As I nuzzled my son and made raspberry noises on his pudgy cheeks, Tristan moved around us to pick up the girls. With one in each arm, he held them as they giggled about seeing him again. I loved it when he did things like that. He may have been even sexier than usual when he was holding our two little girls in his arms.

Over their laughing, he said to Cara, "Our trip has been postponed until tomorrow, so take the night off and if you need to go anywhere, just tell Jensen. I've let him know he's to take you anywhere you need to go tonight. He'll be back from getting the Range Rover soon. We've had an exciting afternoon, so we're staying in tonight with the kids and we'll all fly out tomorrow morning."

"Thank you, Mr. Stone. I think I will take you up on your offer and see if I can find a store open. I'll be back in my rooms later tonight, so if any of the children need anything, just let me know."

Cara turned to walk out of the room, but I caught her by the sleeve and said quietly, "Thank you for everything, Cara. I know you helped my husband to make the trip a surprise. That means a lot to me."

She smiled warmly. "I'm just glad you're all okay. I was worried sick about these little angels losing their mother."

"Thank you. Enjoy some time off tonight. You've earned it."

Cara left the five of us in the nursery to play until dinnertime, and later as we all watched Finding Nemo while we lay on our bed, I couldn't help but think that I was the luckiest woman in the world.

✧　✧　✧

"CLOSE YOUR EYES," TRISTAN ORDERED as we all stood outside the entrance to one of the new villas. Looking at the kids, he said, "Let's do peek-a-boo. I'll tell you when, okay?" The children covered their eyes as they waited to see what lay behind the door, and I squeezed my eyes shut as Tristan opened the door.

"Okay, now everyone look."

I opened my eyes to see a gorgeously decorated villa that reminded me of our hotel rooms at the Richmont Venice. Designed to mimic that hotel, its walls were painted in a rich golden color and a deep red tone used as an accent in the furnishings gave the villa a richness I'd loved so much in Tristan's property in Italy.

"It's so beautiful, honey," I said as I spun around to look at every inch of the main room. "You had them make it look like Venice."

Tristan bent down and kissed me on the cheek as he lifted Diana into his arms. "I wanted it to feel like your favorite place, so I told them to make sure it had the same feeling. I think they got it right."

I looked over on the far wall leading to the hallway and saw a familiar piece of artwork. As I approached it, I realized it was my mother's pencil drawing of Tristan's mother we'd found in the storage unit in Pennsylvania. Done when they were still roommates in college, the portrait had quickly become one of Tristan's favorites because of how wonderfully my mother had portrayed Tressa Stone's gentle nature. Accented by a deep cherry wood frame, it represented what I knew this place meant to him.

"You hung my mother's artwork here? Oh, Tristan, it's beautiful."

"My mother would have loved the idea of this old place becoming villas. She fell in love with the site, so it's only right that she should be here. I couldn't think of a better way to symbolize everything this place is to me than to hang my mother's portrait done by your mother's hand."

"What about when other people rent the villa, though? Won't it seem odd having it here?"

Tristan shook his head and smiled. "This villa is ours. It won't be available for anyone but us, so she'll always be here when we come back." He pointed to a room off to the side where a live seven foot blue spruce Christmas tree stood decorated with lights and ornaments in blue and silver. Dozens of wrapped gifts for the kids sat piled up under the tree. "Merry Christmas everybody! Time to see what Santa brought us."

Ethan led the charge to the presents, nearly crawling over his sisters as they toddled much slower to grab their Christmas gifts. I sat down in the middle of them so I could see how each of them reacted to their new toys while Tristan recorded the whole thing and I helped their little hands open their gifts.

I pulled a big box with Diana's name on it and placed it in front of her. "Santa brought this for you, honey. I wonder what it is."

She beamed at the news that the present was for her, and we tore off the paper to find a barnyard animal set just for her. As I set it up for her away from the mess of the wrapping paper piling up around us, she ran her fingers over each piece, and as she held each one up for me to look at, I told her its name.

Bringing a cow up to her lips, she gave it a kiss as I said, "That's a cow. It goes moo."

That's all she needed. From that point on, moo was all she said while she played with her brand new farm set.

I looked up at Tristan and smiled. "I think she likes it, especially the cow."

He nodded and pointed toward Tressa, who tapped on the brightly colored keys of her kiddie piano. "I think we have a future musician on our hands."

"Tressa, do you like your gift from Santa?" I asked as I crawled over to sit next to her. Giggling, she said her first word ever. "Moo!"

Laughing, Tristan tried to correct her by saying "ma-ma," but she wouldn't hear of it. Moo it was, just like her sister. I turned to him and shrugged. "So the word for the day is moo."

Like the big brother he fashioned himself to be, Ethan brought over his favorite present—a push toy with an elephant's head that contained balls that popped up when it rolled—and said the only word he'd mastered so far. Giving me the handle of his toy to hold, he smiled and said, "Ma-ma. Ma-ma."

I smiled and looked up at Tristan as Ethan threw his arms around me. "Two moos and a ma-ma. Not a bad day."

"Not a bad day at all."

Later, after a Christmas feast fit for a king, we tucked the children into their cribs in the villa next door to ours and returned to sit together on the couch in front of the Christmas tree. Unlike the year before, this holiday had been truly one full of joy.

Tristan wrapped his arm around my shoulder as I leaned my head on his chest. "I think the kids liked their presents, don't you?"

I nodded, loving the memory of their little faces brightening every time they saw a new toy. "I think so. We spoiled them, though."

We sat there quietly until I remembered I hadn't given him his surprise present from me yet. Jumping up, I ran over to my purse and pulled out the box with his cufflinks. "I forgot to give you your surprise."

"Ah, the surprise that got us caught in a blizzard," he joked. He took the box from my hand and held it for a moment. "You know, you didn't have to do this. I have everything I could ever want with you and our kids."

I sat down beside him and curled my legs up under me. "I wanted to get you something just from me to show you that I love you. So when we're having a fight or I'm having a bad day and take it out on you, there's something you can always look at and remember how much I love being your wife. So open it."

He did as I asked, and I watched his eyes light up when he saw the cufflinks. "Nina, they're stunning. You know me too well. I hope when I wear them that you'll be by my side."

"I can see that happening," I said with a giggle.

Tristan put the cufflinks on the table in front of us and leaned over to kiss me. "Now for your surprise."

"My surprise? I thought this trip was my surprise," I said as he stood from the couch.

"It was, but I had another one up my sleeve. Wait there. I'll be right back."

I sat there thinking how wonderful my life had turned out after that first night with Tristan. We'd had our ups and downs, but he was still the most incredible and fascinating man I'd ever met. That he fell in love with me made me feel like the luckiest woman in the world, no matter what surprise gifts he gave me.

He sat down next to me and held out a square box in his palm. "Merry Christmas, Nina."

"Ooooh, I wonder what it is?" I slowly untied the red silk ribbon and removed the gold wrapping paper to see a black velvet box. He'd gotten me jewelry. "Thank you, Tristan. I'm sure I'll love it."

Opening the lid, I saw only a slip of paper sitting where I'd assumed a diamond bracelet or earrings would be. Confused, I took it out and unfolded it, looking at him for some kind of explanation. "It's a copy of a check you wrote to someone else?"

"Read the memo line."

My eyes slowly read down to the bottom left hand corner of the check, and I saw the words "For Nina's studio" written there. "My studio?"

"The builders will break ground as soon as the weather warms a little. They promise me they'll have it complete by your birthday."

My mouth hung open. A studio all of my own? "You got me my own art studio? I can't believe it. My own studio."

"I thought if you had somewhere to go and just do what you love that you'd be happier."

"Oh, Tristan, I'm not unhappy with you and the kids. I hate that you think I am."

He shook his head and cupped my cheek with his hand. "I leave that house every morning and have a life outside their nursery. You don't, for all intents and purposes. Having this studio of your own, even though it will only be a couple hundred yards from the house, will give you a chance to have some time of your own. I think you deserve that."

"I don't want you to think I don't love spending time with my family, but this might be the best gift I've ever gotten. I've been dying to get back to my art after we found my mother's pieces. Thank you so much!"

"If mama's not happy, nobody's happy," he said with a smile.

I pulled him to me and hugged him close, so thankful to have a husband like him. I truly was the luckiest woman on earth.

THE END

CONTINUE READING FOR DETAILS ABOUT MORE GREAT READS!

CLUB X

Meet the gorgeous men of Club X…

Cassian March, the face of Club X, the most exclusive nightspot in Tampa. One of the most eligible men in town, he can have any woman he chooses—and he does as often as he likes. Beneath his cool facade lies a desire for something more, but will his new assistant Olivia have what it takes to fulfill his darkest fantasies?

Stefan March, the manager of Club X, loves the single life. Women are his playground, and this man lives to have fun. Committed to never settling down, he may have met his match in Shay, a bartender at Club X who seems immune to his charms. Stefan loves nothing more than a challenge, though, so let the games begin!

Kane Jackson, half-brother to Cassian and Stefan, he handles the members' fantasies at Club X. Big, bad, and dangerous, his style is hard, like the life he's led. But you know what they say—the bigger they are, the harder they fall and Kane might just fall for Abbi, the one woman able to get beyond his hard exterior to the heart he hides from the world.

Fall in love with the brothers from Club X today! Get Temptation, Surrender, Possession, Satisfaction, and Acceptance and see why readers LOVE their stories!

Love your romance a little darker?
Get the Addicted To You series!

I want her. I crave her. She's my addiction.
The world knows me as Ian Anwell, New York Times bestselling author, but Kristina makes me want more.
Much more.

I need him. I love him. He's my obsession.
Everyone thinks they know Kristina Richards, but I'm more than what they see on the screen.
So much more.

I'm his muse, and this is our story.

Get the four Addicted To You books today!

About the Author

K.M. Scott writes contemporary romance stories of sexy, intense, K.M. Scott writes contemporary romance stories of sexy, intense, and unforgettable love. A New York Times and USA Today bestselling author, she's been in love with romance since reading her first romance novel in junior high (she was a very curious girl!). Under her Gabrielle Bisset name, she writes erotic paranormal and historical romance. She lives in Pennsylvania with a herd of animals and when she's not writing can be found reading or feeding her TV addiction.

Be sure to visit K.M.'s Facebook page at **facebook.com/kmscottauthor** for all the latest on her books, along with giveaways and other goodies! And to hear all the news on K.M. Scott books first, sign up for her newsletter today and be sure to visit her website at **www.kmscottbooks.com**.

BOOKS BY K.M. SCOTT:

If I Dream (Corrupted Love #1)
If You Fight (Corrupted Love #2)
If We Fall (Corrupted Love #3)

Crash Into Me (Heart of Stone #1)
Fall Into Me (Heart of Stone #2)
Give In To Me (Heart of Stone #3)
Heart of Stone Volume One Box Set
Ever After (Heart of Stone #4)
A Heart of Stone Christmas (Heart of Stone #5)
Return To Me (Heart of Stone #6)
Forever With Me (Heart of Stone #7)
Heart of Stone Volume Two Box Set

Temptation (Club X #1)
Surrender (Club X #2)
Possession (Club X #3)
Satisfaction (Club X #4)
Acceptance (Club X #5)
The Complete Club X Series Box Set

Crave (Addicted To You #1)
Adore (Addicted To You #2)
Shatter (Addicted To You #3)
Claim (Addicted To You #4)

K.M.'S BOOKS ARE IN AUDIOBOOK TOO!

Books by Gabrielle Bisset:

Vampire Dreams Revamped
(A Sons of Navarus Prequel)
Blood Avenged (Sons of Navarus #1)
Blood Betrayed (Sons of Navarus #2)
Longing (A Sons of Navarus Short Story)
Blood Spirit (Sons of Navarus #3)
The Deepest Cut (A Sons of Navarus Short Story)
Blood Prophecy (Sons of Navarus #4)
Blood Craving (Sons of Navarus #5)
Blood Eclipse (Sons of Navarus #6)
The Sons of Navarus Box Set #1
The Sons of Navarus Box Set #2

Stolen Destiny (Destined Ones Duology #1)
Destiny Redeemed (Destined Ones Duology #2)

Love's Master
Masquerade
The Victorian Erotic Romance Trilogy

www.ingramcontent.com/pod-product-compliance
Lightning Source LLC
Chambersburg PA
CBHW062021190726
48284CB00014B/1376